**"All you need to know is that if you don't, those captive Levanti die."**

I held my ground though every part of me wanted to step back, hating his closeness and the touch of his breath on my face. "But if you kill them, you'll have nothing left to hold over me to ensure compliance," I said in the same quiet hiss as he. "Kill them and I'll never name you defender."

Leo's eyes narrowed.

"Are you trying to do the controlling thing on me?" I asked, knowing I was pushing it. "That doesn't work anymore, remember? If you wanted to do that you shouldn't have sliced my eyes."

His hand closed around my throat, fingertips digging in hard. "I suggest you reconsider your rash attempt at autonomy, Dishiva," he said, each word spat into my face. "Or I will make sure your people die. One by one. Slowly. Painfully. While you witness every moment."

With a final, meaningful squeeze, he let go and finally stepped back. He smiled then, not so much amused as satisfied. "I know you'll be a good girl," he said, and patted my cheek. "I'll see you tomorrow."

Praise for
# THE REBORN EMPIRE SERIES

"With prose that rises above most novels, Devin Madson paints evocative scenes to build an engaging story. Highly entertaining, *We Ride the Storm* is certainly worth your attention and Madson is an exciting new author in fantasy."
—Mark Lawrence, author of *Red Sister*

"Intricate, compelling, and vividly imagined, this is the first in a new quartet that I am hugely excited about. Visceral battles, complex politics, and fascinating worldbuilding bring Devin's words to life."
—Anna Stephens, author of *Godblind*

"An utterly arresting debut, *Storm*'s heart is in its complex, fascinating characters, each trapped in ever-tightening snarls of war, politics, and magic. Madson's sharp, engaging prose hauls you through an engrossing story that will leave you wishing you'd set aside enough time to read this all in one sitting. One of the best new voices in fantasy."
—Sam Hawke, author of *City of Lies*

"A brutal, nonstop ride through an empire built upon violence and lies, a story as gripping as it is unpredictable. Never shying away from the consequences of the past nor its terrible realities, Madson balances characters you want to love with actions you want to hate while mixing in a delightful amount of magic, political intrigue, and lore. This is not a book you'll be able to put down."
—K. A. Doore, author of *The Perfect Assassin*

# WE DREAM OF GODS

## THE REBORN EMPIRE: BOOK FOUR

## DEVIN MADSON

orbit

orbitbooks.net

Orbit
Hachette Book Group
1290 Avenue of the Americas
New York, NY 10104
orbitbooks.net

First Edition: March 2023
Simultaneously published in Great Britain by Orbit

Orbit is an imprint of Hachette Book Group.
The Orbit name and logo are trademarks of Little, Brown Book Group Limited.

The publisher is not responsible for websites (or their content) that are not owned by the publisher.

The Hachette Speakers Bureau provides a wide range of authors for speaking events. To find out more, go to hachettespeakersbureau.com or email HachetteSpeakers@hbgusa.com.

Orbit books may be purchased in bulk for business, educational, or promotional use. For information, please contact your local bookseller or the Hachette Book Group Special Markets Department at special.markets@hbgusa.com.

Library of Congress Cataloging-in-Publication Data
Names: Madson, Devin, author.
Title: We dream of gods / Devin Madson.
Description: First edition. | New York : Orbit, 2023. | Series: The reborn empire ; book 4
Identifiers: LCCN 2022026620 | ISBN 9780316536455 (trade paperback) |
    ISBN 9780316536431 (ebook)
Subjects: LCGFT: Fantasy fiction. | Novels.
Classification: LCC PR9619.4.M335 W44 2023 | DDC 823/.92—dc23/eng/20220609
LC record available at https://lccn.loc.gov/2022026620

ISBNs: 9780316536455 (trade paperback), 9780316536431 (ebook)

Printed in the United States of America

LSC-C

Printing 1, 2022

*To my Shishi, Calli, who we lost during the journey. I wish you had been with us longer. I wish I could have been there at the end. As you were always there for me.*

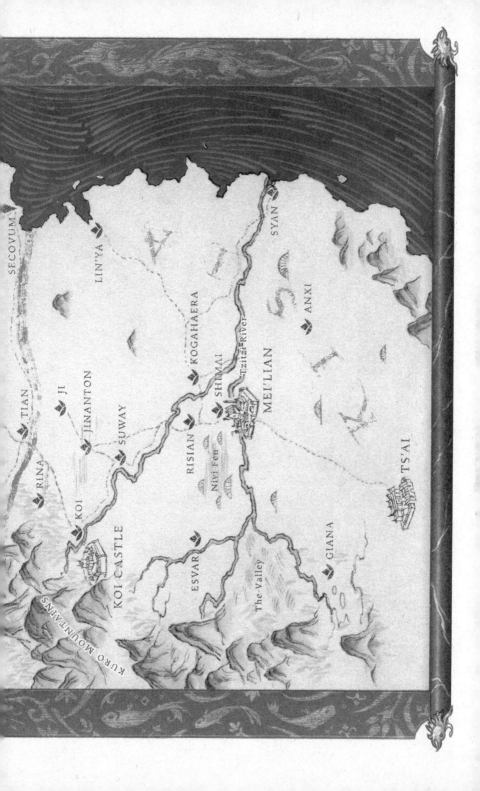

# CHARACTER LIST

### *Levanti*

### Torin

***Rah e'Torin—ousted captain of the Second Swords of Torin***
Eska e'Torin—Rah's second-in-command (deceased, Residing)
Kishava e'Torin—tracker (deceased)
Orun e'Torin—horse master (deceased, Residing)
Yitti e'Torin—the healer (deceased)
Jinso—Rah's horse
Lok, Himi, and Istet—Swords of the Torin
Gideon e'Torin—First Sword of the Torin and former emperor of
    Levanti Kisia
Sett e'Torin—Gideon's second and blood brother (deceased)
Tep e'Torin—healer of the First Swords
Tor, Matsimelar (deceased), and Oshar e'Torin—the saddleboys
    chosen by Gideon to be translators
Nuru e'Torin—self-taught translator never used by the Chiltaens

### Jaroven

***Dishiva e'Jaroven—captain of the Third Swords***
Keka e'Jaroven—Dishiva's second, can't talk. Chiltaens cut out his
    tongue.
Captain Atum e'Jaroven—captain of the First Swords of Jaroven
Loklan e'Jaroven—Dishiva's horse master
Shenyah e'Jaroven—the only Jaroven Made in exile

Ptapha, Massama, Dendek, Anouke, Esi, and Moshe e'Jaroven—
  Dishiva's Swords

## Other Levanti

Ezma e'Topi—exiled horse whisperer
Derkka en'Injit—her apprentice
Jass en'Occha—a Sword of the Occha
Captain Lashak e'Namalaka—First Sword of the Namalaka and
  Dishiva's friend
Captain Yiss en'Oht—First Sword of the Oht, fiercely loyal to
  Gideon
Captain Taga en'Occha—First Sword of the Occha and Jass's captain
Captain Menesor e'Qara—captain of the Second Swords of Qara
Jaesha e'Qara—Captain Menesor's second
Other captains—Captain Dhamara e'Sheth, Captain Bahn e'Bedjuti,
  and Captain Leena en'Injit
Senet en'Occha, Jakan e'Qara, Yafeu en'Injit, Baln en'Oht, Tafa
  en'Oht, and Kehta en'Oht—imperial guards
Diha e'Bedjuti—healer
Nassus—Levanti god of death
Mona—Levanti goddess of justice

## *Kisians*

### *Miko Ts'ai—bastard daughter of Empress Hana Ts'ai and Katashi Otako*

Emperor Kin Ts'ai—the last emperor of Kisia (deceased)
Empress Hana Ts'ai—deposed empress of Kisia (deceased)
Prince Tanaka Ts'ai—Miko's twin brother (deceased)
Shishi—Miko's dog
Jie Ts'ai—Emperor Kin's bastard son (deceased)
Minister Tashi Oyamada—Jie's maternal grandfather and minister
  of the right

Minister Ryo Manshin—minister of the left, chief commander of the Imperial Army

General Kitado—commander of Miko's Imperial Guard (deceased)

General Ryoji—former commander of the Imperial Guard

General Moto, General Rushin, General Mihri, General Yass, and General Alon—southern generals of the Imperial Army

Captain Soku—one of General Moto's men

Lord Hiroto Bahain—duke of Syan

Edo Bahain—duke of Syan's eldest son

Captain Nagai—one of the duke's men

Governor Tianto Koali—governor of Syan

Lord Ichiro Koali—count of Irin Ya

Lord Nishi (Lord Salt)—a wealthy Kisian lord who believes in the One True God

## Chiltaens

**Cassandra Marius—Chiltaen whore and assassin**

The hieromonk, Creos Villius—head of the One True God's church (deceased)

Leo Villius—only child of His Holiness the hieromonk

Captain Aeneas—the hieromonk's head guard (deceased)

Kaysa (She)—Cassandra's second soul

## Others

Torvash—the Witchdoctor

Mistress Saki—Torvash's silent companion

Kocho—Torvash's scribe and servant

Lechati—young man in Torvash's service

# THE STORY SO FAR...

After her failure to destroy the deserter camp, Dishiva is named Defender of the One True God, separating her from her people. With Gideon under Leo's control, she finds allies in Empress Sichi and Lord Edo Bahain and fights to ensure Gideon meets with Secretary Aurus to discuss a peace treaty with Chiltae. Despite the negotiations coming to nothing, she finds a potential ally in the secretary of the Nine.

Still in the body of Empress Hana, Cassandra returns to Torvash's house with Captain Aeneas and Septum, the lifeless seventh twin of Leo Villius. Leo follows, and Captain Aeneas and Cassandra barely escape. When Leo catches up with them, he kills Aeneas and takes Cassandra and Hana captive along with Kaysa and Unus, one of Leo's twins, and another failed assassin, Yakono, whom Cassandra gets to know through the adjoining wall of their cells.

With an army behind her now, Miko makes strategic attacks upon Grace Bahain to weaken Emperor Gideon's support, but when she takes Syan by stealth, she is hemmed in by the city's governors and in danger of being routed. A successful night ambush puts an end to Grace Bahain, but to get out of the city, Miko has to kill the governors and cut her way through her own citizens.

Injured, Rah is left to die by Whisperer Ezma when Gideon's Levanti attack her camp. Saved by one of his old Swords, he convinces the Levanti not to fight one another, with the help of Minister Manshin, who takes them to regroup at Syan. Forced to lead together or risk splitting the remaining Levanti, Rah and Ezma march their people to Kogahaera with Miko's army.

When she returns from negotiations, Dishiva is powerless to stop the execution of Yitti e'Torin and the remainder of Rah's former Swords, a moment that marks the final collapse of the dream that was Levanti Kisia. With Sichi's help, she tries to get through to Gideon, but although they kill Leo, Gideon is a broken man. They have to face the approaching Chiltaen army without him. During the battle, she and Sichi are pursued by another Leo Villius, only for the tower they are retreating up to collapse. Dishiva wakes to find one of her eyes is gone, while the other is damaged. Ezma tells her it was meant to be because she's Veld Reborn, destined to build a holy empire in the name of the One True God. Dishiva refuses, but upon hearing that half a dozen Levanti have been captured by the Chiltaens, she goes to face Leo and save them. But with the death of his father, she is now the hieromonk of Chiltae, and Leo claims her as the false high priest he must kill to complete his prophecy.

The night before the battle of Kogahaera, Rah gets word that Gideon has been broken by Leo Villius and leaves, but while getting Gideon out of the city, they get stuck in a tunnel collapse and have to be rescued. Unwilling to let Ezma lead any longer, Rah calls a Fracturing and takes half the Levanti with him, planning to take them home.

Growing clashes with Minister Manshin over her alliance with the Levanti come to a head when Miko orders her army to march on Kogahaera. Although successful, Miko has to navigate impossible political waters, and when both Rah and Ezma leave, Manshin takes power, leaving her a puppet on her own throne.

When every one of Cassandra's attempts to escape Leo's clutches fails, Empress Hana moves into Septum's body in one final, desperate attempt to turn the situation to their advantage. But Hana's body gives in to her illness and Cassandra dies with it, only to waken inside Septum's mind with Hana. With their final attempt to escape having failed, they dive off a balcony to kill Septum, thus ruining the timing of Leo's prophecy. Before they fall, Kaysa pulls Cassandra back into their shared body, but Empress Hana dies with Septum.

# 1. MIKO

There are no gods. Only men. Emperor Kin had told me so that night in the throne room, lessons spilling unexpected from his lips. What he hadn't said was just how literally he had meant it. No gods. Only *men*.

My divan had been draped in crimson silk, while still more had been gathered behind me, twisted into the shape of the crimson throne. A poor imitation of what had been lost when Mei'lian burned—a loss as hard to swallow as the extra effort Minister Manshin put into my throne now that it was *his* power I displayed.

"I swear on the bones of my forebears. On my name and my honour." Lord Gori had just arrived from the north, possessed of little beyond his name in the wake of the Chiltaen conquest. I would have been glad to have him on my side, but it wasn't me to whom he swore his oath.

Minister Manshin stood at my side, close, towering over me in a way that crushed my authority more than his usurpation of my power already had. In his shadow I truly was just a puppet seated on a false throne. A pretence. A farce.

Lord Gori finished his oath and, bade to rise, looked to my minister. "Your allegiance is welcome, Lord Gori," Manshin said. "Her Imperial Majesty fights for all Kisians, but especially for those who fight for her."

Fights for all Kisians. It was all I could do not to scoff at so great a lie. I wanted to, often, but whenever I thought to denounce his claims, I remembered Sichi and Nuru and our precarious position, and smiled instead. Smile. Always smile. The display of a submissive, non-threatening woman, under which I hid my promise.

I would destroy them all.

"Thank you, Your Excellency. Majesty. I…" The man squirmed, pain and troubles on his tongue. All in the north had suffered through the conquest, and a few words of empathy would strengthen his loyalty, yet Manshin said nothing.

"I know," I said when the man seemed unable to finish. "It has been a tough few seasons, Lord Gori, but we will find our way out of the darkness. Together."

Simple words, yet when he was dismissed, he strode toward the doors straight-backed, lighter than when he had entered despite the mud-stained, frayed hem that danced about his feet.

"Well," Manshin said once he was gone. "Not a very worthy addition to our cause, but an addition nonetheless."

How I wished to tear at his idea of what was worthy, but I took that anger and buried it with the rest.

"He may yet be more useful than he appears," he went on. "That is, if you cease your…attempts at sensitivity. Saying such unnecessary things only displays weakness, Your Majesty."

With my hands in my lap and my back straight, I channelled my mother's impression of the perfect imperial statue.

"Ah," Manshin said with a breathy laugh. "You are giving me the silent treatment, I see."

The urge to clench my hands was almost overwhelming.

"You may, of course, be childish if it gives you joy, Your Majesty, but it is hardly the act of an empress."

I turned to look at him. No scowl, just a stare into which I poured my promise.

*I will destroy you.*

He looked away. He could have acknowledged my anger, have tried to convince me again of his reasons, but why bother when he had already decided how things would be? All he needed was for me to accept and obey.

"Any others?" he asked of Chancellor Likoshi—his choice for the position, of course.

"No, Your Excellency," the man said from the doorway. "A few came with petitions for Minister Oyamada, but he has seen them all."

Minister Manshin grunted. Annoyance? Wishful thinking. My ministers didn't like each other, but that was a far cry from Minister Oyamada being my ally.

"Let the council know we will meet in an hour," Manshin said, dismissing Likoshi and stepping from my side. Without bowing to me, he crossed the floor as Lord Gori had, though his steps were slow and assured, owning the space with ease.

When at last the door slid closed behind him, I slumped, letting out a long breath. Only guards were present to witness my head sink into my hands, two at the door while at my side stood Captain Kiren—General Ryoji's choice of replacement while he was away. The days dragged by and still he hadn't returned. Every day the fear I'd sent him to his death pressed closer.

Needing to move, I got to my feet and strode for the door, leaving Captain Kiren to scurry after me.

Beyond the doors the manor bustled. It was always bustling. People came and went at every hour, my court more alive than Emperor Kin's had usually been. There was an energy, a need to be present for what felt like the building of something new. Old powers sought to retain their positions, while new ones sought opportunities to rise. In different circumstances I would have revelled in it, but instead I walked numb through the halls though people stopped to bow, though they spoke with reverence, though they were, ostensibly, here for me.

I added more anger to my raging core. Manshin had stolen this triumph from me, leaving the only joy that of rebellion.

A circuitous walk through the passages discovered Lord Gori in conversation with one of the chancellor's men, whose sharp shake of the head seemed to refuse what was being requested. Before I could catch a word, the chancellor's man saw me and bowed. "Your Majesty, is there something I can do for you?"

"No, you may go. I require a word with Lord Gori."

A moment of hesitation, then the chancellor's man bowed again, glanced at Lord Gori, and walked away. Once he was out of ear-shot, I turned a smile on the fidgeting lord. "Lord Gori," I said. "Join me for tea. Captain Kiren? Have tea sent up immediately."

Not waiting for acceptance, I swept Lord Gori toward a nearby sitting room filled with old imperial grandeur and a fine layer of dust.

"This is an unlooked-for honour, Your Majesty," Lord Gori said, managing to bow three times between entering the room and kneeling upon the cushion opposite. "I must also apologise for being so importunate just now; it is below my dignity and—"

"You mean it ought to be below your dignity, but desperation makes beggars of us all." I smiled as his eyes widened. "What was it you requested from my chancellor just now?"

Lord Gori swallowed, sending a fleeting glance at Captain Kiren by the door. "I...uh..." The man deflated with a sigh. "Food, Your Majesty. We lost our harvest to the Chiltaen army, and now my people are starving before winter has even begun. Without supplies, I fear much of the north will not make it to the spring."

"Have you spoken to Minister Oyamada?"

"I have not yet had the chance, Your Majesty. It seems he is too busy to see me for the next few days. But I will wait and put my case to him; it's not something you should—"

"It is exactly what I should trouble myself with, Lord Gori. Minister Manshin's only interest is in continuing to steer us toward war and destruction, but I serve my people. That is an empress's job."

Lord Gori frowned, and began words only to swallow them. By the door, Captain Kiren cleared his throat. Time was up.

"I must go now," I said, rising from the table. "But a warning for you, Lord Gori. Minister Manshin is no friend to you, as he is no friend to me; if the time comes to fight, remember that." As he hurriedly scrambled to his feet to bow, I added, "I will tell Minister Oyamada the granting of emergency food stores to you and the people of Hotai has my full approval."

"Th-thank you, Your Majesty."

I was at the door before he finished speaking. Captain Kiren slid it open, and I almost collided with a maid bringing the tea tray. She bowed and apologised and asked if I wished the tea taken elsewhere, while Captain Kiren's eyes bulged with warning. "No," I said. "The tea is for Lord Gori. I must go."

I pushed past, sending the tea tray rattling. A glance both ways along the passage and my heart leapt into my throat. Manshin stood with General Moto at the corner, speaking in a low voice. He'd seen me, but at least he wasn't alone. I spun away, hasty steps propelling me the opposite direction along the passage, Captain Kiren in my wake.

Manshin neither called out nor followed, and slowly my heartbeat returned to normal, though a sick dread kept churning in my gut. I'd been so careful about my meetings with those who came to pledge support, but this time had been too close for comfort.

Forcing a smile for every courtier that halted to bow, I made one more stop on the way to my apartments—a small shrine on the upper floor. My frequent visits there hadn't gone unnoticed, but Sichi's skill for gossip had everyone talking about how admirable it was that I paid my respects to Emperor Kin and Empress Hana so often.

As always, Captain Kiren waited outside the door, leaving me to step alone into the small, dimly lit space filled with guttering lanterns and stubs of incense. A basket of freshly folded prayers sat beside the altar. I took a handful, and laying them out one by one, I lit a fresh candle and rolled back onto my feet. Eyeing the narrow cupboard in the far corner, I took off my sandals and crept toward it, making no sound. Removing the key from its hook beneath was more difficult, even more so to slide it into the lock without scraping the sides. A cough covered the click of the lock, and with a satisfied smile, I eased the door open upon a waft of stale incense. The cupboard was full of candles and incense cones, prayer paper and sashes, and at the bottom beneath the basket of discarded candle stubs was a stack of letters. I drew them out and stuffed them inside my robe before carefully closing the cupboard and locking it again, returning everything to where it had been.

There was no sign of Manshin when I stepped back out into the passage, yet I couldn't but feel watching eyes everywhere. The feeling remained until I stepped into the only safe place I had left. My apartments were grand rooms fit for Kisia's ruler, yet like my mother's apartments had been, they were a finely wrought prison.

Sichi and Nuru sat upon the window seat, their fingers entwined as they talked. The sight was so reminiscent of Edo and Tanaka that a lump of grief swelled, halting my steps abruptly in the middle of the floor. Nuru yanked her hands free, cheeks reddening around her defiant glare.

"I'm sorry, I…" But how could I explain? How could I express a grief that wasn't only about loss but tangled with the pain of always being an afterthought to two people who loved each other? "I just had a thought," I said, the lie so much easier. "Oh, and I've got the letters."

Whatever questions Sichi might have asked, the mention of letters had her up and sweeping toward me, hands outstretched. "How many? From whom?"

"I haven't had a chance to look yet," I said, reaching into my robe. "But it's quite a stack."

Sichi all but snatched them from me as I drew the bundle free. "Lord Iraki," she said, eyeing the seals as she flipped through them. "Governor Uhi, General Raan—"

"Lord Raan," I corrected. "He isn't a general anymore."

"No, you're right, but I assume that's why you wrote to him." She handed it over, along with the other two, sniffing in what I could only take as disapproval. "Ah! Look! Both Lady Zin and the Countess of Hurun have written back!"

Abandoning the rest of the stack, she hurriedly tore open the first of her letters.

"You think I shouldn't have written to Lord Raan?" I said.

"What? No, I mean…" She sighed, lowering her own letter. "No, given what I know of his allegiances he's a good person to court, I just… There are other strengths besides military might."

"Of course there are, but we're in the middle of a war. If we do not soon rid Kisia of the Chiltaens, Kisia as we know it will be gone."

"Yes, but we're also in the middle of social and political change. At least, I hope that's what we're fighting for."

She spoke softly, but I bristled at the hint of censure. "We are, but we can't change anything if we lose the battles."

"And we won't be able to if we fight the wrong way."

I looked down at Lord Raan's letter. "The wrong way? Unless I marry Leo Villius, what other way can we win but by fighting?"

"It's not that I don't think we need to fight," Sichi said. "Just that if we want anything to change, we need to consider other allies as well. Politicians. Priests. Powerful speakers. Women intent on defying history." She lifted her letters with a flourish. "Like Lady Zin and the Countess of Hurun. With the right people on our side, we could rebuild Kisia to be something greater. A society where war isn't the sole ideal we build our identity upon, where culture and learning are valued over division and death."

The words sucked the breath from my body and I stared at her, wrangling with an uncomfortable squirm of emotion. She spoke with such fire, and I couldn't tell if I was more envious of her mind, ashamed of my own failings, or grateful for her guidance. What an empress she would have been to Tanaka had history taken a different course.

"Oh, there's a letter from Edo here," Sichi said, breaking the awkward pause that had followed her impassioned speech. "And there's one sealed with plain wax. It's for you."

Someone had written my name but in a childish hand, and I couldn't think who it could be. Glad to escape our conversation, I broke the seal and unfolded it, sliding my gaze down the page of ragged Kisian to the bottom where breath hitched in my chest. Tor.

*Your Majesty,*

*Please forgive my not good writing. I am learning. I write when I have watched the camp of the Chiltaens and Leo Villius after retreat. They have remained not leave. If you want them not in your land you are lacking time to be gone of them. Many more are coming. Your army is largest now. Not later.*

*Eshenha surveid.*

*Tor*

And that was it. What more had I expected? Some acknowledgement of the awkward way we had parted? Some sentiment?

Truly it was kind of him to write at all, considering how much I had demanded again and again.

That the Chiltaens remained was not news, but that more were on their way? Did he mean the men coming with the secretary of the Nine to sign the treaty? Or others still? Warning Manshin would be admitting I had contacts outside what he controlled and play right into his hands.

I lowered Tor's letter to find Sichi watching me, a small crease between her brows. "What is it?" I said, suddenly breathless. "What's wrong? What's happened?"

"Oh no, nothing, I just..." She held out a letter. "Edo wrote to warn of his impending arrival, and I've...I've had a thought, Miko. You don't want to marry Leo, but marriage can make strong alliances, and marrying someone else would ensure my father can't marry you to Leo—"

"I don't want to marry anyone, Sichi."

"Hear me out, Koko. To marry someone else now while promised to Leo Villius, you would have to marry someone who isn't afraid of my father." Sichi grimaced. "Or of Chiltae. Someone who wouldn't shrink from spitting in Dom Villius's face and risking further war."

My thoughts slid toward Rah. He always did what was right no matter the cost and cared nothing for our power structures, but marriage to him was as impossible as marriage to a songbird. He'd made it clear his heart lay with his people.

"And I cannot but notice," Sichi went on with a brief smile, "that Edo meets every one of those criteria."

"Edo?" I stared, her words not fitting together in my mind.

"My cousin Edo," she said, speaking more slowly. "He meets all of the criteria and is probably the only man who wouldn't try to usurp your power or your position once you were married."

I had dreamed of marrying Edo for a long time, of keeping us all together, of being wanted. Seen. But he had loved Tanaka, and Tanaka had loved him, and all my childish hopes he would one day look at me had fallen somewhere along the way.

"He's on his way," Sichi continued. "Might even arrive today. You could ask him."

"I can't just...ask him to—"

"Yes, Koko, you can. He's been your friend all your life and you need him."

I shook my head. "No, I mean he's the Duke of Syan. He can't be a duke and an emperor, which would mean having to give the dukedom to another. And while I remain under Manshin's thumb, that other would be someone of his choosing."

Sichi bit her nail, sinking deep into thought. Still sitting on the window seat, Nuru fiddled with the hem of her tunic. Our comfortable space had grown tense, and I itched to leave, to move, to do something. Anything. The letters could wait.

I knelt, patting my leg to wake Shishi from her sun-drenched doze before the balcony doors. "Come, girl," I said as she got up and stretched, pushing her paws out in front of her. "We need to check on the army camp."

Sichi clicked her tongue, but left her thoughts unspoken, instead carrying her bundle of letters to the writing table. No doubt she wanted to point out again the foolishness of my focus on soldiers and armies, and I was glad she kept it to herself. Soldiers and armies were what I knew and, in a war, what we needed.

Taking my worries with me, I left them to one another's company and escaped with Shishi into the gardens and from there to the military camp, Captain Kiren a few steps behind me.

For the first time in many days the sun was shining, but a chill breeze gusting from the south stole its warmth. Whether due to the tunnelling wind or the eternal mud, army camps always seemed cold. The soldiers were keeping busy despite or perhaps because of the weather, each camp alive with training drills and all the other military things Manshin could order done in his sleep that I didn't even understand.

With Shishi loping along at my side, I strode into the nearest camp, following Emperor Kin's protocol of always being seen amongst his soldiers. Despite my frequent visits, soldiers and servants alike stopped to bow and murmur "Your Majesty" as I passed, keeping their distance.

"Your Majesty," General Moto said, approaching with more ease than a traitor ought to possess. "What brings you out here to the mud and the sweat?"

"General," I returned coolly. "Surely your spies have informed you that I walk through the camps every day. I would ask what you want, but unless it's to beg forgiveness for committing treason against me, I'll be on my way."

The words owned more heat than was wise, but at least he had the grace to look guilty, even for just a moment. But he made no excuses and attempted no explanation, and that at least I could respect. A murmur of "Your Majesty," and he let me go.

From the ranks of General Moto's soldiers into General Rushin's, I strode through the camps speaking to all who crossed my path, making a show of my existence before moving on toward the tents of the barbarian generals.

As was their way, I found General Yass and General Alon keeping busy, comfortably mixing with even their lowest-ranked soldiers. General Alon had his sleeves rolled up and was sweating through a training bout with a young recruit, while General Yass stood nearby answering all problems brought to him like an emperor seeing petitioners.

"Your Majesty," he said, respect in the title but never awe. "Not just passing through today? To what do we owe this pleasure?"

"A very courtly formality, General," I said.

"It seems apt given the amount of politics happening around here. Are you aware you're being followed? I know all my soldiers and two men who do not belong in this camp are watching you."

By his tone, he might have said something entirely mundane. "I was unaware but am unsurprised. I am watched wherever I go, so be sure to look displeased that I am interrupting your work."

"That's not difficult. Most Kisians think we always look angry. What can I do for you?"

"You can tell me whether you fight for me or for Minister Manshin."

A bold question, but they'd always responded best to honesty.

General Yass turned to look at his fellow general as he caught a training blade upon his shield, filling the air with a reverberant clang. "The situation is difficult," he said, not taking his eyes off the bout. "We need not pretend you don't lack power, and that being the case we cannot risk an outright declaration of support. It would be a death wish, and as much as General Alon and I do not like to dissemble, we have to think of our men."

"And were the situation different?" I said. "If I had more power? More allies? What then?"

"That would depend upon the allies, Your Majesty. And upon..." A moment's silence and I couldn't breathe, anxiety pouring into me until at last he turned back. "Unfortunately, the situation seems..." His gaze flicked over my shoulder to the spies who'd followed me. "Complicated. All I can assure you of is our mutual...dislike...of our esteemed minister of the left and our desire to rid Kisia of Chiltaens rather than bargaining with them."

It was the closest I was going to get to a declaration of support, and it was both enough to make relieved tears prick my eyes and not nearly enough to change anything.

I thanked him and would have left upon the words, but General

Yass had cocked his head in the direction of the chatter growing around us. "What's going on, soldier?" he said, turning to one of his men.

"Bahain flags have been sighted, General."

General Yass grunted, noncommittal. "Interesting development." He threw a sidelong look my way. "Your allies, Your Majesty? Or his?"

"Mine," I said, hoping it was true. Edo and I hadn't parted on the best terms after the battle of Kogahaera, but we would always be the only piece of Tanaka each of us had left.

———————✦———————

Edo stood where Lord Gori had that morning, but he didn't kneel. He spoke no oath. He had understood the hastily scrawled warning I'd sent him—there was no loyalty to me here, only to Manshin.

Beside me, the minister lifted his chin. "Nephew," he said, reminding Edo who had seniority, that here he was but a child. "Your oath?"

There were only guards to witness Edo lift his chin in return. "I'm afraid as Duke of Syan and commander of the fleet, I cannot yet give my oath, *Uncle*. Not without understanding the nature of the alliance you are forging with Chiltae."

How Tanaka would have grinned to see Edo standing so tall and speaking with such assurance, and talking back to someone who was not only the highest power in the land but also an elder of his own family.

Minister Manshin drew himself up, his long intake of breath betraying annoyance. "It is not your place to demand such—"

"With all due respect, Your Excellency," Edo interrupted, "it is my job to ensure the safety of Syan and its people. We need not pretend I can't maintain my land and title without imperial support, as my father did for many years. I do not wish to follow in his shadow, but many of my men fought and died at Kogahaera, *against* the Chiltaens. Chiltaens who still have a substantial military presence within our borders and who are led by a man who doesn't die. Under such circumstances, I cannot give my oath to an empress who would ally herself to them through marriage." His stare slid my way. "We need also not pretend you don't need my army and my ships, so I require a plain answer."

"To what question?" Manshin said, and ice could have formed on the words.

"To the question of what in all the hells you think you're doing to let Her Majesty make such an alliance, Minister."

At my side, Manshin flinched, and it was all I could do not to grin. By the gods, Tanaka would have loved this.

"How dare you stand there and show such disrespect," Manshin said. "You bring disgrace upon our family with your words."

Despite his assurance, Edo flushed. "That isn't an answer, Your Excellency. Leo Villius is Kisia's greatest threat, not someone Her Majesty ought to marry."

"Then it is as well that I have absolutely no intention of marrying him," I said, unsure if I was glad or sorry we had no audience. "And absolutely no intention of signing a treaty with Chiltae."

Buoyed by Edo's powerful presence, I said it as much to see what Manshin would do as because I meant it. By my shoulder, Manshin's hand clenched into a fist—a moment of anger he released with a low laugh. "Very amusing, Your Majesty," he said. "It is clear we are getting nowhere here. This situation would be better served by removing to discuss your...reservations...over tea. Nephew."

Edo bowed. "By all means. Uncle. Allow me to change out of my dirty travel attire, and I shall be ready to discuss the terms of my agreement with Her Majesty."

Manshin didn't rise to the bait, letting both the suggestion of dictating terms and the assumption I would be present slide, his anger covered with a thin smile. "Excellent. It seems we have much to discuss."

It had felt good to make such a declaration, but I didn't doubt Manshin's ability to get his way even if it meant employing threats or risking the rebellion of Edo's soldiers by imprisoning him. I had to warn him, so once we had left the throne room, I doubled back in search of my oldest friend. He seemed to have had the same idea, for instead of retreating to his rooms to change, Edo stood admiring the art in one of the narrower passages off the main hallway. At sight of him, I nodded to Captain Kiren and swept in, bearing an unprotesting Edo into the closest room—a small waiting room by the lack of furnishings.

"I got your message," he said by way of greeting as the good captain slid the door closed behind us, his silhouette a vague outline through the paper panes. "What is Manshin thinking?"

"I don't know, but you have to be careful with him," I whispered. "I have no power. The generals are all on his side, and he has much of the court fooled that I am the one giving orders while he merely advises. Thank you for what you did in there, but tread gently from here; I fear he has come too far now to easily turn back and will remove anyone in his way."

"It's unlikely my complaint will achieve anything unless I follow through with my threats." Edo grimaced. "He doesn't take me seriously. To him, I'm still a child, still the weak young man who fell in love with the man his daughter was meant to marry." Edo pressed a weak smile between his lips. "How angry he would have been the day I married him instead."

"You? But how?"

I'd meant to stay only a few moments, but the grief twisting Edo's smile caught me where I stood. "Before Tanaka..." Edo said only to trail off, and for a moment the ghost of my brother stood with us, all confident and sure and beloved. "Before Tanaka died," he tried again, a small tremor in his voice. "We had plans. We had hoped to be able to put off his marriage to Sichi long enough… We'd spent ages poring over files pulled from the archives, looking at legal precedents and buried marriage documents, and we found two emperors who had married men. Emperor Liu in—"

"You were going to marry Tanaka." It was a truth so obvious I felt like a fool. Yet they had never told me. Never trusted me.

"Yes. That was the plan, not that it can happen now."

He tried to force a smile, but I wasn't so much staring at him as through him, an idea sparking in my mind like it had always been there, waiting. He'd been going to marry Tanaka. There were precedents.

"Koko? Are you all right?"

Outside the door, Captain Kiren coughed, sending my heart into my throat. "Yes, yes," I said, squeezing Edo's arm. "I'm fine, but I have to go. I'm sorry."

I sped for the door. The captain slid it open and closed it behind me swift and quiet, but whatever threat neared, the narrow passage was, for now, empty. With my mind buzzing, I paid no heed to the direction I walked, but out of a mixture of habit and hope, I found myself making for the small shrine. Though I passed people who stopped to bow and murmur, it was all a daze, my thoughts a tangle of half-formed plans and a new, searing hope. Perhaps there was a way forward after all.

The shrine sat at the end of a quiet passage, and though it was unlikely more letters would have arrived in the course of the afternoon, I slid the door open anyway. Again the waft of incense and the flickering of candle flames. Folded prayers sat upon the altar, everything how I had left it except for the cupboard. Its door hung open, the previously neat contents a jumble.

"Looking for something, Your Majesty?"

I spun. Minister Manshin filled the passage, towering over me. I swallowed hard. "I—"

Manshin's fingers closed around my arm, digging into my flesh as he forced me back into the dim space of the shrine. The door slid closed with a bang, leaving only lantern light illuminating Manshin's snarl. "Always in my way," he hissed, spit peppering my face. "Don't you know when to give up, little girl? Anyone else would be grateful to have such a position, such wealth and freedom and none of the responsibilities, but not you, not the damn Otakos obsessed with power."

"Freedom?" I laughed, the sound wild. "I have nothing but—"

"This is not a discussion. This is a warning. Your last warning." He leaned closer, his breath hot upon my face and his fingertips seeming to carve holes in my flesh. "If you value the lives of your... *friends*...you will stop this. I will kill my own daughter if I have to. I will take joy in ending her barbarian friend. I will make sure you marry Dom Villius even if I have to drag you to the ceremony in chains—don't think I won't. You know me better than that."

I could hardly breathe, panic compressing my chest. I wanted to run, to call for help, but I could not move. He filled my world, my future, his height and strength and heat like an assault I couldn't escape. Fear and hate were all I had, and lacking words, I spat in his face.

Manshin flinched but did not let go, just glared silently at me while my spit slowly trailed down his cheek. Unblinking, he released my arm finger by finger and stepped back. His grim stare was no less threatening for the space growing between us. Having slid open the door, Manshin stepped aside for me to leave. "Don't make me your enemy," he said, the words almost calm—fatherly. "This is your last chance, Miko Ts'ai."

I sped out, needing to get away, to escape him, to breathe. Footsteps followed, but when I spun it was only Captain Kiren.

Manshin remained in the doorway to watch my departure, his expression smug and self-satisfied even as he wiped my spit from his cheek with one sleeve.

All that went through my mind as I hurried back to my rooms was that I had to get away from him. Fighting back tears, I flew through the door to my apartments. Nuru looked up from her book. Sichi dropped her letter. Neither was even halfway across the floor before my legs buckled and I fell to my knees. "Edo is here," I said, the words sounding nothing like my voice. "He stood up to your father, but...but he will force my hand by threatening you or by hauling me chained to the altar."

Their joined outcry was little more than a murmur beneath the hammering of my heart. But Manshin's threats had only intensified the spark Edo's words had lit, turning a flicker to a flare. I looked up at Sichi. "I have a plan," I said. "That will protect all of us and make sure they can't take power from our hands."

"What is it?" she whispered, eyes bright.

"Sichi..." I swallowed hard. "Will you marry me?"

2. RAH

It's harder to sever a head than people think, and even harder to feed a hungry Swordherd. Make half of them strangers, some wounded and all angry, and you may as well accept failure as inevitable before you begin. But if I'd been called one thing over the years, it was a stubborn bastard.

So there I sat in a tree, arse numb in the last of the daylight. We had slowly gotten used to the habits of the Kisian animals—the impatient call of the whistling owl, the rising buzz of evening insects, and the crepuscular scurry of the creatures we called *bunnyhounds*, somewhere between a sand cat and a rabbit in size with a long snout. They had the most meat but were hard to track, leaving us having to spread out and wait.

Perched upon a nearby branch, Shenyah wriggled, sending the leaves dancing. She was our youngest Sword, and I felt a degree of responsibility for her I couldn't shake. Guilt, perhaps, over Dishiva. Or Juta. Or all of them.

Something rustled in the undergrowth, and a pig snuffled out, snout to the mud. I readied my javelin, only for the pig to turn back into the bush, leaving only a single trotter visible. Gideon would have been able to get it in the back of the head even through the leaves, but all I could be sure of getting was its rump. Sending a pig squealing off with my javelin stuck in its butt was not a sure way to keep my Swords' respect.

An arrow dove through the leaves, and the pig let out a distressed squeal, thrashing in the undergrowth. Shenyah dropped from her tree with a thud and strode over, bow in hand.

"Pig thief," I said as I dropped to join her. "I had my eye on that one."

"You just wanted to watch it, Captain? That isn't the way I was taught to hunt." The skin around her eyes crinkled, but I felt the rebuke all the same.

"It's a special new technique I'm working on. I call it the death stare."

Shenyah laughed as she dragged the dying animal out of the bushes, tearing the arrow from its neck with quick, practiced movements. "I think maybe it needs more work. By the looks of this pig, the arrow killed it."

"You did well; you're a credit to your training captain."

Mention of Dishiva stole Shenyah's smile, and she sheathed the bow. Dishiva's bow, I recalled, the Jaroven captain having left most of her weapons behind when she'd gone...wherever she had gone.

"Thank you, Captain." Shenyah saluted. "I'll take the pig back to camp now."

I returned the salute and called in the rest of my Swords with a whistle. Distant footfalls grew to a rhythm as my new Swords approached through the trees, not one of them having come to these shores with me.

"It's getting dark," I said as they gathered in the fast-spreading gloom. "Let's head back and get the carcasses cleaned up."

———————◆———————

Once the evening meal was prepared, Amun gathered the Hand. One by one I had lost mine, but their ghosts always sat with me as I watched for hints of dissent, for whispers and troubled looks.

All had been quiet at first, the Levanti who had joined me happy to recover, to be idle and lick their wounds, tend their horses, and just...be. Now they were getting restless.

Amun had been an easy choice as my second; after that, Lashak e'Namalaka, once a First Sword, was named tracker, Diha e'Bedjuti our healer, and Loklan e'Jaroven our horse master. Together, the five of us sat close to the fire. They had brought their meals but were too used to my habits to ask why I wasn't eating with them. Unfortunately, Shenyah had taken to bringing over my plate, though she knew I wouldn't take it. Whether she continued out of a staunch refusal to deviate from our ways or in silent judgement of Gideon's presence in the camp, I wasn't sure.

"We can keep this short tonight," I said, meeting each of their gazes. "Lashak, have your scouts brought any news?"

She licked her fingers and nodded, still chewing. "Nothing exciting or you'd have heard already, but there's still no sign that Dom Villius intends to move, and for some reason the Kisians are still leaving him and his soldiers alone. On the Kisian side, a flood of riders come and go from Kogahaera constantly, and a new group of soldiers arrived today. They're keeping themselves separate and are carrying Bahain banners, so it could be Grace Bahain's son... whatever his name was." She shrugged. "So in short, they're all still keeping to themselves like a bunch of sand cats watching each other through the grass."

"Can't last," Diha said, wiping her fingers on her healer's cloth. "We might not know much about them, but it seems Kisians and Chiltaens can't share the same space for long without ripping each other's throats out. Maybe that new group of Chiltaens will be the spark."

"New group of Chiltaens?" I asked.

"Mentioned them last night, Captain," Lashak said, censure in her glance. "They're led by Secretary Aurus. I understand from the others that Gideon met with him some weeks ago. Although for a man intending only to discuss a peace treaty, he's stayed a long time and now has more soldiers than he did before."

"Oh yes, him. He's moving?"

"Seems to be."

I closed my eyes a moment, wishing something could be simple, just once. "We'd better keep a close watch on them. The moment something turns we need to know. In the meantime, we need a plan to reach Leo if he's not going to budge from inside those walls."

Diha leaned forward. "Just poison their water. Then they're all dead."

"That," Lashak said, grinning at her, "is a great idea. I like the sound of all dead."

"Except we need to talk to him before we kill him," I reminded them.

"Don't worry, he'll come back to life, and then he'll be the only one alive in the camp. Easy." Diha returned Lashak's grin and the woman snorted. "Oops, was that a terrible thing for a healer to say?"

"Since we can't be sure that would actually work," I said, interrupting before they could get too caught up in their plan, "we'll have to think of something else."

Loklan often sat silently watching us while he ate, but tonight he cleared his throat to speak. "We're staying to find out about these Entrancers before we go back, I know, and it's important, but…" He paused, looking around the suddenly still group. "With all respect, Captain, do you really think he will just…tell us everything we want to know? He was—*is* no friend of ours."

He wasn't, but I remembered a different man. One who had wanted the best for those around him. Who had offered us freedom. It had cost so much, but it had felt real. And though I couldn't say so, I felt sure that although he might not tell them, he would tell me. He owed me that much.

"We have to try," I said instead. "The only other person who knows of them is Ezma, and I wouldn't trust her not to stick a blade in my eye, let alone be honest about something she doesn't want me to change."

Mumbled agreement went around the circle, smiles gone. They were in accord, at least for now, but I had watched my Hand fracture once, watched Swords turn on me, and I knew the signs. I was running out of time.

"So...we keep watching?" Amun said, breaking the silence. "And hope to catch him as he's leaving to...do whatever it is that priests do."

"Pray?"

"I think he can do that inside the walls, Diha."

The healer shrugged. "I still think poisoning—"

"Any updates on our supplies, Amun?" I said.

Diha grinned and took up her dinner as all eyes turned to Amun. "The rice and beans we traded for last week will keep us going another week, and enough meat comes in each day for now. But the foragers are reporting the area is nearly cleared of mushrooms and berries and those purple tubers shaped like—well, anyway, they're having to go farther afield each day, and I'm concerned that remaining much longer may not be an option."

"It's getting cold too," Loklan added. "We ought to be stockpiling if we mean to stay through winter. Food will get scarce, especially for the horses."

For a moment we all stared at our hands or our meals, while around us the camp went cheerfully on, our worry allowing others to be at ease.

"We ought to leave before the snow falls," Lashak said. "We spent last winter here and it was terrible. The water freezes over and there's nothing to eat." She spat on the ground. "To think we were almost glad when the Chiltaens found us because at least they had food."

"How long do you think we have left?" Amun asked, his plate sitting abandoned by his foot. "We"—he looked to me—"haven't wintered here. We came after."

Diha gave a little snort, but left Lashak to say, "I don't know. It was colder than this. Much colder. And then one day there was snow on the ground. It was pretty and we didn't hate the little falls."

"But it just kept falling," Diha said.

"You suggest we stockpile supplies and..." Amun glanced at me again, and I knew he wanted to finish the sentence himself, to suggest going home, but loyalty kept the words caught behind his teeth.

"And make for the coast as soon as the first snow falls," Lashak finished for him. "To stay would be dangerous for us and our horses."

Diha nodded. "Some are already saying we should go. That we've been here long enough to care for our injured and our horses and it's time." I made to speak, but she shrugged at me and added, "Not all of them believe in Entrancers, Captain. Or want revenge. And those who do, want revenge against Chiltae, not Leo. Or against Gideon for leading them astray."

Every meeting I tried to avoid this discussion, but every meeting his name came up all the same. "Everyone who chose to follow Gideon must have believed in what he was trying to do," I said as calmly as I could. "If they want revenge for its failure, it's Leo they should hate."

"*We* know that."

"Everyone knows that. Everyone has been told what happened."

Diha grimaced and flicked a glance at Amun as though in

apology. "Knowing doesn't always help when what they lived—what *we* lived—was Gideon failing us."

"And a false horse whisperer trying to use you."

"Don't bring Ezma into this, Captain," Diha snapped. "That she is a disgrace to the title she carries has nothing to do with Gideon's crimes. He does not look better by comparison and must be judged on his own failings."

She was right, but defending Gideon seemed to have become my daily existence. No one challenged me directly, but I saw the glances and the whispers and the wide emptiness around his hut, and over and over I chanted *If only you knew. If only it had been you.*

"You're right, Diha, and I apologise," I said, every one of my bones seeming to grow heavy, sinking me into the ground. "But destroying a man for something that wasn't his fault in the hope of excising grief will not strengthen us."

Diha looked at the ground. Amun at the trees. Lashak and Loklan at their hands. I had brushed through the conversation this time, but next time might not be so easy. The knowledge I would soon have to make a choice between helping my people and helping Gideon squeezed a little tighter.

"If there is nothing else for now, we can meet again tomorrow evening hopefully with some ideas," I said, getting to my feet with more speed than dignity.

"There is one more thing, Captain," Diha said. "We lost Ruhm today. His wounds just wouldn't heal, and fever took him while you were out with the hunt. He's by the shrine."

Not how I had wanted to end my day, but I nodded. "I'll go now. Thank you, Diha."

We broke up, the others taking their half-finished meals and ambling off into the camp to talk and sing and be as joyful as the chill air and the strange surroundings would allow. I buried my envy. It wasn't like I would have been joining them, dead Sword or no.

Ruhm had been laid out before the shrine, little bunches of wilted flowers and sticks carved with prayers placed around him. A lump swelled in my throat at this reminder of home, and for an instant I wanted to shout at everyone to pack because we were leaving, but the reins home kept tightly knotted around my heart had squeezed before and would again. I had to push away the pain with the silent promise of soon. Soon I would go home, when I'd completed the last of my duties here.

I knelt on the cold ground and heaved a sigh, pulling Ruhm's body toward me. Shoulders on my knees. Knees apart. Knife in hand. Not mine, but a Levanti blade, owned by someone who no longer needed it.

Blood oozed out with the first incision, dropping onto the ground. So often had I performed the task that I could let my hands work while my mind wandered, catching snatches of conversation and scents upon the air. The smell of dinner was still present beneath the tang of blood, and despite my current occupation, my stomach grumbled.

At last, Ruhm's head came free, and I let his body slide gently back onto the ground. We would build a pyre in the morning, but for now I got to my feet, knees and ankles aching as I straightened.

Before the shrine, I knelt again to sing our lament. Prayers came next, drawing the gaze of our gods to this Sword who had given his life for his herd and ought to be rewarded with new life. But though it was Ruhm I farewelled, it was Gideon I thought of. I had knelt two days at the Motepheset Shrine to grieve when he hadn't returned from exile. It had broken me more than I had ever admitted, and I never wanted to do it again.

Once finished, I made my way back through the camp, each fire owning a clump of chatting Swords. Amun was deep in conversation around one. Loklan was playing a game of Tiyat against Shenyah at another, the board scratched into the dirt. And Lashak and Diha had their arms wrapped around one another, laughing. Through it all I passed like a ghost, trailed by murmurs of "Captain."

The village of Kuroshima had been all but deserted, yet still we'd chosen to camp in the trees to the north where clusters of long-abandoned buildings spoke of a time the village had been larger. The roofs had needed patching, and we'd had to make do with what tents we'd had with us, but day by day it looked more worthy of being called a camp, spreading out in every direction save one.

Having grabbed two bowls of cold food from beside the cooking coals, I left the chatter behind and made my way toward the lonely hut. Faint light trembled through its narrow linen-hung windows, but despite the appearance of life, my heart hammered as it always did, afraid of what I would find. Too well could I recall his strong, desperate grip as he tried to prise the blade from my hands, tried to force it to his throat. It had been many days since, yet the image lived behind my eyes and I could not shake it.

Scuffing my feet to give warning of my arrival, I pushed through the damp fabric that did duty as a door. Gideon sat against the wall beside the dying fire but didn't look up from the piece of wood in his hands, slowly taking shape.

"Dinner," I said, crossing my ankles and sinking onto the floor in front of him. "It's cold. Sorry. I had to take Ruhm's head before I came."

He kept scraping away curls of wood. I hadn't wanted to give him a knife, but they were everywhere in the camp, and at least carving seemed to occupy his hands if not his mind.

"The mushrooms look good tonight," I said, lifting my bowl. "Slightly browner than last night, but not as brown as the night before. Or the one before that. Really, though, the mushrooms from the night before the night before that were the best. I won't tell Ptoth though. He likes to think he's a really good cook, but Dhamara is better."

He seemed intent on ignoring me, which at least meant I could stare at him as I ate. He hadn't shaved his head since we'd left Koga-haera, and his dark brown hair was just long enough now to own a hint of copper. As a saddleboy it had been long, a dark brown with glints of deep russet best seen in the sun. The firelight on one side of his face brought out tiny flecks, and I was grateful that although time had changed much, it hadn't changed that. What a foolish, tiny thing to cling to.

"You should have eaten with the Hand," he said, as he often did, this interchange as habitual as Shenyah's continuous attempt to bring me my meal.

"Eating and talking at the same time isn't easy. Better to wait."

I made a different excuse each time, but at this one he glanced up, a flicker of humour in his expression. "You seem to be doing just fine with both right now."

Such flashes of life kept me believing he had a future.

"True," I said. "Next time I should eat with the Hand and opine about the brown mushrooms."

He looked at the meal. "They are very brown. You don't have to stay."

"I know."

Setting his knife aside, he took up the bowl and looked through me. There were dark circles beneath his eyes and a slight tremble in his limbs, but worst was the blank, dead way he would sometimes sit staring at nothing, unmoving. I wished I could draw him out to sit by the fire, sure community would help, but these walls weren't only protecting the others from his existence, they also protected Gideon from all that hate.

Once I finished my meal, I took up some of the wood I'd piled in the corner and threw it on the fire. "It's bitter in here," I said, hunting around for a blanket. "And to think it's meant to get colder. What's snow like?"

Gideon looked up. "Cold."

"Oh really? Well, that is a surprise. I thought it would be hot."

"It does burn. Ice too. When you stick your hands in it." He lowered his bowl. "You know that feeling when you've been riding in a chill wind and your fingers feel fat and stiff? And when you try to warm them up, they tingle and burn? It feels like that. And it... crunches."

"Crunches? Like... coals?"

"Yes, but more slippery. The first winter I slipped onto my arse and had one of those deep yellow bruises for days."

I pulled blankets out of the pile around our sleeping mats and threw one to Gideon before wrapping another around my shoulders, not caring that it smelt musty. Standing directly in front of the fire, I wondered if I would ever be truly warm again.

Gideon pushed the unfinished bowl of food aside, ignoring the blanket.

"Don't make me put that blanket over you myself," I said.

"I'm not cold."

"Horseshit. I've been busy and I'm cold."

I crouched in front of him and grabbed both his hands, and it was like clasping chill lumps of metal. "Gods, Gideon, you're colder than cold. Here, come closer to the fire."

"I'm fine."

He resisted my attempt to pull him up, and I made a show of sniffing myself. "Do I smell that bad?"

"Like death."

"Ah, good strong Levanti scent then. Come on, let's—"

"No." He thrust out a shaking hand. "Just leave me. Please."

"Gideon, I'm not going anywhere. I didn't last night. Or the night before. Or the night before that."

"Even though the mushrooms weren't as brown."

I laughed at the unexpected flash of humour and pulled him to his feet. Overbalancing, he stumbled into me, and for a moment the space between us shrank to nothing. There his scent, his warmth, his presence, reminding me not only of old memories, but of new ones. Raw ones. When he had hissed his anger into my face after the massacre at Tian. When he had sat upon a throne and ordered me removed from his sight. When he had kissed my forehead and said goodbye, that his last warning not to get in his way again.

The room felt colder when I stepped back, an apology spilling cheerfully from my lips as he steadied himself and let me throw the blanket around his shoulders. His flash of humour was gone, but at least he was upright.

"We should shave your hair," I said.

"No." Gideon crushed his arms around himself like armour.

"It's getting long for a Sword."

He shrank back, seeming to retreat to that safer place inside himself. "I'm not a Sword anymore."

"Once a Sword, always a Sword," I said. "I can do it for you."

"I said no, Rah."

His hands shook, and as he backed against the wall, I realised I had pushed too hard, tried to be too helpful, too caring, too *much*. "All right," I said, giving him space. "Your hair is lovely as it is."

Surely the stupidest thing I had said so far, but at least it surprised him enough that he glared at me instead of descending into a panic attack. "What?"

"The red. I missed it." I *had* missed it. It connected me to a past we could never reclaim, a boyhood long gone. A time when there had been no estrangement between us, no tension, no unspoken words, no wrongs, and no Leo.

Letting the conversation drop, I knelt to lay out our sleeping mats. No proximity to the fire would render the night comfortable, but I edged the mats as close as I dared and hoped one day, I would feel warm again.

"Are you trying to light us on fire?"

"No," I said. "But I'm sick of being cold and damp. I hate it."

Once I had finished I found him watching me. "You don't have to stay," he said again.

"You tell me that a lot."

"Because I know you're not here because you care," he said, tightening his arms over his chest. "You're here because it's who you are. Because you're always right. Always responsible and virtuous, and I'd rather not have to be grateful for being a burden you suffer through for your own righteousness."

"What?" I flinched like he'd slapped me. "What is this horse-shit? Responsible and perfect? That's you, you fool. I'm the one who ran away from my responsibilities and brought shame to the Torin, remember?"

"Because you wanted to serve your herd," he snorted.

"Because I wanted a life! Because I was selfish! But sure, you put me on whatever pedestal you like so you can punch yourself with my fist."

Gideon stared at me, hints of emotion flitting across his face. My blood pumped too hot and fast and angry to wonder how he felt, and I kicked off my boots so hard they flew across the room.

"I'm sorry you feel like a burden," I snapped. "But I'm here because I want to be. That isn't the same as this being fun."

I wasn't being fair, but neither was he, and in the absence of magic there was no easy fix for this. With a sigh, I went and wrapped my arms around him. He didn't return the embrace, but he stood at ease and let me hold him, and that was all right. "It'll get better," I said by his ear, the same softness with which he had once threatened me. "I know it doesn't seem like it but it will. And I will be here. Because I fucking choose to be here, not out of some sick need to be right about everything."

"Thank you," he said like they were the hardest two words he had ever spoken.

I squeezed tight before letting him go.

We settled on our mats, him silent while I made overly dramatic shivering sounds as though it would help. It was still too fucking cold despite the crackle and roar of the fire, but exhaustion soon tugged me into sleep, lulled by Gideon's even breathing. It was a comforting sound. I should have told him that, perhaps. Told him I felt safe here with him. That his very existence made me feel lighter, despite the tangle of doubts and worries and hurts that came with it. Whatever he had done, whatever he had said, whoever he had been, he was still, and always would be, the Gideon I had looked up to, had followed, had worshipped and relied on. The Gideon I would do anything for.

———————◆———————

I woke feeling I had been covered in cold sand, so completely had the room chilled. Gideon was still asleep, curled upon himself to keep warm.

Voices murmured outside. Hushed. Worried. It was too early for anyone to be setting off on a hunt, and the scouts ought to have been back in the night, so when the low talk became a growing, anxious babble, I reluctantly got up, thrusting my feet into my boots and dragging my blanket with me toward the door.

Ghostly figures filled the centre of the camp, and catching sight of me through the misty dawn, Amun hurried over. He must have been halfway through shaving his head, the smooth half shimmering with damp. "Ezma is on her way."

Even as he spoke, I caught sight of Derkka en'Injit standing beside the main fire. He lifted his hand in a little wave, and every part of me seared hot with anger.

"Why is he here?" I demanded in a low voice. "Ezma is dangerous and so is he."

"I know, but unless you want us to kill them, we can hardly stop either setting foot in the camp."

I sighed, relaxing my grip on the blanket. "Do we know what she wants?"

"Derkka wouldn't say, but"—he gestured toward the trees— "you can ask her yourself."

Usually a herd travelled to a horse whisperer, but on the occasions a horse whisperer travelled to a herd, they did so alone. Not Ezma. She rode into our camp with a dozen Swords in her wake, the headpiece atop her gathered hair rising like a crown while a fine orange robe did service as a travelling cloak. She approached as slowly as her horse would carry her, chin lifted, giving my Swords plenty of time to emerge from their tents to stare.

Thrusting my blanket into Amun's hands, I strode forward to stand in front of her horse. "Ezma," I said, clasping my hands behind my back to make it clear she would get no salute from me.

She reined in closer than was comfortable, the animal's proximity as much a threat as her cold smile. "Rah," she said. "Still here, I see."

"Still here. What do you want?"

"Is that an invitation to dismount and meet with you without risk?"

"If you feel you need that assurance, but your companions cannot." I gestured to the Swords mounted behind her. "I'll have no believers in your god spreading their lies here."

Her smile hardened. "They aren't believers, but if you won't offer hospitality to your own people, so be it." Turning to her closest Sword, she said, "Remain here. Keep your eyes open; it appears this is…unfriendly territory."

Our meeting fire was nothing but cold coals at this time of day, but not wishing to meet anywhere more private, I strode over and sat down in my customary position. A position I ought to have offered her, but she was already lucky I hadn't given in to my impulse to piss on her.

"What do you want?" I repeated as she settled across from me, folds of orange cloth grazing the dirt.

"Gideon." She smiled with her teeth. "You have him. I want him."

"You tried to kill him."

"I was merely seeing justice done, as is required of me."

"No, you cannot take him or anyone else nor dispense any justice here. You are false in every way and don't deserve to be called Levanti, let alone a whisperer."

She laughed, a mocking sound full of genuine amusement. "Will you ever stop being angry that I completed my apprenticeship and you did not? Refusing me my title will not gain you yours."

"I don't want to be a horse whisperer. Better that I left than stayed to twist it into something it's not." I gestured at the Swords still mounted and awaiting her. "Like you with your honour guards. If your only reason for coming here was to parade around and demand Gideon, you have wasted your time."

"And you have condemned your people."

A creeping horror spread through me. "What?"

"I've had word the Chiltaens are blockading the ports. They want Gideon, and you know very well to what lengths they will go for what they want, even if it means killing every Levanti seeking passage across the sea." She folded her arms. "So, it's a simple choice, Rah. Let them take their revenge on Gideon, or watch them kill your people. Again."

Ezma's smile was all too pleased. Around us, Swords watched on from a distance, whispering, waiting, and all I could do was force a smile through my rage. How fine those words must have tasted in her mouth.

"You need to go," I hissed between my teeth. "You ought to be ashamed for even considering such a thing. We don't trade in lives. The Chiltaens don't deserve my horse's shit, let alone a live sacrifice of one of our own, no matter who they are."

"Would you say the same if it was me they wanted?"

"Yes. As tempting as it would be to save people from your influence."

"Funny, because that's exactly what many of my Swords say about Gideon. And you. But you know what, Rah, it's not your choice anyway. It's Gideon's, and I'm sure once you explain he can redeem himself and his honour by dying for his people, he'll—"

I stood abruptly to keep from smashing my fist into her face. "Go. Now. Take your poisonous tongue away."

She rose, all grace and dignity and ease under the watchful gazes of my Swords. "Very well, I will go for now, but if you don't reconsider, if Gideon does not make the honourable sacrifice, I will have no choice but to force your hand."

"A threat? Leave before I have you dragged from my camp."

Ezma adjusted her headpiece, all smiles. "Oh, that would look good, wouldn't it? I'm tempted to stay so you can try it."

Determined to give her no satisfaction, I stood silent.

"No? Maybe if I told you that you're wasting your time here? Getting hold of Leo Villius is easy, but no matter what he tells you, you can't stop what's already happening."

"What *is* happening?"

Her lips twitched. "You'll have to try harder than that."

"Of course, because what would a powerless, exiled old whisperer know? Trapped out here, you're no one."

She leaned close, lowering her voice to a hiss. "I know the plains are changing forever. I know you're too late. You cannot fight people who possess powers you've never even heard of, but you can die trying. That seems like a fitting end for you. Maybe I should tell you how to get to Leo Villius after all."

I wanted to know—needed to know—but I would not beg. Not of her.

Her smile was back, spreading into a self-satisfied smirk. "You're too fun, Rah. Yes, I think I'll tell you after all. Dom Villius has been slowly making his way toward Kogahaera for the last few days, travelling with two companions acting as bodyguards. He travels at night and doesn't want to be found, but what Chiltaen could ever truly hide from Levanti tracking skills?"

"Travelling to Kogahaera? Why?"

Ezma shook her head. "That's all you get, Rah. Do consider my words wisely, however. I'm confident Gideon would appreciate the opportunity to redeem his soul."

No salute. No nod. Just a parting little laugh and she strode away, receiving salutes from my Swords as she went.

I didn't move from the fire pit until she was swallowed by the trees. Whispering broke out around me, but no one dared to approach until Amun came and stood before me, hands upon hips.

"What did she want?"

"To warn me the Chiltaens haven't forgiven us for the slaughter of their army," I said, which was true enough to assuage my twinge of guilt. "It's possible they will blockade ports or attack Levanti attempting to return home."

Amun drew a breath and let it out in a gust, the sound more exhausted than surprised. "Well, better to know, I suppose. Was that all? You didn't exactly look happy during the conversation."

The truth would get out. Ezma would expect me to lie, and Derkka had been here too long, yet the words I should have uttered stuck in my throat. "She wasn't exactly polite," I said instead. "She did, however, tell me where Leo is. It seems he's not in that army camp after all. He's travelling by night, making for Kogahaera."

"Kogahaera? You mean he could be nearby?"

"He could be. She wouldn't give me an exact location, but something tells me Lashak would enjoy the opportunity to flex her tracking skills."

Amun grinned and clapped a hand on my shoulder. "I think we all would—all the more because finding Leo means we can go home. Shall I have tracking parties prepared?"

"Yes, do it," I said. "Let's find the bastard and get out of here."

# 3. CASSANDRA

I had spent much of my adult life sleeping during the day, rolling over and ignoring shouts and hoofbeats and chatter, and the ever-present song of the dead. I hadn't expected sleep to be harder in silence.

*Damn country living,* I grumbled as Kaysa rolled, chasing sleep.

*Maybe I'm just not good at sleeping yet. I struggled at Manshin's house too.*

A breathy laugh emerged through my lips as she returned control to me, forcing me back to the bright evening. *It's not something you have to practice. You just . . . do it.*

*Or don't, in this case.*

I cracked open an eye. On the other side of the room, Unus lay curled upon his tattered mat, his holy robes discarded for a brownish half robe and breeches we'd found. The second mat was empty. My stomach dropped, and sleep having eluded me, I rolled over and got quietly to my feet.

The stairs creaked beneath my weight—the only sound in the house. We had come upon it in the predawn light, a small cottage bearing no sign of life. Dust had covered everything. Food had sat mouldy on the table. Without wondering what had become of the owners, we'd seen to our horses, hunted out mats, and collapsed into uneasy sleep.

Outside, birds chirped cheerfully in the last of the daylight. It would soon have been time to rise and prepare for another night's interminable journey anyway; I was merely getting a head start. I needed to piss. I needed a drink. I needed fresh air.

Unfortunately, the air outside was none too fresh. It held the bitter tang of distant smoke, mixed with stagnant water and the rotting food we'd thrown out that morning. I wrinkled my nose and hurried on toward the small, bushy garden fenced with rotting timbers. Overgrown vegetables and vines of some sort choked the space, and having gone far enough from the house, I crouched to piss—adding to the acrid scents of the evening.

Hana would have made some comment about growing up on a farm and having pissed in the fields with the boys. Or laughed at my desire for privacy despite my total lack of modesty at all other times. Kaysa was silent.

*I can't be her*, she said.

*I didn't ask you to be. I just . . .*

*Miss her.*

Bitterness. I had been cruel to Kaysa for so many years, but had grown so accustomed to Hana's presence, to sharing her body, that her loss had a physical emptiness. When I closed my eyes, I could still see her falling. Still hear the crunch as Septum hit the stones, leaving nothing but a mess.

Forcing the memory from my mind, I stood, straightened my breeches and half robe, and sighed. The fresh air had been a failure, the piss unexciting—time for water, and maybe I could face another night travelling.

A water barrel stood beside the house. It had overflowed, leaving puddles to grow stagnant around it, but the lid had kept the water inside reasonably clean. I prised it off. I'd not thought to bring out a cup so dug my hands in instead, slurping from the fast-escaping water until I was sated. Dropping the lid, I turned back toward the house.

And there he was, limned in evening light as though his bronze flesh had been gilded, his soft, dark hair ruffled in the breeze and that serious, thoughtful look on his face, all thick eyebrows and intense bright eyes. He'd had that same look when we'd unlocked his door back at Manshin's estate. I'd been in such a hurry to free him that I'd not thought about the strangeness of seeing him in the flesh, of being able to put a face to the voice I'd come to rely on hearing through the wall. He'd looked up from his bound hands, everything about him soft and beautiful and young. So young. He had been both more than I had hoped and everything I had feared, and a shameful sort of panic had held me rooted to the floor as he tilted his head and said—

"Cassandra?"

The same twisting, awful feeling weighed me down, and I halted, gazing up at Yakono standing on the veranda. He looked to have been taking some air when I interrupted him by existing.

"I didn't see you there."

A kind smile turned his lips. "I'm sorry. My training makes it second nature to blend in and be quiet."

While I had thudded my way down the stairs and scuffed along the path to the garden. Such a good assassin I was, announcing my presence to the world.

"Yes. You're really good at it," I said, and wanted to sink into the ground at how ridiculous I sounded.

*Do you need me to take over?*

"Thank you," Yakono said, genuinely seeming to mean it. "I worked hard. My master would tell you it didn't come naturally. He said I was a long-clawed hog when he first picked me up."

"You must have been good at other things. To make up for it."

"Oh no, nothing at all, truthfully."

It was just a conversation. There was no reason to panic, yet the thud of my heart would not quieten. I should have left him locked in that room. Or refused to travel with him, whatever our shared purpose. But I hadn't, and now I had to put up with feeling like a child, foolish and gangly and inferior in every way.

"He didn't choose you because you had a talent for your craft?" Kaysa asked, taking over rather than remaining stuck to the ground like a fool. "Surely you had something to recommend you."

"Nothing at all." Yakono shrugged. "My master picked me because I needed a home. Better to help someone who needs a family than give a second family to someone who already has one."

It was exactly the wholesome sort of thing he was always saying, leaving me feeling both in awe and awful.

Wallowing while Kaysa walked back up the stairs, I envied the ease with which she approached him. Spoke to him. Looked at him.

"Did you check the horses?"

Yakono nodded, his gaze ever intent. "We should leave soon."

"Not yet." Kaysa shook our head. "Let him sleep a little longer. He suffers. It takes a toll on one, that sort of pain of the mind."

A question seemed to hover upon Yakono's lips. Kaysa and I had lived a different form of the same abnormality, but I'd kept it secret so long, been called a freak and a monster so often that I couldn't tell him. Couldn't risk his kindness souring to dislike or disgust, or even horror, once he knew what we were. One thing to share an interest in killing people for money, something else entirely to know I could make the bodies get back up again.

"All right," he said, swallowing his question. "But if we don't leave soon, we may add another day to the journey."

He didn't need to say the sooner we finished this the better. It had been all I could do to convince him not to kill Unus on the spot, his desire to complete his contract all that kept him here. Had Unus been more like the Leo we were used to, I doubted he would have believed me, and Kaysa's fear we would turn our back only for

Yakono to stick a blade in Unus anyway was an ever-present fizzle in my stomach.

"We already have to travel slower now that we're close," he went on. "Every day we see more Levanti, and the Chiltaen camp isn't far enough behind us for comfort. If we aren't careful, we won't reach Her Majesty at all."

My stomach flip-flopped. Empress Miko. I had never met her, but now she existed in my heart as a precious child I needed to protect, the daughter I had failed. Even without Hana, the mess of hurts swirled and tugged at my heart with vicious hands, and I wished I had never fallen into her body, wished I could have gone on walking through the world without giving a damn about anyone. Caring hurt too much.

"Cassandra?"

His quiet concern had me back in that room, leaning against the wall as he told his story, the world slowly going dark. I had died alone, but had never felt less alone.

*You could tell him that.*

*No.*

"Are you all right?"

How many people had ever asked me that? So few. Even fewer who had actually cared about the answer. Yakono probably didn't care either, or if he did it was because his perfect upbringing had taught him to care about everyone like we were all special, fragile little bunnies.

"Fine," I said. "Just sick of travelling. And cold. And—"

A scream from the upper floor ripped through the air, and Yakono spun, dashing through the door and toward the stairs like a lithe animal.

"—him."

I didn't give a single damn about Unus, but Kaysa had us following Yakono in a heartbeat.

We found Unus sitting up, his arms folded tightly across his chest as he stared at the far wall like it had grown a monstrous face.

"You're safe," Yakono said, able to dredge up kindness even for this man who had kept him prisoner, who had tried to convert him to the faith, who he had every intention of killing. "There is no one here but us. You were dreaming."

"I saw him. I . . . I couldn't control it. It's hard when I'm sleeping, I'm sorry."

Kaysa knelt on the opposite side of his mat, the touch of her hand to his shoulder a gentle, motherly thing. "None of us can control what we see when we're dreaming. But Yakono is right. You're safe now. He isn't here."

Unus looked from assassin to assassin and, seeing no threat, let out a shaky breath. "It's . . . it's getting worse. I don't know how long I can keep him out. I'm not used to doing it for so long."

It was getting worse all right. Unus had been calm upon Septum's death, sensibly discussing plans, but day by day he weakened. Duos was always there in his head, an ever-present reminder that he could not escape without being hunted by his twin. He didn't even know what and who he was without Duos . . . and that at least I could empathise with.

*You mean I can*, Kaysa said, her bitterness staining all our attempts to find a way forward.

"You saw him?" Yakono said, focussing on what was most important to him. "In your dreams? The . . . other one?"

"Duos. Yes." Unus pressed his hands to his face. "He's trying to find a way to turn everything to his benefit. Even without Septum, he's still plotting. He—*they* never used to be like that, you know. We were more in accord once. We felt the same pull to the faith, the same trust in God, and then . . . I don't even know when it started to change. Or how. I agreed in the beginning. The church did need to change. We did need to fight for those of the faith outside Chiltae. We did need to share the truth with others. And whenever I disagreed with their methods, they talked me around, spoke over me, filled me with their vehemence. Until…"

"You weren't you anymore."

Kaysa's words. The situations weren't the same, but they were comparable enough that as Unus nodded, I knew a deep sense of shame.

*I didn't know what you were,* I said.

*Would it have mattered? Would it have changed the way you treated me?*

I knew the truth, but couldn't give it voice.

"Yes. Not me," Unus said. "I don't know who I am anymore. Every day disconnected from them—from him is…"

Kaysa didn't speak for him this time, but the odd feeling of self-discovery, of both growing and shrinking at the same time, shedding things she was proud of along with things she hated, was so strong I couldn't but feel it to the depth of my bones.

*Our* bones.

As I had been slowly becoming Empress Hana, so Kaysa had become just a ghost of me.

"Yes, but you said you saw him. Where?" Yakono said. "If you tell me, I can end this now."

Unus stared, seeming not to understand the question, before slowly shaking his head. "I don't know exactly—south perhaps—but he…he saw me too."

Kaysa's grip tightened upon his arm. "Are you saying Duos knows where we are?"

His nod was more of a flinch, his gaze darting fearfully to Yakono, who had stilled like the predator he was. Kaysa held tight to control over our body, ready to defend Unus should Yakono lunge at him, but whatever went through the assassin's mind, he soon relaxed. Sat back. "He'll come for you?"

"Not himself," Unus said. "That's too dangerous. He knows you're with me."

"We are not using him as bait to draw Duos out," Kaysa snapped, though it didn't sound like a bad idea to me. "He can read minds, remember? He'll know it's a trap if you try it."

Yakono didn't answer, just rolled back on his heels and rose to his feet. "We have to go. Now."

———————————+———————————

There was comfort in travelling at night, knowing the darkness would hide you like the heaviest cloak, but it was fucking impossible to see. Thankfully my horse seemed able to see better, else we would have been shuffling slowly forward with outstretched arms, twitching at every tiny sound. I was a creature of cities, not forests; of lantern-lit streets, not smothering nothingness; solid stone, not squelchy mud. Unsurprisingly, and annoyingly, Yakono seemed quite at home. Even Unus didn't complain, though I wondered how much he was really with us in mind as he was in body.

Our plan to seek a meeting with Empress Miko had seemed sensible at the outset, but it meant travelling into the most fought-over territory in the empire, where towns and farms and villages had been abandoned to the ever-present Kisian, Chiltaen, and Levanti armies, their supplies stripped bare.

Yakono led the way, Unus in the middle, with us bringing up the rear, taking turns to be the mind in control of our body. It was an odd way to travel, but it made the tension of listening to every sound easier to bear, knowing you could soon rest and let another take over.

*I'll do my stint soon,* Kaysa said.

*I'm good for a little longer,* I replied. *But I think we could have done with a lot more sleep.*

*We don't seem very good at that. I struggle generally, and you lie awake listening to Yakono breathing and wonder what he's thinking.*

*I only do that because I can't get to sleep.*

*Of course.*

I ignored her amusement and glared at the darkness like it would help me see better. I couldn't even see Yakono, only the tail of Unus's horse. The assassin could have been carried off by a giant bird, horse and all, and I wouldn't know until the sun rose for how little Unus seemed to pay attention.

A cry echoed through the trees. We'd heard many strange bird calls while travelling at night, but when the sound didn't come again, Yakono reined in.

"Trouble?" I whispered.

"Sounds like someone got hurt or surprised," he whispered back, his face a featureless shadow. "Let's wait here a while."

We'd halted a few times to see if strange sounds became enemies, and all it achieved was the complete chilling of my limbs and joints until I couldn't think of anything more wonderful than a hot bath. I sat dreaming of sinking into one while Yakono sat, ear cocked to the night. Unus said nothing.

No shouts came. No footsteps or hoofbeats or cries, just the gentle hush of the wind and the myriad animal sounds that defined the night.

Eventually, Yakono nodded and set his horse walking.

"I wouldn't do that if I were you."

The change in Unus's tone sent ice spilling through my veins, and I was back in the Witchdoctor's house, on the run while Leo spoke through Septum's lifeless lips. Slowly Unus turned until his eyes were upon me, bright pinpoints in the darkness.

"Ah, Cassandra, lovely to see you again."

Owning no thought beyond panic, I yanked loose my dagger

and threw it at him. The pommel smacked into his forehead with a sickening sound, throwing him backward off his horse.

"Unus!" Kaysa snatched control and all but fell from the saddle. Mud squelched beneath our knees and damp fronds of undergrowth tangled around us, but she hardly seemed to notice, let alone care. "Unus?" Frantically patting the ground in the gloom, she found his arm and traced it back to his shoulder and up to his neck, feeling for his pulse.

It beat strongly beneath our fingers, and we let go a breath. "Thank God," Kaysa said. "You're so lucky that hit pommel first. You could have killed him!"

From overhead came Yakono's gentle voice. "I'm lucky? I didn't throw it."

*Be careful! We don't want Yakono asking questions!*

"I don't care!"

*You will care when he kills us.*

Seeming to agree, she gave in to my insistent attempts to retake control. Overhead, Yakono was a shadowy outline recognisable only by his scent. "Duos must be close," I said. "Be careful what you say once he wakes up. If Duos can push through his defences at any time, then he can hear us."

Yakono looked about the dark forest as though expecting to see another Leo nearby, but there was nothing beyond the chirrup of insects and the occasional scurry of small creatures in the leaf litter.

Beneath my splayed hand, Unus twitched and let out a groan. I tensed. "Unus or Duos?"

"Ouch," he said. "It feels like you split my head open."

"Unus?"

"Yes, don't hit me again."

"Good to know hitting you in the head can dislodge your brother."

His reply was another groan. "We should keep moving."

Yakono agreed, and having helped Unus groan his way back to his feet and into the saddle, we set off again, all the more alert to every unusual sound. And there were a lot, including the occasional thump or distant crash of falling timber and far-off shouts. Lanterns began to flicker through the trees, and Yakono changed course, moving us away from them.

"Sounds like woodcutters," he said, slowing to let us catch up. "Though why they're working in the middle of the night is anyone's guess. We'll have to circle farther south to avoid them."

Too tired to have an opinion, I let him lead on, but the sound of men working only grew louder. The trees began to thin like we'd reached the edge of the woods, and Yakono halted, faint moonlight creeping in to dust his hair.

"Not just a few woodcutters." He glanced my way as I joined him. "Whatever they're building, it must be important for them to work through the night like this."

"Very important," Unus said, but for the second time that night it wasn't Unus. "They think they're building a pavilion for my wedding to Empress Miko, but since she won't be making it, it's Lady Sichi I'll be marrying."

I froze, hand on my dagger again. "Won't be making it? What do you mean she won't be making it?"

Unus turned, his grin chilling in the shadows. "I mean she'll be dead, Cassandra. Of all the people not to understand my meaning. Dead. Dead. Dead."

I tightened my grip. "When? How?"

"When...when what?" Unus blinked rapidly, and it *was* Unus again. "Oh."

"No! No no no!" I urged my horse alongside him and gripped his shoulders, the same panic that had spurred Hana back at the manor now spilling through my veins. "Get him back! I have to know about Miko! We can't let her die!"

"I...I can't." Unus gripped my arms to keep from falling from his saddle, panic widening his eyes.

"You have to be able to! You—"

Kaysa pushed through my growing fear, steadying our voice and our hands. She let Unus go and sat back, setting a calming hand to our horse's neck. "Sorry, I'm not sure what came over me." She glanced at Yakono, who was little more than a scowl in the shadows. "Perhaps we should start looking for somewhere to stay the night—day."

The assassin nodded and, asking no questions, turned his mount to continue the way we had been travelling.

"I'm sorry, Cassandra," Unus said as he fell in behind Yakono. "I'll let you know if I get anything about Empress Miko."

Kaysa gave him a kind smile and set our horse following his, back into the dark trees.

Despite wanting to call it an early night, it was nearing dawn before we found somewhere safe to stay. There were plenty of small villages with no sign of life, but Yakono refused to stop anywhere out in the open or too close to a road. At last we found a small farmhouse on its own outside a village. Another day in another abandoned house, amid another collection of abandoned junk and some scraps of mouldy food.

"Hopefully the old owners left their sleeping mats when they fled," Yakono said, dismounting. "I don't fancy sleeping on the floorboards again like we had to do back at that other place."

I hadn't gotten much sleep that night. Yakono had. The man seemed able to sleep anywhere and everywhere, his existence perfectly fitting the world no matter the circumstances. I had always felt the wrong shape, my sharp edges tearing at everything I touched.

Unus slid boneless from his horse, gripping the saddle to keep his knees from buckling. "You should head inside and find a mat,"

Yakono said, taking one look at him. "I'll look around for food and water."

Unus nodded slowly and dragged himself toward the door, and without so much as a glance my way, Yakono set off on a circuit of the house. With a scowl, I looked from one horse to another and back to Yakono's and Unus's retreating backs. "Well, fuck you too," I grumbled. "I guess we'll tend to the horses, because as a city girl we're excellent at that." I kicked a stone, sending it bouncing into the dawn light gilding the path. "Fuck all of this and then fuck it off some more."

*Helpful.*

"Shut up. Swearing makes me feel better."

When it didn't help, I gathered up all three sets of reins and led the tired horses into the dark, musty barn. It hadn't been made for horses by the look of the low troughs and small fences, but there was some dry hay, and the doors closed. And it was all there was.

"What are we even doing stopping for the night—day?" I said, looking through a trio of old buckets for the one with the smallest hole. "You heard what Duos said, he wants Miko dead, and if we take our sweet time on the road, we might arrive too late to save her. Or Unus!"

*And if we get found travelling with Leo Villius, that's going to make it faster? If we're found by the wrong people we might not get to her at all.*

There was no answer to that, so I just snatched up the best of the terrible buckets and went in search of a water barrel. When I returned, dripping water, the only thanks I got from the horses was a blank stare as I tipped water into one of the low troughs. "Ungrateful, stinking—"

The words died as Kaysa took over, stilling, a hand to our ear.

*What is it?* I said.

"I'm not sure, but..." She stepped toward the barn door, sitting ajar. Outside, the yard was empty, no sign of either Unus or Yakono or anything else.

"Hmm." Kaysa shook her head. "Nothing. I'll let you get back to cleaning these horses."

"Thanks." The horses seemed not to appreciate my sarcasm. One of them went so far as to eye me with disfavour.

*I think they just want their saddles off,* Kaysa said. *I don't see a brush, but you can rub them down with a handful of hay like Yakono does.*

I bent to collect a handful of hay, back aching after so long in the saddle. I groaned as I straightened, only to draw in a breath and hold it. There *was* a sound, a low rumble beneath the gentle snorts and scuffs of the horses moving about the barn.

"Hoofbeats." I dropped the hay and sped to the door. Outside, the sound was clearer, clear enough that both Yakono and Unus had emerged from the house. Unus glanced our way, but Yakono's gaze was fixed upon the trees.

"Are they coming this way, do you think?" I whispered to Kaysa, not daring to raise my voice to ask Yakono and bring soldiers down upon us.

*I don't know, but I hope not; it sounds like a lot of horses.*

It did. I stepped back into the shadows, though doing so halved our view of the yard. The hoofbeats grew louder. There was no way anyone could know where we were, yet the horses were closing in. Birds squawked, leaping into the skies for safety. Shadows moved in the trees. Yakono and Unus had disappeared back into the house, and I crouched, heart thudding hard as I hoped whoever approached would ride on by.

Like the worst thing that could possibly happen, half a dozen Levanti on horseback burst into the sunlight. Worse still, they slowed. Words passed between them, and like we had been cursed by every god that had ever existed, they reined in and dismounted.

*Shit*, Kaysa hissed as one of the warriors pointed toward the house, Leo's name upon their lips. *We need to do something.*

*Do what? I give as good as I get in a fight, but not against a whole group of Levanti.*

*We can't just sit here.*

The tug of her trying to force her way into our arms and legs was as strong as a tide, but I clenched my hands to fists. *Stop it*, I said. *If we get caught by the Levanti, we'll never make it to Miko before Duos.*

*I don't care about Miko! I care about Unus. If he dies, Cassandra, I'm never going to forgive you.*

Her words carried such promise they were like lead in my chest, but I shook my head. *We can't help anyone if we get caught.* Voices sounded inside the house, and I edged closer to the barn door to peer out. Three of the Levanti had remained in the yard, completing a circuit of the area. One pointed our way.

*Shit.*

I scrambled back, fighting Kaysa's attempts to take over, which sent us stumbling toward our horse as our control flickered. *Stop it! We have to get out of here!*

Our horse snorted as I gripped its reins, thankful I hadn't gotten around to taking off any of their saddles. Climbing up was never graceful, but I clambered into the saddle like a wild thing, panic ringing in my ears.

*Cassandra! Stop this! We can't abandon them!*

*We can save them if we get out of here; we just have to get to Miko first.*

*Cass!*

I ignored her and turned our horse toward freedom. "We're getting out of here," I hissed, and urged it to a trot, speeding as we approached the gap in the doors. The shadow of someone just outside was all the warning I got before the door was tugged open and we sped through, throwing a Levanti off balance. They shouted, but there was no stopping. Speeding out into the yard, I caught a glimpse of Yakono and Unus on the steps, hands raised in surrender, before we dove headlong into the trees.

Levanti shouted after me, but I didn't look back. Digging my feet into its sides, I urged my horse on, caring nothing for the direction we travelled as long as it was away from here. Leaving the animal to choose our path, I could only hold on tight and try not to die, unable to hear anything beyond the thump of hooves and the rush of the wind in my ears. No Levanti seemed to be following, but I wouldn't feel safe until I'd put a lot of distance between us. So gritting my teeth, I pressed my horse faster, hoping it knew how not to run into anything. We needed to get to Miko, and fast.

# 4. DISHIVA

When you've lived your life in the saddle and walking the dry plains, digging in the mud for crabs in the summer and hunting deer in the winter, it is hard to get used to wearing white. To being quiet and calm. To people kissing your feet.

I almost kicked the first Chiltaen who did. It was such a degrading thing that it jarred with my experience of these people. Once I had been held down and raped in the dirt. Now I was being lifted up as an idol.

Dom Villius was enjoying it all too much.

He was often nearby, his presence not so oppressive I couldn't think about escaping, but too watchful to achieve it. He had brought in the trio of young Kisian men who now bowed at my feet, murmuring pious words. Occasionally, I entertained myself imagining devout soldiers were saying ridiculous things like "I achieve piety by eating hair" or "One's arse is holy," but these three looked all too earnest for that. They touched their pendants. They bowed. They kissed my feet, the warmth of their lips unpleasant in the chill. When they were done, they rose and backed away, ignoring my look of desperate entreaty because my mask hid everything. Everything except my damaged eyes.

*Chosen one, whose single vision will build an empire.*

The group stepped out into the weak sunlight, escaping the

musty little makeshift church I now called home. There were few constructions in the camp aside from the palisade walls, but I refused to be grateful for a dry place to sleep, or for having a quiet retreat where Leo's gaze couldn't follow.

I drew a deep breath and held it until my lungs hurt and black spots appeared in my vision. If I kept holding it until I passed out, my body would keep breathing on its own, heedless of my choices, and that was what I had to do. My resigned, gusty exhale rippled the lower half of my mask, and I sank onto one of the chairs. I had to gather the same determination to beat this as the body had to survive. Eventually Leo would slip. Would falter.

My legs twitched, and made restless by the creeping despondence, I was soon up and pacing. Eight steps from one side of the room to the other. Nine from the door to the back wall. The counts were always the same, and that continuity steadied me as nothing else could.

Calmed, I stopped at the door to look out. Nothing had changed. The same tents, Leo's closest with rows growing smaller and smaller as they stretched into the distance. It rained less these days, but the ground was still sodden, and every breath was heavy with the stink of mud and shit, just like the last time I had been a prisoner in a Chiltaen camp.

A legate emerged from a nearby tent, and I flinched, momentarily seeing Legate Andrus in the man's place. Perhaps if I was lucky, he might have the same fate. Gideon was not present to put a blade through him, however, so the legate just stood squinting, a hand raised to shield his eyes. The only difference between him and Andrus was that his surcoat had a blue trim, where Andrus's had been all green, and I couldn't decide if that meant he was higher or lower ranked.

Having gathered himself, the legate strode across the churned earth toward me, and I wished the church had a door I could shut in his face. Instead, I thought of the Swords I had come to protect—Rophet and Tephe e'Bedjuti, Harmara and Jira en'Oht, Ptah en'Injit and Oshar e'Torin—and gripped my hands tight behind my back.

"Your Holiness," the man said. "You well?"

"Yes, I well, you thank," I said, encouraging his butchering of my language. He'd had basic Levanti when I'd arrived, no doubt learned from Gideon and his translators the same as Andrus and Secretary Aurus.

"Good. Uh, inside? Blessing for day?"

I stepped back for him to enter. Many came for my blessing each day, or every few days, and while it amused me to be a heathen speaking nonsense to emptiness, I hated being alone with them. The robe and mask and title felt no more like armour than my armour ever had. Without it, I was still a barbarian who could be chained in the dirt.

The legate strode in, treading mud in with him. Not awaiting an invitation, he knelt at my feet and lowered his head, his hair a wispy nest of sand and grey.

I set my hand lightly upon his head and muttered the prayer I'd memorised without understanding what it meant. It was the one Leo always said—that was my only assurance I wasn't spouting total gibberish.

The man knelt for the whole prayer, its length becoming less and less noticeable now that I spoke it without thought, able to focus on other things, like the balding spot on the legate's head. And the shout of a returning scout. It made the legate twitch, but rather than let him go and discover the latest news, I took petty joy in slowing the blessing to an agonising drone. The man slumped beneath my hand, giving in. He could interrupt, could walk out, could tell me to hurry, but he wouldn't. It hadn't taken long to realise the value these men put on *appearing* to believe. The performance of their religion a higher priority than true faith.

Eventually I couldn't draw out the blessing any longer and lifted my hand from his head, fighting the urge to wipe it on my robe. The legate murmured his own short prayer, bowed his wispy hair to brush my feet, and rose.

"May you find the path to doing the right thing," I said, knowing he wouldn't understand, but needing to add my own plea, my own desperate wish of the gods.

His face twisted in an effort of concentration, but I had only a moment to wish the words unsaid before he nodded. "I try," he said, and headed for the door.

The rest of the day wore on like every other before it. Chiltaens came to the church for blessings or approached me when I stepped out to stretch my legs. "Holiness," they would say, halting as I passed, and I had to swallow the ever-present urge to shout that I was no true priest, no true holiness. I was Levanti and a woman, and neither seemed to fit with their idea of their religion. I didn't even believe in their god. Yet somehow it didn't seem to matter. I walked through the camp untouchable despite Leo's purpose for me.

When the sun began to set on yet another day of useless captivity in service to a monster, despondency set in. I thought of where I could be instead of here, of what choices I could have made instead of these, and had to tell myself that with her people's lives in danger Dishiva e'Jaroven wouldn't have made different choices. It didn't help me feel any better.

My destroyed eye itched. My good one was tired. I was tired. To the very depth of my soul, I was tired and imagined I was lying on a warm mat somewhere with Jass, a fire crackling nearby and nothing to do but exist. No responsibilities. No nagging guilt. Just quiet, blissful existence. It took me a moment to realise there was no herd in this daydream. We were alone, and I wasn't sure how I felt about that.

"Trust you to ruin even a daydream with deep questions," I muttered as I watched the sun set behind the camp wall.

In the fading light, a group of commanders strode past in the direction of the meeting tent. They seemed to hold a meeting almost every evening—the only time I could be sure I was safe from Leo.

One by one every man with any power here made their way to the meeting tent, a well-lit, large pavilionish thing in what seemed to be the centre of the camp. There was no sign of Leo, but neither did he appear to be in his tent, so I slowly breathed out and started to count. One hundred and twenty-two slow seconds—an arbitrary number that somehow felt safe.

One hundred and twenty-two seconds after the last commander entered the meeting tent, I stepped from the chapel doorway. The sun had dropped below the horizon, and a chill breeze tugged at my robe. Even worn over a tunic, the hieromonk's ceremonial attire wasn't warm enough now the weather was getting colder.

With my robe gathered close, I walked quickly despite irregular sources of light. I knew my way, had made this walk many times before.

The sight of the dark shack coalescing from the shadows by the horse pens and latrines always sent dread sliding through me. What if one of them had gotten sick? Or died? What if I never found a way to get them out of here?

The two soldiers standing guard watched me approach, nodding and murmuring "Holiness" as I drew near. Only once had I tried to walk inside, the clash of their respect for me against their orders causing enough consternation that Leo had been summoned. Instead of risking that again, I'd taken to walking around the back, out of sight, and leaning against the rickety wall. There, with only horse pens before me and the cold wind nibbling at my toes, I cleared my throat.

"How are you all tonight?"

Shuffles against the other side of the wall followed a moment of silence, before a rough voice said, "Never been better, Captain."

Someone murmured something I didn't catch, followed by a husky laugh. It was the grim humour of survival, but it was a relief to hear it all the same.

"Food?"

"Same as always, Captain," Oshar said, his voice the only one I could put a name to.

"Fucking awful is what he means." More dry chuckles followed. I didn't comment, merely glad they were being fed at all.

"Water?" I said.

"We're fine, Captain," snapped the original voice. "Just great. Don't you worry about us, we're having a grand time."

I swallowed a flare of annoyance. "I'm trying to get you out of there, I promise."

"Say that any louder and the guards will throw you in here with us."

There was no way the guards couldn't hear me and hadn't guessed what I was up to, though whether they'd told anyone was another matter. I was their hieromonk after all; I could do whatever I wanted. The whole hieromonk thing had seemed too complicated to explain through a wall.

"Don't worry about me," I said. "I'll try to have better or at least more food and water sent in, and I'll get you out of there. I promise."

Oshar's murmured "Thank you, Captain" was the only response I got, and though I wanted more, I couldn't blame them. I'd been promising freedom for weeks.

Pushing off the wall, I took the long way back to the chapel. A walk through the horse pens was steadying even without any Levanti horses, the sounds and smells a reminder of who I really was beneath the mask, despite how hard I'd fought alongside Gideon for a different future. The dream of Levanti Kisia still haunted my dreams some nights, only for me to wake and have to face the man who had been its downfall.

Leo was waiting for me when I stepped into the dimly lit chapel. It took time for my injured eyes to adjust enough to see him, but his scent always gave him away.

"Been out for a walk, Holiness?" he said, his voice deceptively calm. "Been attending to your charitable duties, checking to see that the suffering were still suffering?"

"What do you want?"

"You don't sound happy to see me, Dishiva. I'm hurt."

His words had bite, and when he stepped from the shadows, his grin was fixed and humourless. "Bad meeting?" I said, refusing to give in to my growing fear. "Is that why you're here? To take your bad mood out on me?"

"You think you're so very clever, but you have no idea what is going on here; you're just my little pet until it's time for you to die." He stepped closer, and I fought to keep my feet planted and not think about the tower in Kogahaera and how he'd just kept coming, stalking us like prey. "Tomorrow," he went on, halting in front of me, so close I could feel the warmth radiating from his body, "you are going to name me defender."

"No. I won't."

The last time I'd refused the same demand, he'd grinned knowingly and walked away, leaving me to fret over his intentions. This time there was no smile, no amusement, just a deadly glare as he closed the final step between us. "It wasn't a request," he hissed into my face. "I've let you play your games, but now your time is running out. There will be a ceremony, and you will name me as I once named you."

My heart hammered, thoughts flashing back to our desperate

scuffle in my room at Kogahaera. I had beaten him bloody and left him to die, only for him to come back. But there were cracks in his power. In his plans. He just relied on no one having the courage to take a mallet to them.

"No," I said, swinging the only mallet I owned. "Although I'll reconsider if you tell me why you're insisting *now*. Bad news?"

His glare darkened—a Sword annoyed that I'd picked them up on sloppy work—and for the first time in weeks I thought maybe I wasn't so powerless after all.

"All you need to know is that if you don't, those captive Levanti die."

I held my ground though every part of me wanted to step back, hating his closeness and the touch of his breath on my face. "But if you kill them, you'll have nothing left to hold over me to ensure compliance," I said in the same quiet hiss as he. "Kill them and I'll never name you defender."

Leo's eyes narrowed.

"Are you trying to do the controlling thing on me?" I asked, knowing I was pushing it. "That doesn't work anymore, remember? If you wanted to do that you shouldn't have sliced my eyes."

His hand closed around my throat, fingertips digging in hard. "I suggest you reconsider your rash attempt at autonomy, Dishiva," he said, each word spat into my face. "Or I will make sure your people die. One by one. Slowly. Painfully. While you witness every moment."

With a final, meaningful squeeze, he let go and finally stepped back. He smiled then, not so much amused as satisfied. "I know you'll be a good girl," he said, and patted my cheek. "I'll see you tomorrow."

Drawing up his mask, Leo stepped toward the door. I watched him go, sure every moment that he would turn back and loose more hate my way, but whatever had happened to bring forward his plans seemed to fill his mind, for he didn't so much as glance back.

Once he had disappeared, well beyond sight or sound, I finally let my legs give way and dropped onto the nearest chair. My hands trembled and I wanted to be sick. There was no way out. His need to be named defender was keeping me alive, as his need to keep me in line was all that kept my people alive. The walls were closing in. With him there was no such thing as an empty promise or a step too far—I'd seen too many dead in his wake to believe otherwise.

———————◆———————

I slept poorly, unable to stop imagining the ways Leo could pressure me into compliance. Too well could I remember the dead horses, and Captain Dhamara's body hanging from the rafters, even Gideon lying with froth oozing between his lips—Leo had used the lives of my people against me before and would do it again.

When the rising sun dragged me from my bed, I performed blessings on those waiting before stepping out into the weak morning light. Whatever the weather, the camp was always busy. Messengers and scouts came and went, training bouts and drills filled the air with noise, and someone always seemed to be digging a new latrine, but while that hadn't changed, a tense hush seemed to have fallen over it all like a thick blanket. No drawn weapons, but the usual ease had evaporated. Everywhere I walked, soldiers halted their tasks to bow and murmur prayers, no sign of what had caused the change in the camp's mood. Here and there small groups of men gathered briefly before breaking up again, sending whispers hissing around me like shifting sands. Sands that truly seemed to move beneath my feet, when I caught Secretary Aurus's name.

"Secretary Aurus?" I turned on the knot of soldiers who'd spoken.

Nods and murmurs of "Holiness" were all the reply I got and all the reply I needed. As I walked away, shards of hope wormed their way beneath my skin, yet like shards they cut as they entered, my palpable relief at the arrival of a potential ally causing me no joy. He was Chiltaen. A Chiltaen I couldn't trust, whatever goals we might have in common. That he disliked Leo and spoke my language were all I could allow myself to be grateful for.

At the gates, I found Leo waiting with a collection of legates and commanders. Each made a gesture of respect in my direction, but went on with their low-voiced conversation. Leo paid me no heed, and the creeping suspicion began to grow that his anger the previous night had been triggered by Secretary Aurus's impending arrival. That they didn't like one another was certain. The secretary's arrival might not give me an ally, but it would give Leo an enemy.

Keeping my distance, I watched the bustle around the gates ebb and flow. Scouts and commanders came and went, soldiers gathered to watch, only to be sent about their duties. That Leo and the commanders remained meant the secretary's arrival couldn't be far off, yet minutes passed and the sun rose inexorably higher and higher into the sky.

Eventually, as the sun reached its zenith, a shout from one of the watchtowers sent a pair of soldiers hurrying to unbar the gates. Waving arms and shouting, they cleared space and hauled open the gates, creaking and rattling, to reveal Secretary Aurus perfectly centred within the aperture, waiting. He wore what I'd come to think of as fancy Chiltaen garb, a series of asymmetrical tunics and robes adorned with jewellery that made him appear not only out of place in a military camp, but also out of proportion with his own body.

As the gates swung to a halt, he looked about, eyelids drooping in boredom. Half a dozen men stood behind him, their wariness marked beside his ease. Receiving no welcome, he strode in, gaze flicking between those gathered to greet him before settling on me.

"Ah, Dom Jaroven," the secretary said, striding my way. "How very pleased I am to see you again, Your Holiness." Respect was my due as their hieromonk, but his great show of bowing at my feet seemed more insult to Leo than respect to me. He remained kneeling there so long that I had to speak a blessing over him, which came out stuttered and unsure. This man had sought an alliance with Gideon that Leo had made impossible, but as hieromonk I had power I'd not had before. If I had the nerve to use it.

When Secretary Aurus rose, he turned to approach the gathered legates. Switching back to his own language with ease, he gestured outside the gates to where more Chiltaen soldiers—his, I had to assume—were setting up tents outside the walls. A brief discussion followed. I was unsure where each Chiltaen stood in rank, but that everyone present was below the secretary was clear.

"Secretary," I said, stepping forward as their discussion came to an end. "I require a few minutes of your time."

His lazy gaze swung my way, brows lifting. "But of course, Your Holiness. What can I do for you?"

"In private."

A shrug and he gestured beyond the gates. "My tent is close by if you would do me the honour of joining me, Your Holiness."

It was all I could do not to look at Leo, sure he would find a way to stop me going even so short a distance beyond his influence. But I outranked him, as did Secretary Aurus, so having agreed, I made for the gates, sure I could feel Leo's stare burning into my back. "Safer not to go, don't you think?" he said, soft and threatening.

I almost swallowed my tongue, thinking of what harm he could do while I was away, but Secretary Aurus seemed unimpressed. "I hope you're not suggesting I intend any violence toward either our esteemed hieromonk or any of her people," he said in his bored voice. "Don't worry, Lord Villius, Her Holiness will be returned to your care soon and be able to attend to whatever tasks you require of her."

*Lord Villius.* Leo flinched at the reminder of his diminished position, and foreboding mixed with my hope, turning it sour.

Beyond the walls, most of the small adjoining camp was still in the stage I'd always thought of as beautiful chaos, where everyone had a dozen tasks and people and horses and laden mules were going everywhere, weighed down with tents and sacks and firewood. However, a large tent stood in the centre of it all—one of the only things fully erected amid the bustle.

Having maintained silence all the way, Secretary Aurus invited me inside with nothing but a gesture, and I ducked in beneath the fall of canvas. Inside, three long couches sat around a central table set with fruit and wine. A smaller table and chair covered in papers sat in the corner, while a half-hung curtain divided a bed from the rest of the space.

"Well, now you may speak without worrying about either your words or your thoughts," Secretary Aurus said, dropping onto one of the couches. "Which you quite wisely seem as keen on as I am. I had my men pace the distance between here and the gates three times before deciding where to put my tent."

In his lazy way, he gestured for me to sit, but I remained on the threshold and pulled down my mask. There was a certain degree of satisfaction in the shocked lifting of his brows as he took in my injured eyes. "Why are you here?" I said. "You may be the lesser of two evils, but that doesn't make us allies."

"No, but the enemy of my enemy is my friend, so the saying goes, and I'm here because Lord Villius is…well…let's call him a liability. He has proven himself to be entirely outside the control of the Nine, so as I was already in Kisia, I have been charged with… salvaging the situation."

"Your Levanti has improved."

"Thank you, I have had reason to practice." He gestured again at the couch opposite. "Do sit down; it's not an admission of weakness, it merely saves me getting a crick in my neck from having to look up at you."

I lowered myself onto the edge of the couch. "You don't like Leo, but what are you here to *do*?"

"That I can't tell you. I am confident I can keep him from taking the knowledge from my head, but not yours."

"All right, then tell me why they are here. Leo and his soldiers."

Secretary Aurus tilted his head—a man trying to read me. "You don't know? Yet you came here of your own free will and had yourself named hieromonk."

"I didn't ask to be named hieromonk," I said. "I came here because Dom Villius took half a dozen of my people hostage, and he named me hieromonk so I could be a false priest and die for his prophecy. But whatever his reason, this is a position of power I hold now. A position I can use for my own ends."

The secretary leaned forward, elbows upon his knees. "And what ends are those? You're currently residing in a Chiltaen army camp, their intention the conquest of northern Kisia in the name of the church. I say the church rather than Leo Villius because, while that used to be one and the same thing, your existence makes that not entirely true anymore."

"Surely they don't have enough soldiers to take Kisia. Are you the reinforcements?"

He laughed. "Hardly."

"So you aren't here to finish conquering northern Kisia?"

Secretary Aurus considered me again for some time. "Given our losses so far," he said at last, choosing his words carefully, "it would be foolish not to make the attempt to consolidate what we have taken, should the opportunity arise."

"So that's exactly what you're here to do."

"What I'm here to do will depend greatly upon the actions of everyone else involved, which is why I'm here rather than the Nine having sent a legate with strict orders. Between the number of moving pieces and the divided loyalties of the soldiers currently answering to Leo Villius, this is a ... complicated situation."

I eyed him with the same narrow assessment, annoyed that my scarred vision kept the finer details of his expression from me. "A complicated situation that could be made easier, or harder, by the presence of the hieromonk of the One True God?"

"That depends on what that hieromonk chooses to do. However much some of the Nine have sought to keep the church out of political dealings, it has long now been common for the hieromonk to represent the will of God by marching with our armies and choosing sides in political disagreements."

He met my gaze squarely, not outwardly troubled that such power lay in my hands—a show of faith I had not looked for. No demands, no manipulations; he just sat waiting for me to name my price. A literal price? Money would buy many things, but not what we needed most. I thought of Gideon standing before us offering a new home, a place where we could build away from the troubles of the plains and the slow destruction of our culture. We wouldn't be the same Levanti if we lived away from the plains, but we could choose our own path rather than have change forced upon us by merchant cities that wished we didn't exist.

"Land," I said at last. "A new place we can call home."

Secretary Aurus lifted a brow. "Levanti Kisia?"

"No, we don't want to rule anyone, and Kisia is not a good climate for us or our horses."

I left him to the appropriate realisation and watched for any twitches that might betray how he felt about it. Whether he was particularly skilled at showing little or my vision was too poor to catch the signs, there was nothing. "Chiltaen land," he said.

"Yes, call it reparation for the harm done to us by your people."

Secretary Aurus shook his head. "No, that won't work because you took your revenge in Mei'lian. We are, in effect, equal now."

"That's not true and you know it, but if you must we could look at it another way. Granting us land in return for me standing with you as the will of God will mean your hieromonk won't leave your shores. If I had a home for my people here, I would stay and continue to be of use to you. If not, as soon as my people here are free, I will leave, taking Chiltaen religious authority with me. How would you appoint a new hieromonk? I imagine it might get...chaotic, especially if Leo takes over."

Again he just watched me for some time, eyes bright as his mind turned. "You have an idea of what lands, I assume?" he said at last.

"Lands that we autonomously control," I said. "We won't be kept soldiers forced to live under your rules. They must be on the Eye Sea so we can travel easily to the plains, and be large enough to build or to roam. Space to be free."

It was a big ask, a big risk, and guilt gnawed at me. Kisia was no longer a faceless place, rather the home of Sichi and Edo, where Nuru was sure to stay, but I told myself that my presence at the head of a Chiltaen army would not change the outcome. If the Chiltaens intended to consolidate their hold on northern Kisia, they would do it whether I stood beside them in a white robe and mask or not.

Secretary Aurus eyed me over the top of steepled fingers while I tried not to let the yearning in my heart overrun my good sense. I wanted this, and the more I dwelt on it the more I wanted it, just as I'd wanted so desperately for Gideon to succeed.

"Well?" I prompted when I could wait no longer.

"You would not be allowed to mass an army," he said, once again choosing his words carefully. "Or build warships."

"Beyond protecting ourselves we would have no need of either."

He nodded slowly. "Then, yes, I think so long as your intention is to build a peaceful home for those Levanti who do not wish to return to the plains then you may find that within our borders, protected by the might of Chiltae."

We needed no protection, and yet the promise of it, of not having to live with the constant threat of attack, with the insidious incursions of the city states into our land and our herds, made my breath catch. We could just... *be*. But could I trust him? Or the people—the nation—he represented? Chiltae had forced us to fight, had tortured and abused us, had let us die without care. Could we really trust any of them?

"And what assurance can you give that you wouldn't attack us the moment you felt like it and take the land back?" I asked. "I know better than to just trust your word."

"Why? Because I'm Chiltaen? I could say the same of you after the Levanti slaughtered our army, but I have chosen to understand that choice was made under specific circumstances and by particular Levanti. It isn't wise to judge a whole people by one man or one moment in their history. As you have pointed out, we would not wish our hieromonk to leave our shores, and you're right—however unlikely a candidate you were, you are and, for the length of your life, always will be our hieromonk. Even Leo Villius would struggle to have you set aside, and no one else could. You hold a lot of power. How can I, a mere secretary, betray Dishiva e'Jaroven when she holds the hieromonk of the One True God hostage?"

I stared at him, his meaning sinking slowly into my skin. Leo had given me a powerful position, but since he intended to kill me as soon as his moment came, he'd given little thought to the consequences of his choice should I live. I was both the Chiltaens' greatest weapon and the Levantis' strongest defence.

"That's why he wants me to name him defender," I said.

"Does he? That makes sense. It would give him an unassailable position within the church hierarchy, something he currently lacks, his leadership entirely a matter of..." Aurus waved his hand, looking for the right word. "Momentum. Habit, even."

"I think he is currently working through me," I said. "I'm not entirely sure, but he doesn't want me attending the meetings, and I think it's because he's claiming to be my…spokesperson."

"Interesting, but also not surprising and not difficult to counter-act now I'm here."

"He will try to keep me under his thumb."

Secretary Aurus smothered a yawn. "Of course he will," he said, swallowing the last of it with a blink of watering eyes. "That doesn't mean it will work."

"He has more soldiers than you do," I said.

"Yes, many of whom would refuse to attack God's chosen. Leo is merely holding them by force of personality. You just need to make them want to follow you more."

I tapped a rhythm on my knees. The path to defeating Leo and gaining the lands I'd demanded lay not only through trusting this man, this Chiltaen, but in having to shed as much of my Levanti self as I could to play my part. To lead them. Inspire them. A heavy price, but what were a few more cuts? A few more slivers skimmed from my soul? I'd already given so much, risked so much, that to baulk now would make every other sacrifice meaningless.

While I thought, the secretary reclined once more with a lit-tle groan, as though sitting up had been hard work. He pulled a bowl of nuts toward himself across the patterned brocade and lifted questioning brows. "Something more you wish to say before we agree on this?"

*Wish* was a strong word, yet need was fast overpowering my dis-inclination to speak. "Are any of the commanders here men…" I drew and released a shaking breath. "…men who took part in the subjugation of my people?"

His hand froze part way to the bowl again, his jaw slowing its crunch of the last offering. "I cannot say for sure, not having been present. Legate Andrus is dead, as I'm sure you know, and I doubt any commander who went all the way to Mei'lian with you is still alive, but a good number of those who went with the hieromonk to Koi survived. Many are here with Leo Villius now, having been stringent believers in the church and the myth of Veld. Is there... anyone in particular you are concerned to meet?"

I wished he had not understood my question, or that I had the courage to answer it. Instead, Commander Legus's name went around and around in my head and did not make it to my tongue. If he had survived, I might at least get the joy of jamming a blade between his ribs myself.

"No," I said, an old kernel of anger reopening inside me. I swallowed the urge to let it define my choices. This man was not Legus. My past was not a promise of my future. "Very well," I said. "Lands in return for the exercising of my power as hieromonk on your behalf. I will, however, not be able to work freely while Leo holds my people hostage. He has threatened to kill them should I not name him defender."

"It's time you start giving the orders then, don't you think?"

"But will they listen to me over him? I cannot speak your language."

"No, but I can. So long as you are prepared to fight him for what you want, he can be bested."

I rose from the couch, my hands clenching to fists. "I want nothing more than to fight him. He owes me—owes us—and I will make sure he pays with his blood."

A smile crept across the secretary's features, crinkling the skin around his eyes. "Then I think we have a deal, Dom Jaroven. I look forward to the bloody fruits of our alliance."

# 5. RAH

Derkka had wasted no time. As soon as Ezma left, whispers started spreading through the camp. Our trackers may have left in search of Leo, but even if we found him, going home could be dangerous. Unless of course we gave Gideon to the Chiltaens in return for safe passage.

By the time I sat down with the Hand that afternoon, everyone was talking about it.

"Well," Lashak said, digging a stick into the ground. "Ezma sure made an impression, no doubt exactly what she wanted to do."

"Saviour of the Levanti." Amun spat. "I would not trust her to piss on me."

Loklan shrugged one shoulder, not looking at any of us. "At least she came to warn us. And told us where to find Dom Villius."

"There is that," Lashak agreed, and dropped her stick with a sigh. "You know what? I don't think I'm alone in saying I'm just... tired of all this."

I knew that feeling in my bones. Tired of fighting. Of worrying. Of existing in temporary spaces, never safe, never comfortable, always waiting for the next trouble to come our way. We all needed to go home.

After a short silence, I sighed. "Is there any other news? Any word from the tracking parties yet?"

"No," Amun said. "And no report from Jass yet either, though I don't imagine the Chiltaen army has suddenly decided to move."

"Speaking of reports from Jass." Diha nodded over his shoulder. "You seem to have summoned one."

A figure emerged from the trees near the farthest hut, trailing greetings as Swords called out in welcome. Tor carried his usual frown, all long-legged irritation, his hair caught back in a tight leather band. Having approached, he didn't await an invitation to join us, though Lashak stood to extend one, the tracker always tense when awaiting news of Dishiva.

"Lashak," the young man said, nodding to her. No salute, no title. His gaze slid to me, and he added, "Rah."

"Tor," I returned. "Sit with us."

"Thank you, but I would rather stand." Standing to meet wasn't our way, but neither was folding one's arms and glaring at your leaders. Every time I saw him, Tor seemed to have shed another aspect of Levanti life, starting with respect and ending gods only knew where.

"You have news?" I said, refusing to be drawn on his disrespect, though Amun and Diha shared an exasperated look.

Usually Tor repeated his messages from Jass with great boredom and moved on, but today he stood taut like a bowstring, making me uneasy. "No sign of Dishiva yet," he said first, glancing down at Lashak. "But more Chiltaens have arrived."

"Soldiers?"

"Most seem to be, yes. Jass thinks it's the Chiltaen diplomat who met with Gideon, except he seems to have a bigger army now."

"Oh, him," Diha said. "Or...Orum? Orvus? Whatever it was, more Chiltaen soldiers is never good."

"It's a bit more complicated than that," Tor said, managing to look old and weary despite his long hair and hunched, protective stance. "From what I understand from Jass, Leo and this secretary aren't allies, though whether each other or Kisia or you are the greater enemy I can't say."

*You.* Not *us.* I understood why he felt that way, but the reminder of how completely we had failed him always stung.

"And there's something else." Tor looked at me. "If you would give me a moment alone, Rah."

I bristled more at the intensity of his stare than his lack of respect, but a nod of dismissal sent the others away, grumbling and brushing the dirt from the seats of their breeches. Even with them gone, Tor still didn't sit. "Well," I said. "What is it?"

"It's Empress Miko," Tor said at last, making my heart thud hollowly. "She's marrying Dom Villius."

The words seemed not to fit into my head, and I stared at him for a long time. He just stared back, waiting. "But . . . but she knows about him, doesn't she?" I said at last. "About what he did to Gideon? What he's capable of?"

"She knows."

"Then why?"

Tor scowled at me like it was my fault. "Because we—because *you* abandoned her and left her with no choice but to seek peace on any terms."

I was standing in Mei'lian again, the city burning around me.

*Gideon has many close supporters*, I had shouted at Sett. *People who have been here far longer than I, yet always it is me you spit and shout at, me you expect the world of, my shoulders upon which you drop the weight of responsibility.*

*Because he loves you!*

*That's not how love works!* I had shouted back, only to end up fighting for Gideon because that was exactly how love worked.

Tor's scowl somehow managed to darken without searing his face off. "Well?" he said. "Your play, great Rah e'Torin. What are you going to do about it?"

"Me?"

"You can't tell me you have no stake in this." He jabbed his finger in my face. "That none of this is your responsibility."

He wasn't wrong, yet he wasn't right either. I had no stake, I'd just wanted one. Wanted to be two people. I clenched my fists and gave him back look for look. "No, I care what happens to her, that is true, but her choices are no more my responsibility than my choices are hers."

"You walked away!"

"That's unfair and you know it. You can't take your guilt out on me, Tor. You may have walked out on her, but I gave her a choice. She chose to put her faith in Ezma, not me."

He seemed to shrink as his first outrage bled out. "Damn it, Rah, why are you always so stubborn and righteous?"

"I could say the same of you. Who shouted at me once for trying to help her? Merely following my cock, I think you said on more than one occasion."

At that he finally looked away, a mocking laugh huffing between his lips. "Just let me hate you."

"Also something you've said on more than one occasion. And I'm still not stopping you."

Deflating, he heaved a sigh and finally sat down. "You know if this results in an alliance between Chiltae and Kisia you're going to find it more dangerous here."

I tilted my head. "And you won't? You're still Levanti, however separate you might feel."

His laugh held no humour. "I stopped being Levanti a long time ago. Sharing a skin colour and a language isn't enough when the rest is nothing but scars."

"What are you now then? Kisian?"

"I...I don't really know." Tor looked down into the cold coals between us, his lip caught between his teeth. "I guess I'm not anything, not really. Caught between two worlds but part of neither. No, I don't want your pity," he added when I drew breath to speak. "It's just how it is. I fought so hard to stay Levanti, to be accepted when differences were forced on me, but I was denied every milestone and ignored because my existence was a constant reminder of everyone else's pain. So here I am, untethered, having to find my own place in the world. For now, I am just Tor. I belong nowhere, but at least that means I can go anywhere and be whoever I want, beholden to no one. There's joy in that sort of freedom."

There was nothing I could say, likely nothing he wanted me to say, so for a time we sat in silence, together but not truly in solidarity. We might have remained there a long time, had not a bustle of activity grown at the edge of the camp. Swords were gathering, voices rising, and Shenyah e'Jaroven broke away from the group, sprinting toward us across the grass.

"Captain! Zuph e'Bedjuti and her tracking party are back, and they have Dom Villius!"

Leaping to my feet, I followed her back to where the gathered Swords were growing agitated. "Calm yourselves!" I said, pushing through them to where Zuph and Lok e'Bedjuti stood in the centre of a widening circle. Between them stood Leo, but not the Leo I remembered. Not the Leo, from all I had heard, that I'd expected. He cowered, curling in upon himself, and stared at the ground.

Yet when he looked up, he gave a jolt of recognition. "Rah."

Angry heat coursed through my body, and my skin buzzed. This man had used me. Had used my Swords. Had used Gideon. And now he had the gall to stand in my camp and speak my name.

Clenching both teeth and hands, I turned to the second man they had with them. "And who is this?"

"His name seems to be Yakono, Captain," Zuph said. "We found him protecting Dom Villius, though if you ask me, he doesn't like him any more than we do."

I looked from Zuph to the shrunken Leo to the stranger, who started speaking—not in Levanti. "Damn it. Where is Tor? I need—"

"I'm right here." He stepped forward to assist with a mocking little salute. "He says if it's Leo you want then you have the wrong man. This isn't Leo."

Outcry rose, and Tor lifted his hands in surrender. "I'm just repeating what he said; obviously I can see he looks exactly like Leo Villius."

He did, and yet…in the way that the Gideon I had left sleeping was not the same Gideon I had last seen in Mei'lian, nor the one I had known back home, this Leo didn't stand like the one I'd followed south. There was something impotent about him, something quiet and fractured and strange.

"Ask him to explain."

Tor rolled his eyes, but asked my question. At the sound of Chiltaen words, the stranger let go a relieved sigh.

"He says this isn't going to make a lot of sense," Tor said, eyes narrowed as he concentrated on the words. "And he's going to sound like he's lost his mind, but this Leo is one of seven twins and is not the same as the other six, with something about halves of souls, and honestly, Captain, I think this might take a while to translate properly because it's a bit…odd."

I ran my hand along my scratchy scalp. "All right. Tor, you sit down with this *Yakono* and find out what you can. I'll talk to Leo."

Unhappy muttering spread around us, and I held up my hands. "I know what you fear, which is why I will take this risk alone. And while I do so, I will transfer leadership temporarily to Amun, so Leo Villius cannot make use of my position for his own ends. Does this satisfy you?"

Grumbles were mostly followed by nods and salutes. A few

Swords peeled away to go about their tasks or to just be somewhere else, and in the hush that followed, the full enormity of what I was undertaking fell upon me. Gideon had been alone with Leo. Gideon hadn't been able to fight him. What made me any different?

Safer to just put a blade through the man's throat, but that wouldn't help my people.

"Are you sure about this, Captain?" Amun said. "You can have faith in me, of course, but…"

"But we need this information if we're to have any hope of making a difference back home. Organise a circle of Swords to surround us at a distance with their backs to us."

My second heaved a sigh but nodded, and the remaining Swords began to break up, knots of twos and threes shearing off amid hissed conversation. Tor invited our strange guest toward the cooking fire, and Amun tapped shoulders for guard duty.

Tense though it was, the camp regained some of its former peace as I sat down in the churned dirt, offering the equally uncomfortable dirt before me to Dom Villius. Around us, Swords were turning their backs, far enough away for privacy but close enough that a shout would bring a dozen sharp blades to Leo's throat in an instant.

Whether or not he understood the danger, Leo Villius sat, back curved. He looked like a misbehaving child brought before a herd master to account for their wrongs, but no matter what he said, my people would still hate him.

"I don't expect them to stop hating me," Leo said, wrapping his arms around himself. "They have good reason. *I* hate me."

"You read my mind."

I had wondered before, but it had seemed too wild an idea.

"I did. I'm sorry. It's… hard not to. Especially when you are the only mind close."

I glanced at the backs of my Swords and couldn't but wonder if they were in danger. If, despite my best intentions, this had been a terrible idea.

"I appreciate your honesty at least," I said. "Will you be as honest with every question I ask?"

"If I can. I don't want to die for my brother's crimes."

I leaned forward, elbows on my knees. "Brother?"

"I had six. There is...an anomaly whereby one soul is born into two bodies, but with us it went...wrong. I am the first half. My twin brother ought to have been the second half, except his half split into six. We could all communicate without speaking, but what I didn't realise for a long time is that they could only communicate through me. They had no connection to each other, only to me. And the...noise. I..." He looked at his hands, trembling as Gideon's had trembled of late. "I lost my sense of self. I became a conduit with no thoughts and plans of my own. Until Cassandra killed one. Then Gideon killed another. Dishiva e'Jaroven killed a third, and little by little I began to...find myself. It sounds ridiculous, I know, and I don't expect you to believe me, but it's the truth. I have acted like my brothers for many years, as a puppet dances to his master's strings, but I am not my brother. Now that I have only one left, I am more myself than I have ever been and I don't..."

He seemed to run out of words, and I could only stare as realisations unfolded in my mind.

"The head in the box," I said. "You—*he* hadn't been granted a new body; he was just...showing me his twin's head?"

"Yes. They never came back to life. God gave them no purpose, but the story in the holy book made sense of our odd condition, so we—*they*—tried to live it truthfully. To control it. A kind of grief, perhaps, at how painfully we have experienced life."

It *did* sound ridiculous, but...less ridiculous than a man being brought back to life by his god and granted new bodies. And he spoke not with the pleading tones of one desperate to be believed, but in the matter-of-fact way of someone who didn't care what I thought, who was just stating his truth because to do otherwise was too hard.

"What is an Entrancer?"

A frown crossed Leo's face at the change of topic. "An Entrancer is what Torvash called Thought Thieves who had the ability to control thoughts, not only read them. We're rare. I am one, as were all my brothers, with differing levels of skill."

"You got inside Gideon's head and controlled him."

"One of my brothers did, yes, very slowly and carefully so he wouldn't notice until it was too late."

"Are you doing it to me right now?"

"No. Unlike hearing your thoughts, controlling them requires eye contact." He had not met my gaze once since we'd sat down.

"The Entrancers on the plains," I said, staring at his shoulder instead of his face. "You know about them?"

"Indirectly. They're part of an organisation of…people with special abilities."

"Like you."

"Like me. We are a strange case, but far from unique."

The horror that dawned at such an admission had to be tucked away for later worry.

"I've never met them," Leo went on. "But they tried to recruit me some years ago, and I—we—they—*my brothers* refused, but we kept an ear on the news coming through the ports after that, in case any of them made their way to Chiltae and got in the way of our plans."

"But they came to the plains instead."

The young man shrugged. "Hired, no doubt. They seem to work for money, not for themselves."

"Paid by the city states?"

"Perhaps. I couldn't say."

I leaned in, hungry now. "And how do we fight them?"

"You don't."

"Unfortunately, that isn't an option. They're destroying my home. My people."

For the first time, he met my gaze, a wry apology twisting his lips. "Then my advice is to let them and walk away. Consider for a moment how much trouble my brothers and I have caused. How difficult getting rid of us has been when we are, in truth, tame by the standards of these people. Accept that some people are born stronger than you in ways you cannot even imagine, and walk away."

"Can you tell me how to fight them or not?"

"No. I don't know enough about the different anomalies to have considered how to circumvent them. You could ask Torvash, the Witchdoctor. He studies them, studied me, though he moves around a lot, is notoriously difficult to find, and isn't one to help people."

Of course it wouldn't be as easy as just asking Leo, as Ezma would have known when she told me how to find him. I sighed. "I don't suppose you know where this Torvash is?"

"No. He left the last place I knew he was. The Nine have always kept an eye on him though, should you find a way to ask them."

The very idea of walking into Chiltae and demanding information of their rulers sent a chill through me. Even if I could, this Leo would be my only way in.

I squeezed my eyes shut. I'd kept my Swords here on the understanding that we needed information from Leo; now here he was, but I was no closer to knowing how I could save the plains.

"All right, that's enough for now, but you're staying until I decide what to do. I can offer you protection, but only while you don't harm my people. The moment you seek to manipulate or hurt any of them, you will be dead whether I wish it or not, do you understand?"

"Better than you do," he said, and tapped the side of his head. "I hear. I know."

I could almost pity him. Being able to hear what everyone thought of you in the darkest parts of their mind would have destroyed me.

I got to my feet and gazes turned my way, a hush blooming around us.

Amun waited just outside the protective circle, watchful. "How are you feeling, Captain?" he said as I approached.

"Fine. Angry," I said. "Apparently he needs eye contact to do the controlling thing, which we should let everyone know, but even without that he can read minds if you're close enough."

"Let everyone know? Aren't we...getting rid of him?"

I shook my head. "Not yet. That isn't the man I met travelling with the Chiltaens, not even close. And he doesn't have the information I need, but he may be able to get it for me."

"Do you mean we're not killing him and we're not going home?" Amun's tone was dangerously quiet.

That was what I meant, and when Amun's brows rose in shock, I knew the time had come. My Swords would never accept one of those orders, let alone both. I could put revenge and departure off a few days perhaps, with the right words, but that was all. To do what I had to do to protect the plains, I would have to let my Swords go and fight on alone—a thought more terrifying than I wanted to admit.

Amun gripped my arm. "I know that expression," he said. "Whatever madness you're planning, just...just think it through before you do something you can't take back. Better to be done with that bastard. It's time to go home."

Mouth too dry to thank him, I patted Amun's shoulder and

walked away. I needed a moment of peace, of silence, so I strode toward my hut, sure I was being watched by those who doubted I was still myself after spending time with the hated priest.

Deep in thought, I brushed through the fabric door and almost ran into Gideon. He was pacing back and forth at a furious speed, every breath quick and shallow and rasping. "Oh," I said. "You saw him. But it's not him. I mean it is, but it isn't. It looks like him, but—" I stopped. What difference did it make? They looked the same. The sight of him had triggered Gideon's memories, and what would telling him he was wrong achieve?

"It's all right," I said instead. "I promise. You're safe. He won't come anywhere near you and he—"

"You—" Gideon gasped. "You. You!"

"He didn't do anything to me." I lifted my hands to show I held no threat. "He didn't. I swear. And he won't. Now please, let me help. Breathe with me."

But Gideon thrust me off, his weakness bolstered by panic. Words gusted out on each gasp, "why?" the only one I understood.

"We tracked him down so I could find out about those Entrancers on the plains. He couldn't tell me much, but he told me about his brothers, the ones that died and didn't come back to life, the ones who did this to you. It wasn't him, Gideon, I am sure it wasn't. I wouldn't let him stay if it was. I wouldn't do anything to hurt you."

I wrapped my arms around him, and this time he didn't resist, just let me hold him, a twitching, gasping knot of tightly coiled cord held close. I wished there was more I could do, that I could absorb his pain, could suck it from him like a leech until his breathing slowed, but it didn't work like that. So, while outside my Swords whispered their doubts, I stood and just breathed steadily, in and out, in and out, in and out.

"Rah."

Amun peered around the curtain, exposing as little of himself as possible to the interior of the room. I had my arms around Gideon, but he may as well have not been present for how intently Amun stared only at me—everything about his manner a rejection of my choice.

"What is it?" I said.

"It's getting heated out here. You need to call a meeting. Leo—"

Gideon's muscles tensed and he leapt back, breaking from my hold. "No, no no no," he said, backing across the floor, one hand thrust out, the other across his eyes. "No, not them. No!" He hit the wall and sank down, chest heaving. His shaking hands tried to grip his hair, his fingers writhing like snakes in short grass.

"Gideon."

"Please, no, I'll do anything, just leave them alone! No!"

I stepped slowly toward him.

"Rah..."

Amun hadn't moved from the doorway. No empathy, no understanding, no pity in his gaze. "I'll be there as soon as I can," I said, knowing that while I could ask others to lead, I couldn't ask anyone else to do this. Who else would Gideon trust? Who else had enough past love for him to outweigh their present anger?

"But, Captain—"

"Since you cannot do this, you will have to hold everything together until I can come," I snapped.

Amun stood a while longer, then with a swish of the fabric he was gone, the room darker in his absence. I felt split in two, as I so often had by the wish to help Miko. As I had when Tor had insisted I help her again, her predicament my fault.

"No, no no," Gideon whispered, but his gasps were further apart now, his panic easing. Whether it was my presence or just the passing of time that had helped, I couldn't risk moving when something as simple as existing could ground him.

"You should go," he said at last, finally calm.

"I'll go when you're all right."

"This is why you should have let me die. I'm just in your way. I'm—"

"No," I said. "No. I needed help once. You need it now. No doubt I'll need it again in the future. No captain walks away from a Sword in need."

"I'm not a Sword."

I dropped my forehead onto his shoulder. "We're not having this conversation again. You are a Sword. You are a Levanti. You are everything you ever were, and I will hold that belief for you while you cannot."

He said nothing.

"I do have to go soon," I added. "But I'll be back."

"Giving me to the Chiltaens would be easier."

My head snapped up. "You heard about that."

"I hear whatever people want me to hear, speaking loudly as they walk past the door."

Arms still wrapped around him, I stared at the side of his face. "You should know better than to listen to wilful malice."

"And you should let me go. Better to die protecting people than live and suffer, causing more pain."

"No."

He turned, eyelids heavy. "It's not your choice, Rah."

"Isn't it? It sure isn't yours. Not in this state."

Gideon pulled away. "I can't just do nothing."

"Then don't do nothing, just don't think sacrificing your life will make a difference. Atone. Heal. Help. Dying helps no one."

"It might be easier," he murmured.

"Oh, I'm sure it's easier, but my Gideon never gave a damn about easy."

He huffed a laugh. "Your Gideon."

Outside, someone started shouting, and I could not put off facing my Swords any longer. "Will you be all right?" I said, stepping back.

He nodded, and that would have to do.

Outside, the camp was abuzz with harsh whispers and arguments, with sidelong glances and fracturing groups separated by chasms of muddy grass, the space between their dissenting opinions impassable.

Leo still knelt in the centre of a large circle of grim-faced Swords. The circle had been for our protection, but now it seemed to be for his.

"Rah." Tor had been leaning against a nearby hut waiting. "You wanted me to find out what I could from Yakono. Well, I did, if you want to hear it."

"Of course. What did you learn?"

With an annoyed grunt, he fell in beside me, and I was pitifully glad of the company. "Not a lot," he said, "but he maintains that isn't the Leo we're after, and that we can trust him on that because he was hired to kill the real Leo Villius, so he'd have done it by now if that was him."

"Hired to kill him? By whom?"

"Some Chiltaen; he wouldn't say more, only that he also made a promise to protect this one, though again wouldn't say who he promised. But, Rah, he meant it. He looks calm and quiet and speaks softly, but he's a hired killer. I get the feeling that if you want to harm this Leo you'll have to get Yakono out of the way first."

We had reached the newly lit fire where my Hand waited, and I halted, a nod of thanks to Tor. "I'll keep that in mind. Does he know anything about Entrancers or what's happening on the plains?"

"No, he said he's never heard of them and has never been to the plains. Says he's from the west, the other side of the Kuro Mountains. Had dealings with the Korune once or twice, but that's all."

"Thank you, Tor. Let me know if you find out anything else. Assuming you're staying for now?"

"For tonight. I'll head back to Jass in the morning, and after that I don't know."

I clapped a hand on his shoulder. "You're always welcome to stay."

"Yes, I know, I'm useful to have around."

"Not just because of that."

With a little snort of disbelief, he strode away.

Amun, Lashak, Diha, and Loklan sat waiting around the fire, but there was none of the usual carefree chatter. From all around the camp, Swords watched us, waiting, and tension grew. I drew a deep breath, but it failed to still the flies swirling in my stomach. "All right," I said. "What do I need to know?"

Lashak folded her arms. "No one understands why Leo is still here. Most want him dead. But talk of Leo and of leaving has…" She trailed off, sharing a glance with Amun that sent my stomach plummeting through the ground.

Amun cleared his throat. "It's gotten messy, especially since you…"

"It's brought up Gideon again," Diha said, speaking plainly where the others had failed. "The consensus seems to be that we kill Leo and go home, giving Gideon to the Chiltaens."

Of course. I'd been narrowly dodging the question of Gideon's future for weeks, but it seemed my luck had come to an end all at once.

"If that's what they want, we have a problem," I said, weaving my fingers together and staring at the glowing coals, bright in the hazy grey afternoon. "I can't do any of those things." I looked up, meeting each hard, questioning gaze. "Leo doesn't have the information we need, but he did give me a lead, and with his help, I can follow it."

"And Gideon?"

"Stays with me. Alive. And anyone who suggests we ought to trade him to the Chiltaens for safe passage ought to be ashamed of themselves. The Levanti do not trade in lives."

My harsh words made Diha look away, scowling, while Amun stared at his hands. "And what is this lead?" he asked.

"A witchdoctor who studies Entrancers, among other things. We just need to find out where he is."

*Accept that some people are born stronger than you in ways you cannot imagine, and walk away*, Leo had said. Not a piece of wisdom I wanted to share.

"Shit." Lashak ran a hand over her face. "That's not going to go down well. Half of them hardly even believe in Entrancers and just want to go home, Chiltaen threat or no."

"And they hate Dom Villius," Loklan said, the quiet horse master's expression filled with disgust. "If you're not going to kill him, you have to get rid of him. The longer he's here, the more Swords you'll lose. It doesn't matter that he's a different man; that he looks like the one we suffered under causes enough pain."

Like Gideon, his panic triggered by memories. I needed to give them something, but I could no more give them Gideon or the wrong Leo Villius to tear apart than I could leave without the information we needed.

"It was home and vengeance you promised when you Fractured with Ezma," Loklan went on. "We have lingered long enough."

"I know, but we need to know what we're up against," I said. "We can't fight for the plains if we don't know what our enemy can do, so I'm going to stay."

Amun's head snapped around. "What?"

"You're all right; I can't expect any of these Swords to remain a day longer. I said we'd stay until we found Leo, and now we've found him. You're going home."

Amun pursed his lips. Lashak blew out a heavy breath. "Are you serious, Captain?" she said. "You really think it's so important you'd risk staying here through winter on your own?"

"Yes, it is that important. All I ask is that you give me a day or two to prepare before I step down and we part ways. Keep the Swordherd together that long, even if it means promising we're about to go home."

Diha and Loklan scowled at the fire, determined not to meet my gaze. Perhaps it was the only way they could keep from telling me I was making a stupid mistake. Whatever the reason, one by one my Hand eventually nodded—slow, reluctant nods followed by salutes and murmurs of "Yes, Captain."

They had agreed, but gone was the cheerful accord and the sense of companionship, and I couldn't be sure any of them truly understood the importance of my task.

One by one they got to their feet, the meeting over, the Hand as good as disbanded until their next captain gathered a new one. Amun, Loklan, and Lashak wandered away, all looking like they were in a daze. Only Diha lingered. "Captain," she said, drawing a small pouch from her healer's satchel. With a scowl, she handed it over, its leather soft with age and wear. "One of my small emergency pouches," she said. "Since you tend to get hurt when you do stupid things."

She didn't wait for a reply. Having thrust it into my hand she spun away, her satchel bumping against her hip as she went. "Stupid things," I murmured, watching her go. Gideon had always said I was good at stupid things, but there had always been others there to catch me when I fell. Now I was alone.

# 6. MIKO

Minister Oyamada sipped from his tea bowl, pretending our meeting was a normal part of daily protocol. He seemed to be taking joy in waiting for me to speak, to put myself at risk. He sat across the table, the same man I'd met in my half-brother's company a lifetime ago, and yet not. The lines around his face had deepened, and now he almost never smiled.

"Lovely weather today," he said, adjusting the skirt of his robe at his knee. Outside, grey clouds continued to gather.

I sighed, too exhausted to dance around only picking at truth. "You don't like Minister Manshin," I said.

Another sip. "Whatever gave you that impression, Your Majesty?"

"Your entire demeanour whenever he's in the same room."

He lowered his bowl, some of the humour fading from his eyes. "Ryo is sure of himself and his position, determined to protect the empire, unflinching in his decisions, and has a loud voice."

"Translation: He is controlling and overbearing, doesn't listen to you, and shouts."

"Your words, Your Majesty, not mine."

"I know I am the one at greatest risk here," I said. "And yet it falls to me to be honest because you don't dare. In case you were unaware, Minister Manshin has full control of the court, the council, and the army. He has worked behind my back, behind yours too, I think, to ensure he has every shred of control he can take under the pretence of caring for Kisia."

Oyamada set down his tea bowl, the tap of ceramic on wood momentarily the only sound in the room.

"I was aware of being shut out," he said, brow creasing. "But I was not entirely sure where you stood. Whether you were both trying to be rid of me, or he was trying to be rid of us both."

"A confusion he likely fostered."

"Undoubtedly, because despite what you think, Your Majesty, my position is neither strong nor unassailable. It may have escaped your notice while you were busy worrying about your own standing and wooing Levanti, but the very soldiers I was given this position to ensure the loyalty of are now very firmly behind their minister of the left. Ministers of the right inspire no such loyalty from those with the pointy steel things capable of overturning empires."

He was no longer the emperor's grandfather. No longer a regent. The brief time he had spent helping Jie unite the south had been forgotten. Whatever we personally thought of each other, our fates were tied together more tightly than ever. I held back a relieved sigh and stared intently across the table. "You think he intends to replace you?"

"Wouldn't you?"

I considered, weighing up his family name and wealth compared to Manshin's military loyalty. That Manshin had left Oyamada out of his plans meant he didn't trust him, and had decided any number of ambitious southern lords could fill Oyamada's place. "He might," I said. "I wouldn't."

Minister Oyamada lifted a brow. "No?"

"No. Because I gave you my word and you gave me yours. And you haven't broken yours, no matter how you must feel every time you look at me and see only the hands that killed your grandson."

His lips twisted into a bitter grimace, and he stared at his tea bowl, spinning it slowly. "You are skilled in your use of truths and emotional cuts, Your Majesty. I am yet unsure whether I am more grateful for your acuity, admire your heartless employment of it, or hate you for not being the monster I need you to be."

I could not immediately answer, such raw words akin to a man taking a knife to his heart and slicing it open. He had been allowed to acknowledge his grandson's brief ascendance to the throne, been allowed to uplift his family, been allowed to see Jie properly buried, but he had not been allowed to grieve. There had been too much to do, too many people watching his actions upon this stage. But still that grief lived inside him, heavy, unyielding, its edges all scratchy and spiky like someone had balled up splinters and made him swallow them. I knew because I carried one of my own. So many lives I had not grieved. When would I be able to stop? To rest? To breathe my sorrow, not only my desperation?

I wanted to reach across the table and set my hand on his, to let him know he wasn't alone, but whatever truths we had made space for, that was one step too far. Honesty. Empathy. Compassion. Touch. The things we hadn't allowed ourselves in this court— silent solidarity the best we had.

"I have...a plan," I said after we had sat a moment in silence, sipping our tea. I hadn't meant to come out with it so boldly, but I wanted to trust him. Wanted to believe someone truly was on my side.

"A clever plan or the hopeful gamble sort, Your Majesty?"

"Let's call it both. We need to get the Chiltaens out of Kisia before the winter, or you know as well as I do that they'll dig in and secure their power base here. So, I'm not going to marry Dom Villius. I'm going to marry Sichi."

Minister Oyamada's lips twitched into the beginnings of a laugh even as his gaze raked my face. I had not expected him to take me seriously. Slowly the laugh faded and he sipped more tea. "You're serious."

"I'm serious."

Marry a woman. The idea had felt dangerous, illicit, a thing to be rejected out of hand, and yet how perfect to sit beside an equal who shared the rage that drove me, someone I never had to fear, who couldn't take power from me. A friend.

Oyamada sipped more tea. The bowl must have been close to empty, but I recognised the technique of drinking to hide one's expression and delay speaking. I often used it myself.

"Explain," he said eventually, lowering the bowl.

So I did, and while I spoke, he sat very still, letting the last of his tea cool in with the dregs as I explained all the reasons why marrying a man was dangerous and why Sichi was the best choice.

When I was done, he tapped the edge of his bowl and stared at the tabletop. The maids had brought only tea and dried fruit, no wine or meats, nothing to make anyone think this was a meeting of note. Just a dull discussion about recent supply issues over tea and fruit. Oyamada had even brought a stack of papers that remained untouched on the corner of the table.

"You would be called unnatural," he said at last. "And no doubt many other things."

"Like all the names that were thrown at my mother? That have already been thrown at me? Minister, I could do everything perfectly and people would still hate me because I am a woman determined to have a voice. I am done trying to make people like me. It is time to make them believe in me, or fear me. We have only one more chance at this."

"We?"

"I can't do it without you."

Lies are heavy. It's easy to forget that until you try putting them down. Until you choose to trust, choose the strength that exists beyond vulnerability. Had Emperor Kin known it was there, I wondered as Oyamada's gaze grew bright, almost hungry as he considered his future, or had the Soldier Emperor been too caught up upon the idea that emperors can never be wrong? Lesson five.

"And what's in it for me?" Oyamada said. "Lady Sichi is not my daughter. What is to stop Manshin claiming still more power once his daughter is an empress?"

"He can't. She won't be a Manshin anymore. And what's in it for you is that you'll be on the winning side, on the right side of history. You'll have fought against assimilation by the Chiltaens, for a free Kisia."

His brow furrowed. "Our soldiers may not listen to anyone but Ryo. It could be a very circuitous way of ending up in the same position or worse."

"It might be, yes, but I will gamble on death or success over my current state of imprisonment. I refuse to be a puppet. I refuse to marry a monster. I will give no legitimacy to a holy empire on our land. No peace lies down that road. No future. No Kisia. So, do you stand with me, Minister, or not?"

---

While Oyamada went to undertake the first part of his mission, I ambled slowly back to my apartments, gnawing my lip all the way. Would Manshin think I was running away? Would he suspect Oyamada of lying? Doubts and questions piled up and up as I walked, able to answer none of them.

"Will he do it?" Sichi demanded the moment I slid open the door to my rooms.

I let go a slow, calming breath and nodded. "He's gone to talk to Manshin now, so I suppose we'll soon know what our plan will be."

Sichi mirrored my slow exhale. Her hand had frozen amid Shishi's fur, mid-pat, and Shishi broke the tension by licking and nuzzling Sichi's hand until she went on with the pats. Undertaking a sustained stretching exercise in the middle of the floor, Nuru grinned. A grin that faded when she found me watching. I couldn't blame her. I was marrying the woman she loved.

"A letter came for you, Miko," Nuru said. "Not through the usual route."

Sichi once again abandoned her dog patting to reach for the writing desk. "Oh yes, I almost forgot. Here."

I took it from her hand, careful not to touch her fingers lest Nuru see, though the letter soon drew all my attention. It was unlike any I had ever received, the paper fine like silk and the letters perfectly formed like they had been stamped in place. Embossed in the wax was a single word: *Torvash*.

"Torvash?" I said, turning the letter over.

Sichi shrugged. "I wondered if it was Tor's full name."

From mid-stretch, Nuru snorted. "Only if he has started thinking very highly of himself."

"You know Tor?"

"Of course. We were initiated into the saddle together. We ought to have been Made together." She stopped and stood up, sweat sparkling on her dark brow. "The only reason he was taken by the Chiltaens to be taught your language and I wasn't was because they didn't want girls."

She scowled at the memory, but I could only think how wonderful it must have been to grow up knowing your worth, to be able to see such a society as ours and be confused by it.

"No Levanti would put *vash* on the end of their name," Nuru went on, switching the arm with which she had been working. "It means 'god.'"

"What does your name mean, Nuru?" Sichi asked while I carefully broke the letter's seal.

"It's not easy to translate," she mused. "It's a type of flower with spots on the tips of its petals, but it's also a feeling, a...sense of being home? A...I don't think I've learned a good Kisian word for it, I'm sorry. *Tor* is much easier. His name means 'truth.'"

"What about *Rah*?"

I immediately wished I hadn't asked and lifted the letter to hide my heating cheeks.

"*Rah* means 'plains,'" Nuru said. "Or maybe 'wide-open space.' 'Grasslands'? Something like that, I think, would be the best translation."

"And *Gideon*?" I asked to shift the conversation from Rah, but at Sichi's little intake of breath, I wished I hadn't. Love there might not have been between them, but respect there had. That she'd had to sit by and watch Leo gain power over the man she had entrusted with her future ate at her more than she admitted.

Before I could apologise, Nuru said, "*Gideon* doesn't mean anything in Levanti. It's not a Levanti name, rather one that came from the east, I think? He always used to say his mother named him after a travelling wine merchant, but whether it's true, I'm not sure."

She shrugged and went back to her stretches, and as eager to drop the conversation as Sichi surely was, I looked down at the neatly written letter.

*Your mother requested I pass information on to you*, it began abruptly, and the room faded to nothing but me and the paper and the hollow thud of my heart.

*Yet as I am unconvinced that educating you about soul abnormalities is worth my time or effort, I have instead sent along a copy of my early notes regarding not only the birth and life of Dom Leo Villius and his brothers, but also Entrancers, Thought Thieves, and Mystics and Memaras in general. If your mother was in error and these are not of interest to you, return them via*

*a missive addressed to Kocho at the Red Wheel in Kogahaera.*
*Should the need for more information arise, a letter directed there*
*will also find me, though I cannot guarantee any speed of reply.*

*Torvash*

When I looked up, both Sichi and Nuru were watching me,
Nuru stilled about her task and Sichi all but holding her breath.

"What is it?" she said when I didn't speak.

"I…I don't know. I…I'm not sure I understand it." I looked
down at the letter again, but though the words were still there,
each individual one clear and legible in its perfect handwriting, the
whole was an incomprehensible confusion that swirled across the
page. I thrust it out to her. "You read it. Tell me what he wants."

Sichi took the letter and I began to pace, desperate to expend my
nervous energy before it tore me apart, but the moment she lowered
the letter I stopped. "Is my mother alive?"

"I don't know, Koko. It's…He doesn't say. I think it is best not
to get your hopes up just in case." She reached out a hand though
I was too far away to touch—comfort should I choose to take it. "I
know it's hard. Hope is as terrible as it is precious."

I nodded, and she lowered her untaken hand.

"As for the rest of the letter," she said, heaving a deep breath,
"it seems to be from someone who knows about Leo and the…
unusual things he is capable of. Someone, moreover, whom your
mother trusted. A book did come with it. I tucked it beneath the
writing table."

Hurrying over, I found the slim bound volume Sichi had hidden, and drew it out, unsure what I was holding. Flipping through
a dozen pages didn't enlighten me.

"I…don't understand half of what it says," I admitted. "Or why
Mama thought I would need it. We know Leo is a monster, and I

have no intention of either marrying him or allying myself with him; what else is there to know?"

"I don't know, but if there's any information about how to fight him, that would be good," Nuru said. "Dishiva lost an eye to that bastard. He knows what you're thinking, he can get inside your head, and he just won't die. May I look?"

I gladly handed the book over, and abandoning her exercises, Nuru settled on the window seat, expression growing hungry as she turned the first page. Sichi met my gaze with a sorrowful smile, and I had to fight the urge to burrow into her shoulder and sob. She wasn't mine to touch, as Nuru's continued presence reminded me. We hadn't talked much about our plan to marry, a plan that, while it would allow Nuru to stay, would also thrust me into the middle of a relationship where I was not wanted.

*Not wanted.* Those words nipped at me with their sharp little teeth, hungry for my sorrow. Edo hadn't wanted to marry me. Rah hadn't even wanted to stay. And still I could not think of my mother without remembering the woman who had knelt beside Tanaka's body and told me, without needing words, that I wasn't good enough.

"Are you sure about this?" I said.

"Sure about what?" Sichi replied, having returned to running her hands through Shishi's fur. The lucky dog rolled onto her back in a state of bliss.

"Our marriage."

She didn't glance at Nuru. "You aren't?"

"Oh no, I mean, yes, I am. As strange as it is, I think I will prefer being married to a woman—to someone who understands, but—"

Sichi tilted her head, lantern light shining on the hairpins in her neat bun. Always so perfect and beautiful. How much I had wanted to be her growing up.

"If you are sure, then I am sure. Together, you and I can do anything, and no man will ever be able to put us back in our rightful place."

*Rightful place.* Those two little words rang in my soul, leaving realisation flowing in their wake. I stared at Sichi. "They're afraid of us."

"So afraid," she whispered, as though it were the greatest secret two women could share. "Deep down. Afraid of you. Afraid of me. Afraid of losing the respect and power inherent in their positions to one our society paints as weak. Lesser. Do you remember Empress Tisha Otako?"

"Empress Tisha Otako, wife of Emperor Zashun Otako, Second of his name. A little? He ruled through the first great war, didn't he?"

"So the official histories say. But he died of the imperial disease, and records state he started showing signs of it as early as twenty years before his death."

I thought of my mother, lying propped upon a bank of cushions on her mat, threads of blood trickling from the needles in her arm. "That seems a long time to have the disease."

"It does, doesn't it." Sichi's eyes twinkled. "They don't want people to know these things, Koko, but Emperor Zashun died twelve years before the end of his reign."

"What do you mean?"

"I mean that for twelve years, Empress Tisha sat in her husband's place and ruled the empire. And Empress Lian. The official histories make her sound like a weak, sickly woman, but I was able to dig out firsthand accounts from the archive and…" Sichi blew out a breath. "He didn't rule at all. There were three whole years during which he didn't sit on the throne or take the oath. She didn't pretend to be him, but she did don the male imperial regalia and hold the throne in his place."

We sat a moment in a silence that seemed to ring with new

information, with possibility and fiery hope. Sichi gripped my hand and squeezed it. "We aren't going to rule Kisia by pretending to be men, Koko. We're going to rule as women. And they are going to hate it."

———————————◆———————————

It was hours of pacing the floor and staving off panic before Oyamada returned. Trays of tea had come and gone barely touched, and I'd started a dozen letters, only to ball them up and throw them into the braziers heating the room. A gentle knock was all the warning we got before at last Minister Oyamada slid open the door himself and stepped inside.

"Minister." I sounded strangled, but managed to welcome him with a gesture toward the table.

With murmured thanks he made himself comfortable, his expression impossible to read. Breathless, Sichi and I joined him, leaving Nuru perched on the window seat watching. While Oyamada adjusted his robe and cleared his throat, seeming to have all the time in the world, I held in a demand to know at once what had happened and said as calmly as I could, "Well? How did it go?"

"On one point well and on the rest not so well," he said cryptically, his hand tapping its way across the table as though disturbed by the lack of tea bowl to busy itself with. "Getting his agreement that you, Your Majesty, ought to visit Kuroshima before your marriage ceremony was quickly done. I presented him the historical precedent and emphasised the need for you to be"—Oyamada had the grace to clear his throat and look away—"*cleansed*, given your recent association with the Levanti."

"Cleansed? I do not require cleansing!"

"No, Your Majesty, but I felt Manshin's agreement was more important than . . . accuracy, shall we say."

"Very admirable," Sichi said while I went on seething. "Arguing with my father has never been a wise choice. So Miko is to travel to Kuroshima before her wedding ceremony, Excellency?"

"Yes, and given the ceremony is likely to take place within the next ten days or so, she is to leave in the morning." He glanced my way. "A point I did not argue as I feel the sooner the better is best with Ryo, lest he change his mind. But unfortunately"—he swung his gaze back to Sichi, his hand once again tapping the tabletop—"my recommendation that it would be seemly for Her Majesty to travel with a female companion was rejected without consideration. He says a maid could do the job and that you, Lady Sichi, aren't to leave here under any circumstances."

Sichi blew out a heavy breath and sagged. "I should have known that would be his response. He says I am not his daughter anymore, but he won't let me go while there's a chance I could still be of use to him."

"You are likely right, my lady, especially since he has insisted that Her Majesty take . . . your companion with her."

"Nuru?"

"Yes, Nuru."

Sichi spun to look at the Levanti still perched on the window seat. "Me?" Nuru said. "Why me?"

Oyamada folded his hands together primly, his lips forming a flat line at being addressed without his title. "If I had to guess, Ryo is attempting to remove Lady Sichi's support, leaving her alone and vulnerable to whatever scheme he has in mind."

We sat in silence a moment, contemplating his words. It was, I had to admit, a good estimation of how Manshin thought and worked. "Additionally," Oyamada said, looking not at us but at the table, "Ryo has, in his usual high-handed way, insisted that I accompany you to Kuroshima, Your Majesty. It seems my job as minister of the right is of so little import that I can be absent for up to three days without it making a difference."

Bitterness darkened his face and sharpened his words. "Likely," he went on with a snap, "he wishes me out of the way as well, fearing I will not support whatever plan he wishes to forward next."

"All the more reason for us to remove him from power as soon as we can," I said, hoping my expression conveyed empathy rather than pity. "And if the three of us are already to go, then it is only Sichi we need to worry about."

"Not a worry," Sichi said, smiling mischievously from me to Oyamada. "This will not be the first time I've escaped from a house under my father's nose."

"You have a plan?" I said.

Her smile broadened to a grin. "I always have a plan."

———◆———

Minister Manshin braved the dawn chill to see us off the following morning. No smile, no well wishes, he just stood like an immovable force upon the stairs, a man present merely to ensure a job was done right. While horses were saddled and bags were checked, he watched, gaze sliding over Nuru as though she didn't exist.

When we were at last ready to mount and ride away, leaving Sichi behind, Manshin finally deigned to stride toward me. "We shall ensure everything is prepared for your return, Your Majesty," he said. "You may put absolute faith in me." Words for a watching audience, but as he stepped closer as though to help me into the saddle, he added in a low voice, "I trust you have accepted your place and are not about to attempt something...foolish. Majesty."

He awaited no reply, stepping back before I could recover. A nod to Minister Oyamada, a brief word to Captain Kiren, and he returned to the steps as though determined to watch every moment of our departure. Turning my horse toward the gates, I refused to glance back, my only comfort that Captain Kiren had been allowed to choose the guards who accompanied us.

Riding away from the manor at Kogahaera filled me with relief and dread in equal measure. We'd had to leave Sichi behind for now, but beyond the gates there was freedom; out there the wind whipped into my face and my horse carried me with ease.

So as to arouse no suspicions, Captain Kiren had suggested we ride a full hour in the direction of Kuroshima before doubling back. That way, if Manshin sent out scouts, he would be reassured that everyone as far as the village of Hua had seen us pass.

With Captain Kiren out in front and Nuru brooding darkly in the rear, I was left to the silent company of Minister Oyamada. He had been as expressive as a stone since his meeting with Manshin, but today he looked like a very weathered statue, lines etched deep, every pit and hollow darkened and damp.

"You can talk now, you know," I said, flicking a glance his way. "He isn't going to overhear you."

"I don't know what you mean, Your Majesty. I have nothing I wish to say."

"No? You don't look well."

"I had trouble sleeping. Common before a journey."

And like a stone, I would get nothing out of him. Nothing but fresh, unknown worries to deepen my own anxiety.

The road from Kogahaera to Hua was twisting and mountainous, passing through dozens of smaller villages. They ought to have been bustling at this season as everyone made final preparations for winter, but the first we passed was silent and empty. As was the second. The houses stood neglected, their barn doors wide open and their fences down. Whatever animals had lived in the pens were long gone, and no wood had been gathered.

"Where is everyone?" I said.

Beside me, Minister Oyamada cleared his throat. "This close to a former Levanti capital and a battleground? Those who haven't been conscripted to the Kisian army or killed by our enemies have probably fled, Your Majesty. This is what war looks like for common people."

"You say that as though you were not a lord with a wealthy estate safely tucked away in the south."

He gave me a disdainful look, but at least it was a sign of life. "Ah yes, always the northerner's belief we fight no wars and all have *comfortable lives built on the spilled blood of our tough brethren north of the Tzitzi*. If you truly want to unify Kisia, Your Majesty, I suggest you actually get to know it rather than continuing to perpetuate the stereotypes that helped build the Ts'ai-Otako divide in the first place."

He couldn't have sounded wearier had he been falling asleep.

"You may recall," he added, "that Emperor Kin was elevated to general so quickly due to ongoing skirmishes over the Rokyu Pass."

I stared at him. Minister Oyamada rolled his eyes. "Typical. No doubt your mother ensured you learned a version of history devoid of southern achievement."

"As she would have grown up in a time when lessons were devoid of northern achievement."

"Undoubtedly, Your Majesty, stories are the way we beat each other down so we can climb to the top, but a good leader needs to question every one of them. Has to look for the information they can't yet see."

"And have wise advisors who can point such information out."

"Ryo Manshin is very good at climbing." He glanced my way. "And of jumping to a new mountain when the old one has gotten him as high as it can."

"I think he cares about Kisia in his way."

He snorted. "As a fox cares about ensuring a healthy population of rabbits."

We rode on in silence, each empty house we passed more shell than building. I itched to reach for my bow, disliking the silent, staring windows, but I had wrapped Hacho up on the back of my saddle, looking for all the world like a sleeping roll.

"He came to Achoi to help me, when..." I let the words trail off, wishing I hadn't brought up Jie's death. I had felt so cornered when Oyamada had tried to be rid of me before my execution, sure it had been born of a vicious, untethered hate, rather than love. Loyalty. Family. He had been protecting Jie, fiercely, whatever the consequences, choosing to believe the boy could grow into something the empire needed. Jie couldn't have had a better regent. A better grandfather. A better guide.

"Where else was he supposed to go?" Oyamada said, unaware of the direction of my thoughts. "Manshin was Kin's minister. He was well liked by the army, as you have seen, but however much the elevation of General Kin forever changed the way we saw our emperors, we weren't so far removed from the idea of hereditary power and gods that a general, or a minister, could just take the throne without at least a spark of legitimacy. Emperor Kin used revenge. Manshin could have done the same, had he arrived to find you dead."

While Jie and I fought, Manshin had stood outside those doors. He had called out both our names, had surely heard our struggle, yet he had waited until silence fell to burst in. The realisation made me sick.

"But I wasn't dead."

"No," Oyamada agreed. "You weren't. But you had faith in him. He was your saviour. He still thought it best for Kisia to be rid of the idea of Otakos and Ts'ais and take a more military-centric stance, but he could take his time. He would have taken over at some point regardless of what you did, but you offered him too good an opportunity by insisting on an alliance with the Levanti."

"They helped us."

"I know. I didn't say it was a bad plan."

And he hadn't. Not once. He hadn't railed against any of my

plans. Hadn't gotten in my way. Perhaps because he had felt his position was too precarious, or perhaps because it wasn't his way. Perhaps he had actually trusted me.

"Hindsight is a terrible thing," I said.

"That it is, Your Majesty. That it is."

I began to wonder how different things could have been had Jie and I worked together, only to stop. It was a present I could not attain, so I would not do myself the cruelty of imagining it.

The village of Hua was as desolate as all the others we had passed, yet we stopped to rest the horses as planned. From there, we ought to have continued on toward Kuroshima so as to arrive well before nightfall, but when we remounted our horses, we made our way off the road instead. From stones to boggy grass, our pace slowed considerably, making us a silent, dawdling group circling back toward Kogahaera as the day aged. Captain Kiren led the way, giving every known house or village a wide berth and avoiding scout routes so, with luck, Manshin would never know we'd returned.

It took hours, the squish of hooves in mud our endless companion. With every clod of dirt we churned, Nuru's expression darkened, until she was sure to start her own thunderstorm.

"She'll be fine," I said as we eventually reined in behind Captain Kiren. He'd already leapt down to do a quick scout of our proposed hiding place.

"I know." Nuru's scowl managed to darken still further. "I just wish I could go in there to be sure. I'm so useless here, where everyone recognises me in an instant."

With no words that could console her, I left her to pace about and joined Captain Kiren. "All safe?" I said.

"All safe, Your Majesty. So long as she knows the place, hopefully all we have to do is sit and wait. Although if we're waiting too long, we'll have to make the rest of the journey to Kuroshima in the dark."

"You're worried about bandits on the road?"

"I'm worried about everything, Your Majesty. It's my job."

Rather than join Nuru in pacing, Captain Kiren became a silent statue, watching the incoming track without seeming to even blink. Most of his men were ranged around to keep watch, while one kept an eye on the horses in case we needed to make a quick escape.

The plan had been for Sichi to slip out to Edo's camp with the help of one of the maids and from there go down the hill out of sight of the manor to this very spot. She ought to have made it well before nightfall, yet the sun sank lower and lower into the trees with no sign of her. A night chill set in, further dampening the anxious mood, and soon I was up pacing just to keep warmth in my legs, or at least so I tried to convince myself. My every quiet assurance that Sichi could take care of herself sounded increasingly desperate.

Once the sun had abandoned us, we lit a few covered lanterns, and Captain Kiren brought his troubled expression my way. "If she doesn't come soon, we'll have to decide whether to make camp and see what tomorrow brings or ride on to Kuroshima."

"She'll be here," I replied. "She can look after herself. Trust me, she's coming."

He grimaced but let the conversation drop, leaving me to panic in earnest. Until at long last a hiss came from one of Kiren's men—they'd seen a light upon the track. Before the words were even out of his mouth, Nuru was off, ignoring attempts to call her back. She disappeared into the darkness, and for a few long seconds we held our breath. The flicker of a light appeared, bobbing unsteadily. And from the night, Sichi and Nuru emerged, both grinning with relief.

"I'm sorry I'm so late," Sichi said, out of breath. "It was so hard to find a time to get away with Father so busy about this plan and that, so many robes he wanted me to wear for the dressmakers to alter, I swear I feel like a pincushion."

"A very cold pincushion," Nuru said, rubbing one of her hands. "We should get out of here in case someone followed her."

Captain Kiren couldn't agree fast enough, and leaving barely enough time for me to embrace Sichi in relief, he hurried us to our mounts.

No longer needing to hide our purpose, he led the way across the dark, soggy field to the nearest track. It wasn't the main road to Kuroshima, but it was better than struggling through mud, and we were soon able to speed to a canter beneath the sliver of moonlight.

Riding fast through the night froze my hands to the reins, but I would have suffered twice the discomfort for the elation of escaping Manshin, for having a plan to protect ourselves so we could fight back.

We stopped once to rest the horses along the way. Oyamada grumbled incessantly about the cold and his old bones, yet as we drew closer and closer to the shrine he became insistent that we keep on rather than stop to rest a second time. At last we reached the edge of the old forest where a marker to Kuroshima Shrine pointed the way. Another few miles would bring us to the bridge over the Nuord River. We were almost there. Almost free. It was intolerable to have to slow the horses to a walk while we were so close, but waiting a little longer was better than having them fall from under us.

"Almost there," I said, trying to buoy Oyamada's spirits as I slowed my mount beside his. "Then we can light a very large fire for you to roast yourself atop of."

"That sounds almost inviting," he said through clenched teeth. "You'll be joining me in the flames, I assume?"

A movement out of the corner of my eye drew my head around, playful reply swallowed. It flickered again, a change in texture there and gone. And again. Closer.

"Watch out!" I cried, lunging at Oyamada. I grabbed his sleeve even as the unmistakable twang of a bowstring cut the night. Oya-mada gasped, throwing his arm wide as he fell, arrow caught in the meat of his shoulder. He hit the road with a sharp cry amid Captain Kiren's shouts, every one of my guards drawing their bows and aiming into the trees. More arrows rained down. Some hit the road. One got the rump of a guard's horse. Others sent my men tumbling from their saddles, fletchings trembling in their arms and backs and throats.

"Run!" Nuru shouted, dancing her fearful mount close to Sichi. "Run!"

But Minister Oyamada lay in the road, and I would not aban-don him.

"You go!" I shouted as I pulled Hacho from her wrap. "Take Sichi!"

All was chaos as I nocked my first arrow and loosed at a dark shape in the trees, followed by another, unable to tell how many enemies hid in the shadows.

"We must get out of here!" Captain Kiren said, turning his horse. Blood splattered his face. "We must get you to safety, Your Majesty."

An arrow narrowly grazed his ear and he moved in front of me, jaw set. "Your safety is all that matters, Your Majesty. Please, go!"

It was foolish to stay, but one glance at Oyamada stiffened my resolve. "Get him up and we can go. I will not abandon my minister."

Captain Kiren didn't argue, just dropped from his saddle with his lips pressed into a grim line. Around us, his men went on loos-ing arrows into the dark trees, though few were being loosed back. Something was wrong, but as Captain Kiren hauled Oyamada to his feet, I could give the change no thought. The arrow in Oyama-da's arm was deeply embedded and blood oozed, leaving my minis-ter ghostly pale. "Get him on his horse!"

"He can't ride like this!" the captain shouted. "We have to—"

"Help him up in front of me," Nuru snapped, edging her mount close as she sheathed her blade. "We need to go before—"

A scream rang through the trees, leaving a stillness in its wake—the thud and crack of footsteps in the undergrowth becoming a fading heartbeat. My surviving guards eyed the trees warily, adjusting their stance.

"What is going on?" Sichi whispered, her dagger hand trembling. "Why is it so quiet?"

Another cry came from the night, and a man fell from a high branch to roll down the gentle slope into the road. As he came to rest in the damp leaves, two similarly dressed men burst from the undergrowth and sped toward us. I lifted Hacho, nocked, loosed. An arrow struck one man in the chest and he stumbled, but his companion didn't slow. I nocked again only to catch Sichi's grunt as she threw her blade. At such a distance she couldn't miss, and the dagger sliced the man's shoulder, throwing him off balance. Before he could right himself, I loosed into the side of his face. Thrown back, he hit the road a gasping, blood-splattered mess.

I dropped from my fretting horse as the man started dragging himself toward the treeline. His knee crunched as I stepped on the back of his leg, loosing a muffled, bubbling cry from his throat. Captain Kiren swung a lantern into his face—a face I'd never seen before in my life. The man hissed, dribbling blood.

"Who are you?" I said.

"Fuck you."

"Who hired you?"

The man half rolled, as well as he could with blood oozing everywhere and my foot on the back of his knee. "Did someone have to?"

Here a man I'd never met yet he possessed enough hatred that he would not only die to ensure my end, but not care who he took with me. Enough hatred that he would spit anger at me with his last breaths.

A waft of floral scent laden with sweat and Sichi appeared beside me. "I know this man," she said in a shaking whisper. "He's one of my father's men."

The man bowed, a strange, mocking thing when done lying in the road and bleeding out, an arrow protruding from his cheek like a cruel growth. "My lady," he said, the words as mocking as the bow.

"My father sent you to kill me too, did he?"

"No, though if you ask me it would have been for the best."

Sichi flinched as he spat her way, splattering blood over her feet.

"So it's only me he wants dead," I said.

"Just finish the job," the man growled. "I go knowing there will be someone to finish mine." He glared, the deep hate in his eyes a promise I couldn't but believe. My whole childhood had been stolen by assassins, by the need to see enemies in every shadow even when no enemies ought to exist.

*People will try to shunt you into the darkness*, Mother had said. *Remember you are my daughter.* She had meant it for a boon rather than a curse.

Taking the blade from my sash, I plunged it through the man's throat. He died with a gurgle, blood spilling. I ought to have felt something. Some remorse or disgust or horror at the sensation of the blade piercing paper-like skin, only to meet muscle and the stiff wall of his throat. But I felt nothing. Kneeling, I wiped the blade on his tunic and sheathed it.

"I think he was the last one."

I leapt up, drawing the blade again. A woman stood in the middle of the road beneath the wary gazes of my remaining guards. Blood stained the cuffs of her short robe and splattered her chest, but despite the robe she was Chiltaen. My wariness deepened. "Who are you?"

"I'm Cassandra," she said, the words confident though her gaze flitted warily toward the others. "I came to warn you that the Chilt-aens won't keep an alliance and marrying Leo Villius is a bad idea. No matter what he has promised you, it's a lie."

I tilted my head, examining this strange woman with her blunt warning. "And who do you work for that you, a Chiltaen, would bring me such a warning against your own people?"

"No one." She raised her brows, the answer seeming to surprise her. "I...I knew your mother."

*Knew.*

"Miko," Nuru snapped, her arms still circling the injured Oya-mada up before her on her horse. "We need to go. He needs a healer."

Of all the things to forget. "Yes, yes, of course, but...where? Who can we trust?"

"Surely there are some villages around where the people don't hate you or want you dead."

"Every single one we have ridden past has been empty." I pressed a hand to my forehead. "And we may well find Kuroshima the same but for the shrine, and he can't climb those stairs."

"There are Levanti," the woman—Cassandra—said. "In the village."

"Levanti? Which Levanti?" But she had no answer. I turned to Nuru. "Who would be camped near Kuroshima?"

She shook her head. A gamble then. Rah, I would trust, but run-ning into Whisperer Ezma would not end well.

"We don't have a choice," I said. "We need a healer, and if it's a healer who hates us, we'll just have to deal with that when we get there."

"Agreed," Sichi said.

Not having moved, Cassandra eyed my remaining soldiers. "Allow me to accompany you, Your Majesty, since this unfortunate incident has left you short of a full complement of guards."

My instinct was to refuse, to be indebted to no one, but her mention of my mother gnawed at my thoughts and I nodded. "Very well. You ride ahead where we can see you, and lead the way to these Levanti. Captain Kiren, leave two of your men behind to help our wounded while we ride on ahead."

The captain nodded, but jerked his head at Cassandra. "Are you sure you can trust her, Your Majesty?"

"No, but I am going to for now. There's no time to argue."

With Cassandra riding ahead, we galloped the last stretch to Kuroshima, Nuru in the middle of the group with her arms around the limp form of Oyamada. She grumbled about the saddle not having been made for this and railed at her horse when it protested our speed, but we kept on as the night deepened, stealing the last lingering hints of warmth from the day.

Our breath was condensing in the air by the time we reached the Nuord River, its flow roaring with the season's heavy rain. The bridge was tall and broad, a stone construction as old as the shrine and the village to which it led. Nuru's horse slowed up the incline, but lights twinkled ahead and I pressed on, rising to the zenith and letting my horse hurry down the other side. Where the mountain met the village stood two stone lanterns, both lit, but they were the only sign of life. "The village looks empty," Sichi said, breathless beside me in the gloom. "Where are the..."

She stopped, eyes widening as she stared into the darkness. Figures shifted around us, little more than shadows on night. I didn't want to fight, but I didn't want to die either, so once again I nocked an arrow to Hacho's string and drew it back with weary arms. "Who's there?"

A nearby figure stepped forward. "Miko?"

Only one person said my name like that. I lowered the bow. "Tor." Tears of relief pricked my eyes. "Please," I said. "We need your help."

# 7. CASSANDRA

Heavily armed Levanti flanked us, scowling a lack of welcome. No one spoke as they led us into the trees, though Empress Miko and the long-haired Levanti shared tense looks, leaving the night airless. Ill-ease prickled across my skin on cold fingers.

*These could be the same Levanti who took Yakono and Unus*, I said to break the silence. Kaysa said nothing. She'd said nothing since we'd left Unus, not even during the attack on the road, despite how fast my heart had drummed, drowning out everything but the desperate fear I was about to lose my daughter.

More Levanti appeared as we went deeper into the trees, each a shadowy figure as we passed darkened huts and tents. Empress Miko's guards drew closer. One whispered to her and she shook her head, not drawing her gaze from the Levanti waiting around the closest fire. They watched her approach, blank faced, nothing welcoming here but the lack of drawn weapons.

Leading the way on foot, the long-haired Levanti halted before the firelit group and, gesturing to the empress and her companions, spoke an explanation. Not enough explanation, it seemed, for the one who appeared to be their leader stepped forward. Unlike the long-haired young man, their leader looked more like the other Levanti I had seen, dark-skinned and tall, broad-shouldered and serious, with only a thin dusting of dark stubble across his scalp. He looked from one tired rider in the empress's entourage to another and eventually settled his intent gaze on her.

"Empress," he said, the only word I understood until the long-haired Levanti started to translate. "Why are you here?"

"We were attacked on the road, and my minister is gravely wounded," she replied, her tone taut and high-pitched. "I would not trouble you for anything less serious, I assure you."

Another Levanti from the group around the fire muttered something, loud enough that the empress looked to their translator. "Amun says that's good, because they're full up with helping people right now."

The leader glared at the speaker—Amun, the translator had called him—stretching the tension tighter still. At last the leader turned back and nodded to one of the women standing nearby.

"Diha is their healer," the long-haired translator said, gesturing at the woman. "She'll take a look at your minister."

"Thank you." The empress nodded to her Levanti companion, barely managing to keep the injured man from slipping out of the saddle now. "Go, Nuru."

The young woman set her horse walking in the healer's wake, half a dozen Levanti darting from the shadows to help her with her bleeding burden. Empress Miko watched them go but made no move to follow nor speak again, and amid the growing silence I itched for my blade.

Eventually the Levanti leader spoke. "Are you here for Dom Villius?" he said through his translator, the words seeming to draw all air from the night.

"No, we make for the shrine up the mountain." Empress Miko glanced sidelong at one of her guards. "Is...is Dom Villius here?"

"In a sense." The leader drew himself up. "Our camp is your camp if you wish to remain for the night, Your Majesty."

A small breath of relief eased from one of the empress's guards, and some of the tension relaxed. Or at least it did outside of my skin. Inside, a hand seemed to grip my chest tightly, and like I was retching up bile, words escaped my mouth. "Is Unus here?" Kaysa said, the question bursting across the quiet clearing. "Or Yakono?"

All eyes spun my way, but Kaysa drew us up and glared back.

"I thought you said you weren't here for Dom Villius," the translator said.

"I'm not." The empress bristled. "We met this woman in the woods. She saved us from an attack."

*This woman.* Her gaze upon me was cold and suspicious, and but for Kaysa's determination to stay and find Unus, I might have run away as fast as possible rather than suffer Miko's dislike.

"Tor," the Levanti leader said, giving the translator an order.

The young man sighed. "Make yourselves at home, Your Majesty," he said, speaking to the empress before turning to me. "You may leave your horse here and follow me. I'll take you to your friends."

He sneered the word *friends*, but Kaysa was out of the saddle before I could question the wisdom of trusting them. Looking back only once to be sure we were following, Tor led us across the fire-lit camp, past endless packs of watching eyes and suspicious whispers, toward a hut beyond the largest fire. There, two Levanti stood outside the door like guards, a third sitting nearby watching the curtain-hung hole doing duty as a window.

Outside, the translator spoke to the guards before gesturing for us to enter. No doubt once we did we wouldn't be allowed out again, but that had probably been true since Kaysa had asked about Dom Villius. Without hesitation, Kaysa carried us inside with quick, sure steps. From fire-lit camp to musty interior, the smell of damp was so strong it was like a punch in the face. At least until a fist struck my cheekbone and we reeled back against the rickety wall.

"What the fuck was that for?" I snapped before Kaysa regained control.

Our attacker lowered their fists. "Cassandra?"

"Yakono?"

*See, look*, I said. *Nothing bad happened to them!*

*No thanks to you.*

Unus sat propped against the wall, watching us through lowered lids. "Are you all right?" Kaysa hurried toward him, dropping us onto our knees. "What do they want from you?"

"I don't know," Yakono said when Unus didn't answer. "But we're fine. They've asked him a lot of questions but have left me alone for the most part. Perhaps because I told them killing people is my job."

"So is theirs, I should think," I murmured as Kaysa hunted Unus's face for signs of ill treatment. He looked well, uninjured beyond the dark ring at his hairline where I'd struck him with the hilt of my knife. "Unus or Duos?"

He looked up, a dead stare rebuking us for the question. Kaysa didn't retreat, and eventually he sighed. "Unus. I haven't felt him since we arrived. These Levanti aren't exactly fond of him." He gave a shrug, his tunic scratching against the rough wall. "In an odd way, this is the safest place for me."

Watching the camp through the dark window, Yakono laughed humourlessly. "That might be true for now, but I don't think their forbearance will last. And until they release us, we're stuck here."

"It does seem that way." I rose to join him at the window. "The odds are pretty shit, though you could probably take more of them than I could."

"If we end up fighting them, it won't be for ourselves." Yakono nodded in Unus's direction. "It's him they hate. Rarely have I seen such animosity in an expression. I don't know what he did to them, or what his brothers did, but it must have been bad."

"Used them to get safely into Mei'lian and went back on a promise to free them," Unus said dully from the corner. "Killed one of their translators. Got into their leader's head and turned him against his people. Destroyed their chance for a new home here. Led an attack against them at Kogahaera. Slashed one of their captain's eyes out."

The list was all the more horrible for lacking emotion.

"Well." I sighed. "They really do hate you."

He didn't smile.

"Cassandra," Yakono said, my name rolling beautifully off his tongue. "How is it that you're here?"

"I..." I couldn't meet his gaze. "I came with Empress Miko."

"I thought that was why you ran." He said it so simply, dredging up the guilt I hadn't felt in betraying Kaysa. It would have been easier if he'd been angry. "I'm glad you found her, but why is she here?"

"I was almost too late, and one of her companions was injured on the road, so they came here for help."

"Lucky for us," Yakono said, not a hint of sarcasm in his words.

A shout out in the camp saved me from wallowing even deeper in guilt, and I edged closer to the window. Outside the door, our guards whispered to each other, heads bent close as activity stirred. Miko was out there somewhere, but the gathering crowd was all Levanti, their focus caught to the woman who had called to them.

"The high value Levanti put upon their social rules and structures is impressive," Yakono said, his presence warm beside me at the window. "The only place I've seen anything quite like it is in church gatherings."

"Do you mean being Levanti is a religion?"

"No, they aren't attributing value to the existence of an external power; they are attributing value to themselves and their way of life."

Outside, the woman had started speaking, and already the Levanti were growing restless. Murmuring rose like a tide, and many turned glances upon one another as though to be sure they were all hearing the same thing. "What's going on?"

Yakono shook his head. "I don't know; I never learned Levanti, and my spoken Korune is very rusty."

Of course he knew Korune, while I didn't even know where that language was spoken. The feeling he was not only better at his job but also a superior human reared its head, and I scowled out the window.

As abruptly as it had begun, the speech ended, its last words trailing off into the darkness. The silence thrummed with tension, with the palpable feeling someone was about to shout and draw their blade. Instead, someone near the back of the group turned and walked away. Another followed. They didn't speak, just broke away from the group one by one to go about their tasks in unhappy silence.

A step scuffed at my side and I spun, pulling back my fist just in time to keep from punching Unus in the face. "Don't sneak up on a girl like that," I said, heart racing.

"They're divided," he said, barely registering my complaint. "Unhappy. They want me dead, but their leader, Captain Rah e'Torin, needs me alive to find out more about what's happening on the plains. His tracker, Lashak, just informed them they won't be able to take revenge on me, but that they will soon be going home. It's created a lot of . . . mixed feelings."

"All this is because of you?" I said, the question accusatory.

Unus sighed. "Yes. And no. It's about their old leader, Gideon, as well, I think, but the thoughts are . . . confusing. Noisy. Very . . . hurt."

"We need to get out of here," Yakono said, watching the gathering dissipate into muttering little groups. "If they're this angry about you, they could turn on us at any moment, whatever their leaders say."

"Who was it marvelling at the value of their social something or other just a moment ago?" I said.

"They can have value for their society and still want to kill us, Cassandra. Those two things aren't mutually exclusive." Abruptly he stepped back, loosening his limbs and planting his feet. "Someone is coming."

Levanti voices murmured outside our door before the translator stepped in. Flanked by two warriors, he truly was the most un-Levanti Levanti I'd ever seen, not just for his long hair, but also his slight frame that looked unused to physical labour. He owned no determined confidence either, just a resigned sigh and a stance that seemed to hope no one would look at him.

"Captain Rah wishes to question Dom Villius," he said, eyes on Yakono rather than Unus. "Again. His safe return is assured. You're to remain here."

"What about me?"

The young Levanti's gaze slid my way, still managing to look bored though his brows rose. "I don't know who you are and don't really care, but he is coming with us." He pointed at Leo, and his armed companions edged forward. "And the assassin stays." He turned on the words, stepping back out into the evening gloom. Yakono shifted to a ready stance, all lithe and capable, but I set my hand on his arm.

"Don't," I said. "I'll go with him. Stay here."

He had no time to argue. Resigned to his fate, Unus was already making for the door, so I hurried after him. The translator waited outside, his expression a weary, so-very-done-with-all-this-shit look that I knew well. "You had better not be intending to get in the way," he said. "They're all a bit low on patience."

"As long as you're not planning to hurt him," Kaysa said, riding close inside my mind.

The young man didn't answer, just led us toward the central campfire. Most of the Levanti had dispersed, but not far enough for comfort. From every shadow, wary eyes were drawn to Unus's back.

Standing beside the fire, Captain Rah managed the truly impressive feat of looking even more exhausted than Tor. His companions were a collection of fire-lit scowls, but one pointed at me, Miko's name the only word I understood. At least they seemed to have decided not to hack my head off. Or at least not yet.

Turning from me, Unus became the focus of their attention. None of them looked directly at him, but the captain's questions were sharp and quick and Unus's fluent replies begat more questions. Curious, I turned to the young Levanti, still hovering nearby. "What are they asking him about?"

"The Hand want to understand his…condition, is perhaps the word," Tor said. "His claim of being part of a soul and having… soul brothers. I do not know your words for it."

I looked around the circle of frowning Levanti as the conversation leapt back and forth, the questions biting and harsh.

"They don't believe him?"

Tor gave me an indecipherable look.

*Why do they care?* Kaysa said, the first time she'd sought my opinion since our fight for dominance. *If all they want is revenge for the things his brothers did, why seek to understand him first?*

It made no sense to me either, but any hope they might forgive him once they understood disappeared upon an angry snarl. A nearby Levanti approached spitting hate, only the captain's outstretched arm halting his advance. Unus flinched from the man, and Kaysa took over, propelling us into the fray. "What don't you understand?" she said, the words earning silence. "A soul can be born into more than one body. I have seen his brothers for myself, and I'm walking proof the soul isn't an immutable thing."

All eyes turned to Tor, whose translation left them staring at me in disbelief. How easy for them to dismiss the idea, but all my life this had been my reality, their disbelief denying the very truth of my experience. Freak. Monster. Deathwalker Three.

Even now, the ever-present reminder called from a nearby body. The death song washed unbroken around me, until one of the Levanti cleared their throat. "I believe this man is not the same as the one I met while marching with the Chiltaen army," he said through their translator. "But Dom Villius is too well known for manipulation to accept his... wild explanation so easily."

"Sometimes the strangest things are true."

The man lifted his chin, a gesture of acknowledgement that nevertheless had no intention of bending. I sighed. "All right, let me prove it."

I got up, my blood hot with a lifetime of frustration I'd never been able to express, and strode toward the dead body. It lay singing its empty song from before a shrine of sorts—a pile of stones and branches with symbols painted all over. She looked freshly dead, at least within the last few hours, so kneeling, I set my hand to her forehead.

*Your turn*, Kaysa said.

"My wh—?"

Untethered, I fell forward. The taste of ash bloomed in my mouth, followed by silence. Stillness. No gasp of breath, no ever-present heartbeat. It is hard to overstate how noisy a living body is, how desperate, until those sounds are gone.

Awareness spread through my new limbs like water seeping through cracks, giving me control first of the eyes and the lips and the tongue, then the arms and fingers and finally the legs. Overhead, voices joined and swirled into a storm of sound, but despite the shouting, Kaysa just sat watching me. A faint smile touched the corners of her lips, and for an instant I was sure she would turn and run, leaving me no way to catch her. She didn't. She smiled as I twitched each limb, the discovery not unpleasant.

Sitting up was easier than I had expected. Very freshly dead then, and lacking the stiffness age and ill treatment had built up in my body. Around us people gasped, but I had eyes only for Kaysa. She was enjoying watching me experience something that, while terrifying, was also glorious and freeing, a body protected from all harm by already being dead. It was an experience we both shared now, bringing us closer—this a moment of connection piercing the simmering resentment.

"This," I said, foolishly surprised the voice wasn't mine, "is actually quite nice. Except the ash. I could do without the taste of ash."

Everyone stared. I ought to have felt ashamed perhaps, have known myself for the monster they all saw, but while Kaysa smiled at me with my own lips and my own eyes, I could feel no horror. I was what I was, what the world had accidentally made me, and that was not my fault.

As Kaysa had once done in Jonus's body, I spread my arms for the staring Levanti. "Now do you believe me?" I said, causing a symphony of drawn swords. All eyes darted to Tor, as much accusation as question in their looks.

Their captain was the first to speak, his jaw tense.

"I don't know what Chiltaens believe about death," Tor translated slowly. "But to us, until the soul is released the dead are sacred and you are…" He stopped. Captain Rah was speaking again, fast and worried now, sending a ripple of indrawn breaths around the watching circle.

"How are you in there?" the translator said. "You say you have two souls. What have you done with Lepata's that you can inhabit her skin?"

I looked to Kaysa and saw only the same confusion I felt. Something had changed. The question wasn't curious but charged with fear—and not fear of a walking, talking corpse as one would expect.

"I…didn't do anything with it," I said, looking from Kaysa to the Levanti and wondering if we were going to have to fight our way out after all. "She was dead. There was no soul. Only the body, like…a container."

The young man started translating to growing outcry, and as the Levanti surged forward, I stepped in front of Kaysa, arms outstretched. The power of my invulnerability was like a whole quart of Stiff, and I snarled at them, daring them to cut down one of their own to reach me. No wonder Hana hadn't ever wanted to give up her corpse skins, such strength and—

The blade came fast, one moment a mere glint in the weak light, the next it sliced my neck. No pain, only the pressure of it digging into my flesh, of its sharp edge severing skin and muscle and tendon and bone.

Once again I seemed to fly, not detached like a soul but tumbling over and over. I tried to cry out but had no air, tried to brace but had no limbs, could only watch the Levanti spin by until I hit the ground. Lacking pain, the impact was more sound than feeling and I was lying on the grass, numb from the neck down. No, absent from the neck down. Shouts rang about me like they were coming through water. Feet milled everywhere I looked and—

I flew free again, weightless now, into the warm, loud hum of a living, breathing body, endlessly buzzing.

*Cass? You're all right?*

*I…I think so?*

The palpable sense of relief was the most beautiful thing I had ever felt.

"That," Kaysa said aloud, putting our hands on our hips, "was unnecessary. I can remove my second soul without needing to cut the body open."

The translator said nothing. The Levanti weren't listening, were barely moving. Captain Rah stood with blood dripping from the end of his sword, his chest heaving with more than the effort of so easy a decapitation. Abruptly, he knelt and touched the severed head.

"I'm not in there anymore."

No one seemed to hear us. One by one distressed voices erupted, and the captain rose jabbing a finger at me. I flinched, but he said nothing, just gently gathered up the severed head as though it still owned life.

All eyes tracked him the few steps back to the shrine, where he knelt on the bloodied ground and began to sing. Some of the others joined in, a few loud and clear, some beneath their breath like a prayer.

*They really didn't like that,* I said.

*No,* Kaysa agreed. *Honestly, I think you're lucky to still be here.*

*You think cutting off the head is enough to dislodge a soul from a dead body when you've sat inside one while it rotted?*

*Thank you for the reminder.*

*You're welcome.*

"What did you do?" the young translator said, dragging his gaze from his captain's back with an effort.

"I have two souls in this body," I said. "I can put one of them inside an empty body for a time. It's called Deathwalking."

"But you were released when the head—"

"No, I was pulled back by my other soul. Think of it like two people riding a horse. We take turns who's driving."

"You don't drive horses, and two people on a horse would be—"

"It's an analogy," I snapped. "An example. A cart then. Whatever. We can both lift the hands and move the feet and speak to you, and we can switch over. And one of us is a stuck-up, prudish—"

"—and the other is a cranky old whore," Kaysa finished.

*And proudly so.*

Tor stared, his expression giving nothing away. Did he believe us? Did it matter?

When Captain Rah finally rose from the shrine, he brandished a blade at our throat.

"Whoa." I stepped back as the crowd of Levanti jostled and grumbled and hissed. "I was just showing you proof. I meant no harm."

"You're like Leo?" he said.

"No! I mean, yes, but no. Only in the 'our souls are weird' way."

With his blade still levelled at our throat, Captain Rah pelted his translator with questions, questions the young man disjointedly passed on. "You're one of—Do you know...What do you know about Entrancers? Answer—or about the others on the plains—Tell us everything if you wish to walk away from here alive."

I stared around the fire-lit group. There were more Levanti watching than I could count and no way to push through them and live even if Kaysa would let me abandon Unus. He hadn't moved from his place before the fire, while at the edge of the gathering, Empress Miko stood with her companions, stony-faced. The shame I had refused to feel under Levanti eyes flooded in. Beneath my daughter's gaze, I knew myself for the freak I was.

"I...What?" I said, trying to focus on what they'd asked. "What are Entrancers?"

"He means people like me," Unus said, his dry voice barely audible above the crackle of the fire and the shifting crowd. "He wants to know how to fight people like me. Like us."

*Us.* For so long I'd only ever been a *me.* I'd become an *us* with Hana, sometimes with Kaysa, but never with someone external to my skin. The sense that maybe I wasn't alone, that I could find comfort in the understanding of others as one might in a family, momentarily stunned me. Until the captain's wavering sword tip once again demanded my full attention.

"I don't know anything about Entrancers," I said. "I don't know anything about any other freakish"—I winced at how easily the hateful word leapt to my lips—"abilities, only my own. I can make the dead walk for a short time. The best way to combat that is to incapacitate the corpse, that's all I can tell you."

The translator passed on my answer, sending whispers shifting through the crowd of warriors like rustling leaves. Even before he translated the captain's reply, I caught Torvash's name and tensed.

"Where can we find the Witchdoctor?"

"I don't know! He's more the type who finds you."

Argument followed, punctuated by Kisian voices—Miko and her companions speaking in quick undertones. No doubt Torvash had made himself well-enough known during his time in Kisia that they'd heard of him too.

Despite the back and forth taking place between Captain Rah and his companions, no more questions came my way, and I stood in the middle of a storm, every word raising the anger around me until I couldn't make out anything beyond a roar of argument.

*What are they shouting about?*

I shook my head, looking around at all the angry, fire-lit faces. *I don't know. They're pointing at Unus as much as at us.*

When they'd gathered earlier, they'd been quiet and respectful, but now they all shouted over each other, gesticulating wildly, some spitting as fiercely as the flames that lit the scene. Any moment they were going to tear apart either us or each other. Or both.

"I will take them." Miko stepped into the centre of the gathering, shouldering her way through the throng of warriors. "I will take them!"

Though only Tor could understand, the gathered Levanti quietened, hissing demands at the young man caught in the middle. Tor spilled hurried words to his captain as Miko shouted again. "I will take responsibility for both of them and remove them from your care."

I turned on her. "I'm not a problem. I don't need to be in anyone's *care*."

"Not a problem, just a monstrosity," she said, a flash of disgust in her eyes. "And if there's going to be a freak running loose, I'd rather she was in my debt than not."

"Debt?"

Miko nodded in the direction of the Levanti. "If I don't take you off their hands, you'll be dead within two minutes. Unless of course you're capable of bringing yourself back to life." She lifted her brows, something chilly and calculating in her look that was so much like Hana my stomach clenched. "Well, Cassandra? Your choice."

# 8. DISHIVA

A meeting was called that evening as always, but this time when the first legate strode past the chapel, I drew up my mask and stepped out in his wake. My hands trembled, but I clasped them and walked on, heart beating fast. Murmurs of respect flowed around me with every step, something I appreciated more now that I was making use of the title I'd been given.

It wasn't far to the meeting tent, where light and murmurs spilled through the thin curtains. A young boy stood outside, seeming to await orders. He blanched at sight of me and stared up at the sky— the only person more nervous of my presence than I was. There was still time to turn around, to walk away, but what would that get me beyond regrets?

With a nod to the boy, I rolled my shoulders and stepped inside. In the moment it took my damaged sight to adjust, I got the impression of a close, warm space filled with flickering lanterns and bright colours—a scintillating display of power. The impression didn't change as it came into focus, but a flood of relief spilled through me as Secretary Aurus rose from his chair.

"Dom Jaroven, welcome." As he spoke, he gestured to the chair at the head of the table where Leo sat, giving a start as though surprised to find him there. All conversation ceased. The air chilled. Every eye was on Leo. I needed no clearer proof he had been acting as my spokesperson all this time, that his only claim to power was what Aurus had called a matter of habit.

Expression hidden behind his mask, Leo rose. He spoke a few words in Chiltaen as he unfurled to his full height, and then turned my way. "Am I in your seat, Your Holiness?" he said, the words a soft caress. "Do accept my apologies." His mask rippled as his tongue moved beneath the fabric, across and back as though licking his lip. He seemed to want to say more, and I held my breath, unable to focus on anything beyond him. After a long pause, he bowed. "Holiness, I look forward to tomorrow's ceremony, and I will of course have your orders carried out right away."

Before I could ask what orders he meant, he swept out of the tent, leaving a chill lingering in his wake. One by one the legates and commanders settled, some looking to Secretary Aurus with confidence, others holding on to their wariness. Not recognising them all, I wondered if some had arrived with Aurus's men, the loyalties present impossible to understand.

"I will lead this meeting as though you are leading it," Secretary Aurus said, nodding my way. "You will need to speak so it looks like I'm translating, but not too much. We must try not to remind them too often that you're Levanti."

"I thought I was your hieromonk, not a Levanti," I said, glad the mask hid my face as I looked around the table, the urge to be sick rising once again.

"You are, but this will go much more smoothly if we walk that fine line."

He sounded calm and turned to address the men around the table. Breathing steadily and trying to take comfort from Aurus's ease, I listened to the unknown words swirl about me, the tension amongst the commanders slowly loosening. Wine flowed freely, and some of them even laughed at the secretary's occasional witticisms, my occasional Levanti utterances infrequent enough to maintain good humour.

Having asked what was under discussion only to receive a look from the secretary, I was trying not to fear I'd put my trust in the wrong man when the young boy from outside stepped in and cleared his throat. The eyes of every highly ranked man in the room turned his way, and the boy visibly flinched. Fixing his gaze on me, the boy spoke. From the other end of the table, Secretary Aurus translated. "He says he was sent to inform you that your companions are waiting."

"What companions?"

"You had better go find out, but I have a suspicion Lord Villius has just made a move in response to our little coup."

When I didn't immediately rise from my chair despite the growing murmurs, Secretary Aurus lifted his brows. "You may trust me to finish up here in your name, Your Holiness. I will seek you out after we are done."

With that I had to be satisfied, a small, desperate hope having taken root in my mind that the companions the boy meant were my people released at last from captivity.

I rose to the usual murmur of respect and hurried from the tent as divinely as I could. Outside the boy had disappeared, and the noise of bored soldiers making their own entertainment had grown much louder. Thankfully my robe and mask were like armour for now, protecting me from them whatever their humour, and I sped back to my chapel without being accosted for either entertainment or prayer.

More of the camp boys were hurrying in and out when I arrived, carrying plates of food, armfuls of clothes, and even some buckets of water. Unable to ask what was going on, I pushed my way past.

Inside, six Levanti stood amid the bustle, clumped together for safety as they watched the boys with narrowed, weary eyes.

"Oshar! Rophet! Harmara!" I looked them over as I approached, my heart sinking. Having been bound and brutalised, the captured

Levanti were thin and weak, bruised and battered, their faces speckled with patches of blood. "Oh gods." My words were little more than a whisper as they eyed me as warily as the Chiltaen boys. "I am so sorry."

Stepping forward with his long hair lank and filthy around him, Oshar spoke first. "Captain Dishiva?"

I pulled down my mask, unsure whether the mask or the mess Leo had made of my face would be more horrifying. The Chiltaen healers kept putting patches over my lost eye, but I always took them off. I had tried to tell them I could see better without it, but even if they'd been able to understand my words, they wouldn't have believed me.

"Oshar." I saluted him. "I'm relieved you're all alive, though in a far worse condition than I had hoped."

"What's going on?" He gestured around at the small chapel filling with food and clothing. "One moment chained up, the next we've been released and brought here? Was this you?"

I shook my head, looking at each of them in turn. "No, well, yes, but not directly. I'm not sure why yet, but I think Leo ordered you released and brought here. No doubt he has a reason I won't like, but I'm thankful you're free at last."

"Yes, now that we're free we can rip their throats out," Rophet growled.

"No! You can't hurt them. Our future depends on it."

Harmara en'Oht let out a ragged laugh. "We've heard that argument before, and look where it got us."

Rophet grunted agreement. "I hope Gideon is still alive somewhere so I can stick a blade through his eye myself."

By the door, one of the boys shuffled his feet. "Holiness?"

"*Holiness?*" Rophet spat. "You're even more one of them now?"

"No." I clenched my hands tight. "I have always been Levanti and I always will be, but I do whatever it takes to ensure our safety, even if I hate it. Like wearing this mask, and pretending to be their hieromonk. So please trust me."

Harmara huffed a snort of air. "I trust that you think you mean what you're saying, but I don't trust you not to fail us like Gideon did."

Nods of agreement spread to the others, and for now it was the best I could hope for. I gestured dismissal to the boy and he hurried out, leaving us alone. For a few silent moments, the six released Levanti eyed the food and water the boys had set upon the floor. "This is the safest place in the camp," I said. "You can eat and drink and wash. It looks like there are even clean clothes."

Tephe and Harmara shared a glance before both sped toward the supplies, the others following. I watched them all lunge for the small cups of water, downing one after the other before rubbing the rest over their filthy faces. They took turns cleaning themselves as best they could, limbs shaking and teeth chattering, the cold water making their bruises all the brighter. Having dressed in the plain Chiltaen clothing, food was then shovelled into their faces. There was no time for conversation, but any hope I could make it through the night without having to explain everything was soon dashed. Once they had all washed and changed and eaten and looked at each other's wounds, six pairs of exhausted eyes turned my way, awaiting answers.

"When I heard you had been captured, I came here to get you out," I said, looking at my hands rather than them. "But it was me Leo wanted, not you. I am his false priest."

None of them interrupted as I explained what had happened, how Leo had pursued us up the tower, how Ezma had claimed I was the true Veld, how I had been made their hieromonk—a position that owned power Leo didn't want me to use against him. They listened calmly until mention of Secretary Aurus.

"Another Chiltaen ally?"

Of course it was Rophet who spoke, determined to wield his anger against me. I met his gaze, hoping my scarred eyes would make him look away. They didn't. "Not so much an ally as someone we can use to our own ends."

A step scuffed in the doorway, and someone cleared their throat. I flinched and spun around, cursing my useless peripheral vision as Secretary Aurus strode in without a trace of either smile or frown. "Yes, indeed," he said, the words solemn. "I am absolutely someone who knows how to be useful."

I got to my feet. "Secretary," I said, with all the ease I could muster. "The meeting is over?"

"Yes, but do introduce me to your companions before we talk about that, Dom Jaroven. By the looks on their faces, you perhaps have not had time to warn them I speak Levanti quite well."

In anyone else, such a line, accompanied as it was by a crinkling around his eyes, would have been playful, almost friendly, but he wasn't anyone. He was a Chiltaen leader I could not trust more than I had to.

"As you wish, Secretary. On this side are Rophet and Tephe e'Bedjuti, and Ptah en'Injit. On the other are Harmara and Jira en'Oht, and Oshar e'Torin. This is Secretary Aurus, the man I was just telling you about."

"Good evening," Aurus said when these introductions were met with silence. "It is good to see you all free from Lord Villius's direct malice, though you had better take care as there's no knowing what he may attempt in...in..." He waved a hand vaguely and murmured in Chiltaen, searching for the right word.

"'Retribution' is the best translation for that," Oshar said, not looking up from the flatbread he was tearing into smaller and smaller pieces.

"Yes, retribution, that's the one. Thank you. Might you be one of the Chiltaen-trained translators?"

"That I am."

Still, Oshar didn't look up, but this didn't seem to bother Aurus, who turned to me. "May we continue this conversation in private, Your Holiness?"

Under the suspicious glares of the freed Swords, I walked with him to the farthest corner of the chapel, where in the shadows beyond the flickering lanterns, we could speak undisturbed. "Was it Leo who had them released?" I asked before he could speak.

"I believe so. I must admit it is quite the clever move."

"How so? Now he doesn't have them to hold over me anymore."

"Doesn't he? They're still here, still inside a Chiltaen camp surrounded by Chiltaen soldiers. That they aren't chained up anymore makes little difference to his leverage."

"Then why?"

He spread his hands, the gesture taking in everything inside the chapel and out. "Because it weakens your power. As I said at the meeting, you're our hieromonk, but the degree to which each soldier will want to follow you will depend on how feminine and Levanti you appear or don't appear. The mask and robe hide you well, but—"

"But six Levanti companions will be an eternal reminder I am not who they want me to be. Not who they want to follow."

"Exactly. I told you it was quite a clever plan."

I silently agreed. If Leo could discredit me enough with the Chiltaens here, not only would I be unable to lead them to victory against Kisia, but also no Levanti home this side of the sea could survive unless Chiltaens went on accepting me as their holy leader.

"How about the meeting?" I asked. "Did that go all right?"

"Yes, I kept it light, conveyed the orders from the Nine, spoke much about you leading us to a victory ordained by God and all that. Also sought to make it clear, subtly, that Lord Villius no longer has a strong position in the church. I don't know how much difference it will make to those who follow him, but it started no arguments."

"Are you saying there are legates who would follow him instead of obey orders from the Nine?"

Secretary Aurus sighed. "That is what I'm saying, yes. You see, Chiltae is unnecessarily complicated. Perhaps you've noticed our soldiers wear either green or blue trims? Well, those in green are part of the armies of the Nine; the blue are part of the merchant army, although since trade is money and money grants a place in the Nine, many of the men who fund the merchant army are also our oligarchs and secretaries with control over the armies of the Nine."

"So, the same people command them, but the money comes from a different place?"

"Not all the same people. Enough to mean it doesn't usually matter, but that sometimes it matters a great deal."

"This being one of those times?"

"Why, yes," he said, throwing me an all too cheerful smile. "Just as this is one of those times when it matters whether a commander's loyalty lies with his faith or his country. Those who follow their faith have always answered to the hieromonk, but they also got very used to answering to Lord Villius as his expected successor. Hence his decision to make you look like someone not worth following."

Not worth following. Not Aurus's opinion of our value, I told myself, but the words stung all the same. I turned back to the gathered Levanti still picking at the last of the food, their initial, desperate hunger having dissipated. They looked weak and worn out and so very tired, but that didn't stop a Levanti warrior being worth far more than any Chiltaen on or off the battlefield.

"I will keep working on the commanders," Aurus said eventually. "We have a few days to win them over, before Lord Villius departs for his wedding ceremony."

Still watching my people, I hardly heard his words. "Do Chiltaen soldiers like to be noticed and given the opportunity to talk about themselves and feel special?"

"Most likely, as does everyone. Why? You have a plan?"

"I think perhaps I do," I said. "Maybe we aren't so different after all."

———◆———

I rose with the sun the following morning and, shivering, pulled on as many layers beneath my robe as I could find. From outside came the scent of woodsmoke mingling with the ever-present mud, and my stomach rumbled. The Chiltaen military food was plain and often either over- or undercooked, but I had gotten used to it as I had gotten used to the richer Kisian fare at Kogahaera.

Having dressed, I stared at my masked face in the small bronze mirror, a ghost all that stared back. "Who are you?" I said, and couldn't but wish my reflection would answer the question I could not.

Oshar arrived not long after, dark circles beneath his eyes. "Good morning, Captain," he said, smothering a yawn.

I'd set the mirror against the wall and sat before it, so when Oshar halted behind me all I could see was his leg. There on the side of the reflection he stood uneasy. I looked up. "Is everything all right?"

"I was going to ask you the same question, Captain. I . . . understand what you're doing here, I think, but . . . tell me, how much danger are you—are we—in?"

I stared back at my featureless face in the mirror. "I don't know," I admitted. "But when one is surrounded by enemies . . ."

"Right, so it's as bad as I thought then."

"Probably. I need your help though. Translating," I added, hoping he wouldn't refuse. "I know you don't want to do it, but I need to be able to talk to the soldiers without Secretary Aurus."

The young man shrugged. "Helping is the least I can do. I thought we were going to die here."

He could still die. I thanked him rather than say so.

"Unfortunately, you're also going to have to put on these," I said, picking up the small pile of white attire Secretary Aurus had been able to requisition. "The better to look like my holy assistant than a Levanti."

Oshar screwed his face up as he took the pile. "Does that mean a mask too?"

"Yes. I'm sorry. You do get used to it though, and you don't have to worry about keeping a straight face."

"Hides all disrespect! At least that's something." Clearly trying to be jovial about it, Oshar pulled on the spare robe. I helped him tie it before turning my attention to the mask.

"How can you breathe in this?" he said as I wrapped it around his face.

"Easily; no need to be so dramatic because it feels strange. Just relax."

He did so, and I tied the strings behind his head, trying not to get any strands of his long hair caught in the knots.

"There," I said, stepping back to admire my handiwork. "You look positively godlike."

"Yay?" Oshar got to his feet. "I hope this job comes with extra food rations because I'm starving."

Together we stepped out into the early morning light, the chill air seeming to bite every bit of exposed skin. No doubt thanks to Leo's orders, Oshar's tent had been set up with the others in front of my small chapel, to be visible to all the Chiltaens who came seeking my blessing. I felt tugged two ways, grateful to have my people near me and to not be alone, yet troubled by Leo's plans.

"Surrounded by enemies," Oshar murmured beneath his mask

as we passed the Levanti tents and entered the main camp. "Now I know what caged animals feel like."

"Just keep walking, but maybe fall back a step so you look more deferential."

I hated to ask, but he did so without complaint, not that any fewer soldiers stared as we made our way toward the nearest fire. They were serving up the morning meal, each scoop of rice porridge accompanied by flat, crunchy shards of salted bread. Oshar's stomach rumbled.

"We can't eat yet," I said. "Sorry, but to eat we have to take off our masks, and we can't do that out here."

"You ought to have warned me this job would be cruel to my stomach, Captain," Oshar said.

"We won't be long; we're just going to walk around and talk to people and generally be as leaderly as possible. Then we can go back inside, and you can eat as much as you like."

Having greeted the men gathered around the fire, we walked on along the row of tents away from the central area where they were all big and important. The common soldiers' tents housed two men on mats like the ones the Kisians used, far more the style Levanti were used to.

Despite the lack of anywhere they needed to be, none of the soldiers were still asleep, though some were still sitting in their tents. One we passed was engaged in what sounded like a playful argument with his partner, perched outside the tent shaving. At the sight of us, the shaving soldier hastily got to his feet, pulling on his tunic and managing to drop his razor. Oshar bent to pick it up, spinning it in his hand with ease to pass it back handle first. *Thank you* was one of the few Chiltaen phrases I knew, so I could only assume Oshar's response was to say the man was welcome. More surprising was when he went on speaking, gesturing at the razor now in the soldier's hand and touching his own chin through the cloth mask. The soldier laughed, and as though I wasn't present they talked a few minutes longer before we moved on.

"I think that was the first Chiltaen I've ever just…spoken to for no particular reason," Oshar said as we walked away along the row. "He seemed pretty normal."

"You were expecting a monster?"

Oshar shrugged. "The men who taught us Chiltaen were. I guess the difference was they thought we were beneath them, whereas that man saw an equal." He tapped his mask as he spoke. "Handy thing this piece of white cloth."

We walked on, speaking to soldiers, asking them about themselves, and performing blessings. Oshar was more than a translator; he provided a less intimidating proxy, easing conversations and often having them without involving me at all. He could joke with other young men while I performed blessings, repeating the words over and over as soldier after soldier knelt before me. When at last we headed back toward the chapel, we were both starving but triumphant.

"A solid morning's work," I said. "It's not captaining as I'm used to, but it's not so different either. You make a good second."

"Me? I just—" He halted, staring ahead. "Well, this ought to be good."

Leo stood waiting outside the chapel, his hands clasped before him and his expression hidden behind his own mask. "Ah, Dishiva," he said as we approached. "You've been a busy girl."

Refusing to rise to the bait, I stopped, clasping my hands in the same way. "Merely doing the job you gave me, Lord Villius."

"It's very cute that you think you can make a difference. You aren't going to live long enough for these seeds to bear fruit."

"I'm the hieromonk and you're no one," I said, heart thumping at my own daring. "You can't take that away without destroying belief in the church and its god."

His laugh was dry—humourless. "Oh, can't I? You think you've become quite the expert in our laws and ways these last few days, Dishiva, but no. The church belongs to my family—to me. I am God's chosen, I am Veld, and no upstart little horse breeder is going to stop me building an empire." He stepped close, threatening me with his proximity as well as his words. "You are going to name me defender," he said, the words a hissed threat. "Or I am going to show you for what you really are, peeling away each layer of respectability you've built around that weak, feral, worm of a woman beneath that mask." He leaned closer still, our masks almost touching. "Well?"

"Get. Fucked," I hissed back. "No matter what you threaten me with, I will never name you defender. Find yourself another puppet."

I stepped back, and wishing I didn't have the mask so I could spit at his feet, I strode around him toward the chapel entrance. Oshar hurried after me.

"I do hope you don't come to regret those words, Dishiva," Leo called as I reached the doorway. "That would be so very...unfortunate for your companions."

Heart thumping and blood running hot, I stepped from the bright sunlight into the dim, dusty air of my sanctuary. I would not look back, would not give him the satisfaction of seeing my shaking hands or the hot, angry tears stinging my eyes. Not until Oshar assured me that Leo was gone did I let myself collapse onto the floor and rip off my mask, releasing my fear on a tide of panicked sobs.

———————◆———————

Despite the run-in with Leo, when the evening meeting was called, I left my chapel with more confidence than I had the night before. Oshar followed, grumbling about the mask. Soldiers nodded as we passed, and I hoped I wasn't imagining the increase in voices saying "Your Holiness" and whatever the short prayer was with which they often greeted me.

Stepping into the meeting tent, I once again had to pause on the threshold to let my eyes adjust to the brightness of so many lanterns. Fabric rustled, chairs creaked, and low voices murmured their respect my way, yet the expressions that slowly emerged from the darkness were full of wary confusion, their glances shifting between me and Aurus and Leo. He wasn't sitting in my seat this time, rather had taken another at the table and looked up at me.

"I've informed them that you requested my attendance, Your Holiness," he said brightly. "So that we can discuss the great necessity of naming a defender. In times of war, you know, such things ought never be delayed. Anything could happen."

"Anything indeed," Secretary Aurus said quickly, as though afraid I would make a scene by ordering Leo out. "Join us, Your Holiness; we were just about to begin."

There was no place for Oshar, so when I took my seat he stood behind me as he'd often done for Gideon. By the time I was comfortable, Aurus had begun, and it was all I could do not to look Leo's way and wonder what he had planned. His retaliations were coming swiftly, each one bringing with it the memory of every other time I'd dared to cross him.

The meeting had barely begun when Leo cleared his throat. He spoke in Chiltaen, leaving me to watch the secretary's expression and wait for Oshar's whispered translation.

"He says the most important matter to be discussed is the naming of a Defender of the One True God, since it is the hieromonk's intention to lead the Chiltaen army into battle in the coming days."

Before I could reply, Aurus was speaking, and behind me Oshar went on whispering. "The secretary says that's a matter for the hieromonk and not the legates of the army or a secretary of the Nine."

"I will name a Defender of the One True God when I am ready," I said, interrupting Leo's reply. "When, with the grace of God, the right person is revealed to me."

All around the table, men reached for their wineglasses, looking anywhere but at Leo and me. Except for one man, wearing the blue of the merchant army, who leaned forward. "Surely the right person is here at this table, Your Holiness," he said through Oshar's quick whisper. "Lord Villius has served the faith selflessly for many years, as his father did before him."

"That has never been a reason for God's choice," Secretary Aurus said. "And I must repeat that while it is important that Dom Jaroven make a choice soon, it is not the business of this meeting to choose on her behalf."

Two of the men spoke up at this, and had he not been wearing his mask, I was sure Leo's smile would have been smug. Whatever the outcome, he had created division amongst those present and proved their support for him was strong.

I made to speak over the growing noise, not yet sure what I was going to say, but behind me, Oshar gasped. Something moved in the corner of my vision, and I spun to face the entrance. A newcomer stood in the opening, gilded against the night sky, his face one that still haunted my nightmares.

Looking around the tent before settling his gaze upon me, Commander Legus cleared his throat. "You sent for me, Your Holiness?"

His words and his gaze shuddered through me, and I was back in Chiltae, caught to the ground, every breath full of filth and the stink of his skin. Nearby someone jeered. Darkness swarmed in. I tried to focus on the song, Rah's voice rising like a prayer, but it kept slipping from my mind like water through my fingers.

"Your Holiness?"

Darkness pressed in harder, smothering. Not the darkness of

night but that of eyes screwed shut, of the close pressure of his weight, compressing my chest and stealing my air.

Faces shifted around me. Voices babbled, mingling with the clink of my chains. I was trapped. Drowning. Someone touched my arm and I screamed. Screamed and screamed and lashed out as someone else drew near. My fist connected with bone, but there was no one in front of me, just the suffocating weight crushing me into the ground.

Movement. Air blew around my face. I wanted to be sick, so dizzily did the world spin and sway. "Keep those fools from staring!"

"Make way!"

Tears spilled down my cheeks and every breath was a panicked gasp. Far away, Rah's song was fading. Abandoning me.

"Just try to breathe," someone said, and I did, thinking of Lashak sitting with me back in Kogahaera, counting every breath. I tried to do the same, but I couldn't stop my hiccupping gasps, even when the noise around me calmed to nothing but a murmur.

"No need for you to stay," that same someone said. "She'll be better for peace and quiet." I caught no answer, no shape of a face through my blurred vision, but the same voice encouraged me to breathe again, and I did as it said.

Slowly my racing thoughts calmed enough to concentrate on every breath, then on my dry lips and the comforting flicker of light nearby. Distant voices murmured, unthreatening, while closer to, paper rustled. Unsure where I was, I tried to think back over what had happened, drawing up reluctant memories of the meeting. Of Leo. Of Legus. I couldn't swallow my whimper fast enough and it escaped—a pathetic sound I couldn't hide.

"It's all right, you're safe here," Secretary Aurus said, and so surprising was his voice that I half rose as I turned. But it really was him, sitting on the edge of the next couch, his face a combination of golden light and deep shadows. "And you don't have to explain anything."

He looked back down at the book in his lap, expression inscrutable. I wanted to ask why I was there, why he was watching over me when he could have left me with my people, but they were questions I couldn't utter. No words of gratitude wanted to emerge, only a growl of rage. "I am going to kill that man," I said, my voice hoarse.

"Which one? Lord Villius or the commander?"

I met his gaze, sure my remaining eye burned with tears and hate. "Both of them."

# 9. MIKO

My two prisoners gave me back look for look, though the man who both was and wasn't Dom Villius soon shied to stare at the ground. "So," I said, eyeing each of them in turn. "We have Dom Villius's twin brother, who can read people's minds, and a Deathwalker who knew my mother."

They remained silent as though they'd made a pact not to speak, and I found my gaze drawn to Cassandra. She'd given no other name, but had seemed to know me, had spoken of my mother, and had come to our rescue when she could have left us to die.

"You didn't tell me you were a Deathwalker," I said, keeping my tone even.

"It's—" She cleared the roughness from her throat. "It's not a wise opening. Hello, my name is Cassandra, and I can make dead bodies walk around, how are you?"

"Is that all being a Deathwalker is?"

"No, we are two souls in one body, like we told the Levanti. No," she added, turning her head as though speaking to someone at her side. "This isn't a good time."

I tilted my head, unsure if I found her fascinating or frightening. "And who do you work for?"

"Work for?" Cassandra's brow furrowed.

"Who pays you? Who are you loyal to? Whose side of all this are you on?"

"I'm on my own si—If you're planning to hurt Unus you'll have to go through me."

It was the same voice and yet not the same voice, its tone and diction slightly altered along with her expression. Two souls. It sounded like nonsense, and part of my mind still rebelled against the idea—a deep alarm bell ringing that here was just another person trying to trick me, to take advantage of my desperate need to know what had happened to my mother.

"So you're loyal to this man here?" I said.

"No, I'm loyal to no one, but I care what happens to him because he doesn't deserve to suffer for someone else's crimes."

"And if I threatened his life, would you kill me?"

Her face twisted strangely, every distortion of her handsome features seeming to belong to a different expression.

"Why threaten me when you can use me?" Dom Leo Villius said.

"Use you how?" Fatigue was seeping into my bones, but at least sitting here asking questions meant not being out there having to answer them or having to dig through the ashes of our fine plan.

Dom Villius tilted his head, a sad smile weighing him down. "My brother wants me alive."

"Don't give her a way to use you!" Cassandra snapped—one of the Cassandras. "If you let someone bargain you to him you'll be a dead man."

"Why bargain when she has something he needs and he has nothing she wants? Empress Miko doesn't want to make a deal with him; she wants to be rid of him."

His voice owned the same heavy sadness as his smile, but I couldn't help thinking of all Sichi and Nuru had said about this man. He might not be the one who had hurt them, but he had all the same abilities. The same potential.

Cassandra glared at me. "Is that true? Do you mean to kill Duos?"

"My plans and intentions are my own," I said, disliking her familiarity.

"That's not good enough." Definitely the other Cassandra—her aggression and disdain palpable. "We are not your prisoners, whatever you say, so give us a reason to trust you or we leave."

I looked from one to the other. I hardly even knew what my plans were anymore, let alone how these two might fit into them, only that I needed all the allies I could get. All the power and leverage I could hold.

"My goal is the protection and recovery of Kisia," I said, rubbing a hand over my face and letting out a sigh. "If Dom Villius—the other one—chose to leave my lands, I would not pursue him, but as his goals appear to be directly opposed to mine, I cannot see any way this plays out that doesn't bring us into direct conflict. And should he get in my way, I will not hesitate to end his life. Does that satisfy you?"

Neither answered, and it soon seemed that a slow nod from Not–Leo Villius was the closest they would come to agreement. Footsteps approached outside the hut door, and I was grateful for the interruption until Tor stepped inside with an apologetic grimace.

"Your Majesty," Tor said as the assassin Rah had been questioning was pushed past him. "Rah has asked me to inform you that Dom Villius is not allowed to leave the camp without his permission. I don't know what's in his head since it looks to me like everyone is ready to tear Leo apart, but he says he'll discuss it with you tomorrow."

"He needs me," Dom Villius said, his tone weary. "To find Torvash and get information about the...people taking over the plains."

Surprise flickered across Tor's face, but he squashed it with a frown.

"Did you say Torvash?" I said, thinking of the book tucked into my pack. "*Tor*, Levanti for 'truth,' and *vash*, Levanti for 'god'?"

"Yes. I have long wondered if that was a deliberate choice on his part." Dom Villius tried for a smile. "You probably know him better as the Witchdoctor around here. He studied me and my brothers."

"And Rah needs information from him?"

He tilted his head, eyeing me curiously before an amused smile dawned. With a jolt I recalled that he could read my mind, might now know about the book, and I spun toward the door. "I must go find Sichi."

"Lady Sichi and Nuru are by the fire," Tor said. "Along with your guard captain and his men. There's food waiting for you too, and I understand your injured companion is going on as well as can be expected. He's being tended by many skilled healers."

I glanced back at the three prisoners who didn't think themselves prisoners. I'd wanted to ask about my mother, but with so many other problems pecking at me, I wasn't ready for the answers. They would be the same answers tomorrow.

From Leo Villius and Cassandra, my gaze slid to the assassin. Everything about him was quiet and watchful and entirely forgettable. "Wild is the world where an assassin is the least dangerous person in a room," I said, a laugh covering my own ill-ease as I turned away. Tor held the door open, everything about the stiff way he held his ground reminding me of the night I had forced a kiss on him as though he'd been mine to command.

Thankfully, he said nothing as I passed, but his footsteps fell in beside me as I stepped into the cool night air.

"I got your letter," I said, glad of an easy topic to break the silence. "It was kind of you to write and warn me."

"It was nothing. It allowed me to practice my writing."

"You did well."

"I doubt it, but thank you for your...kindly lies, Your Majesty."

"Kindly lies. I like that. That's the way a lot of people move through life, I think."

There was plenty of chatter and movement out in the fire-lit camp, but compared to the military camps I had been in, it was quiet, owning a feeling of empty space deliberately maintained. And everywhere I looked, Levanti stared back at me, curiosity the kindest of their expressions.

Away from the main fire, Rah sat in a circle with three other Levanti—all familiar, though I knew only Lashak by name. They were their own little group with their backs to everyone else, deep in conversation.

I must have looked at them too long, for Tor followed my gaze. "The Hand are meeting again. Or arguing again, most likely. Rah isn't the easiest captain to work with."

He offered no further explanation, just led me to where Sichi and Nuru sat beside the fire. Nuru's eyes were alight, Levanti words spilling from her lips as men and women of the herd approached to embrace her, now that the first tension of our arrival had passed. Many greeted Sichi as one of their own too, and greetings emerged fluently from her lips. Something she said made a burly warrior laugh, and as she was handed a bowl of food, she sat it on her knee as though born to camp life. The Levanti around her eyed her with approval. I, on the other hand, may as well not have existed. Any gazes I met quickly slid away.

"They really like her," I said.

"They do, yes."

Tor offered no reassurance because there was none to give. Sichi had carved herself a place with Gideon's people, while I felt as awkward as I had when I'd first allied with the Levanti in Syan.

Familiar faces from those days appeared, only to fade away into the night without either a nod or a smile.

Someone held out a bowl of food, and I took it with a little murmur of thanks, realising too late I ought to have spoken in Levanti. "*Elash.*"

No one heard me.

I sat beside Sichi, the sense of being invisible next to the court beauty all too familiar. She wasn't beautiful in the classic way Edo was, but she had the sort of beauty that came together in movement and expression that no portrait could capture. The sort that held the eye and dimmed everyone around her.

Once the initial slew of greetings had faded away, Sichi turned to me, her smile sliding into a grimace as she switched with enviable ease from sociable to practical.

"I had been hoping we had outsmarted my father, but it looks like he outsmarted us," she said. "Taking the opportunity offered to be rid of you."

"Much easier to achieve what he wants without me getting in the way if I'm dead." I thought back to his threats in the shrine. "This way he can take the throne for himself, since he's legally my heir." It had seemed such a wise choice at the battle of Mei'lian. How I could kick my younger self. "Emperor Manshin. How long has he sought the title, I wonder."

"Long enough he probably won't wait around to see your body before declaring himself," Sichi said.

"But when none of his men report back, he'll send more after me."

Nuru pushed food around her plate with her fingers. "How long do you think that will take? Do we have a day? Two? Only a few hours?"

"Until the morning, I should think," Sichi said. "But that also assumes he hasn't discovered I'm missing yet. Again, we should have until morning for that, but we can't be sure."

"And we can't go to the shrine tonight?"

Sichi shook her head. "Shrines are always so strict, and no one can just walk in and demand to be married, so even under the circumstances I don't think they would budge. They may even refuse to help us when they realise neither name in the letter was a mistake."

I blew out a heavy breath, meal forgotten. "So, we hope to the gods that no one comes looking for us tonight, then first thing in the morning we climb to the shrine and hope they'll still marry us. Assuming we get through that, we have to gather allies and stop your father making an alliance with Chiltae before it's too late. I refuse to let Kisia become an extension of Dom Villius's holy empire."

"Killing Dom Villius is something I think we can all agree with," Nuru muttered.

Around the other fire, Rah and his Hand were rising from their meeting, rolling shoulders and brushing down their breeches.

"Do you think—?"

"No," Nuru interrupted. "I'm afraid none of my people have any interest in remaining here any longer than they have to, let alone fighting for you or anyone else."

Her blunt words stung as much as Rah's seeming desire not to look my way as he approached the cooking coals. A nod to the shadowy figures cooking the nightly meal, and taking two tin bowls, he walked away. Silently I willed him to turn around, to look at me, to register with a nod or a smile that he was glad I'd helped with Leo, that he wasn't angry I was here, that we still had something salvageable despite the events at Kogahaera. He walked right to the edge of the firelight before he slowed his steps and turned.

Despite the noise and the laughter, the whole camp faded to nothing, the empire with it. For a brief second there was only him and me in the entire world, then he turned and was gone, swallowed by the night. Beside me, Sichi and Nuru were no longer a comforting presence, just a mockery of what I wished I had.

———————◆

Having checked on Oyamada, a Levanti led us to one of the huts dotted around the camp. There were signs of recent habitation, yet we were alone but for the beginning of a small fire, a pile of discarded storm cloaks, and a pair of sleeping mats. Like they had both been born to this life, Sichi and Nuru rummaged through their bags, chatting quietly to each other, while I stood unsure of my place and my purpose. I was restless, like I was intruding upon Sichi and Nuru's space by being there, but didn't feel any more welcome outside.

Nuru looked up, something kind and yet piercing in her gaze. "*Ki ichasha sorii,*" she said, reminding me of the time Tor had said those same words. "That's what you say to him."

I looked to Sichi, who drew a dark cloak from our salvaged belongings. A small, conspiratorial smile twitched her lips. "We saw you staring," she said somewhat apologetically. "Don't let anyone else make your choices for you. Least of all society."

I understood them as they had understood me. It would be so easy. There was no one here to see. No one here to judge. I had no idea what the future held, but I knew what I wanted in that moment, what I had wanted since that night at the inn on the road to Mei'lian. I shook my head. "He might not want—"

"But he might," Sichi whispered. "You'll never know if you don't go find out."

Refusing the cloak, I let out a deep breath, thrilled and terrified at my own daring. I had crept into his room once. I could do it again.

"*Ki ichasha sorii,*" I said, and Nuru nodded as I brushed nonexistent dust from the front of my robe. "All right. Good. I'm going."

I stepped out before I could stop myself. Cold night air bit my cheeks, and from all around came low chatter. It was late enough that many Levanti had retired for the night, but I hadn't considered what I would do if Rah was asleep or not in his hut, hadn't thought at all. Deciding it was better not to start now, I kept walking.

Rah's hut was on the far side of the camp, warm firelight glimmering through its windows. My steps faltered as I drew near, but the watching Levanti pushed me on, all previous assurance propped up by pride as I strode to the curtain-hung doorway. A quick tap on the wall, and I dove through into the warm interior.

And halted, breath held. From a spot propped against the wall, Gideon e'Torin looked up. I had seen him only briefly after the attack on Kogahaera where he and Rah had been trapped under the ground. Somehow he looked worse now. Dark shadows made pits of his eyes, and I'd never seen a mouth form the opposite of a smile, turning down as though it would require twice the effort to cheer him up.

"Empress?"

Rah stood caught to the floor with one boot on and one off. Everything about him was luminous, his eyes bright, his expression intent, his posture upright and proud. But he didn't smile.

"I'm sorry," I said. "I mean, uh … *korrup* … no, *korrum* … I should—" I turned for the door, only to halt at the sound of my language.

"Don't leave on my account," Gideon said, his Kisian as good as Tor's, though his voice crackled with either illness or ill-use. "Rah could use a break from looking after me."

He tried a smile, but perhaps due to the turned-down edges of his mouth, it looked sad. The sort of sad that gets into your bones. Before I could decide whether to stay or go, whether I could more trust his words or his face, he was on his feet.

"Gideon …" Rah shuffled a step closer, only to stop as the former emperor lifted his hand. This the man I had marched an army against, my great enemy now nothing but a hollow husk.

He spoke in Levanti, whatever he said enough to snap Rah's mouth closed. I wished I had not come, but Gideon was already striding toward the door. The scent of smoke and stale sweat hung about him, yet he bowed to me, all grace and pride, and for an instant I could see a hint of the handsome man Sichi had chosen to follow. Then he brushed past into the night and was gone. The curtain fell back into place.

Rah hadn't moved. I had found him in an awkward situation, yet it was I who fought the urge to look away. "I should go," I said, my heart racing so fast I felt ill. "I should—"

"No." He stepped closer and, bending over, tugged off his second boot. "No." And I needed no more words to know he meant it, that I hadn't been the only one thinking about the moments stolen from us by a want of language. A want of time. A want of freedom.

He glanced at the door only once before approaching, steps silent. A thrill all too like fear trembled through my skin as he drew close, but if he was a hunter, I wanted to be caught, wanted to be touched, to be gathered close, to feel his searing heat.

"*Ki ichasha sorii,*" I said, amazed at the boldness with which I looked up into his eyes. With which I touched his chest. Spoke *please* in Levanti as though it were not the plea it truly was. In that moment I wanted him more than I'd ever wanted anything, as though my whole body was drunk on nothing but his presence. "Please."

His hands were cold through my robe, but it was the confidence with which they trailed up my back that made me shiver. I wanted more, wanted those hands on my skin, and I began to untie my sash. Tomorrow a wedding sash would be tied around my waist, but for now I would live outside the politics and the war and the expectations, outside the responsibility of my title and be just Miko.

My sash slid to the floor, my robe falling open to reveal a sliver of skin. His eyes travelled down, hungry, and still I wanted more. I wanted to be wanted, and had he not slid his hands across my skin I might have dropped the whole robe then and there.

Rah murmured something by my ear, *cold* the only word I understood.

"Then you'll just have to warm them up," I said, turning my lips to his, the words a whisper of breath against his skin.

Despite everything, his kiss was tentative, as much a question as our first kiss in the stable had been, gestures of respect and assurance the only way to communicate consent. It had been a wonder, a man who would not take what he wanted until he was sure I wanted it too. Here again he left space for me to step away from the gentle pressure of his lips, but instead I ran my hands along the bristle of his unshaved scalp and drew him closer. His hands warmed against my back, and the flick of his tongue along my lip was full of such promise that I pressed into him, wanting everything he could give.

Kiss deepening, we stumbled back from the doorway toward the crackling warmth of the fire and the mats laid there, end to end. A moment's thought of Gideon vanished as Rah's hands edged beneath my wrap, setting me alight.

Torn between the desire to experience every moment slowly and my body's desperate need to have him now, I kicked off my sandals and edged him onto the mat. Rah pulled his tunic off over his head, exposing a muscular chest dotted with scars both new and old. Some might have said they marred his skin, but they were a tapestry of his life and possessed a unique beauty. He had pulled out of our kiss to remove his tunic, but his chest was soon pressed against me, as hot as his hands had been cold. His renewed kiss was fierce, his tongue sliding against mine as my skin melted upon his—so glorious a sensation I never wanted to live without it. He expressed my feelings with a groan against my mouth. He wanted me as much as I wanted him, but we had come this far before, and the sudden fear it could again come to nothing flared my impatience. Not knowing how to ask if we should lie down, instinct took over and I knocked his leg out from beneath him at the knee.

Rah hit the mat. He could have saved himself, but he dropped back with a laugh all the more glorious for having been surprised from him. I caught an apology before it reached my tongue and grinned, enjoying this new power. I'd given orders as an empress, but it was a role I inhabited, a skin into which I stepped where pretending confidence and power was expected. This was a whole new realm.

Gripping my hands, Rah pulled me down astride him how I had once seen Tanaka and Edo sit when they had thought me out training. How blissfully unaware they had been. How joyful. Whatever Tanaka had been doing, Edo had arched back, his eyes closed, and I wanted to make Rah gasp like that.

I shifted my weight and he groaned. I wasn't sure what was expected of me, but my hunger to touch him had not yet led me astray, so I lowered my chest to his and renewed our kiss, rewarded with another of his little groans. They were glorious, unconscious things, so free and natural and honest.

The stiff bulge of his breeches had been a shock the first time I'd snuck into his room, but this time fear didn't set in until he wriggled beneath me, fabric shifting as he removed his breeches to lie naked the length of the sleeping mat. The urge to run was more overwhelming than I wanted to admit, though I knew he would be gentle. Knew he would take care of me. Knew my need for him would not be sated until I felt him inside me.

He murmured soft words, and one of his hands ghosted along my inner thigh. His fingers trailed under my wrap and touched me where all my need had been centred, and it was my turn to gasp.

Still speaking his soft words, he touched me gently, flaring my need hot, before slipping his fingers inside.

I cried out. I couldn't have stopped myself. I wanted to keep the feeling forever, for time to stop and leave us connected in such a way for eternity. He smiled and pressed in deeper, seeming to enjoy my gasps as I had enjoyed his. But for me every sensation was new, both strange and marvellous, nothing more so than the moment he withdrew his fingers and it was his hard flesh pressing into me.

My gasps of pure joy became edged with pain. It shocked me, but I didn't want to pull away. I would take pain over emptiness. Over walking away and never knowing what it was my body craved. And when gently he began to move beneath me, his eyes caught to mine, no amount of pain could dispel my fierce need for him.

He bucked his hips gently, thrusting into me, and I wished I could ask him what I ought to do, wished I had landed beneath him, there something so exposed and defiant about sitting so looking down. He was letting me own him, giving me the power should I want it, and that, more than anything else, made me want to wrap my legs around him and never let go.

His hands tightened around my hips, gripping with a need I felt to my core. I'd been loath to remove my robe entirely, but as he thrust rhythmically into me it fell first from one shoulder then the other, sliding into a pool of travel-stained silk around me. My instinct had always been to cover myself, to hide my lack of curves from the world, but he looked at me like I was the most beautiful thing he had ever seen. He ran his hands up my stomach and over my breasts and bit his lip, his little groans of pleasure all I needed.

I bent to kiss his parted lips, to join our bodies chest to chest as his desperation mounted, speeding his movements. I had no idea what it was supposed to feel like, confident only that the lingering pain was stealing something from me. I tried to focus, tried to relax, but wanting him—wanting this—wasn't enough. None of the magical imaginings I'd had of this moment had included pain or confusion, or a yearning centred between my legs and yet filling my body in a way I couldn't explain or sate. It had seemed so simple, so perfect, no thought, only a gracefully produced pleasure that wasn't messy.

But everything about this was messy. We were a sweating, grasping tangle of limbs, him gripping hold of me as I held on to him until he cried out by my ear, a gasp full of pain and pleasure and everything in between.

His body shuddered beneath me, an act of pure reflex so devoid of self-consciousness that I envied him. Envied the way he arched back, so sated, so complete, his expression owning such bliss, envy that mixed with the exultation I felt at having been the cause of such joy.

Unsure what to do, unsure if it was over, I tried to find the words to express my confusion, but before I could think what to say his arms closed around my waist, and caught to his slick chest, he rolled us over. I hit the mat, and as he had before, he slipped his fingers inside me. I gasped at the different sensation, the sense that while it wasn't his manhood it was somehow more intimate. It was the way he looked at me, focussing on me, touching me in a way that had nothing to do with him. And with the wickedest grin I'd ever seen upon his face, he lowered his head between my legs.

With the touch of his tongue upon me I hardly seemed to be in my body any longer, so little did the pleasure feel like anything I knew, and I gave myself up to the sensation, determined to feel what he had, to be sated of this need that filled me like fire. A fire he stoked with every stroke and touch and flick of his tongue until my thoughts shrank to nothing but a hunger for more.

I could not have held in the cry that clawed through me, beginning beneath his tongue and sliding up my body until it burst from my lips, a ragged, wanton thing that was no sooner out than I felt ashamed of it, of how much I had loved it. Of how much I wanted to keep this new me. And there I lay, breathing fast and feeling strange all over, tingling and yet heavy, tense yet relaxed, the pleasure and the pain having mingled so completely I couldn't tell where one ended and the other began. Only that they were both fading now, this, like everything else in life, not something built to last. It was a bittersweet thought for a bittersweet feeling, and I couldn't but wonder when, or if, we would ever get the chance to do this again.

Rah lifted his head, his fingers sliding from my body amid a final shudder of sensation, and his expression told me his thoughts had followed very similar lines. Almost as though apologising, or reassuring me, he drew himself level and gently kissed me, a far cry from the passion we had developed but a lingering thing that perfectly suited my odd mood. It even tasted slightly salty like the tears I fought not to cry. Somehow, without words, we both knew. We had been able to be here, to be nothing but ourselves, untethered from the world around us for this time, but the moment we stepped out that door it would end. He would go back to being a captain of the Levanti, and I would be an empress.

As our lips parted, he said, "I'm sorry," in Kisian, that final mark of respect almost more than I could bear.

"Me too," I replied. And that was it, because even had we been able to communicate more, what was there to say? I could no more ask him to give up who he was than he could ask the same of me.

The urge to get up, to leave before I could not, overwhelmed me, and I got to my feet. I pulled on my discarded robe and drew it closed with shaking hands. Rah sat naked, one knee bent up in the easy way he'd once sat before a food tray at the mountain inn near Anxi. From then to now felt like the completion of something that ought never to have been.

He did not get to his feet, and when I gestured to the door, he made no move to stop me, perhaps knowing as I did that trying to prolong this parting would only make it harder, would only allow hope to rise where no hope ought to live.

His dark skin had started to pimple with the cold when I bent to kiss the top of his head. He looked up then, his lips an offer lacking expectation. I kissed them as gently, trying to communicate all the wishes for his safety, for his people and his future, that I could not say. All the thanks for every moment we had spent together, for being there for me and for all he had shown me and taught me and given me. And almost I was glad I couldn't say the words, for no words would have been sufficient.

I left then, gathering my sash and my sandals and heading out into the cold night. I looked back only once.

The camp had quietened, and I made it back to my hut all but unseen, glad to be alone with the lingering sensations of my body, and with a grief tangled up in so much joy. Nothing had prepared me for it. I had always chased what I wanted, sure if I fought hard enough it would work, but some things cannot be fixed. Some people cannot change, or would not be themselves anymore if they did.

I pushed my way into our hut to the murmur of Nuru's voice and once again stopped on the threshold, cold behind me, warmth ahead. I had planned to drop straight onto my mat, not wanting to talk or to share the experience lest speaking let it flow out into the world and dissipate. I wanted to gather it into my soul and protect it, to never forget a moment no matter how painful it became.

But my mat was denied me. Whether he had come directly here, or they had found him outside, Gideon e'Torin lay with his head in Sichi's lap. "Why—?"

Sichi pressed a finger to her lips and whispered, "He hasn't long fallen asleep. Nuru found him pacing outside like a wild beast."

A deep sadness filled her words, and guilt for having put her in such a position twisted inside me. "I'm sorry."

"What for?" she said. "I'm the one who couldn't save him from Leo."

"Sichi—" Nuru began, but was cut off as Sichi looked up.

"That there was nothing I could do does not make it feel any less true. Run and tell Rah he's here so he doesn't worry, and tell him that he doesn't have to come. Gideon is asleep and can stay until morning."

Sichi's calm imperiousness silenced all Nuru's complaints, and the young woman went out without uttering any more. Silence reigned in her wake.

"He was good to me," Sichi said after a time, not looking up. "Nuru looks at him and sees only her failed captain. The man who made deals with the Chiltaens. Who let himself be manipulated by Leo Villius. She carries too much anger to see anything else."

"Did you want to marry him?"

"Not at first, but after I met him, I did. He doesn't look it now, but he was like an incarnated god. He spoke and people listened. He smiled and everyone smiled back. He was clever. Driven. And he made me laugh. And he knew. About me and Nuru."

She seemed to have more to say, but no more came out, and I couldn't but wonder how differently everything would have turned out without Dom Villius's interference. Would Sichi and I have found ourselves on opposing sides of an ongoing war? Two empresses vying to hold the empire, she with her foreign emperor, me alone.

Footsteps scuffed outside, and Nuru pushed aside the curtain. A sweep of chill air entered, followed by Rah. Our eyes met, a moment of recognition, nothing more, like the twist of a blade in my heart. I'd already had to walk away from him once. This was cruel.

"I hope you told him he didn't have to come," Sichi said.

"Of course I did, but he said Gideon was no one's responsibility but his."

Rah had taken a few steps, only to halt halfway to Sichi's side as though unsure of his welcome. His gaze flitted from Gideon to Sichi and back, his expression unreadable. "Tell him I know I ought to have done better and I'm sorry," Sichi said.

Nuru hesitated, but both Sichi and Rah looked expectantly at her, so she translated. However Nuru might feel about her former captain, Rah nodded to Sichi, the pair of them sharing a moment of grief and hurt with a degree of understanding I couldn't but envy, however foolish it was.

"Thank you," Rah said, and kneeling, set his hand on Gideon's shoulder. "Gideon?"

The one-time emperor must have been barely asleep, for he flinched as though splashed with icy water and jerked back off Sichi's lap. His head struck the floor and he scrambled away, the words *sorry* and *no* escaping between gasps. Frozen in place, we could only stare while Rah slowly crossed the floor toward him, holding his hands out flat and unthreatening.

As Rah drew close, Gideon tried to push him away, palms pressed to the chest I had lain upon, had caressed and kissed and owned for the briefest moment. Rah threw back a foot to steady himself but gave no ground, instead wrapped his arms tightly around the struggling man and held him until eventually he began to calm. He was like a rock in a raging river, still and steady, caring nothing for the tears and the strings of saliva and the mud as Gideon spilled pain upon him. And when he had calmed, Rah helped him to his feet and looked at each of us as though daring comment.

What could I have said but that my heart hurt more than I had ever thought possible, more than when I had left him, more than when I had realised what we had only just begun was already at an end? Here a window into a devotion he could never direct my way.

I had thought myself all right, had been confident in my choice, but the moment Rah and Gideon slipped out into the night leaving the three of us stunned and staring, I could not stop my tears. I had not dared build dreams for a long time, not since Tanaka's head had hit the floor in Koi, but those tiny glimmers of hope that make it through one's defences had held space in my heart for an impossible future.

"Oh, Koko." Sichi wrapped her arms around me. "I'm sorry."

Sorry because she understood what had happened? Sorry because of Gideon? I didn't want to know, only wanted to sob, unable to maintain my own fiction that this was all right, that it would be for the best, that Rah and I could never have worked out and that I'd never thought we would. Because I had. Some small part of me had always hoped.

Another body pressed against my back, and Nuru's arms snaked around us, her chin resting upon my shoulder. Neither of them said any more. They just let me stand there and cry until there were no tears left, until I was empty and numb and exhausted. When we lay down upon our mats, Sichi lay on one side, Nuru on the other, the three of us a comfortable tangle of limbs that ought to have made me smile, so companionable it was. But the memory of Rah I had tucked away had a spiky edge. Just breathing was enough to cut myself on it, to remember his laugh as I knocked him onto the mat, remember his scent and his warmth and the taste of his lips, remember the sad finality with which it had ended.

Even hopes you don't realise you're holding can rip pieces from your heart when they're torn away.

---

We dressed in the early morning chill. Sichi and Nuru moved quickly to warm themselves up, but my mind seemed slow, everything a numb haze. Sleep had come in snatches, the three of us cocooned together against the cold and misery that filled the air, looking for a way in. It had been harder to sleep with Sichi and Nuru moving against me, but while my body had needed sleep, my heart had needed them.

Not able to risk even the Levanti knowing what we were doing, we'd only said we were climbing to the shrine to pray. Captain Kiren and his men had gone ahead, yet my heart beat fast and fearful as we stepped outside our hut. Our robes were plain, our daggers hidden in their soft folds, no outward sign we hoped to change the world beyond the bow I carried upon my back.

"Are you ready?" Nuru said, the first to break the silence.

We looked at one another in the dim morning light, three ghosts moving through history. I patted my dagger and nodded, not trusting my voice. Sichi blew out a long breath. "Second time lucky, right?"

"Can't be any worse than the first time."

Nuru spoke to lighten the oppressive mood, but I could only think of all the ways this could go wrong. Not just at the ceremony, but when it came time to fight. Minister Manshin's attempt on my life had put an end to any hope he could be brought to see my point of view. Or to support me again if I proved myself worthy.

I had been carrying a lot of foolish hopes of late.

Nuru went ahead, Sichi and I following her into the mist. It blanketed the quiet camp, the few figures moving about little more than silhouettes in the pale haze. Captain Kiren stood waiting. "The path to the shrine is clear, Your Majesty," he said. "And while Oyamada had a fitful night, he is going on better this morning. The healers think he will be able to travel soon."

"Well, that's something," Sichi said when I made no answer.

"Also, as there's no food cooked yet, I've packed what I could attain for the climb." He gestured to the little sack he carried hitched to his belt. "Water too."

He was trying so hard. Perhaps he felt responsible for what had happened, that we'd had to be saved by a stranger who'd turned out to be as freakish as Leo Villius.

"Thank you, Captain," Sichi said, while I stared at nothing. No, not at nothing. I couldn't see Rah's hut through the mist, but that didn't stop me looking, from still holding a shred of hope, though it stung just by existing. "We should make a start."

Feeling more ghost than woman, I walked with them away from the camp toward the village and the mountain beyond. The ground was damp and slick with dew, and my sandalled feet were soon icy cold, but it seemed to matter as little as anything else. Just another pain I gathered to me.

Through the trees and the village, the hazy outline of the mountain loomed, its twin stairs hidden beneath overgrown greenery. Expecting us, two priests stood at the bottom beside the stone lanterns, and perched on a rock beside them, his arms propped limply on his bent knees, sat Tor. He wasn't the Levanti I had hoped to see, and yet somehow that was all right.

He slid from the rock and threw his ponytail over his shoulder, something sheepish in the way he approached, with his shoulders hunched and his gaze elsewhere.

"Tor," Nuru said when he came within earshot. "Is everything all right?"

"Yes." He looked at me and immediately looked away. "I was just wondering if you wanted company on the climb, but I see you have guards, so—"

"No, I would like that," I blurted, interrupting his growing stammer. "Sichi has Nuru, but I only have Captain Kiren, so… yes. Your company would be appreciated."

I didn't risk a look at any of my companions, though I wasn't sure what I most feared to see in their faces.

"Then I am at your service, Your Majesty." Tor bowed, stiff and formal, and I wondered then if he had wanted to walk with Nuru or Sichi, not me. Especially given how we had last parted. It seemed so long ago now. So much did.

"Wait, who is that?" Tor said, freezing in place as he straightened, eyes narrowed. "Is that..."

As we all turned in the direction he stared, a shadowy figure broke away from one of the village's abandoned huts and sped toward the trees.

"Stop!" Two of Kiren's men started after the figure, arms and legs pumping, but they weren't going to catch him. I drew my bow, nocking and loosing without once taking my eyes off the fast-retreating figure. He had almost reached the trees when my arrow struck him in the back, throwing him forward.

Sichi gasped and sped after the guards, Captain Kiren and Nuru in her wake. Like the whole was a dream, I followed, numb, unsure whether I ought to hope most that the unknown man was dead or alive—whether I was about to regret my quick instincts.

We found the man face down and unmoving. One of our guards knelt to check him, but shook his head. "Dead, captain."

"Well, let's roll him over and see who he is."

Rolling the dead man exposed a simple, dark grey half robe atop fine, light armour. "Imperial scout," the captain said with a frustrated harrumph of air. "Unfortunately, they usually travel in pairs and the other is probably long gone." He looked from me to Sichi. "It's a few hours back to Kogahaera even if he gallops all the way, but I recommend we move quickly."

"Agreed," Sichi said, a little out of breath. "Good shot," she added, glancing at me, unsmiling, her expression unreadable.

It was an inauspicious start, but by the time we made it back to the stairs Sichi had regained her composure. "Let's get this done," she said, setting a hand upon my shoulder. "Good fortune, Koko. We shall see you at the top, out of breath and wishing to lie down!"

The laugh sounded forced, but her smile was all determination. With a nod to Captain Kiren, she made for her side of the stairs to start the climb.

I followed the second priest to my stairway, Tor behind me and Captain Kiren at the rear, his expression tense and watchful.

I had never been to Kuroshima and had always thought complaints about the height of the stairs were exaggerated, but while one thousand four hundred and forty-four steps start off easy, they don't stay easy.

"Is there a reason this shrine is at the top of a mountain?" Tor said after a time, out of breath.

"It isn't. It's only partway up. It's one thousand four hundred and forty-four steps because that's how many days the goddess Lunyia waited for her husband."

We climbed some steps in silence, until: "Did that really happen?"

I glanced back. Tor's face owned its usual scowl of concentration. "That's what the story says."

"Yes, but is the story true?"

"True? You mean was the goddess real?"

"Yes."

"I...I don't know. Do you believe in gods?"

He said nothing for a time, and again I looked back, surprised by how seriously he was considering my question. "I don't think so," he said at last, brushing a determined fern frond out of the way. "I used to because I had no reason not to, but now I feel like I have no reason to do so either. Has anyone ever seen one? Spoken to one?"

"You don't feel the gods have control over your fate?"

"No. I make my choices. Blaming the gods for them is just... shifting blame. People do it so they can feel better."

"That's very cynical."

"Perhaps."

"If you don't believe in gods, why are you climbing to Kuroshima?"

Again he didn't answer immediately, but this time when I turned to glance back, he met my gaze only to look away. "Because you are. I... didn't get a chance to apologise for walking out the way I did."

"You have nothing to apologise for, Tor. I'm the one who should apologise for having asked so much of you. Not even asked, just... expected it."

"You had more reason to than my own people."

He drew alongside, the stairs just wide enough to accommodate both of us between the damp, reaching hands of the mountain ferns.

"More likely I'm just used to having things my own way," I said, crossing my arms. "There are always servants around for everything. Not that I think of you as—" I broke off, expecting a deep scowl, but he just looked at me. Watchful. Curious. His thoughts impossible to divine.

"I—"

"Do you—?"

We both spoke only to stop at the sound of the other's voice.

"Go on."

"What were you—"

My cheeks reddened and I waved a hand, sure that behind us Captain Kiren would be rolling his eyes, desperate to keep moving. "You first."

"Oh no, I wasn't going to say anything important."

"Neither was I."

The priest leading the way cleared his throat, and murmuring an apology, I continued up the stairs, wishing the mountain would swallow me. No one else had ever made me feel so gangly and ungraceful, so lacking in even the basest intelligence or assurance.

"No," I said abruptly, turning to Tor again. "It *was* important. I was going to ask if you knew why we are climbing to the shrine."

"To seek a blessing before your wedding to Dom Villius, I heard, which, I hope you know, is a terrible idea."

Ahead the priest stopped and turned back and, with a sigh, settled in patiently with his hands clasped before him. Captain Kiren's eyes darted about. The mist had thickened as we climbed, making it feel like we were climbing through the clouds. We needed to hurry, yet drawing a deep breath, I said, "No, I'm marrying Lady Sichi."

"Oh good. That's a much better idea than marrying Leo."

And that was all. No scowl. No surprise. Just a nod like it was normal and fine, and somehow it fanned my annoyance rather than dissipating it. "Leaders do what they have to do," I snapped, and started walking again, fast enough that the priest had to hurry to keep ahead.

"Wait, what? I didn't—"

"No," I threw over my shoulder. "But you would have judged me for marrying Dom Villius."

"Yes, because he's a—"

Tor bit down on his words, and though I agreed, I wanted him to keep arguing so I could keep shouting. He didn't, and we fell into an uncomfortable silence. I glanced back at Captain Kiren only once, annoyed to find his expression inscrutable.

Pointless anger sustained me for the next hundred or so of the damn steps, but I soon began to tire again, my legs like heavy weights it would have been so much easier to cut off and leave behind. Of course I wouldn't have been able to walk then, but I managed another hundred steps imagining how light my body would be without different parts. When I got to thinking about my head, I stopped. Tanaka had seemed so much heavier in death. Perhaps in another life I had lost my head in that throne room, and today he was finally marrying Sichi.

My mother had once made this very climb to marry an emperor she did not love so she could protect an empire she did, and I spent the rest of the climb imagining I was walking in her footsteps. But I wasn't just doing this for the empire, I was doing it for me and for every empress before me who had been forgotten or pushed into the shadows, who had been belittled or ignored or set aside for a younger, prettier wife. For my mother, whose lifetime of being the imperial whore had broken her. It might yet be a mistake. My fight may yet come to nothing, but there was still time. I just needed information, and allies.

I glanced back at Tor. "Why are Rah and his Swords still here?"

"Seeking information," came the wary answer. "Like that Unus said. Information about Leo. Or, not so much about him as about people like him. The others are going home, but Rah wants to find out all he can about the people like Leo who are destroying our homeland. Don't tell him I said so, but I think it's the wisest decision he's ever made—not charging in knowing nothing."

Once again I stopped, swinging around to face him while the priest's steps scuffed to a halt. "So that twin of Leo's was telling the truth. Rah wants information from Torvash?"

"As far as I know. He's some witchdoctor of sorts."

"Right," I said, and started walking again, leaving a plan to coalesce in my mind.

I had seen sketches of the shrine at Kuroshima, but none had done it justice. Small it might be, but it had the feeling of a hidden, secret place, a place where, if gods really did exist, they would live. Tucked away in this hollow, away from the demands and prying eyes of humans.

"Your Majesty." Another priest approached across the stone floor, avoiding the stones painted red like it was second nature to him. "My name is Father Ru. Your . . . *Lady Sichi* has informed me of your purpose here today, and may I say—"

"No, Father, you may not," I said. "This is the decision I am making as Empress of Kisia, and if you would have made no objection to my marriage to anyone else then you may make none now."

He bowed, lips pursed. "As you wish, Your Majesty. Since Lady Sichi has informed me that the marriage I performed between herself and the... *former* Emperor Gideon e'Torin was not consummated at the end of the sevenday, my conscience is free before the gods."

"An insinuation that mine ought not be?"

"Not at all, Your Majesty." Another bow. "Lady Sichi and her companions arrived some minutes ago and are preparing in one of our hollows. If you wish to take a moment to catch your breath, Brother Jia will show you to somewhere you may prepare."

The priest who'd led us up the stairs gestured along a damp mountain path leading to a small outbuilding tucked into the greenery. Captain Kiren offered me the sack he'd been carrying on his belt, and with the promise of a short rest, food, and water, I stepped into the dim, cosy little hollow, leaving him to keep watch outside.

Tor followed me, closing the door softly behind him. "Miko..."

Before he could finish, I turned on him. "Did you really want to climb with me?" I said. "Or with the others?"

"With you." He stilled, hand hovering as though frozen midstep. "Should I not have? I... am still unsure of a lot of your *rushai*... uhh, customs, but I'm trying."

"Did you just want to apologise?"

"I..." Tor's shoulders hunched in on themselves in that protective way he had. "Mostly. But what with us leaving Kisia soon, I... just wanted to... be here. With you."

The words were no invitation, yet his eyes burned into mine with a need I knew in my soul. Dropping the supply sack, I gripped his face roughly and kissed him. The last time I'd done so I'd thought

of nothing but wanting him to know he was more than his ability
to translate; this time I wanted to devour him. Thrusting away
all thought of Rah, I kissed Tor so fiercely he stumbled. His back
hit the wall with a grunt of breath, but he didn't push me away. He
threaded his hands up into my hair and held me to him as intently
as I had him pressed against the wall, the full lengths of our bodies aligned and wanting. It was foolish. Unladylike. The act of a
wanton, not an empress, but I didn't care. In that moment he was a
bandage to a bleeding wound, and I needed him with my entirety,
needed him to want me, would have let him devour me whole if
only he would have enjoyed it.

"Miko," he said, breathless between kisses. "I—"

"If you want me to stop, you're going to have to push me away," I
murmured, running my hands down his chest—slim and lithe, his
tunic damp with sweat from the climb.

He gripped my shoulders, and for a sinking, heart-stopping
moment I was sure he would push me from him, that I would be
left with nothing to do but sink in shame at having forced myself
on him twice, but he moved with me. Half a dozen steps across the
room, and with a thud and an involuntary gasp my back hit wood
and he was kissing me as fiercely, a desperation in both of us as
though the world were about to end.

"*Ki ichasha sorii*," I said as his hands ran over my hips, pulling
me to him. "*Ki ichasha sorii.*"

I might have spoken a spell so suddenly did Tor stop, not stepping back but shifting in a way that meant I could no longer feel
his hardness against me.

"*Sorii yi pham*—" He stopped abruptly and swallowed hard, the
bob of his throat pronounced in the gloom. "I mean I...I have
never—"

"Your Majesty," came Captain Kiren's voice from outside.
"Father Ru says they are ready to begin when you are."

Gripping the waistband of Tor's breeches, I didn't immediately let him go. He licked his lips, chest heaving.

"Your Majesty?"

I let go. "Tell him I'll be out in a moment, Captain."

"Yes, Your Majesty."

Tor stepped back, running both hands through his messy hair. "I'm sorry, I—"

"No, I am," I said. "Can you help me fix my hair?"

I knelt before him as I would have before my maid, only thinking of the implications as he hitched a breath upon a groan. "I... how?" He touched my hair like it was a fragile spider's web. "What do you want me to do?"

"Smooth it. Like you would your ponytail. I don't want to look like we've just been..."

"*Ravuunis.*"

I looked up, causing him to click his tongue as my hair pulled from his hands. "*Ravuunis?*"

He bent and pressed a gentler kiss to my lips, one that lingered with more emotion than I had been prepared for. Our lips parted, slow, sticking like our skin wasn't ready to be apart, and my heart hammered all the more fiercely. Still holding a handful of my hair, he remained bent over me a moment as though reading something in my features.

"Rah turned you down." There was no anger in the words, it wasn't even a question, just a statement, knowing and weary.

"We turned each other down," I said. "It was never going to work. Just like this won't. This is my future. My throne. My home. Not yours."

He straightened slowly, wetting lips already damp from our kiss. A nod, and his fingers were working again, pulling and smoothing strands of hair with more gentleness than he ought to have left for me.

When he had finished, he stepped back, and our moment was gone with our time. Father Ru was waiting.

"Thank you," I said, standing and straightening my simple robe. "For everything. If... if I don't see you again after this, take care of yourself. Live well."

Tor saluted. "*Esvenya lo mote set elvarai*, Your Majesty," he said. "It means... the closest is probably 'May your path be clear and fertile.'"

"*Esvenya lo mote set elvarai*, Tor e'Torin."

Sichi and Nuru were waiting with Father Ru in the main shrine, and as all eyes turned my way I was sure they could see the stolen moments of passion all over me, like Tor's lips and hands had been covered in paint.

Father Ru gestured to the altar. "If you are ready to begin, Your Majesty."

"I am," I said, stepping forward into a new future.

# 10. RAH

We watched the morning hunt return with their kills—a meagre collection of carcasses compared to when we'd first arrived. "Those are some poor pickings," Amun said, holding his hands over the fire to warm them. "This evening's group will have to leave earlier if they're to go farther afield."

I nodded, and when he shuffled his feet, I waited for him to get to what he really wanted to say. "Is it true the empress left this morning?"

"Yes, to visit the shrine, I understand." I held my own hands to warm over the fire. "Considering she left her horse, her belongings, and her minister behind, I'm sure she'll be back."

"Hmm. The sooner she moves on the better. We don't need this getting more complicated."

For a time only the fire crackled, until Amun cleared his throat. "Are you still planning to step down and go in search of that Witchdoctor?"

I didn't meet his gaze. "Yes. I've been considering what I'll need and the best way to go about it, but I don't think I ought to speak until Empress Miko has left. As you say, we don't need this to be more complicated."

"Might be about to get your wish." Amun nodded in the direction of the village. Through the trees, Empress Miko approached with quick, determined steps, Tor trailing in her wake. She'd always possessed fire and assurance, not shying from what stood between her and her goals, but until now I'd not felt like that was me. Somehow, she had returned from the mountain a different woman. Memories of the previous night seeped into my thoughts, unable to be entirely thrust aside.

"Empress," I said as she stopped before me.

"Captain."

Same face, same voice, but this wasn't Miko; this was Her Majesty, the jut of her jaw all the warning I needed.

Tor halted at her side. "Empress Miko wishes to propose a mutually beneficial deal."

The back of my neck prickled, as much from the weight of my herd's gaze as from the sense of impending dread creeping over me. That she had chosen to request publicly, that she stared directly at me as though challenging me to refuse, boded ill. Fighting to hold her stare, I said, "I assume she wishes us to fight for her, but what could Her Majesty have to offer us in return?"

Empress Miko took a book from beneath her arm and held it out. "This."

———————◆———————

I'd expected to sit in negotiations at some point during my tenure as both Sword captain and herd master to this exiled jumble of warriors, but not opposite Miko. Especially not a Miko who looked through me as though we had shared nothing the previous night. Or ever.

Custom allowed both of us to have a second, but necessity made it no choice at all. Tor sat beside me, Nuru beside Miko, our only support in this meeting those who could ensure we understood one another. Tension hummed between us as Tor slowly flipped through the book.

"It seems to be a collection of information about...people like Dom Villius and that woman. Cassandra. Prescients and Deathwalkers and...Time Burners? Prevalence in various areas. A...spectrum of abilities and—"

"Details on each one," Nuru interrupted, fidgeting impatiently with the fraying hem of her tunic. "More than enough information to understand what you'd be up against back home, since that, I understand, is the reason you're still here."

I tilted my head Tor's way without pulling my gaze from the two women sitting opposite. "It does seem so, yes," he said. "There's a lot to get through, and you'd have to decipher strategies for facing any of them from their list of abilities, but...there is a lot of information here."

At that, Empress Miko held out her hand, and with a dismissive shrug, Tor gave back the book. I watched it change hands. Here at last was the information we needed, but what was it worth? What wasn't it worth?

I met Miko's determined stare, unable to suppress the suspicion that she'd been after this the whole time. That we'd never had anything real at all.

"Where did you get it?" I said, leaving Tor to translate.

"It was sent to me," she replied. "By Torvash, the Witchdoctor, on my mother's request. She felt it was important I understand Dom Villius."

"Yet you're willing to give it to me?"

"Nuru has already read all we need to know about him, and little of it was new or surprising. As for the other...abilities..." She let those words hang, a tantalising promise of just how much the book contained. I had been dreading my lone search for the Witchdoctor, and now here was a book containing everything he could tell me. If we paid her price.

We had moved away from the main fires where the day's kills

were being skinned and prepared, but it hadn't stopped most of my Swords from gathering to watch and whisper.

"And what, exactly, does Her Majesty want us to do?" I said, trying for the same cool tone Miko had adopted and hoping it didn't sound bitter.

My voice might betray me, but no emotion crossed her face as she replied. "We require protection. Although we are no longer under the control of Minister Manshin, until we gather allies, we are vulnerable."

"Protection," I repeated. "Manshin is likely to send people after you?"

"Yes."

"Small groups or a whole army?"

"I don't know."

Part of me wanted to agree to whatever she needed, not, I realised, because we'd lain skin to skin. Not even because I loved her, but because I hadn't. "I need more than that," I said. "You are asking me to risk the lives of my Swords."

She stared at me, and once again we were back in her throne room while the echoes of my demands faded around us. She'd refused to protect Gideon, refused to go back on her word to Ezma, and now she was asking for more.

"It would depend on how much of a threat he sees me as," Miko said, Nuru mimicking her tone well. "In a very real sense the presence of a whole group of Levanti will make him think twice about attacking me at all."

Minister Manshin. I'd saved his life, yet he might still end mine. Too well could I recall his fierce anger seething through the prison bars, determined to survive if only to avenge his hate. A hate that had served her well for a time. Now it seemed likely to wash her away.

"How long?" I said.

"If all goes well, no more than six or seven days. Of course, should you choose to remain longer to revenge yourselves upon the Chiltaens, I will gladly have you at my side."

Her gaze flicked Tor's way as she finished, and beside me, he gave the smallest of nods. I realised then that she'd wanted more. She'd wanted us to fight for her, to help her take back her empire, and I had Tor to thank that she'd not made that a condition of this agreement. Wise of him to know I'd never have been able to accept it, while the risk of protecting her for seven days was possible.

I stared back down at the book. Around us the camp was quiet and tense. I'd been about to step down, to let my Swords go home while I continued the search for information alone, but the appearance of the book changed everything.

"You have my agreement, Your Majesty," I said. "The book in return for seven days' protection. I will have to speak with my Hand before we can finalise it, however."

A smile flickered and was gone, crushed beneath the mask of Her Imperial Majesty. A small bow, a murmur of thanks, and she tucked the book out of sight. Beside me Tor made no sign of what he thought, both he and Nuru suddenly finding interesting things to look at elsewhere.

I got to my feet, and all eyes turned my way. Under the weight of so many questioning stares, my chest tightened like someone had wrapped their hands around me and squeezed, a feeling no deep breath could dispel. It was time to gather the Hand.

———◆———

"This is about the empress, isn't it," Loklan said, dropping onto the ground with a scowl. "What does she want?"

It wasn't a good start, but I looked around the circle, meeting the gaze of each member of the Hand. "It's also about the Entrancers and the information we needed. The empress has one of the

Witchdoctor's books and is willing to trade it. I've seen the book," I rushed on before they could speak. "It has detailed information not only about Entrancers but many other strange abilities the city states may send after us."

They looked at one another, no one wanting to speak first. Eventually, Diha folded her arms, sending my already hammering heart racing. "How can you be so sure there are Entrancers after us at all? I've been thinking about it, and I'm not sure Leo Villius and Whisperer Ezma are really worth trusting when they want to lead us astray."

"If you don't believe the city states are undermining us then why are we here?" I said. "Did you deserve to be exiled?"

Diha looked at Lashak, then down into the fire, jaw set hard. Lashak's gaze was on her hands, Amun's on the ground, and as the silence stretched, my hands began to shake. I clenched them tightly, the sensation I was being squeezed in a fist stealing all but my shallowest breaths.

"She's not asking us to fight for her," I said. "I will not lead you into battle. What she needs is to be protected from Minister Manshin while she gathers her allies. I know it's not what we wanted, but seven days' delay in leaving is nothing."

"What happened to stepping down?" Loklan asked quietly, his gaze steely.

It was a punch to the gut, and I couldn't breathe.

"That was under different circumstances," Amun said when I didn't speak. "I'm not saying I want to stay even an hour longer, but that book sounds invaluable."

"How can you be so sure?" Diha asked. "What if the book is useless?"

"It's not," I snapped. "I checked."

The camp had been quiet while I met with Miko, but now a rumble of impatience was growing around us, an impatience fast growing into discontent.

"And what about Leo Villius?" Loklan asked. "Are we keeping him too? Taking him home with us? Crowning Gideon again?"

"I suggested none of those things," I returned coldly. "Gideon stays with me, Leo belongs to the empress now."

"You mean for seven more days he stays with us, and we're stuck with Gideon forever."

I wanted to grip his shoulders and scream that it was just seven days. That he wouldn't have to see either of them. That Gideon didn't deserve the hate they spilled his way. But I could say none of it. "This shouldn't be about either of them," I said, trying to keep my voice calm. "This is about making a small sacrifice of time in return for all the information we need to take back the plains. Is your homeland not worth that? Did you not swear to serve your people when you took the oath?"

While we argued, Swords had been edging closer, our raised voices drawing all too much attention. "Might be time to see what they think," Amun said, gripping my shoulder and gesturing out at the camp.

"We should perform a Fracturing," Loklan said. "Let them choose."

It wasn't a bad suggestion, but if too many left, we wouldn't be able to maintain a camp, let alone protect Miko if Manshin came hunting.

"No, our best chance of survival is together as it has always been. Whatever is decided, we do it as one. I will talk to them."

Loklan said nothing, and I got to my feet. At this movement more Swords gathered, murmuring amongst themselves. I had promised them I would take them home. To stay a little longer ought to be a small thing, but no matter how many times I told myself that, it didn't become true.

I drew a deep breath, heart pounding so hard I might have been charging into battle. "Empress Miko possesses a book containing all the information about Entrancers we need to fight them back home," I called to my Swords, all of them gathered now. "And all she asks in return is our protection for seven days."

A tide of muttering swept through the group, and I went on. "I know you are tired. We all are. We all want to go home, but to a home not destroyed by the sickness that saw us exiled. Seven days is all I ask of you."

Some murmurs of agreement met this, matched by as many grumbles.

"A book? Just take it from her," someone said. "Who's going to stop you?"

"There are more of us than them."

"Is that what we've sunk to?" another returned. "We aren't thieves."

"Nor are we soldiers for hire!"

"Why should we risk bleeding for a book!"

"Why should we help Kisians?"

I lifted my hands for silence. "The oaths we took were to protect our herds, and we need this book to save our people. Our way of life."

Someone barked a laugh, and I was glad I couldn't tell who, my Swords becoming just a wash of unfriendly faces. "A book?" came another voice. "As magical as your Entrancers."

"Didn't you see that woman walk around in Lepata's body?"

Arguments began to swirl around me, discordant and disorienting. I wanted to grip them all by the shoulders and shake them until they could see the looming danger set to crush everything we loved. But we did not rule as the Kisians did. As the Chiltaens did. A captain was only a captain while everyone believed in them, while they were chosen. Neither shaking them nor shouting would change that; it would only hasten my end.

From the crowd, Shenyah e'Jaroven stepped forward. Her jaw

was set, her brows low. "If there is an enemy to fight back home, we cannot fight them if we are all dead."

"Nor can we fight them if we don't know how."

With a disbelieving snort, she stepped closer. "We know how to fight. That's what we're best at and why the Kisians and the Chiltaens keep wanting to use us. Loklan, tell me you don't agree with this."

I held my breath as the young horse master stood. "No," he said. "I don't. But I am not your captain."

"No, Dishiva e'Jaroven is my captain."

"And Dishiva would put her people before herself," Lashak snapped. "As she has done every moment since setting foot on this land. As she is doing right now, sacrificing her freedom for all of us."

This silenced some of the outcry, leaving a hush into which someone cried, "While our captain sacrifices our lives for his cock!"

Not Tor's voice this time, but the same scathing sentiment spat in my direction. I closed my eyes as hate-filled shouts erupted in a chorus, and cresting the wave came the cry I had known was coming.

"Give the bastards Gideon and let us go home!"

"Let *him* bleed for us!"

A roar of agreement rose, cutting over every complaint. Hatred of Gideon—the one thing that went on uniting them and undermining every tenet of Levanti honour.

"We do not trade in lives!" I shouted. "We do not give blood sacrifices to our enemies!"

"And we don't fight for anyone but ourselves!"

The choice to keep Gideon safe and not let them spill Leo's blood had pushed us to a precipice, cracking open fractures that had always been there because, whatever we had been through, Levanti were not one people, not one herd, and that would always be our downfall.

"Challenge! Challenge! Challenge!" The chant rose through the crowd like a thrumming heartbeat. Such goading was not our way, our challenge system steeped in honour and constrained by rules, but as with so much else, our time here had eroded it. We had suffered too much, anger all we had left.

I turned to find Amun weathering the shouts as I was. He met my gaze, sorrow and regret in the twist of his lips. He had no choice, but I would not risk another second dying to my blade. Another friend.

"No." I turned from Amun to the raging crowd of Swords I'd tried to lead. "No. I will not fight for this." I had to shout over the noise. "If you have lost faith in me then I will step aside; I will not fight and further divide us, nor will I risk taking a Levanti life. If you will accept Amun as your captain—" My voice cracked but I fought on. "If you have faith in him and the rest of your Hand, then I will step aside and lead you no more."

It wasn't our way any more than goading a challenge was, but I was done with bloodshed. A few cheers met my words. Some grumbles. And from deep in the heart of the gathered crowd rose another chant. "Amun! Amun! Amun!"

It rose in pitch and volume, swallowing all other cries beneath its insistent demand. I let the noise roll over me like the buffeting of the Eastbore. Once again, I had failed to lead Swords who had put their faith in me, not because I had done wrong but because I had held to principles and duties I could not let go.

A hand fell upon my shoulder, and Amun squeezed it before lifting his hands for quiet. "If it is the will of the herd then I accept the honour of captain—" A cheer cut across his words, but he went on, "We're going home."

The cheer became a roar. He had no choice, but his smile was broad as he spoke those magical words.

"You heard the captain! What are you waiting for?" Lashak shouted into the noise. "This camp won't pack itself!"

That broke the collective fervour, sending them spilling away—the most energetic I'd ever seen a Swordherd about packing a camp. They were going home. Elation filled the air, crackling with a fierce energy like a gathering thunderstorm.

"I'm sorry, Rah," Amun said, only he remaining at my side while Lashak, Diha, and Loklan kept their distance.

"You have nothing to apologise for. I know you'll lead them well, no doubt much better than I."

He grimaced. "I don't think that's true. Being able to bend before the storm is not better than standing firm and refusing to fall."

"It is if the other option is to stand firm and break." Amun made to reply, but I wanted no compliments or platitudes. "No," I interrupted before he could speak. "No, Amun, it's done. Take care. Captain."

I walked away through the buzzing camp. Swords watched me pass, some in silence, others jeering. "Go beg your Kisian for help."

"Traitor!"

"Leave him alone," one said, but such reasonable voices were few as more and more gathered close, stepping into my path. The lightning crackle of tension grew with every step, one after the other all I could focus on. My hut was at the edge of the camp, but at this rate they would snap and tear me to pieces like starving wolves before I got there. Starving for vengeance. For someone to blame.

"You ought to let Gideon bleed!"

I flinched. More Swords piled into my path, and it was all I could do to push gently through, holding my composure as familiar faces turned ugly around me.

"Weak!"

"You can't protect him anymore!"

I made to turn at that, but Lashak's voice once more rose above the noise. "Leave him alone! What are we, city-dwelling monsters or proud warriors of the plains? Step back!"

They didn't obey with alacrity, but they did quieten and edge back enough to let me pass, impeded only by the occasional jutting shoulder or foot set to trip me. One almost sent me face first into the mud, but I managed to maintain my balance, grit my teeth, and walk on, leaving the pack of Swords prowling in my wake.

At last I reached the hut and, feeling numb, brushed through the fabric and into the familiar space, wishing there was a door I could close behind me.

"Rah…" Gideon stood in the centre of the room, eyeing me warily.

"I'm fine." It didn't sound like my voice. "I've stepped aside. Amun is their captain. Better that than being challenged and becoming an exiled exiled exiled whatever I'm up to now."

"That's what bothers you?"

I stared at him, trying to make sense of his question. "Why wouldn't it?"

"Because you were planning to step aside anyway. Now they've made their choice, and that's just how it works." Gideon tilted his head, his eyes narrowing. "You do care. I always wondered."

My laugh was breathy and bitter. "Wondered what?"

"Whether you chose to be a Sword captain instead of a horse whisperer because you wanted glory and admiration, not quiet, solemn reverence."

"Glory and admiration?" My heartbeat sounded hollow in my chest. "Is that what you think of me?"

"It's not wrong to want things, Rah. Even selfish things."

"You would say that."

A hurtful barb I ought not to have thrown, but Gideon pressed an amused smile between thinned lips. "I would, yes, because even in my current state I'm apparently the better balanced of the two of us." He tapped the side of his head meaningfully. "You need to stop deciding what's all right to think and do and feel based on the shame of the child you used to be. Maybe then you'll be a good leader."

"Thank you for that assessment." I'd stoked the fire that morning, but it had since ebbed to a smoulder. Taking up the poker, I jabbed it as much to alleviate annoyance as to get it burning brighter. "Better for everyone that I don't lead then."

Despite the hurt and anger searing through my veins, Gideon just shrugged. "I didn't say that; you're just shit at this part of the job."

"You're calling me shit a lot recently."

"No one else will. You make the mistake of thinking everyone is motivated by the same things you are, and they aren't. You think doing the right thing and holding to our precepts will make people want to risk their lives, but it won't. Most people aren't you, Rah. They weren't born with your core of steel and weren't chosen to train as whisperers. Many of them aren't even motivated by fear their souls will weigh heavy upon Mona's scales. What they want is for *now* to be better. And if not now, then the near future. People will put off joy now for joy later, but you have to promise them joy first. You have to give them something to dream in the darkness, not tell them they're awful for wanting something to look forward to. For thinking of themselves."

My cheeks grew hot and I looked away, hating the picture he painted. "Is that what I do?"

"Not intentionally, but yes. You forget you're the unique one. Most people are driven by self-interest, not martyrdom."

"Is that how you see me? A martyr?"

"No. It's how you see you."

It was the most Gideon had said since I'd found him shaking and wailing beneath Kogahaera. I could not wish he hadn't rediscovered his voice, but he could have chosen a better time or a different target to sharpen his observations upon. Each of his words was a cut, and I could not stem the bleeding, could only decide what to do with the blood. No doubt something stupid and stubborn, just as he expected.

I closed my eyes. "If Swords don't want to hold to our tenets, why choose to follow me in the first place?"

"So they can feel good about themselves for choosing a leader who does hold to tenets."

"That's very cynical."

He shrugged. "You don't need someone to tell you what you think you want to hear."

I leaned against the opposite wall and pressed my hands over my face. "I don't even know what I think I want to hear anymore," I said, the words muffled.

"Yes, Captain. We will fight for Levanti honour, Captain. We will do what is right whatever the cost, Captain. We're with you all the way. How was that?"

"Do you have to mock me?"

His dawning smile dropped. "I wasn't trying to."

"Then by the gods I hope you never try if that's what you achieve when you're not." I jabbed the fire again, breaking a glowing log into bright orange chunks. "It doesn't matter anyway, it's done. Amun is their captain now, and they're leaving."

"Are you going with them?"

I shook my head. "No. Not if there's a chance I can still get the Witchdoctor's book from Miko. Perhaps my protection will be enough."

Gideon tilted his head, his eyes piercing. "Do you love her?"

"I don't want to talk about this," I said, turning away.

"I'll take that as a yes, shall I?"

He sounded like his old self, wry and mocking.

"Does it matter?" I said, stepping to the window to peer out at the busy camp. "There can be no future with her. She knows that. I know that. Everyone knows that."

"That can change. If you love her, you—"

"I don't," I snapped, but while it was true, it was also a lie. I didn't love her. We'd not had enough time for that. Not had enough language for that. But I could have. With time. With the right words and the right circumstances, I might even have stayed, or persuaded her to come back with me to the plains. What a couple we might have been.

With a huff of breath, Gideon settled back onto the floor and took up his knife, carving a golden curl from the rough wood he had been working on. Followed by another. I'd not wanted to talk about Miko, but the absence of further questions felt wrong, like we were holding our breath instead of living, caught outside time.

"That's it?" I said.

"Was there something else you wanted to say?"

"I didn't want to have a conversation at all, but you started it and—"

Gideon sighed, weary. "You've answered the only question it's fair for me to ask."

I turned back to the window rather than answer. Outside, activity was frenetic. Some Swords dashed about packing more hurriedly than was prudent, while others seemed to be doing nothing at all, caught in small groups arguing. The feeling a thunderstorm was brewing hadn't eased, and the longer I watched the more hairs stood up on the back of my neck. From our hut I couldn't see Empress Miko's and could only hope Tor and Nuru had enough sense to keep her out of sight. If Amun could get the Swords away soon, their hate-filled energy could exhaust itself in movement and not strike the first person unwise enough to draw their ire. Or perhaps it was only me they hated. Lady Sichi had certainly been busy as Gideon's wife, making herself a favourite.

"Do you love her?" I said, throwing his question back at him.

Exhaustion had dug deep lines into Gideon's face, yet they cut all the deeper as he frowned. "Who?"

"Your wife."

"You should know the answer to that."

*Because he loves you!*

Sett's words still haunted me in quiet moments. In the wake of their memory, I could not meet Gideon's gaze, and yet to look away in self-consciousness was too much. Instead I stared at the wall behind his shoulder and felt the hard thud of my heart like a drum in an empty cave.

"Rah…"

The room closed in, and I was all too aware of his presence, of his scent and his voice and the sound of his feet shifting upon the floor. Ever since getting caught in the cave, I'd avoided thinking about Sett's words, or about the way Gideon responded to my touch, to the sound of my voice, to my presence. Safer not to think about it, not to have to grapple with the confusion such thoughts brought to my body like a swirling whirlpool.

"Rah?"

Like a hook threaded into my skin, the crack in his voice drew my gaze, and each with our backs to a different wall we stared at one another across the empty floor. There was just him, just that dark, intent gaze and those tired, ringed eyes, just the catch of my breath and the twang of tension in my body like every part of me was made of bowstrings. I felt sick and hot, and yet I never wanted to move, wanted to go on feeling like I was the only person in Gideon's world. Like I belonged to him.

It was, I realised, all I had ever wanted since the first time I'd followed him around as a child. And this was a shitty time to realise it.

"Gideon, I—"

Someone shouted outside, and coward I was, I was grateful. Until I peered back out at the fractious camp.

"Shit," I breathed. "Ezma is back."

Out amid the chaos, the horse whisperer stood by one of the main fires, everything about her tall and grand and imposing as she listened to those gathered around her. They looked to be airing grievances, arguing as much with her as amongst themselves. There was no sign of Amun.

"I don't like the look of this."

I'd hoped that by walking away, by removing myself from view, my former Swords would forget about me and move on, but the arguments outside had grown to swallow any attempt at packing. Had Ezma started it? Or had she been lingering in the area, awaiting the perfect time to make everything worse?

Shifting to the other window brought Amun into sight nearby, he and Lashak facing a shouting Shenyah e'Jaroven. Behind her a crowd was growing.

Gideon's shoulder brushed mine as he joined me at the window. "You ought to have let me die," he said, watching the group draw closer to our hut. "It would have been easier."

"Easier for who?"

"For them. For me. For everyone."

"Except me." I felt his stare, but couldn't pull my attention from the approaching cluster of Swords. "I guess you're right," I added with a bitter laugh. "It turns out I'm a selfish bastard after all."

Outside, the crowd behind Shenyah had grown, and Ezma had joined the young Jaroven still arguing with Amun. It seemed only a matter of time, yet when Amun held up his hands, giving in, my stomach dropped. I had given them my all, but I hadn't given them Gideon. However else I had failed them, this had always been about him.

"You should go," he said, his voice a low rumble at my side.

"No."

I'd fought for them. I'd tried to do what was best, and when that hadn't been enough, I'd stepped aside rather than fight, but it was blood they'd wanted. Hopelessness had been creeping over me, but anger surged back as outside, footsteps and voices closed in.

"Rah!" Amun called. "We want to talk to Gideon."

"You say that, but you know it's not true," I called back. "You know what Ezma tried to do last time, and I won't let her or anyone else do this."

The fabric hanging in the doorway rippled and was pulled aside, Amun barely the first inside as Shenyah e'Jaroven pushed through with her followers. "It's the truth," Shenyah said, stepping to the fore. "We're here to appeal to Gideon e'Torin's sense of honour and responsibility. If he gives himself up to the Chiltaens he can provide us safe passage home."

"So Ezma says," I said, and raised my voice so she could hear me from outside. "She just wants the revenge I robbed her of. Call off your dogs, Whisperer! The answer is no."

"It's not your choi—"

"Yes it is!" I snapped, not daring to look at Gideon nor let him speak lest my hold on the situation slip. "It is my choice to stand between you and let no one pass. My choice not to let this become who we are. Not to let a false whisperer destroy us."

"Put down your damned honour and stand aside," Rorshe e'Bedjuti said.

Ptapha e'Jaroven advanced beside him. "You had better get out of the way," he warned. "Because we're taking Gideon. After everything he's done, ensuring us safe passage home is the least he can do."

Somewhere along the way, reason and honour had been consumed by hurt, leaving us raw and broken. But I stepped into the centre of the room, between Gideon and the angry Swords. "I told you I would not fight," I said, sitting my hand upon my sword hilt. "But I will if you make me."

Gideon shifted behind me. "Rah, don't—"

"Don't you dare say a word," I snapped, drawing my blade an inch from its scabbard. "This isn't about you."

He laughed, but if he spoke again, I didn't hear him, so loudly did my heart thud.

"It is all about him," Ptapha e'Jaroven said, seething as he stepped in, meeting me in the middle of the room. "Gideon is the reason the First Swords of Torin stayed. He's the reason the Chiltaens came rounding us up. He's the reason we fought and died for nothing. Why we attacked other Levanti. Why Yitti and the others died dishonourable deaths. This is all about him, and it always has been. The gods may have forsaken us, but we can still have justice."

"You call this justice? The cold-blooded murder of another Sword?"

Shenyah advanced into the fray. "No, we do not demand his death for justice as Whisperer Ezma did; we demand his life pay for ours. He spent Levanti blood for his own ends"—she jabbed her finger in Gideon's direction—"now we will spend his to ensure no more die. And do not say this is not our way. It is exactly the tenet that underpins *kutum*. Sometimes individuals have to be sacrificed for the preservation of the herd."

"*Kutum* is decreed only in times of great need," I said between gritted teeth. "Because of famine and disaster, not because some Swords don't feel like doing their job."

The crowd in the doorway hissed, and Ptapha closed the distance between us to the length of an arm. "We would do our job if our leaders did theirs. Step aside, *Captain*."

He half drew his blade from its scabbard, the weight of a dozen Swords and more at his back, each stony stare an assurance that I was alone.

I adjusted my grip on my sword hilt. "Don't make me do this," I said.

"Don't make me," Ptapha returned. "He's not worth dying for."

"Then he's not worth killing for."

In better times, our herd matriarchs and patriarchs would have stepped in and ensured sense and empathy prevailed, but those times were long gone. Now there was just anger.

"Challenge him," Shenyah hissed, nudging Ptapha. "If you don't, I will."

Ptapha snorted. "There's nothing to challenge. He's no leader, just a selfish exile we should never have followed."

"Maybe so, but the choice must be left in the hands of the gods."

"No." My anger was building like a stoked fire. "I refuse to leave Gideon's fate to the gods. I will not leave his life in any hands but mine."

Knowing me well enough to be sure I meant it, Amun lifted his hands. "This isn't going to get us anywhere," he said. "You wanted to talk to Gideon and state your case, and now that you have, it's time to step back and walk away. We have no reason to fear the Chiltaens. If they come for us, they will be sorry and that is enough."

His words seemed to drain some of the tension from the room, leaving murmuring in its wake. Footsteps scuffed by the door, some of the Swords turned away, and I breathed out. As the fury ebbed, Amun met my gaze—his wry smile as much apology as it was farewell. The sooner he got them away from us the better.

Shenyah sniffed and turned away, radiating righteous indignation, yet beside her, Ptapha jerked into motion. Instinct kicked in and I made to block, but he hadn't drawn a sword to challenge; he had drawn a knife to kill. The short blade slashed toward my gut, and again my anger flared hot. Gripping his wrist, I twisted hard, forcing him off balance. He crashed head first into the wall, shaking the whole hut.

"Enough!" Amun shouted as Shenyah helped Ptapha to his feet, blood oozing from his nose and the corner of his mouth. "Stand down and get out."

"But he owes us!" Ptapha snarled, spitting a mouthful of blood onto the floor at my feet.

I stared at the blood, heavy breaths barely keeping my anger in check. "I owe you nothing," I said. "Get out, you weak excuses for Levanti."

"Fuck you and your superiority!" Ptapha made to lunge, but his need to shake off Shenyah gave me an opening. Without hesitation, I gripped my sword hilt and drew, bringing the blade up in a deadly arc that cut beneath Ptapha's guard, slicing his stomach, his chest, his arm. Blood sprayed. His sword dropped from his hand and he staggered a step only to fall onto his knees, his chest heaving with desperate breaths. Shock held the room silent, but where I ought to have felt remorse, I felt only a deep, bitter satisfaction.

I adjusted my grip and glared at them all over the tip of my blade. "Anyone else?"

# 11. CASSANDRA

I n the middle of the empty camp, the empress and I sat before a
dying fire. The open space around us lay choked with ghostly
silence, but she just sat and stared at me as I stared at her. And it
was me, not us. Kaysa had retreated, and while I was grateful for
the privacy, I hated that she'd known I needed it.

With the end of her sash wrapped around her hand, Miko lifted
a small ceramic pot from the coals and carefully poured its contents
into two chipped bowls. By her demeanour we could have been in a
palace, drinking the finest tea, rather than sitting amid the desolate
remains of the Levanti camp—fires left smoking, some tents abandoned, and a beheaded body left lying beside their shrine.

"So." In a graceful movement, the empress picked up her tea
bowl and blew away the steam. Once. Twice. Three times. Hana
had often done the same.

"So," I repeated when she said no more. "You have . . . questions,
Your Majesty?"

"Lots. But you know the one I really want answered."

"You want to know about Koi."

"I want to know about my mother."

I wanted to tell her, for her to know how hard her mother had
fought for her, but explaining felt all too difficult, like a wad of fabric sat balled in my mouth. It ought to have been Hana sitting here.

Hana reunited with the daughter she was so proud of. But it was just me, holding tight to the little shards of Hana I had been given. Shards that made me feel like her mother, but were to her nothing but a falsehood. A small, worthless bandage to the gaping wound of her grief.

"Your mother," I began, only to trail off, staring at the steam rising from my untouched bowl. My stomach felt empty and twisted. "Your mother . . . wasn't well."

"The imperial disease," she snapped. "I know." Impatient. Tense. Answers weren't going to make her feel any better.

I took a deep breath. "After . . . after the fall of Koi," I said, carefully avoiding my part in what had happened that night. "The hieromonk sold Empress Hana and me to a man called the Witchdoctor in return for Septum, Leo's seventh twin . . ."

She let me tell the story without interruption, from the day in the clearing when the Witchdoctor had taken us in, to the experiments in the house at Esvar, to the day Empress Hana had almost died upon hearing the Chiltaens had taken Mei'lian and her daughter was missing.

By the time my story travelled back to Koi, where we had burned the castle in our escape, my tea was well and truly cold. Back to the Witchdoctor's house after that with Captain Aeneas and Septum, and telling the story became easier, like I was spilling poison. I hadn't told anyone what had happened there, how we had escaped, how we had been on our way to the capital in search of Miko when Leo had found us. When Captain Aeneas had died. When Hana's body had really started to fail.

Miko listened, staring intently as though determined to experience every moment of her mother's life through story. It was all she had left.

My voice had been steady throughout, but when it came to describing how I had been alone in Hana's body when it died, when I'd died, and how she had fallen inside Septum...for a whole minute I found I couldn't speak. Not since childhood had I felt so full of emotion, like I was that little girl again, begging not to be taken away, promising I would not look at dead bodies anymore, that I would try not to hear them, that I would do anything they wanted me to as long as they let me stay. I had cried so hard I had been sure my chest would burst. I hadn't been able to see for tears, and snot had streamed down over my lips, that grief a force stronger than me.

This time I did not cry, but my chest strained. The empress sat silent. I wondered if she felt the same, if in that moment, in our own ways, we were mourning together without words. I could only guess, for Empress Miko had a mask even more stony than Empress Hana's, and the further I'd gone in my story the less emotion she had shown. Retreating into another place. One that haunted her, perhaps, as the dark places inside my memories haunted me.

"She knew she failed you," I said after a time. "Knew she had made so many wrong decisions. She'd wanted more time. To fix it. To help. To see the woman you've become."

The stony mask fractured, her face twisting only for the pain to vanish, her skin smoothing as she hid herself away again. I might never have sat upon a throne, but I knew the feeling well. To show emotion was to give the world a weakness it could use against you. Judged for too much. Judged for too little. Whether it had been Hana or life that had taught Miko how to guard herself, she did it well. No one seeing her now would have known she was breaking.

I reached out my hand—an offer of comfort. The empathy in the gesture was new to me, but despite the awkwardness I did not pull it back. "Your mother loved you, Miko," I said, daring to use her name, to pretend for a moment she really was my daughter. "She was proud of you. Proud that you would be the one to sit on the throne as she promised your father you would."

At mention of her father, she touched the great bow she wore upon her back, but said nothing.

"I'm sure he would be proud of you too."

Miko looked away. It felt foolish leaving my hand hovering between us, ignored, but telling myself it was more important to offer than to be accepted, I didn't draw back or speak again, just let her fight with the overwhelming emotions as I had done.

"Thank you," she said once all her grief had been tucked neatly away behind the mask. I wished I could tell her that she could cry, that she needn't be ashamed, but they were the words of a mother, and however I might feel, I was not her mother.

I withdrew my hand, closing my fingers around my untouched tea bowl. It was cold. God, what I wouldn't have done for some Stiff.

Around us, the wind picked up, battering the cracked shutters of an abandoned hut. The sound snapped the empress from her reverie. "Thank you," she said again. "Our wise philosophers would have us believe closure and knowledge are important to healing, but I'm afraid I cannot thank you in any way more personal than that, though I am glad she wasn't...wasn't alone."

The empress rose, abandoning her own barely touched tea in the dirt. "Now we have had this conversation you are free to leave at any time. I doubt we will see each other again."

I got to my feet, my nerves prickling. "Thank you, Your Majesty," I said, but where I ought to have demanded some payment or reparation, some compensation for all I had done and suffered for Kisia, for her, for her mother, I kept my mouth shut. Apparently I wasn't that Cassandra anymore. "If there's anything I can do for you—anything to make this easier..." I gestured around, unable to put into words all that had come of her plans.

Miko had begun to turn away, but she looked back at that, her stony expression giving way to contemplation. "Anything?"

"Anything," I said, knowing the moment the word was out of my mouth that I would regret it. But if I could ease the pain from her face and make myself someone in her eyes, I would.

She looked me up and down, assessing. "Perhaps with your skills you will find this mission much easier than anyone else I could send. Well. All right. I need you to go to Dom Villius. The real Dom Villius, the one that is my enemy."

A mix of hope and trepidation swelled inside me. "You want me to kill him?" With Yakono's help it would be much easier than attempting it alone. "I can do that."

"No." The empress shook her head, pressing a wry smile between her lips. "No, don't kill him. Not yet. I need his help."

———————◆———————

I sat staring at the saddlebag I'd brought with me, its contents all supplies. It had been a long time since I'd had anything of my own, all my personal belongings lost when our carriage had crashed on the way to Koi. It wasn't so long ago, but trauma stretches and distorts time, and I couldn't have said if it had happened yesterday or years ago, both true by the way the pain sat in my body.

"She won't really do it," I said as though speaking to the saddlebag. "The last thing she wants is for him to fulfil his prophecy."

*So you say, but it seems to me she would do anything if it meant winning. Getting her throne back isn't our fight, and no one's life should be risked for it.*

"And what is our fight?"

*Getting rid of Duos. Protecting Unus. Both of which also help Miko if she would look beyond the throne to what Kisia's future would be if he becomes Veld. This is a foolish plan.*

That at least I could agree with. I'd almost said so to the empress's face, but for all the risk, her plan had a wild sort of logic no one would expect.

"One's enemy's enemies can be strong allies."

*Even when they're Leo Villius? He can't be trusted to act in the way she's expecting.*

"We're going."

*I know we are, just don't lie about why. This is a terrible and dangerous plan, and you're only agreeing because you want her to like you.*

I looked away from the saddlebag as though it had spoken this painful truth, its strap a lashing tongue. "And you want to help Unus for any other reason?"

*I want to help him because I couldn't help myself.*

"Ouch."

Beside me, someone cleared their throat. "Cassandra?" Yakono had his saddlebag in hand, everything about him neat and sure despite the chaos of our surroundings. "Are you leaving?"

"Wouldn't want to stay," I said, getting to my feet. "You?"

"I have a contract to complete."

"You're going after Duos?"

His nod sank my stomach. "I have to complete my contract, which, considering everything that's happened, seems the right thing to do even if it wasn't a point of honour."

*See? Killing him is the right thing to do,* Kaysa said. *Listen to Yakono if you won't listen to me.*

"If that's still your goal too, we could work together," Yakono went on when I didn't answer. "Given his abilities, two assassins would be better than one."

Meeting Yakono's direct gaze was difficult enough without Kaysa's amusement whenever I struggled for words. I couldn't let Leo be killed while Miko needed him, but to say so to Yakono would be pointless. He'd agree with Kaysa. Leo was too dangerous, too erratic, and since Yakono had been kept from fulfilling his contract this long, no wild plan of the empress's would turn him from his purpose now. He couldn't go home until it was done.

"Sure, the Chiltaen camp is where I was heading," I said, gesturing at my saddlebag. "Once I figure out how to get inside."

*He'll find out, you know. Or kill Leo before you can give him Miko's message. Something tells me he's better at this whole killing people for money thing than you are.*

Thankfully unable to hear Kaysa's words, Yakono smiled, that genuine smile that lit up his eyes and made me feel important. Like I mattered. Like I wasn't entirely invisible.

"Oh good," he said, smile widening. "With two of us this will be much easier. And I think I know how we can get in."

---

I knew fuck all about armies, Chiltaen or otherwise, but it shouldn't have been surprising they needed a supply chain. Yet it was, and Yakono lifted his brows as I stared at the gathered carts and mule trains waiting outside the camp.

"I'm a city girl, all right?" I said. "Excuse me for not knowing how army camps work."

"Men have to eat."

"Yes. I know. It's logical. Can we not argue about it?"

"I'm not." He wasn't. As ever he was calm and rational, and his brows knitted with confusion. "Have I done something to upset you, Cassandra? If it's this ruse you dislike, I am happy to find another way to—"

"No, it's fine. I'm just on edge. Forget it."

*That was very calm. Very professional,* Kaysa said. *He's not going to suspect anything at all after that performance.*

*Well, he shouldn't be so damned considerate.*

*You mean if he was an asshole, you wouldn't feel so bad betraying him? I'm not—*

That was exactly what I was doing. I squeezed my eyes closed, blocking out the cloudy day. *Why does he have to be so decent?* I said. *And have actual ethics and morals.*

I caught myself before saying I too had ethics and morals, because whatever I had once thought I'd had, it had been nothing but survival instincts built upon anger.

*Life sucked*, she said. *You needed to survive.*

I blew out a breath and opened my eyes upon Yakono's anxious gaze, sure my eyes watered only due to the wind. *Thanks. That was what I needed to hear, I think.*

*You don't deserve me being nice to you, but I guess I'm trying something new. And, uh, thanks for not telling me to shut up. That was always your response when I made an observation.*

*I'm sorry.* Those words still felt strange even in my thoughts, yet I felt stronger for saying them.

*I know.*

Yakono had made no reply, instead looking around at the other people in line once more. With the sun slowly sinking, the evening chill was setting in, and all the carters and whores and opportunistic locals waiting outside the Chiltaen camp gathered their cloaks a little tighter. A handful of guards were strolling along checking wares and talking to people, letting some through the gates and turning others away. With no discernible pattern in their choices, we could only wait patiently for our turn, which Yakono managed with characteristic ease. I was barely holding myself together.

I'd thought I would be less stressed having him with me rather than risking him getting to Leo before me, yet the closer we got to our goal the more worried I became. Working side by side meant I either had to tell him what I was doing or trick him—a task that had seemed easy at a distance and now seemed impossible. But Miko needed this. The Levanti had failed her. I could not.

*She's still not going to look at you like a mother even if you succeed.*

I closed my eyes, cold wind whipping through my hair. *I think I told you to shut up so often because while I wield a dagger, you wield the truth, and that hurts more.*

*Oh.*

We edged forward in the line.

*This being honest with each other thing is hard,* she said.

*Right? Who'd have thought? For what it's worth, I'm sorry about running off on Unus.*

*Thank you, but you'd do it again if you had to, and I don't know how to live with someone who cares for my wishes only when they don't get in the way of theirs.*

That bitter truth, cutting into me again, but there was nothing I could say. She was right, and it was pretty fucking terrible.

"What's your cargo?" a guard said to the carter a few places ahead of us.

Beside me, Yakono tilted his head my way. "Are you ready?"

"Of course I'm ready. We've been standing here at least an hour."

"Ready to stop standing here isn't the same as ready to do the job."

"I'm ready, just not used to working with someone else."

"Neither am I. Which is why I asked if you were ready."

The guards moved another step closer, waving the carter on into the camp. I wished I knew if this was a normal level of precaution, but the last few minutes had not increased the amount I knew about army camps.

"Your purpose here?" the guard asked the man ahead of us, and with a shake of my shoulders I let myself slide into character. Not that it was a big change. I was already a bored whore lining up outside an army camp.

The man ahead of us was refused entry, leaving the guard directing his gaze our way. I was used to such men looking me up and down as though they had a right to my body, but such men did not usually look so bored. "The place is already full of whores," he said. "Better you seek your coin elsewhere."

"Elsewhere?" I repeated. "But we're already here. Elsewhere is a waste of our time."

"Unless you want to risk it with our Levanti friends"—the man spat onto the grass—"here is also a waste of your time."

"Are you sure of that?" Yakono said, his light teasing at odds with the challenging look he threw the man. "I can already see one reason it's very worth our time here."

The guard swallowed, his gaze skittering over Yakono before coming to rest somewhere over his shoulder. Taking that as a timely cue, I slid a pair of coins into his hand.

"Fine," the man said, pocketing them without looking at Yakono again. "But don't say you weren't warned." He jerked his head toward the camp. "Go on, in you go."

As we headed for the gates, I said, "For someone who claims not to like sex, you sure did that well."

"Claims?" Yakono frowned. "What has acting a part to do with my feelings about sex?"

"I don't know. It just seems odd."

"I've watched enough people flirt to know what it looks like. I'll take it as a compliment that you find my act accurate."

He sounded bitter, but now was not the time to talk about it. So of course, I talked about it. "Do you really not like sex?"

"Really," he said, gaze sweeping the gathered tents and soldiers as mine ought to have been. "No doubt there are foods and activities you don't like."

"Well, yes, but . . . aren't the pleasures of the body the one thing we all share, you know, because we all have a body?"

"People have tried to tell me so before, but that doesn't make my point any less true. Consider how different all of our bodies are. All of our minds. Our tastes. Our languages. There is nothing we all share, but that's all right as long as we practice respect."

"God, you make me feel like the worst person in the world for even asking, thank you."

He halted abruptly and spun on me, breaking character. "That is unfair," he said. "I answered your questions without judgement even though every time I have to explain it, I'm making an argument merely to exist. If my answers make you uncomfortable that's for you to think on, not for me to apologise for. Now, can we stop having this conversation and do the job we came to do? Let's split up and gather what information we can about his movements and location and meet back here at sundown."

Yakono awaited no agreement, just strode away, the loose half robe he wore hanging suggestively off one shoulder as its skirt fluttered behind him.

"I guess I really am just the worst person in the world," I mumbled.

*I'd offer to take over and give you some time to yourself, but my skill at bending just so to give men the best look at our breasts isn't anywhere near as good as yours. And I'd probably just stab Duos rather than talk to him.*

Ignoring the last jab, I said, "Perhaps you should just take over every time I'm talking to Yakono. He'll like you better than me." I sighed. An army camp seemed a good place to get a drink, drown some sorrows, and disappear, but unfortunately, I had to find Leo before Yakono did.

Not wanting any offers, I didn't bother with the arsing and breasting and trying to catch each soldier's eye, and instead made my way toward the centre of the camp. Though I still knew nothing about army camps, that seemed the most likely place to find the tents belonging to the powerful leader types. A few tents were large enough their tops rose above those around them, even above the roofline of a chapel-shaped building formed from salvaged timber.

Atop a slight rise, we came to the first of the larger tents. The space between them grew, while the number of people around dropped to a few standing in conversation and some boys dashing about their tasks.

"Hey, what are you doing here?" A soldier more decorated than most veered out of his way toward us, brows caught low.

"Just plying my wares, sir." I adjusted my stance and eyed him coquettishly. "Interested?"

The man snorted, looking down his nose. "Keep to the common areas of the camp. No one here is interested in *you*."

A shock of hot mortification spread across my cheeks, and only Kaysa sliding into control kept me from punching the man in the face. "Someone said I ought to try my luck on Dom Villius," she said. "That his tastes ran to... older women."

"Then someone played you for a fool," the man laughed, glancing over his shoulder at a fine tent with a white curtain over the entry-way. "Dom Villius is a man of God and has no interest in earthly... needs." He shooed me with a flap of his hand. "Go on, out of here."

Kaysa thanked him and extracted herself from the conversation more gracefully than I could have done. Like all the times Hana had come to my rescue with her haughty confidence, I thought, and missed her anew. A feeling I'd never expected, especially for a displaced Kisian empress.

"You got to know her because you literally couldn't push her away like you do everyone else," Kaysa murmured, looping back around through the camp to come at the main tents from a different direction.

*This honesty thing,* I said. *I think we need some boundaries. That was too much.*

"Too much truth? I'm not wrong though."

*I look forward to the day I understand you well enough to drop such lovely truths on your head.*

"What makes you think I'm as disastrously lacking in self-awareness?"

*That you don't even know who you are because you've been trapped being me. Oh, look, I can do it too. Gosh, that feels good.*

Our face creased into a scowl. "All right, so, boundaries." *Here, have us back,* she added silently. *Whatever that man thought, most of these soldiers are staring so much they make me uncomfortable.*

*You really should be the one talking to Yakono,* I said, taking over. *You have that whole disliking sex thing in common.*

*And you have the whole enjoying killing people thing. Maybe you just have to stop pushing him away and see what happens.*

"I have not been—"

*Stow it, Cass; you can't lie to me, remember? Although if we get to Leo before him, he won't like us anymore regardless.*

Grateful for the growing darkness, I found a back way into the central circle of tents, past a gathering of flags sprouting from tall poles. We passed a large open tent set up as a meeting space, owning a table and an odd assortment of chairs and wine cups in various states of emptiness. No sign of Leo though, so I sauntered on toward his tent, passing more brightly lit tents far too large for single occupants who didn't also have to accommodate their sense of importance. Leo's, with its white-hung curtain, was in the centre, a pair of guards flanking the entrance.

As I strode toward it, a hiss drew my gaze to the dark recess of a smaller tent wedged between two large ones—the sort belonging to a servant needed close by.

"Cassandra!" the hiss came again, and for a moment I considered ignoring it and walking on, but Yakono would come after me. So, doing my best to look natural, I ambled over and ducked inside. There Yakono crouched in the dim light creeping through the entrance, his features all shadows. "It's too risky to get closer to his tent than this," he said, the note of censure slight but present. "He would recognise you at a glance."

"I know," I snapped. "I know what I'm doing."

Here the moment to admit my plan, to tell him the truth, yet the words remained caught behind my teeth.

"What have you found out?"

"I think I should go in first," I said, ignoring his question. "As a distraction. To pull his attention away."

Yakono's brow furrowed, deepening the shadows. "I don't think that's a good idea. He can read our minds, remember? He'll know it's a diversion."

He was right, and it wasn't a good idea at all if assassination was the goal.

"We need to be careful," he went on. "We're only going to get one chance, and right now he's in his tent and there are guards out front. Any attempt to go in the back or slice our way through would fail because he can hear us coming. I'm beginning to think the only way we're going to get him is in a large crowd where there are so many minds making noise that we can hide. Perhaps if we wait for him to step out and walk about the camp we may get an opportunity, though the aftermath would be dangerous with so many soldiers around."

"Too dangerous, I think. Look, he and I have a history. If I say I want to make a deal with him or that I have a message for him, he'll let me in, and I can take him out as soon as his guard is down."

"That's an even more dangerous plan, especially by yourself."

"There's always a risk in this job," I said.

"If you want to be reckless, we could just charge in there together and stab him, consequences be damned."

It wasn't a serious suggestion, yet the possibility that he would kill Leo before I could give him Miko's message shot panic through me. "No!"

Suspicion darkened the shadows on Yakono's face. "What's going on, Cassandra?"

Always with that gentle way he said my name, always the note of concern. *Just tell him the truth*, Kaysa said.

But the truth would mean explaining what Miko meant to me. Explaining about Hana. About what I was. What *we* were.

"Nothing is going on," I lied, fear hollowing my chest. I ought to have found a way to get here before him, have come up with a believable excuse or at least been better at my job, but I hadn't and I was running out of time. Unable to hold his gaze, I turned and paced the length of the small space, three steps all it took to reach the steep canvas wall and spin back. Gripping the central post, I turned, grateful Yakono was watching people pass outside rather than looking at me.

I needed to get out of there. There was no more time for plans. No more time for thought, only for desperate action. One step. Two. I lunged forward, snaking my arm around Yakono's neck as I'd done a hundred times to people who'd gotten between me and my targets but didn't deserve to die, to the children who'd bullied me at the hospice, to men who'd gotten too handsy without paying, but never to someone whose life I cared about. And at his shocked gasp, at his futile attempt to turn, to struggle, to twist from my hold as my arm tightened across the hard ridges of his throat, I couldn't escape just how much I cared. How much the confused sounds he made as he lost consciousness cut into my heart.

*Cass! What are you doing!*

I wanted to let him go, but this was what Miko needed, so I held fast through his last weak flails, not releasing my hold until Yakono slithered boneless onto the floor.

*Cass!*

My hands shook as I untied Yakono's sash, barely getting it loose before he began to stir. Gratitude he wasn't injured warred with growing panic as I wrapped the sash around and around his wrists before hauling him across the tent floor like a corpse. He tried dopily to separate his hands, but I was stronger and began lashing the other ends of the sash to the central pole. It shook, but was well dug into the ground and would take some effort to shift—time enough for me to get to Leo and see my task through.

"Cass...andra?" he mumbled, trying to move. "What...?"

"I'm sorry." My voice caught, and I dared not move to where he could see me. "I'm sorry. I can't let you kill him yet. Miko needs him."

"I...what?"

"I'm sorry, I'll be right back to let you go, I promise." I edged toward the tent opening as he shook the pole in an attempt to move. "I promise."

As I stepped closer to the entrance, Yakono looked up at me, still blinking and with his brow creased in confusion. That same confusion haunted his eyes, but it was the hurt in them that struck me. The betrayal. He didn't understand—how could he? He knew no more than that someone he'd trusted had turned on him.

"Cassandra..."

Another apology caught on my tongue, but I couldn't voice it, could only turn and stumble out through the opening and into the night, disoriented. Every part of me screamed to go back, like I was as caught to the tent pole as Yakono, every step away an effort, but Miko needed this. Needed me.

Outside Leo's tent, the pair of guards shifted their stance as I approached, hands creeping to sword hilts. I blew out a breath. No going back now. "Leo!" I called. "It's Cassandra. I need to talk to you."

The guards looked at one another, then toward the tent opening, through which an all too familiar voice said, "I thought I heard you out there." The white curtain was brushed aside, and there stood Leo Villius, his pale robes a shining light around which the world turned. I had sought his attention, yet as his gaze fell upon me, I wanted to run, my heartbeat racing in sick panic.

*Remember he's just like Unus,* Kaysa said.

*No,* I said. *He's fucking terrifying, and I'm not ashamed to admit it.*

*That's what makes him powerful. It's not what he can do; it's all the things you imagine he can do.*

A smile flickered on Leo's lips. "Check her for weapons," he said. "She likes to carry a dagger hidden in her boot."

Under their stares, I yanked the boot dagger free with a flourish and held it out, followed by the one strapped to my thigh. I felt unbalanced without them, but I held up my hands to show I had no more, and Leo stepped back through the fall of white cloth, leaving me to follow. I stood a moment on the threshold under the wary gaze of both guards, each holding one of my blades.

*We can still run.*

*And betray Miko as well as Yakono. No.* I clenched my hands into fists and stepped inside.

I'd always thought the saying one was entering a lion's den was overdramatic, but that was how I felt as the curtain fell back into place behind me. For all its external simplicity, the inside of Duos's tent was bright and lavish, with an upright bed on one side, half-screened from the rest of the space by embroidered cloth. Three couches set around a table took up most of the space, like I'd stepped into a rich merchant's entertaining room rather than a tent.

With a broad smile, he gestured for me to sit, exactly as a lion might if food were to make an easy meal of itself.

"I'm not going to eat you, Cassandra," he said. "At least not yet. Do sit and tell me what you came to say."

I perched on the edge of the couch farthest from him. "A message. From Empress Miko."

He stared hard at me. Anyone else might have exclaimed it wasn't possible, that word was she was dead, but Leo didn't waste time with such a show.

"She's alive," I said, hurrying on with words rather than leaving him to read it all from my mind. "She survived the attempt on her life and is now aware that the deal you made with Minister Manshin was for you to marry Lady Sichi, not her. Because she's your consort with two voices or whatever it is you think the Presage says you need to do."

Duos stilled as I spoke, hardly seeming to breathe or blink. "And the message?" he prompted, voice low and threaded with threat. "You cannot have come here just to tell me that she knows."

"No." I drew a deep breath. "I came to propose a deal on Miko's behalf."

"There is nothing I want from Empress Miko except for her to be out of the way, preferably dead, which, somehow, I doubt she intends to give me."

"No, but she has Unus."

I let the words sink in, their weight lowering his brows until he frowned at me across the table. "Do you mean that she would give Unus to me? That seems... unlikely, shall we say."

"It isn't her first choice, but she's running out of options."

Duos fixed his gaze on me, all scowling concentration. "It is a fine offer, should it not be an empty promise. You aren't lying, but was she?"

I'd assured Kaysa as much after Miko had unburdened her fears and her desperation to me. I'd wanted to be useful to her, to feel important, seen, and at last after agreeing to this mission, she had opened up enough for me to see the real Miko beneath the mask. A fierce fighter, idealistic and determined. She didn't want to give Duos something he needed, but she'd grown up in the same environment that had forged Hana. Sometimes a leader has to make terrible choices because they're fighting for their people, not themselves.

"No," I said, hoping Kaysa would keep quiet. "She wasn't."

Duos's eyes brightened, hungry now. "And what is it the empress wishes from me in return?"

"For you to take all your soldiers and leave Kisia. And you must exchange Unus publicly at your wedding to Lady Sichi, for all to see."

"That's no small ask."

"No, but then Unus is no small prize."

*Cass... if she goes ahead with this...*

*Shh! Not now.*

Duos leapt up and started to pace, all energy as he swept about the tent. "Yes," he murmured to himself. "Yes, it just might work. Leaving Aurus..." He chuckled and spun toward us. "Yes, you may tell your beloved empress that she has a deal. I will send all my soldiers marching home in return for Unus, and if she fails to hold up her end of the bargain, I will march them all right back and raze her empire to the ground."

I shivered, the promise in his words tangible.

"And now you go," he said. "Walk straight to the gate and don't linger, or I will take great joy in ordering my guards to throw you out."

I didn't need to be told twice. Jumping up, I sped toward the exit.

"Oh, and Cassandra?"

His voice caught me like my feet had landed in mud, and I looked over my shoulder. "What?"

"Kaysa is right. You'll never be anything to your precious empress. You're no one. Just a desperate old whore carrying a blade in the dark."

His words were just such a blade jammed into my chest, leaching its truth. I was nothing. No one. Yet so desperately did I need Miko to look at me, to make me someone.

*Don't listen to him*, Kaysa said, nudging me toward the doorway. *Let's go.*

Duos's all too satisfied smile was the last thing I saw before I pushed through the curtain and out into the thick night. There I halted, holding out my hand to the guards. "My blades?"

They looked at one another, barely containing smiles. "What blades?"

"You have to be fucking kidding me."

"Watch it," one said. "Whores who make trouble get thrown out around here. If they're lucky."

*Let's go, we can get new ones.*

*It's the principle of the thing*, I said.

*A principle that could get us killed. You can't take a message back to Miko if you're dead.*

With a disgusted snort I walked on, leaving the men laughing behind me. Dying for pride would be the most pathetic of ends—perfect for a desperate old whore carrying a blade in the dark.

*It's not true*, Kaysa said as we made our way toward the tent where we'd left Yakono. *You're nothing to Miko and you always will be, but you're not nothing to me. And if you apologise a lot and explain everything, you might not be to Yakono.*

Her words made me want to run for the gates, but Kaysa kept us striding on toward the tent to face Yakono and my shame.

"I'm back," I said, ducking into the dim tent where I'd left him. "Didn't I say…"

Before my sight adjusted, every other sense felt the emptiness. The space. The silence. Where Yakono had sat tied to the thick central pole, there was nothing but scuff marks on the old rug—no sign even of the sash with which I'd restrained him. Hairs prickled on the back of my neck and I spun, hands raised, but only fears stood behind me. Of course he'd escaped, and why stick around when I'd betrayed him so completely? I could try to find him, but he was not the sort of man to let himself be found unless he wanted to be. He had a contract to complete and a home to return to; I could only hope he wouldn't kill Duos until after the ceremony.

# 12. DISHIVA

I woke to a feeling of heaviness, like every limb had been filled with sand. I'd felt fatigue many times before, but this was new, as though no matter how awake my mind, my body would not move. Outside, the camp was already waking, and soon people would start arriving for blessings and find me curled up beneath my covers—a vision that did nothing to shift me from my mat. Without the sounds from outside, I would have thought time stopped, so still did I lie in the darkness.

The creak of weight on the front step ought to have been like a bolt of lightning, launching me from my bed, but I couldn't even bring myself to crack open an eye.

"Dishiva?" Harmara's voice, followed by a second set of footsteps. "I thought you said she hadn't gone out yet."

"She hasn't." Tephe. "You call yourself a tracker? Open your eyes."

A small grunt and footsteps crossed the floor in my direction. "Dishiva? Captain?" Harmara knelt before me, and I managed to open my remaining eye enough to show I was alive. "Are you sick?"

Was I? I didn't feel sick; I was just caught to the mat, too heavy to move.

"Mind sick," Tephe said, his voice overhead. "Like when you're grieving and you think you'll never move again. You think what Oshar said last—"

"Shh!" Harmara hissed. "If you're right then maybe don't bring it up? Open your eyes," she added, mimicking his former mocking tone.

Tephe grunted. Neither of them was more than a vague shadow through the narrow slit of my gaze. "At least some of the bastards are leaving; maybe that will cheer her up."

"Whether it's good news or not probably depends on where they are going and why."

I licked my lips, surprised to find I could move at all. "Where who is going?" I managed to grumble.

"The Chiltaens," Harmara said. "Some of them woke early and have been packing their tents, while others are just going about like usual."

"Packing? Why?"

The woman shrugged. "We don't know. I was going to wake Oshar and make him go ask, but thought you might already know."

I shook my head, and forcing sheer will through my body, managed to stretch my still weighty limbs. It broke through the sense of paralysis, but did nothing to disperse the sand that seemed to have filled me while I slept. Refusing the helping hand Harmara held out, I rolled over and was able to lever myself upright, body protesting all the way.

More awake than before, I noticed that the sounds from outside became more insistent. Busier. I shuffled toward the window, my legs not yet ready to fully carry my weight. Outside it was exactly as Harmara had said, some of the soldiers sitting by their tents as they usually did at this hour, talking and eating and shouting jokes to one another, while others had collapsed their tents and were in the process of folding and rolling and arguing with their companions. There didn't seem to be a pattern as to who was leaving either, soldiers in both green- and blue-edged tunics preparing to depart.

I sighed and rubbed my face. "You said you hadn't asked Oshar?"

"He's still asleep." Tephe shrugged. "Waking him is like trying to wake the dead."

Harmara snorted, and began to remind Tephe of an incident while they were still chained up, but with my mind buzzing with questions I left them to it and went in search of my robe and mask.

I felt no lighter in my hieromonk garb, but though my legs didn't want to move, I made my way out into the camp. Trying to appear at ease rather than weak, I nodded to soldiers and offered short blessings as I passed, each brief pause giving me the chance to regain my strength. It hadn't improved by the time I reached the gates and covered the last distance out to Secretary Aurus's tent, but the gnawing worry of my health soon collapsed beneath the sound of Leo's raised voice. It emanated through the open curtain, causing both of Secretary Aurus's guards to grimace at me as I approached. Neither sought to keep me from entering, instead stepping aside perhaps in the mistaken belief that my arrival would calm tempers.

Inside, the secretary was lounging on one of his couches, watching Leo pace irritably across the floor. With the argument in Chiltaen, I watched from the entryway, trying to decide if Leo was offensively or defensively angry. He seemed to want to keep me in the dark, for although he acknowledged my presence with a stab of his finger in my direction, he didn't change to Levanti. Neither did Secretary Aurus when he replied, his lazy tone at odds with the tension in his face—no, in his entire body. I'd never seen anyone manage to lounge while looking so thoroughly unrelaxed.

With a second jab of his finger in my direction, Leo stopped pacing to spit out what sounded like an ultimatum. No pause to wait for an answer, no further threat; he turned his back on the secretary and stalked toward me across the floor. "I'm afraid I'm taking rather more of your soldiers with me than planned, so you'll just have to wait on taking Shimai until I'm back. And, Dishiva?" He leaned close, proximity ever his favourite weapon. "I will be back. And when I am, you and I are going to finish what we started." He patted my cheek, and I flinched like he'd slapped me. "Don't go anywhere, will you?"

With those parting words, he strode out of the tent. In his wake, the curtain fluttered.

"Truly a divine man," Aurus said, his tone flat. He had sat up and allowed his brow to furrow, his hands caught together in a tight knot. "Now if only he would die and go to God, everything would be so much easier."

"There are soldiers leaving," I said, gesturing in the direction of the main camp.

"Yes, although hopefully a few less now. He wasn't very happy that I invoked an old law to threaten those commanders who take his side with military discharge."

"Is that what he was shouting about?"

"That and he wanted to tell me he knew what I was up to and that there was no way I could hope to take Shimai without him and his men, but that if I wished to try he would be sure I was remembered as the most foolish military leader in Chiltaen history."

It seemed an odd threat, but the way Aurus's lips compressed into a thin, humourless line told me it meant a lot more to him than it did to me.

"So he's really taking as many soldiers as will follow him and leaving?" I said. "I know he said he would be back, but to willingly walk away when I haven't named him defender yet... Well, it makes me worry what could be more important to him."

"His wedding, I assume," Aurus said, some of his true languor returning. "And taking the soldiers is just to weaken my force and keep me from making any moves in the few days he will be absent."

"Wait, marriage? You said something about that before, but I didn't think you meant *Leo* was getting married."

The secretary took up his wineglass, despite the early hour. "Yes, of course, he's marrying Lady Sichi Mansh—"

"Sichi?" My jaw dropped. "No, she would never marry him, not unless she's being forced. She knows what he is. And he can't wish to marry her, she killed him once."

"Sounds like it will be happier than many marriages," he said grimly. "But no doubt you're right and she is being forced."

I frowned. "And that's all right? You're happy to make an alliance with someone through a forced marriage?"

With an overly dramatic gesture of shock, Aurus sat forward. "I? I am making no alliance."

"Fine, the Nine then."

"The Nine are making no alliance. In case it has escaped your notice, Your Holiness, we are planning to conquer Shimai and then the rest of northern Kisia, not make alliances and treaties with the meagre remnants of their army or their weak court."

"You mean..." I squeezed my eyes shut, trying to think. "The Kisians are making an alliance only with Leo?"

"With Lord Villius and whichever commanders are willing to risk a financially ruinous discharge to support him."

I stared at him, waiting for him to explain, to grant me the piece of knowledge that would make it all sensible, but Aurus just stared back. "But..." I said at last. "Why? Why make an alliance only with him?"

"Because he offered peace, I believe."

His answers weren't helping. "But he doesn't control the Nine, does he?"

"No."

"Or the army?"

"Not most of it, no."

"And he's planning on returning to take Shimai with us?"

"So I understand."

I plonked down on the couch opposite him. "Do you realise none of what you just said makes any sense?"

"You mistake, Holiness, everything I said made perfect sense; it's Lord Villius's plans that are, shall we say, unclear."

"You don't know what he's planning?"

"I don't know what he's planning."

I let out a long sigh. "Then what do we do?"

Aurus rose and began to slowly pace the floor, following in Leo's footsteps. "We march for Shimai in the morning. We hope my threat will ensure more soldiers remain. And we hope my negotiations for a secret weapon do not fail."

"Secret weapon?"

He tapped the side of his nose. "I will get no hopes up. Plan for the worst, hope for the best, as the saying goes. Now, if there's nothing else you wished from me immediately, I ought to go walk around imposing the law of the Nine or at least the threat of it, see if I can't scare some more commanders into remaining with us."

Leaving his wine unfinished, he strode out. I envied his confidence and the quick ease with which he knew what he ought to do next and made it happen. That sort of assurance had belonged to Captain Dishiva e'Jaroven. She had known her place in the world and known what every moment required of her, and then she'd crossed the sea and everything had changed.

I walked back to the chapel deep in thought, paying little heed to the activity swelling around me. Without enough soldiers, we wouldn't be able to take Shimai, and waiting for Leo to return would expose us to whatever he had planned. In order to square all his clashing goals, that likely meant the complete destruction of not only me but also Secretary Aurus and his soldiers, ruining our last chance at a safe haven on the Chiltaen shore. I felt helpless, but every bow and nod and "Your Holiness" that followed my passing reminded me I was not. I was their hieromonk.

Back in the chapel, Oshar and the others sat talking quietly over their morning meal, but all talk ceased at my entrance as six expectant gazes turned my way. "Leo is leaving," I said in answer to the unasked question. "Taking as many of the soldiers loyal to him as he can."

"Good riddance to them all," Rophet said, returning to his food.

Ignoring him, I looked to Oshar. "How do you feel about climbing onto the roof with me?"

"This roof?" he said, pointing upward.

"Yes, this roof."

"Happy to do so, Captain, but we may need some crates or something to help. The walls are very flat."

Harmara swallowed a mouthful and gestured at Rophet. "Ro's shoulders would be easier."

"Why mine?"

"Because you're the tallest."

"By a horse's hair!" He pointed at Jira. "He can do it."

I stepped in. "You can both do it, since both Oshar and I need to get onto the roof. Come on, you can finish your food once you've hoisted us up."

Rophet grumbled, but Jira seemed resigned and rose without complaint. At least until my feet were shifting around on his shoulders as I tried to find a good hold to haul myself up. My robe was in the way, catching on the rough edges of the roof, and the wind kept fluttering my mask and obscuring my sight.

"Come on, Captain," Jira said, voice strained. "I'm not as strong as I used to be. Get up there!"

"I'm trying!"

"And you thought she would be easier," Rophet laughed from down below.

A hand closed around mine. Oshar had already scrambled up, and with him bracing me and Jira giving me a final boost, I managed to drag myself onto the chapel's far too rickety roof. After a moment to catch my breath, I nodded to Oshar and stood up, braving the wind. Down below, a few soldiers nudged one another and pointed up. Others glanced up, only to go on about their tasks. It was now or never.

"My people!" I called out over the camp, leaving space for Oshar to translate at an even greater volume. "It is the will of God that tomorrow we march for Shimai, that at last the great Chiltaen nation conquers this land as its due." Only when I had begun did I realise I wasn't even sure why they wanted northern Kisia, but my vague terms seemed to be enough. Down in the camp, some of the men had lifted fists into the air, while others knelt to pray. Few still went about their tasks. "And so in the name of God, I call upon you all to march with me tomorrow, as through me God leads us all to destiny and glory!"

A few seconds behind my words, Oshar finished the proclamation to a tide of cheering. In all my years leading Swords, never had any group responded with such passion to anything I'd said. The rapturous faces and cries, raised hands and swords and gestures of prayer, sent a thrilled shiver through my skin. The power of this robe and mask, this name, was more than I could ever have imagined. All I had to do was use it.

"Prepare! For tomorrow we march!" At these final words some of them hurriedly dispersed; others remained kneeling in prayer or with their eyes lifted skyward. A few seemed unmoved—likely Leo's men, I told myself, trying not to see the reaction as dissent. I wasn't a captain anymore. No one could challenge me, whatever they thought.

"Well," Oshar said. "That went well, I suppose. Shall we climb down?"

"No, you go. I'm going to just stand here a bit longer, a reminder of all I just said."

"Looking foreboding with your robe flapping in the wind?"

"Something like that."

With a nod, he left me to it. Even as one by one the remaining soldiers dispersed, others who'd missed the scene arrived, and talk spread fast. I stayed as still as I could, trying to appear a godly figure of warning to any commander who thought leaving with Leo a fine idea. I didn't know if my words or my presence would make any difference, but I remained standing on the roof while the sun rose to its zenith and some of those who had been packing their things completed their tasks.

All the while, from the far end of the row before me, Leo stood and stared. Equally silent, we faced off from behind our masks. His unseen glare was a reminder that he could take away what he had given, the moment he was ready for me to die. I didn't flinch. I drew myself up taller and stayed standing there upon the roof looking down at him. Yet when at last he turned to leave, taking his soldiers with him, my knees trembled and I found I was shaking. His long stare had been a promise.

If we failed to take Shimai, I would be worse than dead.

---

Everyone seemed to have something to do except me, so I picked splinters of wood off the windowsill while outside the camp came apart. It looked as chaotic as the packing of a Levanti camp, just with different priorities and patterns.

In Leo's absence, I had expected a sudden shift in the camp's tone, but nothing seemed to have changed. The soldiers who remained were just hastily folding tents and hauling supplies, the air filled with cheerful shouts and the ever-present stink of the latrine pits.

I kept picking at the wooden sill and tapping my foot—more on edge than I'd been for a long time. Behind me, the murmur of Levanti voices wasn't the comfort it ought to have been.

"You know what I'm most looking forward to when we go home?" Tephe said, the whole group gathered around a morning meal. "Good food. No one here knows how to prepare meat properly, and it's such a waste."

Murmurs of agreement were made around mouthfuls. I tried to recall what food had been like back home—the memory coming to me slowly like I had to hack through an overgrown forest to find it. I hadn't been away that long, yet so much had happened it felt like an age, my memories beginning to slip away along with everything else that made me feel Levanti.

Activity sped on outside. There'd been no sign of Secretary Aurus yet, and though he probably had a lot of shouting orders to do elsewhere, I couldn't help but feel he was punishing me for failing to get all the commanders on our side.

*Our* side. What a strange thought. Like I'd ever wanted to march a Chiltaen army to take a Kisian city. For the hundredth time I reminded myself that the Chiltaens would still have marched without me, my presence in their ranks less a betrayal of Sichi than a fight for my people's future.

I opened and closed my fists, keeping myself from pacing, from drawing the attention of the others still murmuring over their meal.

"Captain?"

I flinched, not having heard Oshar approach. "What is it, Oshar?" I said, trying to sound calm though my heart thudded hard.

"The others are, uh . . . wondering what you expect them to do."

A glance over his shoulder found the motley group of Levanti watching on. What did I expect? Beyond requesting Oshar's help, I'd given it no thought, assuming they would do whatever they chose and leave the moment it was safe.

"Nothing," I said. "You're all free to make your own choices. I'm here because I believe I can give us a better future, but I won't walk Gideon's path. I'm not your leader. No one is anymore."

By their expressions they felt as odd hearing such words as I'd felt saying them. "I don't expect you to follow me," I added. "I'm not walking an easy path. If you want to leave, I'm sure the chaos of our departure will cover you, especially without Leo around keeping watch."

They looked at one another, and I found I couldn't breathe. I'd meant what I said, but if they left, if they saw what I was trying to do and walked away, how could I remain confident of my plan?

"I don't know where we would go," Harmara said, the words a whisper as though she didn't want to hear her own admission. "Join Ezma? Gideon? Rah?"

Rophet spat on the floor, a grumble vibrating in his throat. "Fuck all of them."

"I don't want to fight for Chiltaens," Tephe said. "But I don't want to get caught up in their horseshit either."

"You don't have to," I said. "I'm fighting only to leverage the position Leo gave me to get what we need. Reparations for the damage they have done us."

With a snort, Rophet dropped a crust of bread onto the plate, but the expected derision didn't come. He just sat staring at the discarded food, while around him the others met and broke gazes in an awkward dance of indecision. I didn't want to be responsible for them, but neither did I want to be alone.

"I'm staying," Oshar said, shrugging. "It's not like I had other plans."

Even the laughter was awkward, but no one seemed in a hurry to depart. In the end it was Rophet who mirrored Oshar's shrug. "May as well stick around a bit longer and eat their food."

"If you don't leave now, you might not get another chance for a while," I said.

"Then hopefully they'll get better at cooking."

Riding amid a Chiltaen army twanged unpleasant memories. So many towns and villages we'd charged into, laying waste to all around us like we'd truly been the monsters they thought us, drunk upon Gideon's promise of a future. A future I hoped wasn't entirely out of reach.

Oshar rode beside me, but the others had fallen back to give the appearance of mere hangers-on. The only people ahead were Secretary Aurus and the legates, our positions seemingly hierarchical in a way Levanti progress across the plains never was. Behind us, each commander rode with what seemed to be their captains, or some other adjunct, while the lower ranks followed with slaves and supplies bringing up the rear. While herd masters usually led the way, all other leaders from the matriarchs to the sword captains walked or rode wherever they wanted within the group, travelling less a show than a social occasion.

The uncomfortable feeling remained on the second day. I tried to clear my mind, and for a time it worked, but the sense I was reliving horrors I'd already experienced intensified when the city of Shimai came into view, its dark outline emerging through the evening mist. I'd stood here before, looking down at our next target while the city buzzed with panic, and I'd felt only the smallest empathy. Now my vision was less clear, the weather had grown cold, and shame and worry coiled in my stomach.

Some distance beyond the road, another hazy outline sat pressed into the trees, a gathering of sorts perhaps, all small structures and the shifting of life. As we drew closer, figures emerged from it on horseback.

A camp.

"Oshar, my eye hates this low light. Is that another Chiltaen camp? Or Kisians?" The sudden realisation that I could be about to march not only against Sichi's people but Sichi herself sent my stomach plummeting.

"I... I think it's a Levanti camp."

"What? Surely not."

"Definitely a Levanti camp. Their tents aren't all in lines, none of them are big and showy, and there are more horses than Chiltaens tend to have hanging around."

I stared at the approaching figures, while all around us talk grew as the commanders behind us drew level and caught sight of the camp here before us. One of them rode forward, edging past us to reach Secretary Aurus, no doubt to ask the very question I wanted answered—who were these Levanti, and how surprised was he to see them?

"The group approaching," I said, leaning toward Oshar. "Recognise anyone?"

"Unfortunately, yes, Captain," he said. "I'm afraid you aren't going to like this."

They were almost upon us now, but with daylight fast leaching from the sky, it was impossible for me to make out details, except for the horns that seemed to be growing from the front rider's head.

"Oh no. Not..." My voice faltered and I looked helplessly to Oshar, silently begging him to deny my worst fear.

He couldn't. Within moments, the group of Levanti were reining in before Secretary Aurus, and there was no looking away from the bone headpiece rising crown-like from Whisperer Ezma's head.

"Good evening, Secretary," she said, her tone neither surprised nor formal. Her gaze slid my way, locking to my thankfully masked face. "Dishiva." She smiled, the sort of smile that ought to have sent warmth coursing through me rather than the chill of fear I felt. "I'm so glad you have been brought back to me by God's grace. There is much to be done."

# 13. RAH

Rough bark dug into my palms as I tightened my grip and hauled myself up. It had been weeks since I'd last done pull-ups, and my body was already flagging, but I gritted my teeth and fought through the pain. *One more*, I kept saying, but with each I still wasn't satisfied and forced another. The branch trembled and dipped beneath my weight, leaves dancing as I drew myself up once again.

At the top of the next pull-up a movement caught my eye. Gideon stood watching, leaning against a tree with his arms folded. I was glad he didn't have to hide in the hut alone anymore—a thought that brought back fractured memories. The shouting. The hate. The ease with which my blade had sliced into Ptapha's body.

I tensed for another pull-up, but my fingers gave and I dropped from the branch, landing hard. My hands stung as I clenched and unclenched my fingers. With Gideon watching I didn't want to try for more, but neither did I want to stop and invite conversation.

Taking up my sword from the base of the tree, I drew it from its scabbard, its smooth leather hilt like grit against my torn-up palms. Trying to ignore Gideon, I worked through a series of basic exercises with my blade, its sharp edge cutting air. Stepping, turning, and slicing, I followed the mantras drilled into every Sword from an early age and, for the briefest of moments, found peace in being nothing but a blade.

"You're out of practice."

Gideon's criticism cut through my concentration and I stumbled, barely saving myself from an awkward fall. "And you aren't?" I snapped.

"I didn't say that, but I'm not hiding out in the forest getting sloppier with every swing."

Like his words had cut my legs from beneath me, I dropped to my knees, letting go a guttural scream that owned no words. It ripped up my throat, an expulsion of raw emotion that left me feeling no better when I ran out of breath to fuel it. Rage and grief churned in its wake, and when Gideon's footsteps approached it took the last shred of my self-control not to lash out with blade or fist or tongue.

"Better?" he said, crouching beside me.

"No."

"Rah—"

"Don't tell me I made the right choice, that I did the right thing. I'm done with that horseshit."

"Sometimes there is no right choice; there's just the choice you made. Would you be feeling any better if you'd let them take me?"

I glared up at him. "I killed a Sword outside of a challenge."

"No, he killed himself. You stepped aside for Amun. You didn't make them come after me; they made that choice and went on making that choice and now bear the consequences."

"I killed him, Gideon," I snapped, hot tears pricking my eyes. "And I would do it again."

He laughed softly. "I don't doubt you would."

Angry tears spilled, and I could not stop them. Gideon wrapped his arms around me, and protected like a ship in safe harbour, I leaned against him and let out the pain and rage. I thought of Eska, the friend I'd not been able to mourn, dead by my own blade, and of Orun and Kishava, lost to the Chiltaens. I'd lost so many

Swords during that march south and buried all the sorrow beneath a determination to fix everything. I'd not let myself grieve Yitti either, or Sett, not let myself grieve the loss of Levanti unity, of my sense of purpose and place and direction, just pressed on and on without stopping. Without letting myself break.

My tears flowed, grief seeming to leak from my whole face as I gripped tight to Gideon's tunic. I was making a mess, but he didn't pull away, just held me like he was the man drowning.

Only the gods themselves knew how long we sat there, my tears easing only to rage afresh. There was nothing to do but let them all out and slowly, eventually, slip into silence.

"Now do you feel better?" Gideon said, his voice a rumble by my ear.

"A bit," I said, my throat sore and my voice tear-choked. "I've made a mess of your tunic."

He let me go, but didn't look at his clothes. "Life seems to do that."

I wiped my face, feeling lighter than I had before he'd come, like maybe I could walk forward rather than remain caught in this moment like a fly in amber.

"As much as I enjoyed you crying all over me," Gideon said after a time, "I actually came out here to bring you this." He held out a book, its blue cover familiar though I wasn't sure why.

"What is it?" I said.

"I assumed you'd know since Tor said he stole it because you asked him to."

I snatched the book from his hand. "Asked him to—"

"You're welcome," Gideon said dryly. "Not that I want thanks; I only offered to bring it so you'd snap my head off instead of his. Maybe now he'll stop glaring at me all the time."

Ignoring this, I opened the book at random. "Oh, it's Ezma's copy of the holy book," I said, anger seething back as I recalled her triumphant expression. She'd left the camp with Amun and my Swords as though she were their leader now. I tried to swallow my hate and focus, but it thudded like a raging heartbeat in my chest. "I can't believe Tor actually did it."

"He's always been surprising," Gideon said. "Rather like Ezma herself in that regard, only not as unpleasant."

"When did you meet her? Or do you mean because she tried to have you Voided?"

Gideon shook his head. "I met her before that. Not long after we were exiled. She was already here with her apprentice, though she didn't tell us she was a whisperer."

"Didn't tell you? I've never seen her without her headpiece, and the number of times she references—"

"Well, she didn't back then. We didn't know. We thought they were just two exiled Levanti, so we let them stay with us."

"Why didn't you tell me this before?"

"Did it matter?"

I traced lines across the book's cover. "Maybe. I don't know. But if she was with you, how come she wasn't captured by the Chiltaens?"

"Because she wasn't still with us when they came."

Exhausted and with my head aching from all the tears, I struggled to take in this new information. "You're going to have to tell me the whole story from the start, because I'm too tired to piece it together."

Gideon sighed and passed a trembling hand across his face. "One day she and Derkka arrived at our camp, told us they had been exiled alone and asked if they could stay. Of course I agreed; what sort of monster would turn away two Levanti whether they were part of my herd or not? They stayed, they made themselves useful. We had built a camp and were just trying to keep out of the way and hope no one would notice us for the cycle."

"You were planning to return?"

"Then, yes." He looked at me in a way that hollowed my stomach and made my heart thump hard. "Of course I was. Life was hard. We were confused and hurt and angry at having been exiled for doing no wrong, but I was coming back to you. Then."

"What happened?" I hoped he didn't notice how breathless my voice sounded, catching upon the simple question. He'd been coming back, yet I'd had to mourn him.

Gideon shrugged one shoulder, the gesture weary. "She happened, you could say. At least that's where it started. She told stories she'd heard from other herds and explained that our herd master wasn't the only one whose mind had been overset. She was the one who called it a sickness—"

"She called it that?"

"Yes, it seemed appropriate, and I listened because there was truth in all she said, and I needed answers. I ought to have questioned how she knew so much, but I didn't. I didn't question anything until she started talking about Veld."

He sighed and looked up into the tangle of branches dancing above us. "It was just little things at first, testing the waters, I suppose. Then she tried to convince me that Veld Reborn was a Levanti. That they were going to build an empire for our people. A new home. And eventually, that I was Veld." Gideon pressed his hands to his face. "Gods, I was a fool to listen," he said, the words muffled. "But I had been helpless and angry so long that I had to do something. If I couldn't fix the plains, I would build a haven here instead."

He dropped his shaking hands. "I thought a small settlement we could protect and make our own would work, somewhere we could be free of the sickness. It wasn't meant to be an empire. Not then." He shook his head slowly. "We disagreed. Over Veld. She tried so hard to make me believe I had been chosen by the One True God, but you know me, I'm a stubborn ass and I couldn't stop thinking about how different that would make me. You wouldn't have known me. No one would have, not even me.

"In the end she got insistent, I got angry, and they left. We'd been in exile almost a full cycle by then, and it was time to decide if we would stay a bit longer and see if we could make a settlement work, or go home. We were all so torn, but in the end we decided to stay a short while to see if we could get news from the ports of how things were back home, to see if, after the winter, any more Levanti got exiled. Yiss arrived not long after, and then our choice got taken from us."

Again he shrugged, but for all the resignation in that gesture, the effort of reliving so much was showing upon his face. I wished I could spare him the pain, but I needed to understand, every detail about Ezma scratching at my mind like a troublesome grass seed. Every time I thought I finally understood her or her purpose, another layer would be drawn back to reveal something even more complicated beneath.

"The Chiltaens came in the night," he went on. "We'd been here so long we'd gotten lax about keeping watch. Even if we had been expecting a fight, they brought so many soldiers. So I surrendered, as you did, and all the captains who came after.

"I saw her once after that. In her full regalia and claiming her title, and you know, I realise now that the only way she could have gotten in to see me was with the Chiltaens' full knowledge. I don't want to think about what that means, but she gave me one last chance to work with her to build our future or make myself an enemy of a horse whisperer, and I told her to get fucked." He laughed, the sound both wild and weak. "So many herds had started to come. My plans had changed, and if I couldn't get home then I was going to do my utmost to turn the wretched situation we'd found ourselves in to our advantage. But I knew she would be good to her word and stand against me at some point, so I let slip the information about the herd arrivals to the Chiltaens to ensure any exiles came to me, not to her. That didn't work out as well as I had hoped, but there was nothing I could do by the time I realised what joy the Chiltaens took in their cruelty, that however decent some of them were, many saw us as a threat that needed to be beaten into submission."

He closed his eyes, leaning his head back. Weak sunlight dappled his face, the brightness all wrong in the wake of his words, words that had sent my thoughts darting back and forth around the shape of an idea I couldn't grasp, so enormous did it feel.

When I said nothing, Gideon opened his eyes, only to look away from me with a groan of anguish. "Gods, Rah, don't look at me like that. I know I made a lot of terrible decisions."

"I wasn't—"

"I should have listened when you tried to stand up to me instead of having you locked up. Instead of ordering Yitti killed and—"

"Leo did that."

"But I let him in! I was weak. I was trying so hard and he believed in me, he was there for me, and I let my guard down because I didn't want to be alone. Because I wanted someone to tell me I was doing the right thing." Tears tracked down his cheeks and he looked away, our positions reversed from earlier as he clasped his arms tightly around himself.

Leo had gotten into his head, but I remembered the Gideon who had sat beside me at the edge of our camp, his arm around my shoulders as I beat myself up for having abandoned my training. "You wouldn't have needed him if I'd been there for you," I said.

"Horseshit."

"It's not horseshit," I bit back. "Do you know how I got these scars?" I pointed to where my healing wounds had left permanent marks upon my face. "Sett, after he interfered in my challenge to

Yitti. He was so angry at me, said I ought to have been there for you, that you'd needed me and all I'd done was cling to our tenets and be all righteous instead of trusting you, and he was right, Gideon. He was right and he died for it and that was my fault too. He'd pummelled me into the damn road until I wished I was dead and..."

I trailed off, mouth dry. I couldn't bear to admit aloud what I'd done.

"I know what happened," Gideon said. "Lashak told me."

"I didn't mean for him to die. I was just so angry and—"

"I know."

"Fuck, can't you shout at me or something? I killed your brother!"

He breathed out a weary little laugh. "Only if you'll shout at me for killing Yitti and the others, but somehow I don't think you're going to. We're going to have to find someone else to berate us so we can feel bad about ourselves because I'm just...too tired for that. And what right have I to be angry at you?"

I had been so angry with him for so long, as much for his decisions as because he wasn't the Gideon I remembered. I'd been angry at the burning of Mei'lian. At the attack on the deserters. About Yitti's death. I had carried the anger with me like a shield, protecting me from my own guilt, from my own shame at having not seen through Leo's veneer, for having believed in and trusted the wrong people.

"I'm sorry," I said, simple words because nothing more would ever be enough. We had spilled everything, and yet we were still whole, still there, together.

A wry smile turned his lips. "Me too." He sighed. "Well, aren't we a pair, hiding in the forest to cry on each other."

"That's not why I came out here."

"No, you came out here to work yourself to exhaustion so you wouldn't have to do the crying, which you ought to know never works, so you're welcome."

"Oh yes, getting a grief headache is much better, thank you ever so much."

Gideon punched my arm. "Idiot."

"Arsehole."

For a moment we might have been ten years younger back on the plains, something of our former closeness rekindled, but just as I would never be that young man again, neither would he.

I heaved a sigh and got up to fetch my scabbard. A core of anger still roiled deep inside me, but I felt calmer and more centred than before Gideon's arrival. My sense of purpose was slowly recrystallising.

"Oh no," he said when I returned, brushing the dirt off the battered scabbard. "You have that determined look on your face. Should I be worried?"

"No, but Ezma should be."

———◆———

I had walked out into the forest the moment we'd arrived, leaving the others to set up camp and discuss their plans. Miko still had Torvash's book and I still needed it, but I'd had to clear my head. Now determination heated my veins, and I strode into the poorly set up camp ready to make a new deal. I didn't have a camp full of Swords anymore, but we could protect Miko and her companions without them.

Gideon followed me back, our arrival causing everyone to look up, even Empress Miko's sullen minister. He sat with her and Lady Sichi, the three of them having scratched symbols in the dirt as they talked. Nuru and Tor sat nearby beneath one of the tent awnings, while Captain Kiren and his men kept watch and Leo's odd twin sat being watched by all of them.

"Rah," Miko said, the greeting chilly. With a nod she returned to the markings scratched into the dirt, and one by one the others lost interest in us.

Gesturing at Tor with Ezma's book, I said, "May I keep this?"

"If you like," Tor replied. "I've read it and I have the Chiltaen copy, though hopefully I'm done with Leo and his prophetic nonsense." His gaze flicked in the direction of the other Leo, and he shifted uncomfortably.

"One can hope," I said. "Will you translate for me? I need to speak to the empress."

Tor nodded over my shoulder. "Why don't you ask Gideon? His Kisian is as good as mine." His jaw clenched, the expression challenging. "Unless you don't trust him."

He knew trust wasn't the issue. Whenever I thought Tor and I had come to a better understanding, he threw me a rotten apple.

"I can do it." Gideon stepped forward. "With Her Majesty's permission of course." I was no expert on bows, but the one he directed Miko's way seemed as respectful as it was mocking, and by Miko's expression she wasn't sure what to make of it. However, with a glance at her companions, she agreed, and for the second time we sat face to face to treat over the future of my homeland, the book I needed nestled safely in her lap.

Miko began, and having waved aside the need for Nuru to join us, Gideon translated. "What is it her illustrious majesty can do for you?" he said.

I gave him a look, hoping he wasn't planning to embellish every translation. "I want to discuss our deal for the book."

He translated, returning Miko's reply some moments later. "But you have no Swords left to protect me, as much as I appreciate you remaining with us so far." She gestured about the camp, lacking as it was.

"I need the book," I said. "I cannot go home without it. Tell me what I can do in return for it and I will do it."

Possessed of a thoughtful frown, Miko turned to Gideon and spoke to him rather than me. Gideon tilted his head, examining her with the same intensity with which she examined him. My skin prickled. His reply was calm, but I couldn't catch a single word I knew and turned in search of Tor.

"Please," I said, and though he rolled his eyes he slouched over to us.

"What's the problem?"

"They aren't translating."

Gideon and Miko continued their low-voiced discussion, so focussed upon each other they either didn't notice or didn't care that Tor was listening. He stood behind Gideon, brow creased, and after a few exchanges, he said, "She wants Gideon to go to the wedding ceremony with her."

"What? Why?"

"Because he's Gideon e'Torin," Tor said, and a soft laugh brushed past Gideon's lips. "Emperor, invader, enemy"—he was translating for Miko now—"he represents much to those who will be present. Also I fear Sichi will be forced into marriage with Dom Villius despite—"

Miko broke off and drew a deep breath. Tor waited, continuing his explanation only when she again spoke. "I am worried for Sichi, and having the man"—she spat the word bitterly—"she married present ought to make it impossible for Manshin to force her into another marriage."

"But Leo will be there," I said, and turning to Gideon added, "This is ridiculous. You can't face him."

"She has something you need, and she'll give it to you if I do this."

His words made his choice clear, and if our places had been reversed, I would have said the same, but still I shook my head. "We'll find another way. We can negotiate something else."

"She won't take anything else," Tor said. "This is what she needs. You're no use to her, but Gideon's presence at the wedding is. Gideon for the book or you won't get it."

"For someone who continuously berated me for choosing to help her over helping my people, you're quick to take her side," I snapped.

He met my gaze calmly, this the young man who had once thrown his soup bowl at my head and tried to choke me. "I feel closer to her than I do to you," he said. "Neither of us fits where we've been placed, so we have to carve ourselves space in this world."

"Then you protect yours, and I'll protect mine. All Gideon could do at that ceremony is be meat thrown to her enemies. Bait. Ask her if that's what she intends to do."

Slowly, Tor turned back to the empress and began to translate my question. The first flicker of emotion crossed Miko's face, a flare of anger there and gone. She replied in stiff Kisian, which Tor reluctantly translated. "His job would be to overset the reason of those present and make them react with anger. People make poor decisions when they're angry."

It felt as much like a warning as an explanation, but I shook my head. "Everyone who will be there wants Gideon dead." I looked to Lady Sichi sitting nearby, watching along with everyone else. "Do you agree with this? Do you care so little for the life of the man you married that you would let him be bait?"

"Like he is innocent," Nuru scoffed.

"This isn't about who has wronged most," I said. "Just translate the question."

She threw me a disgusted look but translated, speaking my words into an increasingly breathless camp. Even Miko's guards had drawn closer, all eyes flitting from me to her and on to her darkly frowning minister.

"He would not be a sacrifice," Sichi said through Nuru's curt translation. "He would be with us and under our protection, it—"

"And the moment it was expedient you would bargain with his life as you plan to bargain with the life of Leo's twin." I gestured in the man's direction, but he had retreated into himself, curled up and staring at nothing.

"Sometimes difficult decisions have to be made." Nuru's voice, but Lady Sichi's words. It was like watching my Swords turn on me again, on Gideon, deciding as one that his life meant nothing.

"Horseshit!" I rose on the word, furious energy crackling through me. "You are just so desperate that you'll gamble with someone else's life with no real plan."

"You asked for a deal," Miko said, her hand shaking as she gestured with the book. "That means we both risk or sacrifice something."

"What sacrifice?" I bent, snatching the book from her hand and holding it up. "You aren't giving up anything! You don't need this book, but I do. The future of my people, of my home, depends on it, and you want me to sacrifice Gideon's life in return when just handing it over costs you nothing?"

As Tor translated, Miko looked to Gideon as though seeking his opinion on the matter, a dismissal of my answer that flared my anger to fury. "Don't you dare try to manipulate him into sacrificing himself for your cause," I growled. "The answer is no. We are done."

As one, Miko's handful of guards stepped forward. One had drawn a bow, the others swords—all eyeing me as they awaited their empress's instructions. A breathy laugh escaped my lips. "A fitting end," I said. "That you order me killed the moment I stop being a useful tool."

Tor didn't immediately translate, wariness creeping into his bearing. Only when Miko nudged him did he begin, his voice all but a whisper. Once he had finished Miko didn't speak. She stared up at me, seconds stretching tense and breathless.

"Rah," Gideon said softly, rising to his feet. "I can do—"

"No." I didn't look at him, my gaze locked to Miko's. Foolish to ever have thought we had something. That she'd really cared. "If the book really means so much to her, she's going to have to order her guards to strike. Your move, Your Majesty."

Again that whispered translation. A murmur started between Lady Sichi and their injured minister, and from somewhere behind me came Captain Kiren's voice. "Majesty?"

Miko lifted a hand, seeming to pause even the movement of wind through the trees. There she held us, held the world, unspeaking, unmoving, unable to draw breath, until at last she let her hand fall. With the smallest shake of her head, Miko decided my fate. An order from Captain Kiren, and each of the soldiers took a step back, heavy boots cracking sticks in the undergrowth.

Triumph filled my chest like a deep breath, but it was far from pure. Poisoned by anger and self-recrimination, it was hardly triumph at all, more like relief built on desperation. "Sometimes difficult decisions have to be made," I said, amused by my own snark. I tucked the book into my belt and turned away from Miko and from Sichi, from Kisia and all I had sacrificed for it through my misplaced guilt. Behind me, Gideon's expression was unreadable. "Get the horses," I said. "We're leaving. Now."

# 14. MIKO

The arrow sank deep into the cabbage head, sending pieces of vegetable flying. There was little as satisfying as the thud of metal striking deep into coils of hemp, but the density of a cabbage's nested leaves came close. It had crunch.

"What if your targets aren't standing still?" Nuru said, setting the decimated cabbage on the post once more.

"If you hold it and walk around, I'll show you."

"With Your Majesty's permission, or even without, I will pass. Thank you."

Perched on the railing farther along the fence, Tor suppressed a smile. I forced one in response, but it felt all wrong.

Once Nuru stepped back, I nocked another arrow, drew, and sent it flying at the poor cabbage. It looked worse for wear, with chunks missing and flyaway leaves like its hair was a mess. Neither Leo Villius nor Minister Manshin had messy hair, but I would happily put so many arrows in both their faces that they would look like they'd been mauled by goats.

Under the watchful gaze of both young Levanti, I skewered the other cabbages. Waiting for news was the worst part. Mama had always said the best way to understand someone was to watch them wait, to watch as time and uncertainty slowly cracked them open. Memories of her threatened to send tears spilling down my cheeks, but I held them in and gathered my arrows, determined not to let time and uncertainty crack me. Mama was gone. Rah was gone. My last memory of them both would forever be anger and hurt.

I'd pushed him too far. Asked too much.

I thrust the thoughts away and returned to the line I'd scratched in the dirt. We'd stopped only to rest and wait for confirmation of Manshin's movements, and I wasn't the only one struggling to maintain my sanity. Minister Oyamada sat prodding at the ground with a stick in a way more befitting a child than a man of his age and position, while Sichi unpacked and repacked our saddlebags to keep her hands busy. Even Captain Kiren was on edge, pacing while he awaited the return of his men. Only Dom Villius's twin, Unus, appeared untroubled. Hands tied, he sat cross-legged in the grass with his eyes closed and his face turned skyward. Not even our near run-in with a group of Manshin's soldiers had troubled his equanimity. The area seemed to be full of them—small groups combing the countryside in search of us.

I loosed another arrow, sending the scruffy cabbage tumbling off the fence post.

At the sound of approaching footsteps, everyone stilled. Tor and Nuru reached for their blades. "Who's there?" Captain Kiren called, moving to stand between me and the incoming sounds.

"It's Bann and Chiro, Captain!"

Captain Kiren sheathed his blade, shoulders sagging with relief. "About damn time," he grumbled as two of his men appeared through the greenery, their uniforms speckled with mud. "What news?"

"Sorry, Captain," Bann said, bowing to us and then his captain. "We had to hide from one of those damn search parties. They're everywhere!"

Chiro gestured down his armour. "Had to lie flat in the damn mud." He spat. "But they're moving, Captain. All but a handful of soldiers departed Kogahaera this morning, Grace Bahain and his men included. And, ah…" The man glanced my way before resolutely fixing his gaze on the captain. "Talk is Minister Manshin is calling himself Emperor Manshin now."

It wasn't surprising, but the title sent hot fury flooding through me all the same. I was dead and now he didn't have to worry about his puppet empress getting in the way.

I loosed another arrow, the force sending yellowing cabbage leaves flying.

"Are they making for the ceremony ground?" Oyamada asked, standing up and brushing down his robe.

"It appears so, Your Excellency," Bann said. "They were carrying a lot in the way of supplies and camp trappings."

"Travelling fast?"

"No, Your Excellency. They have a few soldiers on horseback besides the generals and some of the lords accompanying them, but most are on foot. It'll likely take three days all told."

Sichi lifted one of her repacked saddlebags onto her horse. "And Lord Edo was definitely with them?"

"Yes, Your Majesty, although he and his men don't appear to be travelling with the main bulk of the force, rather keeping more to themselves. Or at least they were the whole time we were watching them."

I tapped Hacho's tip against my foot. "Perhaps they haven't come to an agreement yet."

"Or he's keeping enough distance so he can send and receive his own messages," Sichi suggested. "We ought to get one to him as soon as possible, before he makes any decisions based on the belief we're dead."

"Agreed," Minister Oyamada said. "We need his support if we want even the hope of being able to oust Ryo. The rest of the army is too firmly under his command."

"Except for the barbarian generals," I said. "Though it sounds like it may be difficult to get a message to them at this stage. We can't risk Manshin discovering where we are and what we're up to until we have more protection."

Nods spread around the small clearing. Protection had been the one thing I'd had settled, until my agreement with Rah had collapsed. Without the Levanti, we were having to waste vital days sneaking around and going without a fire, rather than seeking support and being seen. We needed soldiers.

"Our next step is a message to Grace Bahain then," Oyamada said, turning his attention to the two men who'd just arrived. "Take what supplies you need before you go."

Bann sagged. He'd been eyeing the mat rolled up on the back of his saddle.

"Why can't one of the others go?" Chiro said. "We only just got back."

"Because, as you can see, none of them have returned," Captain Kiren said sharply. "Be grateful I'm not demoting you for that attitude."

"Yes, Captain. Sorry, Captain. We'll get ready to head out at once."

Sichi smiled at the two men. "Your service is much appreciated," she said. "And I can assure you that when we are through this, you will be properly rewarded for your hard work."

A bow to her, murmurs of thanks, and each man stood a little taller. Within ten minutes they had once again ridden away, leaving us to move on, the tiniest sliver of hope having taken root in my mind. If I could just talk to Edo, surely we could find a way through this.

———◆———

We arrived as darkness closed in, and settled in to wait. The old shrine we'd chosen as our meeting place had long since collapsed in upon itself, leaving gashes in the roof through which weak moonlight pooled. Sichi stood in the centre of the draughty space, cloak gathered tightly around herself against the sharp winds. As it gusted through, it made the shadows dance and caught on the wispy parts of Minister Oyamada's thinning hair as he rolled out a square meeting mat.

I stood with my back to one of the remaining walls, watching the night. Nearby, Captain Kiren stood perfectly still amid swaying branches, his eyes trained upon the overgrown path. I couldn't see his men, but it was a comfort knowing many eyes were keeping watch.

"How long do we wait?" Sichi whispered as she approached, still hunched into her cloak. "How long until it's clear he isn't coming?"

"That probably depends on how desperate we are."

"Ah, so we're staying all night then?"

We shared a wry smile barely short of a grimace and went back to staring silently at the night. There was nothing to say. If Edo didn't come, we would be out of options before we'd even begun.

The night dragged on, marked by all too many small noises. Night birds, wind, scurrying creatures—a cacophony that could mask all but the loudest footsteps. Time began to stretch and contract as I fought fatigue, every moment both mere seconds and hours long, so when Captain Kiren at last turned and gestured that someone approached, I had to fight the fear I was dreaming.

Nods and murmurs slowly woke our sleepy group, and before I could convince myself he really was coming, Edo strode through the half-broken arch dressed in full armour, his face all frown.

"Edo, you came!" I threw my arms around him, breathing deep the scent of old memories beneath all that leather and steel. "Tell me, is Shishi safe?"

"She's fine," he said, giving me a tight squeeze before letting me go. "She's begging all my men for scraps and getting very spoiled.

I'm sorry I'm so late; it was difficult to get away and be sure I wasn't followed. Your father has spies in my camp," he added as Sichi stepped forward to embrace him as I had.

"No surprise there," she said. "It's good to see you, Cousin."

"And you, Sichi. Nuru. Tor. Minister." He nodded at each around the group and received greetings in return.

With some difficulty, Minister Oyamada rose to bow. "It's a relief to have you here, Your Grace. We are desperate for news."

*Grace.* One day I would get used to the title as Edo seemed to have, but for now I couldn't but think of his father.

"Well, news I have, Minister," Edo said, returning the bow. "Though whether it's good news or not remains to be seen. You're injured?"

"A mere scratch," Oyamada said with feigned joviality. "Which will be all the better for your news."

While Tor and Nuru continued to keep watch with Captain Kiren's men, we sat upon the meeting mat with Edo, each of us kneeling upon one corner. Oyamada looked regal, Sichi composed, and Edo strong, leaving me feeling out of place at such a gathering despite being the central cause that had brought us all together.

"I truly am glad to see you all well," Edo began once we'd settled, our turned backs managing to shelter the inside of the circle from the worst of the wind. "The news you were dead spread much faster than the whispers that Manshin had men out looking for you. No one seemed to know what had happened to Sichi either, and he shouted at anyone who asked too many questions."

"He's good at that," Sichi muttered.

Minister Oyamada fixed his narrowed gaze on Edo. "What's Ryo up to, eh? Spit it out."

"A lot." Edo sighed. "While he's pretending to everyone that Sichi is travelling with us and just keeping to herself, we all know she isn't. He has more and more search parties out every day, and you can be sure the moment you step out of cover he'll be after her. Whether it's just to protect his honour or for this alliance, he's very focussed on ensuring Sichi marries Dom Villius."

"He'll look like a fool if the marriage doesn't go ahead because she's not there." Oyamada chuckled, seeming to enjoy the scenario he was imagining. "Though he might prefer it to not being able to marry her to Dom Villius because she's already married."

"You did it then?" Edo said, looking from me to Sichi.

"We did," we said almost as one, Sichi adding, "A few more days until our sevenday is up and then he won't be able to do a thing about it."

Edo grinned, looking more like his old self than he had for a long time. "Congratulations. I wish I could have been there. It'll be a momentous occasion in Kisia's history, I'm sure."

"Assuming we can take the throne back from Manshin," I said.

"What do you mean take it back?"

"He's calling himself emperor now, is he not?"

Edo shook his head, perplexed. "Yes, but…you're not dead. He didn't depose you, not even by force. He isn't claiming he's the emperor because you failed to be a good empress, he's claiming to be the emperor because you're dead and he's what's left."

"Yes, but stepping out there and proving I'm not actually dead is hardly going to have everyone rushing to my cause," I said. "Nor make him give up the throne, whether he sits on it himself or rules through me."

Only grimaces answered me. The cold from the stones had begun leaching through the mat, turning my knees to ice and with them my hopes. Wherever we went from here, the road was far from clear. I'd spent so long fighting for this that it was easy to forget why I'd started, what Tanaka and I had wanted to build. To change. Mama would have called them idealistic dreams, but why fight for anything less? To give up was to let Manshin weaken our standing with Chiltae, was to let Kisia keep its internal divisions, remain aggressive toward outsiders, and crumble into its own self-importance. My father's civil war ought to have been the final proof that Kisia had long since stopped functioning, but my mother's marriage to Emperor Kin had been a bandage that kept it limping along in time to the old rhythms.

"There is every chance we'll have to fight Ryo for the throne," Oyamada said, breaking in upon my thoughts. "But I'm not sure how that's to be done unless Grace Bahain here has more soldiers than seems possible."

"I'm afraid not, Minister," Edo said. "What remains of my father's battalions plus those who pledged loyalty to me after the battle at Kogahaera together add up to barely half what Minis— *Emperor* Manshin has at his command. There is some potentially good news on that front, however." He looked around as though expecting fresh soldiers to appear from the dark undergrowth. Sadly, none did. Voice lowered, Edo went on, "Many of Manshin's search parties have talked of finding signs of a small military encampment, Kisian, they think. Most say they must be Sichi's guards and that she has a special group of soldiers."

Sichi laughed. "Wouldn't that be great? Since I don't, however, who are they?"

"Definitely not ours," I muttered.

"In fact, I think they might be yours, Koko."

I stared in confusion from him to Sichi. "Mine?"

"Consider: that they're moving carefully means they have reason not to want to be found by imperial scouts. That they're hiding from Manshin's men means—"

"Means they're not his."

"Exactly. It could, however, be General Ryoji."

Whatever spark of hope I'd kept burning deep, I'd ceased truly believing Ryoji would ever return. "General Ryoji?" I breathed, his name blowing the spark to a flame. "Are you sure?"

"No, but I don't know who else it could be, and the scouts all report they're definitely Kisian camps."

Minister Oyamada made a grumble in his throat. "That's as may be," he said. "But until they're standing here with us we cannot factor them into our plans." Once again he fixed his gaze on Edo. "However, you are here, Your Grace. So do you intend to stand with us or not?"

It was a question I hadn't thought to ask, having assumed the answer. But Edo wasn't just my friend anymore; he was Grace Bahain, and his responsibilities were vast.

"I do," he said upon a sigh. "It's just not as simple as any of us would like. I don't care about the personal danger; no matter where I choose to stand, my life will be at risk, but being labelled a traitor will fall onto people I'm responsible for. For the people of Syan, it's higher trade tariffs or refusal to trade in some places, no access to imperial food stores, no one from Syan able to take ministerial positions, things like that. My father dealt with it for years, but those were relatively prosperous years. We don't know what life will be like under"—he grimaced my way—"apologies, Koko, but under what many see as the beginning of the new imperial government of Emperor Manshin. He has no grounds on which to keep that title, but we all know he'll fight for it, and I have to consider the outcome both ways."

Oyamada nodded slowly. "I feared that might be the case. That Ryo has spies in your camp means he doesn't trust you."

"Hardly surprising given my history," Edo said, and with a small shiver, looked around the dark ruins. I tried not to imagine he was looking at the ruins of our plans. On one of the tumbledown walls, Tor and Nuru sat close together for warmth, watching our meeting in silence as one might sit at vigil with a dying friend.

As silence stretched on between us, Edo grimaced. "I wish I had a plan I could offer, but even with my banner I'm unsure what would be the wisest course for you now. Being seen to be alive would weaken Manshin's position, but it's hard to know how he would react. Stepping down graciously and letting you get on with ruling without him seems...let us say unlikely."

"Ryo is a reasonable man until you don't do what he wants when he wants it," Oyamada grumbled, drawing his cloak tighter about himself. "One must always watch for the change. There isn't much warning."

Sichi agreed, but while talk of Manshin's character went on around me, my thoughts slid away. Being seen to be alive. Such a small thing, yet what consequences it could have. Edo was right; Manshin hadn't deposed me, hadn't taken over where I'd failed. In the eyes of all but a few Kisians in his close circle, I'd been ruling Kisia up until the moment I'd died. Or rather, the moment Manshin had claimed I'd died. Perhaps I didn't need a grand plan, at least not yet. I just needed to be alive.

"Edo," I said abruptly, breaking in upon their desultory conversation. "You cannot stand with us yet, but can you spare us some soldiers for our protection? Loyal men we can be sure would serve our cause?"

"Yes, of course," he said. "I ought to have thought of that; it's the least I can do."

Sichi's eyes brightened as she looked my way. "You have a plan?"

"Not exactly, but we can't decide on a course of action until we know how Manshin will react to the challenge of our existence."

"If you plan to provoke him..." Oyamada began in a warning tone.

"Don't worry, Minister, I intend to provoke him in the smallest way possible." I smiled around at the group of wary expressions, the night having lost some of its former chill. "I will provoke a response merely by continuing to exist as though nothing happened."

"I'm not sure I understand, Your Majesty."

"It's as simple as Edo said, Minister. Manshin hasn't deposed me. He hasn't won a battle; he just took over in my absence. If I fight, he can fight back, but if I just…go on about my tasks as empress and shrug away rumours of my death, he'll need a better plan."

A slow smile dawned across Oyamada's face. "Oh, Ryo is going to hate that."

———————————— ✦ ————————————

Lord Pirin greeted me with a thin smile. He was younger than I'd expected, but of late many sons had taken their father's titles. The old lord had been an ally of Emperor Kin, but whether that meant he had supported the imperial line or the army was impossible to say. It hadn't been an important difference then. It was now.

"Your Majesty," the man said, bowing in welcome. "An honour that you grace my home with your presence."

I'd given him no warning of my arrival, leaving harassed maids hurrying in with tea as we exchanged greetings. They bowed as they backed out, the clink of cups still tinkling in the air.

"Will you join me?" Lord Pirin said, maintaining an almost bored composure. "It would be an honour."

I acquiesced as regally as I could manage, trying to channel something like my mother's demeanour. I'd knelt at tables thousands of times, yet still managed to feel awkward and oversized—entirely out of place. Lord Pirin knelt opposite, expression dull.

The Chiltaen invasion had sent many of central Kisia's lords running for safety, but with the Chiltaen threat seemingly contained, many had returned. Towns and villages were still ruins of their former selves, some empty, others full of refugees from Mei'lian, none with enough supplies to last the winter. Many of the lords and governors I'd seen over the last two days had given up, accepting that famine and illness would ravage their lands and there was nothing they could do about it. Young as Lord Pirin was, he had the same dead expression.

"You must forgive our lack of appropriate hospitality, Your Majesty," he said, pouring two bowls of tea. "We had no warning of your arrival. In truth, the last we heard was that you were dead." He slid my bowl across the table toward me with that same thin smile. "I am, of course, glad to have that news proved false."

Glad enough that he would stand with me against Manshin? A question I could not ask, our current strategy to act as though nothing was amiss between me and my minister.

"Thank you, Lord Pirin," I said, taking up the bowl. "Such unfortunate rumours and misunderstandings seem all too common in times of war."

"War? Kogahaera was liberated weeks ago."

"Indeed, my liberation of Kogahaera was a fine moment, but however quiet the Chiltaens are currently being, they are still our enemy and still camped within our territory."

He looked bemused. "Forgive my confusion, Your Majesty, but I understood a treaty had been negotiated."

"I have heard that," I said, taking a sip of tea still far too hot. "But I have seen no treaty, discussed no treaty, and certainly signed no treaty."

For the first time his bored demeanour cracked, shock leaking through. "No discussion? Your Majesty, I'm sure you must be jesting. There's a pavilion being built for the marriage of Dom Villius and Lady Sichi to seal the treaty; I have seen it myself."

"I wish I were jesting, Lord Pirin, but unfortunately I doubt the remaining Chiltaen army has any inclination to make peace. Why would they? We are weak and divided; there would be no better time to take northern Kisia."

Lord Pirin's eyes widened. His jaw slackened as though he would retort, but while I sipped my tea, he went through the same slow realisation I'd watched a dozen others pass through in the last few days. The rosy picture of our future they'd been sold was built on lies. It was oddly satisfying. A few words of truth and my presence, alive and well, had been all I'd needed.

Once I finished my tea, I took my leave, Lord Pirin not even having time to ask what had brought me there in the first place.

In the manor's front hall, Captain Kiren and half a dozen of Edo's soldiers stood waiting—they my escort on this mission to be seen and heard. Another half dozen had gone with Sichi into the nearby town. "Have they returned?" I asked the captain as we mounted our horses, relieved to be riding away from yet another troubled lord.

"No, Your Majesty. All has been quiet."

For the last two days I'd ridden back to camp to wait for Sichi, too tired from my own tasks to wonder about hers, but I could see thin streams of woodsmoke rising nearby.

"Let's head into the town and see how Lady Sichi is faring," I said. "Then we'll go back to the camp."

"As you wish, Your Majesty."

The nearby town of Esan was almost too small to be called a town, yet too big to be called a village. In close proximity to Lord Pirin's estate, many people from all around had come to winter within its bounds. We found Sichi in the town square, perched on a stone wall with no care to her robe while townsfolk gathered around her. Her guards stood at a distance, alert yet far enough away to keep the people at their ease.

At least until we arrived. At the sound of our hooves, all heads turned, easy conversation fading into wary silence. Dressed all in crimson, I was far more imposing, the image of the emperor they had been brought up to fear and worship in equal measure.

It had been a mistake to come.

"Your Majesty," Sichi said, rising to her feet. "Do join us."

Her cheerful welcome did nothing to ease the growing wariness of those around her. Despite the impending winter, many wore no cloaks, a few no sandals or boots to shield their feet from the icy ground. These were the faces of Kisians left to fend for themselves in the path of war, Kisians who had seen horrors, and who would not survive the winter without help. Would Manshin supply that help? What sort of emperor would he be if I failed?

At an insistent look from Sichi, I dismounted, sending some of the nearest townsfolk scurrying back out of my way. Ragged tunics and short robes, thin faces, muddy streets—Esan was far from the glorious empire we'd always thought ourselves. Fear of their emperor was all that had survived.

"We came to see how you were doing," I said, speaking only to Sichi despite the weight of so many silent gazes on me. "I did not intend to stay."

"Come sit," Sichi said, her voice low as she drew me toward the wall she'd been perched upon. "It will do these people good to know their empress cares about their fates."

"Of course I care, but—"

Low bows spread as Sichi led me through the crowd, and a chill washed over me. I had grown used to the way Kisian nobility bowed to me—all protocol and little respect. Never had they bowed in fear.

With nothing else I could do under Sichi's insistent hand, I sat upon the wall and hoped it wouldn't ruin my only imperial robe. She settled beside me and smiled encouragingly at the people around us, but whatever ease had developed before my arrival, whatever conversation she had achieved, seemed to have fled. Perhaps if I could think of something to say that didn't sound trite, if I could earn their confidence as easily as Sichi, but I was not Sichi.

For what felt like an age, we sat there in silence. Now and then, Sichi would ask something of one of the townsfolk she seemed to have gotten to know, but the answers were monosyllabic, and one by one, those at the back of the crowd began to edge away to go about their business.

"Sadly, we must be going," Sichi said at last, sending relief spilling through me. "If there is anything else you need, be sure to send a message to our camp care of Minister Oyamada. I'll pass on your grievances from today in person though, so don't worry about that. Whatever aid we can provide, we will."

Murmurs of gratitude followed, and all those remaining bowed again as we rose, like a waving sea of muddy wheat trodden down into the dirt.

"My horse," Sichi called to her guards, and within a few moments we had mounted and were escaping the awkwardness.

For a time we rode in silence, words banking up behind my teeth. The urge to apologise mixed with indignation, and nothing came out. When at last one of us spoke, it was indignation that won.

"You need to try to do better connecting to the common people," Sichi said. "We need them."

"What we need is soldiers," I snapped back. "Even with Edo standing with us we don't have enough men to be sure of success against the Chiltaens, let alone your father as well."

"I know, but whatever soldiers these lords have raised already fight for the imperial army. Winning their hearts and minds and ignoring our citizens will get us nowhere, as it got generations of emperors nowhere before you. And even if they could raise more men to fight, what difference will a few more or less make against a many-headed enemy?" Sichi shrugged. "I'm not a tactical expert like my father, but if this comes to a head-on battle, I don't think we can win no matter what clever tactics we employ."

"Which is why we need to undermine him at every opportunity."

She acknowledged this with another shrug. "We're already doing that. We can't appeal to his generals in any way that would make them want to fight for us instead, so it's better to make them come to us because we're winning."

"Winning this war will depend on having soldiers in the first place." I spoke through gritted teeth, frustration heating my veins. "Don't you trust me?"

Shock dropped Sichi's jaw. "I never said that."

"You didn't have to when it was implied."

"You see mistrust because it's what you fear, not because it's there. I implied nothing more than that you don't listen to me."

"I do listen to you, I—"

"Yes, and then do exactly the opposite to what I suggest!" Anger flared in her eyes, and she let out a snort of disdain. "I don't know why I expected any different. After all, I am not an emperor or a general, not even a man, just the foolish woman you married."

Each fierce word was a slap that left me stunned, so easily could they have come from my own tongue. I knew that anger, for it boiled inside me too, ready to spit over anyone who dared look down on me.

A tired sigh blew past Sichi's lips. "I'm sorry, Koko, but you are not the only woman worthy of a voice just because you walk in the men's world; you're simply privileged enough to be one of the few they cannot entirely exclude. You have your way of fighting and I have mine; that should make us stronger, not weaker, but only if we work together. I don't want to be powerless as your wife like I was as Gideon's."

Ahead, Captain Kiren showed no sign of having heard our disagreement, but at those words, I hoped he wasn't just being polite. Gideon hadn't treated her poorly; but her options had been limited by not only politics but also language and culture. She'd have been in the same position married to Dom Villius, or to any Kisian lord—I couldn't fight for freedom while denying hers.

"Sichi, I—"

"Hush," she said, pressing a finger to her smiling lips. "I know. Let's leave it for now. Come to my tent tonight after your discussions with Oyamada, and we can talk some more."

It seemed churlish to push the conversation any further, and I fell gratefully into silence.

The nightly discussion of our progress that Minister Oyamada insisted on took longer that night than usual. A lot of reports of Manshin's movements had come in, along with numerous messages, now word that I was alive was getting out, but I couldn't concentrate on any of it. I kept returning to the trip back from Esan and Sichi's biting words.

"Your Majesty?" Oyamada said for the dozenth time. "Are you listening to a word I'm saying?"

"Yes, Minister, but my thoughts seem intent on wandering." I riffled through the collection of messages that had come during the day, most from minor lords and merchants professing joy that the rumour of my demise was premature. Oyamada thought it a good sign—not that they supported me, but that so few had been part of the plot to put Manshin on the throne.

Taking the pile of papers from my hands with a harrumph, Oyamada eyed me all too sharply. "Everything went well with Lord Pirin?"

"Yes, as I said."

"The rumours that Ryo was last seen riding this way...?"

"Are to be expected. He wasn't going to let me get away with this for more than a few days."

His eyes narrowed. "Ah. Your sevenday is almost up."

I flinched, not having thought about what day it was. "What? Surely not until tomorrow?"

"Given how late it is getting, I imagine it is almost tomorrow already," he said dryly, looking up as though he could see the moon through the fabric of his simple tent. "As I recall, I was also far more nervous than the situation warranted. Don't worry, the knot rarely gets tangled beyond repair, and the rest more than makes up for the frustration."

I parted my lips to point out that my experience was hardly going to be the same, that I wasn't even sure how one lay with a woman, only to snap my jaw shut. No doubt he would have been a font of knowledge and experience, but this was a topic on which I didn't want advice from my minister.

"Let's leave it there for now, Your Majesty," he said. "If any important news comes in the night, you'll be the first to hear about it, but I'm sure there will be nothing exciting enough to interrupt your own… important business."

An embarrassed assurance that there would be nothing to interrupt would not pass my lips, and all I could do was murmur something unintelligible as I escaped into the chill night air, his all too amused expression seeming to follow me like a lingering snicker. From his tent, I could see all the others in our small camp, my own and Sichi's side by side a few steps away, while Edo's soldiers had set up theirs in a protective circle around us. Faint light flickered from within Sichi's tent, while mine was dark and unwelcoming. The urge to return to my own regardless was strong, but the suspicion that Oyamada was right about my nerves made my spine harden like steel.

I let the welcoming light of Sichi's tent draw me in until I stood right outside, staring at the fabric doorway. Ought I call out? Seek permission to enter? Or would that be too formal when she had asked me to come?

I swallowed hard and reached out, only for the fabric to be pulled aside. Sichi stood backlit by lanterns, and let out a sigh of relief. "Koko, I was beginning to worry you weren't coming."

"You wanted to talk, so here I am," I said with all the jovial ease I could manage as I ducked beneath her arm and into a space far more cosy than my own tent. Sichi had a talent for making things comfortable wherever she went, a skill that had no doubt led many people to underestimate her sharp edges and strong will. After today's disagreement, I would have to take care not to fall into the same errors.

"There isn't much left to say, I think," Sichi said, letting the fabric fall back behind her. "We need to work on communicating—both of us—but I know we can do this and forge a path that works for us both. What I wanted to ask is whether you'll come with me to sit and listen to the common people when we ride out to Harnoi tomorrow, rather than making the longer trip to find Governor Kuhuno?"

My first instinct was to explain how important it was that I keep working on spreading the truth and undermining her father's position, but she already knew that.

"Yes," I said. "If you think it's more important then I will."

She smiled and took my hands. "Thank you."

Cheeks reddening, I looked away, freeing my hands from her warm clasp. "Was that all you wanted to talk about?"

"All I wanted to talk about, yes, but I think you'll agree the sooner we end our sevenday, the safer for everyone. I am quite sure it's after midnight by now."

"Oh." I swallowed hard. "But...but what about Nuru, won't she—"

"Nuru understands that we have to ensure this marriage is watertight under the law, and she is also quite happy to share me should we...enjoy ourselves. What a scandalous idea! But with no men around to worry about the continuation of their bloodlines, *we* can decide how we want to live and love, Koko."

So often, talking to her was like taking a hammer to what I

thought I knew and peering through cracks of doubt into another world. A world full of possibilities that frightened and excited me in equal measure.

"You and I chose to eschew the futures built for us by men," she went on. "Part of that means letting go of the idea that womanhood is something to trade, that marriage is an economic transaction to increase a man's power and influence, and building something new."

Sichi stepped closer, grasping my hands again. "Your poor hands are so cold, Koko."

"Sorry."

She chafed my skin in a futile effort to warm them, and I became all too aware of the warmth radiating from her. Of how close she stood and what we were meant to do. I looked at the floor rather than at her, my heart speeding to a frantic pace.

Her kiss was a brush of soft lips over mine, stilling the butterflies inside me for the briefest of moments, only for them to flutter more fiercely as she pulled away. I wanted to return the embrace, but I felt like I had been caught in a tangle of wire that cut into me with every move I thought to take. "I..." My cheeks burned hot. I wished the tent not so warm. Not so bright. "I...I don't..."

Sichi began untying my sash, and as I watched her deft fingers work, I thought of the night with Rah and my breath shortened.

"We'll take it slow," Sichi said.

I could only nod and feel like the foolish little girl she must surely think me. My sash slid to the floor, and Sichi calmly spread my robe open to display the far less bloodstained under-robe beneath. And the white wedding sash, its floral knot flattened against my belly.

Quick work on her own outer robe soon revealed her matching sash, neatly tied at Kuroshima and carried since like the hope we dared hold for the future. This was the moment it had all been for, yet now we had arrived I couldn't think straight.

"I don't know how—"

"It's all right, Koko." She smiled. "Let's untie these sashes before we worry about that."

Face to face we stood in our underclothes, our wedding knots staring at one another as we did.

"Together?" Sichi whispered, touching the loop of my knot.

"Together," I said, finding the same loop on hers. The white silk was warm from her body and smooth like her skin. I let out a long breath. This was no small pledge. No small moment. The choice to walk this path one we might come to regret. Or one that could change the empire.

"Three," Sichi said. "Two. One." She tugged my knot and I pulled hers, and in a tumble of crinkled silk our sashes unravelled onto the carpet between us before falling from about our waists. Without them our under-robes hung loose, barely closed, Sichi's allowing me to glimpse a narrow band of flesh and a pair of full breasts I'd only ever felt pressed against me in a comforting hug. Just as I'd longed to touch Rah's skin, so my fingers twitched to know hers. Yet I couldn't. The idea was the wrong shape in my mind. Tanaka had loved Edo. Sichi loved Nuru. I understood these truths. Whatever was expected of marriage, men could love men and women could love women; that I hungered to touch both surely meant I was broken.

"Are you all right?" Sichi whispered.

I managed a nod.

"You're sure? You have to tell me if you're not comfortable. I'm your wife now, Koko."

Wife. *If only you'd been born a boy*, so many people had said of me over the years. Now I even had the wife to prove it.

"I'm fine. Wife." My laugh sounded wild, but choked in my throat as Sichi let her under-robe slide from her shoulders. I'd always thought the female body beautiful, thought her beautiful, but women's bodies were for men to enjoy. Were for making children. For bargaining treaties and making trade deals and elevating family status. They had nothing to do with joy. Or pleasure. And yet here she stood not for anyone else, only for me and for herself, her curves invitations for my hands, her lips for my kisses.

She eased my robe off my shoulders, her touch more gentle and lingering than Rah's had been, yet no sooner had my robe fallen than her hand was on the small of my back, her breasts pressed to mine as she leaned in to kiss me again. This time the question held more hunger. Lingered longer. And I returned it with the exhilarating sense that we were breaking every rule.

"Let's lie down before we get cold," Sichi said, pulling away.

I wanted to say I doubted I could ever get cold with her nearby, but I let her pull me toward the waiting mat. She kicked the warming pan out as she slid in and lay watching as I dove beneath the protective layer of covers, leaving as much space between us as I could.

Sichi took my hand. "You're allowed to touch me. I'd like you to."

She drew my hand to cup her breast—soft, smoothly curved, its full weight causing my mind to entirely stop functioning. I wanted to run my fingers over it again and again, wanted to press my lips to her skin, nip her flesh between my teeth, wanted to consume her the way I'd let Rah consume me, and it felt both empowering and frightening.

"You're allowed to enjoy yourself, Koko," Sichi whispered. "Just do whatever you feel like."

"I'm not sure I'm ready for that." I drew a shaky breath and let it out upon a little moan. "I'm not sure you are either."

"Oh, you'd be surprised what I'm ready for." The words warmed my ear, sending an uncontrollable shiver through my skin. "But we can keep it simple for now; it has been a long day."

She kissed my neck as she spoke, running one hand down onto my stomach, and toward my legs, sending heat pouring in its wake. Her lips shifted to mine, and I gasped against them as her hand slid between my legs, finding sensitive places I hadn't known I possessed. I arched into her, shedding a layer of inhibition through sudden need. It rushed back full of embarrassment the moment she eased away enough to look at me, seeming to seek permission with her gaze.

"I...know now how this works with a man," I said, growing all the hotter and unable to look at her. "Well, with...Rah, but how do we consummate without..."

"A cock? It's just an appendage on a man's body, isn't it?"

"Well...yes? I suppose so."

"And are my fingers part of my body?"

"Yes."

"Then what is this?" She slid two fingers inside me and I lost all sense, all doubt, just wanted her to push me over the edge as Rah had done and didn't care what anyone thought.

I must have moaned for she laughed and pressed deeper, the skill in her hand and the touch of her breasts against me making me want everything she could do all at once. Fear was washed away beneath a tide of need, every gasp I bit back brightening the hunger in her gaze. I closed my eyes, giving in to the pleasure, to the sense of safety and trust like nothing I had ever known, and the moment my body exploded with pleasure I was sorry to have it over even as I trembled through the lingering shudders, every breath a deep gasp for air like I'd been drowning.

———◆———

The following morning, Sichi and I rode away from the camp side by side. With Tor and Nuru and a pair of Edo's soldiers left to guard the camp, the rest rode behind us—a two-dozen strong wall of crimson and steel to dissuade anyone from getting in our way. The village of Harnoi sat some miles west of Esan, but despite the greater distance we rode at our ease, sharing the occasional shy, knowing smile. In the bright morning light it was almost possible to convince myself I'd imagined the whole thing, but I had only to glance Sichi's way to remember the touch of her skin and joy we'd made together.

"Do you have a plan for once we arrive?" I said, trying to keep my mind on the task at hand.

"No, no plan." She shrugged. "Not everything needs a plan, especially when we don't want anything from these people. What they want from us is to be heard, to know they haven't been abandoned, so just listen. Ask gentle questions so they know they are allowed to speak their minds to you, and then listen to what they say."

"That's it?"

"That's it. Hopefully it will be easier today without the imperial robe."

Knowing our destination, I'd opted for simple armour instead of the robe I'd been wearing like a banner to every lord's and governor's mansion over the last few days. The common folk didn't need to be awed; they needed to be comforted.

Despite the bright morning light, the air was colder than it had been in a long time, a chill made worse by the movement of air past my cheeks. Speeding our pace would get us to Harnoi faster, but make the cold even more unbearable. And cover us in mud. The way to Harnoi was more muddy track than road, few towns and even fewer villages connected to the empire by anything as well built as the Willow Road and its tributaries, filtering everything south toward Mei'lian and Shimai.

"You know," Sichi said, looking around, "I don't think I ever realised half these places were even here. It's like the forgotten centre of the empire."

"Which provides most of the capital's food yet seems to get little in return."

She shook her head in slow disbelief. "So much needs to change. We've let Kisia just go on in the old ways without ever asking if there is a better way we could do it."

As she spoke, Captain Kiren sped his pace to draw alongside. "Your Majesties," he said, the new form of address coming easily from his tongue. "We seem to have company." He nodded to the small rise to the west where a group of riders made a daunting outline against the hazy sky. "What are your orders?"

They were too far away yet to be sure, but Kisian riders in this part of the empire surely meant trouble whether Manshin was amongst them or not. I glanced at Sichi. "I'd say our options are face them or run, and I'm not sure for how long the latter would serve us."

"No," she agreed. "If they're my father's men then they far outnumber us even if we made it back to camp. Better to face them in the open, where they have to consider how they appear to anyone who might be watching."

"If they're Manshin's men they'll want to take you."

"And they'll want to kill you. Neither of us is safe no matter where we go." She grimaced. "I think our time has run out, Koko. Time to see how he reacts."

We could have turned off and made our way back toward Esan without it looking like we were avoiding them, but we kept on toward Harnoi and the ridge upon which they stood, looking more and more imposing the closer we got. My stomach churned and my hands shook, but keeping my back straight and proud, we rode to face those foreboding statues of men.

As we approached, they stretched out, forming a line that blocked the road and any path we might have been able to take around them. At either end, the riders held drawn bows, while those nearest had spears clasped lightly in their hands. At least four dozen, if not more, outnumbering us two to one—and those were only the ones we could see. No doubt there would be more hidden away in the undergrowth, or waiting at a distance to be called if needed.

"Stand aside," Captain Kiren called as we drew close enough to be heard. "You're blocking the road."

No one answered, but right in the middle of the pack on the road a pair of riders edged forward, allowing a third horse to push its way between them. Upon its back sat a memory in crimson and gold—Emperor Kin living and breathing and once again blocking my way. No, not Kin. Just a man in the same mould, filling his boots and his robe with the same assurance grown upon the edge of a blade.

"Good morning, Father," Sichi said as we halted a few lengths out, the sound of our soldiers behind us less comfort than I would have liked. "How surprising that we should have business in the same small town at the same time."

"Sichi. Miko." He growled both our names, but it was our soldiers he stared at, eyeing each man as though committing their faces to memory.

"Minister," I said, grateful my tone sounded even despite my trembling hands. "Is there something you want? Or are you merely blocking our way for the enjoyment of it?"

His gaze snapped back from my soldiers, scowl fixed on me. "I see you have some of Edo's men with you," he said rather than answer, granting Edo no title as he had with us. "I wish I could say I was surprised, but he has always been more emotional than sensible."

"I am not sure how providing soldiers for his empress's protection can be considered anything but sensible given the recent attempt upon my life."

"Empress." He looked as though he wanted to spit upon the road. "I hope you are enjoying your short-lived farce, girl, because—"

"Farce?" I drew myself up. "I am the empress of Kisia. You are my minister of the left, a position I am removing you from at this very moment. From now on, you are no longer my minister, Lord Manshin, only a man dressed in the wrong-coloured robes."

His smile lacked humour. "Clever, but I'm not here for you. You may go on parading yourself about the country for all I care. I am here to take back my daughter."

"Oh, I'm your daughter again now you need me?" Sichi said. "How nice."

"It ill suits you to bandy insults with anyone on the open road," he said. "Let alone your father."

"You are no father of mine."

Manshin's brow lowered, and though he didn't look at his soldiers, something in the way he shifted his weight drew attention to their existence. "We can do this the easy way or the hard way, child. As you can see, my men well outnumber yours, and you have nowhere to run. Fight and I will take you by force, killing as many of your traitorous soldiers as I can. Come with me and they walk free."

At my side, Sichi swallowed hard. We were outnumbered. We had known it might come to this. That he was willing to let me go ought to have been a triumph, but it was a hollow victory. He wouldn't have had he thought me a threat.

Sichi and I shared a long look. There was no other choice. She had to go with him, protected only by the marriage we had made in secret. "I'll be there," I said. "I promise."

"I know you will."

They were all the words we had and all the words we needed. With a nod to Captain Kiren, she clicked her tongue and set her horse walking. A lone sacrifice, she crossed the gulf between enemies.

"Majesty?" Captain Kiren murmured at my side. "Orders?"

"Don't move," I said. "Let her go and don't attack unless they turn on us. If they break their word, give them hell."

"Yes, Your Majesty."

Slowly, Sichi crossed to the other side, Manshin's eyes bright with victory. "A wise choice, Daughter. Better to choose the right side of history and win, rather than go down as a renegade."

I bit my tongue, holding my emotionless mask steady. I would not let him crack it. Would not let him hurt me.

At a gesture from Manshin, his soldiers surrounded Sichi in a formation as much protection as prison. She neither paid them any heed nor glanced back, her head held determinedly high. Without slowing, she continued on along the road, forcing Manshin's soldiers to move to keep up, and with a final, mocking bow, my one-time mentor and minister turned his horse away.

"Do we go after them?" Captain Kiren asked.

"No. This is how it has to be for now."

"Do we head back to camp? Or on to find the governor?"

"Neither," I said, watching Sichi shrink into the distance, soon to vanish from sight beyond the rise. "We keep going to Harnoi. I'm going to listen to the people."

# 15. CASSANDRA

Finding Empress Miko turned out to be easier than expected. Everyone I met on the road talked of nothing but how Kisia now had two emperors, and that they feared more war. I had little interest in the worries of strangers, but by mid-afternoon the collective directions of half a dozen travellers found me standing outside a small Kisian military camp and wishing I wasn't.

Having made myself known to the perimeter guards, I was ushered in under watchful gazes and soon found myself once again sitting across from the empress, she staring at me as I stared at her.

"So." The empress picked up her tea bowl and blew away the steam. Once. Twice. Three times. We had a table this time and a tent to protect from the wind. A white and gold dog lay curled on a collection of pillows in the corner.

"So," I repeated, the way she looked at me over the rim of her bowl causing my insides to twist in joyful agony. "I did what you asked."

"He's going to remove his soldiers from Kisia?"

"He says so, yes."

Miko let out a breath too tense to be called a sigh. "Good," she said. "Good. And did he agree to the specifics?"

Habit more Hana's than mine took my hands to the bowl before me, curling fingers around the warm ceramic. "Yes." I focussed on my hands. On the bowl. On the steam that rose into my face, dampening my skin with its pale, wispy fingers. "But...you can't really intend to give him Unus."

I risked a glance up. Her smile wavered behind the shield of her own bowl. "Can't I?"

"Well...if he has Unus then he's one step closer to his goal."

"True," she agreed. "And though the enemy of my enemy may temporarily be my ally, he is never to be mistaken for a friend." She took a sip, steam rising around her face—each silvery curl a finger with which I wished I could touch her.

"He is...definitely dangerous," I agreed.

Miko tilted her head. "Even to someone like you?"

"Like me?" It took me a moment to remember she knew. "Oh, I'm not sure. He can still read my mind."

"And control it?"

"I don't think he's ever..." I trailed off, returning to the moment I had stood before Leo in Koi, blade in hand, not wanting to kill him. But a fog had fallen over me, owning a heavy voice. Insistent. Tugging. Desperate. And I'd thrust the blade between his ribs. "Once," I said. "When I was on my own."

"On your own?"

"Without—"

The floor seemed to drop, warm clouds rushing up to envelope my thoughts as Kaysa cleared her throat. "Without me," she said, her pointed suspicion and clipped words spilling worry through my smothered mind. "My name is Kaysa."

*What are you doing? Get out of there! She'll think we're—*

"A freak?" she snapped aloud. "Is that what you think of 'people like us'? Why not just—"

"Stop it!" I hissed, spilling tea down my leg as we fought for control. "This isn't helping."

The smile had fallen from Miko's face, but she leaned closer.

"Wait," she said. "Let her talk. Kaysa. Is that her name? The other...soul who shares your body? The one who stepped into the dead Levanti?"

"I did that, but yes, Kaysa—"

"Is right here," she said, taking over again and this time I sank back and let her speak, the avid curiosity on Miko's face a better reaction than I had feared. *"Your Majesty."*

Once again Miko tilted her head to better examine us, tea forgotten. "You don't like me," she said, eyes darting about my face as though reading it.

"I don't know you. Neither does Cass, no matter what she feels to the contrary, and I don't like that you use those feelings to your advantage." Miko flinched, and I wanted to take back Kaysa's terrible words and smooth the hurt from my daughter's brow, but Kaysa thrust aside my weak attempt to take over. "No, Cass, let me speak. She asked to talk to me, and this satisfaction is the least you can give me after what you've forced me to sacrifice for her."

"Forced you to sacrifice?" Miko said, both her smile and her curiosity fading into uncertainty.

"Oh no," Kaysa said, a sneer curling our lips. "I am not fool enough to give you more information to use against us."

Miko's eyes narrowed. "You may not like me, but that doesn't mean you can treat me with such a complete lack of respect. I am the empress of Kisia, which having known my mother, ought to mean something to you."

Kaysa shrugged. "You're not my empress. What happens if people don't bow? Does the world break?"

"All right, that's enough," I said, Kaysa letting herself be pulled away. "I'm sorry," I added, unable to meet Miko's stare. "Things are...complicated."

"So I see. Better to be complicated than useless though, don't you think?"

"I suppose so," I said.

Miko set down her bowl and reached a warm hand to mine, her callused fingers brushing my knuckles. "You have done me a great service, Cassandra, and for that I thank you. Unfortunately, there is still much to do if we're to win back the throne and remove Leo Villius from any position of power, so I hope you will stand with me as my mother would have."

I stared at the hand laid softly over mine, and all words failed me. Hana ought to have been sitting there, ought to have survived, have taken my body and lived on, because unlike me she'd had so much to live for. All I had was this thorn pressed deep in my chest aching with love for a child I'd never had.

*Say no. You're done*, Kaysa said. *We're done. We took Leo her message, and we owe her nothing else. She's using you, Cassandra.*

"Of course I will." My words were little more than a breath, but Miko's smile broadened, and she withdrew her hand.

"She would be as proud of you as I hope she will be of me," she said, and shifting position in readiness to rise, Miko pushed aside the dregs of her tea and gestured at my sodden leg. "Do you need fresh clothes?"

"Oh yes, I suppose so." I could still feel the weight and warmth of her hand. "Nothing Kisian though, if possible. I find moving around in a full robe difficult."

Her smile tightened. "Understandable. I'll see what we have. In the meantime, I'll have my men find you a free tent. The evening meal ought to be served soon." She got to her feet with a small groan of effort, her dog getting up as well and stretching its legs.

*Unus?*

The question hovered unspoken on my lips. It was such a small thing to do for Kaysa, and yet the risk of Miko no longer looking at me with that smile, or never again setting her hand over mine, held me hostage.

"Unus?" Kaysa said, pushing through in my stead.

Miko had turned to speak to the guards outside, but she stilled at that, watching me from the corners of her eyes. "What about him?"

"Where is he?"

"Cassandra or Kaysa?" The wariness in her question cut deeper than I expected. When neither of us answered, Miko shook her head as though dislodging a troublesome thought. "I can have someone take you to him. He's under guard to ensure he doesn't run away or harm anyone."

I swallowed Kaysa's urge to blurt that he would never hurt anyone unless in self-defence, and nodded. "Yes, I would like to see him."

With a lingering look, Miko turned away.

As she had said, we found Unus chained to the ground in a nearby tent, watched by a pair of guards with tense, unhappy expressions. He had only a threadbare blanket between himself and the cold dirt, and he sat curled tightly upon himself as though a chill lived inside his skin.

"Unus," Kaysa said, kneeling in front of him. "Are you all right?"

"Fine." He stared at nothing. "They give me food, and I have warm blankets at night. It's better treatment than I deserve."

"No, it's not. It's nothing like what you deserve." Anger crackled in Kaysa's voice, and I let her take over completely, retreating from the complicated feelings the sight of Unus always produced. Not romantic feelings, thankfully, rather a desperation to fix him, to save him, to prove to herself—to the world—a freak's story didn't need to have a tragic ending.

Unus tilted his head our way, having to squint against the brightness outside. "We're monsters. We deserve all we get."

"You are not a monster. Duos is. Not because he's different, but because he chose to be a monster."

"You went to see him."

"The empress asked Cassandra to go, so of course she did."

He stared at the bright sliver of daylight—all he could see of the camp from where he sat chained. "She's offered me to him. To Duos."

"She won't do it though," Kaysa said, repeating my assurances. "Giving him what he needs is unwise in the circumstances."

"Why? What will it change for her if Duos calls himself a god?"

The realization echoed through my thoughts like the crashing of a rockfall. "Nothing." Kaysa's voice was breathless. "It's just a word unless you believe it means something."

"Exactly. Not believing in the One True God, it changes nothing as far as Empress Miko is concerned."

"So she will give you to him. She has no reason not to."

Hairs rose on the back of my neck like we were being watched, and it took all Kaysa's self-control not to turn around.

"They're always watching," Unus said, lowering his voice to a whisper and tapping the side of his head. "Duos too, always lurking just out of reach."

A footstep scuffed. Someone cleared their throat. "Cassandra?" My name on Miko's lips was like her hand upon mine—a thrill of acknowledgement I wanted to hold tight and never let go. She stood just outside, a folded selection of garments in her hands as though the empress of Kisia had been a laundry maid. "This is all the clothing we have available in something like your size. Some of it is worn Levanti clothing, some Kisian military uniform. I'll let you choose what will suit best."

She held out the pile but came no closer—a treat proffered to draw me in. For all she glanced his way, Unus might not have existed at all.

*She's worried about your allegiance*, Kaysa said.

Your *allegiance.*

*Our allegiance.*

I took the pile of clothes, cleaner and softer than anything I had worn since leaving Chiltae. They felt out of place in a muddy army camp, as out of place as the painted tea bowls and the embroidered edge of Miko's linen robe.

She led me to a tent empty of all but a sleeping mat. "Dinner should be ready when you're changed, and you're welcome to join us," Miko said, leaving me to the comfort of the dark space, its calm a softness against the ragged edge of my racing thoughts.

*We can't let her go through with it*, Kaysa said as I looked through the pile of clothing. *We can't sacrifice Unus. You have put her before him and me again and again, but no more.*

"She may not intend to give him up, whatever Unus says," I said as I pulled a pair of Levanti breeches from the pile and held them against my legs, eyeing their length and waistband.

*That's very wishful thinking. Ask her.*

I grunted rather than answer, still hunting through the clothing. None of their tunics fitted, but a half robe wasn't as difficult to move around in, so I took one in the right size despite its umber hue clashing garishly with my hair.

*Don't worry, it's not like Yakono is here to see it.*

"I wasn't worried about that, and I don't care how he sees me."

*Except seeing us for what we are.*

"That's different."

Had she been separately present she would have given me exactly the sort of look I most enjoyed throwing at every fool I came into contact with, but though I could feel her disdain I didn't rise to the bait, just pulled on the fresh clothes. A boy stood waiting when I stepped back outside. He bowed like we were very important. "Her Imperial Majesty requests your attendance in her tent for the evening meal."

He left no time for refusal, just turned to lead the way through the camp. Miko's tent stood like a silk lantern fighting back the night, and even in clean clothing I felt out of place stepping near it—the performance of her rank reminding me I was not Hana more forcefully than anything else had done. The boy strode in without pause, leaving me to follow, my name announced before I'd passed the golden threshold.

Miko had changed her robe for something fine and shimmering, though her hair remained simply tied and she wore neither paint nor jewels. The man sitting with her wore an embroidered surcoat over his armour, and though he smiled in welcome, a lifelessness dulled his beautiful features.

"Ah, Cassandra," Miko said, rising from the table in a show of great respect. "I don't think you have been introduced to my oldest friend, Lord Edo Bahain, duke of Syan."

"A pleasure to meet you," Lord Bahain said, his fine manners and his strong presence failing to obscure his youth. "Her Majesty has told me rather a lot about you."

"None of it good, I'm sure."

*Don't get drawn in by all this grandeur and kindness, Cass,* Kaysa warned. *It's all false. They just want to make use of us like they'll make use of Unus.*

Both Miko and Lord Edo stared at me as though awaiting a reply, but I hadn't caught their question. "Sorry, I…My mind drifted. What did you say? Your Majesty. I mean, Your Majesty and Your Grace." I'd never felt so out of proportion to the space in which I sat, like a bloated corpse all swollen and clumsy.

"I merely said I was glad you could join us," Miko said, and her smile was as much offer as the clothes she had held out to me, each small moment the sort you take and tuck deep in your soul. A moment of acceptance. Of belonging. Yet the lantern light reflected no accompanying smile in her eyes, and in a far-removed tent, hidden from view, Unus sat staked to the ground alone and cold and hated.

*Someone like you.*

Food arrived, carried in on a collection of fine plates. The two boys who seemed to be doing the work of servants set them down, bowing often, before backing out.

"So what brought you to Kisia, Cassandra?" Lord Edo said, reaching for a cup of wine.

I'd long since left embarrassment about my professions behind, yet the urge to lie and maintain Miko's good opinion was almost overwhelming. "An assassination contract."

Both Kisians stilled and shared a glance. "Not the answer I was expecting," Lord Edo admitted, unfreezing with a smile. "Dare we ask a contract on whom?"

"A servant travelling with Dom Villius on his way to marry Princess Miko."

They both stared. "A servant whose body was picked up by my brother, perhaps," Miko said, her tone determinedly even. "I understand a little better now how you came to meet my mother."

I reached for my own wine rather than speak, rather than risk her discovery that I was the reason Koi had fallen.

"What a small world we live in," Lord Edo said, as calm as Miko at least on the outside. "Will you try some of this fish, Cassandra? It is very well cooked."

*We don't belong here,* Kaysa said as the meal progressed, conversation drifting away from such dangerous topics. *We aren't welcome here.*

*We aren't welcome anywhere.*

*That's not true. Did Unus ever look at us like we were a monster? Did Yakono?*

I twitched a shoulder like I could shrug off her truths. *Yakono still might.*

*And he might not.*

*Doesn't matter now anyway; I made my choice.*

Her voice, her presence, drew closer like she stood before me in my thoughts, obscuring everything else. *The wrong choice, Cassandra. And that's all right, people make bad choices all the time; just don't keep following the wrong path because you started on it. There's still time to go back. To walk another way.*

*What way? You're trying very hard to be wise and poetic for someone who's barely experienced life.*

Silence plucked at my mind and my guilt, stretching it taut between heartbeats.

*Who says living my life through your bad choices doesn't make me wiser than most?* she said at last. *Isn't it true people learn more from failing than from succeeding?*

*Kaysa—*

*Cassandra, listen to me. For once, please. We don't belong here. We aren't welcome here. There is nothing you can ever do to make these people accept you, or to make Miko look at you and see her mother. But I am here. Unus is here. Yakono understands the way you see the world; don't give that up for a false chance at a future you can never have. You are not Hana.*

I closed my eyes, wishing I could block out her words, could wipe away my own doubts, but they all went on spinning through my mind without end. I was not Hana. I knew I was not Hana, but then who was I?

*You're Cassandra Marius.*

*But who is that?* She'd always just been the whore, the act that protected me from the world's hurts. The anger that kept me alive.

"Had you ever been to Kisia before now?" Lord Edo asked, veering the conversation back into the personal. The interrogational. "Or is this your first time this side of the border?"

"No," I said. "I spent time in Lin'ya some years back."

A pause followed, inviting further confidence, but I wanted to explain neither that I'd worked in a whorehouse there nor that it had been in pursuit of a particularly difficult contract. The man had ended up dead on the whorehouse floor, and it had been a job well done—a sense of satisfaction perhaps only Yakono could have appreciated.

"I've never been to Lin'ya myself," Miko said when the silence went unfilled. "Though activities there have long been a thorn in Kisia's side."

"No doubt one's view of that depends what their definition of Kisia is," I said.

My point had been that the poor often acted to survive, their interest in the glory of their nation nonexistent, yet both empress and duke stared at me as though I'd suggested an uprising. The feeling of being out of place increased, and I doubled my focus on my meal.

*Ask them*, Kaysa said. *Ask them what they plan to do with Unus, and don't let Miko brush you off with poetic nonsense again.*

Miko picked at the food on her plate, a momentary lull in the conversation dropping her gaze to the table. In the candid moments she wasn't on show, when she wasn't being Her Imperial Majesty, I was struck by her youth as I had been by Lord Edo's. Mere children, fighting for Kisia's future because no one else would.

*Ask, or I will.*

"Your Majesty." I cleared my throat, struggling to meet her gaze as she looked up. "I have to know if you truly intend to give Unus to his brother."

Her youth vanished behind the hard mask of leadership. "That will depend on what Dom Villius does."

"Yes or no?"

The air in the tent chilled, Lord Edo setting down his wine bowl like a man preparing for anything. Miko's smile was cold. "Yes, if it must be done. Such sacrifices are necessary in times of war."

Kaysa shoved forward, my lips turning into a sneer. "Then

between handing over Unus and letting him marry Lady Sichi, you'll have given him everything he needs to take on the mantle of god."

The empress's eyes narrowed and she leaned forward, meal forgotten. "What does Lady Sichi have to do with it?"

"He can't complete his prophecy without her," Kaysa said, her sneer becoming more pronounced. "She's his consort with two voices."

"And what does that mean?"

Kaysa pushed us to our feet. "No more answers unless you let Unus go."

"I can't do that."

"Then I'll bid you goodnight." Kaysa brushed a hand down the front of our half robe, and unwilling to fight her to remain in that uncomfortable space, I let her carry us toward the entryway.

Neither Miko nor Lord Edo sought to stop us, nor did they call for their guards, though no doubt some would follow us in case we attempted anything...foolish.

Outside, the chill night air felt refreshing against my warm skin, and the sounds of the army camp were enough like Genava's quieter streets that I breathed deep of its comfort. "I don't think she'll change her mind," Kaysa said, striding away from the empress's tent. "Even knowing about Lady Sichi."

*So he really can't complete his prophecy without her? I said. We should kill her.*

"Unfortunately for your bloodthirstiness, he could find another woman who speaks different languages."

*Is that what consort with two voices means?*

"It's what he's using as its meaning."

*But why? Even we fit better.*

Kaysa grimaced. "Let's not give him that idea. Damn, I think I'm getting us lost." She'd walked out of Miko's tent without thought to our destination, and now slid back in our mind, leaving me to save us.

In control once again, I tried to recall the path we'd been led on through the camp rather than dwell on the falsity of Miko's smiles. Yet those cold looks kept intruding like the lingering phantoms of a bad dream.

I sighed. "Who am I, Kaysa?"

*I don't know,* she said. *But it's time to stop hiding behind the identities others gave you and find out. You don't have to be a freak. You don't have to be the child our parents got rid of. You don't have to survive on anger and take only the dregs society allows you. We're more than that.*

Unus's tent came into view. Still under guard, he sat picking at a simple meal. He looked up, his understanding expression catching me between a desire to hide and a dawning relief that here was one person I didn't have to explain anything to. He could see my thoughts and had lived my pain, his identity as much a mystery to him as mine was to me.

Again my skin prickled, and I dared not turn. The feeling I was surrounded by enemies grew, and I threw only a quick glance Unus's way.

*Can you hear me?* I thought. *Cough for yes.*

Pressing a balled fist to his lips, Unus coughed to clear his throat.

*I can't get you out of here with so many people watching, but I promise I won't let Duos take you.*

Unus shrugged, a smile turning one corner of his lips. That would have to do for agreement—to stand there longer was likely to inspire suspicion from the already staring guards. *You're getting into my head,* I grumbled to Kaysa. *What do I care what happens to Unus?*

*You don't, but maybe, just maybe, you care about me.*

I sighed. "Fuck."

From inside the tent, Unus cleared his throat much more loudly, something in the sound chilling my blood. "Don't worry, Cassandra," he called, Duos ringing clear in his tone. "He'll be mine no matter what you do. Walk away while you can."

I spun to snarl at him, but his next words froze me in place. "How long can you live in a dead body, I wonder," he said. "If you get in my way we'll have to find out. It would be an experiment worthy of Torvash himself."

Kaysa had stayed too long in a corpse the first time she'd walked from our skin. The memory lingered, sending dread crawling over my flesh.

"Shut up in there," one of the guards grumbled, knocking the side of the tent with his foot.

"Don't worry, I'm done," Duos said. His laugh faded as we hurried away, fighting the urge to be sick. Kaysa's silent panic fuelled mine, and in the shadows of a random tent I dropped to all fours, the night spinning.

*He'll incapacitate the corpse. He won't let us out. He could bury it with us inside—*

"Stop it," I growled.

*We'd be trapped forever. Forgotten. And—*

Stomach rebelling, I vomited into the grass.

# 16. DISHIVA

Tents were going up and everyone was busy, at least everyone except for Secretary Aurus, who stood in front of his, waiting. The setting sun surrounded him with gold light, but neither his halo nor his mild, patient demeanour worked to calm the worry burning through my veins.

"You are upset that Levanti are here?" he said, his brow creasing. "I admit that's not the reaction I expected."

"If you knew they would be here, why didn't you tell me?"

"I couldn't," he said, ever calm. "I wasn't sure we would come to a fair agreement. Also, whatever you knew was information available to Lord Villius, and whatever else he could know about my plans, he couldn't know this."

"Your secret weapon."

"My secret weapon. I take it from your earlier greeting that you know Whisperer Ezma."

A dry laugh brushed past my lips. "Yes, I know her. That she still calls herself a whisperer is the greatest insult to my people imaginable. She is not even fit to be called a Levanti."

Aurus's brows rose, and he glanced over his shoulder to check the progress of his tent. He waved a hand at the slaves. They'd almost finished with the tent itself and would soon begin the task of carrying in all the furnishings with which Aurus travelled.

"I think we ought to continue this conversation in greater privacy," he said, gesturing me toward the entrance of the empty tent. "Just in case."

Although we were speaking in Levanti, it was perhaps better not to be seen arguing, so I agreed and followed him inside.

Lacking its furnishings and its floor, the secretary's tent was nothing but a square of grass enclosed on all sides with an arc of light spilling in through the open curtain. He grunted with annoyance, but said, "If Whisperer Ezma is so poorly thought of, why do so many Levanti follow her?"

"Why do so many people follow Leo?"

"Because he represents something they want, in his case traditional values and Chiltae ruling over all in a holy empire."

"Not just in his case. They want the same thing; they just use different methods. You cannot ally yourself with her—ally *us* with her."

Hurrying footsteps heralded the return of the slaves, one carrying a lit lantern, the others a rolled-up rug. They dropped it just inside the entry and began to unroll it, halting only when they reached our feet. Aurus sighed and stepped over onto the part that had already been unrolled, and took the lantern from the other man's hand. With a wave of the secretary's hand they were off again, but at least now we had more light. The expression it illuminated on Aurus's face was not comforting.

"You speak like we have a choice," he said, frowning. "Tell me exactly why we shouldn't ally with her when we have made similar alliances out of necessity with Lord Villius. What has she done?"

"She is no true Levanti. She chose to work with—" My jaw snapped shut. How could I say she was connected to the Entrancers who'd had us expelled from our homeland, that she fought for the One True God, when there I stood as hieromonk? The incongruity jarred, and how could I be sure Secretary Aurus wasn't connected to the Entrancers too?

"Work with?" he prompted. "If she has allies I don't know about, that is something I ought to know. Don't you think?"

"You make that sound reasonable, but how do I know I can trust you?"

"I have not proved myself? Have I not done everything you've asked of me? More?"

"And allied yourself with a dangerous fraud!"

Two more men hurried in, bearing one of the secretary's couches between them. They passed between us to set it down in the right place, but Aurus kept his eyes on me, brows caught low. The moment they left, he sighed. "All I know of Ezma e'Topi is that I first met her a few years ago, though most of her communication was with our previous hieromonk, Lord Villius's father. Despite that, as far as I am aware, and I believe as far as the rest of the Nine are aware, she has no other allies. Now, is there something you wish to say?"

I bit my lip, the soft fabric of my mask brushing against my skin. "Have you . . . have you heard of Entrancers?"

His eyes narrowed, and in a slow, wary tone, he said, "Yes. As have you, since you've been fighting one for some time now."

"Fighting one?"

"Lord Villius? Unless we are talking about two different things here."

Pieces that hadn't quite fit together in my head finally clicked into place. "Yes, of course, he's an Entrancer. And Ezma knew his father? I wonder . . ."

"Did you mean Entrancers other than Lord Villius?"

"Yes, on the plains. They are the reason we were exiled, and she knew about it and did nothing—might even have been involved. That's why she was exiled and stripped of her position."

He glanced down at the couch between us, but didn't sit. "I understand why that makes her repugnant to you, as Lord Villius is to us both, but that is not a reason to abandon useful alliances. Rare is the occasion one can afford to be…" He waved a hand, searching for the right word. "Considerate to such things," he settled on with a grimace.

He was right, yet I couldn't agree. She had known about the Entrancers and said nothing, had turned against her people, had tried to convince me that I was Veld and my loss of sight was a gift that had happened for a reason. I pushed out a hand as though I could thrust such memories away, but they all lived at the front of my mind, as visceral as the experiences that made them.

"Dishiva." Aurus glanced at my hand, and I hastily drew it back. "I understand that you're worried, and it sounds like you have every reason to be. She may betray us, but we have no choice. Without her and her Levanti, we have no guarantee of being able to take the city without waiting for Lord Villius's return, and while she *may* betray us, he *will*. We need the numbers and we cannot wait."

Guilt nipped at me. Perhaps if I'd been able to persuade Leo's soldiers to march with us instead, if I'd known better words or had a better idea—I shook my head, refusing to go down the path of ifs and maybes. To weaken Leo's power, we needed to take Shimai before he returned, and this was the only way.

I nodded, glad that the secretary had at least listened to my concerns and understood the possibility of betrayal on both sides.

Aurus looked for a moment like he would say more, but the second of his couches arrived and he shut his jaw hard. With another nod, I left him to direct the placement of his furnishings and escaped into the evening air.

Having no chapel, a tent for me now existed in the central area of the camp. It was standing and, lacking Secretary Aurus's extravagance, seemed already to be lit and furnished. I was all too happy to escape into it, ready to remove my mask and forget my troubles for a few moments and just breathe.

Already tugging on the strings of my mask, I stepped inside only to halt on the threshold. Someone was already there—a familiar someone—though surprise went on holding me hostage until he spoke.

"Nice to see you again too, Di."

"Jass!" I hurried toward him and was gathered into his arms and crushed against his chest. His earthy scent filled my senses, and the beat of his heart sounded by my ear, and for a few blissful moments, I was not carrying the weight of the Levanti future alone.

"I've been so worried about you," I murmured into the side of his neck.

"You've been worried about *me?*" He drew back enough to see my face, his own incredulous. "You're the one who walked into a Chiltaen camp and didn't come out for weeks!"

"I'm sorry! I tried to get a message to you, but I was so trapped when I first arrived. Leo made me the hieromonk and I had to learn to give blessings and—"

"Whoa, slow down, Di," he said, the combination of the nickname and his strong hands grasping my shoulders melting my growing tension. I breathed out shakily and explained what had happened, from the moment we'd parted on that dark road to now, all about Leo's plans and Secretary Aurus and the reparations I had bargained for. The future I sought.

He let me finish without interrupting, only to let out his own shaky breath and pass a hand over his short pelt of hair. "That's . . . and you're sure you can trust this Aurus? That he will deliver what he promised?"

"I don't know," I admitted, breaking free to pace about the tent. "Sometimes I am sure. He hasn't lied to me yet that I know of, and he's been good to me on occasion, but then at other times I'm reminded he's Chiltaen, and how can I trust anything a Chiltaen says?"

"But you are."

"The risk is worth the reward. Just think, Jass. A place we could call our own that's far from the influence of the city states and those Entrancers. Whatever he did wrong, I believed in Gideon's dream, and this is a way to make it work. Even if there's only a handful who want to stay, or who are wary of returning, it's somewhere we could build. Could just... exist."

His slow nod gave little insight into his thoughts, but he folded his arms. "How can I help?"

"Help?"

"I didn't spend weeks sitting on my arse watching that camp for any sign of you just to run away now. Gideon failed because he trusted the wrong people. He failed because he took too much on his own shoulders, because he tried to carry all of us alone. I won't let you walk that path. Tell me how I can help."

For the second time, I wrapped my arms around him and held him close, swallowing a grateful sob. "I'm not sure there's any way you can help. We need to conquer Shimai before Leo returns from his wedding—"

"Wedding?"

His bewilderment made a laugh bubble up my throat. "I think you're going to have to sit down for this one," I said. "And maybe I should send for some wine and food because it's a lot on an empty stomach. But first, is... is Itaghai with you?"

A warm smile spread his lips. "He is. Tephe is brushing him down in one of the pens; he's the one who told me where to find you."

To have Itaghai back and Jass standing there like we'd never parted filled a void in my soul, reconnecting me to a sense of who I was. With them here, getting what we had fought so hard for became all the more important.

"You can go see him now if you like," Jass said, his expression softening to an amused smile. "I'm sure he'll be as happy to see you as you are to see him. That wine and food can wait."

"As must your visit to the horse pens," someone said from the entryway. I spun, heart sinking at the sight of Ezma, a half smile twisting her lips and her bone headdress touching the sloping tent roof. "Your Holiness," she said. "How momentous to see you again and in such a guise."

"Get out," I said, hot anger flowing through me. "Whatever you have to say, I don't want to hear it."

"We need to talk."

"No, we don't. You did your talking at Kogahaera, and the answer is still no."

Ezma turned to Jass. "Good evening, Jass."

"Whisperer," he murmured, making no move to depart.

"If you could give us a few moments, I need to—"

"No," I snapped. "He's not going anywhere. If you insist on speaking then say what you came to say and leave."

Undeterred, she strode in and sat upon one of the two chairs with which my tent had been furnished. "All right." Ezma clasped her hands together, her expression stern. "If that is how it has to be."

"It is."

She gestured to me. "I see your eye has healed well."

"If you mean continues to be gone forever, then yes."

"We all make sacrifices for what's important."

Beside me, Jass flinched, and I was better able to control my own anger knowing he was angry for me. When I didn't answer, Ezma went on, "I know you don't believe in the religion you're representing, Dishiva, but that doesn't mean you are not still fighting for it, not still fulfilling a long-awaited role by being present in this moment. You can be Veld whether you believe in the Presage or not."

"How can I be the chosen of a god I don't believe exists?"

"Because God only has to believe in you for you to serve."

I folded my arms, wishing I'd not let her speak at all. "Tell me why you're here," I said. "Why make an alliance with Secretary Aurus?"

"For the same reason you are here. I'm fighting for my people's future."

"Your people. Do you mean all Levanti or just the ones who follow you?"

"Both."

"Do they believe in Veld?"

"No more than you do, for the most part."

"Yet they are willing to fight with Chiltaens?"

Ezma pursed her lips, her gaze as close to a glare as she would allow herself. "This conversation is getting us nowhere."

"Ah, so you're lying to them."

It was a bow drawn at length, yet her scowl deepened, and I wished I hadn't been right. "What are you telling them? Why do they think they're here?"

The whisperer's gaze slid to Jass, but it was too late to send him away. "I told them the truth. They are here to fight for a safe home. A strong home."

"And how does allying with Chiltaens to destroy a Kisian city achieve that?"

Again she glanced at Jass. "May I finish what I came here to say without being interrupted with a dozen questions? You are Veld, Dishiva. You will build an empire."

"No, I'm—"

"It's time to stop turning away and accept these truths so you can make the right choices. So you can help your people."

"I'm already helping my people."

"So Secretary Aurus informed me. A fine deal you've made with him, though what makes you think you can trust the word of a Chiltaen? He is not your friend."

I closed my eyes, pressing the heels of my palms to my sockets. The empty one still felt strange to touch—an ever-present reminder of all Leo and his damn god had taken from me. "What do you want, Ezma?" I said. "Just tell me why you're here without all the fucking around."

"This isn't a game we're playing, Dishiva," she said. "Your place in history is already written. It's not about what you want or what I want; it's about how things have to be. You are Veld whether you like it or not. That being so, will you or will you not accept the title and lead us into our future?"

"No." I looked up, my remaining eye fuzzy from the pressure of my hand. "I am not Veld. There is no Veld and there will be no empire of the One True God, and the sooner you realise that, the better."

Ezma sighed. "I hoped it wouldn't come to this." She pointed toward the entrance of the tent. "What are your chances of taking the city tomorrow if I withdraw right now with all my Swords?"

"And give up your own deal with Aurus?"

She leaned forward, elbows on knees, her gaze fixed on me. "What do you know of my deal with our dear secretary?"

I realised then that he hadn't told me.

"You didn't consider that perhaps it was you I wanted," she said when I didn't answer. "That your acceptance of your true place is the reason we fight. You are *everything*, Dishiva."

Her words washed over me, their weight threatening to crush me into the ground. My deal with Aurus required taking Shimai, and taking Shimai required Ezma and her followers. The more the options swirled through my mind, the fewer options there seemed to be.

"And what exactly do you want me to do?" I said.

"Di—" Jass began, but broke off, letting the hand he reached toward me fall. He could see as I could that I had no choice.

Ezma leaned farther forward on her chair, eyes bright. "You declare yourself to be Veld in front of everyone, and then go on to lead us to the building of a holy empire."

"A holy empire and someone calling themselves Veld," I said. "Both built on a forced agreement."

"It doesn't matter how it starts, only that you follow it through to the end." A tinge of excitement coloured her voice. "You'll accept your place in history?"

Jass's hand closed around my arm, but he didn't speak. What was there to say? I didn't want to build an empire, I didn't want to be Veld, but for now the only way forward was accepting her terms. An agreement I could walk away from once Aurus gave us what he'd promised and I no longer needed her.

"All right," I said. "I'll be your Veld, but you cannot just use me as a silent figurehead. I need to know what we're doing, how, and why."

"Is that a stipulation you gave Secretary Aurus as well? Or do you trust the Chiltaen more than me? No, don't answer that; we are starting afresh, you and I." She held out her hand. "For the future."

Her hand was worn and lined with hard work like any Levanti's, though I couldn't shake the feeling she'd long ago ceased truly being one of us. With no choice, I took it. "For our people's future. Now get out of my tent."

A sheen of white covered the grass, crunching beneath my boots at every step. Both the sound and the sensation were satisfying, but Jass looked grim. He hovered inside the entrance to my tent, and while it was best for me not to be seen with him even at such an early hour, the way he looked at the grass made it clear he didn't want to step out.

"Is this snow?" I said. "Have you been here over winter?"

A nod, his eyes not straying from the glittering ground. "Just the one. We came as the last one started, about half a cycle before you arrived. But this isn't snow. This is just the warning it's coming. This will melt in an hour or two."

I turned, each stomp making a sound that not only crackled but squeaked. "What is snow then?"

"It's like this but more. It's like... like sand that you can't stand on; you have to wade through it, and it's cold and wet and slippery." His features twisted sourly. "I hoped not to be here for another winter."

"Well," I said, returning to the tent. "If today goes well you might not be."

The sun had only just begun bathing the camp in pale grey light, but tension was already palpable. Most soldiers were awake, either sitting and eating in silence or preparing for what could be a day of battle or a day of boredom. Over in the Levanti camp, things would be more lively, but there was also Ezma.

"What will you do today?" I said when Jass didn't move, his eyes upon the marks I'd left in the not-snow. "Will you fight with Ezma?"

His gaze snapped around. "No. Why would you think so?"

"Because you don't like hanging around feeling useless, and I'm afraid you've had to do rather a lot of that recently."

"I don't like endangering my life for no good purpose either, nor fighting beside Chiltaens." He gave me an odd look. We'd not spoken about my deal with Ezma, preferring the quiet enjoyment of one another's company to worrying about what couldn't be changed. "I'm sorry," he added. "I know you need today to be a success, but I won't be drawing my blade. And since you need to maintain the fiction you're not Levanti, I suppose I'll stick with Harmara and the others."

I turned away, face heating beneath my mask. "You make it sound like I don't want to be Levanti."

"I didn't mean—I just…don't know where we stand anymore. Don't know what I ought to do, what I'm allowed to do, and seeing Chiltaens everywhere brings back memories I'd rather banish forever. And don't say I can leave. Reminding me I can be selfish and bugger off rather than help hasn't worked before, and it won't work now." His hands slid around my shoulders, and he burrowed his face into the back of my neck, sending a shiver through my skin. "You're stuck with me. At least until you need me to carry another desperate message for help."

I laughed and leaned against him. "I won't, I promise."

"Don't make promises you can't keep, Di." He spun me around, his eyes crinkling with laughter. "You'll just want to break them."

He lifted my mask, gently peeling the fabric away from my chin and then my mouth, and holding it there, leaned in to press a warm kiss upon my lips. It was soft, tasting of early morning and the tang of old wine, and I melted against him.

"Good morning, Your Holiness."

I almost bit Jass's lip as I pulled away with a gasp. Secretary Aurus stood in the tent opening, surveying us with a bland expression that made me all too aware of my damp, reddened lips.

"Glad to see you are ready to go," he went on, not waiting for a reply. "Your horse will be here in a few minutes, and it would be quite rude to keep the governor waiting."

He walked out on the words, leaving me standing awkwardly in the middle of the floor, the disconnect between the chill of his abrupt manner and the heat of my body leaving me unsteady.

"I don't think he likes me," Jass said, staring after the secretary.

I pulled my mask back into place. "No, although I don't think he likes anyone. You should go before someone else sees you."

"All right, but you know where I'll be if you need me."

I wanted to say I wouldn't need him, that I could take care of this myself, but all I could manage was a nod. Itaghai was brought to my tent within a few minutes—just enough time to gather something approaching godly composure. "I have missed you so much!" I said, hurrying to Itaghai's head and taking his reins. "You look well. Jass did a good job taking care of you."

I set my face to his, but properly rebonding without my mask would have to wait. Aurus's arrival mounted upon his own horse ended the chance for further reunion. The secretary looked grim, and without exchanging a word, we rode through the grey morning toward the edge of the camp, flanked by murmurs of piety.

As we left the last tent behind, he finally turned my way. "You have to be more careful; you are chosen of God, not a commoner."

It was mild censure, yet it stung all the same. "I know, it's just..."

"Love?" His tone had bite—bitterness even.

"It's hard having to isolate yourself from everyone and everything you know, no matter the reason or the goal," I said, refusing to bring Jass into it.

He made no sign he'd heard me, choosing instead to keep his gaze upon our destination. In the early morning light, the city of Shimai had gathered fog about its roofs like a blanket, appearing otherworldly. A large square of fabric had been erected on poles halfway between the gates and our camp—a poor tent beneath which enemies could meet. To once again call the Kisians enemy tasted unpleasant in my mouth.

"What are you hoping to get out of this meeting?" I said, hating the strained silence. "Surrender?"

"That would be the best outcome, yes, and failing that I will insult the governor until he wants to meet us in battle to avenge the dishonour rather than force us to lay siege to his walls. Kisian leaders are pragmatic only up to a point with us. The easiest way to provoke them is to call them cowards."

"Why do you hate them so much? I don't think anyone has ever explained."

The secretary gave one of his dismissive shrugs. "Trade. Land. History. Culture. Habit. Almost all of what they call Kisia used to be Chiltaen land before the first Otakos crossed the sea to conquer an empire. Some sources claim the land used to be theirs in the first place before we forced them to take refuge on the outer islands, but no one really knows. Either way we are going to fight over this land until one of us wins, no matter how long that takes."

"That's . . . really sad," I said as we approached our waiting escort. "When you consider all you have in common and what you could achieve if you worked together."

"In common?" Aurus looked like I'd told him the sky was green.

"Is that such a strange thing to say? You even share a spoken language."

He lifted a mocking eyebrow at me, our earlier awkwardness seemingly forgotten. "Doesn't your language have enough in common with Tempachi to make communication straightforward? You need not deny it since that's why Levanti was easy for us to pick up. At least those of us with some foundation in Tempachi. They are one of our major trade partners, and you don't get anywhere in the merchant business if you can't tell when you're being mocked and cheated by a foreigner."

"A base language is all we share," I said stiffly. "And is all we will ever share. We have left the city states alone, and they have done nothing but try to destroy us and our way of life. Can you say the same of the Kisians?"

Again with that shrug. "No, but that doesn't change the way we are now. Perhaps we were the same people a long time ago, perhaps we could be better together rather than fighting, but hate feeds societies, Dishiva. Hate drives people more than love. We can hate people we've never met—hate people we'll never meet—whose lives have no bearing upon ours, but we cannot love strangers. Besides, care and empathy create peace and contentment, which would stop people wanting and needing and spending and—"

He stopped when I held up my hand, a protective palm thrust out like a shield. "Your value for life is…terrifying, Secretary. You don't even care for the well-being of your own people, when that is all you should care about."

We'd reached the waiting group of soldiers, but Aurus just rode on, leaving them to fall in behind us. "Then allow me to put it a different way," he said. "If that truth offends you, Your Holiness. The Kisians have harmed us. Often. They have slaughtered our people and destroyed our towns and our churches and our fields. Would you let such offence go without seeking revenge? Would your Swords let you?"

I looked across at the Levanti camp and thought of the camaraderie I'd once had with my Swordherd, because I'd had to care for their opinions to keep my position. Rah had not kept his. He'd cared too much for principles and duty. Perhaps both of us had been wrong in different ways.

"I don't know," I said. "Maybe, if I could explain, if I could make them listen. I would rather try to do what was right for my people than worry it would make me unpopular."

"Then you either are good at convincing people or have a death wish, Your Holiness."

"No, I just don't think about myself as the most important person. I am but one of many."

He gave me an odd, sidelong look, but focussed on the awning ahead rather than answer. It appeared the Kisians were already present—their own small clump of soldiers standing off to one side, leaving only two people sitting at the table.

They grew larger as we approached, their robes becoming two separate garments rather than a blob of colour and their faces slowly growing features, yet thanks to my poor eyesight it wasn't until we were almost upon them that I realised one was a woman. I'd been in Kisia long enough to find it surprising.

"Who's the woman?" I said, keeping my voice low as I dismounted.

"I am not entirely certain," Aurus admitted as he too slid from his saddle. "But if I had to guess I would say she's probably Mother Li, since she's the only woman to ever hold a religious position in Kisia as far as I'm aware. You have rather a lot in common."

Leaving our horses with the servants, we approached the pair who had risen from the table. Mother Li wore a plain grey robe with a high neck, tied closed with a white sash simply knotted, but it was the straight line of her severe lips that drew my attention. Since this was the second time we'd sought to claim her home, I couldn't blame her.

In contrast, her companion had donned a bright, shimmering robe in deep blue and silver, perhaps hoping to dazzle us with his importance, just as his welcoming scowl sought to shame. Secretary Aurus, dressed equally fine and possessed of untouchable equanimity, seemed to notice neither.

As we joined them at the table, two servants performed introductions in Kisian. Since Aurus had insisted I attend the meeting without Oshar, I could only nod when my name was spoken, before sitting down to a game of guess that expression—body language and tone all I had by which to gauge how well the meeting was going.

The governor spoke first. I'd missed his name, but found I didn't care, my gaze caught to Mother Li. She possessed all the calm piety in her bearing that I lacked, yet the look she fixed upon me ought to have scorched the mask from my face. Hate for everything I stood for burned in her eyes, all the fiercer for how still she held herself.

When Aurus spoke, it was in his usual calm manner, and unable to keep holding Mother Li's gaze, I turned to the governor instead. Exchanging pleasantries, perhaps, each with a fixed smile, while behind them the gates stood resolutely closed. Patched, worn gates, the wood blackened around the edges. They hadn't stood long last time, the Chiltaen war machines soon battering through them and forcing the city to surrender or be slaughtered. Hopefully they would remember that and surrender rather than fight.

A frown creasing the governor's brow was the first sign of discord. Aurus's tone hadn't changed, but the man's frown deepened. He flinched. And drawing a sharp breath, Mother Li interrupted. "No." It was one of the few words I'd picked up, and though the rest of her speech meant nothing to me, her determination and refusal were clear. Whatever terms Aurus had offered were not acceptable to the Kisian dignity.

Secretary Aurus seemed untroubled, and I wondered if any amount of anger or hate could break through his calm. As he replied, Mother Li got to her feet with the speed of one who'd accidentally sat on a candle.

"Not surrendering then?" I said, glancing at the secretary.

"No, I'm—"

"Levanti?" Mother Li had been ready to stride away, but at the sound of my voice she peered closely at me.

"Yes," I said, hoping the Kisian word wouldn't sound too mangled upon my lips.

Mother Li's brows flew up. I didn't understand her next question, though it was equally penetrating.

This time it was Aurus who said "Yes," causing the governor to stare at me as intently as Mother Li. But while he just stared, she leaned over the table, palms flat upon it. I tried not to flinch or move, even as her eyes bored into mine and her lips pulled back from her teeth in a snarl. I didn't need to understand her words to feel their venom, their bite, their disgust. She finished with a final snap of fury and spat in my face. Droplets hit my mask and I gasped, and before I could shake off my shock she had thrown a final glare at Aurus and spun away, striding back toward the city gates.

"Well," Aurus said, unperturbed. "That was unexpected. However, I think it went quite well."

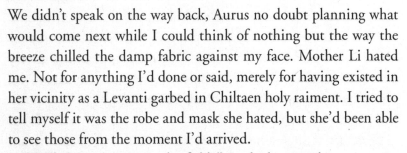

We didn't speak on the way back, Aurus no doubt planning what would come next while I could think of nothing but the way the breeze chilled the damp fabric against my face. Mother Li hated me. Not for anything I'd done or said, merely for having existed in her vicinity as a Levanti garbed in Chiltaen holy raiment. I tried to tell myself it was the robe and mask she hated, but she'd been able to see those from the moment I'd arrived.

"Will they meet us in the field?" I asked as we drew near our camp, dragging our entourage behind us.

"I believe so, yes." He glanced my way. "You must lead the soldiers into battle, but then fall back and protect yourself. I have picked some riders to act as your guards. They aren't as skilled as Levanti, I'm sure, but hopefully they will do as well until you can get yourself out of there."

"You don't think I can fight?"

"That isn't what I said. You were a Sword captain; I assume you fight extremely well, but between your injured eyes and your importance, I don't think it's wise to fight more than is absolutely necessary for the look of the thing."

We were fast approaching the edge of the camp and fast running out of time. Clearing my throat, I said, "I don't know what deal you made with Whisperer Ezma, but she threatened to take her Swords and walk away if I did not accept my position as Veld and

announce it before the battle. I had no choice but to agree; I just...
wanted to warn you."

Heedless of his horse carrying him on toward the growing noise
of the camp, Aurus stared at me, a small crease between his brows.
"Interesting," he said. "I wonder..." He trailed off, disappearing
into his own thoughts.

"You wonder?" I prompted.

He flinched, seeming to have forgotten I was there. "Thank you
for trusting me with that. Knowledge is how we best prepare for all
eventualities."

Back at the camp, everything was soon chaos. Soldiers scurried
about, messengers were sent running to the Levanti camp, and
everyone was shouting. I understood nothing of what was being
said around me; standing with Itaghai in the middle of the busy
camp was akin to a waking dream. Every now and then I caught
sight of Jass and the others reluctantly helping with the horses, but
for the most part I was alone. It didn't seem to matter how many
Chiltaen soldiers knelt before me for a blessing; I felt increasingly
invisible. I was but a robe and a mask, a lifeless white husk no one
wanted to see through. Only Mother Li, hissing her hate viciously
into my face.

Swept along upon a tide of my own decisions, we were all too
soon marching out from the camp toward Shimai. Kisian soldiers
were already on the ground. They had a strong number and would
have given the Chiltaen force trouble, but to a herd of mounted
Levanti they would be folded like bloodied paper.

I had been in many battles, had taken part in ambushes and
hunts and protected my herd on numerous occasions, never shying
from danger, yet somehow sitting at the head of a joint Levanti and
Chiltaen force outside a city we'd already conquered once made my
heart thump with a fear I'd never known. This was it. This had to
work. The future I dreamed of relied on shedding Kisian blood.

As I halted our advance and turned back to face my army, I thought of Mother Li. Of Ezma and Rah and Gideon and our herd masters back home. What Rah had never realised but Gideon had always known was that there were no gods doling out fairness, that ideals were for an ideal world, and that to hold to them when no one else did was the fastest road to death and destruction. It wasn't right, but of all the things I'd done in the service of my people, lifting my voice to lie as I led them to attack a city that had done us no harm was the easiest thing of all.

"I stand before you as Veld, chosen of the One True God," I began, and nearby Ezma's voice rose in triumphant translation. Farther away, Oshar soon added his voice to ensure everyone could hear me. "I lead you now to victory against this city, that we might take our first step toward the rebuilding of our holy empire. History is with us! Faith is with us! God is with us! This is our destiny!"

Cheers rose. Swords and bows and spears were lifted and shaken to the sky as though we challenged the gods themselves. Thunder spread upon the banging of shields and boots and hooves, connecting us all to a single cause.

Heart soaring, I turned Itaghai back toward the city and the waiting army, and upon a tide of bloodthirsty roars, we charged.

# 17. RAH

We rode south, taking care to keep our horses well rested. A well-rested horse was one ready for anything, a wise precaution when Ezma was our only certainty—where she was, how many Swords were with her, and what she was planning all unknown. With every passing moment the details seemed to matter less and less, consumed by the need to rid the Levanti of her once and for all.

Gideon rode ahead, able to call out to any Kisians we happened across in the hope of directions. It turned out that following Ezma was easy. Since she took no pains to blend in and made no attempt to hide what I'd come to think of as her crown, everyone Gideon asked could point us in the right direction.

After one such interaction with an old man out tending his pigs, we rode on a way side by side—south again. Always south. An inkling of where she had gone was beginning to gnaw at my thoughts.

"Tell me," Gideon said abruptly, pulling a bug out of Orha's mane rather than looking my way. "What are you planning to do when we find her?"

"I'm not entirely sure," I lied.

Having flicked away the offending bug, the look he threw me was sceptical at best. "You stood up to her and called a Fracturing once," he went on. "And those who wanted to listen to you already did. This time won't be any different, not now she has almost everyone turned against you."

There seemed nothing to say to that. He was right, but it didn't matter.

We rode on a little way in silence. It ought to have been companionable, but there was something more Gideon wanted to say, and it tugged at my comfort like a nagging child.

Eventually he spat it out. "She won't like you getting in her way again."

More warning than question. Thankfully, I hadn't told him about Ezma declaring a *kutum* or Derkka drugging me, or his warning would have been much stronger.

When I didn't answer, Gideon sighed. "Whatever you do, they're going to hate you for this, you know," he said, staring between his horse's ears. "If you stand up to her again. If you challenge her or kill her even in self-defence, you will carry this forever. It doesn't matter that she's exiled. It doesn't matter that she's lost her way. She's still a horse whisperer. No one has ever clashed with one like this."

Worry rippled beneath his determined calm. "It doesn't matter that someone probably needs to do it," he went on. "Whoever does will forever be branded dishonourable. You know that, don't you?"

I had been thinking about it a lot, surprised how little I cared now that anger seemed to be all I had left. "Rah Whisperer Slayer," I said, nodding with mock appreciation. "It has a nice ring to it, don't you think?"

He gave me a dry, unamused look. "I'm being serious."

"So am I."

He eyed me, brow furrowed. "Dead dead?"

"As dead as I can manage."

Gideon snorted a breathy laugh. "Rah Whisperer Slayer. Sounds ridiculous. Honestly, Rah, she's dangerous and a threat to all Levanti, but you don't have to do this. You don't need revenge for what happened with Ptapha—we can't even be sure she had anything to do with it."

I stopped Jinso in his tracks and scowled at Gideon until he too stopped, turning Orha back to face me. "Revenge has nothing to do with it," I said. "Yes, I'm angry, and it's an anger that no longer seems to subside, but she has to be dealt with, and not just because I want to. She knew about the Entrancers on the plains getting into our herd master's heads and causing mass exile; she knew, and she did nothing because it furthered her plans. Whatever those plans are, they don't involve the strengthening of the Levanti people, rather our destruction to make way for a holy empire."

"I know that," Gideon said. "But it doesn't mean you or anyone has to do anything about it."

He may as well have been speaking a different language. "What do you mean no one has to do anything about it? If we don't do anything, our people and our way of life will be gone."

"Happens to people and places all the time," he said with a shrug.

"Do you really not care?"

"Should I?" His eyebrows drew together, both rising at the outer edges like eagle wings. "It's been a long time since I felt welcome among the Levanti here, felt like I belonged. Even when I was their leader I wasn't one of them." He snorted a laugh. "Do you really think we'll go home and find it all as we left it? That we haven't changed so much that we won't be able to live *the Levanti way* anymore? Even if the Torin who came here could forgive me, I was an emperor; I can't just go back to doing whatever a herd leader says. Could you?"

What ought to have been the right answer was on my tongue in an instant, but it was a lie. Gideon had been right, back in our small hut outside Kuroshima—I didn't want to follow anyone. I wanted to be seen, to lead, to be admired for being the indomitable Sword who did what was right when everyone else failed.

Though I hadn't spoken, Gideon breathed out a soft laugh and turned Orha back the direction we'd been travelling, leaving me with my thoughts.

———◆———

In the middle of the afternoon we stopped to rest our horses. For all the chill that had been building, the day had been uncomfortably hot in the thick, soupy way Kisia carried its heat. It sapped energy faster than the dry, and despite our slow speed the horses were sweating and so were we.

We dismounted at a stream and let the horses drink their fill while we stretched tired limbs and picked at our meagre supplies. Gideon flopped down in the shade, his back against a convenient tree trunk, but I was too restless to relax. Since Gideon had asked whether I could go back to the plains and be part of a herd again, my thoughts had been whirling. I felt untethered from my sense of self, of place and purpose, yet there was something almost exciting about it. Tor's words kept repeating in my mind.

*I belong nowhere*, he had said. *But at least that means I can go anywhere and be whoever I want, beholden to no one. There's joy in that sort of freedom.*

In losing the path I'd been walking, I'd gained endless possibility, and it set my mind buzzing. I told myself I ought to feel lost and un-Levanti, that I ought to feel ashamed for having lost my herd, but it changed nothing.

"You're making me tired just listening to you stride around," Gideon grumbled, his eyes closed and his hands clasped loosely in his lap. "Sit down or go pace somewhere else."

Like my legs had been cut from beneath me, I dropped onto the ground in front of him. "I seem able to piss off everyone without trying."

He cracked open an eye. "Because you make people feel bad. You don't bend or break, and it's really frustrating but demands respect. You even challenged me for leadership of the herd, remember?"

"That's not what I meant, but yes, I remember. You weren't very happy about it."

Both eyes opened at that and he looked more tired than ever. "I'd worked hard. Sacrificed a lot. Tried to build the foundations of something new, and you couldn't see it. Of course I wasn't happy. Doesn't mean you were wrong."

"Doesn't mean you were either."

That got a chuckle and he closed his eyes again, resting his head back against the tree. Throat bared, a line of sweat made its way down his skin, and I had the sudden, intense desire to trace it with my tongue. It was as though I'd drunk too much wine. It had grown harder to ignore him, harder to avoid how I felt in his presence, and with each layer of lies about myself I stripped away, my feelings strengthened, threatening to take over.

"Get it together," I muttered to myself, dragging my gaze from his throat and his lips and the soft sweep of his hair. I ought to look about for food to add to our supplies, ought to fill our water skins and check the horses, but I didn't move.

Gideon was watching me when I looked back, his head tilted and a fine crease between his brows. "Are you talking to yourself?"

"Yes. Since you were too tired to properly berate me just now, I have to do it myself."

He shrugged. "I can berate you if you want. What do you want me to say? You're terrible with a javelin, although in your defence you hated practicing because it hurt your shoulder. You also aren't as accurate with a bow as you could be."

"You're not doing a very good job."

"All right, fine, you're a stubborn, dense fool who has made me furious more times than I can count, and you—"

He gasped and my lips were against his, pressing him back against the tree. Drunk on fatigue or hunger or *him*, I ignored his small sound of protest and slid one hand into his hair, the other down his neck, wanting to touch every part of him at once in case he suddenly ceased to be present. To be mine.

"Rah," he managed, pulling away enough to speak. "What are you doing?"

The question jolted me from my need and I stared into his eyes, hunting understanding. He looked shocked and weary, the flicker of something like my own heat there and gone, a mere figment of my imagination. What *was* I doing? This wasn't the time and I wasn't ready—neither of us was—

And now I'd forced it to the front of our minds anyway.

"I..." My voice betrayed me as a new panic bubbled up. "I..." I'd ruined our peace, like the needy child I'd always been, relying on him for things it wasn't his place to provide.

I wanted to be sick.

In an instant, I was on my feet, fighting the urge to run. I'd never run from a fight, never backed down, but somehow all it took was Gideon's blank expression to make my knees want to drop from beneath me.

"Rah," Gideon said, my name mixing in with the buzz of panicked thoughts filling my mind. "Rah?" He wasn't looking at me anymore. He had risen to a crouch and turned, one hand on the tree trunk's rough bark. "Rah, I think someone is coming."

His warning hiss broke through where my name had not. "What?" I stepped closer, trying to see what he had seen, but nothing moved beyond his chosen tree. Nothing but the sway of leaves and branches in the wind.

Gideon raised a hand. "There, hear it?"

I held my breath to listen. And there it was—voices. Heading this way. "Travellers?" I whispered, not daring to look down at him as I spoke.

"We haven't passed a road or track in the last few hours."

Yet the voices were definitely drawing closer—not loud, but a continuous stream of low conversation like a distant murmur. Footsteps followed. Heavy. Slow. The rhythm that of horses.

"Watch it," someone snapped, the words loud enough to make out. "You let that branch slap right into my face."

The reply was lost to the distance, or to the heavy thud of my heart. "Shit," I hissed.

"Shit indeed," Gideon agreed. "Levanti probably aren't a good sign at this point."

"No."

Either they were just happening to go the same way, also in search of Ezma, or they were following us. Neither heralded Levanti I wanted to meet in a shadowy Kisian glade.

"Let's get out of here," I said, looking around for Jinso and Orha. Orha was drinking from the nearby stream, but Jinso had followed a trail of grass a little way into the trees. To call him or whistle would give our presence away. "Shit," I whispered again. "Get our bags, take Orha, and get out of here as fast as you can. I'll be right behind you."

I sped off on light steps across the damp grass, gaze flitting from Jinso to the trees and back. Even over my movement, I could hear the approaching Levanti. They weren't making any attempt to hide their presence, and while they weren't yet close enough to recognise any voices, there were at least three of them.

"There!" one cried out, louder still. "The tracks start again there, look."

"Fresh too. We must be close."

The excitement drew Jinso's attention from his grass and then to me as I neared, holding up a hand to keep him calm. But the voices had ceased now, replaced with the sound of rapid movement through the undergrowth, and Jinso backed even as I reached for his bridle.

"There they are!"

I spun as four riders burst into the glade, snapping thin branches from the tree Gideon had been leaning against. Thankfully he had made it to Orha, bags slung over his shoulder.

"Go!" I shouted.

If we both mounted now and tried to run they'd give chase, but there was still time for Gideon to get away if I kept them busy. I let go of Jinso's bridle. "Shenyah e'Jaroven," I called, walking toward the group. "And Rorshe e'Bedjuti. To what do we owe this great pleasure?"

The young Jaroven and her three companions, only one of whom I recognised, reined in. "You're not as funny as you think you are, *Captain*," she sneered. "You know why we're here."

"To apologise?"

Rorshe spat upon the grass and jabbed a finger at Gideon, who hadn't mounted, hadn't run. He'd attached the bags to Orha's saddle and now stood watching, arms loose by his sides. "That man is a blight upon all Levanti," Rorshe said. "And it is our solemn duty as Swords to protect our people from such curses. He cannot be allowed to lead anyone astray again."

They might have been my own words, spitting hatred toward Ezma as I followed her south with only one goal in mind, but where I had made the right judgement, they had not.

I drew my blade, arm steady. "You really think I'll let you take him this time?"

"Oh no," Shenyah said, leaping out of her saddle with ease. "We're hoping you'll fight so we can kill you both. You have proven yourself to be little better, Rah e'Torin. We should have listened to Whisperer Ezma the first time she warned us about you."

It was their hatred I faced, yet Ezma's name that sent cold anger roaring through me. She had wanted me dead because I'd been in the way; now, whether she'd explicitly sent these Swords after me or not, she was the reason they were here. Here with one purpose in mind. But in the choice between life and death, I'd chosen life again and again, and I would do it now even if it meant the lives of four more Swords. It ought to have been a difficult decision; I ought to have tried to talk to them first, to negotiate, but as the other three dismounted and drew their blades I just wanted them dead. I would beg no mercy from Swords twisted to Ezma's path.

"Rah..." Gideon said, his sentence hanging unfinished.

"Yeah, well, you should have run when you had the chance," I said, keeping my gaze hooked to the advancing Swords.

"You know I was never going to do that. You wouldn't have."

I let go a breathy laugh. "No, I wouldn't have."

"Well?" Shenyah said, standing to the fore as the group formed a small semicircle around us. "Are you going to give up quietly? Or make this fun?"

She held Dishiva's bow firm and ready, the fingers of her free hand itching to reach for an arrow. Rorshe adjusted his grip and shifted into a defensive stance, eyes unblinking, but the unknown Sword closest to me still had his guard down.

I lunged into motion, sprinting the half-dozen steps to the nameless one. Keeping low in case his instincts kicked in, I slid past, blade held firm as its edge cut into cloth and skin and flesh. Someone shouted. A strangled cry rasped from the man's throat and he staggered back, just as something whistled overhead, so close the shifting air caressed my scalp.

"Fuck!" Shenyah was reaching for another arrow as I spun, footsteps halting midcharge as I dodged one blade and parried another, all instinct. Time blurred, slow and fast all at once as I defended myself from Rorshe and the second nameless one's jabs, both men baring their teeth in hate. Somewhere behind them, Shenyah went on shouting. "You ruined everything, Gideon! We lost everything because of you, and now you don't even have the decency to face me!"

I fought the urge to turn and hunt the silence behind me. Had he run?

"Ha!" Shenyah barked as I narrowly missed a slice down my arm, so close it could have taken skin. "I ought to have known you would just keep hiding behind Rah. Fight your own battles, you coward!"

A step. The shifting of fabric. The sense of warmth and breath no matter how imagined. To turn and be sure would be to take a blade through the gut, so I went on parrying and dodging and side-stepping, each movement bringing me closer to the moment my body would flag. Yet I could do no more with two of them on me, intently focussed. Until Rorshe's gaze flitted over my shoulder— that the final assurance I needed that Gideon hadn't run at all.

"Rah, go left."

The strength of Gideon's command seemed to reach deep inside me to a trust we'd once had, always able to be sure where the other was in the heat of any battle. It had been years. Too many. Yet on his word I went left, lunging at a dangerous opening in Rorshe's guard that would leave my right side unprotected. My blade slid into Rorshe's gut, and every second I pushed deeper I knew Nameless's blade was just about to skewer me through the side, leaving Rorshe and I coming to the same bloody end.

A body hit the ground. Panic spiked through my veins, and lifting a foot I kicked Rorshe off my blade and turned, a demand to know if Gideon was all right already parting my lips. The question went unspoken. Nameless lay spilling blood through his gashed throat, coating the grass.

"This is over. Done," Gideon called to Shenyah, bloody sword still in hand. "Go before we have to farewell four souls."

She had an arrow nocked. Her hands trembled as she pulled back the string. "Fuck you!"

Shenyah loosed. Gideon shoved me hard, and I hit the ground, pain pulsing through me to end in the all too familiar spike in my ear. It made me never want to move again, but at the rattle of another arrow being drawn from its quiver, I rolled.

The stabbing ear pain made me want to retch, but I leapt to my feet, the clearing spinning as Shenyah came into focus. Too far away to reach her before she loosed again, but my fury owned only one instinct and I charged. Letting out a guttural roar made of pain and anger, I sped toward her, no thought of what I would do when I got there except tear her apart. She could have loosed an arrow through me, and I wouldn't have slowed.

Shenyah lowered the bow and ran. She was quick, but I had a head start, thundering after her like a single-minded predator.

"Rah!" Gideon shouted, his voice emerging through gritted teeth. "Let her go!"

The plea planted my feet and I spun back, leaving Shenyah's footsteps to crash on into the trees. Gideon knelt near the fallen bodies, his face tilted to the sky and blood covering his arm.

"Shit." I hurried back, dazed and with my ear still throbbing its complaints.

"Just let her go," Gideon repeated when I drew near. He hadn't moved, face still skyward, baring the ridges of his throat as he had before I'd forced that kiss upon him. Not the time to worry about it, yet as I knelt at his side to look at his arm, the memory kept forcing itself to the front of my mind.

"You're losing a lot of blood," I said, ignoring his pained hiss as I lifted the edge of his torn sleeve. "But it doesn't look too deep. Did you take the arrow out?"

That made him fix his attention on me rather than the sky. "No, what kind of idiot do you think I am? The damn thing tore right past, ripping flesh like I'd been bitten by an animal."

"It needs sewing, but we can't stay here in case she comes back."

As I got to my feet, Gideon nodded in the direction of the bodies. "What about their heads?"

I looked at the three Swords who'd come to end our lives. Would they have given us the honour?

"Leave them," I said. "Shenyah will be back for her horse and she can do it, since it's her fault they died." Pulling a length of rope from one of our packs, I tied a makeshift torniquet above Gideon's wound and pulled it tight. "Come on," I said, nudging him toward Orha. "We need to get out of here in case she comes back with more friends."

With a nod and a long string of hisses, Gideon let me help him into the saddle.

———◆———

An hour later, Gideon tumbled from his saddle. He landed on his knees and rolled, mud smearing the fabric I'd tied around his arm. My own pains had been exacerbated by the brief ride, but with no one else to help, I got to work. I propped Gideon against a broad tree trunk and went scouting for firewood. No Hand, no herd, just the two of us in the Kisian wilds far from home or safety. I kept moving. No one else could build a fire. No one else could gather water. Or food. Or clean and sew Gideon's wound. There was just me, and so I worked.

Fire. Water. Food. There wasn't time to hunt, so I gathered some of the mushrooms Miko had cooked back in the hills and dug out dry rice cakes from Jinso's pack. And between every task, I checked on Gideon. Pale, but still with me.

It was early evening by the time I had water heating over the fire.

Without a pot, I'd resorted to building a cone of sticks to hang a waterskin over the flames. It would probably ruin the skin and the water wouldn't boil, but warm water was better than nothing.

"All right, time for the fun part," I said, setting a hand upon Gideon's shoulder. His eyelids fluttered open. "I'm sure you've been waiting your whole life for me to stick a needle into you over and over again, and finally here we are. My turn to leave a mark on you with my excellent stitching."

"Do you have to?"

"Yes. I'm not just doing this for fun. Let's move closer to the fire."

"You built a fire already?" He blinked hazily, his words thick.

"No, I was feeling lazy so I used my magic powers, but magic fire is far warmer than normal fire anyway. Come closer and see."

He narrowed a suspicious look my way. "Are you making fun of me?"

"No, I'm trying to keep the mood from getting despondent by employing ridiculous horseshit; now come near the fucking fire so I can do my job."

That moved him. He shuffled toward the flames, grimacing and gritting his teeth at every movement and arriving with the appearance of a man who was about to be sick. "Excellent," I said. "Now how do you feel about sitting up while I do this? It will be easier if you do, but if you're planning to pass out on me then maybe not."

"This is hardly my first time."

"That's what everyone says."

The confusion that creased his features and parted his lips was so glorious that I grinned despite everything. "I'm going to try to take your tunic off without having to cut it because it's already too cold around here, but I'm not sure how well that'll go."

He nodded, and helping where he could, we wrestled through the slow peeling away of his tunic, caught to his skin by dried sweat and dirt and blood. With much pained hissing on his part, the wound in his arm was soon laid bare before me. It could have been worse, I reminded myself as I examined it, it could have been deeper, or through the centre of his arm, or his back, or his throat. He could already be dead. But it could have been better too. It could have not happened, or have happened near a healer so someone else could do this part.

Seeming to follow my thoughts, he said, "How long has it been since you sewed anyone up?"

"You don't want me to answer that."

"Oh. Good. Where did you find the needle and thread?"

"Diha gave it to me," I said, extracting the small healing pouch from Jinso's saddlebag. "Because I tend to get hurt when I do foolish things."

Taking a strip of fabric from the pouch, I dusted it with salt and poured warm water over it, inordinately proud of the very makeshift healer's cloth I had contrived. Gideon eyed it with disfavour. He didn't complain, just gritted his teeth as I began cleaning his wound. It had been a couple of hours, and some blood had crusted in an attempt to scab, but the cut was too long and deep for that to be enough. So once it was clean, I took out the needle. Taking my time, I held first one end and then the other to the flames, singeing the tips of my fingers.

All Swords learned how to tend basic wounds, but while many went on to learn more and a few were taught by a herd's healers, I had never been interested.

"You need a longer tail of thread than that," Gideon said as I threaded the needle. "Here."

I held it out and he pulled more thread through the eye until he was satisfied. "If you're not sure how much, go with the length of your arm. More than that will get tangled."

"You are welcome to do it yourself if you prefer."

"No. I trust you."

He closed his eyes and let out a breath, keeping his arm propped loosely upon his knee. I set the needle to his skin. Moved it. Decided a little to the left would be a better place to start. Changed my mind. Thought of Yitti and wanted to scream. Gideon didn't tell me to hurry, even if he wanted to.

He grunted when at last I pressed the curved needle into his skin, but he neither flinched nor opened his eyes. I'd forgotten how thick flesh felt, the resistance like warmed leather yet with the unique reminders it still lived. The seeping of blood. The shifting of his hairs and the dimpling of his skin whenever a cold wind blew. And the deep pulse of his heart beneath my fingers as I gripped his arm tight.

Gideon was good to his word and didn't faint though I worked slowly and carefully, not having the confidence of Tep or Yitti or Diha to work any faster or to think of anything beyond where the next stitch would go. When at last I was done, I cleaned my handiwork and took the last of the fabric strips from the pouch to bind it tightly. And when that was done, I breathed for what felt like the first time since we had stopped. For now, there was nothing I needed to do. It wouldn't last, but when Gideon lay down, a cloak thrown over him like a blanket, I just sat and enjoyed not needing to move. Not needing to think. Not even needing to listen to the sounds of my Swords and wonder how much longer they would trust me to lead them.

We weren't safe enough for us both to sleep, so I sat at Gideon's side, nibbling on charred mushrooms and staring at the flames. Beside me, Gideon's breathing evened as he fell into a deep sleep, and I soon found myself staring at him instead of the fire. At the shallow crease between his brows. At the mahogany sweep of his growing hair and the patchy stubble around his chin. At the dark notch between his collarbones and the curve of his neck and the long fingers gripping the edge of his makeshift blanket. And little by little, a heavy sadness crept over me. Not the unwelcome sort, but the sort that comes with understanding, with acknowledgement of something long denied.

"Gideon," I whispered to see if he would wake. Even at the sound of his name he went on sleeping, that crease between his brows ever-present. I touched his hair, letting the soft threads slide through my fingers, and still he did not wake. "I'm not ready for you to know," I said, my heart hammering. "But...I love you. I think I've always loved you; I just got very good at telling myself you were my friend. My hero. My brother." I heaved a deep breath. "That's why I kissed you when I shouldn't have, and I'm sorry."

He made no reply. Around us the forest went on buzzing with evening life. Nothing changed, and yet despite everything, I felt a little lighter.

## 18. MIKO

Minister Oyamada tapped his fingers on the lap table that was the only piece of furniture left in my tent. At least he'd stopped pacing the short distance space allowed.

"If Your Majesty would please sit still," asked the maid behind me for the dozenth time. She was no imperial-trained dresser, but a one-time maid to a rich merchant's wife was better than trying to do my hair myself, or asking Oyamada to do it. Imagining him trying to set pins in my hair and getting increasingly frustrated made me smile.

"I cannot promise my best work if Your Majesty will not sit still."

"Her Majesty is merely nervous," Oyamada said, continuing his rhythmic tapping. "You are dressing her for a wedding after all."

"And I have no lap table to drum on since His Excellency has commandeered it," I said.

Minister Oyamada's fingers stilled abruptly. "Mere boredom, Your Majesty."

I made to turn a satirical look on him, only to stop myself. The maid clicked her tongue and went on working.

For a short time, we sat in silence while the woman worked, until the silence became as unbearable as his tapping had been. "You know Manshin better than many," I said, taking care not to even twitch as I spoke. "What do you really think he'll do?"

"As I've said before, I'm not sure," Oyamada replied, brushing his dry, wrinkled hand over the small tabletop. "He's both a very predictable man and one who will do...unexpected things. No doubt the combination is what makes him an excellent general, staid but with a flair for the occasional surprise."

"That isn't very comforting," I said, gritting my teeth against the pain of pulled hair and sharp pins.

"I wasn't aware Your Majesty was after comfort; were that the case you perhaps ought not to have asked what I think Ryo will do. You are about to embarrass him in front of a lot of important people."

I drew a deep breath and let it out slowly, but all the tension in my body remained. I was about to ride to a wedding pavilion and destroy his attempted alliance with Dom Villius not only by claiming Sichi as my wife, but also by completing my own deal with the Chiltaen religious leader. Many things could go wrong. Manshin could try to arrest me. Dom Villius could turn on me despite the agreement Cassandra had brokered. Even Cassandra might yet turn out to be trouble if that second voice of hers got in the way.

I bit my lip. "Are the others ready to go? Dom Villius's brother and Cassandra, I mean."

"We've commandeered a palanquin and four carriers so they can go unseen on the journey," Oyamada said, returning to his tapping and giving me the urge to snap his fingers. "Whether they are ready or not to depart seems irrelevant. It's not as though either needs to be finely dressed or make a grand appearance."

"No, but I wouldn't want to present a prisoner in filthy clothes or looking as though he had been poorly treated. Especially not one who looks exactly like Dom Villius—something it would also be good if everyone could see."

"Very well, Your Majesty. Before we depart, I will ensure neither of our...guests has a dirty face."

I gave him a look, earning another cluck from the maid. "You had better tell me, Minister, if you think I am making a big mistake. You are fast running out of chances."

Oyamada sighed, fabric rustling as he shook his head. "No, Your Majesty, I do not think you are making a big mistake, but we seem doomed to troubling times in which there is no safe path through anything. Truly, I ought never to have left Ts'ai! To think, I could be even now sitting in my library with a roaring fire and warmed wine."

"Instead, we're about to do something that cannot be taken back," I said. "Which could be either the beginning of something new and powerful, or the beginning of the end."

"Succinct and depressing, Your Majesty." He groaned with effort as he got to his feet. "I'll go check everything is ready. I do hope you don't mean to take too much longer about Her Majesty's hair," he added to the maid. "We are running out of time."

On that admonition, he swept from the tent, demands for updates already issuing from his lips.

After having sat for what felt like hours having my hair brushed and tugged and knotted and pinned, the task was done all too soon, the maid's departure leaving me sitting alone in my tent. I was ready to go, yet to stand up and step outside would be to set my feet upon a path I could never walk back. I laughed humourlessly into the flickering light. That had been true for a long time and would go on being true for the rest of my life. There was no point in delaying that inevitability to stay invisible and safe, succumbing to a mere mirage constructed of canvas.

I got to my feet, muscles sore after kneeling for so long in one place. Outside, the camp was full of noise and activity, horses neighing and bridles clinking as the small contingent of guards Edo had provided organised themselves into my escort. With a deep breath, I stepped out into the bright sunlight to face yet another fight I refused to run from.

"Captain," I said, catching Captain Kiren's attention. "Are we ready to depart?"

He gestured at the gathered group of soldiers. "Whenever you are, Your Majesty. We weren't able to find enough horses for everyone to ride, but since we have to keep to the palanquin's pace it hardly matters."

Minister Oyamada had been busy. Along with the palanquin, horses, and ongoing supplies, he had even managed to find some crimson surcoats and belts, sashes and banners. With half of my soldiers riding and the other half on foot, and with a glorious if faded palanquin in tow, my arrival would be impossible to miss.

"If you're ready, Your Majesty, we can set forth," the captain said, breaking in upon my imaginings of making a grand scene.

"Almost," I said. "First I need your assistance strapping on my bow sheath and quiver."

His cheeks reddened. "Surely such a task ought to be done by a..." Captain Kiren trailed off into a grimace.

"Exactly so, Captain. This camp is not only sadly lacking in women, but especially lacking in women who know how such things work."

A wry smile broke through his discomfort. "True enough, Your Majesty, but are you sure you wish to carry your bow? It is not customary for weapons to be carried with ceremonial robes, especially not to a wedding."

"That's no problem since I'm hardly a customary emperor. Do it and we may go, before the ceremony starts without us."

Managing only a nod, the captain set about tightening and tying the straps on my sheath, making sure that despite the mountains of silk I wore, Hacho would stand straight and tall and my quiver wouldn't shake. It took longer than it ought with Captain Kiren being not only meticulous but careful not to touch me any more than was absolutely required to get the task done. When at last he stepped back with a satisfied nod, I was ready.

The journey to the pavilion was slow going, the palanquin carriers struggling to keep pace with the weight of two passengers and the seemingly endless patches of boggy ground. Stringent complaints emerged from behind the vehicle's curtains every time there was a rough bump or one of the men adjusted his grip and nearly dropped a corner. It wasn't helping, but at least Cassandra's voice reassured me she hadn't made a run for it, taking my valuable prisoner with her.

When at last we joined the road, our pace evened and the complaints from inside the palanquin subsided. At my side, Captain Kiren maintained silence all the way, focussed on getting me to the pavilion safely so I could focus on what I would do when I got there. Sichi and I had talked it over again and again, but too much relied on Manshin's response to my arrival. Would I be allowed in? It seemed impossible to refuse the empress of Kisia entry when everything would be seen by the noble guests. It would be even more dangerous to attack me, yet I couldn't set aside the fear he would do just that, damn the consequences. With the right lies he could probably get away with it.

Despite my inner turmoil, the gods had provided a beautiful day for a wedding. It wasn't warm, but the sun shone bright in the crisp air, and at any other time I would have enjoyed the slow ride and taken in the scenery. Instead I chafed at our pace and wanted to arrive both at once and never. I could not even lose my thoughts in the dour rhythm of our horses' hooves or the dance of birds enjoying the sunshine. My fears lived too close. Without Oyamada, without even Tor or Nuru for support, success or failure hung upon my shoulders alone.

The closer we got to our destination the more sick I felt, until the peak of the pavilion roof came into sight upon the horizon and determination hardened around me like armour. I would not let anyone make me afraid.

I touched Hacho at my shoulder. "I hope you're ready," I said, thinking of my father. He would not have been afraid.

"Ready for any outcome," Captain Kiren said, breaking our silence. "And it looks like, despite our setbacks, we've arrived in good time."

Once the home of a grand shrine, the plain south of Kuroshima now held a pavilion that, even at first sight, looked like a collection of hastily assembled parts. People the size of ants seemed to be milling around outside; many were dull coloured—most likely soldiers—while the rest shone and twinkled in a variety of bright colours.

As we approached, a group of the dull soldier ants broke away from the rest, heading our way. I drew a deep breath. "Here we go."

A guest sure of their welcome might have slowed to greet the incoming men, but I maintained my pace, the pavilion growing larger as we neared. Behind the clump of soldiers, guests in a variety of coloured robes were stepping out of carriages and being helped from palanquins—prolonged war having done little to change the way the nobility chose to present themselves. The marriage of a new emperor's daughter was not to be missed if one wanted to ensure influence for their family. One by one they turned to stare at our arrival. We were on show, and I drew myself up in the saddle and tried to look as Emperor Kin had—like he owned everything he laid eyes upon.

"Halt there!" called a soldier striding to meet us. "What is your business here?"

Any louder and some of the guests might have heard him. Already we had quite the audience watching on, pointing and chattering.

"This is Her Majesty Empress Miko Ts'ai," Captain Kiren returned, and one of the soldiers before us visibly flinched. "On what authority do you command your empress to halt her progress?"

"On the orders of His Imperial Majesty Emperor Ryo Manshin."

"Her Majesty's heir?" the captain said in the haughtiest voice I'd ever heard come from his lips. "Does not something seem odd about that to you, given here Her Majesty sits, very clearly alive? I recommend you step aside. Now."

Ill-ease rippled through the group. There were only a dozen of them, and none were mounted, but while I would not hesitate to fight my way through them, with so many people watching it would have to be clear they'd struck the first blow. So, lifting my chin, I said, "We must continue on, Captain. It is ill-mannered even for an empress to be late for a wedding."

"Indeed, Your Majesty." At that he clicked his tongue and set his horse walking. I let him pull ahead to clear the way, holding my breath as he reached the line of enemy soldiers. Time seemed to still as both he and Manshin's men held their ground, and a flash of memory took me back to General Kitado lying on the side of the road in the rain, having given his life to protect me. A cry hung silent on my tongue, and I reached out, like I could pull Captain Kiren back, saving him where I'd failed to save Kitado.

Then the line broke and I let my breath go. Manshin's soldiers stepped aside just enough to let Captain Kiren through, but they remained close and glaring as I approached, swallowing a sob of relief. Once I had passed through the fire of their dislike, the group dispersed to watch on from a distance, no doubt wondering how Manshin would respond to their failure to keep me out. Too many witnesses. Too much talk.

For all its hodgepodge architecture, the closer we drew to the pavilion, the more it loomed with menace. My guards seemed to feel it too, the relieved chatter that had followed the retreat of Manshin's soldiers soon fading into a tense silence.

From the grand pavilion entrance, a path of folded paper prayers led back to a pair of mounting stones. There, guests recently alighted from carriages and palanquins milled around exchanging greetings before ambling along the prayer path to the stairs. All talk faded and all eyes turned as we approached. "Captain Kiren," I said, reining in my horse. "Have half of your men remain with the horses and the other half stay with the palanquin." As I spoke the faded silk box was set down upon one of the mounting stones, causing necks to crane. "They remain here until required," I added. "That is, *if* they are required."

A final check of my bow and blade, and I dismounted as gracefully as I could, down into the crowd of guests with eyes for no one else. A wave of bows rippled through the group, followed by respectful murmurs of "Your Majesty," and upon that tide of reverence I floated along the path with Captain Kiren a step behind me, leaving whispering in our wake.

Servants stood at the base of the stairs, but though they bowed deeply and welcomed me, it was General Moto who caught my gaze. Standing in the doorway, he seemed merely to be overseeing the orderly arrival of all the guests, yet he came forward as I mounted the bottom step. "Your Majesty, I—"

"I seem not to be the only one you are calling Majesty now, General. Excuse me."

"Your Majesty," he repeated as I reached the top step. "You cannot carry a bow into—"

"Cannot?" I rounded on him. "The only thing I cannot do is accept traitors, General."

I walked on, heart racing as clumps of Kisian nobility stepped aside. I knew most by sight, but it was an odd feeling, like I was looking at people I'd once met in the illustrated pages of a past life.

With every step, paper prayers crumpled beneath my feet, while all around me winks of light reflected off jewels. The whole space seemed full to bursting with lantern light and braziers, incense and storm flowers. And people. People whose eyes darted from me to the far end of the room, where a throne had been ensconced—the blasphemy of a throne in a sacred space not seeming to trouble my former minister perched upon it.

The crowd grew quiet, the feeling that even the room was holding its breath taking me back to the day Tanaka had stood before Emperor Kin. Then as now, a guest who had arrived before me stepped forward to bow, yet despite their obeisance Manshin paid them no heed. Over the nobleman's curved back, Manshin and I stared at one another, both determined to show no emotion. No surprise. No anger. Whatever happened now, the story would spread faster than any wildfire.

When the nobleman arose from his bow, it was into the sort of silence than pulls at you like a current. He looked around, and his face paled at sight of me. Upon the throne, Manshin seemed to be waiting for me to speak, to attack, no doubt so he could hold the defensive high ground against the over-emotional woman. I shot him a challenging smile. My presence was attack enough. The next move was his.

Turning away, I walked on through the crowd. Away from the throne sat an altar laid with a white sash. Rows of silk cushions sat facing it, a few already occupied by men and women determined to get the best view. Many had small tea bowls in their hands, and they were chatting amongst themselves like a flock of important chickens.

"Do you wish me to acquire you the frontmost spot, Your Majesty?" Captain Kiren said, his voice little more than a whisper at my side.

I turned, murmuring my reply into my shoulder. "No, I will remain standing."

"Ah." The word had a grim tone, and I couldn't keep the flash of a mischievous smile from my lips.

"You're quite right, General. My choice has nothing at all to do with being able to escape more easily."

The stream of arriving guests began to slow, and little by little talk buried the silence that had accompanied my arrival. People still threw glances my way or took pains to keep their distance, but the sense of impending danger no longer held them prisoner. I could not let myself sink into such ease, however. I'd made my move, and now it was time for Manshin to counter—it was just a matter of when.

Granting many smiles and nods, I wound my way through the crowd of guests, even stopping a few minutes here and there to exchange words with people I recognised. Many members of Emperor Kin's court had been lost in Koi, but in Kisia there was always someone waiting to replace a fallen lord. No one asked me why there were two emperors in the room or why they had heard I died; the peace seemed too fragile. Smiles and bows and compliments of robes were all that it allowed, and sinking into the vapidity I made a full circuit of the room. There was no sign of either Sichi or Dom Villius—no doubt both somewhere deeper inside the pavilion getting ready for Manshin's big show.

"Captain?" I said as a general move toward the cushions began. "Have you seen any Chiltaens at all?"

"No, Your Majesty. Not one."

With guests bowing and nodding as they flooded past us, there was no time to say more, only to wonder whether anyone else thought it odd that Dom Villius had brought none of his countrymen to his own wedding ceremony.

In a storm of clacking sandals and swishing silks, the gathered nobility of Kisia knelt upon the cushions, a few glances all that were thrown at me, standing at the back of the room. Upon assured steps, Manshin rose and made his way toward the altar, everything about his demeanour seeming to deny my existence.

As though triggered by his movement, a pair of sliding doors opened and Dom Villius stepped out, accompanied by a second figure—a man in the white mask of a Chiltaen priest. I had known Dom Villius would be present, yet still I flinched at sight of him, thinking of all the things Sichi and Nuru had told me he was capable of.

Perhaps reading my thoughts, his gaze swung my way, and he acknowledged my presence with a nod and a smile that was almost a smirk. I could only hope such beneficence meant he intended to keep our bargain. Were there no Chiltaens present except his priest because he'd already sent his army home?

"If you cause trouble," a deep voice whispered in my ear, "you will regret it."

Manshin stepped back, but I could still feel the warmth of his breath on my skin and supressed a shudder. For an instant that seemed to stretch into eternity, we met each other's hard stare, the rest of the room ceasing to exist. Hate lived in his dark eyes, disdain in the lines about his mouth, both giving the lie to his eventual smile. "We can talk after the ceremony," he said. "After all, Kisia must come first."

On those words, he lifted his chin and walked on toward the altar. There Dom Villius stood, eyes on me though everyone else had once again turned at the opening of the sliding doors. Sichi stepped through, gloriously attired in one of the finest robes I had ever seen, its lilac silk lavishly embroidered and set with jewels. Despite the fear we surely both carried, she looked both serene and beautiful, smiling upon the gathered audience before gliding forward.

"Ah, my daughter," Manshin said, greeting her with every sign of being a doting father. "Dom Villius. Father Tawo." The priest bowed deeply, and with everyone and everything now in place, my heart started to thud fast and heavy. Manshin had said I would regret making a scene, but he hadn't considered how much more I would regret doing nothing.

"It is with great honour that I welcome you," Manshin began, addressing the gathered nobility. "To witness the marriage of my daughter, Lady Sichi Manshin, to His Eminence Dom Leo Villius of Chiltae, the sealing of a treaty long overdue."

I cleared my throat. "Of what treaty do you speak, Lord Manshin?" I said, stepping forward into a sea of staring eyes.

From beside the altar, Manshin's jaw set in warning. "The treaty making peace with Chiltae, of course."

"I have signed no treaty. I have signed nothing. I have not even been presented with the terms of such a treaty to consider."

"It is customary for an imperial council to take care of such things." It was almost a croon, but his eyes darted toward the stairs where General Moto stood. "This is hardly the time to contest it."

I glanced at Sichi, her small nod and smile a burst of warmth that eased the tension in my chest. I took another step forward. "Surely this is the best time, Lord Manshin, before anyone is made to go through with this farce of a wedding."

Excited whispers spread through the crowd, all hauteur thrown to the wind. Before the end of the day, half the empire would have heard the story of this momentous occasion.

"You agreed to this wedding—"

"No, I did not," I interrupted, the power of that truth seeming to lift me from my body. "What honour would there be in begging peace with our aggressors? Or in agreeing to the marriage of my own wife to another?"

Sharp gasps swallowed the whispers and air fled the room. Heads turned toward Sichi, who stood smiling beside her father as his face reddened.

"Married to Sichi?" he said. "What nonsense is this? You're a woman."

"It's not nonsense," Sichi said, turning to the priest. "Father Tawo, you must be aware such a thing is legal, and if you're not I can recite many precedents. Such as the marriage of Lady Chimiki and Kaeko—"

"That will not be necessary, my lady—"

"Your Majesty," Sichi corrected, causing Manshin to scoff. On his other side, Dom Villius stood glassy-eyed like a man stuffed. No wedding guests could have paid for better entertainment. Mama had taught me to be careful of what I let people see, to protect my dignity like it was a fragile bird, but she had also taught me to be ruthless.

The priest cleared his throat amid rising chatter. "That will not be necessary, *Your Majesty*," he corrected. "It is not often done and is not encouraged, but the precedent has long been established, and the law is sound."

"What?" Manshin hissed, an eye upon their audience. "Then you must annul it at once."

Again the priest cleared his throat. "I'm afraid the only grounds upon which I can do so are if one or other is already married—"

"Which is not the case," Sichi said, seeming not to even notice the noble guests leaning hungrily closer to hear her every word. "Since you already had my marriage to Gideon e'Torin annulled."

"If one or other was coerced against their will—"

"Which we were not."

"Or the sevenday wasn't consummated," the priest finished.

Manshin barked a laugh. "Well, since they can't do that, it is—"

"Can't?" Sichi's voice rang with challenge. "Unless you want your affairs spread all over the empire, I recommend you take my word for it rather than ask for details here."

"You are the one bringing shame on our family again," he snarled low. "You are marrying Dom Villius right now or—"

At the sound of his name, Dom Villius seemed to come to life, drawing his absent stare away from me and swinging it Sichi's way. "It would seem that we are not to be married today after all, Lady Sichi. Allow me to express my…disappointment. Both at this outcome and that it may now be some time before our treaty is recognised." He turned back my way. "A fine play, Your Majesty."

"You see what struggles this Otako usurper seeks to bring upon us?" Manshin said, spreading his arms like crimson wings as he stepped forward, speaking to the gathered nobility now. "She seeks to destroy any chance at peace and plunge us back into endless war for nothing."

I smiled through the angry murmuring. "You mean I will not grovel to our enemies, will not accept peace if the price is not only our land but also our honour. Captain?" I kept my eyes locked to Manshin as I spoke. "Have my guest brought in at once."

"Yes, Your Majesty."

With a bow he spun away, leaving me standing alone before the stares, some curious, others laced with anger. Dom Villius possessed the only smile, an amused, curious thing that was more chilling than Manshin's glares. Behind him, his masked priest stood unmoving—an ominous statue.

"If you will excuse me, Father," Sichi said, nodding to the priest before making her way through the still kneeling guests, the skirt of her robe brushing shoulders as she passed. Manshin made to grab her hand, only to think better of it, his scowl following her instead. He nodded to General Moto, still standing near the door, and with talk once again rising from the audience, I could feel the moment slipping from my grasp. People would talk about this day for a long time, but embarrassing Manshin would mean nothing if I couldn't prove myself more worthy at the same time.

Captain Kiren hadn't returned, so I cleared my throat and spoke over the growing noise. "You do, I hope, intend to hold up your part in our understanding, Dom Villius."

"And what part might that be, Your Majesty?" came his cold reply, silencing the room more completely than I had managed.

"Your brother," I said, pushing on though my heart seemed to fill my throat. "In return for the removal of your soldiers from our lands." Without awaiting a reply, I turned a triumphant smile Manshin's way. "You see, Lord Manshin, there are many roads to peace that do not leave Kisia weak and poor."

A parade of expressions crossed his face before he buried them all beneath a cold, regal smile. "I think we are all quite tired of this petty farce you have thrown us into, child. We might as well all go and enjoy the waiting food and music, wedding or no."

His words animated some of the guests like magic, the promise of food pulling many a lord and lady from their silk cushion. Talk swelled, and clenching my hands to fists, I turned again in search of Captain Kiren. A few guests were already stepping out, lingering glances thrown back my way, but there was no sign of the captain or Unus.

"You ought to have heeded my warning," Manshin growled, and I turned back to find him all too close. "I will not let you get in my way."

"No? Planning to send thugs after me again?" My hands shook. "You can threaten me all you like; it won't make this alliance you're planning any wiser. I warned you weeks ago, and now I've just saved you from having to hear me say that I told you so."

He barked a laugh, drawing the attention of a passing lord, who stared at us with interest. "You think you've won something?" he hissed, lowering his voice. "You may have drawn Edo onto your side and made me look like a fool today, but Kisia's generals still fight for me. I will have your marriage annulled, and Sichi will marry Dom Villius. And no, I will not send thugs after you, not after this. You walked in here a free woman, but you will leave a prisoner to be executed for treason. Moto!"

"With so many people watching?" I asked. "What reason do you intend to give?"

"Need I give more than the treason of striding in here and ruining Kisia's future? Mot—"

Manshin's jaw dropped, and I spun to see what had caught his eye. General Moto hadn't moved from the doorway, seemed not to have heard his emperor's command at all. His gaze was fixed upon Captain Kiren or, more accurately, to the man shuffling in his wake.

"But that's..." Manshin turned back to where Dom Villius stood to find he hadn't moved, yet here was a man with an identical face entering with my captain. "How...?"

"Ah, here he is at last," I said as guests stopped making for the door to stare. "Dom Villius, will you honour our bargain? Your brother in return for peace?"

"No," Cassandra said, appearing in Unus's wake. "You can't give him up."

"Cassandra, wait outside," I said. "This is not your concern. Dom Villius? Your answer?"

A collection of lords and ladies stared at him, and Manshin seemed to be trying to burn a hole through his skull with a look, but Dom Villius had eyes only for Unus. "My army removed from Kisia," he said, "is a small price to pay for my brother's life."

Cassandra snorted. "Literally, since you mean to kill him. Miko, you can't let him—"

"Your Majesty?" Captain Kiren said.

Manshin joined in the rising chorus demanding my attention. "This is ridiculous. Moto, get them all out of here."

But as talk swirled around me, full of demands and opinions that thickened the air, another sound rose outside. Hoofbeats. In the distance, someone shouted. Having remained in the doorway, General Moto descended the few steps in search of answers.

"General Moto," Manshin repeated amid the questions some of the lords were throwing Dom Villius's way, one even going so far as to prod Unus as though doubting he was real. Dom Villius ignored it all, trying to push through the thickening chaos to reach his twin, but like a nightmare that wouldn't end, Cassandra—or Kaysa—kept putting herself in his way.

"Let him go, Cassandra, please!" I said, finding my voice. "This is the only way. This is the deal I made, and you cannot dishonour me now."

She spun around, jaw dropped, and for a moment we stared at one another through gathered bodies, she seeing her daughter, I seeing nothing but someone in my way. "Captain Kiren," I said. "Make sure Unus goes with his brother as promised. Dom Villius, I think it is time we stepped out of this crush, don't you?"

"Indeed, *Your Majesty*," he said. "Lead the way."

From outside, the shouting rose in volume. A glance at Sichi earned a shrug, but she started threading her way toward the door at speed, only to halt as General Moto strode back in. "Your Majesty!" His strident voice rolled over everyone else's, owning an edge of panic that silenced all. "Your Majesty," he repeated, swallowing hard as all eyes turned upon him.

"What? Spit it out," Manshin said. "What's going on?"

"It's...it's Shimai, Your Majesty." His gaze slipped my way as he spoke, his expression sinking my stomach. "Shimai has fallen, Your Majesty. To the Chiltaens."

# 19. CASSANDRA

Shouts erupted. The wedding that wasn't to be had descended into a mockery, but nothing was quite as ridiculous as everyone pointing fingers at one another with cries of "You lied!" and "Traitor!" and "This is all your fault!"

"Why the fuck do they all sound so shocked?" I said, looking around at the chaos. "They're all rich and powerful people; of course they lie and stab people in the back."

*And you don't?*

"This is not the time."

Although not standing in the room's centre, Miko was its centrepiece, a furious goddess in crimson and rage. She had both Leo and Emperor Manshin trapped beneath a torrent of accusations and demands that shifted in and out of hearing as worried guests swept around us like a rising tide.

"Your army *is* the Chiltaen army!" Miko shouted. "We will not stand for such trickery! *This* is the man that you sought to ally yourself with!"

*We need to get out of here*, Kaysa said. *No one is paying any attention to us, or to Unus. Just walk over and grab him and walk out.*

"They won't just let us go," I murmured back.

*Which is why we have to take the opportunity while we have it. Please, Cass. Unus is in danger here. We are in danger here.*

One of Miko's guards still had hold of Unus's arm, his other on a dagger hilt as he awaited the inevitable trouble. He wasn't watching me though. For once I was one of the least dangerous people in the room.

*Ha!* Kaysa laughed. *Says the assassin.*

*Not much of an assassin*, I said. It had been a long time since anyone had hired me for a contract, not since I'd been hired to kill Leo. And he was still alive, standing calm before Miko's onslaught, smiling faintly as he denied all her accusations and refuted all knowledge of the attack on Shimai.

*It seems odd that Emperor Manshin isn't joining in, though surely having Chiltaens attack the city wasn't part of his proposed alliance with Dom Villius.*

"Mmm," I said, only half listening. If Miko kept Leo focussed on her, perhaps...

*Which does make one wonder, if Dom Villius and Secretary Aurus aren't working together, did Emperor Manshin know he wasn't making an alliance with Chiltae, only with Dom Villius?*

Attempting to look like I had every reason to be there, I started across the floor.

*Cass! What are you doing? Unus is over there!*

"Just shut up for a minute so I can concentrate," I hissed beneath my breath.

*But Cass—*

*No buts, Kaysa*, I said as I walked on, keeping Duos in the corner of my vision. *There's never going to be a better time. He's distracted, and there are so many people here he surely can't discern individual thoughts. We can end this.*

*For Yakono?*

*For all of us, including Unus.*

Anxiety bubbled inside me, but she kept her worries to herself as I moved on, almost in place. None of the fancy Kisians paid me any heed. Arguments went on swirling around the room, not only between Miko and Leo, everyone seeming to have an opinion everyone else needed to hear. The priest whose job it ought to have been to do the whole marrying people thing kept glancing at the door, his expression that of a man wishing to be anywhere else.

Leo still hadn't noticed me. The masked priest he had with him seemed equally oblivious, taking no interest in anything happening around him, let alone my approach through the crowd.

Waiting could ruin my chance, any pause enough to draw attention my way, so I did what I was best at and didn't stop to think. A step in, followed by another, my hand sliding to the blade tucked against my hip. Leo went on talking, explaining something to Miko in the most condescending way, that would have made me want to slit his throat had it not already been my plan.

Two more steps and then—

The masked priest behind Leo lifted his arm. I let out a shocked cry and, unable to stop, slammed into the man's elbow with a crack that echoed through my skull on a quake of pain. I staggered back, almost losing my footing as my vision sparked. A few whispers shifted around me and people craned their necks to stare, but even when I spat blood Leo didn't turn.

Desperate to finish this, I tried to push aside the pain and hurried toward the little shit. This time the masked priest didn't move to stop me, and for a glorious moment I knew I had him. Until the priest's arm once again shattered all momentum as though I'd run into a stone wall. I threw a foot back to steady myself, shaking off the daze. Leo was right there, so close I could almost gut him but for this fucking asshole in a mask.

Thankfully I knew more dirty street tricks than any priest.

I walked slowly forward, and the moment he moved to strike, I dropped and slammed my foot into his ankle. Between that and his momentum, he ought to have hit the floor face first, but the bastard had good balance and merely staggered, his mask falling from his face. Righting himself, the priest drew a short, deadly, and all too familiar blade as he turned.

"Yakono?"

No recognition softened his grim expression as all around us the previously curious guests let out panicked cries and sped for the door. Shouting and brawling was one thing, sharp blades another. Running seemed like an excellent plan, and it was all I could do to stand my ground as Yakono approached, every step a threat.

"Are you going to attack me?" I said, desperately hoping the answer was no. "I know it was shitty of me to tie you up in that tent, but I'm...I'm sorry. You know, for whatever that's worth."

He made no sign of hearing me, let alone caring, and I sighed, not liking my chances. I drew my blade, risking a hesitant step forward. "Yakono, it's Cassandra." Another step. "You don't really want to do this." Step. "Just put the blade down and we can—"

He lunged, lodging a gasp in my throat. I threw myself awkwardly to the floor and rolled, every part of me hurting. A vibration in the wooden boards was all the warning I got as he came at me again, and I rolled back the other way. His blade pierced the air beside me.

*Be careful! I don't want to die yet!*

"Neither do I!" I said, scurrying to my feet and spinning, block ready. But the strike I braced for didn't come. Yakono had returned to Leo's side like a dog that wouldn't stray beyond its leash.

"You're not going to get through him," Duos said, grinning like this was the most amusing thing he'd ever seen. "This man isn't just any puppet; he's one of the famed Jackals all the way from Suon on the other side of the Kuro Mountains. The Nine paid very handsomely indeed to have me assassinated, and still they failed."

"Yakono!" I called, trying to draw his attention. "Snap out of it!"

"What makes you think that's even his real name, Cassandra?" Duos grinned, all teeth and mockery. "He's a professional after all, unlike you. I'm enjoying the irony of being protected by the man sent to end my life."

I had never considered it might not be his real name, and the realisation I didn't really know him struck hard. Duos chuckled, and wanting nothing more than to stick a blade through his face, I lunged. Yakono moved fast, every defence a precise and economical takedown. His blade slid close and he blocked all my attempts to get under his guard, and though I was soon gasping he wasn't the slightest out of breath. Most of the fancy Kisians had fled outside, leaving only a handful of highly ranked soldiers having a conversation in the corner that wasn't quite a discussion nor quite an argument. Somewhere beyond the sliding doors, Lady Sichi's voice was being wielded like a whip, while outside shouts for horses and palanquins all merged into one desperate plea to get out of here.

"Giving up, Cassandra?" Duos said from safely behind Yakono. He stood alone now, Miko and Emperor Manshin both having disappeared about far more important business.

"No," I said, wishing my lungs didn't ache with the effort. "But why don't you fight me yourself instead of hiding? Are you afraid of me?"

"Afraid?" Duos laughed, the sound echoing into the tangle of rafters rising above. "No, not afraid. You're just not worth the effort. And it's far more entertaining to stand here and let your Yakono kill you and capture my brother while I do nothing. How kind of you it was to bring me so perfect a tool."

"You—"

My reply was cut short as I spun—Kaysa hunting for sight of Unus. He hadn't moved, but none of Miko's guards were watching him now.

*What's the idiot doing just standing there?* I said, which Kaysa translated as: "Unus! Run!"

Control returned like a flood of cold water pouring down my

spine and spreading into every limb as I spun back to face Yakono's blank stare. Neither he nor Duos had moved, Duos continuing to smile like he was enjoying a show.

*We should go with Unus*, Kaysa said.

*We can't leave Yakono here!*

*We have to, Cassandra! You've tried getting through to him, and it isn't working!*

I ignored her and stepped in again, but there was no sign of the Yakono I'd thought I knew in his eyes, not even when I almost got under his guard and we were briefly close enough to touch. "Time to snap out of it," I said, more plea than order. "We—"

A powerful shove in the chest and I fell back, unable to keep my feet on the ground as I toppled. Landing hard, I slid, tunic riding up as I skidded along the floor, burning my skin. Breathing was an effort. Pain filled my chest. My head came to rest against something—not a wall, but a foot, unmoving and stinking of mud.

I looked up. Unus. He should have run; instead he stood there with his eyes closed and his fists clenched tight. His whole body trembled with effort.

A sharp gasp was cut short. Duos staggered, a hand pressed to his head like someone had hit him. "Try now," Unus growled through gritted teeth.

The blade dropped from Yakono's hand with a heavy clang and he blinked rapidly, a man trying to dispel a waking dream.

"Yakono." I rolled back onto my feet. "Can you hear me now? It's Cassandra."

He swayed, a hand pressed to his forehead.

"Yakono?" I risked a step closer, followed by another, sure he would lunge at me again at any moment. "Yakono, can you hear me?"

"I can't hold it!" Unus cried, real pain behind his words.

"Shit!" No time left. "I'm sorry," I said, and stepped past to kick

346 • *Devin Madson*

the back of Yakono's leg. He dropped, knees striking the floor—his skills finally contained. It was the work of muscle memory to twist him onto his back and pin him there between my knees, and never would I admit how cathartic it felt to slap him hard across the face. I brought my hand back the other way, catching his cheekbone with my knuckles.

"How about now?" I said. "Can you hear me now?"

A concerned notch cut between his brows. "Cassandra?" he whispered, my name the only sound in the sudden silence. "Where...?" Realisation slowly dawned across his face, fear pushing all concern aside. "I attacked you. I...I almost..."

He pushed me off, scrabbling to his feet. Once upright he backed across the floor, eyes darting as he sought to contain his panic.

*Cassandra!*

"Not the time," I murmured, eyes on Yakono.

*Yes, it is about fucking time you listened to me—they've gone!*

"They've..." I spun. The room was empty. No arguing Kisian soldiers, no cowering priest, and definitely no Duos. Or Unus. "Fuck!"

I sped to the door, taking the steps in one leap. The field around the pavilion contained far fewer guests than I'd expected, and even fewer soldiers. Some servants milled about, averting their gazes as I swept a look around. No Unus. No Duos. No Miko.

"Unus!" I called, trying not to give in to Kaysa's rising panic. "Unus!"

Rounding the corner of the building, hope flared only to immediately die. A few servants were picking up the crushed paper prayers off the grass, while at the mounting stones a lady in a fine green robe argued with her head carrier.

"Unus!"

I made a quick circuit of the building, getting no reply nor finding any sign of him or Duos. They might as well have evaporated.

I found Miko, however, or rather her distant, retreating back. Crimson-clad, she made the shining centre of a group of mounted soldiers shrinking as they rode up the slope to the road. Other groups of soldiers were departing too, one surely led by Emperor Manshin. Every Kisian had run, escaping like rats from a sinking ship.

"Get the fuck back here!" I shouted after the retreating empress. "You fucking brought us out here, and now you're just leaving us?" I spat on the grass and found I was trembling with a fury I couldn't contain. How I had wanted to trust her, to help her, to be there for her as Hana would have wanted me to be, and after everything I'd tried to do she'd let Duos take Unus and then fucked off about her own suddenly more pressing business.

"Fucking stupid place with its fucking stupid people," I said, turning to look back at the pavilion, now little but an abandoned monument to the most ridiculous wedding that had ever been attempted. "Fuck!"

Deep inside my mind, Kaysa started to laugh. "Don't you start," I said, making my way back to the main entrance, still holding the tiniest sliver of hope I would find them inside. "I don't want to hear it."

*No, what you don't want to hear is I fucking told you so! I told you we ought to have gone with Unus, have gotten him to safety while we had the chance, but no. It's always about you and what you need, and I'm sick of it, Cassandra. So sick of it. Of always being the last person you think of.*

As I reached the steps, I almost ran into Yakono, striding down them with his face set in a determined scowl.

"Feeling better?" I said, but he didn't stop or speak, just strode on. "Yakono?"

He waved a dismissive hand, which for him was as good as telling someone to fuck off, and rounded the corner out of sight.

"Great," I said, starting after him. "Just great."

*Clearly he doesn't want to have anything to do with you, and I can't blame him. Just leave him alone.*

"No, that's the stupidest suggestion you've ever made."

*What? I—*

"You want to find Unus, and Unus will be with Duos. And who needs to find Duos and kill him so he can go home?"

I didn't wait for an answer, just heaved an exhausted sigh and jogged after the scowling assassin.

# 20. DISHIVA

I had fought as little as was necessary in the battle, yet my part in the aftermath seemed endless. I had to perform blessings on both the conquered city and the injured soldiers taken to a pair of grand manors, make a short proclamation of our success, and have my few minor wounds cleaned—all before checking that Itaghai had been properly tended in my absence. And everywhere I went, Mother Li followed, her sharp gaze unwavering in its censure.

It had long been dark by the time I could escape her to wash and change, after which one of the young boys who always seemed to be around led me in search of food. I followed him through the busy passages of yet another Kisian manor taken over by people who had no reason to be there. Whether we had been welcomed by its owners or they had run didn't matter; every step we'd taken since first entering Kisia had been ornamented with stolen grandeur. The room the boy led me to even reminded me of Gideon's room in the manor at Kogahaera.

But it wasn't Gideon who awaited me; it was Secretary Aurus, kneeling at a Kisian table spread with Kisian food. Without couches upon which he could lounge he looked uncomfortable and out of place. But at least Mother Li hadn't insisted on being present to go on glaring at us.

"Ah, Your Holiness," he said as the boy closed the door behind me. "I had begun to fear you had fallen asleep and wouldn't be joining me."

"My apologies, Secretary. There was much to do, and I didn't know you were waiting." I knelt, hoping I did Sichi justice in looking more at home at a Kisian table than he did. At least all the dishes looked familiar, and my mouth watered. Out beyond the shutters, the conquered city was in the grip of a wary hush.

Aurus slid a wine bowl across the table as I untied the strings of my mask and let it fall, the first easy breath without it always a joy.

"To our success," he said, serving himself from a dish of steamed vegetables. "How does it feel to have conquered a city?"

"You make it sound like it was my first time when this is the second time I have taken part in conquering *this* city."

"Ah, of course, though I imagine this is a little different from last time."

"Yes, it's lonelier. Chiltaens on the whole have given me little reason to enjoy their company."

He pressed a hand to his chest, brows raised in astonishment.

"Not you personally, all of you. As a people."

"And we are to be more pleased by yours when so many of our soldiers were slaughtered at your hands?"

"Truly it is astounding we made it to the end of the day without fighting each other instead of the Kisians. And for it to have reached such a late hour before you brought that up."

He lifted his wine bowl in salute, amusement crinkling the skin around his eyes. "There are still a few hours until midnight. Plenty of time for us to turn on one another."

I shuddered theatrically. "Don't even suggest it, I'm far too tired."

"You did very well today. Your Veld speech was particularly moving and, more importantly, convincing."

I grimaced. "You must hate that I'm making use of a Chiltaen religious figure I don't believe in."

"Me? Oh no, not in the slightest. Faith is not my forte, and if it were I'd be very glad you had returned to lead us back to our holy imperial roots and all that."

"Did you used to have a holy empire?"

"No idea." He drank deeply from his wine bowl. "Some scholars say we did, some say we didn't; some say it's a reference to something coming in the future, while others say it's merely...I don't know a good word for it. Uh, pretend? Explaining something through something else."

"I'm not sure we have a good word for that, but I know what you mean. It's like how every story has another meaning hidden inside it."

"Exactly." He finished the wine and poured himself more. "That makes the most sense to me. Whether or not we were once part of a holy empire, I think the time for such things has passed, and anyone who thinks one can be conquered now is a fool."

I looked down into my wine bowl, spinning it absently. "Do you think Whisperer Ezma is a fool then?"

"Either your whisperer is the cleverest and most patient person I've ever met, or she's a fool ensnared by faith and idealism. Take this Veld thing for example. Before she got you involved, she tried to convince Gideon e'Torin that he was Veld, and assured us she could turn him to good use. Of course the old hieromonk and a collection of my fellow oligarchs found a way to turn him to good use on their own, though it came back to bite us harder than we were prepared for."

My hands trembled, and I clenched them to fists to make them stop. Ezma had told them Gideon was Veld. Had told them she could use him. "When was that?" I tried to sound merely curious, but the words came out as a thin breath.

"When he was the only one here with his warriors, an interesting anomaly a few of us thought could be put to good use in, uh...

*theatrical* politics. Another claimant to Veld would have hampered Leo Villius and thrown doubt over what his supporters were saying about him."

That Ezma had been exiled before us I knew, but that she had been here making deals with the Chiltaens and perhaps even pulling the strings behind our suffering on this side of the Eye Sea... I found I could not speak, could not think, could only stare at Aurus, my mind a blank hollow void of all but a feeling I was going to be sick. "Did she... did she genuinely believe Gideon was Veld?" I said, swallowing hard. "Is she truly a believer in your God, or is... is that a lie too?"

The secretary gave one of his eloquent shrugs. "I couldn't say. She is certainly very well versed in scripture, but she wouldn't be the first person to use religion as a weapon because it suited her ends. No member of the Nine is a believer, not really, whatever face we show when people are watching. Uncompromising merchant practice does not fit with the empathy and generosity the faith demands. We would not long be oligarchs if we were truly devout."

"You know," I said, spinning my wine bowl faster now, all he had said so far collecting in my ears to buzz like angry wasps. "You never told me what deal you made with her. What does she want from you?"

He looked speculatively at me over the top of his own wine bowl. "Our alliance is built on an understanding we've long had with her, though as the situation changed it's gone through many variations. Essentially it is her assistance when required in return for Chiltaen ships and soldiers."

I stared, trying to fit this information into my mind. "Chiltaen ships and soldiers," I repeated. "But why?"

Aurus spread his hands. "She has never said, though one only has to consider what one generally uses soldiers and ships for to hazard a guess."

"She wants to attack someone."

"That is the logical conclusion, yes."

I gnawed my lip. "So your deal had nothing to do with me?"

A clump of rice froze halfway to his lips. "With you?"

"Forcing me into claiming my destiny as Veld."

"My dear Dishiva," he said with lazy humour. "The Nine have no need of Veld. We don't need a religious excuse to conquer Kisian cities; we've been doing it quite happily and without provocation for decades and without Veld for even longer."

"And if you succeed in conquering Kisia, what will you do with Empress Miko and Lady Sichi?"

He considered this question in silence for a time, chewing his food as he chewed his thoughts. Outside the doors, the silhouettes of his guards rocked gently back and forth as they shifted their weight. "That depends on where and how they are captured," he said. "And what use we can find for them. If it comforts you, killing them would not be our first choice."

Was that comforting? How horrified Sichi would be to see me now, but Kisia was her responsibility. My people were mine.

Outside in the compound, someone shouted. It seemed at one with the general hubbub around the manor, but it pulled Aurus from his cushion. Quick strides took him to the window.

"What did they say?" I said, his concern making anxiety flutter through me.

He pressed a finger to the glass. "Come here and tell me what you can see."

I moved to his side, and for a few long seconds a deep foreboding held us silent. Levanti filled the street outside our gates, Ezma unmistakable at the front with her jawbone headpiece reaching for the night sky.

"She's trying to look intimidating," I said, more to myself than my companion.

"She's succeeding." Secretary Aurus heaved a sigh. "After all the trouble I went through convincing my soldiers they were safe marching with Levanti despite what happened in Mei'lian. They will want my head for this."

As the Levanti drew closer, I tried to recognise figures within their ranks. Was Oshar with them? Was Jass? I hadn't seen any of them since I'd first charged toward the city.

"Was there any warning or ultimatum before you killed my countrymen in the capital?" Secretary Aurus asked with a sidelong look my way.

"No. Every Chiltaen soldier was just...struck down. Gideon said surprise was the most important weapon we had."

The secretary grunted. "I'm not sure if that is comforting or not. Or whether your whisperer is a stronger or a weaker enemy. I thought we had a strong alliance, but so Legate Andrus thought of Gideon."

"Gideon stabbed him in the back. Literally."

"I did know that, yes. Are you about to do the same to me, Dishiva? I am, as you can see, entirely at your mercy, but if that is your plan I would rather you gave me a moment to pray first."

"I didn't think you were religious."

A wry smile turned his lips. "I'm not, but nothing converts men faster than facing death."

The Levanti mob had reached the gates and halted with their reins gathered. Every Chiltaen soldier in the yard watched on warily, hands hovering near their weapons.

"I would prefer if this didn't end with your people slaughtering mine, Secretary," I said.

"I was going to say much the same thing, Holiness," he returned. "A replay of that particular moment in history would not further the creation of a Levanti nation state upon Chiltaen territory. That offer rather relied on you not attacking us. Once is a moment of violent opportunism; twice is a pattern we cannot trust."

I crunched my hands to fists. Ezma knew what was at stake, what I had marched with the Chiltaens to earn, and she was spitting upon my sacrifice by gathering her Swords outside the gates. It didn't matter what her purpose was; it looked bad, and that was enough.

One of Aurus's soldiers hurried from the gatehouse toward the manor doors. "Well," Aurus said. "It looks like we're about to find out what she wants. With luck we may yet be able to defuse this situation. Shall we?"

Despite Aurus's optimism, the walk along the passage was so much like a walk to one's execution that I couldn't speak, could only force one foot in front of the other. Halfway, we met the guard who'd come running, his brief words to Aurus merely that Whisperer Ezma wished to speak to us. Both of us. At the gates. She had refused to step inside.

When we arrived, the courtyard was full of muttering soldiers and slowly moving lanterns as men patrolled the compound's perimeter. The secretary stepped out first, leaving me to follow, the eyes that fell upon him anxious and unkind. More than one soldier glared and muttered.

A short watchtower sat to one side of the gates, and rather than shout through the stout wood, Secretary Aurus climbed it. Reaching the top in Aurus's wake, I looked out over the road. It was full of Levanti and their horses, of lit torches and scowling faces.

"Secretary Aurus," Ezma called up to him. "Your Holiness. You need not worry we intend you harm, at least so long as you stay quietly where you are and don't get yourselves in trouble."

"At the risk of sounding like a cliché," the secretary said, managing to sound bored despite everything, "what, may I ask, is the meaning of this?"

"You are our prisoners, Secretary. You and your hieromonk and your soldiers. We already have the city gates locked down and are in the process of forming a perimeter around your compound to ensure you remain where you are."

I set my hands on the parapet. "This was never part of our understanding," I hissed. "I agree to be your Veld so you can trap me? You are ruining everything I've fought for!"

"You dreamed so small, Dishiva," she said, shaking her head. "Why accept a small gift of land and always have to be grateful when you could conquer an empire? Your heart was in the right place, but *this* is what our people need. What we deserve."

"How does going back on our understanding get you what you need to achieve that?" Aurus said, his calm sounding increasingly forced. "None of my soldiers understand what you're saying, so you can still walk away now before you irrevocably destroy our alliance."

Her smile chilled me to my bones. "I'm afraid our alliance offers me nothing of value, Secretary."

"Nothing of value?" His teeth were clenched now.

"My people were never going to be able to conquer our rightful empire alongside Chiltaens. It's gold I need."

Aurus stiffened. "You're holding us ransom."

"Very clever, Secretary. Too bad the possibility didn't occur to you earlier. You were so busy worrying about what Dom Villius had planned that I seemed the safer bet."

"And who are you going to demand this ransom of?"

"Whoever will pay me. The Nine, perhaps, since I have a large portion of their army, one of their oligarchs, and their beloved hieromonk at my mercy, a hieromonk who has not yet named a successor. Failing the Nine, perhaps the Kisians would pay handsomely for me to open the gates and hand them an easy victory."

Beyond our sphere of torchlight, the city was quiet. Shimai had been conquered, had eventually surrendered, yet even so precarious a situation was about to be overturned to the soft sounds of crackling torches and shifting hooves.

Secretary Aurus could have argued, could have negotiated or even begged, but with a final glare down at Ezma he showed he knew none of those things would work. Turning his back, he strode to the ladder and was out of sight in a flurry of colourful linen.

When I looked back, Ezma had her sharp gaze fixed on me. "If you want him to get out of this alive, persuade him to send a plea to the Nine. If not, I will offer you all up to the Kisians."

"Why are you doing this?"

"I told you: to conquer an empire."

"But how can you conquer this place if you give it back to the Kisians?"

A frown flickered across her features, leaving bemusement in its wake. Soldiers and ships, Aurus had said. Soldiers and *ships*.

Realisation slammed into me like an arrow, and I staggered back a step, breath caught. "You're not conquering Kisia. You're conquering the plains."

Her silence was all the admission I needed.

"You said you were going to fight for our future, for our people, not against them," I said, my voice shaking. "You—you—" I stared down at her, shock and anger temporarily stealing all words. How could the Levanti standing with her hear such words and not turn on her? Had she convinced them with her easily peddled lies?

"Careful what you say, Dishiva," Ezma said, voice low and vibrant.

"No. Everything I have done has been for my people. To stand between the Levanti and the destruction Leo Villius tried to bring upon us. To give up every part of myself in return for the land and protection Secretary Aurus has promised. That you seek to take that from us, from me, to enact violence against your own people, is despicable. You are no whisperer. You are a scalebreaker."

A few gasps broke the silence, but Ezma just gathered her reins. "This discussion is over," she said, and spitting upon the stones, she turned her horse. With a whole group of Swords left to guard our gate she rode away, leaving us trapped within our walls.

Somehow I got down from the watchtower, but the night was a blur as panic seared through me. From nearby, Aurus shouted orders, and the sleepy courtyard was soon alive with running steps. None of the soldiers sounded panicked, but when I turned to ask Aurus what he had told them, I caught only the hem of one of his tunics as he disappeared back inside.

I hurried after him. "Secretary!" I called, sense and feeling slowly returning to my body like spreading warmth. He didn't turn, didn't answer, just sped up the stairs from the entryway in the opposite direction from which we'd come minutes earlier.

Unsure what else to do, I followed. "Secretary?" The farther I walked from the entry hall the quieter the manor got, what life it possessed silent in the wake of this new confusion. How long until the soldiers realised we were all prisoners now?

"Secretary?" Every room and passage I glanced in was empty, most dark, but as I reached the end of a gallery, a rasping sound drew me on. Thoroughly lost, all I could do was follow the sound, though it bounced oddly in some of the spaces, finally growing louder only when I slid open the door to a room much like every other. Inside Aurus stood leaning against the wall, each drawn breath a harsh, desperate rattle. He exhaled, only to immediately suck in more air like he was drowning. Uncomfortable memories surfaced. I'd sat on the floor of my room in Kogahaera unable to breathe, but I'd had Lashak to wrap me in her arms and coax me to calm.

Aurus slid to the floor, gasping. This was far from the Aurus I'd thought I knew or the Aurus I needed, but unable to let him suffer alone, I sat down beside him.

"You need to breathe," I said, setting a tentative hand upon his shoulder. "Here, repeat after me and breathe at the end of each line. We are the Swords that hunt."

He turned a reddened face toward me, adding confusion to his panic.

"Look, it's all I can think of right now, so just repeat it, it'll help. We are the Swords that hunt." I breathed deeply after the words and let it out to say the next line. "So your hands may be clean."

"So—so your—" He drew a sharp breath, but there had been more space between them, and I nodded encouragingly.

"We are the Swords that kill," I went on, drawing another deep breath and letting it go. "So your soul may be light."

"So your soul—your soul may be—be light."

"We are the Swords that die." Deep breath. "So that you may live."

"So that you may—may live."

"Good! We'll make a Levanti of you yet," I said, patting his shoulder. "Let's go again."

I repeated the words over again and he spoke more of them, the rhythm of his breathing slowing enough to ease the fear he would pass out on me. Another round through, and he had almost all the phrases and his breaths were deeper. By the end of the fourth he had regained something akin to calm, however fragile and temporary it might be.

"Better?" I said.

"Much. Is that an oath you take?"

"Yes, when you get Made as a Sword, that's what you pledge to do in service to your herd, after you've been branded."

"Branded."

"Yes, branded. No, it is not barbaric. It means that no matter what happens to me, the gods will know I made this sacrifice for my people and weigh that in my favour when I die."

He sighed, shifting into a more comfortable position now the worst of his panic was over. "How nice it must be to believe in something," he said, his voice regaining some of its usual drawl.

"When you believe in nothing, this life and this world is all there is, and that makes failure harder to bear. I am quite ruined."

"We can find a way out of here. And if not, you can ask the Nine for the ransom."

He threw his hands up, huffing out a breath that smelled strongly of wine. "Reputation is everything in Chiltae. The only way to earn power and influence is through earning money, and that requires trade and investment and personal relationships, and the development of those requires reputation. It is the foundation of everything, and should it shake the rest falls." Aurus met my gaze, wryly amused. "How good do you think my reputation will be when people find out I was tricked by a Levanti holy woman and imprisoned in the city I just conquered?"

"I...admit it doesn't make you sound like the wisest man, but surely this is an unusual circumstance."

"You're too kind." Definitely a drawl. "I don't think my countrymen would agree with you even if we survive. However, if she deals with the Kisians, and Chiltae is humiliated by the loss of the army and the city to them, my reputation would be such that I may as well be dead."

"That's very dramatic."

"Think of it as being like your sense of honour. You may not consider failure a dishonour, but we do."

"Not a dishonour, but..." My words trailed away upon my own returning fears. The consequences of this failure were much greater than dishonour. Thanks to Ezma's fervent belief in a holy empire, the Levanti were about to lose everything. "You know those ships and soldiers you promised Whisperer Ezma? She wants to conquer the plains in the name of the One True God, destroying everything we are and everything we have. Did you know?"

Slowly, he shook his head. "No, well...yes and no," he said. "I guessed she wished to conquer land she could call a holy empire, but while I imagine the oligarchs who first made the deal might have known where and considered it to their benefit to be directly involved, I was never informed."

"Would it have made a difference to your plans if you had been?"

"Probably not. We each must look after our own."

"Barring the hundreds, even thousands of Chiltaen soldiers you would have been sending to the plains to die."

He grimaced. "Someone always has to lose. Usually the poor. Although since it will now most likely be mercenaries crossing the sea to fight, perhaps our soldiers actually won this time. They'll remain alive a bit longer."

Mercenaries. The possibility was far more frightening than Chiltaen soldiers because it was full of unknowns. Between Ezma's knowledge of our land and our lack of cohesion, how easy it would be.

"If we were to escape," I began, staring unfocussed at the far wall, "she wouldn't be able to get a ransom for us, and you wouldn't have to give her any soldiers, yes?"

"Yes, although since that's the single weakness in her plan, I imagine she has done everything possible to ensure we cannot. I ordered my men to do a thorough search of the whole palace, including hunting for underground passages. The Kisian imperial family has always been very keen on escape tunnels."

"This is a palace?"

"It is, yes. In fact, in the throne room here stands the last copy of the crimson throne in the empire, which is part of what gives Shimai its present degree of importance. And is also why the Kisians would pay well to oust us."

I turned to look at him, though with my thoughts churning I might as well have been looking right through him. "If there's a tunnel, what then?"

"Depends where it goes. I am not hopeful, however. And even if we could get out into the city, we'd still be trapped inside the walls." Aurus lowered his head into his hands, drawing deep breaths to keep fresh panic at bay. "You should make peace with your whisperer and get out of here while you can."

"No." The speed and vehemence of the word surprised me as much as him. "No," I repeated more calmly. "I will not take part in her plans, no matter how she intends to force me to keep playing Veld. That is not what I want. Tell me, if I can find a way to get us all out of here alive with no sacrifice of reputation, will I still be able to leverage my position as hieromonk to get lands for my people?"

Panic in abeyance, he watched me thoughtfully for a time, the tapping of two fingers against one another the only movement he made. "If I lose no reputation in the process...if we can spin this just so, then yes, yes, I think we could do that."

"I save you, you save us. Do we need to make some sort of formal pact?"

Aurus chuckled, all breath. "I think we've come far enough to be able to dispense with that, don't you? I trust you with all the resources I have available if you will trust me to pay you back in full as originally agreed."

A small voice in the back of my mind screamed that I ought not trust him, that he was a Chiltaen, but I pushed it away. Whatever that lingering fear, I did trust him. I wasn't sure when I'd begun to do so, but I trusted this powerful Chiltaen man more than many of my own people. I would fight to save him, not only to get the lands he'd promised, but also because I wanted to.

The small notch between his brows smoothed as I held out my hand. "That's a deal, Secretary. We are in this together."

He took my hand. His was soft and smooth, unchafed by labour, while mine was all roughness and calluses and skill. "A deal," he said. "Dishiva."

# 21. MIKO

I lay staring at the play of dappled light on the roof of my tent. I had barely slept, but we'd needed to stop and rest, or we would reach Shimai too exhausted to act.

There had been no time the previous day to think, only to move, to find Edo and gather up our camps and make it as far south as we could before dark, leaving the cursed pavilion far behind.

"Miko?" came a soft voice from outside, and curled up at my feet, Shishi lifted her head. "Are you awake?"

"Unfortunately," I replied.

With a rustle of fabric, Sichi stuck her head into the small space, agreeing with a wry grimace. "I had trouble sleeping too. Edo's men have made some kind of millet porridge with dry berries that actually smells quite good. Nuru and Tor have ridden out with the scouts, but Edo has found some tea if you want to join us."

I got up and drew an overlarge cloak on over my hodgepodge of under-robe and tunics, before stepping out into the crisp morning. Shishi followed, stopping on the threshold to stretch all four legs and give herself a shake.

"How simple life must be as a dog," I said. "I'm quite envious."

Sichi led the way through the camp we'd set down in haste the previous evening, the whole thing a shambles compared to the proper way Kisian battalions usually camped. Some tents were already in the process of being rolled up, carts were being repacked and horses saddled, yet despite all the activity a tense hush hung as though we feared to wake the dead. Following at my heels, Shishi's carefree amble through their midst seemed all that was able to draw brief smiles from the soldiers we passed. It was like the fear inside me had manifested outside my skin.

We found Edo sitting on a mat before what was left of a fire. He hadn't yet dressed in the many layers of armour that would cover his simple tunic and breeches, and in the soft fabric he looked far more like the Edo I had grown up with rather than the soldier he had become of late. The pangs of old heartache resurfaced, piercing my skin like needles. How different everything would have been had Tanaka lived. Edo might even have smiled, rather than glancing around and finding our camp empty of the man he loved.

"Tea?" he said, pouring three bowls as we knelt to join him. Despite being outside, Edo had chosen a private spot tucked away behind two of the larger tents, where only the occasional soldier passed by.

Having knelt and taken up my bowl, I sat blowing away the steam while one of Edo's men brought our food. Three tin bowls full of millet porridge. It had never been my favourite, but the smell made my stomach grumble impatiently.

"Thank you, Wen," Edo said, and with a bow the man departed, leaving the three of us alone with our porridge, a large quantity of stale tea, and each other's morose company.

We hadn't spoken much the previous evening beyond what had been necessary for organisation, but now that we had the time and space to do so, none of us uttered a word. For a time we sipped our tea, took spoonfuls of porridge, and stared into the dying embers.

Eventually, I blew out a deep breath. "We need a plan."

"At the moment I don't think we can decide on one until we reach Shimai and see how things lie there," Edo said, swallowing a mouthful of porridge. "The news came with very little information about what had happened and how, and without knowing what defences they destroyed and how big the Chiltaen army is, there's not much we can do."

He spoke with such easy authority and competence that I found myself watching him rather than listening to his words, unable to shake the bitter sorrow of Tanaka missing out on this moment. What a pair of emperors they would have made.

"Miko?"

I blinked. "Sorry, did you say something?"

"You were staring oddly at me," Edo said. "You disagree with my estimation?"

"I…" I hesitated upon the truth, knowing it would bring pain. "No, I was thinking about Tanaka. About how much he would have loved this. Have… have loved to see you leading a whole army as though you'd been doing it all your life."

Edo looked away, and reaching over the embers, I laid my hand on his. Tears welled in my eyes, and I couldn't blink them away. "He would have been so proud of you, Edo. Of both of us, I hope, but… I'm sorry, I shouldn't have said anything."

"No, no," he said thickly. "I… I have been thinking about him often. I always do, but… oh gods, Koko, I miss him. I miss him so much it's like my entire body is nothing but an ache of grief, and it's all I have and all I am and will ever be, this walking emptiness."

Abandoning my breakfast, I shuffled around the dying fire and wrapped my arms around him. He buried his face into my shoulder and shuddered with soundless grief he'd been holding in as I had, assuring myself I would feel when there was time, when this was done, when I could rest. But with my arms wrapped around his shaking body, I realised there never would be a good time.

Sichi's arms wrapped around us, her softness and her scent and her warmth added to the moment, and I let my tears fall. I'd kept thrusting my emotions away, crushing them down and denying them, but as my tears flowed freely I found myself sucking in ragged breaths, my chest shuddering. Tanaka and Mama, gone where I could not say goodbye. Rah, lost to me in a different way. General Kitado and General Ryoji, who I hoped would not join the list of those I had to grieve. Mei'lian. Koi. The only homes I had ever known. The empire had been a solid thing once, something Emperor Kin could have handed to me, carefully, as one passes on a precious heirloom. Instead he and Mama had fought over it, and it had smashed upon the ground at my feet, leaving me to pick up the pieces.

There together in that quiet space the three of us were a ball of tears and sorrow and hurt, and yet because it was a hurt we shared, somehow that made it all right.

Eventually there were no more tears. Our cheeks dried and our shoulders steadied and we gave each other space in which to breathe again. It felt good to have let out so much shared pain, but it hadn't budged the rock of hopelessness I'd been carrying in my heart since the previous day. Had Manshin known what the Chiltaens were doing? That he wasn't making an alliance with anyone but Dom Villius? Or had his attempts at a treaty just hidden Chiltae's true intentions from us both? I wasn't sure which possibility frightened me most. With a united Kisia behind me I could have faced any enemy with confidence. Divided we were weak. And I couldn't let go of the fear that Manshin had betrayed more than just me.

"Ah! There you are, Your Grace." Catching sight of us, one of Edo's generals strode over, halting with a deep bow. "Your Majesties," he said, sending a pleasant little shiver down my spine. "Your Grace, we'll be ready to leave as soon as these last tents go down, should you wish to give the order."

"Yes. Yes, General," Edo said, shaking himself back into the role life had forced upon him. "The sooner we set off, the sooner we reach Shimai."

"As you wish, Your Grace. Oh, and the scouts have returned with news of Lord Manshin."

Hardly were the words out of his mouth than Nuru appeared around the corner of the tent, Tor slouching along in her wake. No matter where he was or what he was doing, he always looked like he was trying not to be so tall, trying to draw as little attention as he could.

"What news?" Sichi said, leaping to her feet to grip Nuru's hands in welcome. For an instant I feared that Tor expected me to do the same—our moment of passion at the shrine having gone unspoken for so many days it was beginning to take up space between us like a giant spectre.

"We found him," Nuru said. "About a quarter of a day's march south. He seems to have mobilised his men at great speed."

Tor had crouched to pat Shishi, but looked up at that. "Or he already knew they were going to take Shimai and was ready to depart the moment the news came."

"That is what I've been fearing," I said. "That we might arrive outside Shimai to find ourselves outnumbered by an alliance of Chiltaen and Kisian soldiers. What if all of this was somehow part of his plan? What if we've already lost?"

Tor went on patting Shishi, everyone silent as they contemplated the horror of my suggestion. The moment was shattered as the tent beside us deflated in a rush of air, two soldiers standing ready to roll it for transportation.

Shaken from my contagious despondency, Edo shook his head. "I refuse to believe that, whatever Manshin himself might do, all his generals would agree to fight with Chiltaens against their own people. Minister Oyamada might be able to give us better insights there, but at the very least he'd lose the barbarian generals the moment he gave such an order."

With a thoughtful frown, Sichi looked at Nuru. "His army," she said. "Is it still the size it was at Kogahaera?"

"Hard to say as the camp was more haphazard than at Koga-haera," Nuru returned. "What do you think, Tor?"

"I didn't see your camps at Kogahaera," he said. "But I was with the Chiltaen and Levanti force that captured Shimai before the rains, and if he doesn't have an alliance with the Chiltaens hold-ing the city he doesn't have the numbers to take it. Not without those... siege weapons the Chiltaens had."

"You need to meet with him."

I spun to stare at Edo. "What?"

"You need to meet with him," he repeated, getting to his feet as the tent behind him began deflating. His men were almost ready to leave. "Think about it, Koko; the only way we can hope to find out what his plans are is by asking."

"Asking?" Sichi said with a little laugh. "You should know my father is as good at lying as yours was, Cousin. He won't admit to betraying Kisia."

"No, but he also won't accept a temporary alliance to oust the Chiltaens if he wants them to keep hold of the city."

"You don't think so? What better way to sabotage our plans? He is very good at subtle manipulation."

"Yes, but if so it would still be better to have him where we can see him."

Sichi hummed in thought. "There is something in that. What do you think, Miko?"

The only one still sitting, I ran my hand through Shishi's long fur and tried to think clearly, to imagine all the ways the next two days could go. It was like peering into fog, all possibilities and motives obscured.

"You're right," I said, nodding slowly. "We need all the information we can get, and he's the only one we can get to. Edo, send your fastest rider with a message and see if Manshin will meet me tonight. If he refuses that'll at least tell us something before we march to Shimai."

Edo brushed himself down. "I'll send someone at once. In the meantime we'd better prepare to depart."

He strode away on the words, leaving me prey to doubts. Meeting with Manshin might provide useful information, but was it safe? He'd already tried to have me killed once to get me out of his way; what was to stop him doing so again now that I was proving to be a persistent thorn in his side?

"Gods," I said, running my hands over my face. "I wish General Ryoji were here; he always knew what was best in such situations."

"Still no word on whether it was him roaming around the area?" Sichi asked.

"Nothing. At least nothing I've heard."

Having stepped back from our small group, Tor cleared his throat. "I could find him for you."

I spun around. "What?"

"I am a Levanti, and if Levanti are good at anything it's tracking," he said with a wry smile. "And while your general may be avoiding Kisians, he won't see much threat in a lone Levanti."

It was a simple fix for at least one of my worries, but also something I couldn't ask him to do. "No," I said. "It's too much to ask."

"You aren't asking. I'm offering."

I wanted to say that he'd already offered too much, that I'd already asked too much and expected too much and that I didn't want him to think he was only able to stay while he was useful, but none of those words came out. Instead I just stared at him and he stared back, sending an uncomfortable prickling sensation cascading through my stomach.

Nuru cleared her throat, and I flinched like I'd been struck. "I'll go with you, Tor," she said. "Two of us will have a better chance of finding him than one."

Sichi didn't ask if she was sure, didn't say she'd rather Nuru didn't go. Whatever understanding they had was stronger than the mess Tor and I had made of...whatever existed between us. Had I kissed him at the shrine because I couldn't kiss Rah? Perhaps, but it hadn't been the first time. Yet what future was there that didn't involve asking still more of him without any assurance his sacrifice would ever be reciprocated? A wise woman was one stepping back from this unexpected ledge, as an honourable woman wouldn't let him take such a risk under the mistaken belief we had a future together.

I did neither. Instead I stood there and smiled and thanked them both, holding tight to my shame until they'd turned to leave. Until it was too late to call them back.

———————————◆———————————

When our messenger returned, he carried Manshin's agreement. He would not push on to Shimai that day, but make camp outside the town of Dizen, some miles north of the city, and meet me there. It was a courteous reply and one I ought to have been happy with, well did it bode for the possibility of a temporary alliance, yet that was exactly what made me wary. If Manshin didn't need me, if he feared I would get in the way, he would have refused. No matter how I thought it through, dread was the end result.

We reached the outskirts of Dizen as the sun was setting. Manshin's army had already made camp, the scent of cooking on the air making my stomach growl. But there was no time for food and no time for rest—not even to get out of the saddle. Time only to share a tense look with Sichi and Edo, tell them to look after Shishi, and ride on with Captain Kiren at my side. He was my quiet, stoic protector now, as General Kitado had once been. It was how they had been trained, yet I couldn't but wish in that moment for General Ryoji—he the closest thing to a father I never realised I had.

Manshin's chosen meeting place was no manor or fine house,

rather a walled garden on the outskirts of the town. We arrived just as the last sliver of sunlight sank below the horizon, the air fast taking on a biting chill.

"It would appear Lord Manshin is already here, Majesty," Captain Kiren said, nodding to a shadowy figure by the gate. As we approached, the man stepped forward, the single hanging lantern illuminating General Moto's features.

"Majesty," he said with a slight bow as we reined in.

"Odd you should insist on still calling me so when you serve another, General," I said. "He is waiting?"

"Inside, yes. Alone." He glanced significantly at Kiren as we dismounted.

"I will speak to him alone, but Captain Kiren will stand within the wall. If that is not allowed then I have serious doubts as to your intentions."

Annoyance flickered over his face, but he nodded and led the way inside.

The garden beyond the gate was little more than a grassy hill dotted with flowers and carved stones, with a small pavilion sitting atop it like a hat. The solitary figure kneeling inside grew larger as we approached, but Manshin showed no sign he heard us coming, not even when General Moto halted a dozen paces out and said, "This is close enough for us, Captain, don't you think?"

I met Captain Kiren's questioning look with a nod, and nerves swirling in my gut, I walked the rest of the way alone, the skirt of my dark robe catching on the unkempt grass.

When I stepped in beneath the low roof, Manshin at last looked up, and it was both the same and a very different man who faced me across the table. He had all the same assurance, the same belief in his place and his worth, but where he had always been calm, anger now simmered before I even opened my mouth.

"Miko," he said, eyeing me up and down. If he hoped to put me out of countenance with such a ploy, he reckoned without the years I had spent at court being the object of every woman's pity.

"Ryo," I said, pleased with the calm tone I achieved. He had chosen to wear imperial robes to our meeting, complete with as many fine jewels as could be pinned around him, like a manufactured aura of power. Beside my simple attire I couldn't have said whether he looked gaudy or I looked plain.

Not waiting to be offered a seat, I gathered my skirt and knelt opposite. Tea sat steaming upon the table, but there were no other refreshments. Despite his promising reply, it seemed neither of us wished to extend this meeting beyond what was necessary.

Showing a bored disinterest in his tea bowl, Manshin leaned back against the latticework. "I ought to have known you would come running for help the moment things got too difficult."

"No," I snapped. "You don't get to play that game. But for your actions in dividing Kisia by proclaiming yourself emperor, this wouldn't be a difficult situation. In fact, had you not cosied up to Dom Villius, this might not have happened at all."

A small sneer stretched his lips. "What do you want?"

"I want to retake Shimai and get the Chiltaens out of Kisia for good, but first I want to know if that's what you want too, or if we are greater enemies than I knew. Was this your doing? Did you betray Kisia?"

I hadn't meant to be so forthright, but the flash of annoyance that crossed his face was deeply satisfying. Perhaps treating our discission like an exchange of punches would work better than employing the twisty double-talk we both despised.

"Betray Kisia?" he repeated. "You mean like when you chose to break an agreement of great benefit to the empire by claiming to have married my daughter."

"Claiming?"

"Sichi is not your wife."

My anger flared, but I would not let him bait me; I had promised myself that dignity at least. "I'm not sure how you can say so when we took oaths and consummated our sevenday. If you wish precedents, I can give you precedents."

"Nonsense. She is my daughter, and without my permission the union is meaningless."

"She is not underage."

"No, but you are."

Some shock must have shown on my face for he leaned forward, a grinning wolf moving in for the kill.

"But you aren't my guardian," I said, regathering calm. "In fact, I have no guardian because I am the Empress of Kisia. You may not like it, but my marriage to your daughter is legal, binding, and very happy."

His grin turned into bared teeth. "You dare to lay hands upon her?"

"Why not? She's my wife."

"You—" Manshin began and halted, seemingly unable to find the words to express all that was wrong with what I'd said, with our marriage, with the very idea of two women who had no need of a man. And while he clenched his teeth and glared at me, I saw anew this man I had looked up to and admired. He had been less furious at Sichi's marriage to Gideon. Had happily thrown her at an unpredictable Chiltaen holy man, but her marriage to me went against his view of how the world ought to work.

Gathering himself somewhat, he smoothed his features and said, "I will not allow anyone to make a mockery of the Manshin name. As Emperor of Kisia I decree your union invalid."

"You can't. By your claim, we have the same rank, and I will keep my wife."

I had come to speak of war, yet here he sat unable to move beyond this grievance. Still glaring at me, Manshin reached for the teapot and poured tea into both bowls. Before he set the pot back down, I slid my bowl across the table and, gripping the edge of his, drew it toward me. He eyed the swap, his stare unpleasant. "You think I would poison you?"

"You've already tried to kill me, don't pretend. Now, are we to discuss the Chiltaen invasion of Shimai? If not, this is a waste of my time."

"Then speak," he said, taking a sip from my former bowl with a defiant look. "I assume you need my help?"

His tone was so superior that I clenched a fist beneath the table. "Only as much as you need mine. Neither of us has the numbers to take the city alone—"

"Only thanks to you getting your claws into Edo. Were you to let him go, I could oust the Chiltaens from Shimai before the first snowfall."

"Then you do intend to fight for Shimai?"

"That depends on whether you are the greater enemy or not."

"Me? If you think I am the greater enemy I would say your priorities are poor, but I am flattered."

Manshin leaned forward, his stare pinning me. "That depends on whether you will do the right thing for the empire and declare your marriage to Sichi invalid."

"What?" My bowl nearly slipped from my fingers. "Right for the empire how?"

He tilted his head, seeming to be trying to see if I was joking. "So she can marry Dom Villius and seal the peace treaty."

"Peace?" I set my bowl down with a harsh clack. "They took Shimai. Any treaty you are trying to negotiate with Chiltae has been spat upon, unless—"

"Unless?"

I glared across the table, disliking his challenging smirk. He wanted me to accuse him of what seemed both utterly ridiculous and yet all too possible, but I swallowed the words rather than let myself be provoked. Lifting my chin, I said, "No, I will not declare my marriage with Sichi invalid."

"Well, if that is your decision." Manshin spread his hands in a magnanimous gesture, his smile unpleasant. "Since you're the Empress of Kisia, routing the Chiltaens is your sole responsibility."

"Then you are stepping aside?"

"Oh no, if we're speaking of what's best for Kisia, that cannot be considered."

"Ah." I tapped my chin. "So either I declare my marriage invalid or you will disengage from this fight, perhaps hoping I'll fail at retaking Shimai so you can sweep in and clean up the mess, saving everyone. How pathetic. I once thought you were the most dedicated and responsible man I knew, ready to do what was best for Kisia even if it was not personally in your best interests."

"This is best for Kisia. This empire needs stability. Tradition. Strength."

"You mean needs to return to the way everything used to be with men in power and women subservient and no empresses getting in the way of the correct ordering of things? Or perhaps you mean returning to the poor treatment of anyone not born Kisian? Or to letting Chiltae raid our borders whenever they like so long as there's a pretence of peace?"

Manshin sat back, smiling like a man watching a kitten fight. "You have my terms. Take them or leave them. It makes no difference to me."

It might make no difference to him, but it did to me. Whether he fought to retake Shimai or stepped back to let me fail, I was the one at risk of being destroyed or forgotten. If in the aftermath he then ousted the Chiltaens and saved the city, it would be so much easier for him to follow in General Kin's footsteps and take the throne for good whether I was alive or not.

"Well?" he said.

I let go a long, pained breath. "I will not use the word *invalid*, but if we can find a phrasing that achieves the same ends, will that be enough of a sacrifice on my part to make you do your duty to the empire?"

Manshin smiled, all too satisfied, and turning toward the garden called, "General Moto! Fetch more tea."

# 22. CASSANDRA

My legs ached, my hip joint twinged, and every part of my body seemed to be seizing up with the growing cold, but I'd always been a stubborn bitch so I kept walking. Yakono hadn't so much as slowed, damn him, not even now the sun was sinking fast. More surprising was that Kaysa hadn't spent the whole afternoon berating me. She had hardly spoken at all.

In the last light of the shadowy evening, my toe caught on rock, and it was almost more effort than I had left to keep myself from tumbling over. Every part of me already hurt, what were a few extra bruises? Not having so much as paused or glanced back, Yakono pulled even farther ahead.

"This is getting ridiculous," I muttered, and jogged to catch up. Falling in beside him drew as little attention. I may as well not have existed at all.

"So, are we going to just...walk all night then?" I said.

Yakono said nothing. Didn't even turn. At least he was being consistent—consistently an ass.

*You tied him up and left—*

"Not only is walking all night a stupid idea from the viewpoint of your body needing rest," I said, ignoring Kaysa. "But it's also a stupid idea in a 'fuck it's cold in Kisia' way, and a 'whoops I got lost in the dark' way." Kicking another unseen rock, I added,

"And also in an 'I tripped over and smashed my head and now I'm dead' way."

Yakono kept on walking as though he hadn't heard me, so I sped in front of him and held my hands to his shoulders. For a moment it felt like he would push through me and tread on toward Shimai over my fallen body, but the pressure against my hands was there and gone, leaving Yakono standing awkwardly before me. It was as though without the angry momentum he had no idea how to stand. How to be. I'd never seen him look so out of place. So unsure.

"Come on," I said, stomach squirming uneasily. "Let's find somewhere more sheltered and build a fire; that way at least we won't freeze to death."

Eyes on the ground, Yakono finally nodded.

———————————◆———————————

It wasn't a great fire, and the only thing around to eat was grass and mud, but at least we'd stopped walking. Had we stopped walking earlier there might have been time to hunt for food, but I kept my mouth shut and stared into the flames.

*You need to say something*, Kaysa said.

*I have been saying things*, I returned. *He's the one not replying.*

*Snarking at him about not wanting to freeze to death isn't what I had in mind. You need to apologise for what happened.*

*I did! Back at that fucking wedding.*

*When he couldn't hear you properly and couldn't respond! Come on, Cassandra, you care about him, so perhaps it's time you showed it.*

I pulled a face, glad Yakono was focussed on the fire.

Kaysa sighed. *Go ahead and fuck this up for good if you like; it makes no difference to me.*

*Then why give advice at all?*

*Because* he *deserves an apology.*

In the firelight, Yakono's face owned more lines and shadows than usual, aging him years. In the time since I'd first met him, I'd never seen him look so...heavy, like it was an effort to even lift his head. Days travelling without good sleep hadn't troubled him, nor had long distances on foot or tense situations. Yakono was a man ready for anything and everything, a kind word always waiting on his tongue. He did deserve an apology, but he also deserved someone better than me to give it.

"Yakono," I said, and immediately thought of Duos's jeer that Yakono wasn't his real name. I swallowed hard and pressed on, trying to ignore the sudden bitterness that memory dredged up. "I'm not sure if...if you heard me, back at...back there, but—" He looked up abruptly, and I almost swallowed my tongue. "Well, I said that I was sorry, and I wanted to mention it in case you don't remember or didn't hear me. I'm, well, sorry. For the whole tying you up in the tent and leaving you there thing. I mean I did come back, but you were gone."

On the other side of the fire, Yakono closed his eyes.

"Not that me coming back made it all right that I did it, I just wanted you to know," I added in a rush, feeling more naked than I ever had without clothes on. "I should have just told you that I needed to talk to Leo, rather than kill him. Miko had—"

"Then why didn't you?"

"Because—" I snapped my jaw shut. How could I explain about Miko? Yet how could I not? Lit by the firelight, his penetrating gaze seemed to glow, searing deep. "Because...because I didn't want to explain about...about Miko. Empress Miko."

Making no demands, Yakono just waited for me to go on. Or not. He wasn't the sort to browbeat until he got the answers he wanted, but his disappointed expression was a far more dangerous weapon.

I looked away into the darkness. "I...I knew her mother—a long story that one—and I owed her a debt. So when Mi—Empress

Miko asked me to carry a message to him and offer an agreement, I couldn't refuse."

"But you didn't want to tell me?"

There was something plaintive in the way he asked that made it feel like I'd kicked a puppy. "Not because I don't trust you," I said, able only to glance at him, not hold his gaze. "It's just the whole thing with Empress Hana is...well...personal."

He nodded, the gesture solemn and full of understanding.

*Cassandra!* Kaysa exclaimed. *You weren't meant to lie about it!*

*I didn't. It is personal. I took a break from my body and hung out in the body of an empress for a while and then died in it; there's not much more personal than that!*

"I wish you had told me even just that much," Yakono said, regarding me steadily over the flickering flames. "But I understand. You don't really know me, after all, and I don't know you. We just got...thrown together upon this very odd journey."

There seemed nothing else to say, and I would happily have returned to staring into the fire in silence for the rest of the evening had Yakono not sat there biting his lip, holding on to words as I had been. Eventually, once my anxiety had risen to a truly uncomfortable level, he said, "I must thank you. Without your help, I'm not sure I ever would have gotten out of that. Gotten away. From him."

His words grew increasingly restricted, like they were an effort, and having finished he sank back into the tense silence of a man with much to say who didn't wish to speak.

"Don't blame yourself," I said, snapping twigs and throwing them into the fire. "You aren't the first person he's done that to. It's one of his favourite games, controlling minds. I got the feeling that was why no one wanted to have anything to do with that Levanti who left with Captain Rah when he stole Miko's book."

"Emperor Gideon? Yes, I heard that too."

"He was an emperor? Did I know that?" The question was more for myself than him, the tangle of memories and thoughts that had come from being disembodied with an empress opaque at times. "Not that it matters," I went on. "The point is that succumbing to it doesn't make you weak."

He shook his head slowly. "It was awful," he whispered, and I had to strain to hear him over the flames. "I was awake and yet not, able to feel every living process in my body though it seemed to belong to someone else. And he was there, in my head, filling up all the spaces I'd never known I had until I could hear nothing else— none of my own thoughts. He...his voice became my thoughts."

Having started talking, he seemed unable to stop. "I didn't want to hurt you," he sped on, the words a flood breaking the banks of his control. "I didn't want to hurt anyone, to attack anyone. I tried so hard to stop, willed myself dead so I couldn't hurt you, but there was nothing I could do. Nothing but watch as I hit you with my own fist and tried to gut you with my own blade, no amount of screaming inside able to make it out."

Tears trickled down his cheeks and he let them fall, looking small and lonely and helpless. The heart I'd always told myself I didn't have ached for him, and hardly thinking, I got up and moved around the fire to sit at his side. "I will take great joy in watching him die for the last damn time," I growled.

Any elaboration on how I would like to see it and what I wanted to do to Leo evaporated from my mind the moment Yakono set his head on my shoulder. It was like a lightning strike, stunning and unexpected, and I could only hope I hadn't physically flinched.

"I'm sorry," he whispered, his lithe warmth leaning into me and his breath close.

"You don't have to be," I said, my voice a throaty rasp I tried to clear with a cough. "You don't have to be. I'm the one who is sorry."

He said no more, just kept his head upon my shoulder like it was his pillow for the night. And like it was the most natural thing in the world, I slid my arm around his shoulder and held him there.

———————◆———————

Having once again spent far more time walking than I ever wanted to do again, we finally reached the city of Shimai in the afternoon. Despite the speed with which both Kisian leaders had departed the shambles of a wedding, no army of any kind sat camped outside the city gates. There were plenty of carts, however, backed up along the mud-smeared road and interspersed with enough mule trains that the road wasn't going to get any cleaner.

"Are we just…walking in then?" I said, breaking the silence that had stretched all morning. After our conversation the night before, Yakono seemed disinclined to risk more words than necessary.

"Too dangerous," he said, not glancing back. "Without knowing whether Duos is already here, we'll need a better plan than that." He pointed at a large clump of trees ahead, sitting amid a collection of abandoned fields. Debris lay scattered across the ground, everything from broken fenceposts to lost sandals, horseshoes and snapped arrows churning in with the hoofprints to destroy once neat rows. It was like a battlefield within a battlefield, and empty as it was, it felt wrong to cross it.

Yakono didn't seem to feel my discomfort, for he leapt over one of the few upright fences and strode on across the littered field toward the trees.

It had been still out on the fields, but stepping into the copse brought a rustle of leaves to my ears. Yakono stopped, hand raised in warning.

*That's not wind*, Kaysa said.

Turning an ear in the direction of the sound, Yakono stalked forward a few steps before crouching in the undergrowth. Voices. At least two, yet even straining to hear, I couldn't make out a single word.

Yakono crept forward, ears still pricked like he was stalking prey. Perhaps he thought it might be Duos, but sure it wasn't, I took half a dozen far from quiet steps forward, craning my neck. Behind me, Yakono hissed. Ahead, bushes rustled. Inside my mind, Kaysa had begun to protest my lack of care when two men came into view through the narrowing tree trunks. "Just as I thought," I said, giving their drawn blades a disdainful look before turning back to Yakono. "Levanti. The two who stole Torvash's book and walked off on Miko."

A crease appeared between Yakono's brows as he straightened. "You mean Captain Rah?"

"Yeah, and the one you said was an emperor." I gestured toward them as Yakono joined me. Both Levanti still had their blades drawn, but they'd lowered them amid a hissed conversation. They had both looked worse for wear the last time we'd seen them, yet somehow they looked even worse now. The last few days hadn't been kind to them, their faces drawn with fatigue and smears of dried blood covering both their tunics.

"Captain Rah," Yakono said, nodding respectfully to him.

"I'm not sure if he's a captain anymore after what happened," I murmured.

"No reason not to be polite, especially since they could be of use."

"Not unless that long-haired translator is around."

The Levanti who wasn't Captain Rah nicked the back of a finger with his blade and sheathed it. "That long-haired translator you're referring to has a name," he said coldly. "Tor e'Torin. But since I imagine he's still following Empress Miko around, you should already know that. Let me guess, you're here scouting ahead for her?"

"No," I said, the word far more of a snap than I'd intended. "Unlike your *long-haired translator*, we aren't following her around anymore."

"What Cassandra means," Yakono said, stepping into the fray

as a deep scowl darkened the Levanti's face, "is that we are here on our own mission. We need to get inside the city."

Thankfully, Captain Rah sheathed his blade too, since I had no interest in fighting two Levanti even with Yakono at my side. Yet despite the lack of weapons now on show, the air in the copse felt cold and unfriendly.

"Gideon?" Captain Rah said, glancing at his companion.

Gideon didn't shift his gaze from us, but replied in a low voice. That I couldn't understand his words made me uncomfortable. Doubly so when he gestured my way.

"What is your mission inside the city?" Gideon asked at last, turning his full attention back our way.

"What is yours?" I said before Yakono could answer.

To my surprise, the Levanti warrior grinned. "Spiky," he said. "I respect that. Our business inside the city is with another Levanti. We have no interest in this battle or in helping anyone take or keep this city. Your turn."

I eyed him, reluctantly appreciative of his directness after spending so much time with empresses who hardly ever said what they meant. "We're here for a friend. And to kill Dom Villius."

Gideon flinched at the name, but kept a smile fixed to his face. "That we can agree on."

Gesturing my way, Captain Rah spoke again. "Why is he pointing at me?" I said. "Is there something on my face?"

"Dirt, yes," Gideon replied. "But he was pointing out that you're Chiltaen."

"Oh, am I? I hadn't noticed."

*Cassandra, please, I don't want to be run through by grumpy Levanti after getting this close. Let me take over if you can't play nice.*

"You, Chiltaen." Gideon spoke slowly as though explaining something to a child. "City, taken by Chiltaens. You may be our best chance of getting inside."

I snorted a laugh. "Oh yes, I'm sure if I just walk up there and demand to be let in, no one would ask any questions at all, especially about the three very un-Chiltaen men I have with me."

"Cassandra," Yakono whispered by my ear, halting my ill humour with a shiver. "These men might be useful; they might even have food they will share. Why don't you go scope out the city gates while I talk to them?"

He wanted me out of the way, and I couldn't blame him. My stomach was rumbling and I was in an irascible mood, more interested in ripping people to pieces than forcing polite and diplomatic words past my snarky lips.

"Fine," I said. "I'll let you boys talk, and I'll go keep an eye on some walls that won't have moved." I stomped off without awaiting a reply, managing to hope both that Yakono would call me back and that he wouldn't at the same time.

The copse wasn't all that big—walking to the edge escaped neither sight nor sound of the others. Trying not to hear what they were saying, I crouched down amid the low bushes to examine the prospect. At first glance, Shimai was like the Kisian equivalent of Genava—an old city straddling the empire's most important river. Unlike Genava, there was only one bridge joining the north and south banks of Shimai, and the city walls had been so battered by war it was a wonder they still stood.

As I had snarkily told Yakono, the walls weren't moving. Neither were the gates. The whole city was just sitting there in its hollow being a city. At first glance all the people waiting to get in through the gates had been Kisian, and a second glance didn't change that assessment. More were slowly arriving, coming together outside the gates from all directions to sit and await entry. One at a time was being allowed through, and I wondered what the Chiltaen army was worried about. Hidden Kisian soldiers? No Kisian army had even shown up yet, and when they did, it would be to stomp around outside and let everyone know how angry they were. Assuming Miko and her false emperor didn't rip each other apart first.

*Cassandra,* Kaysa said slowly. *That man there, beside the cart at the front with the black wheels. He doesn't look Chiltaen, does he?*

I'd been staring at the gates while my thoughts wandered, but she drew my attention sharply to the people—small, distant people— working around the gatehouse. Not just small and distant, but wearing what looked far more like Kisian uniforms.

"Kisian?" I said. "But why would any Chiltaen legate let Kisian guards work the gate? Unless the whole conquered city story was a lie?"

*Seems unlikely. There's all that debris back in the fields around the copse, and there are no Kisian flags or banners flying.*

The ground between us and the city looked churned too, the movement of many feet and hooves not yet having been smoothed by rain.

Attention caught, I peered at the gatehouse and along the top of the city wall, looking for any sign of Chiltaen soldiers. There were far fewer lookouts than would usually guard the walls of Genava even in peacetime, but not one of them wore Chiltaen colours. There were no Chiltaen flags either, not even at the gatehouse, the only splash of colour there the saddlecloth of a very grand Levanti horse.

"Oh."

*That makes even less sense,* Kaysa said. *Why would—*

"I don't know, but I know who we can ask."

I was on my feet so fast my head spun, but a dozen long strides brought me back to where Yakono and the two Levanti were deep in conversation. "So," I said, breaking in without ceremony. "The walls might not move, but the people on top of them and around the gates sure do, and none of them are Chiltaen."

Yakono's brows drew close in sickeningly adorable confusion.

"Not Chiltaen? Do you mean the Kisians fended off the attack after all? But—"

"No, there are a few Kisian guards working amongst the people trying to get their carts through the gates, but the rest..." I turned to Gideon and Captain Rah. "They're Levanti. So, new plan. *You* walk up to the gates and ask them to let us inside."

A smile flickered at the corner of Gideon's lips as he turned to translate this. Somehow, what I'd said was so funny that he couldn't contain the smile long, and both Levanti started to laugh. I glanced at Yakono, who shrugged, before folding my arms and waiting for the mirth to die down. Unfortunately they had only to look at one another to break out in fresh laughter, tears wetting their eyes as they gasped.

When Gideon at last wiped his eyes with the back of his hand, he said, "Sorry, but as the two most hated Levanti to ever live, your suggestion was very funny."

"They wouldn't let you in?"

"No, they wouldn't let us in and might even fill us all with arrows for the fun of it."

As he spoke, Captain Rah turned away, wiping his own eyes, and headed off through the copse as I had done. Gideon and Yakono made to follow, leaving me to bring up the rear, stomach still growling.

At the edge of the copse where I'd recently crouched to watch the city gates, all three men got down on their bellies and lay silently in the undergrowth. Lying on the cold ground was the last thing I wanted to do, so I leaned against a nearby tree and waited for them to come to the conclusion I had—Levanti, not Chiltaens, had control of that city. It made no sense, but one couldn't argue with numerous dark-skinned and over-equipped men and women striding about the place, each easier to see once you knew what you were looking for.

In a low whisper, Captain Rah and Gideon discussed what they could see, or what it meant, or just admired the local bird songs for all I knew—their language nothing like Chiltaen. Leaving them to it, Yakono slid back before rising to join me, his long-fingered hands brushing leaves from the front of his clothes. "You're right, all the guards keeping watch and checking people at the gates are Levanti with a smattering of Kisian men."

"Were you expecting me to be wrong?"

"No, I just...it's important to be sure of information, Cassandra." He looked away. "I need to get it right this time. No more mistakes, no more...fuck-ups."

He so rarely swore that I laughed. "Like you've ever fucked up anything in your life."

"I let him get inside my head."

I pressed my hands to his cheeks with more ferocity than I had intended. "That was not your fault. I'll keep repeating that as often as I must until you believe it too."

"I should have been able to fight him, should have been stronger," he said, shaking his head slowly despite my hold. "It's my mind; surely you can't say I don't have full control over it."

Snorting a laugh, I said, "I can and I do. Trust me on that."

His gaze flicked from one of my eyes to the other as though trying to read a lie, but for all the lies I'd told in my life that wasn't one of them.

"Trust me," I repeated. "This time I know what I'm talking about."

Yakono nodded but didn't pull out of my hold, just stood meeting my gaze with all the directness and honesty and heart I was incapable of. He said nothing, yet I stepped back, dropping my hands as though he'd stung me.

"Cassandra..." My name rumbled throatily off his tongue, and I couldn't tell if I most wanted to run or stay, to hear his words or not.

A stick snapped, and we both flinched. "Hey, lovebirds," Gideon said, boots crushing undergrowth as he approached. "We have a plan. I think."

"What is it?" Yakono said, remarkably calm considering the rapid tattoo of my heart and my intense feeling of horror at having been called a lovebird.

It had been Yakono who asked, yet it was me Gideon looked to. "We could get inside in the back of one of those carts if you'll get yourself a Kisian body."

"What?" Yakono said.

"Rah says that Cassandra—"

"Yes, thank you, we've got it," I interrupted, heart slamming even harder into my ribs. "You don't need to explain."

Gideon glanced curiously between us, but thankfully kept his mouth shut. I had never wanted to do anything less in my life than reveal my freakishness to Yakono, yet the refusal sitting on my tongue went unspoken. What other way could we get inside the city? Not only so Yakono could finally fulfil his contract and be able to go home, but so we could save Unus's life. After everything I'd done, I owed Kaysa that much.

She said nothing, but I could feel her close. Watching. Waiting. If Unus died, I wouldn't deserve anyone's forgiveness, least of all hers.

"All right," I said at last, rubbing a hand over my face. "I'll do it. All of you keep your mouths shut and stay here. I'll be back as soon as I can."

I spun away on the words, wanting to answer no questions. None followed, only Kaysa's presence remaining with me as I headed for the edge of the copse.

*I'm taking the corpse,* she said. *I'm not going to let you mess this up.*

# 23. RAH

The cart stank of damp vegetables and rotting straw, but somehow that wasn't the worst part. The oppressive silence was worse. It seemed to have nothing to do with not wanting to be found and everything to do with no one wanting to talk about what had just happened.

Cassandra had left only to return soon after, gesturing for us to follow. I had known exactly what to expect, yet I'd cringed at the sight of a Kisian man leaning against the side of a cart pulled just off the road, a scarf neatly knotted around his neck. It had been done well, leaving no sign of blood or the slit it surely hid, but a deep, uncomfortable silence seemed the only possible response.

"So that's... her as well?" Gideon had whispered as we'd made for the back of the cart. "The cart driver?"

"More or less," I'd said. "It's complicated and I don't really understand it, but yes, he's dead and she's walking around in him."

"How many dead people can she walk around in at once?"

I'd whacked his uninjured arm. "We're not asking her to do anything more after this. Gods, I hope it's only one."

The only good thing to be said about hiding in a pile of straw and vegetable sacks with three other people is that at least it's not cold. Gideon lay distractingly close, each steady exhale brushing past my arm. The other Cassandra and the assassin had lain down at the other end, seemingly as far apart as they could manage.

Almost from the moment we'd stepped into the back of the cart, the vehicle had started moving, leaving us to hide ourselves as best we could while being drawn toward what felt like something inevitable. These city walls through which I'd once burst as part of a conquering force were now all that stood between me and the final act I owed my homeland, that would free me from the shame of failure I'd carried all too long.

My hip ground against the wooden boards as the cart bumped over a pothole, only to lurch right into another. I suspected our dead driver was deliberately searching for them. In the darkness, the other Cassandra muttered something that sounded like a complaint laced with swear words. The assassin said nothing.

Outside our foul-smelling darkness, a babble of voices started to build.

Taking a deep breath, I let it out slowly, willing myself to remain calm. It was hard with so many unanswered questions swirling through my mind, their answers able to change everything to come. Did the Kisians plan to retake the city? Were Amun and my other former Swords in there? What had happened to the Chiltaen soldiers? And most of all, what the fuck was Ezma hoping to achieve by taking over a Kisian city?

The lack of answers gnawed at me.

Outside, Kisian voices grew louder, closer and more numerous with every turn of the wheels. Our pace slowed and my heart started to thud heavy beats. We were close, but it might still be hours of waiting to be let in, so I closed my eyes and recited a silent mantra to keep myself from getting twitchy.

The cart halted with a sudden, sickening jerk. The voices around us didn't change, only my heartbeat increasing to a rapid rate. We repeated the pattern of starting to move only to stop again half a dozen times over what felt like an hour, but still we seemed no closer to our destination than we had before. I barely smothered the urge to peer out and see where we were and went back to chanting the mantra, not only to keep me calm but to stop me scratching. The straw was starting to make every inch of my skin itch.

Forward again only to halt, and it was beginning to feel like a waking nightmare.

"Do you think she knows what she's doing?" someone said, and it took me a moment to realise they'd spoken in Levanti. From outside the cart.

"Better than any of us do," came the dour reply. "Why? This is a bad time to start doubting, Jahat."

Jahat grunted in response as the pair moved past, their conversation fading into the overwhelmingly Kisian babble.

Another jerk forward changed something about the way the sound moved around us. Had we made it beneath the stone arch of the gatehouse?

Our dead driver had been so quiet the whole way that it was a shock to hear a deep voice rumble from the front of the cart. Another deep voice replied, tone more bored than troubled. I held my breath. Someone laughed. A second man snorted. Beside the cart, boots scraped as someone turned on the spot. And with another jolt, the cart started forward again.

I let my breath go, easing tension from my body. We were inside the city.

"Hey, whoa," a Levanti woman said, her surprised tone nothing to the shock that flinched through me. "Are you all right? He doesn't look so good."

"Is that blood?"

Voices gathered upon a collection of shuffled footsteps, but the deep voice of our dead driver mumbled and muttered and failed to disperse the interested onlookers.

"Hey, Vihaya!" someone called out nearby. "What was it you were telling me the other day about that woman who made a body get up and walk around?"

Shit. I closed my eyes tight. This wasn't going to end well. Already more footsteps were approaching, and the cart slammed to a halt.

"Who let this cart through? I want it searched!"

Beside me, Gideon tensed. "I guess that's our cue," he muttered. "Over the left side and run for the closest street."

A hissed question came from the other end of the cart, but there was no time to explain. Gideon moved first, his bunching muscles powering him upright in a burst of straw and leafy greens. I followed, leaping over the side of the cart to land heavily amid shocked cries and shouts.

"This way!" Gideon yanked me toward the closest street.

"It's Rah! Rah e'Torin!"

"What the fuck is Gideon doing here? He should be dead!"

I didn't dare glance back. Speeding on in Gideon's wake, I dodged around curious Kisians and other carts stopped to unpack their goods. The small square before the gates felt choked and breathless, crammed with people coming and going, surprise all that was getting us through. Pushing people aside or ramming between them shoulder first got us to the nearest street amid a chorus of complaints, Levanti shouts close behind.

The street was far less packed, and we sped along, no thought to direction as footsteps thundered after us. At the first corner, Gideon skidded right. Holding his injured arm close to his body, he ran on, darting left at the next opportunity. Close rows of shops and houses whipped by in a flurry of wood and stone and brightly coloured flags, people leaping out of our way and shouting after us as a rack of candles went tumbling. Another turn seemingly at random, and we were speeding right toward what looked like a Levanti camp—a square teeming with tents and horses and warriors from the plains.

Gideon turned again and, for the first time, risked a look back as he took the corner. Following his gaze, I caught a momentary flash of a street empty of Levanti pursuit.

Gideon slowed, jogging along the narrow alley with his chest heaving. "We need to hide," he said on an exhale. "Lie low until they stop looking for us."

"Any ideas where?"

He shook his head. "Not yet, but it needs to be somewhere we can see what's going on. There's no point hiding in a hole for an ambush."

I'd not heard that expression since leaving the plains, the realisation making me smile even as the pain of homesickness twisted my heart. It was a unique combination of pain and joy with which Gideon always seemed to infuse me.

"Maybe one of these buildings that looks out onto that square," he said, looking up at one nearby with three floors and a brightly coloured sign. "They look like shops of some kind."

He was still looking up when a Levanti stepped out of the next street, knife in hand. "Idi!" I cried as the man lunged. Gideon spun, taking the edge of the blade along his shoulder rather than through it, but for a man already injured it was little comfort. I reached for the knife I'd carried since losing my own, barely getting it free of my belt before running footsteps approached from behind. Out of breath, the two Levanti who'd been following us through the streets finally caught up. "Well, fuck," I muttered, the same anger from the clearing returning like hot water bubbling up through a well. That we existed seemed to be all it took for every Levanti to want us dead.

At least there was freedom in the knowledge that talk would be pointless. I kicked over a nearby rain barrel, sending stale-smelling water gushing into the alley. The two new arrivals tried to stop, only for one to push the other into it, feet sliding. Able only to hear the scuffle behind me and hope Gideon was all right, I grabbed a cracked tile from the barrel's plinth, lifting as I swung. With all the force of my gathering anger, I slammed it into the head of Gideon's attacker, covering them both in a rain of sharp ceramic shards.

Gideon's assailant staggered, but just as I'd taken no chances back in that forest clearing, I would take none now and plunged my knife into his throat. Without waiting for him to fall, I yanked the blade free and spun to lunge at the other two—one was already down, a stomach wound staining the water red. The other had her foot stuck in the cracked barrel, snarling with pain and frustration as she tried to wriggle it free. It was an easy kill and I lunged, only to be yanked back, snapped off balance.

"Just leave them!" Gideon hissed, pulling me away. "Let's go!"

I almost slid my hand from his grip, wanting to finish the fight they'd brought to us, but Gideon set off at a run without waiting. Spitting on the ground, I set off after him, no thought for where he was going or why, only for the anger that came so quickly to my veins.

In a haze, I followed him back through the twisting streets, occasionally slowing to look up at the tall buildings and duck into side alleys to test for open doors. Finally seeming to have found a house he liked, Gideon shoved me into a dimly lit shop with shuttered windows, closing the door firmly behind us. For good measure he threw the bolt home. "Right, this should be safe. And if I've worked it out right, the upper floor at the front should look out over that square where Ezma is camped."

Throwing a cursory glance around the dusty shop with its empty shelves, I headed for the stairs. They creaked beneath my weight, protests doubling when Gideon followed. Thankfully, the sound brought no one from farther inside the building, and the second floor was as dim and bare and dusty as the shop floor had been, an old table and two chests all that was left of the furniture.

"We should hunt out what supplies we can find," Gideon said, making for one of the chests. "There might be food or warmer clothes. Rah?"

Daylight seeped through the panes of a sliding door at the other end of the main room. I walked toward it, not hearing him, only the call of Levanti chatter and activity beyond. Undoing the poor excuse for a latch, I slid the balcony door open.

"Rah!" Gideon grabbed my arm, yanking me down with a hiss of pain. "Don't just walk out there," he growled. "They'll see you. Peer through the fucking fretwork."

"Clever," I said, and having recovered from the shock, added, "Are you all right?"

"Fine." He let go and, keeping his injured arm crooked against his chest, approached the balcony at a crouch.

I joined him, peering out through the gaps in the ornate fretwork that framed the balcony. There, down in the square, Levanti moved about as though in a camp made of wood and stone and other people's lives. Some horses had been stabled in a building with a wide door, others tied to poles beneath shelters made from cleared-out market stalls, while tents of all kinds and piles of supplies sat everywhere, lacking organisation. Smoke rose from half a dozen campfires, bringing us the scent of cooking, but even my stomach's needs meant nothing when I laid eyes on Ezma. Ezma, walking about with the slow pace of someone supremely confident in their surroundings, spreading wisdom with her orders, and faith in a false god with her very presence. A false god in whose name she would destroy our homeland. Our way of life.

The same rage that had overtaken me down in the street crashed over me again, and I made to rise. How easy it would be to draw my blade and jump down there to thrust it into her gut, her neck, her eye. It would be over and—

For the second time, Gideon gripped my arm and yanked me

down, my forehead narrowly missing the top of the fretwork. "What are you doing?" he hissed. "They'll see you."

"Then they can see me stick my knife into their whisperer."

I drew my blade, only for Gideon to twist it from my hand, dropping it between us with a thud. "They won't see that; they'll see you getting skewered the moment you jump down. Or at best, the moment you attempt to kill her."

"I came here to end her, Gideon, I—"

"I know! Just think up a better damn plan, because fuck you and your sacrificial glory. I didn't come all this way to watch you be a martyr."

A fierce shove overbalanced me, and I landed hard on my arse, pain jolting through my tailbone. Moving away from the balcony, Gideon got to his feet and started pacing, his movements bordering on frantic.

"Gideon—"

"No," he interrupted, holding up a hand as though to block my words. "I don't want to hear it right now. Just...don't be an idiot. For once. Do that for me if you can't do that for yourself. Either we leave here together, or not at all."

"Killing her is a risk no matter how careful I am!"

He ran a hand down his face. "For once, the Rah you need is the stubborn ass who does everything by the proper tenets."

I stared at him, realisation of his meaning slowly trickling through me, only to land with a thud of iron in my gut. "I have to challenge her."

"You have to challenge her."

# 24. DISHIVA

I paced back and forth along the short passage, through fingers of weak grey daylight that had started to creep in. They were a cruel reminder that time had kept passing, that the quiet night was about to give way to a day I didn't yet know how to navigate. Or even if I could.

I paced on as the sun rose. My legs seemed full of a frantic energy I couldn't disperse, but my eye stung, dry and tired, eyelid heavy like my mood. At the beginning of the night I'd been sure we'd find a way out, some passage or side gate Ezma hadn't thought to guard, but as the night wore on, our options slimmed to only the very worst available. In the darkest hours, I'd started searching the palace myself, running my hand along each wall I passed in the vain hope of finding a hidden doorway everyone else had missed.

At the scuff of a step, I spun, flinching as though I'd been near to sleeping on my feet. Rapid, aching blinks brought Secretary Aurus into view. He'd donned the finest clothes I'd seen him wear since our first meeting, seeking the power and confidence in cloth and jewels that he didn't have in the approaching day.

"You couldn't sleep either?" he said, voice a little ragged in the early morning chill.

"No. Neither have I yet figured out what we're going to do."

He set his hand upon my shoulder, gentle, his smile wry and

apologetic. "It shouldn't have to be your burden, Dishiva. I've sent a message to Whisperer Ezma. I'm going to negotiate."

I nodded, but the weight hanging over me grew heavier with dread. I hid it behind a grin. "And if she doesn't agree, we can always just kill her."

Secretary Aurus let his hand fall on a bark of laughter. "I'm not sure the bloodthirsty option is the best idea while her followers are the ones guarding our escape routes."

"I'll find a way to make it work."

He didn't answer, and as the seconds stretched, I realised he was just staring at me, brow creased. "What?" I said.

"Do you ever give up, Dishiva?"

"No, not when it's important. Why? Do you?"

His brow creased all the more. "I didn't used to think so, but you've made me wonder. About a lot of things, actually. Who'd have thought I could learn so much from a barbarian."

A challenging grin accompanied the final word, his eyes creased with mocking amusement. I punched his arm. "You're the barbarians. You bury dead people in the ground and then grow food out of it."

Aurus's smile froze. "I...never thought of it like that. How unpleasant."

For a time, we stood in companionable silence, watching the courtyard come to life through the narrow slits that did for windows in this low stone section of the palace. Chiltaen soldiers, as uncertain of what the day would bring as we were, ambled around, lost and unsure what they ought to be doing, and whether we were prisoners or conquerors.

Without turning his head my way, Secretary Aurus cleared his throat. "Whatever happens today, there is no one else I would rather face such troubles with, so thank you."

I flicked him a glance, sure he was joking again, but even in profile his expression was set and serious. There were dozens of people I would rather have been facing difficulties alongside—Jass, Lashak, hells, even Rah if it came down to it, someone I knew well enough to trust their word, who understood what any outcome would mean for our future. I'd come to trust Aurus, but his words struck less gratitude in me than pity. To have so few people in one's life that one could trust, could fight with, could strive with, vulnerable, toward a goal…what an empty life that must be.

"I guess you're pretty good for a Chiltaen," I said, trying for the same mocking tone with which he had called me a barbarian. Perhaps I didn't quite get it right, or my pause had betrayed me, for there was no smile when he at last turned my way.

"Dishiva…"

He left my name hanging, his incomplete words prickling at my skin and setting my heart thumping in something all too like fear and yet not entirely. I ought to have spoken, to have asked what he wanted to say, but I couldn't make my lips move or my mind turn, frozen there in the pale morning light.

Running footsteps shattered our strained silence, heralding the arrival of one of Aurus's soldiers. Aurus turned, demanding to know what the man wanted, but before the soldier had even come to a complete stop, news spilled from his lips. At the sound of Ezma's name, I needed no translation. She had arrived.

———————◆———————

The crimson throne was the least comfortable thing I'd ever sat on. Its twisting back protruded in bumps and spikes, making slouching unthinkable, while the seat owned the iron hardness only long-dead wood can achieve.

"There should be a cushion," I said, trying to find a comfortable position. "*You* get a cushion."

Secretary Aurus turned his head, even so small a movement

making his jewels clink. Between his encrusted belt and the bright colours of his numerous long, layered tunics, he looked too grand even for a throne room. "I get a cushion because this is the empress's seat, at the emperor's side."

"Why does the empress get a cushion? I thought Kisians didn't like women."

He scrunched up his nose. "That's an overdramatic way to put it. I'm sure they like women very well, just—"

"Not in any position of power where they can tell men what to do, yes, but then why give the woman the only cushion?"

"I don't see the purpose of this discussion," he said coolly. "This meeting with Whisperer Ezma is critical, and we can't let it get out of hand. In which case, I think it will be best if you let me do most of the talking. I'm a lot less likely to get enraged."

I narrowed my eyes—eye—at him. "Is this like the cushion? Some kind of protective thing?"

"No, I don't think you require my protection in the slightest, but she might leave if we shout at her."

I reluctantly agreed and went back to staring at the closed doors. The throne room in Shimai looked very like the one in Mei'lian, the likeness so striking I expected every moment to hear Legate Andrus or Leo, to smell the blood and feel the rush of victory as Gideon proclaimed himself emperor. But I was the one sitting upon the throne looking down at the empty throne room—two Chiltaen soldiers standing by the doors our only company. Despite the discomfort, a thrill of possibility had shivered through me as I'd sat down, and I couldn't but wonder if Gideon had felt the same. He'd once sat just so and tried to change our lives, and only now did I fully understand the weight of all he had carried.

At last, after waiting far too long, footsteps echoed beyond the doors.

"Finally," Aurus muttered as we both sat up straighter.

The great carved doors swung ponderously open upon a squeal of protesting metal, and into the throne room's red-tinted light strode Ezma. She wore her usual attire—a bright orange half robe flecked with gold and her headpiece, more crown than anything a true emperor of Kisia would have worn. She had no sword at her side this time, but she walked with the confidence of one who has no need of edged weapons. In her wake, Derkka's robe had no gold and was not as bright, but neither was it Levanti, and nor was the self-satisfaction with which he wore his circlet of worn knucklebones.

I'd promised myself I wouldn't let them anger me, but I clenched my teeth at the very sight of her, my fury growing when she favoured me with an amused smile. "Hardly an accurate position for you to sit in, Dishiva," she said, striding past the stone where visitors were meant to stop. "In that guise more so than just as a Levanti." She halted halfway between the stone and the edge of our dais. "Secretary." She gave him a nod of respect before she went on in quick and meaningless Chiltaen.

When she'd finished, Aurus lazily leaned forward, an elbow on his knee. "You are going to have to repeat that, Whisperer," he said. "Since I refuse to converse in Chiltaen."

A mocking smile flickered on Ezma's lips. "Very well. I said the position of consort to a false Levanti priest ill becomes you, Secretary. How uncomfortable it must feel to be put in a lesser place by a foreign woman. Twice."

"I assure you I am managing quite well," he said. "I'm rather more adaptable than you think."

"That's good, given the situation you've found yourself in."

"Indeed."

Ezma lifted her chin. "I assume by now you have tested your capacity to escape and found it lacking, and have realised you will have to deal with me to get out of this mess. And since your safety and the safety of your soldiers is entirely in my hands, you have no choice but to accede to my wishes. Send a plea for help to the Nine requesting gold, supplies, and slaves, which you will give to me in return for your freedom."

"I find your demand very interesting," Aurus said, propping his chin upon his palm. "It didn't occur to me until this morning, but I have to wonder why you would have *me* send a plea for help rather than sending your terms directly to the Nine yourself. Perhaps you have considered Chiltae's history and realised we do not take threats kindly."

"And if I have? You must admit this is the wiser course."

"The wisest course is not waiting the weeks it would take to get a message to Genava and back at this season."

Ezma had been about to speak, but words abandoned her, and for a moment she just stared at Aurus as he stared at her, a challenge from which neither was willing to look away. "What then are you suggesting instead, Secretary? So far you are making a powerful argument for selling you to the Kisians instead."

"But selling us for what?"

She seemed to slump just a little and scowled up at him. "What do you mean?"

"Soldiers? Money? Ships? How much of such things do you think the Kisians can afford after all that's happened?"

"And you can?"

"Unless you slaughter the largest portion of my army that remains."

Ezma stared at him, and slowly, a smile spread her lips. "You're a clever shit, Aurus, but you know as well as I do that no Chiltaen soldier will take orders from a Levanti, and no Levanti will willingly fight alongside a Chiltaen for longer than necessary. The only reason we fought with you here was because my people all knew they weren't really fighting with you at all. If your offer is Chiltaen soldiers—"

"You have something else in mind?" Aurus interrupted. I was succeeding in keeping my mouth shut and not enraging her, but my heart hammered so fast my limbs felt like mere buzzing appendages as Ezma lifted her chin, all triumph.

"Gold," she said. "For mercenaries."

I'd walked into this meeting knowing she intended to conquer the plains, that mercenaries had been an option, but to hear her speak so boldly of them shocked me onto my feet. "You would conquer your homeland with warriors who want nothing but gold and spoils? Who have no morals to stay their hand against innocents?"

"Would turning Levanti on Levanti be better, do you think?" The words didn't even seem to trouble her, so easily did they fall from her lips. "Or taking Aurus's soldiers and letting the Chiltaens have their revenge?"

Standing, my hands clenched tight, I realised I didn't have an answer. How precarious the safety of the plains had become. If she didn't conquer them, the city states eventually would, my bid for new lands and a new home fast becoming the only way I could protect our way of life. Yet to do that would mean letting her win so Aurus lived.

"We all do what we have to do," Ezma said. "I play my part, as do you. You rail against it now, Dishiva, but Veld is your destiny, and this is your path I'm laying down."

"No."

Ezma's smile was humourless. "So you've said before, Dishiva, but destiny will find a way to change your mind; it always does." She looked to Secretary Aurus with the same predatory look. "To which end, Your Excellency, I must humbly decline any offer you might make me. I understand from my scouts that a Kisian army is on its way as we speak—may even have arrived already—and despite your doubts I'm sure they will be able to provide everything I need in return for being let into the city for an easy victory."

Aurus stiffened, producing no confident response. Fear rose

around me like twisting vines wrapping tighter and tighter about my chest, increasing the hopeless feeling there was nothing I could do and it was my own fault. She would destroy the Chiltaens to destroy my plans, leaving me nothing to do but fulfil the destiny she was setting in place for me.

"I see you both understand me," she said. "And now this meeting is finished, and I will leave you to whatever it was you were wasting your time with before I arrived. Derkka?"

A nod from her apprentice and she spun around. The throne room doors began their creaking journey from closed to open, and as Ezma strode toward the aperture, I wished I could reach out and pull her back, could close the doors in her face. I'd said we could always kill her if things didn't go the way we wanted, but with so many of Aurus's men under Levanti watch, harming her was the quickest route to even quicker destruction. Yet with every step she took toward the doors, my goal slipped away and the prospect of a conquered plains grew stronger.

"Wait!" I stepped to the edge of the dais as the word leapt from my lips. "Wait."

Ezma halted, turning an amused look over her shoulder. "What can I do for you, Your Holiness?"

"Do your Swords, the ones who chose to follow you, really believe in all this?"

"Who chose to follow me? They're all here now, Dishiva. Captain Amun e'Torin and his Swords have joined us as well, formerly Rah's Swords of course, but it seems he finally went too far and killed one of them, so they walked away."

"Killed—"

"One of yours, I believe. Ptapha e'Jaroven? Dead by a captain's hand without challenge or cause."

My knees wobbled. Ptapha? He'd deserted to join Ezma's camp during Gideon's rule, but...what could possibly have happened?

"You're shocked," Ezma went on. "That's a more humane response than I was expecting from one who has always taken Rah e'Torin's side. Thankfully his Swords are now free of him, and they may yet find new purpose through faith and be able to let the past go. As must you. Goodbye, Dishiva. Secretary."

Head held high and carrying her self-satisfied smile, Ezma walked out. Only then did I realise she hadn't answered my question.

---

The secretary wouldn't sit still. He would perch on the worn couch for a few seconds before getting back to his feet and pacing. Sometimes back and forth, other times just to the window and back, muttering and twisting his fingers.

After the meeting with Ezma, we'd sought the highest room in the palace we could find with a good view of Shimai's northern gate. Outside which the Kisians were already a dark clump amid the mist.

"They're just standing around," Aurus said, dropping once again onto the couch beside me, making the old thing creak and sag. "Are you asleep?"

I'd closed my aching eye, but that he thought it possible to doze off with a gut full of foreboding and his incessant movement was laughable. "I am quite awake," I said.

I began counting in my head, and as I reached five he was up again, springing to his feet with a nervous energy that banged the couch back against the wall. His feet scuffed as he paced. "Why wouldn't they immediately either attack or seek a meeting? And if Ezma is so keen to make this deal with them, why hasn't she strode out there to demand one?"

"You ask these questions like you expect me to have an answer."

"Perhaps she has another plan. Or do you think despite what she said she's worried they won't be able to give her what she wants?"

Letting out a deep sigh, I let him keep trying to talk himself out of his fear like a saddleboy or saddlegirl before their first fight. Somewhere along the way I'd started to rely on him. On his easy confidence. That was what I needed now.

"At least Lord Villius isn't here to mess things up even more."

I opened my eye, squinting at the change from dark to light. "Are you afraid of him?"

Aurus snorted. "No, my precautions are to protect my interests, not myself, interests he seems determined to overturn. I need a stronger word. Refresh me on Levanti swear words."

"You're not afraid of him?" I repeated.

"No." His brows rose. "Are you?"

"Yes. If you're not you can't really know what he's capable of. I spent enough time with him in Kogahaera that no matter how old I live to be, I will shudder at the mere thought of him. And that's before he cut my eyes."

Aurus opened his mouth to retort, but snapped it shut. "He did that to you?"

"Yes."

"I'm sorry."

"Sorry? Why? You didn't do it."

"No, but we ought to have been able to deal with our own monster without dragging anyone else into the fight."

An apology was the last thing I'd expected, and I leaned back, wishing I was elsewhere. "Perhaps you should have thought of that before you decided to . . . what was the phrase? Make good use of us?"

He grimaced and poured the entire contents of his wine bowl down his throat. "An excellent point as always, Dishiva. If I spend much more time with you, I'll be in grave danger of developing a conscience."

"How terrible."

"Truly. Merchants with a conscience are poor men, and poor men aren't oligarchs of Chiltae." Aurus strode back to the window and froze. "They're moving."

"Who is?" I got up and squeezed into the narrow space beside him. "Ah, the Kisians." Riders had broken away from the mass and were making for the gates—half a dozen perhaps, a meeting party, not a charge.

"Imperial banners," Aurus said. "Although whether that's Empress Miko or Emperor Manshin, or perhaps miraculously both or neither, is unclear."

Closer to and not as blurry, the city's northern gate started to open. A pair of riders emerged—Levanti, though their identities were stolen by distance. "I assume that's Ezma riding out to greet them," I said. "Which means we're fucked."

"There, that's a Levanti swear word, isn't it? I'll remember that one. *Fucked*. Yes, Dishiva, we are utterly fucked."

The Kisian riders grew larger as I glared at them, unable to make out anything more than shapes. Miko...Would that mean Sichi? Nuru? There was nothing I could seek from Emperor Manshin, but if I could get a message to Sichi there might yet be a chance we could get out of this alive. It was a small, desperate chance I clung to with the last shreds of my hope. Yet we were still as trapped within the palace walls as we had been before.

It was my turn to pace, striding back and forth with slow, deliberate steps as my mind turned. Sichi couldn't speak Levanti that well, and Empress Miko not at all. Aurus could translate, but of all those trapped inside the palace, he was the one least likely to be let out. What I needed was a servant I could trust. Or a priest.

I slammed to a halt. "A priest," I said.

"A priest?" Aurus's eyes narrowed. "Why do we want a priest?"

"Because she may be the only one who can save us."

———◆———

We found Mother Li sitting in the small chapel. At the sound of our far from quiet footfalls, she rose from her cushion and turned, the slow movements of an old woman but also of one in no hurry, who was still seething at our very existence. No bow, no smile, no nod, nothing; she just came to stand right before me, shoulders back, eyes narrowed. Waiting.

Secretary Aurus cleared his throat and addressed her in Kisian, seeking permission to speak. She didn't look at him, but her slow, solemn nod my way was all I needed.

"I need your help," I said, leaving a pause so Aurus could translate. He did so a little haltingly compared to the speed at which Oshar could work, but his tone was respectful, as was his bearing, and it would have to do. "You...you may have noticed," I went on haltingly when she didn't reply, "that we have been trapped inside this palace by Levanti. By...my people, but they're led by someone...bad."

I let the words hover as Aurus translated, hopefully more elegantly than my blundering search for an explanation. How I could explain Ezma to this woman? How I could explain the danger she posed to the future of so many, not just the Chiltaen soldiers we had conquered Shimai with?

Mother Li's expression didn't change. I drew a breath and let it out slowly. "I think you and I are rather more alike than it at first appears," I said. "You were shocked, I think, to find a Levanti wearing the attire of the hieromonk, but what angered you was hearing the voice of a woman behind the mask. Here, women are the overlooked, the used, the left behind—the ones who suffer most when enemies seek to conquer your land."

As Aurus translated that last part, her face creased, an expression of grim sorrow crushing her skin like velvet. I pressed on. "My home is being destroyed. I am only here, only accepted these robes and this position, as a way to help my people. With your help, I can still do that and at the same time can walk every last one of these Chiltaen soldiers out of your city without a fight—without anyone having to get hurt at all."

A frown drew her brows close as she looked from me to Aurus and back, assessing. Considering.

"Please help me," I said. "You are the last hope I have."

For a long time we stood staring at one another, she considering while I waited. It took all my self-control to stand still and be patient, to let her read what she could of my intentions in my face. Eventually she nodded, and relief spilled through me as strong as the sort of grief that weakens your knees and steals your voice. "We shall talk," Aurus translated when she spoke. "But first... tell me about your home."

# 25. MIKO

The city emerged from the morning mist like the prow of a mythical ship. In all the illustrations of the first Otakos crossing the sea, their ships looked as grand, limned in light and accompanied by scaly creatures of the deep. There were no scaly creatures here, only the churned grass of fields abandoned for the winter, but for a brief, quiet moment there was something mystical about the scene, like the promise of a grand future.

Sichi halted her horse alongside, drawing her cloak closer about her. The chilly morning had turned the tip of her nose red. "There aren't very many guards on the walls," she said, critically scanning Shimai's defences. "And they've not done much to shore up the gates. Seems odd unless they didn't think we were coming."

"Surely they would have known we'd not let them keep the city through the winter if we could oust them," I said, hunting the scene for any other oddities that could make sense of the first. "With Mei'lian gone and Koi still in Chiltaen hands, Shimai is more than just a city and an important river crossing."

Sichi nodded slowly, brows caught low. "No Chiltaen scouts on the way, no one making any move to come and greet us, and a city that doesn't look ready to defend itself." She turned my way. "I don't like this, Koko."

"No," I agreed. "But whatever is going on, we need to retake the city and fast."

We rode the short way back to the ranks of our joint army to find Edo and Manshin being meticulously polite over details—the kind of politeness that's more like the repeated sticking of a thin blade into one another's skin. "If that is what you think best, Your Grace," Manshin was saying, seeming happy to sit in his saddle and admire the view.

"They haven't fortified the gates," I said, joining them with only a chill glance for the man who'd once been my greatest ally. "Nor are there many guards."

"And there's no sign they're intending to ride out and treat with us," Sichi added. "At least not yet."

Manshin smiled, but said nothing.

Gritting her teeth at his seeming amusement, Sichi said, "We ought to decide what our immediate plan is."

I had expected Manshin to be overbearing, to push me around and make sure he got his own way, so everyone would see who the true leader of this army was and by whose hand the city would be retaken. Instead, he seemed to have veered the other way, refusing to so much as give an opinion that might help, intent on letting me fail on my own terms. No wonder he had been keeping his generals at a distance since we'd set out together, not wanting them to hear him say things like "We'll do whatever you think is best, Your Majesty."

I gritted my teeth, hating how he managed to unbalance me at every turn. When I thought we might finally work together for the sake of Kisia, he threw the responsibility on my shoulders alone; where I hoped I might get the chance to speak to the generals he'd stolen from me, he wouldn't let them come near—it was like playing an Errant master who'd thought ten steps ahead before you even knew there was a game.

"We'll stop here for a bit and see if anything changes," I said, forcing my voice to sound more decisive than I felt. "Don't let the men get too comfortable, but rest and food while we consider our options would be beneficial."

Manshin nodded solemnly. "Very wise. I'll spread the word."

"And take credit for your good idea," Edo muttered as he rode away. "I don't know what he's planning, but I don't like it."

"I think he's just planning to do exactly that," I said. "Take credit for the wins and throw the failures in my face so when this is done I have no choice but to concede to his better management. I'd be left with the same decision my mother had—accept rule by a dictatorial man or risk years of civil war."

Mention of my mother brought up all the old memories, and for a moment Edo's face creased as he crushed down grief. "Your mother was a tough woman."

"She was," I agreed. "But she shouldn't have had to be. She shouldn't have been trying to hold the empire together even as its breaking pieces sliced through her bare hands. And she shouldn't have had to do that alone."

"No, she shouldn't have," Sichi said. "And that's what we're fighting for. A Kisia where that isn't the way power works, just because it always has."

"Burn it all down!" Edo cried in a perfect imitation of how Tanaka would speak when he got in one of his moods. "Let's just burn it all down and take a ship back to those icy islands and never come back."

I laughed, tears pricking my eyes at the mixture of joy and grief, and the knowledge of how different everything would have been had Tanaka been riding with us.

Still chuckling and wiping our eyes, the three of us split up to mingle amongst the soldiers as food was prepared. Manshin had disappeared, likely to wherever General Moto was hiding. Even without him nearby, eyes seemed constantly to watch me, and all the soldiers I spoke to who weren't loyal to Edo were wary and quiet, murmuring a "Your Majesty" but little more. Some even got up and moved away rather than find themselves in my path.

I ate, I drank, and I let my horse rest, gaze constantly pulled back to the poorly fortified city like a lodestone. Sichi was right. Something was amiss, but I couldn't put my finger on what it was and how much it ought to be worrying me. Perhaps the Chiltaens had lost more men than expected and were awaiting backup, or were just planning to hold out as long as they could or even torch the city as Gideon had torched Mei'lian. Once I started thinking it over, the options were endless, and the only way to find out was to ride down there.

Leaving Sichi and General Rushin to oversee the packing of the food and preparations for battle, Edo, Manshin, General Moto, and I—accompanied by half a dozen riders and a flag bearer—set out toward the city. There had been no sign of movement either upon the walls or around the gates since we'd arrived, and still nothing now that we had started across the empty fields.

"How close do you think is safe?" I whispered, leaning Edo's way as I eyed the gates. "I don't want to look like a coward, but I also don't want to become a pincushion."

"Halfway seems to be the accepted compromise," he said. "It looks strong and forces them to come just as far to talk to you."

"Assuming they want to talk."

"They may not, but surely they would rather talk than take part in a prolonged siege. It would take a few days to march to the next crossing, but we could quite easily set up a second camp outside the south gate and shut them in for the winter."

On his other side, General Moto made a disgusted sound. "Military camps in winter. I hope it won't come to that."

It seemed such a cheerful, friendly thing to say for a man who'd stabbed me in the back. Thankfully, he didn't seem to expect an answer.

With flags flapping at our backs, we approached the small rise that marked the halfway point, but the gates remained determinedly closed. No potential battlefield ought to be so quiet and no conquered city so peaceful.

In a show of unity that had nothing to do with reality, the four of us halted in a line along the rise. Needing something to do with my nervous energy, I patted my horse's neck and adjusted my bridle and didn't look at the others. "How long do we wait?"

"I'm not sure," Manshin admitted, the first time he'd spoken anything beyond an agreeable pleasantry. "I've never been in a situation where no one came to parley."

We waited. And we waited some more. My legs got stiff and my back was determined to keep slumping, while the constant shift of the clouds left us alternately in bright sunlight and gloomy chill. Our horses grew restless. For a while, Manshin and General Moto passed the time with a low, murmured conversation, but soon even that faded, leaving nothing but the wind and the increasingly desperate flap of our flags.

"This is ridiculous," I said, glancing up to find the sun had made considerable progress toward the sky's zenith. "The longer we sit here, the stupider it is," I added in a muttered under voice, but though Manshin turned a reproving eye my way, it was General Moto who spoke.

Nodding toward the gates, he said, "Looks like something is finally happening."

A thrill half relief, half worry wormed through me as the city gates finally started to move, yawning slowly open with the ponderousness of people in no hurry. From the widening gap, riders emerged. Levanti riders.

"What—?" General Moto's exclamation could have burst from any of our lips, but I was glad he was the one to give voice to my confusion.

"Well, that was unexpected," Manshin murmured.

It was, but the grimace I shared with Edo had nothing to do with Levanti in general and everything to do with the woman leading the small group. Whisperer Ezma rode proudly ahead, her crown of jawbones impossible to miss at any distance. I closed my eyes and let out a sigh. My heart knew not whether to sink or lift, for it was possible she could be both better and worse to deal with than a force of Chiltaens, depending on what had gone on inside that silent city.

"Ah, Your Majesty," the whisperer called as she approached. Glancing at Manshin, she added, "Or possibly Your Majesties. How overcrowded your empire seems to be getting." She reined in, her companions halting behind her with their hands all too close to sword hilts and bows.

"You aren't helping in that respect, honoured Whisperer," I said, determined to have the first say before Manshin could take over. "When you left Kogahaera I was quite certain you intended to make your way home, yet here you are. I expected to find a Chiltaen army holding my city."

"Oh they did, briefly, but now we are holding them."

Her smile had a self-congratulatory edge—the smile of one keen on their own intelligence. "That sounds very clever," I said, playing along to keep control of the conversation in my hands. "But you're going to have to be a bit more explicit if you want me to follow your meaning."

"Why, only that once they had settled down for the night in their barracks, we barricaded them in and took control of the city, capturing their oligarch and their hieromonk."

"I see, that is quite the play. Are you intending to hold the city through the winter?"

Ezma tilted her head, her curious gaze crawling Manshin's way.

"Well?" I snapped.

"Tsk, how high and mighty you play, child," she said, her tone making me clench my hands tight upon my reins. "Don't worry, I have no interest in holding your city a moment longer than I must to get what I want."

"And what is it you want?" Edo asked.

She straightened in her saddle, dragging her defiant stare from one to the other of us along the line. "Gold," she said. "And ships."

"Why?"

Her amused glance my way was almost pitying. "For mercenaries and supplies, so Veld Reborn can conquer the Levanti plains in the name of the One True God."

Manshin barked out a cruel laugh as my stomach curdled. Rah had given and given and given again, and I had sworn the last time I'd asked too much of him that it would be the last, yet still it hadn't been. Here I was again, the path to saving my empire, to reclaiming my throne without loss of life, went through the heart of his people. But if I didn't, if I refused, Manshin would take the deal anyway.

He didn't speak, waiting for me to make the decision, this time with an amused crease at the corner of his mouth. He had hated Rah from the beginning, hated the Levanti, refusing to see value in what they brought to our cause, and he was loving this.

The Levanti were strong. Perhaps we could warn them of what was coming, could yet change the course of Ezma's plans—weak excuses I knew for the consolations they were. Yet I nodded. "Very well," I said, trying for a shrug and a carefree tone. "I think we can come to some agreement. Gold and ships in return for you opening the city gates and letting us retake Shimai without a fight, Chiltaen army and all."

"Chiltaen army and all," she agreed. "So long as you can offer a greater payment than the Nine would give to see that same army safely home again. Or, perhaps safely left to hold the city." She raised an eyebrow at General Moto as he grumbled something under his breath. "You don't like that idea, General," she said. "Well, then, shall we negotiate?"

———————————————◆———————————————

I checked Hacho over half a dozen times, needing something to do. The deal with Whisperer Ezma meant we could retake the city without a battle, without further loss of life or destruction, yet the details of it gnawed at my bones. We were sending further misery home with the Levanti, and at the end of the day I would still have to fight for my right to the throne. It was small mercy that neither Tor nor Nuru had yet returned from their search for General Ryoji and so knew nothing of my perfidy.

I ran my hand over Hacho's blackened wood. Her presence and the power in the smooth curve of her limbs was a comfort little else gave me. Every day I felt more and more like a drawn string, but like strings, people aren't made to be drawn and held until they break. How long could I go on like this if I failed?

It had been impossible not to see similarities between my present and my father's past. Katashi Otako, true heir to the throne, had once stood with his army outside Shimai with Hacho in his hands and sought to unmake the empire with flame. Now here I stood, seeking to unmake it through peace so it could be remade stronger.

Preparations sped around me, the short time we'd given ourselves to make ready to take the city fast running out. Riders mounted, foot soldiers formed into lines, discipline a little marred by the thrill of being able to win without a fight. Only the supply trains would remain behind to ensure their safety in the event of something going terribly wrong.

"General Rushin and Lord Edo and their men will ride ahead with me," Manshin called to the massed army, riding up and back before the front ranks with the ease of a man born to the saddle. "General Yass, your men will follow, along with—"

"And I—" I began, only to bite down on the desperate squeak as Manshin went on, ignoring my existence as he outlined the straightforward plan of attack, such as it was. Edo was to secure the bridge, the barbarian generals were to secure the areas along the riverbank where the wealthiest and most important citizens lived, while Rushin's men were to secure the lower city around the gates. Nowhere in his plan was there any task for me, and too late I realised he'd played me well. He'd let me make all the decisions that hadn't mattered, lulling me into a false sense of importance, before ripping it all out from underneath me by taking command with ease. The army even cheered as he finished, Edo's soldiers included, what was left of the day promising a fine and glorious victory for us and deep shame for the Chiltaens.

I shared a grimace with Sichi, but before I could give voice to my ill-ease, a shadow fell between us. "Sichi," Manshin said as the ranks started shifting into their places behind him. "You'll be riding with me and my soldiers since you're no longer under the protection of... your former wife."

"Former—?" Sichi turned, her face a mask of shock. Of course he had chosen now to stake his claim upon her again. "Miko?"

I'd not found time or words to explain the only condition upon which he had agreed to our alliance, but now that we were being allowed to just walk in, I wished I had. I'd hoped never to have to tell her, that by some chance I would be able to deny our agreement, to renege on the dissolution of my marriage, but it seemed there were still many lessons in honesty and humility I needed to learn.

"Sichi, I—" What could I say? She wasn't a fool. Realisation spread across her features, ending in a sharp, humourless laugh she directed at both the architects of her situation.

"I ought to have known you wouldn't let it go," she said, spitting bitterness at her father. "Still want me to marry Leo to assure an alliance with the people who keep conquering our cities?" She tittered rather than let him answer. "I spit on any marriage you would try to force me into." Having spent her anger on her unmoved father, Sichi looked my way with a disappointed huff of air. "I get it, I do, but I deserved to know. I really thought we were going to do this together."

She didn't stay to hear my excuses, letting herself be ushered away by a hovering General Moto and a group of his men. At least whatever happened, I could be sure she would be well protected.

"May the best emperor win, child," Manshin said, turning his grand mount toward the city amid the passing ranks of his soldiers. "Too bad you weren't born a boy after all."

A last, biting strike like a whip to my flank. His words left me momentarily breathless, staring at the flick of his horse's tail as he departed.

"Your Majesty?"

I flinched at the nearby voice, relief at the sight of Captain Kiren bringing me back to myself. "Captain."

"We ought to be getting on, don't you think?" He nodded in the direction of the city. Where before, as we waited outside Shimai, time had barely seemed to pass, now it raced along. The front lines of our joint army, carrying both imperial and Bahain banners, were almost to the gates.

"Shit," I hissed like air leaking from an angry bellows. "Are your men ready, Captain?"

"Ready as always, Your Majesty."

"Then let's go!"

I jammed my heels hard into my horse's sides, and it leaped into motion. All around us the army charged, even the foot soldiers sprinting for the open gates, covering the ground at a speed that was leaving me behind.

Not checking that Captain Kiren and his men were with me, I sped on, only to have to slow amid the crowded field. The gates were a bottleneck, ranks pressing to get through in an undignified rush. No doubt Manshin was already inside, already playing grand saviour of the empire. The knowledge tasted bitter on my tongue, as bitter as the realisation I had no idea what I was going to do once I got inside the walls. How could I challenge him? Sichi would have had advice, but Sichi wasn't here. I was on my own.

Eventually, surrounded by the push and shove of excited soldiers, I drew near the open gates. But there progress slowed and I had to rein in or risk trampling my own army. "What's the hold-up?" I snapped, looking around to find that Captain Kiren had kept close. Behind him, the field was far emptier than I had thought possible, the only soldiers left a group making for the city at a walk rather than a run. They had no general with them, and perhaps I ought to have shouted at them to get them moving, asserting some author-ity, but the discomfort of being alone stayed my tongue.

"Move it! What's holding us up?" Captain Kiren shouted, the mass of soldiers in the gateway having thinned but not dispersed. "Don't make us trample you. Make way for Her Imperial Majesty! Make way!"

He might as well have been shouting at the walls for all the response he got. Some of the soldiers just stood there, no longer pushing and shoving, just there like they'd decided to go no farther.

"Make way!" Captain Kiren shouted again, rising in his stirrups. "Make way for Her Imperial Majesty!"

Some of them started to move, glancing back at us before pushing their own way through the remaining soldiers, but most planted their feet and didn't budge.

"Manshin," I hissed beneath my breath. "He's trying to stop me getting into the city so he can take all the glory for himself. We're going to have to push through."

"Captain!"

We both spun. One of Kiren's men had turned, sword drawn, to face the foot soldiers behind us. They'd been sauntering toward the city but were nearly upon us now, one man out in front leading the way. Four dozen? Five? It could even have been a hundred men, but any desire to count them died when their leader removed his helmet.

Beneath the Kisian armour walked Dom Villius, unmistakable in his white mask. It covered his mouth, yet somehow seemed to smile. Around him, his soldiers drew bows, nocking arrows to their strings amid the tense silence of an indrawn breath. Captain Kiren shouted orders, but in that frozen moment it wasn't his words I heard, only the sharp whispers of steel being drawn behind me.

# 26. CASSANDRA

The woman with the fucking bones on her head wouldn't stop staring at me. She hadn't said anything, just bent down and peered at me like she could pierce my head with her gaze. She'd done the same to Kaysa, kneeling out of reach to my right, surrounded by Levanti with drawn blades. That the body she wore was already dead seemed not to concern them.

"Are you just going to stare or what?" I said, knees starting to ache. "I'm getting bored."

Bone Lady straightened, glancing around at the swell of activity surrounding us. North from the Levanti camp, the city gates were being hauled open once again, while the citizens of Shimai were pouring into the streets amid excited gabble. "Bored?" she said, speaking at last. "What a time to be bored. Destiny is about to change everything, and here you are to witness it, or perhaps to mess it all up."

"Just tell me what you want; I'm too tired for talking around the point."

"Very well. You entered this city with Rah and Gideon e'Torin—"

I barked a laugh. "And a walking, talking corpse, but by all means let's focus on what is most important."

The woman scowled, her annoyance warming me to the depths

of my icy soul. "I will get to that part," she said coolly. "But first I want to know why you entered this city with them and where they went."

"How the fuck should I know? Is this why you've kept us under guard all fucking night, so we might go soft and help you find your fugitives?" I hadn't planned to laugh at her, given the number of Levanti around with sharp, pointy swords, but between the sleepless night and the lack of Kaysa's stabilising presence, I was beginning to feel delirious. "I don't know either of them. Your captain Rah cut my head off the first time I met him, so I wouldn't say we're friends. We needed to get inside the city, they needed to get inside the city, that's it. Just like Yakono told you when you asked him."

Yakono had his eyes closed, but he nodded, proving he hadn't managed to fall asleep while kneeling on stone. He'd hardly moved at all, speaking only to the Bone Lady when she'd asked him questions, but not to me. He hadn't said a word since I'd gone to find a Kisian corpse for Kaysa to walk in, and I couldn't say I blamed him. This was exactly why I'd tried so hard never to let him find out.

"Very well," the woman said as the first Kisian soldiers strode through the open gates—the size of toy figures for now, but we would soon be swamped. "Why were you so desperate to get inside the city that you would work with two Levanti outcasts?"

She'd asked Yakono the same question during the night, but he'd refused to answer. Perhaps because it was against his code or because he was being cautious, or for some other wise reason I couldn't think of. "We have a contract on Dom Villius and we're here to kill him," I said.

Bone Lady laughed, glancing around to see if anyone shared her amusement, though I was pretty sure none of the other Levanti understood a damn word I was saying. "He isn't here," she said, turning her attention back to me. "As amusing as it would be to see him fail at his final hurdle with a knife in his back."

"Not here *yet*," I said. "There's a thing called an ambush we were going to try, have you heard of it?"

The amused smile dropped from her face, and I knew I'd gone too far, just couldn't find the will to care. Nothing had gone right since I'd left Genava, yet here I was, kneeling before a Levanti wearing a crown of bones in the middle of a Kisian city about to be reconquered by Kisian soldiers. I'd have said I just wanted to go home, but somewhere along the way I'd stopped thinking of anywhere as home.

The heavy footfalls of a whole army approaching rose amid people cheering. God, I was tired.

"You seem to have very few survival instincts for someone who is still alive," the woman said, the words biting. "So, let's make a deal. You answer one last question to my satisfaction and I'll let you go, uh...ambush Dom Villius. If not, I hand you all over to the first Kisian soldiers who walk through this camp. Your choice."

"That rather depends on the question, doesn't it?"

A humourless smile spread her lips. "The issue of the...what did you call it? Walking, talking corpse?" She gestured at the very dead Kisian cart driver, and my gaze slid Kaysa's way. After her first desperate fight to be set free, she'd settled into as deep a silence as Yakono, though whether due to hopelessness or growing discomfort in her dead flesh, I couldn't say. "Explain what this"—she waved her hands around vaguely—"is. Or I'll let the Kisians decide what to do with you."

Around us the Levanti had quietened, eyes upon the gates. The Kisian army was spreading out into the streets, securing the city or whatever it was that armies did, but the bulk of them still seemed to be heading this way and were too close for Levanti comfort. For once, I agreed with them. Kisian soldiers or telling the truth. It ought to have been an easy decision, and in any other situation it would have been. But Yakono was right there. He still had his eyes closed, but I knew he was listening as intently as Kaysa was attempting to communicate via her unblinking, dead stare.

"Cass," she rumbled, voice crackling and dry. "Do it or I will."

We'd been prisoners of these Levanti since being found in the cart, had been kept awake through the night, unable to talk to anyone unless this woman was present to understand us, and now with an unfriendly army bearing down upon an already unfriendly situation, freedom was an admission away. Not an admission to Bone Lady. To Yakono.

Damn.

I closed my eyes and drew a deep breath. "I'm a Deathwalker," I said, and looking at Yakono rather than the angry Levanti lady, I went on, "I was born with a...voice...inside my head, only it wasn't a voice like what some people hear; it was another person. Another soul. People are meant to have one soul in their one body, but I was...made wrong. I have two."

It sounded like nonsense, pathetic nonsense, but Yakono opened his eyes, squarely meeting mine. No reply, no questions, he was just waiting for me to go on. The Levanti woman had a far hungrier look, one I'd started to see more often when admitting my odd ability. Some people were horrified, others wondered to what uses I could be put.

Kisian soldiers were flooding past now, slowing through the Levanti camp, but not stopping. The Kisians weren't at all surprised to see the Levanti, and their gazes slid over the three of us like we didn't exist, like I hadn't just flayed myself open so we could get on with killing one fucking Leo and saving another fucking Leo.

"The rest is obvious really," I hurried on. "Deathwalker because we can move one of our souls into a recently dead corpse for a time and then bring them back when that body gets useless. Very handy for getting into places, or out of them, having a body that can't be killed because it's already dead. Give the nice lady a wave, Kaysa."

Glaring as only a corpse can, with half the man's face refusing to cooperate, Kaysa lifted a stiff hand. "Can we go now?" she croaked.

"So your other soul is in that body right now, but you could bring it back into your—into that one?" Bone Lady's eyes were bright and curious. "Show me."

"You'll have to tell your brutes not to stab me the moment I move, then," I said, nodding at the Levanti encircling us.

A few words to them and she nodded. There was nothing for it. I needed to pull Kaysa back before the corpse froze up completely, but I would have preferred not to top off this disastrous admission to Yakono with a demonstration. "Fuck," I sighed. "Guess it's too late now."

I shuffled forward, keeping an eye on the armed Levanti, and reached for Kaysa's hand. I'd gotten so used to the feeling of her or Hana coming and going from my body that I hardly thought about it now, about how the sensation was like breathing so deeply and yet not deeply enough, filling an emptiness that could never truly be filled. It took a mere second yet could feel like a lifetime—Yakono's heavy gaze upon me the whole time.

Robbed of a soul, the Kisian carter's corpse fell slowly sideways, refusing to bend, only to topple like a felled tree.

*Thank God, that was getting uncomfortable*, Kaysa said, relief spilling through me at the sound of her mind.

"Fascinating," Bone Lady said when I sat back. "If you're ever in search of work outside Kisia or Chiltae, there's a group of other... talented people who work for hire. They're currently across the Eye Sea, but I'm sure if you asked the right people someone like you could find them easily enough."

Someone like me. I would always be the accident I had been born and nothing else.

"That's great," I said. "Can we go now? Have I performed enough for your curiosity?"

Bone Lady saluted in the Levanti way, long hair shifting around her crown. "You have, and answered the question of why you are so connected to Dom Villius's destiny. No wonder he would take an interest in someone literally walking around with two voices."

Kaysa gasped like she'd been struck, and with a dismissive wave and few words, the Levanti around us stepped back. A few nicked their skin and sheathed their blades, stretching and yawning, while the others kept their weapons drawn and watched the passing Kisians warily.

*The consort with two voices,* Kaysa said as I got to my feet, knees aching so much I had to wait for them to be able to hold me. *She knows about the prophecy.*

Yakono stood far more easily than I had, his gaze shying to the now discarded corpse of the Kisian carter lying on the stones. "Am I..." he began, "the only person who didn't know that you were—are—two people?" He drew his gaze back from the corpse, the hurt and sadness in his eyes like a gut punch. "Is that even what it is? Are you... two different people?"

"I... I suppose you could say that, yes."

"And Captain Rah e'Torin is allowed to know but not me? Why?"

"Because I don't care if he hates me!"

His jaw dropped. "You were worried I would hate you?"

"People always do. I'm an unnatural freak, like Duos and his brothers."

"Are you trying to become a reborn god and kill everyone in the process?"

"Well, no—"

Kaysa shoved forward, taking over. "This is lovely and all," she said. "But there are suddenly a lot of very worried Levanti around here. We should move before they decide we're their enemies after all. Getting caught again is not an option if we're to have any chance of saving Unus."

Even through the fogginess of being buried beneath her control, the noise around us was rising. The excited cheers of the Kisian citizens had given way to confusion, and the Levanti were shouting to one another in something akin to a panic, pulling away from the soldiers still pouring through the square.

Thrust back into control, I had the sensation of staggering within my own skin. "What the fuck is going on?" I said as all heads turned toward the gates. Weapons that had just been sheathed were being drawn again as the Levanti contracted into a defensive formation.

Both Yakono and I stared around, seeking what had changed. No Kisian soldier seemed interested in attacking them, yet still panic heated the air, filling it with a buzz. One didn't need to understand Levanti to eventually catch the name spreading through them like a hissed expletive.

Dom Villius.

"Quick," Yakono said, catching the name as I did. "We have to hide before he sees us. We need a plan."

He sprinted off across the square, dodging tents and fires and brandished blades. I followed, wishing I had anything like his graceful ease. My knees screamed the whole way, refusing to let me forget for how long they'd been pressed into the stones.

Seeming to know where he was going, or at least able to remember which way was north, Yakono ducked into a street and took a sharp turn down an alleyway, almost colliding with a small knot of children arguing over whether they ought to go home or stay to watch the excitement. Yakono's sudden appearance sent them running, hopefully for safety. With an apology for frightening them still tripping off his tongue, he slid to a halt at the alley opening, beyond which the children had been getting an excellent view of the incoming Kisian soldiers. They too had slowed, some turning as confusion spread through the ranks.

"Looks like no one was expecting him to show up," Yakono said as I joined him at the corner.

"Except for us."

He agreed with a half shrug, eyes still on the passing soldiers. "He needs to see his prophecy through, and everything he needs is here."

*Everything he needs,* Kaysa mused. *Except for Lady Sichi free to marry him.*

*You keep harping on about the marriage thing,* I said. *I hope you aren't thinking of marrying the bastard now he's so close to becoming Veld.*

*No...*

Her lack of conviction was not comforting.

"I wonder if—ah! There he is!" Yakono crouched as Duos came into sight, striding at the head of a group of Kisian soldiers who seemed like the only people in the whole city who weren't upset to see him. Heads proudly lifted, they followed the Chiltaen holy man like he was their god—and dressed in the full hieromonk's regalia, he could have been. He'd always worn variants of a high priest's garb and always had his mask at hand, but I'd never before seen him in ceremonial cloth. His father had worn it only on certain occasions and never when on the road with the army, yet here Duos was, already dressing for his new job as God incarnate—Veld Reborn.

A little shiver ran through my skin, deepening to horror as a formation of soldiers came into view. They followed in his wake, marching in a protective block around a hooded figure. Chains and manacles hung from around the figure's neck, joining to wrists and ankles so all they could do was shuffle forward, shoved onward by the soldiers behind.

*Unus*, Kaysa breathed. *We have to get him out of here.*

"If Duos is with the Kisian army then we're in trouble," Yakono whispered as the chained and hooded figure of Unus shuffled on out of sight, replaced by still more soldiers striding past.

"Yes, but why?" I said.

"Because I'm good at my job and so are you, but that's a lot of soldiers."

"No, I mean... why would the Kisians want anything to do with him and his god pretentions?" I straightened up, knees continuing their protest. "It makes no sense. Their alliance ended in shambles at that stupid wedding, and he's Chiltaen!"

Still crouching at the corner of the alley, he peered up at me through a loose fall of hair, all confusion. "Did the Chiltaens conquer this city or not?"

"No fucking idea, it's all—"

*Cass!* Kaysa cried. *I have an idea. It's not the greatest, but I can't think of any other way we can stay close to him.*

*What? How can we—*

"He needs a consort," Kaysa blurted aloud. "He needs a consort with two voices to complete his prophecy and Lady Sichi is taken and we're a better choice anyway."

"I... What?" Yakono said, slowly getting to his feet. "Consort?"

"Yes, it's in the holy book. That's why he wanted to marry Lady Sichi and made the deal with her father and—" Kaysa broke off, pacing the short width of the alley like a leaf caught in a spinning wind. "Yes, yes!" She stopped abruptly. "If we offer ourselves he'll take us with him and we can stay close to Unus, ready to strike should there be an opportunity to kill him. You can stay as close as you safely can. One of us on the inside and one on the outside, yes?"

"He'll kill you!"

"No, at least not until after marrying us and proclaiming himself a god. And he can't get into our mind the same way as yours because it's already rather crowded."

Yakono looked away, many different expressions crossing his face before settling on shameful frustration. "Is this Cassandra I'm talking to, or... the other—"

"Kaysa," Kaysa snapped. "Yes, you're talking to Kaysa because Cassandra isn't very good at plans or at thinking straight when you're around, so until it's time to stab someone, I'm in charge. Now, I'm going to walk out there before Duos gets away and offer myself as his consort, and you're going to do what assassins do and follow us or whatever, all right?"

*Kaysa, what the fuck?*

I tried to shout, but Kaysa held tight to control, blocking me out with gritted teeth.

*Kaysa! We can't marry him! There's no one I want to marry less!*

She ignored me, intent gaze caught to Yakono. "All right?" she repeated. "You do want to finish this contract, don't you?"

A nod.

"Then this is how we're doing it. Keep out of sight; the last thing Cassandra needs is to have to fight you again."

I winced, as Yakono did, but full of determination, Kaysa just spun on her heel and strode out into the street, leaving Yakono nothing to do but obey and me nothing to do but scream.

"Quit it, Cassandra," she said, our heart racing as she sped along the street, not fighting the flow of soldiers but rushing with them. "You've done much stupider things."

*Stupider than chasing after someone who wants us dead and begging him to marry us?*

She barked a short laugh. "How romantic you make it sound."

The movement of soldiers slowed as they reached the Levanti

camp, ill-ease staining the air with whispers and growls. No one seemed to know who was on what side or even how many sides there were, hatred of Dom Villius the only unifying force. He had stopped with his procession of Kisian soldiers and, heedless of the dislike around him, stood talking to the woman with the bone crown. It didn't look friendly, but neither did it look unfriendly, something of the respect of rivals in their stances.

"Leo!" Kaysa called, making me want to shrink even further down into our subconscious. Every head in the square turned our way, eyes widening, fingers pointing. Whisper, whisper, *Such a freak*. Under so many stares I couldn't but feel the truth of it.

"Ah, you're back already, Deathwalker," Bone Lady said, emphasising the title with a glance Duos's way. "Something I can do for you?"

"No." Kaysa stood tall and sure and did not look away, did not buckle, and as much as I hated the entire plan, I couldn't but be proud of her. "I require nothing from you. I'm here to make Lord Villius a proposition."

He'd been watching us since we'd arrived, but only at that did he pull down his mask to eye us over the pale fabric. "Kaysa," he said, her name all but a croon. "How unusual to see you so in command. By all means, proposition me. Although if it's about my brother you'll be wasting your breath."

"No. Not Unus. Me and you. You need a consort to see this through."

The hundreds of stares faded to nothing. There was just us and the deep, heavy thud of our heart as Duos slid his mask down the rest of the way, a small smile turning his lips. "I see. A literal translation of the original words rather than a metaphorical one. I've always said you were the clever one, Kaysa."

She made a mocking little curtsey, but Duos wasn't watching; he looked around, ears pricked for sounds only he could hear. Minds.

Thoughts. Hopefully Yakono wasn't too close, but even thinking such a thought could bring him to Duos's attention.

"Oh, don't worry," Duos said, finally looking back. "I already know everything that's in your mind, and I can tell you that your plan won't work. My soldiers will be on the watch for our . . . friend, and there is no way you are getting near enough to Unus to so much as shout at him. But you're right about the consort, so I will have to take the small risk that you have a cleverer plan than it appears." He gestured to one of his men. "Captain? We're bringing this one too. And send someone to find a priest. I'm getting married."

## 27. RAH

Sleep had been hard to come by, the night filled with increasingly delirious rehearsals of what I could say to win over the Levanti who hated me. Whenever my exhausted body dragged me into a doze, my dreams were the same, vivid, swirling nightmares of how it could all go wrong. Long before the sun rose, I had given up on my mat.

Sitting on the balcony with a blanket wrapped around my shoulders, I watched the Levanti encampment through the fretwork—watched as it slumbered and as it came slowly to life with the rising sun. Fires were stoked and sleepy figures moved about the mist like ghosts, wavering in and out of existence. I felt akin to their ethereal forms, as insubstantial and veiled as my sense of who I was. I couldn't remember what being completely at one with a herd had felt like, trusting them all and knowing we were family. Even if we made it back to the plains, it would never again be like that. At least not for us.

A yawn and some shuffling steps behind me heralded Gideon's arrival, as insubstantial as those down in the square so long as I didn't turn around, so long as I let him exist as nothing but small sounds of life. We ought to have talked, but as always it had been easier not to. Easier to sit in our separate spaces and get caught in our own thoughts.

"Do you have a plan?" Gideon asked, insistent on existing. I wasn't sure whether I was more discomforted by his refusal to bend to my sombre imagination or comforted by it.

"As much of one as is possible."

We sat awhile in silence, both watching the Levanti camp in the square come to life. Food was soon cooking, laughter rising with the smoke. Only the movement of Kisian citizens warily going about their business around the edges made the camp seem out of place.

"When will you go down there?" Gideon asked.

"Soon," I said, hoping he wouldn't guess that the very thought made my limbs feel heavy, yesterday's rage having dissipated enough to let in doubts. "When I'm ready. I can hardly go down there with a blanket around my shoulders."

"If you plan to wait until the day warms up, I think you might be waiting a while; the mist looks heavy."

Minutes slid by, questions beginning to bank up against my tongue. Could I really challenge a horse whisperer? What would we do after all this? Who would we be? Where would we go? I wasn't sure I wanted the answers.

"Something is going on." Gideon's words brought me out of my reverie, a pit so deep I had to swim against a tide of confusion to return.

"What?"

He gestured at the camp. "Something has changed. The mood is off."

"Everything looks normal."

"Bad news, perhaps."

"But what could..." My voice abandoned me as a possibility filled all the space in my mind. Leaping to my feet, I was across the abandoned living space in seconds, taking the stairs to the attic rooms two at a time. One room looked out on the square like the balcony below, but the other looked out toward the city walls. Not quite toward the gate, but throwing open the window and sticking my head out fixed that. "Ah, shit," I hissed. "Just what we need."

"Let me guess," Gideon called up the stairs. "Her Imperial Majesty has finally deigned to show up."

There had been a time when Miko's arrival would have been a relief, but that time had long gone. And if she was still fighting for sole possession of the throne, one wrong move could send the whole situation to the hells.

I was out of time.

Gideon stood waiting at the bottom of the stairs, his expression so much the disapproving First Sword he'd once been that I stopped in my tracks. He folded his arms. "Tell me you're sure this will work."

"I'm sure it needs to be done," I said, folding my own arms.

"That's exactly what I told myself, and look how that went," he said with a laugh that seemed to mock both of us.

"You have a different suggestion you'd like to share?"

He rolled his eyes. "No."

"Then this conversation is pointless. If Ezma isn't stopped, if she gets out of this with everything she wants, then there will be no more plains to go home to, no more Levanti as we know them. We will be the last of a dying culture no one cared enough to save."

"That's what I thought I was doing too." Gideon turned and strode away across the room, giving up the conversation, and yet the moment he stopped pressing me to account for myself, everything felt wrong. With words unsaid and thoughts unshared, I followed.

"Gideon?" He didn't stop. "Gideon, stop walking away. It's done. What went wrong is in the past. Let go of your mistakes."

"Mistakes?" Gideon spun back. "Mistakes? You weren't there!" he cried, pressing a fist to his chest. "You have no idea what it was like. What I had to do. What I had to *be* to protect the lives of my Swords. When someone hits and hits and hits at everything you care about, you can't think about tenets or tradition or honour. There is only the determination to survive. I may not have achieved anything worth being proud of, but I would do it again in a heartbeat."

His chest heaved as he thumped it, heedless of the wound in his arm, and once again I stood before the Gideon who had fearlessly carved a path for his people, had weighed his soul heavy to save his herd, not letting even me stand in his way. I could not breathe. I stared at him like something inside me had broken. He stared back, all intense dark eyes.

"And what do you think I did?" I said, spilling the first words that came to my tongue, anything to stop him looking at me like that. "Do you think I've just been—"

"I have no fucking idea what you've been doing, Rah, but by the gods I wish you would make up your mind."

All the air was sucked out of the room. "What do you mean?"

Gideon laughed bitterly. "You know what I mean, but by all means let's just keep shouting until we feel better."

"I . . . I'm sorry. I shouldn't have kissed you, I—"

"I don't want you to be sorry, I want you to mean it!"

Breath abandoned me and my insides knotted. There were so many things I wanted to say, things I'd said to him while he slept, but standing before him in that moment I was nothing but an empty shell full of such fire I feared I would burn him.

Gideon closed his eyes, a sigh brushing past his lips. "First you have the worst timing of anyone ever, and now this? Just . . . *do* something, Rah. Tell me I'm wrong if I'm wrong, but for the love of all the gods don't just stand there staring at me."

"You gave me no permission. I . . . I shouldn't have—"

"What more permission do you need now?" He ran a hand

through his mahogany-tinged hair and looked away. "What more can I do but have loved you all my life, even when you couldn't see me?"

"I could always see you."

He met my gaze with such mocking disbelief that anger flared me to motion. "Don't look at me like that," I snapped, stepping closer. "Gods, Gideon, you were my whole world. You were my hero! My brother! The fath—"

I broke off, realising I'd just spewed the narrative I'd long buried my feelings beneath. Gideon rolled his eyes. "You are so shit at this," he said, shaking his head and turning away.

I gripped his arm. "Don't walk away from me." My heart thumped hard as fear and hope mixed in Gideon's eyes. "You want me to mean it. You want me to prove myself." He didn't draw back as I closed the space between us, though I could feel the rapid racing of his pulse beneath my fingers, and as my nose brushed against his, breath caught in his throat. "You want to see what fire I carry for you?" I said, so close to his lips I could almost taste them. "I'll try not to burn you."

"No, don't try," he whispered. "Burn me. Please."

Our kiss back at the camp had been unexpected and tentative and all wrong, but this time I had a heart to prove. Taking his face in my hands, I kissed him, not a gentle kiss, but one full of fury and need and fire, ferocious and hot, and gods how had I convinced myself for so long I'd not wanted this. Wanted him. He'd asked me to burn him, yet still I held back, afraid he didn't know what he was asking for. Until, kissing me as hungrily, he shoved me back against the wall. The uneven woodwork dug into my spine, yet like it was the key to a part of me I'd never let anyone see, I stopped thinking. There was just him and me and the heat of our bodies together as I spun us around and threw him against the wall in my place.

Swallowing his short gasp, I deepened our kiss, consuming him. This man who had long been my world, who I'd never let myself see as more than a brother for fear of losing him, hot and vital and mine. All his strength and his glory, every muscle and scar and scratch of unshaved stubble. Mine.

"Rah," he gasped, pulling away enough to speak, his lips red raw from my passion. "If this is just your pity—"

"Pity?" I slid my fingers around his throat. "Shut. Up." I pressed against him, sure he could feel my hardness as I could feel his. "Does this feel like pity?"

His throat bulged beneath my palm as he swallowed. I watched the flick of his tongue as he licked his lips, felt the swelling of his chest as he drew breath, everything about him so vulnerable in that moment, and yet his eyes begged. I'd spent so long trying to find the old Gideon that I'd failed to see the new one.

"This is your chance to tell me to stop," I said in a whisper against his lips.

I hadn't loosened my hold on his throat, and he strained against it as he leaned close, glaring a challenge. "I said burn. Me."

The air was cold, yet his skin seared hot as I gripped his tunic and ripped it off over his head, owning just enough self-control to consider which arm was injured. My own tunic followed. We needed to talk. We needed to work through so much pain and confusion, so much history, but neither of us seemed to have any words, any sense of time or place, just a searing need that had to be sated. It might be the only chance we ever got.

With our tunics tossed aside, I turned him to the wall and yanked down his breeches. Part of me expected him to pull away then, for the fragility of his mind to rebel at such vulnerability, but when I loosened my own breeches, he slid his hand below the band and closed his fingers around me, his every movement a challenge, goading me on.

He bit down a cry as I slid slowly into him, part gentle beginning, part drawing out the sensation, savouring it as I savoured the hitch of his breath and the low moan of a curse brushing past his lips. I wanted to take him slowly apart and put him back together, to possess him, to peel back every layer of this new experience and take my time enjoying it, but we had come too far, had been too heated to allow for anything but the furious sating of our first, burning need. It was no gentle lovemaking, no sweet moment. Perhaps that would come later if we walked out of this cursed city alive.

Pressing away from the wall, he leaned against me, arching back so his head rested on my shoulder as we hurried our way to satiation. With the bulging line of his throat bared, I slid my hand around it as I closed my other around him, squeezing both, the delighted moan by my ear almost enough to end me then and there.

It was the shuddering of his body that did it, his hot seed covering my fingers as he cried out my name, a pained notch between his brows as he reached his climax. I soon followed, pleasure ripping through me. But once I found I could breathe and think again, the glorious feeling was all too soon chased away by shame at how brutally I had used him.

I closed my arms around him, and there I stayed, catching my breath and calming my heart, the clarity of the moment muddying second by second with every intrusive thought. That he hadn't been ready for this. That I hadn't been. That I ought to have been gentle. That we ought to have talked. That no one could look at the way I had acted and see an honourable man, let alone a caring lover.

When I let him go, he stayed leaning against the wall, arms shaking.

"Shit, Gideon," I said, pulling out of him. "I'm sorry, I don't know what came over me. I . . ."

He turned, leaning on one arm, his other hand shakily drawing up his breeches. "Rah. Are you ever going to stop apologising for who you are and what you want? It's insulting."

The words that leapt to my tongue were less defence than self-denial, and I snapped my jaw shut.

He took on a superior *I told you so* expression as he retied his breeches, leaving me only his torso to stare at while I struggled with this new idea. "I'd have told you to stop if I wanted you to stop," he said, reaching for his tunic. "Feel ashamed if you want to, but don't you dare make me feel I ought to be for enjoying it."

"I didn't mean..."

But it didn't matter what I'd meant. I'd apologised for something we'd both enjoyed because it didn't conform to my ideal of myself. "I guess...I guess I'm not the paragon I like to think I am."

"You can close your fingers around my throat while you fuck me and still be a paragon of Levanti honour. In fact, I'm pretty sure you're still about to go be all self-sacrificing for your people in a moment. Are you blushing? Gods, Rah, if you're about to tell me you genuinely wish you hadn't done that or didn't enjoy it, I swear—"

"If I didn't enjoy it, I wouldn't be fucking blushing at how hot the thought of doing it again makes me, all right? I just want to—"

"Want to what?" he said, taking a challenging step toward me. "Want to hold me down? Want to choke me? Want to have me in any way you want?"

I groaned. "Stop."

"Stop what? Don't you want to do those things?"

"Why are we even talking about this? There's a horse whisperer problem I have to go solve."

Gideon snorted. "Because hiding behind duty is always easier."

"What do you want me to say?" I cried.

"I want you to tell me how much you want me so I don't feel like a fool! Tell me I am not alone, that this wasn't a one-time thing, that I haven't loved you forever for one amazing fuck up against a wall and goodbye."

"Oh, are you saying there's something I'm not shit at?"

His brows slammed down. "I'm being serious."

"So am I. You've been telling me I'm shit at everything lately; it's nice to know there's one thing I do well."

"Gods, go back to beating yourself up, it was more attractive."

"Look, I'm sorry, I don't know what to do about...about this. This thing. This us. I'm meant to be walking out there and challenging a horse whisperer, not thinking about all the things I want to do to you. I mean, gods, you had a breakdown, Gideon, you're injured."

"I am, but this conversation is hurting me more than your dick ever could. Fuck off. Go be a hero."

He turned away, drawing his tunic on carefully, hissing at his injury. I ought to have helped, but all I could do was stare at his back, hearing his words over and over in my mind. This thing he had awakened in me, had it always been there? Had I been repressing it like I'd repressed my feelings for him, holding tight to honour and duty because it was safer than admitting there were things I wanted? Did I even know myself at all?

"Gideon," I said.

He didn't look around. "What?"

"I have to go, you know, army at the gates and all, but...I love you."

A wary profile turned my way.

"I've loved you for a long time," I went on, the words easier to say once I had started. "Only I'm...an idiot. I convinced myself I just admired and looked up to you, that I had to give myself only to the herd to make up for all the ways I'd failed. You're right. Hiding behind duty has been safer."

Having stared at me a long time, Gideon slowly nodded. "You really do have the shittiest timing."

I had to laugh. "I do."

"I love you, now goodbye, I'm off to challenge an egomaniacal horse whisperer who's already tried to kill us both."

"Something like that, yes. I'd say I'm sorry, but you'd bite me."

"Look at you learning." He strode toward me, sweat glistening in the notch between his collarbones. He stopped so close I could feel the warmth radiating from him and feel his breath upon my lips. "I wish I could say you haven't made it easy to love you, but loving you has always been easy. It was not being loved back, not being seen, that has been torture."

"You could have said something."

"I did," he said. "Every day. In everything I did and everything I said. Everyone else knew, which meant the only reason you didn't was because you didn't want to." He shrugged. "Would a confession in words have achieved anything more than scaring you away?"

I couldn't answer, because there was no answer. It might have, my old self as far removed now as his, a totally different Rah I didn't know anymore.

Gideon seemed to understand and leant close, touching his nose to mine. "Go do your hero thing, but you had better come back. We're not done here."

He kissed me, drawing breath like he was trying to fill himself with my scent, with my whole being, and never in a single moment of time had I felt so completely seen and valued and desired for everything I was, right down into the dark depths I'd pretended not to have.

Having drawn his fill, he shoved me away and I stumbled back a step. "Go on," he said, looking away. "Before I stop you."

What could I do? To stand there assuring him I didn't want to go was more cruelty than kindness, so I grabbed my tunic and turned away. Every step my feet grew heavier, numbness spreading through me, but I couldn't turn back. Couldn't stop. I might have been hiding my feelings behind duty, but that didn't mean the duty wasn't real.

"You're sure she'll let a challenge happen?" Gideon said as I reached the stairway down into the shop.

I didn't turn, wouldn't do myself the cruelty of looking at him again. "She's Levanti leading Levanti," I said. "She can't refuse a challenge, especially not in the position of a herd master. And then . . . I just have to make them listen."

Just as I'd once sat across the fire from him, only needing to make them listen. I wondered if it was in his mind as it was in mine, this odd juxtaposition of then and now likely to stay with us wherever we went from here.

My footsteps sounded loud on the stairs, hollow like the thud of my heartbeat. In the shadowy store below, I paused to check I had all I needed, one final preparation for one final battle. While I stood there in the dim light, I half expected to be called back or for Gideon to follow, but more than anyone Gideon knew about determination and sacrifice.

Stepping out into the street was like walking into a different world, everything wrong, from the bright sunlight now ripping through the mist to the sounds and the smells, the street alive with the buzz of excited Kisian chatter. Their empress had come to liberate them.

Setting off along the street, I did my best not to make eye contact with anyone, to not be a threat. I had to not worry about Shimai's people, not think about Gideon or Miko, instead narrowing my focus down to one person—one purpose. She was out there in the square, commanding, leading, being everything she shouldn't be. She was a spit in the face of every whisperer who had come before her.

I needed that rage, needed to hold on to it, to keep it burning in my chest, building with each step. Without it, it would be all too easy to consign the Levanti to the hells and turn back. They'd given me plenty of reasons to walk away.

I'd taken the long way rather than stepping into the unknown through the shop door, but my path grew increasingly crowded as I neared the city gates. Cheers and shouts, hurrying footsteps—it rose to a deafening roar as I caught sight of the first flash of crimson. The Kisians were already inside the walls.

"Shit!" I sped to a run, dodging in and out of people gathered to watch Kisian soldiers spill into the city. Ahead, Levanti tents. Smoke rose from campfires. I slowed at the final curve in the road and slammed into someone coming the other way.

"Rah!"

Stunned, I stepped back, blinking. "Amun! What are you doing here?"

"I…"

Of course they'd followed Ezma. He would have had no choice after what had happened, would have had to listen to Shenyah's demands. Gods, had she made it back? Did he know what had happened in that clearing?

Each thought sped by, but it was sorrow that creased Amun's brow. "I'm here because Ezma is here," he said at last. "Lashak wanted to try to talk some of her followers into coming back with us before we left. The better question is why the fuck are you here? If Ezma finds you—she was so angry yesterday when you got away—damn it, Rah you should have just gotten the fuck out of here while you could."

"I'm going to challenge her."

Amun's jaw dropped, and gripping my arms he tried to hustle me back out of the square, looking over his shoulder in case anyone had heard me. "No, you're fucking not. Have you forgotten she called a *kutum* on you? That Derkka drugged you? They aren't going to let you lead even a single Sword out of here or anywhere ever again."

"Amun, I'm no longer your captain and can give you no orders, but if you still think of me as a friend, you'll let me do what I came here to do."

He opened his mouth, only to shut it again, pain shooting across his features. Behind him, someone cleared their throat, and Amun closed his eyes. "Ah, Rah e'Torin." Derkka strode up behind Amun, the bow in his hand reminding me of the night he had drawn it at my back, only to kill Grace Bahain instead. "We've missed you."

"Yes," I said. "You did."

His lips quirked a smile of acknowledgement, and he gestured for me to walk with him. "Our esteemed horse whisperer is waiting for you."

Without awaiting a reply, he turned back through the small crowd of gathering Levanti, leaving me to follow. A nod was all the reassurance I could give Amun that I understood the danger, that after everything, I was grateful he'd tried to warn me.

Most of the Kisian soldiers seemed to be moving on into the city, but even those passing through the square seemed to exist in another world. Levanti closed in as I followed Derkka, whispers running like hissing sands beneath the sounds of the city, each pointing finger and glare a reminder of how much hate they had already spent upon me.

In the centre of the square, Whisperer Ezma stood watching us approach, her jawbone headpiece rising to the sky. She clasped her hands behind her back and lifted her chin. "Rah e'Torin. I see you've finally decided that hiding is only for cockroaches—those who are unwanted and yet impossible to get rid of."

I halted before her. "Lovely to see you too, Ezma."

Levanti ranged around us, closing in like predators. Some of them had called me captain once.

"Are you here to help us this time, I wonder?" Ezma asked.

"No." I stepped back and swept a look around the watching Swords. "I am here to challenge you, Ezma e'Topi, in your capacity as a herd master of the Levanti. Too long have I watched you lead faithful Swords astray with lies while you seek an army with which to conquer your own homeland. Do you accept my challenge? Or will you step aside?"

Murmuring buzzed around us, but it suddenly seemed very far away as Ezma's lips spread into a broad smile. "I've been waiting so long to hear you say those words, Rah e'Torin. So yes, I accept your challenge."

## 28. DISHIVA

I had been trying not to pace, but all it had achieved was bouncing on the balls of my feet instead. Secretary Aurus flicked sidelong reproaches my way, keeping his mouth shut. Ezma had ridden out to meet the Kisians—had stayed out there a long time in negotiations—but nothing else had happened. No one had joined them, no one had walked out the gates—nothing. Even once Ezma had ridden back to the city, leaving the fucking gates open—nothing.

"Come on," I murmured under my breath like a prayer. "Come on, come on, get out there. No army is going to stand outside open gates for more than a few minutes arguing about their plans."

Beside me, Aurus's silence had weight.

"Come on," I said, trying not to think through all that could have gone wrong between Mother Li being allowed out of the palace and now. Had she been accosted? Had someone guessed my plan? Had she lied about intending to help us? "Get out there, this is it. Come on." I didn't want to even think about the last option.

"Dishiva..."

Whatever Aurus had been about to say, he thought better of it, falling back into his hefty silence.

Seconds crept by. I wished I could stop them, yet to stand forever in limbo would have been no better. Like slowly rising water, a chill of cold dread stole up my legs and settled in my gut.

"She's not going out there, is she," I said, voice hollow.

"I don't think so." There was kindness in his tone and a twist of pity on his lips, not pity for me so much as for the situation in which we had found ourselves, pity that this was how our last play for survival—for a future—had ended. "It was a very good idea, but sometimes good ideas are ruined by the smallest things."

"And sometimes bad ideas are salvaged by the smallest piece of luck," I agreed. "I was hoping this would be one of those times instead."

He pressed out a wry smile. "Would have been nice, yes. Perhaps we should have prayed more. Or at all?"

For a moment I just stared at him, before laughter bubbled unbidden to my lips. Aurus managed to keep a straight face for a few commendable seconds before he broke into a grin, a chuckle vibrating deep in his throat. "Imagine," he said. "The hieromonk—praying!"

"Ridiculous!" I laughed. "Utterly ridiculous!"

And for a few joyful minutes at what felt like the end of the world, all we could do was laugh. Laugh until tears sprang from our eyes and our stomachs hurt, nothing seeming to matter anymore. Even when the laughter started to fade, relief spread in its wake. Relief that I could stop thinking, stop trying, stop fighting. There was peace in such failure.

We slid into a companionable silence, standing there watching the Kisian army finally make their way through the open city gates. I wondered vaguely, in the way of one not entirely inhabiting their body, what would happen when they reached us. Would it be like a wave crashing over the shore? Would they want every Chiltaen soldier dead or captured? Aurus would be a prize worth holding for political leverage, but would they think the same of me or see me for the fraud I was? Perhaps they would kill me on sight and ruin all of Whisperer Ezma's carefully laid plans for Veld's return. Imagining her face upon hearing the news almost made me start laughing again. I'd be dead, but it would almost be worth it.

Once the army was making its way through the gate and into the city, it became impossible to follow their movements, to know if they were spreading through the streets like blood through veins or making a direct path toward us. Would it be Emperor Manshin or Empress Miko who first stepped into the square before the palace gates? Would it matter?

There were so many ways the next few hours could go, yet I found I didn't want answers, didn't want to discuss it, preferring the calm, companionable silence that had fallen between us, the most unlikely of allies.

When at last the first Kisian soldiers stepped into the square, Aurus turned. "Well, Dishiva, it has been an honour."

"That it has, Secretary," I said. "That it—"

I broke off, blinking, my remaining eye surely deceiving me. No emperor or general had entered the square in the wake of the leading soldiers, rather a figure dressed in layers of white cloth, a white mask covering his face. A hieromonk in everything but name.

Leo.

"Oh shit," I whispered. "Shit."

"That's another swear word, isn't it? I didn't think it was that terrible getting stuck spending time with me, but there you go."

"Not that!" I gripped his arm, as much to steady my suddenly shaking legs as to get his attention.

Aurus shifted to better see down into the square. "What is it?"

Down below, the white-clad figure slowly lifted his hand and waved, a gesture that had sent me into a panic before and might have again had not an idea struck me with greater force. "I think..." I said slowly. "I think I may have one final really bad idea that, with a little bit of luck, might work."

There wasn't time to construct a scene in the throne room like what we'd performed for Whisperer Ezma, but we made it down to the palace courtyard before the gates swung open, and stood waiting with Aurus's soldiers. That Leo's arrival coincided with the Levanti opening the gates seemed the ultimate in cruel jokes. Perhaps Aurus had been right after all—we should have prayed. Anything to keep the gods from playing such tricks.

Ignoring the Levanti who opened the gates as though just for him, Leo strode in. Flanked by Kisian soldiers and with at least three dozen more at his back, he made a grand sight. They'd even brought a prisoner—perhaps two—though one was hooded and shackled while the other was surrounded but walked free, a strikingly handsome Chiltaen woman with a sour expression.

"Ah, Dishiva, Secretary," Leo said, approaching with spread arms as one might greet an old friend. "How very good it is to see you both looking so well cared for." He spoke in Levanti, words only for us. "Also that I have a moment to gloat before Emperor Manshin arrives to make whatever use of you he will." Even with his mask on, the smug look radiated in Aurus's direction. "How very easily you let Whisperer Ezma play you, Secretary. I ought to have thanked her for the amusement."

"Even if that amusement comes at the price of Chiltaen lives?" I said.

Leo tilted his head. "You think I care about your soldiers? Men who would rather follow the commands of a secretary than their god?"

"One might also wonder what cause any Kisian soldier has to follow you."

"Kisians?" Drawing down his mask to better see, Leo looked around, his gaze sliding over his soldiers as though they weren't there. "I wasn't aware I had any with me, although I'm sure that will soon change."

"No Kisi—" My sight hadn't been good since he'd sliced my eyes, but I ought to have noticed earlier that the soldiers with him weren't attired in the imperial army's flawless Kisian garb, and they weren't Kisian. Beneath the helmets, their faces were, for the most part, a shade too pale.

Beside me, Aurus clasped his hands behind his back in the manner of a disapproving patriarch. "Is such a deception undertaken with the emperor's knowledge? Or are you playing a very dangerous game with Chiltae's reputation?"

Leo slid his mask back up, covering a smile. "You seem to be under the mistaken impression I'm here to converse with you, Secretary."

"You should be here to save your people from being slaughtered," I snapped.

"Dishiva, don't tell me you want to save Chiltaens now?"

"Yes. I do."

His brows rose. "Even Commander Legus?" He gestured back toward his small army again, and this time I was grateful my eyes had failed me. I'd not recognised Legus in the ranks surrounding the Chiltaen woman, but at the sound of his name he stepped forward.

"Holiness?"

I flinched. He was looking at me, not Leo. Back in the meeting tent, he'd seemed to have no idea who I was beyond his hieromonk, but something in his expression now made me wonder, some twist of triumph about his lips. Fear I could not control slid down my spine and held me frozen, mind blank.

"Is something wrong, Dishiva?" Leo said, his feigned solicitude almost as chilling. This wasn't how this meeting ought to have gone. I had meant to stride up to him, fearless, and demand his help in return for the only thing he still needed from me besides my death. Instead I stood still and silent, holding panic down because I could not let it break free. Not again.

"Dishiva?" Aurus's breath was warm by my ear, and I suppressed a shudder at bad memories. Not him, I told myself, not him. But what was the difference between two Chiltaen men? Why had I set out to help them at all?

"I think we're done here," Leo said. "Time I was getting on with my own business. Don't worry, Emperor Manshin will be along soon to take care of yours."

With a nod to his men he made to move past us. One soldier shoved the surrounded woman in the back, sending her stumbling into a walk with a growl, the other prisoner drawn on with clinking chains. They'd locked manacles around our wrists and marched us until we fell. They'd hammered our chains into the hard earth, and there had been no escape. No escape when they'd held me down, weight smothering, scent filling my nose. How much I had wanted to be breathing in poison. Such shame I wanted no Levanti to ever feel again.

"Wait!" The word burst from my lips like it had sped from a long away. "Wait."

Shuffling footsteps halted, and though it felt like the world was spinning, I gathered the last of my courage. "You need me to name you Defender of the One True God."

Leo stopped, turning his masked face my way. "Or I could claim the position by right when you die."

"And do your god prophecy in the wrong order?"

He went on staring at me through the slits in his mask, and I could only hope I was right. When the silence carried so far that the Chiltaen woman started to hum, I pressed, "Better to do it all the right way rather than take the risk, don't you think?"

"And what would you want in return? Since I assume this is a deal you wish to make with me, Dishiva."

"Yes." I drew myself up, though my spine seemed to want nothing more than to curl in upon itself for protection. "I'll name you

Defender of the One True God if you get Secretary Aurus and every single one of his soldiers out of this city alive."

Leo laughed. "I am no worker of miracles. I—"

"No? Isn't that what a god is?"

His teeth snapped shut behind his mask, a glare flashing through the slits. "And your life, Dishiva?" he said. "Do you sacrifice that too, my false high priest?"

*False high priest*—my death the final step upon his prophetic ascension. But first he needed to be named defender. He needed his consort. Needed a self to sacrifice. If I agreed, there might still be time to come up with yet another last-ditch, desperate plan.

"I do not give myself in sacrifice," I said. "But I will remain behind while Secretary Aurus and his men leave the city."

"Dishi—Your Holiness," Aurus gasped. "It is not your job to sacrifice yourself for us."

"Actually, as your hieromonk, it probably is. Either way, that's the deal I'm offering, Lord Villius. Take it or leave it."

"How very tough you sound talking like that while your knees shake," Leo said. "As though there's any way you have real leverage over me."

"That's not an answer."

"No wonder Aurus likes you. Very well, Your Holiness. I accept. You name me Defender of the One True God and I get Aurus out of here."

"And his soldiers."

"And his soldiers," Leo amended. "At least those who haven't already been killed or captured by the Kisians." He spun to Commander Legus. "Commander, my marriage will have to wait a few minutes. I have a new position to take first. Have everyone gather around that plinth in the square—the more people we have to witness this momentous occasion, the better."

"Marriage?" I said, having hardly taken in another word.

Leo drew his mask down, once again revealing that all too familiar smile. "Why, yes, perhaps you have not been introduced to Cassandra Marius, my consort with two voices." He gestured to the handsome Chiltaen woman, who scowled back. As though drawn by an invisible hand, my head turned slowly toward the hooded and shackled figure, dread crawling through my gut.

"And who is that?" I said.

His lips split into a toothy grin. "You know the answer, Dishiva. No more dawdling now; let's make a show of this before it's too late to save your precious secretary."

He strode back out into the square, leaving me to follow with the rest of his entourage. I could have run, but he knew the inside of my mind too well to fear I would.

"You don't have to do this," Aurus said at my side. "I would rather accept failure than see you sacrifice yourself for his plans. If you prefer that thought not to be sentimental, then let's say that the Nine aren't prepared for Veld Reborn to truly exist."

"Better to lose still more of their army and one of their leaders?"

Aurus shrugged one shoulder. "Perhaps."

"Sometimes you're a bad liar."

Flanked by soldiers, we walked out through the palace gates and into the empty streets. Leo had set the pace of a man who might have run if not for dignity, and the semi-jog with which his soldiers kept up sent thuds and clanks echoing around the square. My own breathlessness had nothing to do with speed. Doubt had long been my companion, its voice growing louder the more alone I felt, and now it drowned everything. Trusting Leo was the worst idea I'd ever had. He'd always been the one holding all the reins.

"This is the last time I'm going to ask," Aurus said as we were hurried in Leo's wake. "But are you sure you want to do this?"

"No, but it's what we're doing."

He pursed his lips, a man who wished he hadn't said it was the last time he would ask.

To one side of the square sat a raised platform like those the Tempachi town criers used, but there were no criers here, only the distant shouts of approaching trouble echoing up from the heart of Shimai's north bank. As we arrived, one of Leo's soldiers gestured down the hill and then back toward the palace, heavily frowning.

"Captain Venute seems to think doing this here in the open is not wise," Aurus murmured, leaning my way. "He says returning to the safety of the palace walls would be better."

Leo's vigorous shake of the head needed no translation. "Don't tell me," I said. "He will take the risk if it means having an audience?"

"However did you guess?" Secretary Aurus looked around as Leo's small contingent of soldiers took up protective positions, spread thin by the number of smaller streets and alleys opening onto the square. There was no sign of any real Kisian soldiers yet, but as we were standing outside the palace, it seemed only a matter of time.

"We might get some trouble," Aurus murmured, nodding in the direction of a group of Kisian citizens gathered outside a barricaded building. None of them carried any obvious weapons, but they had the look of men who knew where to get some and weren't afraid to use them. "I wonder if they've realised these aren't Kisian soldiers yet."

"Seems likely, unless their eyes are as bad as mine." Safer not to stare, I looked around the rest of the all too open area Leo had chosen for the ceremony and found more knots of watching citizens who could be trouble. The question I couldn't answer was whether I wanted there to be trouble, whether going through with this was such a good idea when Leo had his consort with two voices right here with us. She had as many soldiers around her as were spreading out to watch the streets, another large clump remaining with the chained figure whose probable identity made it impossible to look his way for more than a few moments without shuddering.

A hand gripped my arm, urging me toward the platform with a grunt of Chiltaen. Aurus snapped something and the hand let go, Commander Legus stepping back with a mocking bow in the secretary's direction. I couldn't thank him, couldn't think. Heart hammering, I stepped up onto the platform beside Leo, who beckoned me with a smile almost as shudder-worthy as Commander Legus's touch.

"Let's finally get this done, Dishiva," he said. "And stop playing this game."

"A game you started," I returned. It felt so long since our roles had been reversed, when in punishment for failing to destroy the deserter camp Leo had named me defender. I had been stripped of all connection to my people and set adrift, and in one last desperate attempt to lead them into a new future, here I was again.

"All right, you remember the words?" Leo said.

"Yes, I think so."

"Good, let's finish this."

He knelt before me as I had once knelt before him, and I let out a deep breath to calm my racing pulse. From places all around the small square, Chiltaen soldiers watched on from beneath Kisian helmets, watched in turn by whispering citizens, the tension akin to the moment before an ambush when no one can breathe.

"I—" I swallowed, disliking the strange shape the Chiltaen words made in my mouth. "I call upon the blessing of the One True God," I said, closing my eyes to focus on the words rather than those watching, rather than think what would happen when I finished. If it all went wrong, Aurus's freedom could come at the cost of my life before I could find a way out. "That he may protect this warrior who gives himself body and soul into his service, as he fights to protect him and his humble servants upon this mortal plane."

I drew a breath. Our audience stood perfectly still, making the sound of many approaching footfalls all the louder. "Do you, Lord Leo Villius," I went on, hurrying through the last of the words, "swear upon life and honour to uphold and defend the faith of the One True God?"

Leo bowed his head. "I swear upon my life and honour to uphold and defend the faith of the One True God."

"Then as Her Holiness the hieromonk of Chiltae, it is my great honour to accept your pledge on behalf of the One True God, in whose service you will make your family proud. Rise, Defender."

The thunder of approaching footsteps grew with every word I spoke, forcing me to all but shout the last pronouncement. Kisian soldiers—real Kisian soldiers this time—were pouring along the street and spreading into the square, their leader a tall man in imperial crimson.

"Your Majesty!" Leo cried, rising to his feet with spread arms. The rest of his words meant nothing to me, but they sent confusion spilling through the approaching soldiers. From one group of watching citizens, a man stepped forward, calling out a challenge. Another joined him, and in the growing furore, Leo's soldiers drew their swords. Unsure where to point them first, they closed protectively around Leo, throwing glares at every potential enemy.

All at once, everyone seemed to be shouting, and amid the rising chaos, Cassandra kicked the nearest soldier in the shin. Yanking a short blade from one of their belts, she followed up by plunging it into the man's gut. They all turned on her. Leo shouted, an edge of panic in his tone, but as he jumped down from the narrow platform to hurry into the fray, I followed.

"Leo!" I shouted. "You have to get us out of here now before the emperor takes the palace!"

Leo turned, eyes laughing. "Really, Dishiva, you ought to know better. No one but a Levanti gives a damn about honour." He gripped my wrist, fingers digging into my skin as he leaned close. "You are my false high priest and I'm not going to fail. My destiny has been waiting far too long. Commander Legus! Take *Her Holiness* inside."

Leo strode away shouting orders, heedless of the fights erupting around him. Legus's hand closed upon my arm, tightening to a cuff when I tried to pull away. "Holiness," he said, leering, his breath hot. The rest of his words meant nothing, but even had I been able to understand him, memories rang in my ears, mingling with the shouts all around us, and I couldn't move.

"Commander!"

The man spun, and a fist connected with Legus's jaw with a vicious and satisfying crack. Reeling back, his grip ripped from my arm, his face replaced with that of Secretary Aurus.

"Dishiva! Go!" He shoved my shoulder. "Get out of here. Run!"

"But what about—?"

"Just run! We'll go the other way as a distraction!"

He shoved me in the back, and I staggered forward into motion more out of instinct and a desire not to fall flat on my face. One of my knees buckled, but I managed to stay upright and moving, every direction a blur. Shouts and clashing steel crashed over me in a disorienting wave as I sped on, robe whipping about my feet, no plan beyond desperation.

Nearing one side of the square, the chaos thinned enough that I could hear my own footsteps and I risked a glance back. The crimson-clad emperor seemed to be getting the situation under control, but Secretary Aurus was nowhere to be seen. Only one Chiltaen seemed to have noted my escape amid the chaos—Commander Legus, blood leaking from his nose as he gave chase.

Panic jolted through my chest and I ran on, knees trying to

buckle at every step. I could not let him catch me, could not relive it, could not have this be how it ended after fighting so hard. I was a Levanti. A Sword of the Jaroven. I ought to have died in battle, yet I was running away, fear spilling weakness through me.

From the edge of the square, I sped into a street, dodging a pair of soldiers tending an injured comrade while two others lay dead upon the stones. One didn't even seem to have drawn a weapon, but the other had died with his sword in his hand like a true warrior, and at the sight of the bloodied hilt, I stopped like my feet had rooted into the ground. No. I would not run. I would not hide. I would not let a worm decide who I was or how I would die. Snatching up the dead man's sword, I turned to face the approaching footfalls speeding in my wake.

Commander Legus slowed as he caught sight of me standing my ground beyond the injured soldiers. It had seemed like a good idea, important, yet as he stalked nearer on a predator's soft steps, I had only doubts. The sword was no Levanti blade, its grip strange to my hand, and I had no armour, no backup, nothing but myself. That used to be more than enough, a realisation that brought with it a flare of anger. I pulled off my mask.

"You think you're better than me," I growled, not caring that he wouldn't understand the words. They weren't for him. "I was chained and starved, but there are no chains now."

No chains but those that tightened around my chest as I held my ground at his steady, smiling approach, his sword held loose and sure in one strong hand. The strong hand that had held me down by the throat, that hadn't cared whether I could breathe so long as he had all the power.

I hefted my stolen blade. "Fuck. You," I hissed through gritted teeth. "You are nothing."

He lunged, darting a sudden thrust toward my gut and grinning when I flinched back. Catching the corner of a building with my shoulder, I staggered to regain my footing and almost tripped on a step. The fucking city was closing in on me, as much an enemy as the man taking all too much joy in stalking me on slow, deliberate steps. He said something as I backed up, glancing over my shoulder to be sure nothing was in my way. Thankfully, apart from the few soldiers near the mouth of the street, the stones were empty, the skirmish in the square having either drawn people in or sent them running.

Commander Legus kept talking, seeming to like the sound of his own voice—a voice that rang in my head, twanging every bad memory. How he had laughed, offering me to his men like I had been nothing but a tool to share around, worse than an animal, chained down to be shamed and broken. Again he lunged forward with a sudden jolt, and I dodged rather than counter, a spike of panic lancing through my chest. He had only to exist to send my heart racing so fast that I couldn't concentrate, couldn't find the reflexes I had honed to such perfection over many years as a Sword of the Jaroven. I was a saddlegirl again, tripping over her footwork and flinching from every attack.

He laughed, seeming to understand what was going through my mind, and upon his grin the beginnings of a true, deep fury began to break. How dare he make me feel so small, make me forget who I was and what I could do, that I was strong, valuable, honoured. I was not the animal he had chained and never had been. That Dishiva had been his version of me, his idea of Levanti and of women, seen through the fractured lens of his own weakness.

Legus thrust again at my gut, eyes bright with laughter, but this time I didn't dodge. Didn't step back. Didn't flinch. I would not, not for such a man. My blade met his with a sharp clang that reverberated around the empty street, stealing the smile from his face.

"I am not who you see," I said, disengaging the blade to parry as he struck again, his enjoyment turned now to naked anger and disgust that I dared stand up to him. Seeing his tiny soul for what it was made me want to laugh, and rather than strike my own blow, I countered his again, and again, each assault and thrust getting wilder and more desperate, peppered with spat insults.

"You are nothing," I said, feeling my body slide into an easy rhythm of instincts I hadn't found for a long time. "You are a worm. I am a warrior from the plains, and you cannot touch me."

Hissing his own retort, Commander Legus threw out his arms in challenge—a challenge to strike him if I thought I was so good.

"With pleasure," I muttered. "May Nassus guide this blade to its just end."

Feinting one way and jabbing the other, I sent him stumbling back at the first strike, his teeth bared in a snarl. He came at me again, ever the aggressor, and when I caught his blade on the flat of mine it was the work of a twist, a step, and a breath, to turn and slide the point of the heavy blade into his stomach. A pop of resistance as it pierced his skin, his flesh, his guts. I didn't hold it there, didn't prolong his death or hold his gaze to make a point. I'd already made it.

Amused by the combination of shock and anger still colouring his features, I withdrew the blade and let him stumble back, legs weak. I watched him buckle, blood pouring over his hands. His eyes widened as I set my stolen blade upon his shoulder, but he deserved no freedom for his soul. Instead, I wiped the blade clean on his surcoat and stepped back. Checking I still had my mask, I slid the sword into the loops of my hieromonk's belt and walked away. He gurgled something, calling after me, but I didn't turn. Didn't run. I would never run again.

# 29. CASSANDRA

Blood oozed from my nose like I was a drunkard stuck in a bar brawl, and one of my teeth was hanging loose. It turned out Duos's orders to keep me alive hadn't extended to not breaking my face.

*Did she get away?* Kaysa asked.

*Fucking better have.* I lifted my throbbing head, hunting the quieting square for any sign of the Levanti hieromonk. *She's fucked our plan up good and proper already.*

Emperor Manshin's orders finally seemed to have gotten through to the gathered soldiers, though not before he'd shouted himself hoarse to be heard over the chaos. It had been glorious, setting that keg of tension alight with a swift kick to the shin. Watching them all turn on one another had almost been worth getting fists to the face.

"Inside the palace!" the emperor roared as he passed. "Everyone inside! General Moto, get your men moving."

The great bear of a Kisian strode our way, trailing crimson silk. "Dom Villius," he said. "Get your men off the streets before we have any more incidents like that. The situation is too fragile for this nonsense."

"I'm afraid that'll have to wait, Your Majesty," Duos said in his smoothest tone. "Thanks to Secretary Aurus, my high priest has escaped, and I can't finish this without her. If you want my men off the streets sooner rather than later, then by all means send some of your own in search of her as well."

"No, I've already had to split my most loyal soldiers to deal with Miko and slow down my foolish nephew. I need all I have here to ensure I can hold the throne."

"This is turning out somewhat riskier than you assured me it would be, *Your Majesty*. I hope I'm not going to regret choosing the wrong Kisian leader."

Emperor Manshin snorted. "Unlikely. The risk is small, but we'd be better off not letting it grow any bigger. Leave your men out hunting if you must, but get off the street and inside so your presence raises no more questions."

Duos made him a mocking bow. The tall Kisian stared down at him a moment, before spinning away shouting still more orders as he strode toward the palace. Duos chuckled, sending a chill shuddering through my skin as he glanced my way. "Bring her," he said to the two soldiers unlucky enough to have been given the task of holding me captive. One also had blood streaming from his nose. "Let's get inside and finish this. Commander Legus?" Duos turned, running his gaze around the small square and finding that the only people not already moving toward the palace gates were corpses. "Damn it. Get her inside, then one of you get me a fucking priest."

He strode off on the words, a gesture all it took to get the men guarding Unus moving in his wake. He'd remained still through the whole ordeal, perhaps having retreated into himself rather than hear and feel the chaos, or suffer his brother's hateful control.

*What's our plan now?* Kaysa asked, her nerves bubbling in my gut as we let ourselves be walked toward the palace.

*How am I supposed to know?* I said. *Offering to marry the monster was your idea.*

*To get closer to Unus!*

*Well, we've done that, he's right there; he's just still in chains, and even with most of Duos's soldiers off hunting for that damn hieromonk there are still too many of them.*

I felt her frown. *Half a dozen is too many? Come on, Cass, you're better than that, aren't you?*

It was half vote of confidence, half challenge, her memory flashing to moments we'd taken on great odds and somehow made it out alive. At any other time, her belief in me might have been elating, but now it was just another failing piercing my insides. *These are all highly trained soldiers*, I said. *And they all know I'm a threat, and we won't get another chance at surprise. And with Unus chained up too, we can't exactly expect any help.*

*Then we'll just have to wait for Yakono.* Her tone was so sure he would come that it robbed me of any reply.

In the palace courtyard, the new emperor of Kisia was still calling out orders, servants and soldiers running everywhere about a dozen tasks. Lanterns, silks, messengers—he had something planned that needed the arrival of as many nobles and city leaders as they could find. Leaders, always with their grand gestures and ceremonies, like they really believed that stories could change the world. In truth it was the world that changed the stories, the winners who chose what got written down for future generations to learn, by which they could know their place in the world and the paths they could walk.

*You're becoming profound in your old age*, Kaysa teased.

"Shut up," I muttered, but the words owned far less malice than they'd once had.

"Get those two out of the courtyard," Emperor Manshin was saying to Duos when we arrived. "This won't work if the first thing everyone does is run into your...woman."

"That's all very well, but I need a priest," Duos hissed back. "Find me one, or there will be nothing for any of your nobles to see."

Emperor Manshin opened his mouth to argue, only to grunt and nod instead. "Very well. Any priest? Or do you need me to scour the city for a Chiltaen?"

"Any, just make it fast. I need to be ready the moment my men come back with Dishiva." He laughed abruptly, eyes alight. "Or failing that, I'll just have to kill the priest you find me. Better make sure it's not someone you like."

"As though I am friends with priests," the emperor muttered. "Take your business through to the shrine until I call for you. No one will disturb you there, and you can marry as many whores as you like."

"Why, thank you for your generosity, Your Majesty," Duos said with another of his mocking bows. "I shall, of course, keep out of sight until the moment my existence suits you."

"You know we have to play this carefully. Keep the risk low, reap the rewards. It'll be worth it once the day is through."

He walked away on the words, only to stop and turn back. "You might want to hold off on your whore, however, if you wish to truly build the alliance we agreed on. Sichi is on her way."

"Lady Sichi?" I spat the name like it was poison, which in a way it was since her arrival could be deadly.

"My daughter, yes," the emperor said. "Her previous marriage has been dissolved, and she's once again free and in need of a…strong male presence in her life." He turned away once again, striding toward the palace doors through a sea of Kisian soldiers— real Kisian soldiers, each bowing deeply to their emperor as they took up protective positions around the walls and outbuildings. Half a dozen stood on either side of the palace doors, thrown open to let the sounds of activity, of change, echo out into the courtyard.

Lady Sichi. Fuck.

Without a word, Duos strode away, traversing a patch of sunlight on his way to the shrine on the far side of the courtyard. It sat tucked behind a screen of latticework and vines, a private, secret space. Leo had never been one for hiding himself, but he did like dramatic entrances.

*Do you think he'll marry her instead?* Kaysa asked as our long-suffering guards shoved us back to a walk in Duos's wake. *We're still a far better choice given the words in the presage.*

"Yes, but it's not like we want to marry him," I muttered, not caring if the soldiers thought I was talking to myself.

*And you think she does?*

"No, but she's the daughter of an emperor, not an old whore from common stock."

Kaysa grimaced, though they were words she'd often said to me in the past, belittling me whenever I'd run low on Stiff and she reclaimed her voice. For so many years, we'd used all our strength to fight a war within our own skin, leaving no energy to live a real life beyond it. Really, it had been pretty fucking stupid looking back now.

The air inside the shrine was musty like damp clothing, and by the state of the braziers no one had been through to clear out the old coals or light them in a while. The only light was that provided by the weak winter sun, cut into dozens of tiny squares as it poured through the latticework.

It wasn't a large space, yet the handful of soldiers who had remained to guard Unus and me seemed out of proportion, tiny men in a vast space unsure what they ought to be doing with themselves. Fighting they could do; knowing how to act at what could turn out to be a forced wedding hadn't been part of their training. Probably.

As much to annoy Duos as because my body ached all over, I slumped onto the nearest step, trying for calm despite the possibility that this was about to go very poorly. "Well, this is fun," I said as Duos took a turn about the confined space, his bright eyes revealing a level of energy and excitement that wouldn't let him stop. "Should be quite the party," I added. "That is, should your new father-in-law be a fool and not immediately behead you the moment you cease being useful."

Duos spun, teeth bared in a hard smile. "You think you're very clever and will get me to tell you all about our plans, but no. You are not here for conversation, only to be my consort in the event Lady Sichi once again slips through my fingers."

"Why her? There must be plenty of women in Kisia who speak more than one language. One of them somewhere might even have hit her head on something and not mind the idea of marrying you. That way you could do without all this..." I waved a hand at the guards standing awkwardly about. "Forcing someone to the altar at knifepoint surely doesn't look very good even for holy men."

"Your opinions are hardly of interest to me."

"That's a shame," I said. "I have such a lot of them."

He ignored me, instead looking around the shrine as though in search of something. Beyond the lattice walls, soldiers finally seemed to have stopped arriving and milling around, although the glimpse of a brightly coloured silk robe was no improvement. Silk and murmuring chatter meant nobility and city leaders, rich fucks with their grand clothes and superior sneers—at least one knew where you stood with soldiers, even if it was at the pointy end of a weapon.

"Here," Duos said, gesturing to a place on the floor that looked no different to the rest. "Hold him down here."

Unus was shunted forward, almost tripping on his own chains.

"What are you doing?" I said, Kaysa's fear spurring the words from my lips.

"Finishing what I started," Duos replied as one of the soldiers kicked the back of Unus's knees, sending him to the stones with a crack of kneecaps.

Lunging to the forefront of our mind, Kaysa leapt us to our feet. "You cannot sacrifice him yet!"

"Can't I? I thought your knowledge of the presage was better than that, Kaysa."

She had retained far more of its words and meaning than I had, but struggled now to bring the passages to the fore of her mind. The consort with two voices, the sacrifice of self, the ending of the false high priest...surely it had to go in that order?

Duos clicked his tongue. "Not specifically, though there is safety in keeping to the order things are mentioned. In this case, however, with Dishiva having escaped, it is wiser to get on with the things still in my power before something else goes wrong. So..." He drew a short knife from inside his robe and held it up to the sunlight. It glinted on the sharp edge—a moment of theatrical drama as one of the soldiers yanked the hood from Unus's head.

Full of static, his hair puffed up atop his head only to slowly settle around his reddened face, mouth caught in a pained rictus. Duos leaned close, his whispered promises too quiet to make out though they made Unus squirm.

"It will be a relief to finally be rid of you," he said as he straightened up. "Such a thorn in my side, yet necessary to the end."

Out in the courtyard, more finely dressed Kisians were arriving amid a rising hubbub of curious chatter, but of Yakono there was no sign.

*Shit*, I hissed as Kaysa strode toward the twin Leos, causing the guards to step protectively into our path.

"You're making a mistake to do this now," she said, voice vibrant. "A mistake that, like the loss of Septum, could ruin everything."

"I know what I'm doing," Duos snapped. "I am Veld Reborn. I will build a holy empire that spreads beyond Chiltae, that reclaims our former lands and takes what is owed to God. Hold him. Tightly," he added, nodding to the men keeping Unus in their firm grips.

I had no weapons, and guards stood between us and Duos, but unless Yakono was about to make a very timely arrival, we were out of choices. I glanced around one last time and was still alone.

*Not alone*, Kaysa said. *Never alone.*

A lump formed in my throat as I thought of dying in Hana's body. Yakono had been there, but inside my mind it had been the most alone I had ever felt. At least this time Kaysa and I would die together.

Ducking around the guards, I charged at Duos. As I'd known he would, he leapt aside at the last moment, slashing a line of fire along my arm with his sacrificial blade. "Oh, you want to play, Cassandra?" He laughed as I spun back to face him again. "You want to see just how misplaced my father's faith in your skills was?"

He darted in, all grins and glinting blade. His soldiers hovered, kept at bay by Duos's enjoyment—small comfort when his knife punched into the flesh of my arm. Spinning, I ripped it from his hold, sending it flying across the shrine. Blood spilled from the gash it left, but to stop and stem it meant letting him retrieve the blade. Letting him kill Unus. Letting him win.

I charged in again, but able to read my mind, he anticipated every strike and every opening. Speed didn't matter. Skill didn't matter. One on one, it was like fighting a wall. A wall with sharp fists and quick footwork, who knew the most vulnerable places where we were already hurting. Punch after punch, our scuffle took us back and forth across the shrine floor while Unus knelt unmoving, surely able to feel every shred of wild joy his twin felt at our slow destruction.

"You think even if you could kill me, it would make any difference?" he laughed. "Your precious Miko is already dead, Cassandra. You can't save her anymore."

For the dozenth time, I dragged myself up off the stones, none of my limbs wanting to move and the taste of blood hot and tinny in my mouth. "People keep saying that," I said, the words slurred. "People keep saying she's dead, and she just keeps disappointing everyone." My punch was wild, all motion and no power, but this had never really been about beating him.

His foot connected with my gut, sending us sprawling, skin tearing on the stones. "Perhaps that's so, but even if she makes it here, she won't live, and your sacrifice will have been for nothing. She's better off dying in battle out there than making it this far only to be executed as a traitor."

"No!" The word emerged as a growl and I refused to stay down, refused to give up. "I will not let him do that. And I won't let you." I dragged my feet toward him again, swaying and weak, but it had stopped mattering. The pain was nothing to the emptiness of my heart and my life. Perhaps dying in pain was worth it if you had something, or someone, to die for.

I charged in again, feeling more like a wall of meat than a person, but as he met us exactly where he knew we'd strike, a scuffle broke out.

One of Duos's soldiers staggered into view, his hands pressed to his head and his eyes squeezed shut. Chains clanked. Steps scuffed. And Duos sent me howling to the ground with a swift kick to my right knee.

"Don't let him get inside your heads, you fools!" Duos snapped. "Get him back now, or it'll be your necks on the block!"

Running steps vibrated the stone floor beneath our cheek as the guards sped after Unus. A vague sense of satisfaction that he'd escaped broke the monotony of pain, though it was sure to be short-lived. Unus had nowhere to go and no weapon, the whole palace now a nest of enemies of various kinds.

Gripping a handful of our hair, Duos pulled our head up off

the stones, making our scalp burn. "How sad," he said. "You give your life for him, and he doesn't even have the decency to help save yours." He clicked his tongue. "And like Dishiva, he won't get far." With his other hand he gripped my jaw, squeezing until I was sure it would snap. "You are all going to die."

# 30. MIKO

F orm up!"
Captain Kiren's shout broke me from my shocked stupor, and I yanked Hacho from her sheath. Turning my horse, I nocked and loosed an arrow just as the first volley came flying our way.

"Form up! Protect Her Majesty!"

My guards seemed to be everywhere and nowhere, enemies on every side. Instinct was all I had, nocking arrows and loosing until blades drew close. One shaved the rump of my horse, and it was all I could do to keep her from bolting into my own soldiers as I drew my sword. With every hack down into a Kisian soldier, I hoped they were not mine, that I was fighting the right battle, sending blood spraying. Throats and faces and arms and heads, I lay about me with everything I had, and the sounds of death mounted around me. Cries of pain and shock, the squeal of a horse cut from beneath its rider—it was like being back at the battle of Risian, except it was my army that had turned on me.

"There's too many!" Captain Kiren's shout was close by, though I couldn't see him amid the whirl of beasts and bodies. "Run, Your Majesty! Run!"

I could kick my horse to a gallop and dash away across the fields, might even be able to dodge arrows by weaving a safer path, but for the chance I'd have to secure my throne after such a flight, I might as well die fighting—a martyr to hang like a dead weight around Manshin's throat.

"Your Majesty!"

"I'm not going anywhere, Captain," I shouted back, tasting blood as some sprayed into my face, hot and bitter. "This is my gods-be-damned empire even if I have to die for it!"

Turning my increasingly reluctant horse, I swung my increasingly reluctant arm. My sword was starting to feel heavy with the blood of Kisians who shouldn't have had to die, their lives spent in nothing but the service of Manshin's power.

"Majesty!" came Captain Kiren's desperate cry again. "More!"

I spun to find him at the edge of the battle farthest from the gates, where Dom Villius and his soldiers had disappeared. But while he may have gotten inside the city, more soldiers were bearing down on us—riders and foot soldiers, banners snapping.

"Your orders?" Captain Kiren asked, his glance my way drawing his gaze from the fray as a blade thrust toward him.

"Captain!"

I couldn't reach Hacho in time, couldn't loose an arrow into the enemy Kisian's eye, yet even as I lunged forward like I could stop him with my bare hands, an arrow punched into his chest, sending him reeling. Granted a moment of time, Captain Kiren thrust down, piercing the next soldier through the neck. Around us, Manshin's men started to run amid the approaching thunder of fresh enemies.

Gripping my sword so hard my fingers hurt, I spun to face them. Ranks of Kisian soldiers flying imperial banners. For a moment I was sure they were more Chiltaens, the rest of Dom Villius's army come to end me, but pulling ahead were two riders with long dark hair flying in their wake, their horses the largest and strongest by far.

Tor and Nuru.

"Yes!" I cried, spilling relieved tears as I punched a fist into the air. "Yes! They found him! It's General Ryoji!" On a paroxysm of thankful sobs, my sword fell from my hand and I bent forward, pressing my forehead to my horse's sweat-lathered mane in the closest thing to a prayer of thanks I could manage.

"You came!" I called as they came within earshot. "Thank all the gods that you came!"

"Miko! Are you all right?" Nuru demanded, reining in before me with her bow still in hand. "Who were they? What is going on?"

"Where is everyone else?" Tor added, but I could answer none of their questions before General Ryoji joined us, brow creased.

"Your Majesty, you are unhurt?"

"I...I think so, but—" I looked around at the bloody slaughter tainting the ground and wanted to be sick.

Captain Kiren trotted over, far too calmly for a man who would have lost his life but for Nuru's bow. "General."

"Captain. What has happened here?"

"We were blockaded getting inside the city," the captain said. "And set upon by Dom Villius—"

His name sent me plummeting back to earth, all the thrill at their arrival vanishing. "Dom Villius. Shit! There's no time to explain," I said. "Sichi is in trouble and Manshin might be about to give the whole damn empire to Chiltae for all I know. He'll have made for the palace. Are these men all yours, General?"

"All yours, Your Majesty," Ryoji said. "But I see my story will have to wait for another time. We will follow where you lead."

Whatever other questions they might have had were swallowed, leaving me staring at their expectant faces and realising I had no idea what I was going to do or even what we would find inside the city.

"To the palace," I said, urging myself and my new army into motion.

"Right, I'll lead the way just in case he's laid any further traps for you," General Ryoji said, slipping easily back into his former role. A few orders shouted to his men and we were moving, in through the now clear gates and across the entry square, our horses' hooves clattering over the scorch-blackened stones. There was no time to stop and look around, only to take in the city as a collection of impressions—knots of people warily watching us pass, the smell of woodsmoke thick on the air, shuttered windows, and barricaded doors. Of the remaining soldiers who'd blocked our way there was no sign. Nor did any of the ones we passed look like Leo's Chiltaens in disguise, but they would have had to move quickly to avoid being noticed in the daylight.

We rode on, General Ryoji leading the way. A nearby square looked to be filled with tents and Levanti, but neither Tor nor Nuru paid it any heed. That Whisperer Ezma and her followers had lingered would soon prompt questions of what she was waiting for, questions I wasn't ready to answer.

As we drew near the first of the military barracks once used by Shimai's standing battalion, I had expected to find blood and chaos, for the front ranks of our joint army to have torn open the gates and slaughtered every Chiltaen inside, but though a large group of soldiers stood outside it, the gates were still shut. In front of them stood half a dozen priests, arm in arm, humming a prayer.

"What in all the hells is going on?"

At the head of the group of soldiers, General Rushin seemed to be attempting to negotiate, but he turned at the sound of my voice. "Your Majesty," he said, happy to acknowledge my rank and my existence now it might help him. "Perhaps your command may make the difference."

"Perhaps, but first tell me, General, were you aware that Dom Villius was travelling secretly in Lord Manshin's ranks?"

"There is no time to—What?" He looked genuinely shocked,

and he'd never been Moto's calibre of liar. "I am not sure I understand."

"Neither do I, but I am hoping your master will explain it to me. Also why he had men blockade the gates in front of me and attack, in his second attempt to end my life by devious means."

"Your Majesty, I—"

"Don't try to convince me you had no knowledge that Manshin took all the power of the throne for himself even before he declared himself emperor in my absence," I interrupted, pulling no punches and sparing him no guilt. "I will hear no excuses. If you are truly loyal to Kisia and to the throne, you are going to have to prove it. Now, what's going on here?"

General Rushin swallowed hard, seemed ready to start any number of exclamations and protestations, but thought better of it. "Your Majesty," he said instead. "It would appear that revered Mother Li has given these priests orders not to let us into the barracks."

"Why?" General Ryoji demanded, having walked his horse to my side.

"That I could not tell you, Hade," Rushin said. "Something about the Levanti and a future home, and to be honest I have started to wonder if they're all about in their heads—something they ate perhaps that has scrambled their minds."

"Your Majesty!" one of the priests said, stepping forward from the line. No, not just any priest, Mother Li, the only woman to have been given such an exalted position within the priesthood.

"Mother Li," I said, though I couldn't recall having met her in the flesh before, only heard stories of her tenacity and wisdom. "An explanation would be appreciated. I have somewhere I rather desperately need to be, yet you seem to be getting in the way of General Rushin doing his job."

With the determination of one who would have marched the

length of an entire battlefield, she walked through the knot of soldiers before the barracks to reach my side. "Your Majesty," she said again, bowing deeply. "I stand here on the plea of Dishiva e'Jaroven, one of the Levanti brought here by the Chiltaens. She rode with them as their hieromonk when they took this city, but not for glory or hatred."

"I'm sorry, did you say as their hieromonk?" I said. "A Levanti? Woman?"

"Yes, Your Majesty, it is quite miraculous, and as one holy woman to another she begged my assistance. I tried to reach you outside the gates but was not allowed through, nor were any others, so I could not treat with you on her behalf."

Dishiva. The name sounded familiar, perhaps one I'd heard Rah speak before, but there was little time to wonder as the aged priestess went on. "She desires only safe passage out of the city for Secretary Aurus and his soldiers, promising that they would leave freely without bloodshed and walk away should they be allowed."

"Why would they do that? They've a great victory in conquering the city."

Behind me, General Ryoji's mount was getting restless along with its rider. "Majesty," he said. "We need to get to the palace. Who knows what Manshin might not already be up to."

He was right, I had to find out what he had planned with Dom Villius, had to save Sichi from being forced to marry him, yet I didn't move. "Explain," I said instead, turning back to the priestess. "What would happen if I gave the order to let the Chiltaen soldiers walk out of here unharmed?"

"What? You cannot be considering it, Your Majesty!" General Rushin exclaimed, but I turned my shoulder on him and stared expectantly at Mother Li.

"Secretary Aurus has promised the Levanti land in reparation," Mother Li said, ignoring the general. "But if he dies here or loses all face with the Nine, he will not be able to uphold his side of their bargain."

"Land in reparation," I whispered, the words so stark a contrast to Whisperer Ezma's plans to conquer the plains.

General Rushin grunted. "Like any member of the Nine would ever promise such a thing. You have been fooled, Mother Li. If we let these soldiers walk free, blood will run in the streets! Majesty, these men conquered our city, we cannot just let them go."

Emperor Kin would never have done so, nor Emperor Lan before him. Even my father might have been too caught in the ways of old power to consider a different course. Sichi had said we needed to find new ways, new paths, new structures, and doing exactly the opposite of what Kin would have done seemed a damn good start. I had come to re-create the world, not destroy it further.

"We owe the Levanti a debt," I said, speaking loudly enough for all around me to hear. "Not only here in the salvaging of this city, but in the protection of Kogahaera and Syan. They have not always been allies and may never be again, but if this is their wish from us then it is my decree that these Chiltaen soldiers are allowed to go free and unharmed so the Levanti may earn their just reparations. May Chiltae's generosity weaken them rather than our allies."

"But Your Majesty—" General Rushin spat, eyes wide.

"General Rushin, you grant me my title yet not the respect and obedience it deserves. Those are my orders. If you would disobey them then by all means do so now while everyone is watching so I may take the pleasure of removing you from command."

He opened his mouth and closed it, only to open it again and stand there gawping like a fish, the triumph of having silenced him rushing hot through my veins. "I'm glad I've made myself clear, General," I said. "I now feel I can confidently leave this matter in Mother Li's capable hands. Captain Kiren and a small contingent of his men will remain with you for protection, Mother. And, General, on this matter, you now take your orders from Mother Li."

"From—"

"Yes, General. And assuming there are more soldiers in the other barracks, I do not want to hear that they were conveniently forgotten. Once the Chiltaen soldiers are all safely out of the city, report to me at the palace."

"And...and if they don't leave peacefully, Your Majesty?" the general asked, swallowing hard. "What are we then to do?"

"Then you have my permission to do what is necessary in protection of Shimai and her people, though I feel quite sure that if you let Mother Li do the talking, she will be able to convince them it isn't in their best interests to try it."

Stepping back from my horse, Mother Li bowed deeply. "Your Imperial Majesty," she said, reminding me of what Sichi had said about power residing not merely in swords and armies.

A buzzing sense of triumph and possibility filled my veins as I returned to where General Ryoji and his men waited in the street, Tor and Nuru in their midst. Both were smiling, and their approval buoyed me all the more. "To the palace now, General Ryoji," I said. "Keep on your guard though, there's no saying what else Manshin has planned."

Once again following in the general's wake, we set off through Shimai's winding streets, our concert of hoofbeats enough warning for anyone—soldier or civilian—to get out of our way. Where it was needed, General Ryoji or one of his men shouted a warning, sending people scurrying, but for all the chaos I had expected, the streets were oddly calm. We'd left many soldiers behind waiting to see the Chiltaens escorted out, and Manshin had sent Edo to secure the bridge, but there ought to have been more soldiers from other battalions and more people cheering them on—joyful in their salvation. Instead we passed few on the way to the palace, and those we did I eyed with suspicion, expecting more to turn on me at any moment. General Rushin hadn't, but though I tried to convince myself that was because he'd had no part in such plans, it could have easily been because there had been too many people watching outside the barracks.

There had been little sign of fighting in the streets, Ezma's Levanti seeming to have kept their word and gotten out of the way, yet as General Ryoji slowed to a trot at the small square outside the palace gates, he immediately had to dodge a pair of dead men face down on the stones. Others were strewn about, and a couple of unlucky soldiers seemed to have been given the job of clearing the way, dragging bodies off the street.

"All Kisian," General Ryoji said, glancing around.

"No, General." I pointed at the nearest he'd almost trampled. "Look closer. All Kisian uniforms. These are Dom Villius's men, the ones who attacked me outside the gates."

"Another there," Nuru said, nodding in the direction of the central mounting block.

Tor looked around, jaw set. "I wonder what happened."

"What's happening," I corrected. "This is far from over, and to make things worse those finely dressed citizens seem to be making their way to the palace."

"At least we can be sure where Manshin is," Ryoji said, setting his horse walking again. "He always did like an audience. Grand stories make grand men, he used to say when I was but a captain."

He made for the open gates, where some dozen definitely Kisian soldiers stood guard. Half watched us approach, throwing wary glances at General Moto, who seemed to be in command. He wasn't paying us any heed, however, too focussed on an argument he was having with another general. The man looked up and was for a moment both my old friend and someone completely new, confident and sure of his position.

"Koko!" Relief split Edo's face, but only for an instant. It clouded over again, his lips setting into a thin, grim line. "Thank the gods you're here. General Moto will not let me in nor explain why the city is abuzz with talk of Dom Villius."

"I told you, young cub, there's nothing to get excited over. If he's inside the gates, I'm sure he'll soon be found and sent packing."

"Bullshit," Edo said, his ferocity a joy to behold. "You're refusing to let me in because I'm loyal to the true empress, and you and your usurper are hiding something."

"A high flight, boy. I am not letting you in because you have work to do out here. It's the people of Shimai who have been invited to meet with His Majesty."

Edo spat on the stones at the man's feet, sending a flash of annoyance across Moto's face. "Charming," he drawled.

"General Moto," I said. "As the empress of Kisia I command that you and your men step aside so we may pass, or I'll have no choice but to remove you from your position."

Unfortunately, Moto was made of sterner stuff than General Rushin, or he cared less what the few people watching thought of him. "I'm afraid I cannot do that," he said. "I take my orders from His Imperial Majesty—"

Running steps scuffed behind him and he broke off, already drawing his blade as he turned. A soldier's instinct, but the sight of Dom Villius dashing my way would have made me draw my blade too. Moto's men moved without needing orders, blocking the open gates so the sprinting priest couldn't get out without being caught. Panic-stricken, Dom Villius seemed not to care.

"No, wait!" I threw out a hand to stay theirs. "Stop! That's not him."

"Not him?" General Moto sneered as the closest soldier grabbed hold of the sprinting priest, finally stilling him with a blade held to the young man's throat.

"Not him," I repeated, and slid out of the saddle to land with a thud back on solid earth amid solid troubles, the triumph of my win over General Rushin fading to nothing. "This is his twin, Unus. That's right, isn't it?"

The young man with the monster's face nodded, trying to catch his breath and looking back toward the palace every few seconds. If someone had been following him, perhaps they didn't want to be seen. The real Dom Villius perhaps? His purpose in Kisia seemed to tangle more by the moment. "Tell me," I said, speaking gently to the man Cassandra and her mind-twin had so fiercely defended at every turn. "Is your brother after you? Is he here?"

"Yes, yes, he's here," he said, looking around so wildly I could see only the whites of his eyes. "He has almost everything he needs to become a god."

"A god," I repeated, ignoring General Moto's snort. "Your faith means nothing here. Tell me, in what way will that help what Lord Manshin is planning and why does he want Lady Sichi?"

The young man drew in a deep, shaky breath as though pulling courage from the air, only to let the breath go on a laugh. "You mean Veld's consort with two voices, and Emperor Manshin of the combined imperial expanse of Kisia and Chiltae?"

*The combined imperial expanse of Kisia and Chiltae.* The words rang through me like a gong, and I stiffened. General Rushin had laughed at the idea that the Chiltaens would give anyone land in reparation. If only he had known they would soon be expected to give their entire country to Manshin and Dom Villius—something they wouldn't do without a fight. A long, bloody fight that could still end with our total destruction, all for Manshin's ambition. And what an ambition. How long had he worked toward such a goal, churning those who got in his way beneath his wheels? This son of the infamous traitor general, committing the ultimate treason.

There in the shadow of Shimai's palace, I came face-to-face with the depths of my own naivete. What a gift I must have been when I'd first begged his help, and how well he had kept playing me as he shored up his plans behind my back. He had kept placing his pieces on the board and moving them around even as the shifting sands stirred beneath us. He'd taken Ezma in his stride. He'd recovered from the disaster of the wedding. He'd taken every opportunity to get me out of the way, clearing the road for his ascension to the highest possible imperial state. But if he wanted to keep his throne, he was going to have to go through me one last time.

I glared at General Moto. "The only way you're stopping me from walking in there right now is if you kill me, General. Your choice."

## 31. RAH

In the centre of the square, a dying campfire was stoked to a blaze. Two sticks were brought, their ends held to the flames to blacken, while as much space as possible was cleared in what wasn't just a camp but a main square in a city under attack from within. Most of the Kisian soldiers seemed to have passed through, but enough remained—a reminder we ought never to have been there at all.

Amid the bustle, Ezma stood faintly smiling, her hands clasped behind her back as she surveyed the preparations. Whisperer Jinnit had often stood so, watching me go about my daily tasks at the grove, always ready with a stern word should I make even the smallest mistake. *Fierce pruning makes the best flowers*, he had often said, and I couldn't but wonder if Ezma had been taught the same way. Broken the same way. Pity fluttered feeble wings in my chest, but it was far too late now for it to make any difference.

It was Amun who handed me the stick that would be my speaker's rod, his expression grim. "Are you sure you want to do this?"

Yitti had asked the same before my challenge to Gideon a lifetime ago, my conviction that something had to be done as strong then as it was now—a hard core inside myself that I took comfort in recognising.

"No," I said. "But if I don't, will someone else do it?"

Amun grimaced. "She's a horse whisperer."

"An exiled horse whisperer with no right to leadership. We have no kings, remember?" I took the stick. "Whatever happens, take care of Jinso for me. I had to leave him out in a copse north of the city."

His nod was solemn. "Of course."

With nothing else to be said and no more preparations to make, he stepped back with the rest of the herd—this strange mix of Levanti from different places with different brandings who'd once had different leaders.

Space around the fire opened like a yawning maw, leaving only Ezma still faintly smiling. "Shall we?" she said, gesturing to the fire with her own blackened stick.

Despite the warmth of the flames, the stones were cold. I couldn't remember the last time I'd truly been warm, when ice hadn't grown in my joints or clouded my mind, when I could have revelled in the relief of cool stones against which to press my skin. There was no relief sitting opposite Ezma, only the cold, hard rock digging into worn-out ankles.

Stepping into the widening circle, Amun cleared his throat. "We call upon the gods to watch over this moment, to bring wisdom to the lips of those who would lead us and strength to the hearts of those who must choose the right path." It was the traditional prayer and had been said by Yiss en'Oht before my challenge with Gideon, yet here in this faraway city, where I sat facing a Levanti threat to a Levanti future, it was almost funny. Like any of the gods gave a single shit about any of us.

Done, Amun stepped back, fading into the faceless crowd. After all the activity, the sudden silence around us was like fog in my ears, the only sounds those of the city coming from far away.

With a triumphant thrust, Ezma raised her talking stick into the air, sending a murmur of shock rippling through the herd. As the challenger, I had the first right to speak, a right she stole as she said, "This challenger, Rah e'Torin, is well known to most of you, but for those who do not know, he is an exiled exile who has failed to lead time and time again. He has been removed from every position of authority granted him by your good faith and has undermined every attempt made to give you all the justice you deserve. With all of that, the fact he sits here challenging me now is surely evidence of an unsound mind."

She lowered her stick and adjusted her bone headdress. The watching Swords absorbed her words in silence, as was laid out in our tenets.

Into that silence, I lifted my own stick, anger simmering. "You don't like me," I said, fixing my gaze on Ezma. "You all have reason not to like me or to wish to follow me. I have made many mistakes since setting foot this side of the Eye Sea, mistakes I acknowledge openly. My determination to hold to our old ways saw many of my Swords die before ever we reached Mei'lian, saw me challenge Gideon when he was giving every last part of himself to build you all a future. But when I saved him from being Voided at Ezma's hands, it wasn't justice I was undermining, but hate. You see, your horse whisperer hates everything Levanti"—Ezma snorted—"she hates the democracy of our herds, the transience of a leader's power, and the separation of horse whisperer and herd. She hates our way of life and our gods and seeks to change everything that makes us who we are."

I hadn't finished nor lowered my stick, but she lifted hers again. "What evidence do—"

A handful of Swords behind her hissed, making Ezma flinch and lower her stick, triumphant smile vanishing at the rebuke. The Swords who'd stepped in to uphold the rules could have been anyone, the crowd all one to me, yet my heart warmed with pride that even here, even now, some of our ways still stood and everyone had the right to a voice.

Arm beginning to shake with the effort of holding the stick up, I went on, "What evidence do I have that you hate all that we are? You knew about Entrancers like Dom Villius getting into our herd masters' heads back home and you did nothing. You hold beliefs so counter to our ways that you were exiled for life. And the only reason you are here playing war with the Kisians and the Chiltaens is to leverage everything you can to be able to sail back to the plains with your own army and conquer your own people in the name of your Chiltaen god." Rumblings of shock passed through the watching Swords, and again Ezma stuck her stick into the air, this time waiting as I continued, "I have never claimed to be perfect, but what I promise is that I don't actually want to lead anyone, I don't want to conquer my homeland; I just want to go home and for there to still be a home to return to."

I lowered my hand, fingers so tightly gripped around the stick I wasn't sure I could pry them free. Swords were beginning to shuffle around us, making their move to one side of the fire or the other with their decision—a decision that could still be changed as, with wide eyes, Ezma kept her stick in the air.

"I see it all now," she said, more dawning horror than the defensive retort I'd expected. "It's just like what happened with Gideon. I should have seen the signs earlier, and with poor Dishiva too, as Dom Villius took over more and more of her mind."

"That's a lie!" A jostling in the crowd spat forth Jass en'Occha, jabbing a finger in Ezma's direction. "Dishiva made a deal with the Chiltaens for land in reparation for how they treated us, and by selling her out to the Kisians, you've destroyed any chance of that and doomed her for her selfless sacrifice."

More murmuring spread, the rules of the challenge breaking down under so strange a situation. A few Swords hissed at him as they had at Ezma, but Jass held his ground. Gesturing my way, he said, "Rah e'Torin pisses me off and I don't want him for my captain, but by all the gods he is the only one trying to save us from ourselves."

Having hurried into the circle in Jass's wake, Derkka gripped the stocky Sword's arm to tug him away, but he may as well have tried to pull a tree. Talk was rising all around us, nothing Ezma's apprentice could do now to get the challenge back on track. Into the confusion, Ezma started to laugh. "The Chiltaens give us land?" she said, lowering her stick to press her hands to her cheeks. "That anyone could believe they would ever do such a thing is all the proof you need that Dishiva's mind has been wholly taken over, just as Gideon's was before her." Ezma got to her feet, lifting her arms to the herd. "No one is going to give us what we want; no one is going to give us the future we deserve. It has to be taken. It has to be guarded, even and especially when the enemy comes to us in familiar clothes to take it from us." She pointed down at me. "He fell under Dom Villius's spell once before, leading his Swords to their deaths, and has fought again and again to protect Dom Villius's greatest triumph from justice. That Gideon e'Torin still lives, still works against us all, is due only to actions Rah has undertaken on Dom Villius's orders."

I leapt up, all shreds of the challenge gone in the growing chaos. "Nothing I have said even benefits Dom Villius, let alone came from his lips." I threw my arms wide. "He isn't even here!"

"Yes, he is," Ezma said, quietly enough that the watching Swords had to stop talking to hear her. "He walked through here mere minutes before you arrived. And he was on his way to the palace, no doubt to speak with Dishiva."

The creeping dread she slid into those words rippled through the watching Swords, and from somewhere in the crowd, a voice cried, "He killed Ptapha without a challenge!"

"And Retta, when he snuck in the gates yesterday!"

From Ezma's silence, rumblings grew once again as more names were added to my list of wrongs. "I had no choice!" I said, turning around to glare at the group as some of them edged in. "Had I not, they would have killed me. Every Levanti has the right to protect their own life!"

"You mean Gideon's life!"

For a brief moment, I closed my eyes, wishing the world away. Always it came back to Gideon, to his failure in their eyes and the error of my loyalty. He had dreamed too big and pushed too hard, and then not been strong enough to hold Leo at bay.

"This has nothing to do with Gideon!" I shouted, though it never seemed to be true. "I challenged your whisperer because she plans to conquer the plains for a foreign god. Will you fight for her and destroy your own people? Will you choose your path now even more poorly than when you put your faith in Gideon? Have you learned nothing?"

Like a Tempachi preacher, Ezma raised her arms, supplicating the gods. "Always it is Gideon on your mind and Dom Villius on your tongue," she said, her voice breaking over the noise of the crowd. "Your wild stories are as fanciful as Dishiva's belief in Chiltaen generosity! My people! Do not be drawn in by such evil magic as is before you. Rah e'Torin is following where Gideon led, giving his soul to a man who wants to destroy our unity, our future. I am a horse whisperer, honoured amongst Levanti, chosen for my strength of character and wisdom to advise where no other can, to make impossible choices and guide our steps—"

"You were exiled!" I shouted, but my voice hardly rose above the noise. Half anger, half cheering, some of the crowd didn't seem to be paying us any heed as they began to argue amongst themselves. My plan had been so simple and ought to have ended in a quiet, considered decision of individuals, only it had turned into this. Though Gideon wasn't with me, I had the urge to turn to him, to say I'd told him I should have just stabbed her.

"See this disharmony?" Ezma went on preaching to her followers, eyes wide and wild. "This man is its sole cause. He is the embodiment of our fractured souls, sent here to turn us from our purpose, and he will not stop until Dom Villius has every one of us under his spell, until he can turn all of us on one another and make sure none of us ever get home. No Levanti will be safe until his influence has been purged. As a threat to the very essence of Levanti spirit, Rah e'Torin must be destroyed, removed not only from our herd and our land and our hearts, but from our pain. A pain that must be visited upon his body and his soul, so he alone carries it with him into the darkness."

Ptapha and Loklan and Shenyah had been so angry, so full of righteous rage at my refusal to give them Gideon's blood. I'd fought them and I would have fought again, but upon the rising tones of Ezma's voice too many Swords stepped forward from the crowd. Dozens of fearful, angry Levanti, twisted by Ezma's mania and their own pain.

While Ezma went on crying her lies to the sky, Swords closed in, some familiar, others not. In the distance, shouts of disagreement melded into the thump of my fear, and I closed my eyes. To fight would be useless, would only make me into the traitor she'd painted me, yet to not fight would be my end.

How long would it take Gideon to realise I wasn't coming back? It ought to have been a depressing thought, yet where sorrow and panic ought to have lived there was just nothing. Until the first fist punched into my gut. After that there was only pain.

## 32. DISHIVA

I didn't run, but as I left Legus's corpse behind, I did realise I had no idea where I ought to go or even where I was. The city was a maze, and there was no saying where Aurus might be or if he would even be alive after what had happened outside the palace. No, best not to dwell on the possibility all this might still be for nothing. Without him the Nine would never listen.

I walked on, trying to follow the shouts and clashes of battle, but they echoed oddly about the streets, leaving me sure I was going in circles. Looking up at the sun, I gave up on sounds and headed north. North was toward the gates, and from there I could find my way back toward the palace in search of Aurus.

A man wearing the blue trim of a Chiltaen soldier sped past the end of the street and with a shout I hurried after him, only to skid to a stop as three Kisian soldiers darted by, giving chase. "Shit," I hissed, pulling back into the shadow of a shop awning. A brown cat eyed me with disdain, wishing me gone from its hiding place. Chiltaens free from their barracks ought to have been a good thing, but not with the Kisian army roaming at large. It seemed whatever alliance Emperor Manshin and Dom Villius had didn't extend to their men.

Once the Kisians had passed, I jogged to the end of the street and turned to follow them, glad of the heavy sword in my hand. It wasn't very holy, but was better than getting holey. I laughed, the sound breathy and wild. Jass would have punched my arm for even thinking of that one.

Keeping to a safe distance, I followed the running soldiers. Those citizens who were braving the streets leapt out of the way as they passed, only to then find me barrelling toward them like a white-robed fury. The farther we went from the palace, the louder the sounds of battle became—pained cries and shouts, scraping hooves and the rhythmic thud of swords banging upon shields rising like a collective war cry.

Nearby shouts pierced the noise, and hope flared in my chest at the sound of a familiar voice. Taking a sharp turn in its direction, I stepped out into a crowded street only to halt abruptly, sword in hand and chest heaving. Chiltaen soldiers filled one side of the road edge to edge, Kisian soldiers the other. In the middle stood Secretary Aurus and Mother Li, along with a handful of armed Kisians who seemed to be on their side.

"Secretary!" I called, holding my courage close as every gaze turned my way. "Might I be of some assistance?"

"Dishiva!" Aurus's jaw dropped, and something like pride flared in his eyes. "You most certainly can, Your Holiness," he said, recovering from the shock. "It appears that Her Imperial Majesty got your message after all and ordered our release, but her generals don't take orders well."

Some of my confident swagger fled as I looked upon the soldiers blocking the way, and at the tense face of Mother Li and her priests. The Kisian leader growled something I was glad I couldn't understand, and I shrank a little more. After dealing with Legus I'd felt like I could take on anything, but now doubts were seeping back in.

"Dishiva," Aurus said quietly. "You can get us out of the city. You have the greatest power of anyone here."

"Me? What can I—?"

"What we kept forgetting is that you are the hieromonk of Chiltae, Dishiva," he said, bright eyes boring into mine. "You carry with you the weight and power of hundreds of years of the Chiltaen church, respected even by the Kisians. They may not believe in our god, but their society is also built on a foundation of priestly reverence. Lead us out of the city."

The Kisian army hadn't let Aurus pass, but I wasn't Aurus. I wasn't even Chiltaen; I was the closest thing there was to a bridge between so many disparate people.

"Trust me," Aurus said. And despite everything that had happened since I'd landed on this cursed shore, I did. I took a deep breath and dropped my sword. It hit the road with a clang, leaving me with no weapon and no armour, just the robe that had so far protected me from harm. Taking off the mask was a risk, but to make this work I needed to be both Chiltaen and Levanti, both warrior and priest, to be the bridge I'd never wanted to be. With a final deep breath, I lifted my arms to the sky.

"Witness!" I called, shouting above the grunts and clangs and cries, the running steps and the panicked babble as Kisian citizens sped away from the renewed fighting. "Witness me!" And keeping my arms up in the act of one supplicating the gods, I started to walk, lifting my voice to the heavens in song. Loud and clear and stronger than I had ever sung before, the Levanti lament that called the gods to witness our suffering.

Behind me, Aurus shouted orders, drawing his soldiers to us from all around. With their shields up, they fell in behind us like an armoured tail as I slowly advanced along the street. The Kisians blocking the way edged back, unsure. Their weapons remained in their hands but not one of them lunged at me, at least not yet. They may not have believed in the Chiltaen god, but I hoped their sense of honour would keep them from striking down a defenceless priest singing her way through the streets.

"It's working," Aurus murmured at my back. "It's working. We just need to make it to the gates with as many men as we can!"

The gates seemed an impossibly long way away. The initial shock was already wearing off. Some of the Kisian soldiers muttered to one another, others pointed toward the gate or behind me at the gathering Chiltaen soldiers.

Unable to risk breaking the spell, I kept singing. A white robe flickered in the corner of my vision, and another voice joined me. Not Levanti, but at the slightly crackled tones of Mother Li lifting her voice with mine in a different song, tears sprang to my eyes. I'd thought she'd walked away, had tricked me, had just said what she needed to say in order to get out of the palace, yet here she was, risking her life for a future that wasn't hers.

In a repetitive dance of confusion, the Kisian soldiers fell back only to regroup, following us toward the gates in shifting clumps. Nothing about them seemed unified. No one was giving orders. And the farther we went, the more citizens joined their ranks to hassle our flank.

We just needed to make it to the gates.

As we neared the main square, another, deeper voice joined my song, and I turned to find Jass beside me. He winked, and for a moment shock suspended my voice, leaving him carrying the lament alone. Until another voice joined—Harmara, soon followed by Rophet, Tephe, and Oshar, walking with me in our last hope to gain a future.

More Levanti joined us as we approached the gates. Tears pricked my eyes at the sight of Lashak and Diha, followed by many more I didn't know, who didn't want me to carry this burden alone.

It was going to work. Kisians all along the street were stepping back, still gripping their weapons, but letting our odd parade roll by now. I hadn't felt so strong a sense of belonging since I'd been exiled, and I flew, singing all the louder as behind us ranks of Chiltaen soldiers followed, trusting us with their fate. Wild though it was, there was beauty in this fragile moment, walking and singing and changing this one moment in history.

At the top of a rise, the gates came into view. Not close, but not so far that hope didn't spill through me. Fewer Kisians lined the streets ahead, but in the main square, a dense gathering of Levanti blocked the way. Our song had grown loud with many voices, the beat carried by an army of Chiltaen boots, yet the roar swelling from the crowd crashed over us. Shouting. Screaming. Levanti were pressing forward, punching their fists into the air.

Beside me, Jass punctuated the next line of the song with hissed curses, stretching onto his toes in the hope of a better view. Unable to ask, I could only glance a question his way.

"Rah," he mouthed, turning my blood to ice.

I sped my pace, more panic than plan. Some Levanti at the back of the screaming crowd turned our way, nudging their companions. A few folded their arms, intent on blocking the road, and behind me it was Aurus's turn to swear. It had been working; now it was my own people who were going to destroy the moment and our future with it.

As we approached, Levanti at the back of the crowd turned, and the unmistakable figure of Whisperer Ezma in her bone crown appeared upon the plinth around which they'd gathered. Before her knelt Rah, blood dripping from his brow and dark bruises marring his face. His arms. His neck. But that would soon mean nothing. Behind him, Derkka held an executioner's sword and grinned at the crowd of bloodthirsty Levanti shouting and crying for justice as though Rah had led them astray.

At the back of the crowd, Amun e'Torin was trying to push through, screaming hoarsely, but he kept getting pushed back, a swimmer clawing against a raging tide. Halting my steps, I let the song fade from my lips. "Ezma!" I shouted. "Ezma! Stop this madness!"

Treating the plinth like a stage, she held up her arms, seeming to call for calm, yet the baying for blood went on. Rah hadn't moved. Or couldn't, his body too battered to fight anymore. Not even when Derkka stepped forward, ready to swing.

"What is going on?" Aurus hissed at my back. "We need to keep moving before the Kisians wake up and slice us into tiny pieces."

I didn't answer, just pushed my way into the crowd. "Ezma!" Like for Amun, getting through was near impossible as Sword after Sword stepped in my way.

She was going to give the order. I couldn't stop her. Couldn't stop us becoming this, and as Derkka lifted the blade I held my breath. I was back in that courtyard facing Gideon while Yitti and his Swords lost their lives, nothing I could do to stop it.

A familiar scent snatched at my attention, and I truly was back in that moment, facing Gideon. Except he was there beside me, not in crimson but in simple Kisian armour, his short crop of dark hair dusted with shades of red. He was our grand, strong leader again, willed into existence by my desperation. He didn't look at me, his whole attention upon the platform. Eyes narrowed, he drew back a javelin and let it fly.

It flew fast and true, its tip burying deep into Derkka's throat. Thrown back by the force, the apprentice fell out of sight, blade dropping from his hands. A second javelin followed, speeding for Ezma, but Gideon had lost the moment of surprise and she stepped aside, letting it fly past her shoulder like it was nothing.

"Gideon e'Torin, traitor to his people," she called as she took Derkka's place standing over Rah. "How fine a day for the Levanti when we can rid ourselves of two such poisonous wounds. Bring him to me!"

Spurred on, angry Swords surged toward us. Upon the platform, Ezma took up Derkka's blade, ready to finish the job herself. Rah had not moved, and but for the rise and fall of his chest I could have believed him already dead.

Gideon didn't budge as hissing Swords closed in. "Rah!" he shouted. "Rah! Get up and fight!"

For the first time, Rah lifted his head. Blood dripped from his nose and his lip, and his tight grimace was all pain, yet he hunted Gideon in the crowd, and something like hope flared within me. "Go on, get up," I said, as Gideon snatched another javelin from a nearby Sword. Again he pushed forward, calling to Rah, but if he was hoping to reach the platform, he wasn't going to make it. Ezma had the blade, her revenge close.

Planting his feet, Gideon threw the javelin. It flew by Ezma's ear and she flinched, pausing the execution to point at Gideon, turning more of her followers our way. They'd just been shouting before, but now blades were drawn, every face a mask of hate.

"Shit!" Gripping Gideon's arm, I dragged him back and thrust him into the flock of Levanti who had been singing behind me. "If you want him, you're going to have to go through me," I snarled, glaring at Ezma's followers.

"Through *us*," Jass corrected, stepping up beside me. Lashak was with him, Diha too. Amun had drawn his swords and was shouting to Rah as Gideon had, urging him to get on his feet, to fight back, to not let the fallen whisperer win. And for the first time since I had landed on these cursed shores, I felt like I wasn't alone. Whatever part he had played in our pain, we would protect Gideon because we were part of something far larger than ourselves. We weren't protecting just him; we were protecting every shred of hope for a brighter future.

"Rah!"

At Gideon's ragged gasp, I braced for the worst, but the stone platform was empty. No Rah. No Ezma. Just Derkka lying forgotten, blood oozing from his throat.

Even without their leader, Ezma's followers went on pressing toward us, bellowing hate and rage and demanding Gideon's blood. "We need to get through," I said as Aurus shouted something behind me. "But we can't cut them down."

This seemed to jerk Gideon to action, and dragging his gaze from the empty platform, he spun toward Aurus. "You," he said. "You are the man in command of these soldiers?"

"Yes, you have a plan?"

"I do if your soldiers will listen to me."

"I'm afraid they don't have my language skills."

Gideon answered in Chiltaen, widening Aurus's eyes. "Holy God," the secretary said. "I thought you looked familiar. Emperor Gideon, how far the mighty have fallen."

"Fuck you too. Tell your men to listen to me, and we might be able to get out of here."

Gideon didn't wait for a reply, just barked out orders in Chiltaen. Once again he was the man we had followed, had believed in, his broad shoulders squared as he drew his sword. Whether it was his commanding tone or the heat of the moment, the Chiltaens didn't need their secretary's reassurance, just obeyed as though Gideon had been their leader.

For a moment all was motion. The front ranks slipped between us, their shields raised against the Levanti onslaught. Others drew alongside, while a second row joined the first, their shields held at an angle like the beginnings of a roof. Shuffled back from the fray, it was like standing in a metal hull, each Chiltaen soldier holding their ground with a steady arm. There they waited—*waited*—for Gideon's next instructions. What an emperor he could have been. What a home he could have built. Now we could only grieve the future Leo had stolen and stand behind Gideon one last time.

With everyone in place, Gideon shouted again, and in unison the Chiltaen soldiers took one step, followed by another and another, slowly pressing forward with their shields. Levanti thumped upon them, shouted, screamed with disgust at those hiding behind sheets of metal, but they could not stand their ground. Shunted slowly back, they had to move out of the way or be trampled beneath Chiltaen boots, and step by step we edged toward the gate.

A couple of arrows bounced off the shields, followed by a javelin. My anger boiled. It wasn't the Chiltaens they were trying to hit, not the Chiltaens they'd wanted to stop; it was me and Gideon and all those who'd stood with me, and I hated them for it. But they were my people too. We owed them the same future.

"Stop," I said, turning to Gideon. "Order them to stop walking."

"Stop? The gate isn't far—aren't you trying to get out of here alive?"

I gave him a withering look—this man I'd once taken orders from now taking orders from me. "Just do it. And tell them to let me through."

Gideon shrugged, and with a few sharp words of Chiltaen, the soldiers stopped their slow, inevitable walk toward freedom.

"What are you doing, Dishiva?" Aurus hissed. "It's too dangerous to step out there."

"Like how it was too dangerous to stand in the centre of the road and walk your army out of here? That worked, didn't it? Have faith in me, Secretary."

He looked like he wanted to argue, and glanced at Gideon and Jass for backup. Both shrugged, too used to my determination to dissuade me. "Good," I said. "Now, if anything goes wrong, get out of here as fast as this walking shield can get you. Once beyond the gates, you should be safe; they don't have the numbers to face you on open ground."

Not awaiting a response, I threaded through the ranks of Chiltaens in front of us until I stood behind the frontmost wall of shields. At a word, the shields parted just enough that I could draw a deep breath and step out onto the sun-lit road. In an instant, all eyes and arrows were trained upon me. Some in the crowd shouted and shoved and sneered, spat and swore, and my fury took over.

"Throw down your weapons and step aside!" I shouted, glaring at them all. "This stops now! We may not have deserved exile when we came here, but witnessed by all the gods, we do now. This is not our city. These Chiltaens are not our enemies. You are not my enemies and I am not yours, and nor is Whisperer Ezma a leader worthy of half the name. She lied to you all so she could take an army from these lands to conquer our home, because otherwise she could not go back. But you, my herd, my people, my friends, you are free. Lay down your weapons and walk away."

I'd made no threat, given them no ultimatum to rage against, just spoken the truth. And whatever our allegiance, we all carried a deep, draining exhaustion.

It was time to go home.

Some went on shouting, but enough grew quiet that bit by bit, silence swallowed everything. They wouldn't all agree. Some would stand by Ezma no matter what she did, but my words meant just enough in that moment that they began to fracture, those who stood their ground increasingly alone as one after another stepped aside. Those who moved didn't smile, didn't salute or thank me or even acknowledge my words, just glared and made space for the possibility of a better choice. An honourable choice. I'd once jeered at Rah's obsession with honour and duty, but now I'd seen far too much of what we looked like without them.

"Walk," I said, and trusting my people not to attack me, I started forward. Step after slow step, the shield wall followed, but I did not step back through it, refusing to hide from those who had sought to take out their anger upon us.

Holding myself together, I walked through the glaring crowd toward the open gates, leading our one-time enemy to freedom. I didn't let myself think I'd won, didn't let myself dwell upon the future I'd been fighting for, just focussed on each individual step and sang the lament of our people.

Echoing from behind the shields, the others picked it up once more, but we were not alone. All around the square, Levanti joined in, some murmuring, others lifting their voices like a cry to the heavens, a wail upon which they finally let out their pain. And for a time, there in that foreign city amongst dead and dying soldiers, we were united.

Only once we were well clear of the city walls did I stop singing, my throat raw. My feet faltered and my knees buckled, dropping me onto the cold grass.

"Dishiva?" Jass hovered before me. "Dishiva, are you all right?"

"Don't fuss," Gideon said, nearby though I couldn't see him. "She's coming down off more adrenaline than you'll ever feel in your life."

Jass grumbled at him, and I found myself laughing. The breath wheezed up my throat, dry like the last laugh of a dying old woman, and gods did I feel like one.

Around us Chiltaens jogged past, all clanking armour and thudding footsteps. From somewhere orders were being shouted, but getting out of there as fast as possible seemed to be the only plan.

"Dishiva." In the fading daylight, Aurus knelt before me, but whatever words he'd had upon the tip of his tongue shrivelled under Jass's gaze. "Well done, Your Holiness," he said. "I'll take it from here."

Before he could rise, I gripped his hand, holding him in place. "Did we do it? Do we have a future?"

Aurus's lips twitched. "I think I can salvage something. Yes."

I let him go. "Thank you."

"No," he said. "Thank you."

# 33. MIKO

I strode in through the throne room doors, Hacho an angry shard of history in my hand. At the head of the room, upon the dais, Manshin sat upon the throne, at ease in his stolen place. A place stolen from my father. From my brother. From me.

A scattering of men in fine robes filled the blood-coloured space, the few women seemingly present as a decorative afterthought. Whispers rose and they contracted into small, protective groups as I passed. Had they acceded to their new emperor's summons because they believed in his right to the throne? Or so they could tell their grandchildren they'd been present at the beginning of a new dynasty?

"Dodging your attempts to kill me is getting tiresome, Lord Manshin," I said, causing the soldiers around him to shift their stances and adjust their sword grips.

"Kill you? We were in a battle," he returned, sitting forward on the spiky throne of my ancestors. "Death and injury are constant friends at such times and are no one's fault."

Lifting Hacho, I nocked an arrow to her string, aiming at his left eye. "Do not think I won't do to you what I did to Grace Bachita when he sought to take my throne from me."

At the first creak of the bow, a dozen soldiers sped forward, lining up in front of their emperor amid a collective gasp. Behind me,

General Moto's heavy steps finally caught up. "Your Majesty, this is hardly the appropriate—"

"General!" Manshin snapped from behind his wall of steel and flesh. "Arrest this traitor at once."

On Moto's heels came dozens more footsteps, each set the thud of heavy boots and armour. Soldiers poured through the open doors. Moto's men, most likely, though it didn't matter. General Ryoji would soon be here with mine, and then there would be a bloodbath. We could each make an end of the other in the dramatic style Mama and Emperor Kin had perfected, leaving Kisia still more fractured and vulnerable.

Or we could try something new.

I lowered Hacho. My mother had once been given a choice to marry the man who had destroyed her family or condemn the empire to civil war. I'd never been sure whether she'd made the right choice or what the other path might have looked like, but my error had been not wondering whether there had been another way. A third choice she hadn't seen.

Crouching, I set Hacho and her scabbard gently on the floor.

"Miko!" Sichi gasped, stepping from a knot of noblemen near the dais. It was good to see her safe, to know she cared, but I held up my hand to stop her coming forward. Behind me, more hasty steps heralded the arrival of General Ryoji and Edo, their voices rising upon the hubbub. I didn't turn.

"Lord Ryo Manshin," I said, the stage fully set now. "You are waiting upon the arrival of Dom Villius. Your first attempt to marry him to your daughter failed, yet you doubled down on your determination to have him for a son-in-law, even when it was made clear by the very taking of this city that he has no control over the Nine. Tell me, why is that?"

"This throne room is neither a courtroom nor a meeting table," came his cold reply.

"No, Emperor Kin proved that when he killed my brother in cold blood on his throne room floor. And you and I proved that again when we forged Kin's will after his death so Grace Bachita couldn't take the throne."

Murmurs raced around the room, but I kept my gaze fixed on the scowling man upon my throne. "I have nothing to hide," I said, spreading my arms. "No hidden blades, no hidden plans, just a heart that belongs to the empire, as has the heart of every one of my ancestors before me. So tell me, Lord Manshin, why the determination to marry Dom Villius to your daughter?"

"You ask that question like it is strange for rich men to contract marriages between their children," he said, throwing a laughing glance at the noblemen in the room, encouraging them to enjoy his mirth. "It has been common practice in Kisia for—"

"Why. Marry. Dom Villius. To. Your daughter," I enunciated slowly, stepping forward as much to take me out of reach of Hacho as for the threatening effect.

Manshin's amusement vanished. "General Moto, I believe I ordered you to arrest this traitor once already, yet still she stands here. She has already confessed to forging her way to the throne after Emperor Kin's death, which she both caused *and* hid from the court. Do you need more crimes?"

I clenched my hands to fists and released them, easing a slow breath between my lips. I would not let anger win. Could not.

Behind me, General Moto made no move.

Beyond his protective wall of guards, Manshin got to his feet. "General Moto, I said, arrest her!"

"First I would hear the answer to her question. Your Majesty." That the general added his title almost as an afterthought was a better outcome than I dared hope for, but a vote of no confidence in one leader wasn't a vote of confidence for another. Oyamada had feared Moto's rivalry for Jie's throne, and swapping one military emperor for another would be as easy as blinking.

Manshin scowled over the entire room, a man who wished he could set us all alight. "Arrest her," he barked at his guards.

Where General Moto would not budge, the guards stepped off the dais as one. "Stand your ground!" Moto snapped to his own soldiers as the doorway into the throne room became a mass of shifting men. "Stand your ground!"

General Ryoji pushed through with the judicious use of his shoulder, leading a handful of his men into Kisia's last throne room. "If Your Majesty will excuse the interruption," he said, not making it clear which majesty he was speaking to. "It would seem your awaited guest has arrived."

From the knot of guards he'd led inside, Dom Villius stepped forward. Or rather, his twin did, yet so completely had Unus taken on his brother's persona that I flinched, heart leaping into my throat for a horrified moment fearing I'd got it all wrong.

At the sight of Dom Villius, noise swirled about the room like he was a whirlwind, bringing danger and distrust wherever he went. "Have you all been waiting for me?" Unus said, once again making me glance Ryoji's way to be sure he hadn't brought the wrong man. "Is it time for me to finally take my bride? Or shall I first pronounce you, Emperor Manshin, lord of the unified territories of Kisia and Chiltae, ruler of the holy empire?"

His words landed with a thud, their echo leaving a moment of silence before exclamation rose around us. All at once, everyone had demands and questions, and even the guards Manshin had ordered to arrest me seemed hesitant to step into the storm.

"Lies!" Manshin shouted over the noise. "General—"

"It is not a lie," I said, stepping past the humble stone. "You wanted to marry Sichi to Dom Villius to strengthen the ties between Kisia and Chiltae, not on a political level so much as on a religious one. When did he convince you that you'd be better off helping him become Veld Reborn and rebuilding a holy empire than getting in his way? Were you working behind Kin's back too?"

Manshin snorted, looking down at me as one would look at a worm. "Such nonsense only proves you have lost your mind. I will not let you turn everything I seek to do for Kisia into a farce. Kisia needs no idealistic Otako girl to lead it—"

"Nor does it need a power-hungry, ambitious general bent only on war! Kisia is starving. Kisia is dying. Kisia will not last the winter if you spend its food and its energy and its people fighting Chiltae for a holy empire. Kisia needs to heal."

"Then it needs neither an Otako nor a Ts'ai to lead it," he spat.

"No," I agreed. "It needs someone who listens to what the people need. The days of raging endless wars and ruling from a palace disconnected from the world are gone, and we need to change with it." I looked around at each of the noblemen and -women present as I spoke. It would make no difference to them who sat on the throne at the end of the day, but perhaps for a brief moment they might have empathy for the majority of Kisia's citizens, who were not so fortunate. The ones who would die when famine came, and who would be sent to fight our wars. "I do not want to claim that throne on the shoulders of my forebears," I went on, speaking to them as much as to Manshin. "I do not want to rule as an Otako or a Ts'ai, but as someone who has dreamed of a better future."

Silence had grown as we spoke, and now behind me, someone stepped into it, boot scuffing stone. "I stand with Her Imperial Majesty," General Ryoji said, his voice rising to the rafters.

"Of course you do," Manshin said. "Your relationship with—"

"I stand with Her Imperial Majesty."

I turned as a second and third voice echoed the pronouncement, to find both General Alon and General Yass standing beside Ryoji. My heart swelled at the sight of them. Too many times had I sought their support against Manshin, putting them at risk, that to have them feel safe enough to stand with me in that moment was the boost of confidence I needed. Yet when I swung my gaze toward General Moto, brows raised, he said nothing.

"General Moto," Manshin said, his tone that of a man whose patience was running out. "Perhaps now you will do as I ordered and arrest her."

But Moto didn't move; he stood staring up at the man he'd chosen to follow. Moto wasn't a man fast to anger, but the set of his jaw held an edge of rage. These men who'd long ruled Kisia from around the meeting table didn't like to be lied to, didn't like to be kept in the dark, didn't like to be made a fool. Perhaps Manshin had never realised that ambitious men could be relied upon only while they were part of one's plans, and never again from the moment you took a step without them. He had taught me that.

For a long moment Manshin and General Moto stared at one another, before General Moto spun to face those of his soldiers standing at his back. "Get that man out of here," he ordered, pointing at Unus. "And do a full sweep of the palace grounds for his supporters. I want them all rounded up and brought here at once. Go! Now!"

Moto's men hurried off about their general's orders, while upon the dais Manshin stood motionless, frozen in a moment of indecision. Without the support of General Moto, without General Yass or General Alon, without the vehement backing of the nobility, who stood silent like mere watchers of history, he had nothing. I knew that feeling all too well. I hoped he felt the floor buckle beneath him as I had back in Kogahaera, when he had taken everything from me.

With one last look around the room for support that didn't come, he spun on his heel and made for a narrow door hidden in the wall behind the throne. The escape hatch, Mama had always called it. I'd never seen Kin use it, to do so surely an act of surrender.

I sped after him, all the dried blood from battle cracking and flaking as I moved. A glance back assured me no one was following, and I slipped out of sight in his wake. Almost immediately the narrow passage turned back upon itself, dimly lit by small windows as it twisted toward the heart of the palace. Even had it been dark, I could have followed his heavy, furious treads.

"Manshin!"

He flicked a look back over his shoulder but didn't stop. Didn't speak.

"Manshin! You know it doesn't have to end like this. You were once the best minister of the left the empire ever had, a staunch and selfless protector. Why not commit yourself to the empire—"

"And be pardoned?" he laughed. "I know how you all think. Ts'ai, Otako, it doesn't matter, you're all the same. But of course it's honourable when you have to make hard choices and monstrous whenever anyone else does the same."

Abruptly, Manshin stopped. Sichi stood at the other end of the passage, Hacho held inexpertly in her hands and her eyes bright like pools of flame. "Miko might be able to find it in her heart to be merciful, Father, but I cannot," she said, nocking an arrow to the string. It wasn't quite the motion of one who has never done such a thing, but it wasn't far off.

"Put that down, girl," Manshin snapped. "That cursed thing ought to have gone into the ground with Katashi."

"Are you giving me an order?" she said, taking a step closer.

He clasped his hands behind his back and looked down at her. "As your father I have the right to do that. Just as your father is the one who always has your best interests at heart. I ensured you could marry the man who would become hieromonk of both Kisia *and* Chiltae and this is what I get? The power and wealth you could have commanded would have been beyond anything."

"My best interests," she repeated, and gritting her teeth, she loosed the arrow. I ducked, hands over my head in fear of her aim, but the arrow thunked into the wall and fell with a clatter at Manshin's feet.

"This is very entertaining, my dear," he said as she calmly nocked another arrow, "but—"

She loosed. This time I didn't duck, and was rewarded with the meaty thwack of pointy steel meeting muscle. Manshin hissed, looking at the arrow in his arm.

"There," he said through gritted teeth. "You've had your fun, now put that down."

Sichi seemed to be in a whole other world for how little heed she paid him, drawing another arrow from the scabbard and setting it to the string. That left only one more arrow, and I wasn't sure whether I was more glad or sorry I hadn't had time to replenish them.

She loosed again, the increased force of her growing confidence sending him reeling back. On instinct, I caught him as he fell against me with a grunt. "Sichi!" he snapped, touching the arrow in his shoulder. "Stop this. Now."

Sichi loosed the last arrow into his knee and Manshin screamed.

"Sichi," I gasped, sliding to the floor beneath his thrashing weight. "Are you sure you want to do this?"

I'd been asked that question so many times since I'd stepped out from beneath my mother's protection that summer back in Koi. My answer had always been yes, but never had I felt the degree of certainty I saw in her eyes. No rage, no flair, she just pulled the dagger from his belt and pressed its tip to the underside of his jaw as he struggled to rise. She hardly needed to even push.

I scrabbled out from beneath him as he bled, blood bubbling to his lips in place of the curses he tried to scream upon us. Not that we were listening. Not really. His death would be a great weight off both our shoulders and off the empire, but I didn't watch his life end. Instead, I reached for Sichi's hand, and together we sat there needing no words. There would be time later for apologies, for promises and for plans. For now though, there was just an end.

And when at last Manshin stopped breathing, we breathed a little easier.

34. CASSANDRA

The stone floor of the shrine was the warmest, most comfortable thing I'd ever lain on. It shouldn't have been, I had just enough sense left to know that, yet it didn't seem to matter. My whole body and soul—both of them—were adrift on a tide of blood and pain. It was the happiest I'd ever felt.

"Staying down this time?" Duos said, his voice disembodied somewhere above me. "It's a wise choice. If you're still alive when I get back from pronouncing His Imperial Majesty lord of all the lands, then we can keep playing this ever so fun game. Ah," he added at the sound of footsteps. "My cue, I—"

He broke off with a growl. I ought to have been worried, have looked up to see what had upset him, but every part of me felt heavy. I just wanted to go on lying there and never move again. There on the warm, comfortable stone.

"You sent for a priest?"

The voice was familiar, but the stones were still comfortable.

*It's Yakono!* Kaysa shouted in my head. *He's here! With two of you, surely you can kill him!*

It sounded hard.

"Pathetic," Duos said. "Are you here to try, *again*, to complete your contract, or did you come to save her? Don't bother answering, your mind is an open book."

*Get up!*

Kaysa pressed forward, and happy to slide into the still more comfortable and warm recesses of our mind, I let her take over. Groaning, she managed to get us onto our knees, the shrine spinning slowly around us.

"Cassandra." Yakono's hand was there, and she took it, letting his strong grip pull us to our feet. His jaw was set and his eyes hard, not shifting from Duos even as he steadied our balance.

*Right, now get back out there and kill the shit,* Kaysa said, leaving me in control of the aching body again. What I wouldn't have given to lie back down.

"How do you want to do this?" I whispered, the words slurring as they passed my swollen lips. "Shall we just rush him?"

He didn't answer.

"Yakono?"

He turned, and with Kaysa's warning shout ringing in my head, Yakono's tightly balled fist struck me in the face. Blood spurted from my nose, and I staggered back, Duos's laughter ringing through the shrine. "Did you really think he would be able to fight me? No matter how much a path might overgrow, once you make it, it's always there."

I spat a mouthful of blood as Yakono came at me again, a one-two punch to the gut that doubled me over, bile adding to the blood already spilling from my lips. Everything seemed hazy again, but his next strike owned a blade, and I narrowly dodged a thrust at my face. "Fight it!" I shouted, trying to wipe the blood from my nose and failing to stem it. "Don't listen to him! Think of your precepts!"

Shouting hadn't worked last time, so I backed up, only to run into one of the shrine's central pillars. "Shit!" I hissed, ducking and scurrying awkwardly aside as Yakono lunged. "Where the fuck is Unus and his magic shit when we need it!"

*It's too dangerous for him to come back! He might die!*

"And we definitely will if he doesn't!" I said, still backing away from Yakono. "Right, we need another plan."

"Just give up, Cassandra," Duos said. "Consider it a beautiful end. Dying for love, or is it…from love, perhaps. Really, you are the most pathetic whore I've ever met."

I clenched my shaking hands tight, and keeping an eye on Yakono, I edged around the echoing space toward Duos.

"You're a terrible assassin too," he went on, as step after step, the dull-eyed Yakono followed me as though I had him on a leash. "Really, Cassandra, you've let Kaysa weasel her way into your mind and turn it all soft."

I kept backing up, edging near enough to Duos that I had to watch him too, trying to keep both him and Yakono in sight with every step.

"I can keep this up all day and all night," Duos said as I drew closer. "But you are old and tired, Cassandra. Just let him kill you and put us all out of our misery."

In the corner of my vision, Yakono kept pace, seeming to move without Duos having to give the act of control much thought.

"Oh, it's not hard when you've had as much practice as I have," Duos said, folding his arms.

Another step toward him. Closer. Closer. Trusting that Yakono would keep following, I stared only at Leo, watching for any twitch or flicker that might precede an attack. My field of vision slid slowly out of focus, Yakono nothing but a hazy shape behind Dom Villius now.

One more step and as a crease wrinkled Duos's brow, Yakono swung his fist. He'd been aiming for me, and a good strong punch from behind with that much follow-through ought to have felled Duos, but my angle had been off. He caught only the shit's ear, sending him stumbling.

With Duos's concentration momentarily shattered, Yakono blinked, shaking his head to clear the haze.

"Yes!" I cried. "Now let's—"

With a roar, Duos swung, slamming his fist into the side of Yakono's head and sending him sprawling all tangled limbs.

"No!" I started forward as he hit the stones hard, but Duos blocked the way, his teeth bared. He stared into my eyes, and a scream like the one that had ripped from Septum's lips tore through my head, freezing me in place. I staggered, knees buckling as I tried to focus. *Oh no you don't*, Kaysa hissed, and tore through the barrage, taking over. The scream came again, clogging Kaysa's mind this time, but though it was like pushing through a fierce wind, I took back control and strode forward.

Duos laughed, not a shred of humour in the sound. "How slippery you Deathwalkers are. Freaks, just like me."

"We are not," Kaysa snapped, fists clenched. "People might not understand us, but we'll never be like you."

"Such morality! Such idealism! Really, Cassandra, this one has much more fire than you. But all freaks are the same, Kaysa, and no matter how kind people might sometimes be, they'll never truly understand you. Never truly accept you. Not like I do. We are the same, you and I."

Kaysa spat at him, the glob of saliva almost hitting his feet. "Never. You have exactly the amount of humanity one would expect from a man with one twelfth of a soul." She advanced, sending him edging back, teeth bared. Defensive. "You're a weak, pitiful monster."

"And like I said, we are the same."

Without a dagger, we had only our fists and knees and anger, and we unleashed them all upon him without thought. I had done the same to an older boy at the hospice once, had snapped and lashed out, biting and scratching and pummelling his face into the stones, and there had been so much blood when the Blessed Guards had finally pulled me away.

The same flame of hatred flared now, but Leo blocked or dodged every punch, sidestepped every kick, retaliating with greater speed over and over again until all I could taste was blood and bile, and the shrine grew hazy before my eyes.

"Come on, Cassandra," Leo taunted, his grin a hateful thing. "You're meant to be so good at this. And to think, you are the only two assassins Aurus hired who even survived."

I blinked through a wave of exhaustion that tugged at me like an ocean current, before I was charging in again upon Kaysa's fury. She didn't have my skill, but our shared body knew the right movements, and each of her strikes ought to have landed. But Duos dodged and blocked, laughing as he protected himself from her fists.

Focussing upon one of our legs, I took control and kicked his shin. My boot connected hard and he hissed, flinching back, only for Kaysa to land a fist upon his jaw.

*Cass! He can't read what we're going to do if we keep switching!*

Duos stumbled, but he regained his balance, wiping blood from his lip with his pale sleeve. "How stupid do you think I am?" he said.

"Stupid enough to knock down your best weapon," I said, gesturing at Yakono, groaning now upon the floor, hands to his head.

Duos snarled, but I saw his anger for what it was—an admission of weakness, that moment of doubt all we needed. We had grown so used to sharing this body, of being able to slide in and out of control, that it became like a dance—not of fighting but of pulling the levers that made our body move. A punch, a kick, a step, fists to face and gut and throat, and everywhere he tried to block he failed because he could not see us coming. He had not trained to fight by reacting but by reading his opponent's mind, and with two voices dancing around one another he flailed and stumbled, blood leaking from his lip and his nose and a cut above his eye. Yet for all the bruises he would have come morning, he moved too quick for me to grab his throat or snap his neck, and I had no blade, no way to end this before he found another way to overpower us. To outwit us. To win.

But I had come too far to let Hana down now, so I clenched my aching fists ready to fight on no matter how long it took.

From the moment I'd first hit the stones, the world outside the shrine had ceased existing, everything narrowing to this man in this moment. Until upon a tide of running steps that illusion shattered. "Your Holiness!" One of Leo's men sped in, out of breath. "Your Holiness! We have to go!"

Five more followed, each face a mask of fear. "Keep watch," one hissed to another as they faced Duos's frozen fury.

He stepped back out of my range and snapped, "Well? What is it?"

"It's Emperor Manshin," the first man said, shoved forward by the others. "He's...dead. Empress Miko has the throne now and they know we're here."

"Dead?" Duos spoke quietly, but he could have roared the word for all the rage it held. "Dead? And my consort? My high priest? My twin? I will have you all gutted for this!"

"Your Holiness—"

"Kill that one." Duos jabbed a finger at Yakono. "And bring her. *Alive.*"

Six armed soldiers approached across the floor, and though every part of me was exhausted and broken, I shifted my weight, ready to fight. "The empress's guards will find you if you don't run now," I said. "And just think what they'll do to you."

Grimaces flashed across their faces only to freeze in place. Mid-stride, eyes open, as though time had ceased to turn.

Kaysa spun around. Wherever he had been, Unus now stood in the doorway with his arms spread like an avenging god, a god who stared right through me, seeing nothing. His arms trembled and he gritted his teeth with the effort of holding six men still.

Duos began to laugh. "That's it, Unus," he called, voice echoing around us. "Use the power, remember how strong we are, how much better we are, born for a single purpose we're now so close to fulfilling."

"Don't listen to him," I said. "Remember that without him you're free."

"I know you believe in everything I plan to build," Duos went on, addressing Unus, though it was us he watched. "All you have to do is sacrifice me and take on the mantle of Veld, fulfilling the prophecy we were born for."

"I can't—hold—them—long—" Unus ground the words out between clenched teeth. "You—have to get him—now!" His last word dragged, rising upon an ascending scream like someone had gripped each of his arms and was slowly tearing him down the centre.

Duos filled my vision as he filled the future, a future fast shortening toward the moment seconds from now when Unus would lose his grip on the soldiers and I would get hacked apart by six angry men who wanted to get out of here.

Kaysa screamed. The sound was trapped inside my head, but it filled every space, raw and loud and all-encompassing. Her glance flicked to the floor behind Duos, and realising Yakono no long lay there, I joined in.

Duos pressed his hands to his ears as the assassin appeared behind him. Catching some thought, Duos spun, locking his gaze to Yakono's. "No!" I reached out, as though I could stop Duos from getting inside Yakono's mind again, but while I reached, Kaysa lunged forward, slamming our foot into the back of Duos's leg.

His knees buckled, striking the ground, but though the floor vibrated it was nothing to the shaking of the world when Yakono plunged his dagger into Dom Leo Villius's neck. I felt it pierce the skin and crack into bone as though it were my hand that wielded it, every sensation owning a sound. And when he yanked it free and plunged it back in, there was no kindness in Yakono's eyes, not even professional indifference, only the bright, hot anger of a man made to fear his own mind.

Blood sprayed as again and again Yakono pierced Leo's body, not stopping even when the priest ceased to breathe. Not until he fell, spilling blood from a dozen increasingly wild gouges, never to rise again.

A wretched sob leapt from Yakono's lips, and he dropped the dagger, stumbling back, his eyes wild. "I'm sorry," he gasped. "I'm so sorry, I tried not to hurt you. I tried so hard not to hit you but he was just...in my head and I couldn't stop and—"

"I know." I gripped his shaking shoulders. "I know, I know."

"What...what happened? Is that...?" The deep voice caught upon confusion. Duos's six soldiers stood blinking, one furiously rubbing his eyes, his gaze shifting from Unus breathing heavily in the doorway to Duos's bloody corpse.

"It sure is," I said, fighting the urge to laugh. "You should probably run while you can. Empress Miko isn't the merciful type."

The soldiers looked at one another, remaining frozen a few seconds longer until at last one backed toward the door. That broke their trance and they sped out, shoving to be the first to escape. I hoped they would run into a whole host of angry Kisians.

Shoved clear of the doorway, Unus had dropped onto the floor and lay there unmoving, every breath coming fast and hard—everything about him so alive beside his fallen brother. His soul twin. Part of me kept expecting Duos to twitch. To groan. To breathe. To live. He'd never come back to life; it had always been just another brother ready to die for the cause, but I couldn't shake the fear Duos was different.

"We should probably go before the empress's guards find us," Yakono said. "I don't think I have the energy to explain...this."

"Unus needs a few minutes, I think," Kaysa said, crawling across the floor to lie at Unus's side. "Besides, I want to be totally sure Duos is really dead and not going anywhere."

Having eyed us a moment, Yakono joined us, and together we lay listening to distant sounds of change going on around us. Side by side our chests rose and fell, Unus's rapid breaths eventually slowing. After a time, Yakono slid his hand into mine, and though it felt strange, it was the good sort of strange I'd not felt for a long time. On the other side, Kaysa reached out a hand to take Unus's. He squeezed back weakly, and there the three of us lay, unwilling to move for as long as the world would allow.

# 35. RAH

R ah!" The distant voice nagged at my consciousness, broken upon the seething pain of my own people. "Rah!" The voice came again, intent on denying my end.

"Rah!"

Not just any voice. I looked up, everything hurting just to achieve so small a movement. I blinked, but the haze of sweat and blood and pain would not clear.

"Rah! Get up and fight!"

A foot scuffed close. A blade scraped the stones beneath my hands with a metallic whisper.

"Rah!"

Panic now in Gideon's voice. He was there in the crowd, amid a tide of screaming Levanti and white-clad priests, and a great column of soldiers like an armoured snake. I blinked, sure it was all a dream brought on by pain, Gideon the only one that seemed real. He had a javelin in his hand, but his face was a rictus of pain and fear.

Memory of how I'd got there started to seep in along with the scent of nearby blood, and the shadow of a lifting blade caressed the ground.

Something ripped through the air over my head. Ezma gasped and her feet shifted, pulling the blade's shadow out of sight. "Grab him!" she snapped, the command shrill over the noise. "They can both die here together, ridding us of their curse forever."

I'd fought again and again not to die, to keep going, keep breathing. Beneath the punches and kicks and cuts of my people, I'd found a dark ocean of acceptance. As a martyr to a grander cause, I could let myself go, but not Gideon. Never Gideon.

Pushing through the pain with a roar, I kicked out, catching Ezma's ankle. She hissed and stepped back, and in her moment of shock, I spun and launched myself at her knees. The all too familiar piercing pain cut through my ear as my shoulder hit her legs, but Ezma fell, crying out as she landed upon the stones, grasping her left arm. The impact sent her jawbone headpiece flying. It landed with a rattling smash, scattering shards of bone. The sight held me captive a shocked moment, but Ezma paid it no heed. She rolled to the edge of the platform and, still holding her arm, slid out of sight. Behind me the square was a chaotic mess of shouting and shoving, but there was no time to see what was going on, only to snatch up Ezma's fallen blade and pull the javelin from Derkka's throat.

Leaping from the edge of the platform after Ezma almost sent me tumbling onto my face. She had fared little better. Still clutching her arm, she had scrambled up only to stumble, momentum all that kept her from falling again as she found her balance and ran.

I sped after her, my attention narrowing to nothing and no one else. At the end of the street, she slowed to glance back, before darting out of sight through an arch. I followed, slowing, but not enough. A chunk of stone slammed into my shoulder, tearing fabric and skin. I almost dropped the javelin, and Ezma lunged as though to catch it, only to hastily back up when I straightened, adjusting my grip. "Going to kill me, Rah?" she said, backing along the path, still holding her arm. "Going to weigh your soul heavy on Mona's scales by ending a horse whisperer?"

"As you were willing to end me when all I'd done was exist?"

I said, breathless from the run and the pain. With every step she took back, I took one forward, wary despite her lack of weapon. "Why didn't you try to convince me I was Veld? Why didn't you try to get me on your side as you tried to get Gideon?"

She barked a laugh, glancing back as she went on retreating step by step. We were alone in this narrow road, the buildings all shut up and the sounds of chaos growing distant.

"That would have been a waste of time when I knew you by reputation," Ezma said. "Rah e'Torin, the honourable one, he who stood up to Gideon, who had become something more than just a man in the eyes of desperate Swords needing a leader. I could count on Gideon losing loyalty over time, but not you."

She threw another glance back over her shoulder, and I threw the javelin. The overarm motion twinged my ear, and I gasped, pulling the throw. Instead of hitting her throat it stuck in her arm, gouging flesh as its weight ripped it free.

Pale and hissing pain, Ezma ran, leaving me breathing sharp gasps with my hand pressed to my ear and my head spinning. Fuck Sett and fuck her and fuck it all. So useless and pathetic a pain, so completely immobilising whenever it struck.

It took a few seconds for it to fade to an ache, and drawing the stolen sword from my belt, I took off after her again. She couldn't have gotten far, so I slowed at every corner and doorway, holding my breath to listen. The end of the road gave way to courtyard, where a small shrine sat beneath a towering, twisted tree. Two narrow archways led into other courtyards that looked like copies of the first, houses facing inward, their welcoming balconies belied by their barricaded doors. There might have been people inside, but the courtyard was empty but for a small flock of chickens pecking around the base of the tree. They ignored me as I turned in a slow circle, hunting signs of movement.

As I backed toward the shrine, bark crackled overhead and

something hit my neck, only to smash upon the ground, scattering shards of painted wood. At a heavy thud behind me, I stepped back, slamming Ezma into the tree trunk. Pinned, she flailed a short blade toward my face, but I gripped her wrist and twisted.

Teeth sank into my shoulder and I yelped, my hold loosened before I could wrench the blade from her hand. She spun free, knife brandished. "Perhaps I should have tried to win you over rather than fight you," she said, once more backing away from me, scattering chickens. "We are both determined dreamers of a better world, and what a world we could have built had we shared the same dream."

"You don't have a dream, you have a god."

Sweat glistened on her skin and blood smeared her ashen face, yet still she laughed. "So do you, only yours is yourself."

"Horseshit," I spat. "I've only ever fought for my people, never for myself. You're the one who wants to destroy the plains to build an empire."

She bared her teeth in something I couldn't call a smile. "You think you know me so well."

"I do," I said as she retreated slowly back through the narrow arch into the next courtyard. "I wish I didn't. I wish I could just hate you, could say I don't understand you, but in another life, I could have been you, and that hurts more than anything you can throw at me."

Ezma went on backing up, her blade brandished and her eyes on me.

"I gave up my training because I didn't want to be alone," I went on, wondering if here at last I would get through to her, if maybe we could forge a different ending after all. "Because I wanted things. Because my soul yearned. If I had stayed, the isolation would have fed my resentment until it twisted into hate, my responsibility an open wound. You don't have to be this. You don't have to do this."

She tilted her head to the side, all pity. "Oh, come on, we both know it's too late for that. You don't trust me. I don't trust you. We've chosen our paths. How I once felt doesn't matter." She pressed a closed fist to her chest. "I found somewhere to belong. Something to fight for. Something that matters more than me and that gives me peace. You sneer, but every sneer only pushes me closer to my purpose."

"Your purpose of destroying your own people."

"That you think that's my goal just shows how narrow your mind is."

Her slow retreat brought us out into the next courtyard, where a washing line hung low with damp clothing. Snatching a tunic, she threw it in my face. Instinctively I parried with my sword, sending my ear ringing. A sleeping mat shook loose from the line to flop on the ground before me, while across the courtyard Ezma was already halfway up some stairs, wild laughter in the glance she threw me.

Once my ear settled, I took off after her, leaping up the stairs two at a time, determined not to let her win. And in that moment I understood. I hadn't tried to bridge our differences with empathy because I wanted to save her. My anger was too deep for that. I had done it so when I slid my blade through her throat, I could tell myself I had tried.

Keeping my tread light and quiet, I followed her along an upper veranda. She seemed to be heading for a rickety ladder leading to the roof, a challenging look back like she thought I wouldn't follow. But as her hands closed around the parched wooden rungs and she looked skyward, I charged. She had no time to climb and no space to dodge, only to catch my full weight as I slammed into her. She hit the low railing and toppled back, the pair of us falling head first onto an awning below. It tore, sending us spilling back into the courtyard, winded and bruised.

The sword jolted from my hand, skidding away as I struggled

to my feet, gasping for breath. Ezma looked as bad as I felt. Worse. The arm she'd held earlier now hung at a horrific angle, her face pale. Her good hand still clutched her knife, and with a guttural cry she lunged. Expecting her to go for my throat, her jab at my thigh took me off guard and I tripped, falling hard and taking a slice across the knee.

Before I could roll, Ezma loomed over me, triumph curling her lips. I lifted my boot between her legs as hard as I could. I'd seen many a Sword drop from such a kick, and she didn't disappoint, staggering back a pace, her face contorted. A man might have hit the ground, but her shock was at least enough for me to kick the blade from her hand. It flew across the courtyard and slid away, clattering.

I rolled after it, but as I rose, she leapt on my back. My elbows gave way, slamming my chin into the stones.

"You might not be able to kill me, but I can kill you," she snarled, smashing a palm into the side of my head. My bleeding chin scraped back across the stones, and the familiar pain cut through my ear. Only my deep, stubborn determination to give her no satisfaction brought me through it, and I rolled, gritting my teeth as I tried to buck her off.

Ezma gasped as she overbalanced, her broken arm unable to save her as she sprawled sideways.

"You think I won't kill you," I hissed, wiping my bleeding chin and finding the skin torn. "You think I won't save the plains from you, especially when it will give me so much joy?"

She shuffled back as I rolled to my feet, hot blood trailing down my neck.

"You think I care for the title you have no right to cling to?"

"Oh no," she said, staggering up though she rocked on her feet, ashen and unbalanced. "I see you, Rah. I have always seen you. You aren't just a threat to everything I've given my life for; you are a threat to yourself and everyone who comes in your way. You are a pit of darkness with no end. A destroyer with no soul. You would strike me down even were I still a full horse whisperer, but you cannot because that's not how it's written."

One of her feet dragged as she hobbled back, passing through the shadow of an overhead branch. The courtyard could have been a circle formed for a challenge, the space our own—just me and her and her knowing little smile. "What do you mean, isn't how it's written?" I said.

She laughed. "You think I ever planned to live through this? That it was ever *my* hand that would build the holy empire?" She spread her good arm, inviting witness. "I am but a wheel turning the present toward the future. I'm going to die, yes, oh yes, but not by your hand. I am Dishiva's false high priest."

"What?" The word was out before I could bite it back, twisting her expression into such satisfaction.

"I love telling you things when it's too late for you to change them," she said. "The tingle of joy I get down my spine is finer than the warm morning sun after a cold night."

I squeezed my eyes shut for a moment, trying to slot this new information into what I already knew, but it wouldn't fit. It had to be the other way around, that Ezma would kill Dishiva, ensuring her final elevation to the position of Veld.

Ezma seemed to sense my confusion, for she laughed all the harder. "I am not Veld. I told Dishiva that when I revealed her destiny; I just never told her how our story would end."

"But Leo made her his false high priest."

"A mistake on his part. *He* might never have followed her, might never have believed her real, but you have only to look at how the Chiltaens treat her to know she is no fake. It doesn't matter that she's Levanti. Doesn't matter that she's a woman. Their hieromonks are above any such considerations, and once they have the position, they have it for life. No. She was never a false anything, but me, walking about and calling myself a whisperer when I have had that title stripped from me, I am as false as a Levanti comes. You have said so yourself, many times."

She had stopped backing away when I had stopped advancing, the pair of us caught in this moment while the world went on without us. Elsewhere in the city, Dishiva and Amun and Lashak were fighting different battles. They fought for their lives and their futures, while far beyond these walls other people went on living ordinary lives doing ordinary tasks, the sun rising and setting upon a day of no importance.

"Does knowing I am going to die anyway satisfy your petty need for revenge?" Ezma said.

"Petty—? No. I have watched you do everything in your power to tear us apart. All these deaths are on your hands. Petty revenge." I spat on the stones between us. "Whatever satisfaction I will take in killing you, this long ago stopped being about me."

"But you aren't going to kill me."

"You keep saying that," I said, taking a slow step forward and enjoying her flinch. "But I know something Dishiva doesn't know. You didn't always think she was Veld, did you? You told Gideon it was him, and when he wouldn't play along, you sent the Chiltaens after him and his Swords, and everything that followed was your fault."

"Oh, you can't absolve him so easily." She stood her ground when next I advanced, standing as tall and proud as someone near fainting from a broken arm can. "You cannot throw all the blame at me. I did what I did because I had to, but Gideon chose his own path. You think I condemned him to Voiding just to hurt you, but no. He deserved it."

"Says the false whisperer," I spat. "Who were you lying to? Gideon? Or Dishiva?"

"Neither. I made a mistake in my original translation. I thought Veld was a man, not realising it had to be a woman because the faith doesn't allow men to have male partners."

She bumped into the veranda post. "But Veld isn't Chiltaen," I said. "Isn't of the faith. How can you be sure the same rules apply?"

A flicker of annoyance flashed across her features, and I leapt forward, slamming her against the post. Gripping hold of her good arm, I closed my other hand around her throat, squeezing the ropey cords of her bulging neck. I tightened my hold, her widening eyes and panicked gasps filling me with joy. With nothing more I wanted to say, I gritted my teeth and crushed her throat with all my strength.

Until she swung her broken arm at my head. It was no punch, not even close, but the surprise loosened my hold enough for her to tear away, and drawing a desperate gasp of air, she kicked me in the shin.

I fell back, an uneven stone sending me stumbling as her breath rasped in and out and she hacked a cough. The ground struck me as I fell, an exhausted wreck of pain upon the stones.

Her laugh was a terrible, racking thing as she dragged herself toward me. "Can't. Kill me," she said. "Only. Veld. Can."

I rolled and caught sight of her fallen blade, its hilt inlaid with carnelian like a promise of blood. I dragged myself toward it, one elbow after another, the torn fabric of my clothing catching on the stones.

Her trailing steps followed as my fingertips caressed the blade's edge and I pulled myself closer one last time. Reaching out, I closed my hand around its hilt. No time to look, only to let instinct carry me through pain one last time.

Perhaps in another time, another place, another world, I thrust out that blade and found only air. Or caught the edge of her arm or shoulder, only to collapse and be unable to fight on. But as I turned, punching out the blade with every last ounce of effort my body possessed, it was solid flesh I met. Its tip drove through skin and sinew, spilling blood with which I could cleanse the world.

Her good hand shook as it touched the wound, feeling for the knife—her knife. How familiar it would feel stuck there, promising an end that wouldn't come until I drew it out. This final moment less gift than torture, awash with pain as I stared into her eyes and made sure she understood she was about to die. That there was nothing she could do. That her prophecy had been wrong.

"Veld," I spat. "You put your faith in nothing but a story."

Ezma's eyes widened and she gripped my fingers, a convulsive hold that seemed to seek reassurance I was real. "Rah," she said, my name little more than a strained gasp on her pale lips. "Rah. Rah."

"What?"

"Wide. Wide open plains. Rah."

The meaning of my name in our tongue. It was no revelation, yet her tight squeeze around my wrist and her unblinking stare made me uneasy. I could have withdrawn the blade, could have let her fall and expire upon the stones at my feet, but I did not.

"Rah," she repeated, ending my name on something of a choked laugh. "Rah, wide open plain. Veld. Wide open... Wide open plain."

Her laugh was a rasping, hideous thing, making the blade shake with her body. "It's you. You will build... the empire. You. All along. The name... right there in front... of me. May God—"

I yanked the knife out. Her mouth sagged open and her eyes widened as blood spilled free. Her tongue moved within the cavity of her mouth as she tried to speak, but her voice was a mere breath. Still, I flinched. Every sound was a truth she sought to pour upon me, dragging me back into the mess her death ought to have freed me from.

"No." The knife fell from my hand to clatter once more upon

the stones. "No. I don't believe in your god. I don't believe in your purpose. There is no Veld. No holy empire. It was all lies written down long ago and twisted into whatever you wanted them to mean."

The hand with which Ezma had been trying to stem her mortal wound stretched shakily toward me, her wide eyes unblinking. "You," her lips mouthed, the word but a breath and yet the loudest thing I had ever heard. "You."

One of her knees buckled, dropping her leg beneath her and sending her sprawling, a gasping, bleeding, broken woman I'd wanted to watch die, only for the deep, visceral joy of it to turn to ashes. She pointed at me no longer, looked at me no longer, and yet even expiring there upon the stones, just a collection of bones and skin and organs, I felt her pronouncement like the vibrations of a scream in my flesh.

I stepped back, but my legs wouldn't hold me. I hit the stones harder than I'd expected, every part of my body seeming to recall the bruises and the cuts and the wounds, every joint and muscle a raw sear of pain like I was burning from the inside. Bile rose up my throat and the world spun. Nearby, someone spoke. Kisian. It made no sense until I recalled we'd been in a city. Important information slid away whenever I tried to grasp it. I had the feeling I needed to be somewhere, that something was just out of reach, but as more voices gathered in a babble around me, all I could do was stare up at the sky and float away upon a tide of my body's sufferings.

# EPILOGUES

 36. DISHIVA

The small table was covered in the finest tablecloth I had ever seen, its green weave filled with intricate patterns made of tiny gold stitches. Two scrolls had been spread across it, edge to edge, held down by colourful polished stones, yet beside the tiny cups seemingly made for mice, even the fancy stones seemed normal.

In the chair opposite, Secretary Aurus sat reading one of the scrolls, though he surely knew its contents by heart. Perhaps he wanted to appear diligent, or perhaps he just didn't know what to say to me anymore.

While Aurus read, or at least pretended to, I admired the view. The field in which the Chiltaen delegation had set up was upon the east side of Harg, the all but abandoned port town that had, according to Aurus, once serviced a copper industry before deposits in the surrounding mountains dried up. Enough of the town was still standing to help us make a start, and while the waters weren't deep, the wharf comfortably took the shallow sloops most traders used around the Eye Sea. The first traders had already started arriving.

The scribe standing beside the table scratched his nose. At his side, the servant Aurus had brought with him could have been hewn from stone.

Eventually, Secretary Aurus cleared his throat. "This all seems to be in order," he said, finally meeting my gaze. He had come attired in three layers of asymmetrical embroidered garments, belted in fine gems and edged in gold thread. A ring on every finger glinted in the afternoon sunlight. "Shall we sign, Your Holiness?"

"Whenever you're ready, your fanciness."

His lips twitched. "It is as well for us both that no one else here knows what you just said." He took up his quill.

"Is that all we have to do? Sign?" I said.

"You sign yours, then we swap seats, and sign each other's."

"How intimate."

"Are you ever serious?"

"As I recall you once—"

"All right, thank you. I shall remember to visit whenever I want my ego deflated. Are you going to sign, or are you going to make me look like a fool?"

"I was about to ask you the same question."

We stared at one another across the table, part challenge, part understanding, the complexity of him and of this moment an illicit thrill. "At the same time then, perhaps," he said with a twitch of a smile that made him look boyish. "If we cannot trust one another."

I took up my quill and dipped it in the ink, only to hold it poised and drying while he did the same. Then, at an infinitesimal nod from him, we each set quill to parchment. I'd practiced a signature over and over the night before, both Oshar and Jass having endless suggestions for how to best shape the letters. It turned out only half as well as I'd hoped.

Setting down his quill, Aurus rose from his chair and I followed, circling around the table to sit in the seat he had already warmed. The second signing was easier, neither of us needing the reassurance of simultaneously setting ink to page. Our quills made little clatters as we set them down.

"Is that it then?" I said as the scribe began sprinkling sand over the pages. "It's all done?"

"All done. The head scribe of the church is expected tomorrow, along with the church chancellor, who you will be able to boss around all you like. They are men set in their ways, but I don't doubt you will twist their reverence for your title into getting everything you want. If I could offer a piece of advice?"

"Of course."

"The Nine do not like things to move so quickly and may be... prickly for some time. Take care not to make too much noise and remind them too often that you exist."

I lifted my brows. "Them? Do you discount yourself from that assessment?"

"No, but nothing is ever stable in Chiltae. I may not always be a secretary of the Nine and so may not always be here to fight for your interests and argue for having Levanti allies—Levanti citizens even—rather than Levanti enemies. If this is to work out well, you must build your own strength, quietly, with the church as your rock."

However he tried to frame it, I knew his advice had little to do with his own interests or even Chiltae's and found I couldn't meet his gaze. The possibility that I might never see him again after what we had been through together sat wrong in my chest, its shape both pointed and swollen. I watched the scribe roll the scrolls. He had a green wax candle already lit, ready to seal them, but nodded first to the little cups. Aurus's servant was pouring a viscous liquid into each from a small, plain bottle. "What is that?" I asked.

"It's a very potent mix of honey and wine with some spices or other that I always forget the names of. It tastes fine, but you have to put your blood into it."

"What?"

"Your blood. You Levanti cut yourselves before you put your

weapons away; we seal important contracts the same way. Well, we did, now it's mostly alcohol with just a drop of blood for the sake of tradition."

The servant laid a small knife in front of me, hardly large enough to have slain a butterfly. "And you think we are backward and strange."

Aurus shrugged and pricked his left forefinger with the knife tip. Holding it above the closer cup, he waited until two drops fell. Unsure if the choice of hand and finger were significant, I copied, puncturing my fingertip and letting my blood drip into the cup. It didn't so much mix into the liquid as sit upon the top slowly spreading.

I made to take the cup, but Aurus grabbed it first. "You don't drink your own, Dishiva," he said. "That would be pointless." And meeting my gaze a moment over the top of the cup, he tipped it to his lips and downed the contents, my blood and all, in a single gulp. He set it down empty, and slid it like a challenge across the table. "Your turn."

"Very well."

Mixed in with the spices and the honey and the bite of alcohol, I shouldn't have been able to taste his blood, and maybe I couldn't, the taste all in my mind as I swallowed and licked sticky lips. "Tasty."

"Thank you."

I set the cup down. "Why are you doing this?"

"Doing what? My job?"

"No. The other things. Pressing to make sure this was done as fast as possible. Traveling out here to sign it rather than demanding I come to you, which I assume is more usual. Even the advice. Surely no secretary of the Nine can truly want a powerful Levanti state within their borders, yet you have made sure I have access to the reach of the church and the Villius estate funds—why?"

"Because I am a man who believes in playing both sides," he said. "Especially in such troubled times as these. I'm beginning to feel there is no way to be sure tomorrow will be the same as today, and in an uncertain future, I expect you not to forget."

"That's a good lie. I like it."

"Lie?"

I sat back in my chair, enjoying his confused frown. "Yes. But don't worry, I promise I won't tell anyone you actually have a heart and a soul. It must be quite the burden in your position."

He laughed, but all too soon crushed it with a grimace. "You have no idea. But also, I have no idea what you could possibly be talking about."

Aurus rose from his chair and bowed to me. "Your Holiness."

"Your fanciness."

No smile flickered this time.

"Goodbye, Dishiva."

———————♦———————

Jass and Amun were waiting for me back at the main house. It felt odd having a house, let alone a main house, but after a week I was starting to finally think of it as mine. I had so few belongings, yet there was a definite... *me*ness about the place that owned warmth.

"Well?" Jass was on his feet the moment I stepped through the door. "How did it go?"

I held up the scroll. "All done. No hitch at all."

"He didn't go back on any of the agreements?"

"None."

"You'll pardon me for being suspicious that he plans something."

I let him take the scroll, though he wouldn't be able to read it any better than I could. Oshar had promised to write a translation when he had time. "I certainly thought he might have been pressured into changing it," I said. "But no, it went exactly as he said it would. He has more heart than he would like anyone to suspect, but I also think he is playing both sides. Chiltae has been left weak, and while Empress Miko isn't in any position at present to take advantage of that, I don't think the time is far off when they'll have to contend with the full weight of Kisia seeking revenge. Cultivating some Levanti goodwill is not a terrible plan for the Nine."

"Oh, like we'd fight for them again," Amun snorted, taking a gulp of wine. "But let them go on believing we might if it gets us what we want, huh?" He gestured to a pile of letters on the table. "More letters came while you were away. Oshar said he would be back soon."

"And another boat is leaving on this evening's tide," Jass added. "Lashak and Diha are going to be on board, if you want to..."

He trailed off with a grimace as though he could feel my heart sinking. Of course they were going home. Had I not been caught here, thrust upon a new path, I would have gone with them. Too long had I been a warrior of the plains to let it go from my heart. I nodded. "I'll go now so I don't miss them. The letters can wait, I'm sure. Even the hieromonk of Chiltae is allowed time off."

"I'll come with you," Amun said, pushing aside his wineglass. "See if there's been any news of Rah yet."

I gripped his arm as he strode toward the door. "You know we would have heard if there had been," I said. "Stop worrying. They'll come. Rah was so badly injured there is no way they can travel at the speed many of us did."

"I know." He ran a hand along his freshly shaved scalp, perhaps enjoying the bite of the sharp regrowth as I always did. "And with groups of injured Swords still arriving, I have hope, but... I ought not to have let them travel alone, both so... weak."

We had the same conversation daily, Amun unable to let go of the guilt and responsibility. "It was what they wanted," I reminded him. "What they needed."

"I know."

"They'll come."

The look Amun gave me was full of sorrow. "How can you be sure? What if they decide to find somewhere else to get on a ship?"

"Then they do. You can't fix how they feel; you can only make peace with it."

Jass ambled over, the scroll still in his hand. "If I was Rah, I'm not sure I could face any of us again. I mean, not *us* specifically, but... Levanti."

Amun nodded, grimaced, and unable to find words to reply, made for the door.

We walked in silence down to the wharf, the bustling activity of Harg making up for all the things we couldn't say. Horses and tents and familiar faces were everywhere I looked, and though many turned away rather than deal with what I was and what I was trying to achieve, I received as many salutes as scowls as I passed. Some of the Swords staying were doing so only to see out the last of their exile, others too injured to risk the voyage, but Gideon had ignited a dream of a different Levanti future that could never be forgotten, and bright were the eyes that looked upon what we had won and found a path worth walking. We would always be Levanti, but being Levanti meant many things, not all of which were caught to the high veldt and the deltas, the groves and wintering places. To build a life here would take work, as did all that was worthwhile.

A ship had arrived from Genava that morning bearing tools and cloth, leather goods and food, and having been emptied and resupplied, it sat wallowing in the water waiting to take passengers across the sea.

We found Lashak and Diha preparing to board, their horses' reins looped tightly around their hands to keep the nervous animals from bolting. Lashak's eyes brightened at sight of me. "Di!" she cried, stuffing her reins into Diha's hand, but where she would once have hugged me, she held back. "Am I allowed to touch you? Is that not a thing now you're all...holy and stuff?"

"Probably not, but if you don't, I will call down God's wrath upon you, or whatever it is that Chiltaens curse with."

She laughed and wrapped her strong arms around me, the hug long and heartfelt, ending in tears. "I'm going to miss you," she said, wiping her eyes when she finally let go. "If the godding thing doesn't work out, you know where to find us."

"Always. In the meantime, send pottun, huh? Not just the leaves but some seeds; I don't know how well it will grow here, but I am damn well going to try."

"I'll do that, yeah."

There had been so much I wanted to say, so much I wanted to thank her for, but as I stood there upon the dock, I realised she knew it all. This might be the last time we ever saw each other. She might return to the plains to find everything had changed in our absence. Or nothing had. Such worries would have been in her mind as they were in mine, but to acknowledge them would turn this moment into something different. So instead, I returned her embrace, breathing deeply of her scent and her warmth and locking her in my memory, before I stepped back and let her go.

———————◆———————

Jass was warm and I was tired, content to lie against him in the darkness and never move again. Often at such times we chatted, learning about one another as we ought to have done along the way, the usual progress of such things denied us. Tonight, however, we just lay in silence, listening to the quieting chatter of the town and watching moonlight flicker across the ceiling.

"Is this just...life now, do you think?" he said eventually, the kind of thought he must have been mulling over for a while. "Or is everything going to change again?"

"I don't know," I said, shifting so the words wouldn't come out smushed against his shoulder. "I suppose it depends what you mean?"

"I mean..." He drew back enough to turn, his short hair scratching on the pillow. "This. Here. The town and the plans and...us."

*Us.* We had just fallen into this thing, unplanned and unconsidered, and now here we were. "Do you want it to be? If you want to go back—"

"No, I don't. I'm here, and I'm not going anywhere while there's a here to be."

"Then yes. I guess this is life now."

"Will it last though? Not us, you couldn't get rid of me if you tried, but...this...whole place, this idea. Whatever you think of Secretary Aurus, do you really think the Chiltaens will hold up their side of the bargain?"

I propped myself up on an elbow. "Who am I?"

"Dishiva e'Jaroven."

"That's who I am to you. Who am I to them?"

"The hieromonk of Chiltae."

"Exactly. I walked out of that city and survived because people believed in me, or at least in my title. If this is where the hieromonk resides, they'll have to respect that. They'll bring trade and we'll make allies, the whole of this venture protected by the veneration they have for their church. I am the hieromonk for the rest of my life, and if I live long enough, perhaps that will be enough to sow strong seeds."

"One final lifelong sacrifice, huh?"

I shook my head. "Not sacrifice. Service. To the herd. To our people. To ensure a future. It is what any Levanti would do were they in my position."

"No, it's not, but it's what you have chosen, and for that we are fortunate."

"You would have done the same."

"You think so? I'm not so sure. Amun asked me today if I'm planning to put myself forward as herd master for the town, and I just laughed."

I rested my head on his chest. "Not interested?"

"No. I am quite done with being responsible. No more complications, just hunting and fishing and...building, whatever I'm needed for and can do, and then coming home to you at the end of the day."

"That does sound nice, yes. Do that. So long as I am the one you want to come home to, that is."

"I'll let you know if I change my mind, shall I?"

"Please do."

He wrapped his arms around me, crushing me against the sleeping mat. "I was kidding! I already said I'm not going anywhere. You're stuck with me."

"Oh no," I said between the kisses he planted upon my lips. "What a shame."

# 37. CASSANDRA

We didn't say goodbye. Miko had asked after me, so I'd heard, and that would have to be enough. I'd wanted to hold her. To tell her I was proud of her. To see her take her place upon the throne as her mother had promised her father she would, but to do so would have torn open more wounds than it healed, and I was a coward.

There had been no reason to linger. In all my years, I had developed no connection to anywhere or anyone I would be sorry not to see again. At least none who still lived. It was Empress Hana and Captain Aeneas I thought of as we took horses and rode west, they the only two people for whom I would have given my own life to have brought back theirs.

And Yakono.

He rode at my side, a quiet companion rather than one who needed to fill every silence, though we often fell to talking over old contracts or descriptions of his home. I'd never thought about what lay beyond the Kuro Mountains, but now I was going to see it with my own eyes. Unus followed, somewhere behind us. He'd wanted more than anything to leave Kisia and Chiltae and build a new life, but he'd chosen to travel separately. He needed the silence, he'd said. The peace. To finally be alone.

Yakono turned, the bitter wind fluttering his hood. "It'll be dark soon. Shall we continue in the hope of finding an inn or give up and camp, Kaysa?"

"How do you always know when it's me and always point it out?" she said.

He shrugged. "I'm getting used to the difference in facial expressions. And . . . based on all our recent conversations, I say your name to make sure you feel as seen."

Neither of us had an answer to that. He had a talent for saying such things, and I wasn't sure I would ever be comfortable as the object of his attention when he did. Or when he poured all his heart into his gaze and watched me, waiting, a little bit wary, a little unsure, a man who has been stung before but keeps returning all the same.

"Thank you," I managed, swallowing the hurt with which I so often lashed out. I wasn't very good at being earnest, but I was trying. Sometimes. "Let's ride on a bit farther. I really want to sleep in a bed tonight."

"That I can agree with. Cassandra."

I didn't ask him again how he knew.

———————◆———————

Luck was on our side for once. An inn came into sight before the last of the day's light leached from the winter sky. It had not yet snowed more than a dusting, but the sleet-grey sky had been promising it all day. Perhaps we would wake up to find ourselves snowed in. At least there would be warm beds. Or bed, as it turned out.

The innkeeper greeted us with a grimace. "What with the weather turning poorly, we have only the one room left, I'm afraid."

"That's all right," Yakono said. "We can share."

"There's, uh, only one bed, but I can ask the missus to roll out one of them mats the—"

"No need to go to the trouble. We can share."

He said it calmly, showing not the smallest degree of embarrassment or ill-ease, yet there was a warmth in his tone perhaps only I caught. And for all my extra years, my cheeks reddened, and I found the ceiling full of very interesting knots of wood.

The innkeeper bowed and smiled and seemed as devoid of speech as I often felt in Yakono's presence, leading us up the stairs with the occasional glance back to be sure we followed. The inn was small but warm and cosy and full of the scents of cooking, the exact opposite to the chill darkness gathering outside the windows. There was nothing grand about the room, just a single bed and a small table, its threadbare chair having seen better days.

Having shown us in, the innkeeper stood in the doorway wringing his hands. "It's perfect, thank you," Yakono said, all sincerity. "How much for the night? And a hot meal and the stabling of our horses?"

Yakono didn't even haggle, just paid the man the stated sum and smiled at him until he went away.

Warm water came and we washed. Food arrived and we ate, drawing the table close to the bed so we could eat together, one of us perched on the mattress, the other on the rickety chair, both warm and comfortable and full of good food.

I'd never felt nervous getting into bed with a man, but it turns out there's a first time for everything. In the absence of sex, I wasn't even sure what one was supposed to do when sharing a bed with someone, but all the ideas that crossed my mind were intimate and vulnerable and terrifying. Yet when Yakono stripped to his waist and slid into the bed beside me, setting his chest to my back and wrapping me in his arms, it was good. He was strong and gentle and nuzzled into the back of my neck, and it would have been really nice had the snow fallen so deep we were trapped there for days.

"Is there going to be a dearth of beds when we reach your home too?" I said.

"Not usually, but there could be." His breath was warm against the back of my neck. "If you would like that."

"I think," I said, tightening my hold on the arm curled around me, "that would be...nice. Yes."

There was no guarantee of what the future held, no guarantee there even was one, yet for the first time there was a sense of open space, of possibility, and I curled up against Yakono's warmth and just existed. Outside the wind blew and the snow fell, and no one needed me. No one even wanted me dead. Out here I didn't have to be Cassandra Marius anymore; I could be whoever I wanted to be, and there would be Yakono with his kind eyes and his whole heart.

*I really like him, Cass,* Kaysa said as we both drifted off. *I really like...this. This everything.*

*Yes, I like him too, but...Kaysa?*

*Yes, Cassandra?*

*I really like you too.*

And for the first time, I had deprived her of all power of speech.

# 38. MIKO

Manshin had once said that Emperor Kin kept the throne with the power of a good story. A story that *felt* right, however little truth it might contain. People rebel at loose threads even though it's the neat, scripted tales of which they should be wary, the ones that fit together with nary a crack between their pieces, each cog turning toward the future. The *right* future. Manshin's death at the hands of his brutally used and underappreciated daughter was just one more cog turning toward a new future. And so grew the story.

In the wake of the chaos within Shimai so many decisions needed to be made, proclamations declared and messages sent, orders given and meetings attended, that Sichi and I barely had time to snatch moments to breathe and tell each other we could do this. But we could do this, we had to, because to fail would be to let Kisia fall back into its old, stale patterns, suffocating change. There was a future where god emperors were no longer needed. Where wars with Chiltae were not an annual occurrence. Where the people of the mountain tribes would truly call Kisia home, but it would not come if we did not fight for it. Every day. With every breath.

———————✦———————

A few days after the retaking of Shimai, we met the last few Levanti outside their nearby camp. It was no formal thing with banners and tents and courtiers, rather the meeting of old friends upon the side of the road.

Many had already left, heading north at full speed. Others had lingered a night or two, while those who had been injured remained longer. Now they were all leaving and had come to say a final farewell to Nuru and Tor.

A dozen Levanti awaited us in a nondescript field that blustery afternoon, every face familiar, though I didn't know all their names. Nuru and Tor leapt from their saddles the moment they reined in, crushing each of those who had come to say goodbye in fierce hugs, tears flowing freely. It wasn't until I'd dismounted, gaze flitting around the gathered warriors, that I saw Rah. He sat propped against a convenient tree, his head leaning back, the stubble of his short hair the same colour as the bark and not all that much darker than the bruises covering his face.

I stepped forward, only to halt, gaze skittering to Gideon standing guard nearby. "What happened?"

"He fought for us," he said, lifting his chin. "As he always does. Even when it is a bad idea and we aren't worth it."

"Gideon," Sichi said, and was gathered into the tall man's embrace, the pair holding to each other with their entire souls for a moment I envied, so deep was their understanding and acceptance.

I'd wanted such a parting with Rah, but he didn't even open his eyes, let alone get to his feet. He breathed—that the only comfort I could take. As I drew near, more and more wounds caught my eye, so many he might have been held together by bandages and hope.

"Rah," I said softly, kneeling beside him on the damp grass while behind me the others chattered on in Levanti. "Rah?"

His eyelids flickered, and for a moment he was there, peering through swollen sockets. A smile twitched his lips. "Miko," he said, bringing tears to my eyes.

As gently as I could, I ran my hand across his scalp, just wanting to touch him, to be connected this one last time. If it hurt, he didn't show it.

"You have as much to thank him for as we do," Gideon said behind me. "Although," he added with a shrug, "he didn't do any of it for you."

"I know." I turned to face him, this fearless warrior who had divided my empire. Had stolen my throne. To whom Rah had always been devoted. "He did it for you."

Gideon e'Torin's brows rose, brows that lacked the red tinge of his hair. "I doubt that," he said. "He loves me and I love him, but that does not make me ignorant of what he's always been."

"And what is that?"

"Very selfish."

I stared at Rah, thinking of the man who had helped me reach Syan in the hope of safety, who had climbed into a rickety boat with me so I wouldn't be alone, who had walked the breadth of Kisia at my side without tiring or complaint, and I shook my head. "How can you say so? He sacrifices so much. You said yourself he is injured because he fought for his people even when they didn't deserve it."

"He did." Gideon tilted his head, eyeing me with something all too like amusement. "That doesn't mean he did it for a selfless reason."

"I thought you said you loved him."

"I do. Didn't you?"

The amusement in his penetrating gaze made my cheeks redden, and I tried to remember the broken Gideon I had met at Kuroshima, his head in Sichi's lap as she tried to keep him calm. I'd pitied him then, this great enemy of mine, and I couldn't but wish I could still pity him now instead of feeling small and foolish beneath his gaze. "Too well to ever say such a mean thing of him," I said, hoping to wipe away his smile.

Instead, it deepened. "True is the love that sees fault and does not waver."

His gaze slid to Rah as he spoke, warmth in his eyes. Rah looked back, and though he could not have understood our conversation, such understanding hung between them that my heart constricted. I'd never stood between two people who made the air boil.

"I have a message for you from Dom Dishiva e'Jaroven," Gideon said, finally turning back my way. "She is Chiltae's new hieromonk and will be remaining to build a settlement on the coast. She says she looks forward to seeing you again soon and is sure you will deal well together."

I couldn't tell if the absent hieromonk had meant the words as a threat or if the way Gideon spoke them just sounded like one, everything about him spiky and dangerous. Rah blinked slowly up at us. I had wanted to say goodbye, to see him one last time, but now I wanted nothing more than to retreat to the safety of my own world, so I bent and pressed my lips to his forehead in the least injured spot I could find. "Goodbye, Rah," I said. "Be well."

He looked up, his smile vague and hazy, only one of his eyes open. "Goodbye, Miko. I'm sorry. *Eshenha surveid.*"

We parted soon after, Tor and Nuru having bade their last farewells. Rah was helped into his saddle, pale and gritting his teeth, while the others kept their distance.

The four of us were silent as we rode away, but as we reached the hill where our guards waited, I had the feeling I was being watched and looked back, hoping to share one last fond smile with Rah. But it was Gideon who had turned. Riding close by Rah, he focussed all his attention upon me for a moment. He did not glare, did not speak, did nothing but watch us depart, yet I couldn't suppress the shiver that trickled through me. Of course he was not only the broken Gideon I had met at Kuroshima, he was also the man who had slaughtered a whole army of Chiltaens calling him their ally, who had massacred thousands of Kisians, burned our cities and sought to build an empire upon the bones of mine. Ruthless. Single-minded. Opportunistic.

I forced myself to turn away, to look ahead and listen to Sichi's conversation and think about the future, yet my thoughts kept being dragged back to that stare and the amused smile with which he had torn me apart. Rah was lucky to have the devotion of such a man, but perhaps the plains were not. To what lengths would such a man not go for the one he loved?

———————◆———————

Mei'lian had burned. Anything that had survived had been taken apart for supplies and building materials, like the remains of a corpse picked over by hungry animals. Yet somehow between all the ruins and the debris, the scorched stones and the empty shells, were patches of surviving beauty that had refused to die.

I walked alone through the remains of the palace gardens, the buildings themselves little more than jagged stone arches and fallen beams, like a giant hand had crushed them all. Yet the pond where Tanaka and Edo and I had pretended to be pirates was still there, as was my favourite tree, and out in the imperial graveyard lay the father I'd never been allowed to mourn.

Sichi was waiting, General Ryoji too, not as the head of our imperial guard today but as himself. It had taken many days for Cassandra's information to bear fruit, but at last Mama's body had been found and brought home. Home was gone, if one thought of home as the buildings and the city, but there is always another kind of home with the one you love.

I threaded my hand into Sichi's as we stood beside the freshly dug grave. Space had been left next to Katashi Otako, and I had to wonder now if she had always meant to take it, if in death they could have the eternity they never got in life. I'd hoped to be able to find Tanaka too, but Koi was still under Chiltaen control, so he was going to have to wait for me a little longer.

With a few grunts of effort, a pair of servants approached

through the ruins of the stable yard carrying the burial box. I looked down at the gravestone. Katashi Otako. How that name had hung over me like a blade all my life, daring me to be proud of it. To own it. Sichi squeezed my hand, giving comfort, while beside me Ryoji shifted his feet, his jaw set.

That afternoon, Empress Hana Ts'ai, the last child of Emperor Lan Otako, was laid to rest beside the man she had always loved. The priest spoke his prayers. The seeds of kanashimi blossoms were sown. And in the wake of the quietest of formal proceedings, the three of us were left by the graveside with our grief.

"She was coming back to me, you know," I said. "Cassandra told me. She was on her way back."

Tears tracked down my cheeks. If only she could have made it. If only we could have had a few minutes to look at one another, to sit and nurse our tea bowls and just look. For me to see the complicated, determined woman who had always been there, and for her to see what I had become and be proud. But that moment had been stolen from us along with so much else.

"She's home now," Sichi said, once more squeezing my hand. "And we'll find Tanaka. I know we will. And we'll bring him home too."

"I just wish I could have told her—could have told her that I understand now," I said. "That I am sorry I didn't listen. Sorry I always fought so hard and resented everything she gave Tanaka. I wish ... I wish I could have told her that I loved her."

"She would have liked that," Ryoji said, his voice thick. "More than anything. But she knew, Miko. She knew."

I had no more words, only tears, and the three of us stood there in silence for a long time, grieving what felt as much like the end of an era as the end of a life, surrounded by ruins and covered in scars. But if we wanted to build something new, something strong, something whole, we couldn't do it on top of our pain. We had to build it atop our dreams.

39. RAH

I ran my finger along the line of Tempachi words, reading slowly. The paper had a fragile quality, perhaps because it had belonged to Ezma, and I could think only of her lifeless, dry skin. I had to keep telling myself she was dead, reminding myself I would not turn around to find her watching me, so close did she haunt my every waking thought. Everywhere I went I could feel her gaze.

*One*, she had written, making her own notes upon the page. *Veld is broken by their leader.* Gideon's name had been crossed out, leaving the rest to say, *Dishiva was exiled by her herd master.*

I had read through the original passage twice, hoping to find something she had missed, some specification of what sort of leader had been meant, but there was nothing.

*Two*, the notes went on. *Veld is broken in a throne room. Some reference to Dishiva's part in the coup?*

Had she ever asked Dishiva about that day? Only I had broken, staring up at Gideon on the throne and seeing a stranger condemning me while he walked a path I couldn't follow.

*Three. Broken in a cave.* I didn't like to dwell on our time trapped beneath the ground. Fear crowded close these days.

*Four. Stabbed in the back by an empress, otherwise denoted as one who is both leader and god.*

I'd read the original account of the fourth death half a dozen times, trying to find ways I could wriggle free of it. Miko hadn't betrayed me, not in the way we tended to think of betrayal. She'd been caught to a decision she'd made and couldn't change, having promised Ezma Gideon's life, but the account in the book wasn't clear on the idea of it being an empress. Leader and god meant a lot of things. It could have been Leo, whose use and betrayal of my initial friendship still hurt to recall, or even Ezma herself when she'd left me to die.

*Five—*

The book was yanked from my hands, its tangle of scrawled words replaced with Gideon's scowl. "Rah." He tucked the book behind his back. "You're not going to find anything new in there you haven't already read. And you're not going to heal if you don't eat."

He dropped the book next to his saddlebag on the opposite side of the fire and sat down, taking up one of the scratched ceramic plates he'd picked up somewhere. A lot of the last few weeks had vanished in exhaustion or been replaced with Tempachi words as I scoured the book again and again. I needed to let it go, but every time I closed my eyes, Ezma was there pointing at me, her slackening face sliding into horror. *You.*

Gideon sat chewing and watching me, his brows caught low. He had changed again since Shimai. Not that he was better, or fixed, or had returned to his old self. Such things didn't happen. That wasn't how trauma worked, however much we wished it did. Perhaps it hadn't been Leo he'd needed to face, but his people and the pain of his failure. Now he walked with a little more purpose. He was a man with a future once more.

He pointed at the plate in front of me. "Eat."

I laughed softly and took up the plate. Laughing any harder still hurt my ribs. "I feel like you're enjoying getting me back for all the time I spent telling you what to do when you weren't well."

He didn't answer, just went on eating and watching.

We'd carried a lot of silence with us upon this journey north, a slow trek through the plains of memory as we passed places we'd fought, places we'd camped, places we'd suffered, and places we'd lost people we could never reclaim. Going home was harder than I'd expected.

I slid a small clump of rice between my teeth and chewed slowly, resenting how much even so simple a task still hurt. Day by day it got a little better, bruises turning from angry black wounds that covered my flesh to lingering patches of discolouration. Diha had stitched me up. Unless the memory of her clicking her tongue over me as she worked had slipped from my time in the deserter camp, filling a space in my head that had needed a face. I'd been far too injured to get up and move, she'd said, to chase Ezma down, to fight, yet I had torn myself to pieces to end her and almost ended myself. Her look had been wary, and she hadn't lingered.

Though we travelled farther north each day, the weather was getting colder. I hated it, but we were moving as fast as we could when sitting in the saddle for even an hour was a struggle. Keeping a good fire going was hard too, wood difficult to come by when Gideon was the only one able to hunt and gather and tend the horses. All I was good for at the end of a ride was to tumble out of the saddle and lie upon the ground feeling sorry for myself. And read Ezma's book.

Once we'd finished eating and the fire had begun to die, Gideon unrolled our mats and dumped out our blankets. We picked them up whenever we found them and now had two saddlebags full, tightly rolled. Still, the early hours of the morning would creep their bitter fingers into my bones.

"Here." Gideon dropped the last blanket on the pile beside me. "Make yourself a nest. I'm going to check the horses."

The blankets were warm, some were even soft, but as I watched

Gideon stride away across our meagre campsite to where Jinso and Orha were but faint outlines in the night, it was to Ezma's book my thoughts strayed. He'd left it beside his saddlebag. Hardly any distance at all, and worth the brief flare of pain for a few minutes of checking her notes before he returned.

Whenever I didn't move for a time, I forgot how bad moving could feel, and having crawled to the other side of the fire, I couldn't crawl back. So, I sat on the hard ground and opened the book where I had left off.

*Four. Stabbed in the back by an empress.* I worried about that one more than I ought, coming back to it again and again, each memory of Miko owning many different emotions.

*Five,* the next line said. *Veld is broken by betrayal, abandoned when they need their followers most.* That one made me laugh, so often had it happened to me.

*Six. Veld is broken by himself, given in sacrifice.* The one my gaze always stuck upon, where I found I could read no further, only sit and wonder if Ezma had realised in those dying moments that she had made this one all too true. I was still wearing the pain of it, and even when my bruises faded and my wounds healed, the memory would live on, an ever-present scar upon my mind like the one Gideon carried with him.

Thought of Gideon seemed to manifest him before me, but he didn't snatch the book out of my hands this time, just looked down from his great height, weary and sad. "Do you need help getting back to the blankets?"

I did but shook my head, preferring to wince and grit my teeth and suffer the short crawl than admit it had been a bad idea. Or that I couldn't stop thinking about the book. *Broken by himself, given in sacrifice.* Even as I reached my mat and rolled onto it, a shiver spread through my skin that had nothing to do with the chill night air.

Gideon threw a last chunk of wood on the fire and spread out our blankets, making a warm cocoon. I was thankful for the blankets, but it was his warmth pressed against my back every night that made it possible to sleep, his arm draped around me.

Back in Shimai, Gideon had found me as the last of the sunlight stretched orange fingers across the sky. His hand had slid into mine as he dropped his forehead to my chest, whispering a prayer of thanks. I knew that gratitude from when I'd kept his blade from slicing open his throat. We were both broken, I thought as I slid into sleep, but at least we had each other.

———————◆———————

It took another ten days to reach the coast at our slow pace. Day by day I'd been able to ride longer and help more, though it would be weeks before I would regain anything like my old strength or agility. For now, I was content to be able to walk without hissing and spitting pain like an overfilled kettle.

We'd been able to smell the salt spray and hear the call of seabirds since early morning, but it was nearing evening before we caught the first glimpse of blue upon the horizon. Torin had no particular connection to the sea, and I'd had enough of it in that little boat off the coast of Syan to last a lifetime, yet the sight brought a lump to my throat I couldn't immediately swallow.

Gideon halted Orha upon the hilltop and stared down at it, the wind catching the ever-lengthening strands of his dark hair. "Are you sure you want to do this?" he said, not turning.

I cleared my throat, hoping emotion wouldn't sound in my voice. "Yes. Aren't you?"

He pierced me with one of his earnest, intent stares. My stomach flipped, as it so often did when his brows notched just so. "I'm not sure," he said. "I made peace with never seeing the plains again a long time ago."

"You've come a long way north for someone unsure if they want to cross the sea."

"It's one thing to ride a direction, another to reach a destination. And besides, I kept thinking this couldn't be real, that because I couldn't imagine myself going home the coast would always be another day away. And another. And another."

The thought that we could have come this far only to say good-bye lodged an even larger lump in my throat. "Gideon, I..."

"You cannot stay here," he interrupted. "Even if it is where I am. I know. Else perhaps you would have learned Kisian and stayed with your empress. *Ver brii a senaii.*"

"What does that mean?"

He smiled, a soft smile made all the softer by the evening light and his windswept hair. "It means 'I will go where you go.' Or more accurately it ought to translate as 'You are my home,' but that sounded too sappy."

"Nice though."

I wished it was a thought I could return, but no matter how much I wanted to keep him now I'd found him, the plains were calling me, like a string had been knotted around my heart to pull me back across the Eye Sea. Had Gideon wished to stay, I would have been caught between two loves and sure only of pain.

"It is nice," he agreed. "But we can't have your ego getting too big."

"That seems unlikely. If I wasn't already a shell stuffed with doubts, I always have you to tell me when I'm shit at something."

He lifted his brows, his smile managing to be both suggestive and yet innocently shocked at the same time, and I wondered if his thoughts went to that abandoned shop in Shimai as mine did. For all we'd said we needed to talk, for all it had felt like the bumpy beginnings of a new path, it was one we'd not yet walked, neither of us quite ready for more than knowing the other was there, every injury still too raw to allow for the spilling of our hearts and souls and minds even to each other.

"Well," he sighed, looking back at the sea. "Shall we keep going? Or camp a night here and make the rest of the journey in the morning?"

I'd been keen to reach what felt like the end of the road, to touch the salty waters of the Eye Sea, but I shook my head. "No, let's... let's camp here tonight. One day isn't going to change anything."

That night I didn't dig Ezma's book out of the saddlebag. Gideon and I made a meagre fire and sat talking, not of anything specific, just of whatever came to mind, the conversation flowing like the wind and the waves with an ease we hadn't been able to find for a long time. He was my old friend again in that moment, but now I could see the glint in his eyes as the night wore on, and when we lay down in our nest of blankets we were warmed as much by passion as the tight weaves of wool laid over us.

"*Verii a sena yii,*" I said as we lay twisted up together beneath the moon, not caring that my hurts all ached anew.

Gideon laughed. "*Ver brii a senaii.* But no. Never say something to me because it's what you think you should say or what you think I want to hear. Promise, huh? I've had enough lies and pretence for a lifetime. As long as you love me, your love doesn't have to come in the same form as mine."

"All right, then how do I say 'I will always fight for you' in Kisian?"

"*Esh torii kiis ur ver,*" he said, propping himself up on an elbow and kissing my neck. My cheek. The scars on my chin. "*Qi'ash ur ver. Qi'wor ur ver. Scorsh a senaii ur ver.*"

"That was too many words, even I know that."

"I said I will always fight for you. Die for you. Kill for you. Burn the world for you."

A shiver of mixed delight and fear trickled through my skin, and

I found myself pressing up against him, desire flaring anew. "Why are all your words so much better than mine?"

"Because you, my sun, my moon, my earth, my soul, are shit at this."

———————◆———————

The sun had not yet burned off the morning chill when we rode into Harg, Jinso and Orha seeming to sense our hesitation and slowing to an amble as tents and pens rose around us. This was the land Dishiva had fought for, and I'd known there would be Levanti present, some staying, others travelling home, yet I'd not prepared myself for so many. Or for so many stares. Conversations broke off. Heads turned. Whispers spread, rushing like a wave ahead of us.

"Oh good," Gideon said. "We've been completely forgotten."

"We could make this a game and bet on which of us they're staring at the most."

He grunted a laugh. "You're the whisperer killer."

"Nothing to you, Your Imperial Majesty."

Whatever the gathered Levanti whispered, their stares followed us into the town proper, some Swords even choosing to walk in our wake, wary like they thought we might suddenly draw our weapons and lay waste to them all. Gideon let out a heavy sigh.

Harg was more port than town, sitting at the base of high hills like its houses were tumbling into the sea. Up there, the fields were verdant and horses were already grazing, little gatherings of tents popping up like distant mushrooms across the veldt. I'd been sceptical of Dishiva's plans, but wherever Levanti hadn't stopped to stare at us, they were busily occupied, some fishing or building or cooking by one of the many fires. There was even a hoya game taking place at the edge of the water, barefoot Swords diving for the sack, only to land upon dark sands.

"Rah, you dog!" came a shout, and Amun hurried down the

steps of a nearby house. "There you are! How long must you keep a man waiting!"

"As long as he can," Gideon murmured under his breath.

There was no time to retort before Amun wound through the gathered onlookers, his grin likely to split his head in two, so wide did it spread. He threw open his arms, and dismounting, I fell into them to be crushed so tightly I was sure I had more broken ribs by the time he let go. "You took so long I thought for sure you'd been eaten by wild rabbits."

"Oh no, I am not so poorly I couldn't have eaten the rabbits first. Although to be fair, Gideon did all the hunting and I did all the complaining."

Having drawn attention to Gideon, Amun looked up and saluted stiffly. "Gideon."

"Amun."

A few awkward seconds hung, before Amun turned to all those watching and waved his hands. "What are you all staring at? No entertainment here, go on."

With grumbles and lingering glances, the group dispersed, taking their whispers away to spread through the settlement. Soon, not a soul would be unaware the whisperer killer and the emperor had arrived.

"I see we are famous," I said, looking at a nearby group of Swords rather than at Amun. "The bad kind of famous." When I looked back, a grimace twisted his expression. It tightened into a wince when I added, "Do they have a name for me yet?"

"You don't want to know," he said. "It's ridiculous and makes no sense, and I'm sure they'll stop using it as soon as you're..."

"Out of sight?" I finished for him, but it was exhaustion rather than anger I felt. How poorly things might have turned out for them all had I made a different choice, but it was so much easier to pretend they'd not laid hands upon me or made their own poor choices. Easier to brand me a pariah, burying their gratitude with their guilt. I squeezed his arm. "Go on, out with it. Better to know."

His grimace had become a permanent feature of his face, and he glanced up at Gideon as though begging help. No help was forthcoming.

Amun sighed. "It's... They're calling you Godslayer."

"What?"

*Brave before God, this Godslayer kneels, falls, rises, lives to walk the path of the one chosen to build their home anew.*

"I don't know who started it, but I think it's because between the talk of that... holy Veld Leo was trying to become and Dishiva's new position, everything that happened here felt... important? Anyway, ignore them. I am sure they will soon forget it and move on."

"Mmm, Godslayer," Gideon said like he was savouring a taste. "I like it. It's very dramatic. Though it makes you sound like you're taller than me, and you're not."

I heard the words, heard Amun's reluctant snort, and yet it was Ezma who stood before me once again, her finger outstretched in that final, horrified realisation. *You.*

*This Godslayer kneels, falls, rises, lives to walk the path of the one chosen to build their home anew.*

"Rah?" Amun tilted his head into my line of sight. "Are you all right? Hey, Lashak and Diha have already gone home, but I'm sure Dishiva will be pleased to see you. Do you want—"

"No."

I'd thought to stay, to linger and relax into the memory of what having a herd had been like, but the words of the damn book rang on in my head, and I stepped back. "No. If there's a ship leaving, we should go."

"There are always ships. Word seems to have gotten around that the hieromonk is here with her fat Chiltaen purse and she's buying a lot of supplies, so they just keep coming. Most are happy to make a little extra coin carrying Levanti back across the sea."

"We don't have any coin."

Gideon leaned forward, the saddle creaking under his shifting weight. "Godslayers don't get paid well."

*Godslayer.* The word was like a hammer strike.

"Dishiva's secretary man is paying for that too. She thinks he wants to make sure as many Levanti leave as possible so the rest of the Nine don't get too scared."

"We're sorry for what we did to you, now go away?"

"Fuck no, they're never going to apologise, but they'll sure get rid of us as fast as they can in case we stay angry."

I said nothing. Jinso tossed his head, breaking the awkward silence. "Are you sure you won't stay even a night?" Amun said.

For all that he had shooed the gathered Swords away, all too many still stood watching from a distance, my name and crimes upon their lips. Fighting for my people so they could have a home to return to had made me even more of an outsider, and I would have to make peace with that. Later. For now, I just wanted to get away as fast as I could. Away from the name they had given me.

I set my hand upon Amun's shoulder. "No, but thank you. That you wished me to will have to be enough. I can't…"

I couldn't find the words to explain without cutting myself open, but he nodded, seeming to understand. "I'll see you back home then, I guess," he said. "Take care." Amun looked up. "You too, Gideon. Keep this idiot out of trouble, at least until I'm back, eh?"

"A heavy and difficult responsibility, but I'll try."

Amun pressed out a wry smile, thumped my shoulder, and stepped back, giving me space to climb back into the saddle. Not an easy task when every limb still felt like it was being held together with string, but I did my best with so many people watching. There were even Chiltaen fishermen sitting on the docks, and some of the sailors hanging around waiting for the tide wore Tempachi attire—the first time I'd seen their like since leaving home a lifetime ago.

A nod to Amun and I set Jinso walking, glad he could carry me where my own legs would have failed. "Are you all right?" Gideon said, keeping pace alongside.

"Fine, let's just find a ship that'll take us and get out of here."

There were three shallow-hulled ships docked at the wharf, and a fourth anchored out in the deeper waters ferrying goods in by rowboat. Levanti were everywhere, horses and supplies and packs and bales of straw making a tangle of activity and a wealth of familiar smells to counteract the bite of the sea. A pair of Swords were arguing with a Tempachi merchant, while Oshar was trying to translate between a harried Chiltaen man and a trio of Levanti, their horses heavy with packs. The third ship looked to have just docked, and dark-skinned sailors were carrying crates down the broad gangplank. "Afternoon," Gideon said, trying Levanti first as he approached their captain.

The man looked us up and down and eyed our horses before answering in Chiltaen. His brows rose when Gideon replied in kind, and I was glad to leave the discussion to him and look around, drinking my fill of this land and the people who chose to remain. Soon the high pastures would fill with horses, and Levanti could farm and hunt and use the trees to build more houses, adding to those already lining the shore. Before one such house a figure stood watching, dressed all in white. Dishiva. It was cowardly to leave without saying goodbye, but today I was a coward and if anyone would understand, it was her. I lifted my hand in salute and she lifted hers in return, a shared acknowledgement that bridged the gulf that now lay between us. We'd started along the same path, but it had diverged long ago.

With our horses to tend and supplies to manage, it was late by the time we were settled in the ship's hold with the handful of other

Levanti making the journey. They kept their distance, a reminder that even when we were short on space, they would rather not get too close to the Godslayer. At least the merchants were used to trading in horses, so each of our mounts had their own narrow berth to help keep them upright in rough seas.

Gideon sat quietly in the straw, leaning against the side of the ship as close to Orha's feet as he dared. His way of dealing with the whispering Levanti was to stare at them until they looked away, though whether he was doing it for himself or for me I wasn't sure.

"Come, sit," he said, holding wide an arm. In the space beside him I could be nothing more than what I was, but I didn't take it.

"I need some air," I said, and shouldered my saddlebag. In the lantern-lit gloom he eyed it rather than me. He knew but said nothing, just watched me leave with his usual intent stare.

The sun was setting as I climbed the slick steps onto the deck where the crew hurried about, glaring at my intrusion. The coast of Chiltae was not yet distant, and I could still see the small figures of my people moving about the town, the sight oddly melancholy.

I leaned against the railing. The sailors made a sort of music as they moved around me with their footsteps and chatter, their orders called to the beat of a heavy drum at the prow. None of them paid me any heed now that I was out of their way, leaving the sea breeze my only companion as I drew out Ezma's book and opened it to the familiar pages.

*One. Veld is broken by their leader.*
*Two. Veld is broken in a throne room.*
*Three. Broken in a cave.*
*Four. Stabbed in the back by an empress, otherwise denoted as one who is both leader and god.*
*Five. Veld is broken by betrayal.*
*Six. Veld is broken by himself, given in sacrifice.*

*And then to ascend to godhood and the position of Veld Reborn as foretold, they must slay a false high priest and be forevermore a Godslayer.*

I closed my eyes, yet the words were still there, imprinted inside my eyelids. They were just words, just words someone had written long ago in the holy book of a religion I didn't follow, of a god I didn't believe in. Leo had tried to make it true. Ezma had tried to make it true. That I had trodden every one of the steps was nothing more than the deliberate twisting of events to fit the foretelling, or at best a coincidence. Such things happened all the time.

I closed the book with a snap. Harg had melded into its surroundings now, no individuals discernible amid its shadowy existence here at the edge of our world, stretching our homeland and our ways a new direction. Below me the dark waves churned like hungry animals. I could drop the book. I could let it go, could watch it hit the water and sink to be eaten by whatever creatures lived in the deeps. It might live on a time in my thoughts, but time makes shadows where clear memories once stood, and one day I might be free even of that. It would be so easy.

I shoved the book back into my saddlebag. Not today; perhaps tomorrow I would be ready to let it go. Carrying it with me like the weight it was, I went back down into the hold, stinking of sweat and salt and horse and shit, and sank onto the straw beside Gideon. The weight of his arm fell across my shoulders and he asked no questions, just held me against him. His Imperial Majesty and the Godslayer were finally going home.

# ACKNOWLEDGEMENTS

What a journey this whole series has been since I started it back in 2017 as a self-publisher. Now in 2022, I'm unsure how I feel about it coming to an end. There is a lot of relief that it's finished after so much work and so many long hours, torn pages, frustration, rewrites, rewrites, edits, and rewrites, but having lived with Rah and Miko, Cassandra and Dishiva for all these years, it's emotional to step away. I can only hope that they travel well from the moment in which I left them all in charge of their own destinies, at least for now. Thank you so much for travelling upon this journey with all of us.

There are, of course, so many people to thank after working on this for many years, so please bear with me as I spill gratitude from my heart. I'm going to try to do this semi-chronologically to look vaguely like I'm organised.

Amanda! The first person to ever read *We Ride the Storm* and to throw edits at it. You've always believed in me and my work and always been there to pick me up whenever I fell into the Pit of Despair. Thank you!

Chris! My love, my rock, my best friend, it is impossible to overstate how much harder this would be without you. I mean... I'd have to choreograph my own fight scenes, for one—ew.

Nivia! I shall forever be grateful not only that you emailed me out of the blue and changed my life, but also that you have been the greatest help in making sure these books were the best they could be, pulling no punches and making me do better to get my story and my voice across. Also for being patient and understanding as I went through the onset of chronic illnesses that set dates back repeatedly. Thank you!

Julie! My wonderful agent who is always ready to go into battle for me because dear gods that's hard to do for oneself! You are a bright and illuminating ray of light in the murky and opaque publishing world, always ready with an answer or a plan and a kind word. Thank you!

Belle and Tam! The sheer volume of whinging you both put up with from me is staggering. I cannot count how many times I've complained about writing YET ANOTHER action scene or asked you both to finish writing the book for me, even if it meant Belle would kill Leo off at the earliest opportunity. Thank you for hangouts, chats, listening to dramatic flops and woes and health whinges; you are both AMAZING. Thank you!

The entire Orbit team! Always so many people to thank because it takes a village (or an army!) to put out a book like this, and Orbit have been wonderful through the whole of this series, and I couldn't have asked for a better experience upon entering the traditional publishing waters. Also special thanks to Ellen Wright and Angela Man, Publicists Extraordinaire, for all their hard work.

Nico Delort! Charis Loke! Lisa Marie Pompilio! The artists who turn my bare words into beautiful books, I couldn't have asked for a more stunning product to sit proudly upon my shelves. You all brought the world and the characters to life in the way I could not.

Sam! Every creative person in a difficult industry needs a best bestie who they can both celebrate even the smallest of wins with and be grumpily petty with, and I couldn't have asked for a better one. Thanks so much for always being there and always checking in to be sure I'm all right.

Sara! Always there for emotional support or weird conversations about the sexual status of sacrificial goats—I couldn't do this without you!

Hui, Jared, Kop, and Adam! My SPFBO judging team at The Fantasy Inn, who have been a joyful lifeline this last year while I worked through edits. It's been a while since I had so much fun while reading, so thank you!

The Bunker. All that needs to be said.

There are always so many people who help in small ways even if they don't realise it, and I'm very sure that, here at the end of the series, I've forgotten some special ones. Unfortunately, I've reached the point past which I'm not allowed to edit this beast anymore, so in case you're one of these people, I'll just shout "I'M SORRY" and "THANK YOU" into the void. Thank you all for sharing this journey with me. I'm very much looking forward to the next adventure.

# extras

orbit

# meet the author

*Leah Ladson*

DEVIN MADSON is an Aurealis Award–winning fantasy author from Australia. After some sucky teenage years, she gave up reality and is now a dual-wielding rogue who works through every tiny side-quest and always ends up too over-powered for the final boss. Anything but Zen, Devin subsists on tea and chocolate and so much fried zucchini she ought to have turned into one by now. Her fantasy novels come in all shades of grey and are populated with characters of questionable morals and a liking for witty banter.

Find out more about Devin Madson and other Orbit authors by registering for the free monthly newsletter at orbitbooks.net.

# if you enjoyed
## WE DREAM OF GODS
### look out for

# THE BLADED FAITH
## Vagrant Gods: Book One

### by

# David Dalglish

*Cyrus was fourteen when his gods were slain, his country invaded, and his parents—the king and queen—beheaded in front of him. Held prisoner in the invader's court for years, Cyrus is suddenly given a chance to escape and claim his revenge when a mysterious group of revolutionaries comes looking for a figurehead. They need a hero to strike fear into the hearts of the imperials and to inspire and unite the people. They need someone to take up the skull mask and swords and to become the legendary "Vagrant"—an unparalleled hero and assassin of otherworldly skill.*

*But not all is as it seems. Creating the illusion of a hero is the work of many, and Cyrus will soon discover the true price of his vengeance.*

# Chapter 1

# CYRUS

All his life, Cyrus Lythan had been told his parents' armada was the greatest in the world, unmatched by any fleet from the mainland continent of Gadir. It was the pride of his family, the jewel of the island kingdom of Thanet. Standing at the edge of the castle balcony, his hands white-knuckling the balustrade, Cyrus watched their ships burn and knew it for a lie.

"Their surprise will only gain them so much," said Rayan. The older man and dearest family friend stood beside Cyrus as the fires spread across the docks. "Hold faith. Our gods will protect us."

Smoke blotted out the harbor, but along the edges of the billowing black he saw the empire's ships firing flaming spears from ballistae mounted to their decks. Thanet's boats could not counter such power with their meager archers, not even if they had fought on equal numbers. Those numbers, however, were far from equal. Thanet's vaunted armada had counted fifty ships in total, though only thirty had been in the vicinity of Vallessau when two hundred imperial ships emerged from the morning fog, their hulls painted black and their gray sails marked with two red hands clenched in prayer.

"Shouldn't you be down there with the rest of the paladins?" Cyrus asked. "Or are you too old for battle?"

The man's white plate rattled as he crossed his arms. He was a paladin of Lycaena, a holy warrior who'd dedicated his life to one of Thanet's two gods. It was she and Endarius whom the island now relied upon to withstand the coming invasion. The castle was set upon the tallest hill in the city of Vallessau, protected by a wide outer wall that circled the base of its foundational hill. Thanet's soldiers massed along the outer wall, their padded leather armor seeming woefully inadequate. Paladins of the two gods gathered in the courtyard between the outer wall and the castle itself. Despite there being less than sixty, the sight of them gave Cyrus hope. The finely polished weapons of those men and women shone brightly, and the morning light reflected off their armor, be it the gilded chain of Endarius's paladins or the white plate of Lycaena's. As for the god and goddess, they both waited inside the castle.

"You are brave to call me old when you yourself are not yet a man," Rayan said. His skin was as dark as his hair was white, and when he smiled, it stretched his smartly trimmed beard. That smile was both heartfelt and fleeting. "His Highness ordered me to protect you."

Cyrus tried to remain optimistic. He tried to hold faith in the divine beings pledged to protect Thanet. A seemingly endless tide of soldiers disembarking from the ships and marching the main thoroughfare toward the outer castle walls broke that faith.

"Tell me, Rayan, if the walls fall and our gods die, how will you protect me?"

Rayan looked to the distant congregation of his fellow paladins of Lycaena at the outer gate, and his thoughts clearly echoed Cyrus's.

"Poorly," he said. "Stay here, and pray for us all. We will need every bit of help this cruel world can muster."

The paladin exited the balcony. The heavy thud of the shutting door quickened Cyrus's pulse, and he swallowed down his lingering fear. A cowardly part of him shouted to find somewhere in the castle to bury his head and hide. Stubborn pride kept his feet firmly in place. He was the fourteen-year-old Prince of Thanet, and he would bear witness to the fate of his kingdom.

The assault began with the arrival of the ladders, dozens of thick planks of wood with metal hooks bolted onto their tops so they could lock tightly onto the walls. The defenders rushed to shove them off, but the empire's crossbowmen punished them with volley after volley. Swords clashed, and though the empire's losses were heavy, nothing slowed the ascent of the invaders. What started as a few scattered soldiers fighting atop the walls became a mile-long battlefield. It did not take long before the gray tunics overwhelmed the blue tabards of Vallessau.

Next came the battering ram. How the enemy had built it in such short a time baffled Cyrus, but there was no denying its steady hammering on the opposite side of the outer gate. Even the intervals were maddeningly consistent. Every four seconds, the gate would rattle, the wood would crack, and the imperial army grew that much closer to flooding into the courtyard.

"It doesn't matter," Cyrus whispered to himself. "The gods protect us. The gods will save us."

The fight along the walls was growing thicker, with more ladders managing to stay upright with every passing moment. Cyrus could spare no glance in their direction, for with one last shuddering blast, the battering ram knocked open the outer gate. The invading army flooded through, and should have easily overrun the vastly outnumbered defenders, but at long last, the castle doors opened and Thanet's divine made their presence known.

The goddess Lycaena fluttered above an accompaniment of her priests. Her skin was black as midnight, her eyes brilliant rainbows of ever-shifting color. Long, flowing silk cascaded down from her arms and waist, its hue a brilliant orange that transitioned to yellow, green, and blue depending on the ruffle of the fabric. The dress billowed outward in all directions, and no matter how hard Cyrus looked, he couldn't tell where the fabric ended and the goddess's enormous wings began. She held a rod topped with an enormous ruby in her left hand; in the right, a golden harp whose strings shimmered all colors of the visible spectrum. Cyrus's heart ached at the sight of her. He'd witnessed Lycaena's physical form only a few times in his life, and each left him breathless and in awe.

"Be gone, locusts of a foreign land," Lycaena decreed. She did not shout, nor raise her voice, but all the city heard her words. "We will not break before a wave of hate and steel."

Fire lashed from the ruby atop her rod in a conical torrent that filled the broken gateway. The screams of the dying combined into a singular wail. The other god of Thanet, Endarius the Lion, charged into the ashen heap left in her attack's wake. His fur was gold, his claws obsidian, his mane a brilliant collection of feathers that ran the full gamut of the rainbow. Wings stretched from his back, the feathers there several feet long and shifting from a crimson red along the base to pale white at the tip. Those wings beat with his every stride, adding to his speed and power.

Endarius's paladins joined him in his charge. They did not wield swords and shields like their Lycaenan counterparts, nor did they share their long cloaks of interlocking colors resembling stained glass. Instead their gilded armor bore necklaces of fangs across their arms, and they wielded twin jagged swords to better support their ferocity. They bellowed as they ran, their version of a prayer, and they tore into the ranks of the invaders, the spray of blood and breaking of bones their worship.

In those first few minutes, Cyrus truly believed victory would be theirs. Thanet had never been conquered in all her history. Lycaena and Endarius protected their beloved people. The two divine beings rewarded their faithful subjects with safety and guidance. And as the imperial soldiers rushed through the gate with their swords and spears, the gods filled the courtyard with fire and blood. From such a height, Cyrus could only guess at the identities of the individual defenders, but he swore he saw Rayan fighting alongside his goddess, his sword lit with holy light as he kept his beloved deity safe with his rainbow shield.

*You burned our fleets*, Cyrus thought, and a vengeful thrill shot through him. *But we'll crush your armies. You'll never return, never, not after this defeat.*

The arrival of the twelve tempered his joy. The men appeared remarkably similar to Thanet's paladins, bearing thick golden platemail and wielding much larger weapons adorned with decorative hilts and handles. Unlike the rest of the imperial army, they did not wear gray tabards but instead colorful tunics and cloaks bearing differing animals. The twelve pushed through the blasted gate, flanked on either side by a contingent of soldiers. They showed no fear of the two divine beings leading the slaughter. They charged into the thick of things without hesitation, their shields held high and their weapons gleaming.

Cyrus knew little of the Everlorn Empire. Journey to the mainland took several months by boat, and its ruling emperor, arrogantly named the God-Incarnate, had issued an embargo upon Thanet lasting centuries. The empire worshiped and acknowledged no gods but their emperor, and claimed faith in him allowed humanity to transcend mortal limits. Seeing those twelve fight, Cyrus understood that belief for the first time in his life. Those twelve...they couldn't be human. Whatever they were, it was monstrous, it was impossible, and it was beyond even what Thanet's paladins could withstand.

God and invader clashed, and somehow these horrifying twelve endured the wrath of the immortal beings. Their armor held against fire and claw. Their weapons punched through armor as if it were glass. Soldiers and paladins from both sides attempted to intervene, but they were flies buzzing about fighting bulls. Each movement, each strike of an invader's sword or swipe of Endarius's paw, claimed the lives of foes with almost incidental ease. The battlefield ascended beyond the mortal, and these elite, these invading monsters, defied all reason as they stood their ground against Thanet's gods.

"No," Cyrus whispered. "It's not possible."

Endarius clenched his teeth about the long blade of one of the invaders, yet could not crunch through the metal. His foe ripped it free, and a crossbow brigade unleashed dozens of bolts to pelt the Lion as he danced away. The arrowheads couldn't find purchase, but they marked little black welts akin to bruises and frayed the edges of Endarius's increasingly ragged wings.

"This isn't right," Cyrus said. The battle had started so grand, yet now the defenders were scattered, the walls overrun, and the paladins struggling to maintain their attacks against wave after wave of soldiers coming through the broken gate. In the center of it all raged gods and the inhuman elite, and the world shook from their wrath. Thanet's troops attempted to seal off the wall entrance and isolate the battle against the gods. It briefly worked, at least until the men and women in red robes took to the front of enemy lines. Their lack of weapons and armor confused Cyrus at first, but then they lifted their hands in prayer. Golden weapons blistering with light burst into existence, hovering in the air and wielded by invisible hands. The weapons tore through the soldiers' ranks, the defense faltered, and Cyrus's last hope withered. What horrid power did these invaders command?

Time lost meaning. Blood flowed, bodies fell, the armies meeting and striking and dying with seemingly nihilistic determination. A spear-wielding member of those elite twelve leaped into the air, a single lunge of his legs carrying him dozens of feet heavenward. Lycaena was not prepared, and when the spear lodged deep into her side, her scream echoed for miles. It was right then, hearing that scream, that Cyrus knew his kingdom was lost.

"How dare you!" Endarius roared. Though one invader smashed a hammer into the Lion's side, and another knocked loose a fang from his jaw, the god cared only for the wound suffered by the Butterfly goddess. Two mighty beats of his wings carried him into the air, where his teeth closed about the elite still clinging to the embedded spear. All three crashed to the ground, but it was the invader who suffered most. Endarius crushed him in his jaws, punching through the man's armor, smashing bones, and spilling blood upon a silver tongue.

A casual flick of Endarius's neck tossed the body aside, but that was merely one of twelve. Eleven more remained, and they closed the space with calm, steady precision. No soldiers attempted to fill the gap, for what battles remained were scattered and chaotic. There was too much blood, too much death, and above it all, like a sick backdrop in the world's cruelest painting, rose the billowing smoke of Thanet's burning fleet.

"Flee from here!" Endarius bellowed as a bleeding Lycaena fluttered higher into the air.

"Only if you come with me," the goddess urged, but the

Lion would not be moved. He prepared to pounce and bared his obsidian teeth.

"For the lives of the faithful," Endarius roared. His wings spread wide, unbridled power crackling like lightning across the feathers.

Cyrus dropped to his knees and clutched the side of the balustrade. He could feel it on his skin. He could smell it in the air. The overwhelming danger. The growing fury of a god who could never imagine defeat.

"Strike me with your blades," the Lion mocked the remaining eleven. "Come die as the vermin you are."

They were happy to oblige. The eleven clashed with the god in a coordinated effort, their swords, axes, and spears tearing into his golden flesh. The god could not avoid them, could not win, only buy time for Lycaena's escape. No matter how badly Cyrus pleaded under his breath for the Lion to flee, he would not. Endarius had been, above all, a stubborn god.

A blue-armored elite was the one to strike the killing blow. A spear pierced through Endarius's eye and sank to the hilt. His fur rumbled, his dying roar shook the land, and then the Lion's body split in half. A maelstrom of stars tore free of his body like floodwaters released from a dam. Whatever otherworldly essence comprised the existence of a god burned through the eleven like a swirling, rainbow fire before rolling outward in a great flare of blinding light. Cyrus crouched down and screamed. The death of something so beautiful, so noble and inseparably linked to Thanet's identity, shook him in a way he could not fathom.

At last the noise and light faded from the suddenly quiet battlefield. Two of the eleven elites died from the eruption of divine energy, their armor melted to their bodies as they lay upon the cobblestone path leading from the main gate to the castle entrance. Nothing remained of Endarius's body, for it had dissolved into light and crystal and floated away like scattered dust. Lycaena was long gone, having taken to the skies during the divine explosion. The paladins and priests of both gods likewise fled. A few entered the castle before it locked its gates, while the rest took to the distant portions of the outer wall not yet besieged by the invaders, seeking stairs and ladders that might allow them to escape out into Vallessau.

The soldiers of the Everlorn Empire filled the courtyard to face what was left of Thanet's defenses. Cyrus guessed maybe a dozen archers, and twice that in armed soldiers, remained inside the castle. Opposing thoughts rattled inside his head. What to do. Where to go. None of it seemed to matter. His mind couldn't process the shock. Last night he'd gone to bed having heard only rumors of imperial ships sailing the area. No one had known it was a full-scale invasion. No one had known Thanet's navy would fall in a single afternoon, and the capital along with it.

The nine remaining imperial elites gathered, joined by the men and women in red robes who Cyrus assumed to be some manner of priest. One of the nine trudged to the front and stood before the locked gateway. He showed no fear of an archer's arrow, which wasn't surprising given the enormous gray slab of steel he carried as his shield. His face was hidden underneath a gigantic bull helmet with horns that stretched a full foot to either side of his head. He said something in his imperial tongue, and then one of the priests came forward holding a blue medallion. The gigantic man took it, slipped it over his neck, and then addressed the castle.

"I am Imperator Magus of Eldrid!" the man shouted, and though his lips moved wrong, there was no doubt that he somehow spoke the native Thanese language. "Paragon of Shields, servant of the Uplifted Church, and faithful child of the God-Incarnate. I command this conquest. My word is law, and so shall it be until this island bends its knee and accepts the wisdom of the Everlorn Empire. I say this not out of pride, but so you may understand that none challenge my word. Should I make a promise, I shall keep it, even unto the breaking of the world."

Magus drew a sword from his waist and lifted it high above him. He spoke again, the blue medallion flaring with light at his every word.

"I make you one offer, and it shall not be amended nor changed. Bring me the royal family who call this castle home. Cast them to the dirt at my feet, and I shall spare the lives of every single man, woman, and child within your walls. But if you will not..."

The Imperator lowered his blade.

"Then I shall execute every last one of you, so that only vermin remain to walk your halls."

And with that, silence followed, but that silence was like the held breath between seeing a flash of lightning and feeling its thunder rumble against your bones. Shouts soon erupted within the castle, scattered at first, then numerous. Screams. Steel striking steel.

*Mother! Father!* Cyrus's parents were both on a lower floor, watching the battle unfold from the castle windows. That their servants and soldiers would so easily turn upon them seemed unthinkable, but the sounds of battle were undeniable. Cyrus turned to the door to the balcony, still slightly ajar from when Rayan left.

"Oh no," he whispered, and then broke into a sprint. The door wasn't lockable, not from the outside, but if he could wedge it closed with something, even brace it with his weight...

The door opened right as he arrived, the wood ramming hard enough into him that he feared it might break his shoulder. Cyrus fell and rolled across the white stone, biting down a cry as his elbow and knees bruised. When he staggered to his feet, he found one of his guard captains, a woman named Nessa, blocking the doorway with her sword and shield drawn.

"I'm sorry, Cyrus," the woman said. "Maybe they'll spare you like they promised."

"You're a traitor."

"You saw it, prince. Endarius is dead. They're killing gods. What hope do we have? Now stand up. I will drag you if I must."

Nessa suddenly jerked forward, her jaw opening and closing in a noiseless death scream. When she collapsed, Rayan stood over her body. Blood soaked his white armor and stained his flowing cloak. His hand outstretched for Cyrus to take.

"Come," Rayan said. "We have little time."

They ran through the hall to the stairs. Cyrus pretended not to see the bodies strewn across the blue carpet. Some were soldiers. Some were servants. The king and queen still lived, yet the people of Thanet were already tearing one another apart. Was this how quickly their nation would fall?

Once at the bottom of the stairs, Rayan guided him through rooms and ducked along slender servant corridors hidden behind curtains. During their flight, treacherous Thanet soldiers ordered them to halt twice, and twice Rayan cut them down with an expert swing of his sword. Cyrus stepped over their bodies without truly seeing them. He felt like a stranger in his own skin. The entire world seemed unreal, a cruel dream no amount of biting his tongue allowed him to awake from.

Within minutes they were running down a lengthy corridor that connected a portion of the western wall to the castle proper. The corridor ran parallel to the courtyard, and at the first door they passed, Cyrus spotted the enormous gathering of soldiers surrounding Magus of Eldrid.

"I had feared the worst," Magus shouted as Cyrus continued. "Come before me, and kneel. I would hear your names."

Cyrus skidded to a halt at the next doorway. He pressed his chest against the cold stone and peered around the edge. It couldn't be. His parents, they were meant to escape like him. They had their own royal guard. Their own protectors. Yet there they stood before the Imperator, flanked on either side by blood-soaked traitors. His father was the first to bow his head and address their conqueror. With each proclamation, the empire's soldiers cheered and clattered their swords against their shields.

"Cleon Lythan," said his father. "King of Thanet."

"Berniss Lythan," said his mother. "Queen of Thanet."

Cyrus's stomach twisted into acidic knots. How could the world turn so dark and cruel within the span of a single day? Magus lifted his shield and slammed it back down hard enough to crack a full foot-deep groove into the stone and wedge his shield permanently upright. With only his sword swinging in his relaxed grip, he approached the pair.

"Cleon and Berniss," he said. "We are not ignorant of your kingdom and its history. Where is your son? The young man by the name of Cyrus?"

"I suspect he fled," Cleon said. The courtyard had grown deathly quiet. "Please, it was not by our order. We don't know where Cyrus has gone."

The Imperator removed his bull helmet. Cyrus had expected more of a monster, but Magus seemed remarkably human, with deeply tanned skin, silver eyes, and a magnificent smile. His long black hair cascaded down either side of his face as he spoke.

"I requested the entire royal line. Was I not clear? Did my word-lace mistranslate?"

"No," Berniss said. "Please, we looked, we did."

The man shook his head.

"Lies, and more lies," he said. "Do you stall for his safety? Feign at ignorance, as if your boy stands a chance of survival once this castle falls?"

Cyrus took a step, one single step out the doorway toward his parents, before Rayan grabbed him by his neck.

"We must escape while there is still time," the paladin whispered. Cyrus resisted his pull to safety. He would watch this. He must.

"I gave my word," Magus continued once it was clear neither would offer up Cyrus's location. "A clear word, and a true promise. Accept this blood as a sacrifice to your memory. May it sear across your conscience in the eternal lands beyond."

Cyrus knew fleeing with Rayan was the wiser decision. He knew it was what his parents wanted. But it seemed so simple to Cyrus, so obvious what the right course of action must be. He turned away from the door, pretending to go with the paladin. The moment Rayan's hand released from his neck, Cyrus shoved the man's chest, separating them. A heartbeat later he was out the door, legs and arms flailing as he willed his body to run faster. The distance between them felt like miles. His voice sounded quiet, insignificant, but he screamed it nonetheless.

"I'm here!" It didn't matter if he put his own life at risk. He wouldn't leave his family behind. He wouldn't let them die for his sake. He ran, crossing the green grass of the courtyard between him and the gathered soldiers. "I'm here, I'm here, I'm—"

Magus swung once for the both of them. His sword passed through blood and bone to halt upon the white brick. Only

Cyrus's mother's injuries weren't instantly lethal, for the sword cut across her arm and waist instead of cleaving her in half. Her anguished scream pierced the courtyard. Her pain ripped daggers through Cyrus's horror-locked mind. Magus, however, twirled his sword in his fingers and shook his head with disappointment.

"Why do I bother?" he said as he cut the head from Berniss's shoulders. "It's always easier to rebuild from nothing."

Cyrus couldn't banish the sight. He couldn't stop seeing that killing stroke. His legs weakened, limbs becoming wobbling jelly that could not support him. His whole family, gone. Slain. Bleeding upon the courtyard stones with their blood pooling into the groove Magus had carved with his shield. Crossbow bolts hammered into the men and women who had turned traitor and brought the royal family out in custody. No reward for their betrayal. Only death.

*Too late*, he thought. Too late, too late, he ran too late, revealed himself too late. A scream ripped out of Cyrus's chest. No words, just a heartbroken protest against the brutality of the day and the terror sweeping through him as the ground seemed to shake at the approach of the Paragon of Shields. Too late, he had gained the attention of the monster from the boats. Too late to save his parents. Too late to mean anything but a cruel death. Cyrus prayed he would meet his father and mother on the rolling green fields of Endarius's paradise. Face wet with tears, he stared up at Magus and slowly climbed to his feet. He would die meeting the gaze of his executioner; this he swore. Not on his knees. Not begging for his life.

The golden-armored paragon grabbed Cyrus by the throat and lifted him into the air. Instinct had Cyrus clutching at the heavy gauntlet. How easily he carried him. As if he were nothing. Just a ghost. Magus, this man, this monster, towered above the other soldiers come to join him. Cyrus stared into the man's silver eyes and promised vengeance, even if it meant coming back as a spirit. Not even the grave would deny him his due.

"Cyrus?" Magus asked him. The necklace at his throat shimmered with pale blue light. "Prince Cyrus Lythan?"

Cyrus sucked in a shallow breath as the gauntlet loosened.

"I am," he said. "Now do it, bastard. I'm not scared."

One of the soldiers beside Magus asked a question in his foreign tongue. Magus thought for a moment and then shook his head. He tossed Cyrus to the stone, dropping him beside the bodies. Cyrus tried not to look. He tried to not let the blood and bone and spilled innards of his beloved parents sear into his memory for the rest of his life, however long or short it might be. He failed.

"Lock him in his room," Magus said. "We have much to do to prepare this wretched island, and too few years to do it. And one thing I've learned is that when it comes to keeping a populace in line, well..."

His giant boot settled atop Cyrus's chest, grinding him into the stone, smearing him upon the blood of his slain parents.

"It never hurts to have a hostage."

# if you enjoyed
## WE DREAM OF GODS
### look out for

# ENGINES OF EMPIRE
## The Age of Uprising: Book One
### by

# R. S. Ford

*The nation of Torwyn is run on the power of industry, and industry is run by the Guilds. Chief among them are the Hawkspurs, whose responsibility it is to keep the gears of the empire turning. That's exactly why matriarch Rosomon Hawkspur sends each of her heirs to the far reaches of the nation.*

*Conall, the eldest son, is dispatched to the distant frontier to earn his stripes in the military. It is here that he faces a threat he could never have seen coming: the first rumblings of revolution.*

*Tyreta is a sorceress with the ability to channel the power of pyrestone, the magical resource that fuels the empire's machines. She is sent to the mines to learn more about how pyrestone is harvested—but instead, she finds the dark horrors of industry that the empire would prefer to keep hidden.*

*The youngest, Fulren, is a talented artificer and finds himself acting as a guide to a mysterious foreign emissary. Soon after, he is framed for a crime he never committed. A crime that could start a war.*

*As the Hawkspurs grapple with the many threats that face the nation within and without, they must finally prove themselves worthy—or their empire will fall apart.*

# PROLOGUE

Courage. That ever-elusive virtue. Willet had once been told a man could never possess true courage without first knowing true fear. If that was so, he must be the bravest man in all Torwyn, as fear gnawed at him like a starving hound, cracking his bones and licking at the marrow.

He knew this was not courage. More likely it was madness, but then only the mad would have walked so readily into the Drift. It was a thousand miles of wasteland cut through the midst of an entire continent, leaving a scar from the Dolur Peaks in the north to the Ungulf Sea on the southern coast. A scar that would never heal. The remnant of an ancient war, and a stark reminder that sorcery was the unholiest of sins.

Willet glanced over his shoulder, squinting against the midday sun toward Fort Karvan as it loomed on the distant ridge like a grim sentinel. Had there ever been built a more forbidding bastion of stone and iron?

Five vast fortresses lined the border between Torwyn and the Drift, each one garrisoned by a different Armiger Battalion, the last line of defence against the raiding tribes and twisted beasts of the wasteland. Fort Karvan was home to the grim and proud Mantid Battalion, and though Willet hated it with every fibre, he would have given anything to be safe within its walls right now. Instead he was traipsing through the blasted landscape, and the only things to protect him were a drab grey robe and his faith in the Great Wyrms. Well, perhaps not the only things.

"Pick up your feet, Legate Kinloth," Captain Jarrell hissed from the head of the patrol. "If you fall behind, you'll be left behind." The captain scowled from within the open visor of his mantis helm, greying beard reaching over the gorget of his armour.

Willet quickened his pace, sandals padding along the dusty ground. Captain Jarrell was a man whose bite was most definitely worse than his bark, and Willet wasn't sure whether he was more afraid of him or of the denizens of the Drift. The only person he'd ever known with sharper teeth was his own mother, though it was a close-run thing.

By the time he caught up, Willet was short of breath, but he felt some relief as he continued his trek within the sizeable shadow of Jarrell's lieutenant, Terrick. The big man was the only inhabitant of Fort Karvan who'd ever offered Willet so much as the time of day. He was quick to laugh and generous with his mirth, but not today. Terrick's eyes were fixed on the trail ahead, his expression stern as he gripped tight to sword and shield, wary of any danger.

At the head of their patrol, Lethann scouted the way. In contrast to Terrick she was the very definition of mirthless. She wore the tan leather garb of a Talon scout, travelling cloak rendering her almost invisible against the dusty landscape. A splintbow was strapped to her back, a clip of bolts on her hip alongside the long hunting knife. Every now and then she would kneel, searching for sign, following the trail like a hunting dog.

Three other troopers of the Mantid Battalion marched with them but, to his shame, Willet had no idea what they were called. In fairness, each of their faces was concealed beneath the visor of a mantis helm, but even so they were still part of his brood, and he their stalwart priest. Willet was charged with enforcing their faith in the Great Wyrms, and when would they need that more than now, out here in the deadly wilds? How was he to provide sacrament without even knowing their names? It reminded him once again of the impossibility of the task he'd been given.

Since his first day at Fort Karvan, Willet had been ignored and disrespected. The Draconate Ministry had sent him to instil faith in the fort's stout defenders, and Willet had gone about that role with all the zeal his position demanded. It soon became clear no one was going to take him seriously. Over the days and weeks his sermons had been met with indifference at best. At worst outright derision. The disrespect had worsened, rising to a tumult, until the occasion when he had drunk deeply from a waterskin only to find it had been filled with tepid piss when he wasn't looking.

Had Willet been posted at another fort in another part of the Drift, perhaps he would have been received with more enthusiasm. The Corvus at Ravenscrag or the Ursus Battalion at Fort Arbelus would have provided him a much warmer welcome. For the Mantid Battalion, it seemed faith in the Guilds of Torwyn far outweighed faith in the Ministry. But what had he truly expected? It was not the Draconate Ministry that fuelled the nation's commerce. It was not the legates who built artifice and supplied the military with its arms and armour. It was not Willet Kinloth who had brought about the greatest technological advancements in Torwyn's history.

His sudden despondency provoked a groundswell of guilt. As Saphenodon decreed, those who suffer the greatest hardship are due the highest reward. And who was Willet Kinloth to question the wisdom of the Draconate?

"That lookout can't be much farther ahead," Terrick grumbled, to himself as much as to anyone else. It was enough to shake Willet from his malaise, forcing him to concentrate on the job at hand.

They had first spied their quarry four days ago from the battlements of Fort Karvan. The figure had been distant and indistinct, and at first the lookouts had dismissed it as a wanderer, lost in the Drift. When they spotted the lone figure again a second and third day there was only one conclusion—the fort was being watched, which could herald a raid from one of the many marauding bands that dogged the border of Torwyn.

Raiding parties had been harrying the forts along the Drift for centuries. Mostly they were small warbands grown so hungry and desperate they risked their lives to pillage Torwyn's abundant fields and forests. But some were vast armies, disparate tribes gathered together by a warlord powerful enough to threaten the might of the Armiger Battalions. No such armies had risen for over a decade, the last having been quelled with merciless violence by a united front of Guild, Armiger and Ministry. But it still paid to be cautious. If this scout was part of a larger force, it was imperative they be captured and questioned.

The ground sloped ever downward as they followed the trail, and the grim sight of Fort Karvan was soon lost beyond the ridge behind them. Willet stuck close to Terrick, but the hulk-ing trooper provided less and less reassurance the deeper they ventured into the Drift.

Willet's hand toyed with the medallions about his neck, the five charms bringing him little comfort. The sapphire of Vermitrix imparted no peace, the jade of Saphenodon no keen insight. The jet pendant of Ravenothrax did not grant him solace in the face of imminent death, and neither did the solid steel of Ammenodus Rex give him the strength to face this battle. His hand finally caressed the red ruby pendant of Undometh. The Great Wyrm of Vengeance. That was the most useless of all—for who would avenge Willet if he was slain out here? Would Undometh himself come to take vengeance on behalf of a lowly legate? Not likely.

Lethann waved from up ahead. Her hand flashed in a sequence of swift signals before she gestured ahead into a steep valley. Willet had no idea how to decipher the silent message, but the rest of the patrol adopted a tight formation, Captain Jarrell leading his men with an added sense of urgency.

Their route funnelled into a narrow path, bare red rock ris-ing on both sides as they descended into a shallow valley. Here lay the remnants of a civilisation that had died a thousand years before. Relics from the age of the Archmages, before their war and their magics had blasted the continent apart.

Willet stared at the broken and derelict buildings scattered about the valley floor. Alien architecture clawed its way from the earth, the tops of ancient spires lying alongside the weath-ered corpses of vast statues. He trod carefully in his sandals, as here and there lay broken and rusted weapons, evidence of the battle fought here centuries before. Cadaverous remnants of plate and mail lay half-reclaimed in the dirt, the remains of their wearers long since rotted to dust.

Up ahead, Lethann paused at the threshold of a ruined archway. It was the entrance to a dead temple, its remaining walls standing askew on the valley floor, blocking the way ahead. She knelt, and her hand traced the outline of something in the dust before she turned to Jarrell and nodded.

Terrick and the three other troopers moved up beside their captain as Willet hung back, listening to Jarrell's whispered orders. As one, the troopers spread out, Jarrell leading the way as they moved toward the arch. Lethann unstrapped her splintbow and checked the breech before slotting a clip of bolts into the stock, and the patrol entered the brooding archway.

Willet followed them across the threshold into what had once been the vast atrium of a temple. Jarrell and his men spread out, swords drawn, shields braced in front of them. Lethann lurked at the periphery, aiming her splintbow across the wideopen space. At first Willet didn't notice what had made them so skittish. Then his eyes fell on the lone figure perched on a broken altar at the opposite end of the temple.

She knelt as though in prayer. Her left hand rested on a sheathed greatsword almost as tall as she was, and the other covered her right eye. The left eye was closed as though she were deep in meditation. She wore no armour, but a tight-fitting leather jerkin and leggings covered her from neck to bare feet. Her arms were exposed, and Willet could make out faint traces of the tattoos that wheeled about her bare flesh.

"There's nowhere to run," Jarrell pronounced, voice echoing across the open ground of the temple. "Surrender to us, and we'll see you're treated fairly."

Willet doubted the truth of that, but he still hoped this would end without violence. This woman stood little chance against six opponents.

Slowly she opened her left eye, hand still pressed over the

right, and regarded them without emotion. If she was intimidated by the odds against her, she didn't show it.

"You should turn back to your fort," she answered in a thick Maladoran accent. "And run."

Lethann released the safety catch on her splintbow, sighting across the open ground at the kneeling woman. With a sweep of his hand, Jarrell ordered his men to advance.

Terrick was the first to step forward, the brittle earth crunching beneath his boots. Two of the troopers approached from the flanks, closing on the woman's position. Lethann moved along the side of the atrium, barely visible in the shadow of the temple wall.

"I tried," the woman breathed, slowly lowering the hand that covered her eye.

Willet stifled a gasp as he saw a baleful red light where her right eye should have been. Stories of demons and foul sorceries flooded his memory, and his hand shook as it moved to grasp the pendants about his neck.

Terrick was unperturbed, closing on her position with his sword braced atop his shield. When he advanced to within five feet, the woman moved.

With shocking speed she wrenched the greatsword from its sheath and leapt to her feet, blade sweeping the air faster than the eye could comprehend. Terrick halted his advance before toppling back like a statue and landing on his back in the dirt.

Willet let out a gasp as blood pooled from Terrick's neck, turning the sand black. The other two troopers charged in, the first yelling in rage from within his mantis helm, sword raised high. The woman leapt from atop her rocky perch, sword sweeping that mantis helm from the trooper's shoulders. Her dance continued, bare feet sending clouds of dust into the air as she sidestepped a crushing sweep of the next trooper's blade before thrusting the tip of her greatsword into his stomach beneath the breastplate. Willet saw it sprout from his back in a crimson bloom before she wrenched it free, never slowing her momentum, swift as an eagle in flight.

The clacking report of bolts echoed across the temple as Lethann unleashed a salvo from her splintbow. Willet's lips mouthed a litany to Ammenodus Rex as the woman sprinted around the edge of the temple wall, closing the gap on Lethann. Every bolt missed, ricocheting off the decayed rocks as the woman ate up the distance between them at a frightening rate. Lethann fumbled at her belt for a second clip, desperate to reload, but the woman was on her. A brutal hack of the greatsword, and Lethann's body collapsed to the dirt.

"Ammenodus, grant me salvation that I might be delivered from your enemies," Willet whispered, pressing the steel pendant to his lips as he did so. He found himself backing away, sandals scuffing across the dusty floor, as the woman casually strode toward the centre of the atrium. Captain Jarrell and his one remaining trooper moved to flank her, crouching defensively behind their shields.

They circled as she stood impassively between them. For the first time Willet noted the white jewel glowing at the centre of her greatsword's cross-guard. It throbbed with sickly light, mimicking the pulsing red orb sunk within her right eye socket.

This truly was a demon of the most corrupt kind, and Willet's hand fumbled at the pendants about his neck, fingers closing around the one made of jet. "O great Ravenothrax," he mumbled. "The Unvanquished. Convey me to your lair that I might be spared the evil propagated by mine enemies."

In the centre of the atrium, the three fighters paid little heed to Willet's prayers. The last trooper's patience gave out, and with a grunt he darted to attack. Captain Jarrell bellowed at him to "Hold!" but it was too late. The woman's greatsword seemed to move of its own accord, the white jewel flashing hungrily as the blade skewered the eye socket of the trooper's helmet.

Jarrell took the initiative as his last ally died, charging desperately, hacking at the woman before she ducked, spun, twisted in the air and kicked him full in the chest. Willet held his breath, all thought of prayer forgotten as he saw Jarrell lose his footing and fall on his back.

The woman leapt in the air, impossibly high, that greatsword lancing down to impale the centre of Jarrell's prone body, driving through his breastplate like a hammered nail.

It was only then that Willet's knees gave out. He collapsed to the dirt, feeling a tear roll from his eye. The pendants in his fist felt useless as the woman slowly stood and turned toward him.

"Vermitrix, Great Wyrm of Peace, bring me a painless end," he whispered as she drew closer, leaving her demon sword still skewered through Jarrell's chest. "And may Undometh grant me vengeance against this wicked foe."

She stood over him, hand covering that sinister red eye once more. The jewel that sat in the centre of the greatsword's crossguard had dulled to nothing but clear glass, but Willet could still feel its evil from across the atrium.

"Your dragon gods will not save you, little priest," the woman said. Her voice was calm and gentle, as though she were coaxing a child to sleep.

Willet tried to look at her face but couldn't. He tried to speak, but all that came out was a whimper, a mumbled cry for his mother. He could almost have laughed at the irony. Here he was at the end, and for all his pious observance he was crying for a woman who had made his life a misery with her spiteful and poisonous tongue.

"Your mother is not coming either," the woman said. "But the voice is quiet, for now. So you should run, little priest. Before it speaks again."

Somehow Willet rose to his feet, legs trembling like a newborn foal's. He took a tentative step away from the woman, who kept her hand clamped tight over her eye. The white jewel in her sword, still skewered through Jarrell's chest, shone with sudden malevolence. It was enough to set Willet to flight.

He ran, losing a sandal on the rough ground, ignoring the sudden pain in his foot. He would not stop until he was back at the gates of Fort Karvan. Would not slow no matter the ache in his legs nor lack of breath in his lungs. He could not stop. If he did, there would be nothing left for him but the Five Lairs. And he was not ready for them yet.

orbit

Follow us:

**f** **/orbitbooksUS**

**🐦** **/orbitbooks**

**▶** **/orbitbooks**

Join our mailing list
to receive alerts on our
latest releases and deals.

**orbitbooks.net**

Enter our monthly
giveaway for the chance
to win some epic prizes.

**orbitloot.com**